Decepti

DECEPTION GAME

WILL JORDAN

CANELO

First published in United Kingdom in 2015 by Canelo

This edition published in Great Britain in 2019 by

Canelo Digital Publishing Limited
57 Shepherds Lane
Beaconsfield, Bucks HP9 2DU
United Kingdom

A CIP catalogue record for this book is available from the British Library.

Print ISBN 978 1 78863 459 5
Ebook ISBN 978 1 910859 04 9

Look for more great books at www.canelo.co

For Matthew – who ensures life is never dull

Prologue

Drake took a breath, the scorching dry air searing his throat, tiny grains of wind-blown sand stinging his eyes. Overhead, the sun beat down mercilessly from a cloudless sky, raising beads of sweat on his already burned and reddened skin.

Around him, locals and small groups of tourists moved back and forth through the crowded central square, paying little attention to the Westerner in dishevelled clothes leaning against the wall beside a small cafe. Perhaps the cuts and bruises marked him out as someone to studiously avoid, or perhaps the dangerous flicker in his eyes was what really kept them away. Whatever the reason, the ebb and flow of humanity seemed to part around him like a river slipping past an implacable boulder.

Glancing up, Drake turned his gaze towards the low hilltop about half a mile away overlooking the bustling town centre, where the weathered and tumbled walls of the ancient settlement still rose up against the pristine blue sky, heavy stone blocks jutting from the parched earth.

That was the place where it was supposed to happen; the place where the tumultuous events of the past week would reach their final, deadly conclusion. Everything he had fought for, everything he had sacrificed, every compromise he had made… it had all led him here.

He would live or die by what happened today.

His pulse was pounding strong and urgent in his ears, almost drowning out the tinny ring of the cell phone as he held it against his head. The man he was trying to reach would be wary of calls like this. He wouldn't answer readily, might not answer at all in fact. Either way, there was nothing he could do to change it.

All he could do was wait, and hope.

And just like that, the ringing stopped. He was connected.

'So you're still alive, Ryan,' a voice remarked on the other end of the line. A smooth, confident, controlled voice. Not the voice of a man whose own future hung in the balance just as much as Drake's. 'And you're late. Didn't I make it clear what was at stake?'

'You did,' Drake replied, his eyes scanning the crowds around him. 'I have what you want.'

'Then I suggest you bring it to me, so we can finish our business.'

Drake knew this was the moment of choice. His last chance to back out.

'No,' he said, speaking with calm finality.

I

There was a pause. A moment of confusion and doubt; a chink in the armour momentarily exposed. 'Excuse me?'

'We both know I'm dead the second I hand it over. You'd never let me live after everything I've seen, everything I know.' He was committed now. There was no going back – the only choice was to move forward. 'So I suggest you remember this moment, because this is as close as you're ever going to get to what you want.'

To his credit, his adversary remained surprisingly composed in the wake of this blatant act of defiance. A different man might have railed against him, shouted down the line about how foolish Drake's actions were and how he would surely be punished for them.

But this man was another sort.

'Ryan, maybe you've forgotten the reason we're in this position,' the calm, pleasant voice went on. 'If you need reminding, I'm quite prepared to leave behind a piece of her at our meeting place. And believe me, it'll be a piece she'll miss.'

Drake closed his eyes for a moment, swallowing down the fear and horror at what he was hearing, because he knew well enough that this was a threat his adversary was quite prepared to make good on. A sadist who took pleasure in inflicting suffering on others.

'You won't do that,' he replied, sounding more confident than he felt.

'Really? Enlighten me.'

'I'm offering you something better.'

'And what would that be?'

'There are three ways this could go. First, you kill her, I release the files across the internet, then I turn all my attention to hunting you down. Believe me, I'm good at finding people, and I'm prepared to devote every waking moment of my life to finding you. And when I do, anything you do to her will be nothing but a happy memory compared to what I do to you. Second, you kill me before I can get to you. The files have been uploaded to an automatic email server, and without me to stop it, everything you've worked to cover up gets released within two hours of my death.' He allowed that prospect to hang there for a moment or two. 'Either way, you lose.'

'As do you, Ryan,' he reminded him.

'There's more at stake here than you and me. We both know what you're really playing for. Are you ready to give all that up, watch it fall down around you?'

There was a pause. A gambler weighing the risks against the potential rewards. 'I presume there's a third option?'

Drake took another breath of the sandy, stifling air. 'You give her back to me, unharmed. I agree not to interfere with your plans or tell anyone what we found, you agree not to come looking for me, and everyone walks away. It's that simple.'

'Very heroic of you,' he remarked with dour humour.

'I'm no hero. Never was,' Drake said, truly meaning it. 'And this isn't my war. I just want it to end.'

This was it. He had said and done everything he could. The rest depended on the man on the other end of the line.

And then he heard it. Not some vicious curse, not a growl of anger or even a muttered promise that he would pay for this one day.

What Drake heard instead was a low chuckle of amusement. The laugh of a man finally springing a trap that had been long in the making.

'Come now, Ryan. We both know this can only end one way.' He paused a moment, allowing his words to sink in. 'Look down.'

Glancing down, Drake saw something on his stained and crumpled shirt. A splash of red light that hadn't been there before. The glow of a laser sight.

'Wouldn't run if I were you. You're covered from two different directions, and my friends are just itching to pull those triggers.'

They had found him. Somehow they had tracked him here, predicted this move, known exactly what he was going to do. And now they had him out in the open, the time had come to spring their trap.

No sooner had this thought crossed his mind than a black SUV pulled up nearby. The rear doors flew open and a pair of men leapt out. Men Drake had encountered before. Men who had tried to kill him more than once over the past few days, and who wouldn't hesitate to do so now if they were given the order. Their hands were on weapons hidden just inside their jackets, ready to draw down on him if he so much as twitched.

'Like I said, Ryan,' the voice on the line said, filled with the confidence of a man in total control of the situation. 'This can only end one way.'

Drake lowered the phone as the retrieval team closed in on him.

Part I

Rendition

To date, at least fifty-four countries are known to have participated in the CIA's extraordinary-rendition programme, many playing host to so-called 'black sites' where detainees are held and interrogated for an unlimited period of time without any legal rights. The number of people imprisoned in this fashion may never be known.

Chapter 1

The sheer scale of Arlington Cemetery never ceased to amaze Drake. Occupying more than 600 acres of land on the west bank of the Potomac and located a mere twenty-minute walk from the White House, the immense complex was both physically and symbolically close to the heart of the nation. Its size and scale served as an eternal reminder of the sacrifices made by generations of Americans, from the Civil War all the way up to the present day. And it was here, beneath the gentle shade of blossoming trees, that 400,000 of America's war dead rested, their graves laid out in neat rows of white headstones that stretched almost beyond sight.

It was a sobering, reflective sort of place, and one that Drake had visited more than once in the past few years, either to pay respects to fallen comrades or just to be alone with his thoughts.

Today however he had a different purpose here.

Turning left off Roosevelt Drive, he began his ascent up a steep grassy hill towards the memorial complex at the top, passing a group of people heading in the opposite direction. A mixture of ages and genders, but comfortable enough around each other that they almost certainly belonged to the same family. An old man in the centre of the group, leaning heavily on a walking stick as he made his way down the hill, was likely the reason for their visit. He was wearing a dark blue navy cap with the name of some warship emblazoned in frayed gold lettering, though he'd passed by before Drake could get a close look at it.

He didn't suppose it mattered. It meant something to its owner, and that was what counted.

Strange how differently America regarded its war veterans, he thought with a fleeting sense of regret as he ascended the steps. Here they were treated with respect, even reverence. The old cliché that a man in uniform could walk into any bar in the country and have at least one guy buy him a beer was, in Drake's experience, still alive and kicking. Back in the UK, the best they could hope for was a shoddy state pension and bingo night down at the ex-servicemen's club.

He did his best to push these thoughts from his mind as he reached the top of the steps, taking in the scene beyond. Standing in the centre of the wide open plaza was an immense marble sarcophagus, its white surface bright in the afternoon sun.

The Tomb of the Unknown Soldier was one of the most sacred places in the whole of Arlington; an eternal monument to the thousands of soldiers who had perished unknown on the battlefields of the world, their identities forever lost.

It was guarded twenty-four hours a day, no matter the weather, by the Sentinels – elite members of the 3rd US Infantry Regiment known as the 'Old Guard' – and today was no exception. Uniform immaculate, back ramrod straight, sunlight gleaming off his mirrored sunglasses, a single soldier carrying an old M14 rifle paced slowly back and forth in front of the tomb. So precise were his movements, and those of every other Sentinel who had come US before him, that a perfect square had been worn into the marble paving by the long decades of their watch.

A few tourists were there taking pictures of the spectacle, probably viewing it as a curiosity akin to the Queen's Guard standing motionless outside Buckingham Palace. Drake was content to bypass them as he headed for the Memorial Amphitheatre located behind the tomb.

To a casual observer his demeanour was little different from any of the hundreds of other people milling around the cemetery that day. He walked with the easy, comfortable pace of a man heading somewhere with no great urgency, neither hurrying nor dawdling. His posture was relaxed without appearing nonchalant, confident without swagger, his expression conveying little beyond the superficial interest of an average visitor.

Only his eyes, hidden behind dark sunglasses that didn't look the least bit out of place on that warm sunny afternoon, betrayed the keen, eager gaze of a trained operative, drinking in every detail of his environment and the people within it. His gaze leapt from face to face, looking for any hint, any telltale clue that they weren't who they were pretending to be.

Drake had made a living out of finding people, many of whom didn't want to be found, and he'd become very good at spotting something out of place. A gaze that lingered a little too long, a twitch that betrayed tension and intensity where none were warranted, an involuntary shift of posture to accommodate the uncomfortable bulk of a concealed weapon. He'd seen it all in his time, and his senses were on alert for it now.

He relaxed a little as he drew closer to the amphitheatre, content for now that no one amongst the spectators had shown undue interest in him. That didn't mean no one was watching, of course, but Drake had grown used to covering his back over the past couple of years.

He'd grown used to a lot of things over the last couple of years.

Normally reserved for Veteran's Day services and other public events, for the most part the massive outdoor theatre stood empty and unused. There was little for tourists to see or do inside, and no monuments stood within its columned walls, so few people lingered there long.

In short, it was a good place to talk without fear of interruption or eavesdropping. And this was one conversation he didn't want overheard.

Edging around one of the big stone columns that formed the outer boundary of the theatre, Drake paused a moment to survey the space within. Rows of benches radiated outward from the main stage, rising up gradually towards the outer periphery of the theatre.

Not one of them was occupied.

Drake glanced at his watch and took a breath, considering his next move. He could break cover and venture out into the centre of the theatre, making his presence known to anyone who might be waiting, but doing so would leave him exposed and vulnerable. It went against his instincts to go into a situation like this at a disadvantage.

On the other hand, he could remain where he was and see if his contact decided to take the initiative. However, meetings like this often lived or died based on mutual trust, and it was possible his contact was harbouring similar doubts. The last thing he wanted was for them to get cold feet and walk away, especially since he had gone to such pains to make this happen in the first place.

He was about to begin a circle of the theatre's outer wall when he heard footsteps on the stone floor, coming his way. Slow and heavy, accompanied by slightly laboured breathing. An older man, overweight, perhaps not in good health.

Gripping the Browning high-powered automatic hidden in a pancake holster at the small of his back, Drake readied himself for the hundred different ways this could go wrong, and slipped out from behind the pillar.

The man standing facing him was in his early sixties, black, of average height and above average weight, his close-cropped hair and moustache speckled with silver. Even a cursory glance revealed a man who wore his years with some discomfort; his shoulders were stooped, his forehead deeply lined by years of care and worry. The collar of his expensive suit was loosened, and there was a visible sheen of sweat on his brow.

The climb up here had clearly not been a pleasant one for him.

He tensed for a moment at Drake's sudden appearance, but quickly regained his composure at the realization this was the man he'd come here to meet. The young Shepherd team leader who had contacted him covertly through an intermediary, who had insisted on a face-to-face meeting away from Langley, who had promised he possessed information of great importance to the Agency.

'I hope you didn't drag me all the way out here just to shoot me, son,' he remarked coolly, his dark eyes flicking downward, indicating the hand that Drake was keeping behind his back. 'I'm sure they've got a nice spot picked out for me at Arlington, but I'd rather not take it just yet.'

Drake's grip on the weapon relaxed, some of the tension easing, though he didn't let go of it yet. 'Director Hunt.'

'So they tell me.'

Charles Hunt was the officer in charge of the CIA's Counterproliferation Division, tasked with monitoring and intercepting the flow of illegal arms worldwide, from missing ammunition crates at Russian supply depots all the way up to Iranian attempts at purchasing nuclear secrets. Their job was stop weapons from ending up in the hands of America's enemies.

'Are you here alone?' Drake asked.

'As alone as any of us can be these days,' he said, glancing upward, as if they might glimpse a surveillance drone circling overhead.

Drake's eyes hardened. 'I'm not playing games. If you were followed here—'

Hunt's greying brows drew together in a frown. 'Mr Drake, I'm not in the habit of lying to people. And I'm also not in the habit of dragging my fat ass out of my very comfortable office for secret meetings at national monuments with every crackpot who tries to contact me. But I know who you are, so I chose to show some faith in you today. Maybe you should do the same with me, and lose the attitude, along with the gun.'

Reluctantly Drake let go of the weapon.

'Better,' Hunt remarked.

'You said you knew who I was,' Drake prompted him.

'You made a name for yourself with that business in Russia last year. Whether that's a good or a bad thing remains to be seen, but you can bet your ass people are taking notice. That makes you either an enemy to be destroyed, or a commodity to be used.' He surveyed Drake with a critical eye. 'Personally, I'm not sure whether you deserve a commendation or a firing squad after the shit you pulled.'

Drake decided to let that one pass. His actions the previous year technically amounted to treason; he'd aligned himself with a foreign intelligence service without any kind of authorization, not to mention aiding and abetting a wanted terrorist. Not for the first time, he caught himself wondering just how many enemies he'd made over the past couple of years.

'I'd settle for ten minutes of your time,' he said instead. Despite the tension of their initial meeting, he was very much aware that a divisional director of the CIA wasn't the sort of man to be trifled with. Simply getting access to him without alerting a dozen different department heads had been an ordeal in itself, forcing Drake to negotiate a minefield of protocol and hidden lines of reporting, not to mention calling in a few favours.

Whether or not it had been a wasted effort hinged on what happened in the next ten minutes.

Hunt glanced at his watch – an old model bearing the US Marine Corps seal – then turned his dark eyes back on Drake. 'All right, Mr Drake. Ten minutes. I suggest you make it good.'

Drake certainly couldn't promise that. The only thing he could guarantee was that it would be worth hearing.

Reaching into his pocket, he produced an electronic device that resembled a small walkie-talkie with several aerials affixed to it, and flicked a switch mounted on the side. A single green light was the only indication that the signal jammer was now active, though anyone trying to use a cell phone or any other communications device within fifty yards would certainly know about it.

Hunt regarded the device with a raised eyebrow. 'That bad, huh?'

Drake gestured to one of the benches nearby. 'You might want to sit down for this.'

He did, and he listened for a lot longer than ten minutes as Drake related the events of the past two years, from the operation to rescue a prisoner named Maras from a Russian jail, to the dirty war being waged by a private military company in Afghanistan and the death of the chief of Russian intelligence last year. And all of it tied together by the legacy of one man: Marcus Cain.

Cain, who was now the Deputy Director of the CIA, and next in line for the top position if the current leader stepped down.

'That's quite a story, son,' Hunt remarked when Drake finally brought his extended narrative to an end. Despite his flippant choice of words, it was clear Drake's tale had nonetheless made an impression on him. 'But why tell it to me?'

The enemy of my enemy is my friend. A very old saying, and one that was often misused in trivial rivalries. In this case however, Drake could only hope that the adage proved true.

If so, he could think of no better enemy for Cain than the man whose position he had usurped two years ago. Hunt himself had once occupied the post of Deputy Director, and been hotly tipped to assume the mantle of leading the world's foremost intelligence agency before too long. That was until an abrupt reshuffle of the Agency's executive level had seen Hunt effectively demoted to divisional leader. Still a position of some power and influence, to be sure, but the message was clear – there was a new star player on the field, and his name was Marcus Cain.

Drake was certain that such a demotion, especially in the closing years of Hunt's career, must have left a deep impact on him. Deep enough, perhaps, for him to aid Drake in destroying the man who had so derailed his plans. It was a rotten trick to use a man's bitterness and resentment for one's own ends, but the chance to win an ally in the highest levels of the Agency's power structure was something Drake couldn't pass up.

'Because I'm not the only one who wants to see Cain take a fall,' Drake answered. 'I know he replaced you as Deputy Director, and I'm guessing it wasn't your decision to step down. He fucked you over, just like he fucked over everyone else he's ever come into contact with. Whatever you were expecting to do with the rest of your life, it's all been taken away because of him. Well, this is your chance to take something back. Help me expose the things he's done. Help me stop him before more innocent people get killed. I can't promise you'll get back everything you've lost, but I can promise he'll lose a lot more than you ever did.'

Drake had never been one for stirring speeches or impassioned monologues. All he could do was set out what he knew, what we wanted, and what Hunt could do to make it happen. It was a gamble, to be sure – this whole meeting had been a leap of faith, in fact – but it was a gamble he felt he had to make.

And now, his sentiments delivered, all he could do was wait for Hunt's reply. It wasn't long in coming.

Whatever reaction he'd expected, it wasn't the fit of laughter that suddenly overcame the man seated beside him. 'And I'm supposed to just take you at your word on all this, right? Some random field agent contacts me out of the blue with wild stories of secret conspiracies and an offer to resurrect my career, and I just leap in with both feet and hope for the best?' Hunt shook his head in disbelief. 'Mr Drake, you're still a young man, so I can forgive a little naiveté on your part, but what you're asking is ridiculous.'

9

And yet, Drake couldn't help but notice that Hunt had made no effort to defend Cain, or to warn him of the treasonous nature of his proposal. Taking his lack of reprimand as tacit acknowledgement that his accusations had merit, Drake pressed on.

'You said you were willing to show a little faith.'

'Faith and blind faith are two different things, son. So far you're not giving me a hell of a lot to put my faith in.'

Drake couldn't blame him for that. 'I'm here. We both know you could have me arrested after everything I've said to you. But I came anyway because I'm willing to risk my life to bring that fucker down. I want to do that, but I can't do it alone. I need people in positions of influence. People who still have the power to hurt him. People I can rely on. People like you.'

'Very touching, but what makes you think you could trust me even if – and this is a big if – I agreed to help you?' Hunt asked.

Drake nodded to the watch on Hunt's left wrist. 'That's a nice watch. You were with the 2nd Battalion, 7th Marine Division in Vietnam. Did two tours. Wounded at Khe Sanh while trying to rescue a squad that was cut off and surrounded, even though you'd been ordered to wait for support. Before that, you petitioned to bring charges against a fellow Marine for terrorizing Vietnamese civilians, even if it meant betraying one of your own.'

If it was important to know your enemy, it was even more so to know a potential friend, as Drake had learned through bitter experience. When he'd first conceived of this plan, he'd spent weeks learning every aspect of Hunt's life and career, probing as deep as he could without being flagged by the Agency. By now he felt as if he knew the man as well as Hunt knew himself.

Reaching into his jacket pocket, the divisional director produced a handkerchief and used it to wipe the perspiration from his brow. 'You've done your homework. Bravo. What's your point?'

'My point is that everything I've learned about you so far tells me you're a good man. You're ready to stand up for what's right, and you're not afraid to risk your own arse to do it. And the fact you still wear that watch tells me you haven't forgotten that. That's why I took the risk to contact you. That's why you haven't walked away, and I think that's why you want to believe in me now.'

'A good man,' Hunt repeated, snorting in derision. 'That's a real nice sentiment, but those things happened a long time ago. Things were different then. There were rules to follow, a code of conduct, a line between right and wrong. Sure, we might step over it on occasion, but it was always there, no matter what.'

He sighed then. A weary sigh of a man fighting an unwinnable battle for far too long. 'Then you get into… this line of work. And you realize the line you put so much faith in never really existed. It only existed in your mind, because *you* wanted to believe in it. You *needed* to believe in it. But all the belief in the world doesn't make something true. The truth is, people can do just about anything they want and get away with it. All they need are three things – the will, the brains, and the right friends. And believe me, Marcus Cain has plenty of all three.' He flashed a grim smile. 'How do you think he became Deputy Director in the first place?'

Drake clenched his fists as he regarded the man seated beside him. 'So he gets away with everything he's done? Is that what you're saying?'

Hunt shot him a piercing look, as if to remind him of who was the more senior here. 'No, that's what *you're* saying. *I'm* saying that you don't take on a man like Cain by making a few half-assed accusations and expecting the world to fall in line behind you.'

'I don't need the world behind me,' Drake insisted. 'But I do need you.'

'To do what, exactly?' Again that weary smile. 'Call the President and have him fire Cain this afternoon? Or maybe haul him up in front of a Congressional hearing, air all the dirty laundry in public?'

'That would work for starters.'

'I'm sure it would, but we both know that's not going to happen. If anything at all is going to come of this, I need to know what you know. First, tell me what actual evidence you've got against Cain.'

'Eyewitness testimonies. Field operatives and Agency personnel that have been coerced into silence by him. All of them are prepared to testify against him.'

'Which means jack shit in situations like this,' Hunt countered. 'Witnesses can be discredited, blackmailed or just made to disappear. I need something real.'

Drake said nothing for several seconds, weighing up how much he could reveal, how much to risk. There was one final card he could play, but it was the kind that could only be played once. There was no telling what reaction it might provoke, but he sensed this was a critical moment. Hunt's faith in him was wavering, his initial interest giving way to scepticism and doubt.

He had to offer something meaningful, and there was only one way to do that.

'I've got Anya,' he said at last.

That was when Hunt's demeanour changed. Like a lucky punch delivered in a losing fight, the tide seemed to turn at that moment. 'She's still alive?' he asked, his voice hushed.

Drake nodded.

'Jesus Christ,' he breathed, letting out a long sigh. 'Where is she?'

Drake gave him a look that made it plain he wasn't going to give such information away to a man he'd just met, no matter how good his character appeared to be. In any case, he couldn't tell Hunt even if he'd wanted to. Anya was a ghost, appearing where and when it served her purpose, and vanishing into the shadows when it didn't. She might have been an ally, but only on her own terms.

'Point taken,' Hunt conceded. 'But will she help?'

Drake glanced away, running a hand through his hair. 'She wants to see Cain go down as much as we do.'

'That's not the same thing.'

'She'll help,' Drake assured him.

Hunt regarded him in thoughtful silence for a few moments. 'Let's say you're right; that everything you've told me is true and that I should trust your word. Even you must understand that it's not about whether you're right or wrong, it's about who's willing to *say* you're right. Who's willing to stand by you, and who's willing to stand by Cain. Who knows they stand to lose so much if he goes down that they'll do everything in their power, take any risk, to stop it happening, because they know that if his lies and secrets are exposed to the world, theirs will be too.'

Drake had heard such dire warnings before. 'I know Cain's got friends in the Agency—'

'I'm not talking about the Agency,' Hunt cut in. 'I'm not talking about Congress or the Pentagon or the White House, or any other building you care to mention.'

'So what *are* you talking about?'

'Wake up, Mr Drake. The real power in this country doesn't lie in buildings that give guided tours, or men who have to answer to oversight committees or voter groups. The real decision makers are the ones you *can't* see, that you don't know about because that's exactly how they choose to make it. They're the ones who stand to lose the most if Cain goes down, and they're the ones who'll do anything it takes to stop it from happening.'

Drake was silent for a moment, searching for a diplomatic way of saying what was on his mind. He was rapidly tiring of the game Hunt seemed to be playing. He'd come here to enlist this man's help, not to listen to riddles and innuendo.

'So who are these people?'

'One step at a time, Mr Drake,' Hunt cautioned him. 'Even I don't know all of them, and I'm certainly not dumb enough to tell you the few I do know. But they're the people who will fight hardest to stop Cain going down, and they're the people we should both be extremely afraid of.'

Drake looked at him. 'And yet, you're still here.'

'I am,' he admitted. 'Because despite everything, despite all the compromises and the little bits of myself I've had to give away over the years, I still remember that line in the sand. I believe... no, I *want* to believe it's still there. And I think you do too.' He rose to his feet with the deliberate effort that his age and build demanded. 'Find me something I can use. Then we'll talk, Mr Drake. For now, that's the best I can offer you.'

Drake sighed and nodded, recognizing Hunt's offer for what it was. He had an ally, a reluctant one who wasn't ready to risk his own neck just yet, but an ally all the same. It certainly wasn't everything he'd hoped for, but it was the best he was going to get.

For now, it would have to suffice.

'I'll be in touch,' Drake promised, slipping his sunglasses back on.

Chapter 2

Freya Shaw blinked her eyes open, her mind returning to awareness.

She was lying on her side in the cargo compartment of a small van. There were no windows that she could see. The sides and floor were simple metal; thin outer panels bolted onto steel reinforcing ribs, interspersed with small holes for latching bungee cords or other devices to stop things rolling around. A single electric light burned overhead; harsh and bright and relentless.

It was obviously a well-used vehicle. The paintwork on the walls had been dented and scratched in countless places by heavy jostling cargo, exposing the dull gleam of bare metal beneath. The floor was covered with dried mud, discarded cigarette butts and pieces of paper that had long since decayed into dried, yellowed pulp. Rust was taking hold in places, slowly eating away at the vehicle's frame like a cancer.

But for all the van's unkempt condition, her captor had clearly taken care to leave nothing in the cargo compartment that could aid a possible escape attempt. No sharp pieces of metal that could slice through the plasticuffs, no tools that could be used as improvized weapons, nothing.

Another hard jolt, this one violent enough to slam her head painfully against the floor. Reluctant to take another pounding, she managed to get her feet beneath her and forced herself up into a sitting position, bracing her back against the side of the van. Each jolting movement seemed to reverberate down her spine, but it was better than being knocked unconscious again.

She flicked her tongue over her lower lip, tasting blood. The left side of her face was throbbing with the dull pain of bruising where she'd been struck by a heavy object. That was the last thing she remembered before darkness had engulfed her.

She closed her eyes for a moment, letting out a silent cry of frustration and fear and impotent anger. She could guess where all this was leading, could anticipate the end that was coming for her, and knew there was nothing she could do to prevent it.

With a final shuddering lurch, the van halted. The rough growl of the engine ceased a moment later, and the light went out, plunging the cabin into darkness.

Trying to still her wildly beating heart, Freya held her breath and strained to listen. She could hear footsteps outside, and the jangle of keys being removed from a pocket. With a click, a lock was disengaged and the rear doors swung open on creaking hinges. Cool night air rushed in, and she could feel moisture on her exposed skin.

A dark figure clambered up into the cabin and strong hands grabbed her under her armpits, hauling her to her feet. She could do little to resist as she was forced out of the van and into the waiting darkness beyond.

They had halted in a patch of waste ground; Freya knew that right away, from the towering walls of an old factory in the distance, broken concrete crumbling away to expose rusted steel reinforcing rods beneath. Gravel and loose stones crunched beneath her feet as she was led down a slope away from the van. The ground was treacherous, and she briefly lost her footing as the stones beneath her gave way, only for her captor to pull her upright.

'It doesn't have to be this way, you know. You don't have to do this. I'm worth more to you alive,' she said, knowing how futile and pathetic her words must have sounded. How many times had her captor heard those same words, uttered by desperate men and women in the final moments of their lives?

At the bottom of the slope, dark muddy water glimmered in the faint moonlight. Rainwater that had collected over time in the depression. A yank at her arm brought her to a halt about half way down.

'Get on your knees,' a cold, clinical voice instructed her.

Freya swallowed hard, knowing what was coming. She'd known the moment she'd awoken in that van. This was where she'd been brought to die.

For a moment she caught herself wondering who would eventually find her body out here. A labourer on his way to work? A kid out playing with friends? Some guy taking his dog for a walk?

She knew it was ludicrous to be thinking of such things, yet she couldn't stop herself. She had faced danger more than once in what had been a long and eventful life, had even seen death up close and personal, yet for all those experiences she never could have imagined such an end for herself.

Dying out here in some muddy hole in the ground, unmarked, unknown, uncared for. It didn't seem real. It was a dream, a nightmare, a feverish imagining conjured up by a restless mind.

'No,' she said, forcing the word out through gritted teeth even as her heart thundered in her chest. 'I won't.'

Yanking her arm free, Freya turned around to face her adversary, eyes gleaming with defiance. She wouldn't give them the satisfaction of putting a bullet through her head from behind.

'You look me in the eye, you coward,' she said, staring right at them. 'Look me in the eye when you pull the trigger.'

If she'd expected her words to strike a chord, to engender some kind of reaction, she was to be disappointed. A second came and went. A second broken only by the sigh of the evening breeze, and distant hoot of an owl, and the hammering of Freya's heart.

'You shouldn't have come looking for me.'

She saw the barrel of a weapon raised, saw the long snout of a silencer gleaming in the thin sliver of moonlight.

Freya let out a breath. 'Of all the people, I never—'

A 9mm slug passing through her chest silenced that sentence before she had a chance to complete it. She let out a strangled gasp, as if in surprise, then fell backward and collapsed to the ground, her body skidding down the rocky slope until it came to rest in the pool of stagnant water.

As darkness closed in around her, Freya's last thought was one of simple, heartfelt regret.

Ryan, I'm sorry.

--

George Washington University Hospital, Virginia

Like most people, Drake had no great love of hospitals. He'd spent more than his share of time in them over the course of his career, having been wounded numerous times in the line of duty, and had few pleasant memories of those stays.

Today however he was here not for himself, but for a friend.

'You know, it doesn't matter how much plastic surgery you get,' he said, pasting on some fake joviality as he entered the private room. 'You'll always be an ugly bastard.'

Dan Franklin, the current head of the Agency's Special Activities Division, and a man Drake had long considered a close friend, was sitting upright in the bed, propped up by several pillows while he flicked idly through the channels of the wall-mounted TV opposite. He looked about as bored and listless as a man could be, and yet seemed to perk up immediately on Drake's arrival.

'Well, shit. And here was me thinking how much I'd kill for some intelligent conversation. Be sure to send someone in when you leave, okay?'

He was grinning at the playful banter, but Drake could see the pain etched into his features. It seemed to have become a constant companion of his in recent years, and the toll it was taking was becoming harder to ignore.

'I'll do that.' Reaching into the plastic bag he'd brought with him, Drake laid some issues of *Time* and *Newsweek* on the bedside table. 'Here, this should keep you going for a while. Now, there's some big words in there, so if you get stuck, be sure to call one of the nurses to help you.'

Franklin made a face. 'Wasn't planning on being here that long.'

Pulling up a chair, Drake sat down opposite him.

'Seriously, though, how are you doing, mate?' he asked, surveying his friend honestly for the first time in a long time. He'd aged noticeably, Drake realized almost in surprise. Franklin was only a few years older than himself, but he looked at least a decade more. There were lines around the corners of his mouth and eyes that hadn't been there a just a few short years ago, his dark blonde hair now had faint streaks of silver at the sides, and recent weight-loss had left his face looking sallow and gaunt.

He shrugged with grim resignation. 'The consultants came in today. Apparently I have the vertebrae of a 90-year-old with arthritis. They're recommending spinal-fusion surgery.'

Drake felt his heart sink. The two of them had once served together in Afghanistan. Both young, both strong and ambitious and competitive, until a roadside bomb had ended Franklin's military career. Shrapnel embedded in his spine had required hours of surgery and months of difficult rehab, and left him in near-constant pain that had worsened noticeably in recent years.

Proud to the last and weary of rehabilitation, he'd refused further medical intervention until the bitter end. Only when he'd started experiencing numbness in his legs and difficulty walking had he finally ceded to the inevitable and sought treatment.

'Will that fix it?' he asked, knowing how stupid and simplistic such a question must have sounded, as if the human body were a car engine in which one could just swap out defective parts.

Franklin gave him a weary smile. 'Maybe. That's what they told me – maybe. Then again, it could also leave me paralysed from the chest down. Either way, I'd be out of action with the Agency for weeks, if not months.'

At this, Drake actually let out a laugh. 'Dan, the free world will survive without you for a few weeks. If that's what you're worried about, put it out of your head right now.'

'And where will that leave you?' Franklin asked, lowering his voice. 'We both know the deal here. If I'm laid up in a hospital bed, I can't protect you.'

Drake was all too aware that the man sitting before him was about the only thing that had kept Cain from having him assassinated these past couple of years. The deal he had struck not to reveal Cain's part in the hijacking of American drones and the subsequent murder of innocent civilians had maintained an uneasy status quo. But both parties were starting to realize that this truce couldn't last forever.

And if something happened to Franklin, it wouldn't take long for the sword to fall.

Leaning in closer, Drake looked his friend hard in the eye. 'Mate, I want you to listen to me very carefully. This isn't about me now. This isn't about the Agency or Cain or any of that other stuff – this is about you. You're hurting, I can see that, and you need help. You can't go on like this. So get yourself sorted out before it's too late, for God sake. We'll deal with the rest later.'

Franklin swallowed and looked away for a moment. 'That's not the only reason, Ryan,' he admitted. 'Ever since this happened, I feel like I've been living on borrowed time, like there was a bomb ticking away inside me and every day I've been waiting for it to go off. Now we're down to it, I'm... scared shitless. Not of dying, but living as a cripple, pissing into a bag for the rest of my life, having people pity me. I can't live like that. I don't... I don't have what it takes to make it through that.'

Drake felt terrible for his friend. He shared some of the man's apprehension of what lay ahead, felt his frustration at watching his physical abilities slowly dwindle.

And beneath it all, he felt something else. Guilt. Guilt that it had happened to Franklin and not him. Guilt that it had been his friend's Humvee that had triggered that roadside bomb. Guilt that Franklin had put off this surgery for so long out of loyalty and duty, when Drake had done so little for him in return.

What could he possibly say to the man? If it were him, would he have the courage to go through with surgery that could leave him paralysed for life? What reassurance could he offer?

'You deserve your life back, mate,' he said at last. 'If this is your best – your only – chance to get it, then there's no choice to make, is there?'

Franklin held his gaze for a long moment, as if still wrestling with the matter in his mind. Then, reluctantly, he reached for the magazines that Drake had brought him.

'Let's see what crap you brought,' he conceded, his voice carrying an undertone of grim determination. 'Might need it if I'm going to be here a while.'

–

Drake was in a less than jovial mood when he returned to his home in Fairfax just west of central DC later that evening, having stopped off to buy a crate of beer and enough burgers, steaks and sausages to feed a small army; which in reality was pretty much what he was about to do.

A busy day at Langley followed by his visit to Franklin's hospital room had left him running late, and as he pulled into his driveway he let out a sigh of exasperation at the sight of two cars and a motorbike already parked up in front of his house.

'Shit.'

There was no sign of the drivers, and for a moment he wondered if his teammates had decided to bin the whole thing and head to the nearest bar instead. However, as soon as he killed the engine and stepped out into the evening air, the sound of music blaring from the back yard told him they had decided to start the party of their own accord.

Grabbing the beers from the passenger seat and piling the pre-packed food awkwardly on top, Drake hurried around the side of the house, nudging open the side gate with his foot.

Sure enough, Cole Mason, Samantha McKnight and Keira Frost were already in the unkempt square of grass that he called a back yard, armed with drinks of their own. The rear door of the house was wide open, the hi-fi from his kitchen resting awkwardly on a chair with a power cord trailing back inside.

'Well, look who decided to show up!' Mason said when he spotted Drake. He held his beer up in a mock salute. 'Good of you to arrive late for your own party, man. I was getting ready to order take-out.'

'I was getting ready to raid your fridge,' Frost chipped in.

'Looks like you already started,' Drake said, glancing at the beer she'd apparently helped herself to. 'I don't remember giving you a key.'

The young woman shrugged, entirely unconcerned. 'It's our job to break into places. As far as it goes, yours was pretty easy. You should get someone to look into that.' She downed a mouthful of beer as if to emphasize her point. 'By the way, your music collection sucks. Had to resort to the radio.'

Drake cocked his head, listening to the Black Eyed Peas blaring out. 'This what the kids are listening to these days?' he asked with a wry grin.

He saw a flash of anger in her eyes at his implied insult. 'How the fuck should I know, Ryan?'

Keira Frost was now in her early thirties, but her short stature and diminutive frame made her look years younger. Much to her annoyance, she was often still asked for ID when buying alcohol – something that provided Drake no end of amusement, and which he made a point of reminding her about at every opportunity.

'Anyway, you were the one who arranged this thing,' she reminded him. 'Then you disappear and stop answering your cell. What happened?'

Drake glanced away. He'd turned off his cell phone in the hospital and must have forgotten to switch it back on again. 'I was visiting Dan.'

McKnight approached him. 'How's he doing?'

'Ask me in a few days when he gets out of surgery,' he said, powering his phone up.

'That bad, huh?' Mason asked. Having been wounded in the line of duty himself, and endured a difficult and lengthy rehabilitation, he understood Franklin's situation better than most.

Drake said nothing to this.

'Well, you're here now,' McKnight said, sensing his discomfort and moving to change the subject. 'What do you say we get drunk and burn some food?'

Despite the tension of his earlier meeting with his friend, Drake couldn't help but smile a little. God knew, he could use a drink after today.

In short order, Drake had fired up the gas barbecue set against one wall of the yard, and set some of the meat to cooking on the grill. He hardly considered himself a gourmet chef, but even he could work a barbecue without too much difficulty, and before long the group descended on the grilled meat like they hadn't eaten in a week.

Food, drink and banter are a good combination at any time, and the atmosphere soon became relaxed and jovial, Drake's earlier tardiness quite forgotten. With the drink flowing, it wasn't long before they were swapping old stories of past exploits, many of which they'd heard before, but which always seemed to get more entertaining the more they had to drink.

Even Drake found himself enjoying the company, and was beginning to appreciate the merits of hosting such a get-together with his teammates. It was an idea borrowed from their fallen companion John Keegan, who had been killed during a mission in Afghanistan the previous year.

Keegan had made a point of inviting the team to his place for dinner, either to celebrate the successful end of another operation, or just as an excuse to eat and drink. In truth, most of the food he produced looked like it had seen the business end of a flame-thrower, usually prompting mockery and jibes from the rest of the team, but perhaps that had been part of the fun. Perhaps it had even been Keegan's intention all along, Drake reflected as he sat on his back doorstep, comfortably full and slightly drunk as he stared up at the evening sky.

If nothing else, he hoped the man himself approved of his efforts.

His philosophical musings were interrupted when McKnight approached, easing herself down next to him.

'So what's the verdict?' Drake asked.

'Nobody's dead yet,' she acknowledged with a sly smile. 'Could have been worse.'

Drake glanced at her. 'You're flattering me. I don't suppose Jamie Oliver needs to start job-hunting just yet.'

'Who?'

'He's a British...' Drake began, then thought better of it. 'Never mind.'

She seemed content to let that slide. Instead she took a drink of beer and glanced over at Mason and Frost, who were in the midst of an animated conversation that seemed to lie somewhere between the shared telling of an anecdote and a full-blown argument. Knowing Frost, it was probably a little of both.

Still, both of them seemed to be enjoying it.

'Thanks for doing this, Ryan,' McKnight said quietly. 'Having everyone here. It's... well, it means something.'

'You've all done a lot for me – more than I had any right to ask.' He flashed a grin. 'The least I can do is burn some cheap burgers for you.'

This prompted a laugh, though it soon quietened as her expression turned more serious. She leaned a little closer, her hazel-coloured eyes searching his. 'Did you hear anything more from Hunt?'

Drake shook his head. It had been several days since his meeting with the former Deputy Director at Arlington; days that had been ominously quiet for all of them. In truth, he didn't expect to hear much from the man, when he'd made it plain he wouldn't act until Drake had something concrete he could use.

'Do you really trust him? What if tries to screw us over?'

The thought had crossed his mind more than a few times. Despite his rigorous background checks, despite the research and the observation and even the gut instinct that told him Charles Hunt was of a different sort from Cain, he couldn't deny the possibility that this could all go terribly wrong.

'As far as he knows, I'm working alone,' he said, knowing that wasn't what she was really asking him. 'I'm the only one he can screw over.'

'You know you're not alone, right?' she said, her voice soft and quiet now.

He could feel McKnight's eyes on him, but tried not to look at her. He knew his answer wouldn't have satisfied her, and that she might mistake his effort to protect her for mistrust, but it was better than the alternative. Until he knew where things led with Hunt, the rest of the team stayed out of it.

McKnight opened her mouth to say something else, but before she could speak, Drake felt his cell phone vibrating in his pocket. He reached in and fished it out, ready to reject the call if it was anything work-related, but instead frowned when he saw the caller ID.

'What is it, George?' Drake answered, making no effort to hide his irritation.

With Franklin out of action, George Breckenridge had taken over as head of the Shepherd Programme, effectively becoming Drake's immediate superior. Drake knew little of the man's background except that he'd never been a field agent, his talents lying instead in management and administrative work. In a nutshell, this meant climbing the corporate ladder, taking credit for other people's work and ingratiating himself with the Agency's higher echelons of command.

His new – if temporary – position saw him managing half a dozen Shepherd teams and coordinating all regional activity within the programme. In Drake's opinion, they couldn't have picked a worse candidate for the job.

A difficult and fractious man at the best of times, Breckenridge had taken an immediate dislike to Drake and his team. The animosity between the two men had only intensified since Franklin's admission to hospital. Without Dan there to mediate, Drake had a feeling things were only going to get worse.

'Drake, we need you to come into the office,' came the brisk summons. 'As soon as you can.'

Breckenridge always made a point of calling him Drake, for the same reason Drake called him George – because he knew it pissed him off.

'I'm busy,' Drake replied, feeling neither the desire nor the responsibility to elaborate. Fuck it – it had been a long day, he was tired and in no mood for talking shop, especially not with a man like this.

'Do I sound like I give a shit?' Breckenridge hit back. 'I'll make this simple. Find your way here within the hour, or find yourself a new job.'

Without waiting for a reply, he hung up.

Drake let out an exasperated breath, along with a muttered curse. He could have sworn the bastard timed these calls specifically to cause maximum irritation.

'That was... to the point,' McKnight remarked. 'What did he want?'

'Take one guess,' Drake said, rising from his makeshift seat.

Chapter 3

Despite having only clocked off a few hours earlier, Drake once more found himself back at Langley, nursing a cup of coffee and a bad attitude as he made his way through the labyrinth of corridors and small offices that made up the New Headquarters Building. Being on the wrong end of several beers, he'd been forced to hire a taxi from his home in Fairfax. His government security clearance might have worked in his favour at times, but he suspected it didn't cover drink-driving.

Breckenridge had messaged him advising him to report to his office rather than one of the briefing or conference rooms in the building's upper levels, which puzzled Drake. Then again, it could just have been his boss wanting to show off.

Halting outside the door, Drake took another deep swig of strong, bitter-tasting coffee. He'd rather have downed a glass of whisky before dealing with a man like this, but doubted it would do many favours for his professional conduct.

Thus armed, he pushed open the door and strode in without bothering to knock.

His first impression was how different this office was from the cramped, cluttered, untidy cubicle in which he did much of his own work. There were no handwritten sticky notes plastered everywhere, no printed sheets and case files cluttering his desk, no coffee-cup stains on the expensive wood surfaces. Everything was very neat, very tidy, very clinical and precise.

Unlike himself, Breckenridge had embraced the digital revolution with open arms, and was happy to use his government expense account to indulge his passion for technology.

Everywhere Drake looked he saw high-end laptops and associated paraphernalia, the latest iPhone charging on Breckenridge's desk, and the ubiquitous tablet computer he carried around like a preacher's bible. On one occasion Drake had even witnessed him conducting a call via Bluetooth headset despite both his hands being free.

The big plasma-screen TV mounted on the wall behind him was tuned to Bloomberg, with the latest share prices flashing across the bottom of the screen. Breckenridge liked to stay on top of his business news, though God only knew why. As Drake had learned through Frost's online snooping, he had no investment portfolio to speak of.

'Didn't you ever learn to knock?' he demanded, distracted from whatever he'd been working on by Drake's sudden arrival.

In stark contrast to the pristine office and high technology that surrounded him, Breckenridge himself looked very much like what he was – a tired and stressed man fighting a losing battle against middle age. Paunchy, with greying hair, a florid complexion and perpetually furrowed brow, he'd always reminded Drake of Richard Nixon on a bad day.

Drake shrugged. 'You said you needed me here as soon as possible. Here I am.'

The older man regarded him for a long moment in strained, uncomfortable silence. Then, perhaps trying to assert his professional cool, he gestured to an empty chair.

'Take a seat.'

Drake did so, feeling like an unruly student hauled into the principal's office. 'What can I do for you, George?' he asked, laying his coffee down on the desk.

'You can start by using a goddamn coaster,' his superior replied irritably, sliding one his way. 'That desk is Carpathian elm, and it costs more than your monthly salary.'

'It's a very nice desk,' Drake said, making no move to use the coaster. 'Now would you care to tell me why I'm here?'

Breckenridge eyed him in brooding silence for a few moments longer before turning his attention back to his computer. With a few keystrokes, Bloomberg disappeared from the TV behind him, replaced by what looked like a surveillance picture of a man leaving a rundown apartment building.

The subject in question looked to be Middle Eastern, in his mid thirties, well-built and with a few days of stubble coating his jaw. His hair was long and unruly, tied back in a crude ponytail. He had a cell phone pressed against his ear, but seemed to be keeping a wary eye on his surroundings.

'Say hello to Khaled Arazi. Or, as we know him, Ifzal Fayed,' Breckenridge began. 'He's a captain in the Libyan army, and a former asset of ours.'

Drake glanced at his boss. 'What's his deal?'

'We recruited him about a year ago on the promise that he had contacts within their military-intelligence service. He claimed he could supply viable intel about ISI commanders operating out of Libya, supported by Gaddafi.'

The mention of ISI was enough to get Drake's attention. al-Qaeda might have been decimated by eight years of attritional warfare, coordinated assassinations and drone strikes, but where one enemy fell, a new one was always waiting in the wings – in this case, the Islamic State of Iraq, better known as ISI.

Less a terrorist network and more a legitimate military force in their own right, they had risen seemingly out of nowhere in the chaos of post-invasion Iraq, capturing key cities and vast swathes of territory, and forcing the US to once more deploy troops in the region to help the beleaguered Iraqi army. A hard-fought campaign had seen them driven out of their desert strongholds, but the victory had been a hollow one at best. Lacking the resources and the political will to pursue their fleeing enemy, the US could do little more than consolidate their position.

Meanwhile ISI's central leadership were rumoured to have retreated into Syria, Jordan and even North Africa, where they were reorganizing and rebuilding their forces for a renewed campaign.

'Supported by Gaddafi?' Drake repeated. 'I thought he was on our side now. Why help ISI when he knows it would incite a war against us?'

Breckenridge snorted in amusement. 'Gaddafi's on no one's side but his own. He might have cozied up to us since we toppled Hussein, but it's no secret that he still sponsors terrorist networks and revolutionaries all across the world. He spends more money financing foreign groups than he does on his own people. The stupid bastard probably doesn't even know who he supports from one day to the next. In any case, even if he's not in on it, there could well be elements within his government who are. Fayed was supposed to be our way of separating fact from fiction.'

'So what happened?'

'The Agency paid him generously for leads on key ISI commanders operating in the country, but after six months of feeding us useless, outdated bullshit, he went dark, took the money and ran. Since then we've tracked him sporadically through Romania, Hungary and Austria, but this is the first time he's stayed anywhere longer than a day or two. NSA intercepted a phone call matching his voice signature in Paris earlier today, and we think we have a location. Looks like he's set up shop there.'

Drake imagined it had taken no small measure of hard work and resourcefulness to track a man like Fayed, who clearly wanted to disappear. Then again, the Agency was known to be very hard-working when it came to finding people who took their money and fucked them over.

'So you want Fayed brought in,' he said, feeling no need to phrase it as a question.

Breckenridge nodded. 'We need him alive and talking, and preferably without the French government's knowledge. Maybe then we can get some real answers from him, and our money back.'

It didn't take a genius to guess what would happen to Fayed after that. The Agency weren't exactly known for their forgiving attitude towards traitors.

Drake didn't care too much about the man's fate, if he was honest with himself. Live by the sword, and all that. What he did care about was why he of all people had been summoned here for what seemed like a simple snatch-and-grab operation.

'Why us?' he asked. 'Surely there must be other teams that can handle this?'

Breckenridge tilted his head. 'Oh, I'm sorry. Is this sort of thing beneath you, Drake?'

'That's not what I meant.'

'Good, because after the crap you pulled last year, you're lucky you're not pacing a cell in Guantanamo Bay, never mind still working for the Agency.' He let out a sigh of frustration. 'And as it happens, there isn't anyone else available. The directors don't like all the floating resources we're taking up, so a lot of our specialists are being siphoned off into other programmes. We're down on manpower, and as much as it pains me to say this, you're the best of what we've got.'

The Shepherd programme maintained a cadre of permanent team leaders like Drake, but the bulk of their manpower was made up of specialists who could be brought in as and when they were needed. The downside was that these skilled operatives were therefore unavailable for other tasks.

'That makes me feel very special, George. Thanks.'

Breckenridge gave him a disdainful look, then slid a printed dossier across the desk to him. 'Everything you need on Fayed is in there. We have a plane standing by at Andrews; wheels up in four hours. Get your team together and get on it. Questions?'

How the fuck did you get this job? That was the most pertinent and polite question that came to mind, though Drake decided not to voice it.

'Good,' Breckenridge said, taking his silence for compliance. 'Don't forget to take your coffee with you.'

Chapter 4

With its wide, tree-lined boulevards and rich architectural heritage dating back over a thousand years, Paris had long been considered a jewel amongst Europe's capital cities; a place that had inspired the dreams of romantics, artists and connoisseurs of every kind, from every country.

But for Drake, crouched in the shadows of a dimly lit stairwell that smelled of stale urine and damp, it was an entirely different prospect. The rundown residential apartment block in which he found himself was, in contrast to the ornate architecture the city was known for, a product of cheap 1940s utilitarianism. Stark, bleak and inhabited by people who clearly wished they were living somewhere else, it certainly wasn't the kind of place he'd visit by choice.

But sightseeing was the last thing on his mind tonight. If the Agency's intelligence was to be believed, then his target, Ifzal Fayed, was living in one of these shitty apartments at this very moment.

So here they were in the city's 18th arrondissement; one of the least desirable areas of Paris due to its high crime rates, low-quality housing and sheer distance from the city centre. But with a high proportion of North African immigrants, he supposed Fayed's choice of safe house made sense.

Drake was disturbed from these thoughts by noises coming from one of the apartments that backed onto the stairwell; a rhythmic pounding accompanied by strained grunts and cries that could only mean one thing. Either the walls here were paper-thin, or the couple going at it were trying to put their neighbours to shame.

'Someone give her a medal,' Cole Mason remarked, flashing a wry grin in the gloomy stairwell as the woman's cries reached a merciful crescendo. 'Sounds like she earned it tonight.'

Like Drake, he was wearing a dark brown shirt, trousers and jacket that wouldn't win any awards in the style stakes, but which neatly completed their cover as delivery men. True, not many companies delivered packages at two o'clock in the morning, but they needed some kind of reason for being here in case a curious resident spotted them.

It also explained why McKnight and Frost, the other two members of his team, were parked in an alleyway outside in a truck commonly used by delivery firms. The cargo they were here to collect was likely to be a little less cooperative than what FedEx were used to transporting, but then that was what the Agency paid them for.

'What do you think?' Mason prompted, nodding toward the source of the noise. 'Girlfriend, or paid for?'

'Could be married, for all you know,' Drake mumbled.

Mason gave him a look of pity. 'Dude, no married couple makes that kind of noise.'

'Wouldn't know,' he replied, reaching for the little radio unit fixed to his throat. Right now he had far more important matters on his mind. 'Unit One to Overwatch, do you have eyes on target?'

In the rain-soaked alleyway down below, their technical specialist, Frost, was seated in the cargo compartment of the delivery truck, hunched over a portable computer terminal while water drummed on the truck's steel roof. In her hands was a remote-control unit of the kind normally used to pilot radio-controlled planes, and in this case the reality wasn't much different.

Hovering in the night sky under her guidance was a miniature surveillance drone, designed for use in urban environments just like this. About a foot wide, roughly diamond-shaped and with a rotor blade mounted at each corner, it certainly wasn't an elegant-looking aircraft. In fact, to a casual observer it probably resembled a child's toy rather than an advanced piece of remote-surveillance equipment, but its role in situations like this made it invaluable.

The little four-bladed helicopter was hovering about fifteen feet out from the wall of Fayed's apartment building; close enough to allow its operator to see into the dwellings but far enough away that the faint whir of its electric engines wouldn't disturb the inhabitants.

'Stand by, One,' Frost replied, gently manipulating the drone's guidance stick to increase its altitude.

Staring intently at the grainy image being transmitted from the drone's digital video camera, Frost watched as weathered brickwork gave way to a window ledge, its paintwork noticeably peeling and covered with bird droppings.

She had to hurry. With a battery life of less than thirty minutes to consider, she couldn't afford to leave the drone on station for long, but hopefully it would stay aloft long enough to give them the confirmation that Fayed was on site.

'Shit,' she said under her breath, applying left stick to steady the drone as a sudden breeze blew it slightly off course. One of the drawbacks to these little aircraft was that it didn't take much to bring them down.

'Problems?' McKnight called from the cab up front.

'Nothing I can't handle.'

Keeping the drone under tight control, she resumed her climb, slowly bringing the aircraft level with Fayed's window. As she'd hoped, a set of blinds had been lowered but not closed, permitting her a slightly truncated view of the living room beyond. The overhead lights were switched off, most of the illumination coming from the glow of a TV screen or computer monitor.

'Overwatch has eyes on the apartment,' she said over the radio.

'Any sign of him?'

'Not yet. I see a laptop switched on. Stand by, One.'

'Copy that.'

Up front, McKnight was sitting in the truck's driver seat, waiting in anxious silence for confirmation from Frost that they could move. The delivery truck was about as good a ruse as they could hope for in an urban area like this, but every moment they spent here increased the chance of being compromised.

She was quite certain that Drake and Mason were entertaining similar thoughts. At such an early hour, there wasn't much chance of encountering anyone on the stairwell, but that didn't mean it couldn't happen.

At least the poor weather conditions would help keep people indoors. The steady drumming of rain against the windshield had been their constant companion since they'd started tonight's operation, and it showed no signs of slacking off.

No sooner had this thought crossed her mind than life stepped in to prove her wrong.

Catching movement in her rear-view mirror, McKnight glanced around in time to see a figure moving through the shadows of the alleyway. Straightaway her hand went for the silenced automatic hidden beneath her seat.

Their orders were to avoid armed confrontations at all costs. That being said, Shepherd teams were trained to defend themselves if need be. There was no telling if Fayed had people watching his back, if this was some local thug out looking for trouble, or simply an innocent bystander on his way home.

'Three has eyes on possible contact,' she said, keeping her voice calm and controlled. There was no need to panic at this stage; she knew what she was dealing with. 'In the alleyway, moving up.'

'Hostile?' That was Drake, an edge of tension in his voice now.

'Unknown. Stand by.'

In the back, Frost leaned a little closer to the screen, straining to make out details through the poor-quality video feed. The drone's modest size meant it could only carry a small payload, which in this case translated into low image-quality. Still, it was enough for her to make out the basic layout of the sparsely furnished apartment.

Suddenly the interior of the truck resounded with a heavy metallic *thunk* as something struck the outer panelling hard. Frost jerked back on instinct, momentarily losing control of the drone, which pitched sideways and threatened to impact the building.

'What the fuck?' she hissed, struggling to regain control. It went against her instincts to sit there and do nothing with a possible confrontation brewing outside, but in this case there was little choice. It was her job to pilot the drone, and McKnight's job to watch her back while she did so.

'Just some drunken asshole,' McKnight called back as the truck reverberated once again, accompanied by a jeering call from outside.

'Well, I'm having kind of a hard time concentrating,' Frost said tersely. 'Can you do something about it?'

McKnight was already moving. Leaving the automatic where it was, she selected a different weapon from the glove compartment, swung open her door and leapt down from the cab to face the intruder.

The source of the disturbance, an overweight man in his mid thirties, was clearly on the wrong end of a heavy night out, judging by his dishevelled hair, unsteady gait and beer stains on his shirt and jeans. At least, she assumed it was beer.

He was leaning heavily against the side of the van, balancing himself with one hand while he urinated against the rear wheel with the other. The banging seemed to be caused by his head lolling forward and striking the metal panelling as he struggled to stay awake.

'What do you think you're doing?' she demanded, employing the slightly rusty French she'd learned in school years earlier. One hand was behind her back, gripping the electric taser that she'd pushed down the back of her trousers. 'Get out of here before I call the police.'

Unfocussed, bloodshot eyes turned slowly in her direction, registering a moment of surprise before moving up and down her body with the brazen disregard for modesty that only alcohol could impart. Zipping himself up with difficulty, he turned to face her.

'Sorry, I was… I couldn't find the restroom.' He laughed at what he seemed to think was blinding humour. 'What's a beautiful girl like you doing out here so late?'

'Working,' she retorted, trying to mask her distaste. 'Now get lost.'

'But we only just met.'

'And now we part ways. Go home and leave the van alone.'

With that, she turned and made to return to the cab. Come on, just fuck off now, she silently prayed.

'Hold on! Don't go yet, we were just getting to know each other,' he called out, stumbling to catch up. 'I'm sorry for pissing on your truck. I didn't mean to—'

He was silenced abruptly as McKnight whirled around, jabbed the taser into the centre of his chest and pulled the trigger. There was no thought of resisting or fighting her off; thousands of volts of electricity were coursing through his nervous system, overriding whatever signals his drunken brain was still sending out.

He went down straightaway, collapsing in a heap amongst the discarded trash that littered the alleyway. Unable to cry out, he could manage only a low groan as his body continued to convulse.

McKnight kept the trigger held down for a few more seconds before finally releasing him. She'd given him a fair chance to leave, but he hadn't taken it. His loss.

'When a girl asks you to leave, you leave,' she said under her breath.

Kneeling down beside him, she wrapped one arm around his neck, braced herself and pulled tight on it. It didn't take him long to realize that something bad was happening, but his panicked struggles amounted to little more than some weak and incoherent flailing that certainly wouldn't break her hold.

She kept up the pressure until his struggles eased as the oxygen supply to his brain was interrupted, and finally he blacked out. Satisfied that she'd done enough, she released her grip and reached out to feel for a pulse. It was fast and shallow, but it was there.

With luck, he'd wake up in a couple of hours, groggy and hung over, and probably with no memory of the encounter.

She and the rest of the team would be long gone by then.

Reaching up, she keyed her radio. 'All clear here.'

Meanwhile Frost had guided the drone back into position to resume its electronic vigil by the apartment window.

'Come on, asshole,' she whispered, staring intently at the screen as if she could will him to appear. 'Come out, come out, wherever you are.'

'Overwatch, sitrep,' Drake prompted. She could tell he was getting impatient. He and Mason were geared up and ready to move, adrenaline flowing, nerves taut, but instead they were being forced to stand by and do nothing.

'Still waiting for – shit, got movement!' she hissed, spotting a figure moving through the dimly lit apartment. She would have killed for night vision at that moment.

'Overwatch, what do you see?'

'Stand by.' Clenching her teeth, Frost forced herself to stay calm as she gently adjusted the drone's position, correcting for little swirls of air that were moving it back and forth.

There! A figure suddenly moved into frame, settling himself into a chair facing the laptop, his features now cast into sharp relief by the electronic glow. A man, late thirties, muscular build with a thickening midsection, his head crowned by an unruly tangle of dark curls. In the space of two seconds she compared the face in the grainy video feed with the one she had committed to memory before the operation, looking for differences, variations, distinguishing features that might separate them.

She found none.

'Confirmed. Target on site.'

That was all the confirmation Drake needed. 'Copy that. Moving in.'

Signalling to Mason that they were good to go, he ascended the stairwell to the level just above them, and pushed open the fire door to the dimly lit hallway beyond. Mason was close behind, carrying a few essential tools in a canvas holdall slung over one shoulder.

The door they were looking for was apartment 313. Counting down the numbers on each side, Drake moved forward at a steady, confident pace. There was little sense in creeping along inch by inch, since the chances of the hallway being booby trapped were remote to say the least.

'Coming up,' Mason said quietly, indicating the next door on their left.

They had rehearsed the next part several times, so there was no need to talk. Laying the holdall down, he unzipped it and pulled the top open. Stowed inside were a pair of heavy-duty bolt cutters, a taser, and a single concrete brick.

Mason took the taser while Drake helped himself to the other items, and together the two men advanced the last few feet to the apartment door.

'Call it out, Overwatch,' Drake prompted, lowering himself into a crouching position and placing the brick on the floor beside his left foot. Mason hunkered down beside him, keeping the taser at the ready.

Hollywood would have people believe that they could use some kind of tranquiliser gun to immobilise their target within seconds, but if such a weapon existed then Drake had yet to hear about it. Even the best sedatives designed to bring down big-game animals took several minutes to kick in; minutes during which Fayed could scream, call for help, grab for a concealed weapon or do any one of a hundred things to completely ruin their day.

No, the only reliable methods of taking someone down quickly were either to shoot them or tase them. Since they'd been instructed to return Fayed alive, their choice for this job was obvious.

'Copy, One. Ready when you are.'

Mason gave a nod to confirm the taser was primed and ready to fire. Gripping the bolt cutters and checking that his foot was just touching the brick, Drake reached out and knocked on the door. Not loud or aggressive; just the simple knock of a new arrival announcing their presence.

A few seconds of strained silence passed.

'He's moving, One,' Frost announced. 'Heading for the door.'

Drake paused, readying himself. When it happened, he would have to act fast. A mistake from either himself or Mason might give Fayed time to barricade himself into his apartment, forcing them to use a far louder and more dangerous method of entry. Since their briefing had been to effect a covert extraction of the target, that would not be a good thing. It would also drastically increase their chances of being apprehended by the local gendarme, which would be an even worse thing.

Shepherd teams were by their nature deniable operators, meaning they could expect no support from the Agency, the State Department or anyone else in the US government if they were captured. Drake had little desire to sit out the rest of his career in a French prison.

The next several seconds passed in silence, save for the loud thumping of Drake's heart as he gripped the bolt cutters, ready to spring into action. The waiting was always the hardest part of any op like this. Danger and problems he could deal with, but waiting for something to happen was enough to test anyone's nerves.

'He's at the door.'

The seconds stretched out, yet Fayed gave no sign of opening up.

Drake caught Mason's eye, the simple look conveying everything he needed to say. What was Fayed waiting for?

'Target's on the move, heading back to the living room,' Frost reported.

Drake glanced up at the door, taking note of the spy hole mounted in the centre. Likely Fayed had glanced out into the corridor, seen nobody and assumed it had simply been a prank.

Fortunately the solution to this kind of stubbornness was simple. *If at first you don't succeed*, Drake thought, knocking again.

'Target's on the move again,' Frost advised. 'Watch yourself, One. He could be armed.'

Drake almost smiled. In situations like this, the power of frustration is never to be underestimated. It usually doesn't take much to annoy most people into dropping their guard, even if they're not aware of it.

'Almost at the door.'

Their limited intel on Fayed suggested he had travelled alone, and had neither a wife nor a girlfriend, but there was no telling who might be here. For all they knew, the nominees for lovers of the year that they'd heard from the stairwell earlier could have been Fayed and a local lady of the night.

Drake tensed and flexed his fingers as he heard the click of a lock being undone. A moment later, the door moved inward a couple of inches before stopping on its security chain. In the gap, Drake saw a fleshy, unshaven face staring out into the hallway.

It happened fast, just as they had rehearsed. Kicking his foot out, Drake shoved the brick into the gap between the door and the frame, preventing it from closing, while at the same moment, Mason tilted the taser upward and fired.

That was when things stopped going to plan.

There was a pop as the pair of spring-loaded prongs mounted at the front of the weapon were propelled forward, followed a moment later by a loud, almost mechanical clicking sound as the weapon delivered its incapacitating charge.

But instead of embedding themselves in the muscle of Fayed's thigh, the conducting prongs sailed right past to strike the wall beyond. Fayed had ducked back out of the way, causing Mason's shot to miss him by mere inches.

How had he known? Was he ready for them?

There was a crunch of splintering wood as Fayed shoved the door from the other side, trying to close it on them only to find the gap blocked by the solid concrete brick. No way was he getting it closed as long as that brick was wedged against the frame.

In any case, Drake wasn't about to let him try again. He was moving even before Fayed tried to lock them out, jumping to his feet and gripping the security chain in the blades of the bolt cutters. A single, powerful yank was all it took to snap the chain.

Realizing the door was compromised and that he couldn't hope to hold it closed against two men, Fayed abandoned his efforts and sprinted away even as Drake shouldered his way into the apartment, dropping the bolt cutters and reaching for his concealed sidearm.

'Two, on me,' he called out.

The prospect of a calm, orderly takedown was rapidly fading into the distance. He was firmly in damage-control mode now, trying to regain control of the situation before it turned into a complete fuck-up.

Advancing into the narrow main hallway with the weapon up and ready, he found himself facing out into the apartment's cramped living room. Sure enough, he caught the flickering glow of a computer screen – probably a laptop – off to his left.

He was also just in time to see Fayed launch himself at the living-room window, throwing up his arms to protect himself. There was an audible bang, followed by the tinkle of shattered glass as the window gave way beneath the impact, and suddenly Fayed had disappeared into the darkness beyond.

'Shit!' Drake hissed, sprinting forward to witness what he expected to be Fayed's broken body lying on the street thirty feet below. Had the man just thrown himself to his death to avoid being captured?

Leaning out, he found that the window faced out onto an alleyway running between this building and another residential block right next to it. However, his view of the alleyway below was partially blocked by the steel grating of a fire escape, now covered with broken glass. Fayed must have launched himself out onto it.

Sure enough, the man was stumbling down the stairs one level below, heading for ground level.

'Unit One. Target heading for the alleyway on the north side,' Drake spoke into his radio even as he vaulted over the broken window frame. 'I'm going after him.'

'Negative, One,' McKnight countered. 'I'm en route. Wait for backup.'

'No time. He'll be gone.' Even as he said this, he was leaping down the first set of steps, taking them two at a time. 'Two, secure the apartment, grab any intel you can find and evac now!'

The laptop he'd spotted while making entry, plus any cell phones, electronic storage devices and even printed documents scattered around the apartment could be a potential gold mine of information in the right hands.

'On it,' Mason replied.

Drake was hot on Fayed's heels, but the target had a head start on him. Disengaging the safety latch that held the lowermost fire ladder in place, he waited a moment while it extended to ground level, gripped the rungs and allowed himself to slide down.

Drake knew right then that he'd never catch the man if he descended in similar fashion. Leaning out over the rail, he surveyed the darkened alley below. A number of steel dumpsters had been pushed up against the walls on both sides, all heavily filled with plastic bags of trash, including one almost directly below.

With no time to think about other options, Drake took aim, drew a breath and launched himself over the railing.

What followed was a second or two of tumbling, sickening weightlessness as he plummeted through the air, powerless to do anything about his trajectory now. If he'd misjudged his leap by a mere foot or two, he was going to slam into the pavement or the side of the dumpster. Either way, he was looking at broken bones and a failed mission, neither of which appealed to him.

His thoughts were cut short by a violent, jarring impact as he made contact. He braced himself, expecting to feel the faint pop as bone snapped followed by the first wave of pain, but none came. Instead he felt himself enveloped by a lumpy, yielding softness, while his nostrils were suddenly filled with the nauseating stench of rotting garbage.

His aim had proved true. Twisting around, he reached for the edge of the dumpster and used it to heave himself out, leaping down onto firm ground and drawing his weapon once more.

The narrow space between the two buildings was occupied by half a dozen containers just like the one he'd leapt into, all overflowing with garbage as if nobody bothered to empty them. The smell of it was overpowering despite the rain. More plastic bags were scattered haphazardly around, some ripped open by scavenging animals. Miniature waterfalls cascaded down from the broken guttering above, adding to the ambient noise and making footing treacherous. There were no working lights in the area; what little illumination there was came from the street lights on the nearby road.

It was into this dark, rain-slicked world that Drake advanced, weapon at the ready. Fayed was here somewhere with him, waiting to make his move.

'Unit One, Overwatch,' he whispered into his radio unit. 'I'm in the alley. Any sign of him?'

'I'm looking, One,' came Frost's reply. 'Stand by.'

He could hear the faint buzz of the drone's electric motors moving overhead, but the low ambient light made it impossible to see the little aircraft itself. Hopefully Fayed couldn't see it either.

'Got him, One!' Frost called out. 'He's hiding in an alcove. Twenty yards, on your right.'

Drake was moving before she'd even finished speaking, heading straight to where she'd indicated. Their eyes in the sky might well have made the difference between success or failure on this mission.

Hearing the splash of boots in the puddles up ahead, he looked up in time to see a figure suddenly leap from behind cover, bolting through the shadows towards the far end of the alley. He must have heard Drake's approach and guessed that retreat was the only option. Swearing under his breath, Drake gave chase.

'Stop or I'll fire!' he warned, though he knew it was almost impossible to fire accurately while running, never mind in questionable lighting conditions against a target he'd been ordered to bring home alive. Fayed perhaps knew it too, and paid him no heed.

In a moment, he had disappeared around a corner.

Drake hit his radio pressel even as he sprinted to catch up. 'Target heading down the north alleyway. One is in pursuit.'

'I'm almost on you, One,' McKnight replied, breathless from running.

'No time. He'll be gone before you get here.' Exerting himself, Drake rushed to catch up. But no sooner had he rounded the corner than a dark figure leapt at him from an alcove to his right.

He knew right away that he'd made a mistake by rushing in without thinking. It went against everything he'd been trained to do, but excitement and eagerness to take down the target had overridden his judgement.

Fayed wasn't running after all. He was fighting.

He whirled right and brought the pistol to bear, finger tightening on the trigger. He might have been ordered to bring the man in alive, but when his own life was at stake he had no choice but to defend himself.

However, before he could fire, Fayed's arm swept up and knocked the pistol from his grasp. The weapon flew through the air to land several yards away, skittering across the slick ground before coming to rest next to a pile of sodden cardboard boxes.

Seeing Fayed draw back his arm to take a swing at him, Drake dodged aside and struck out, feeling his fist connect hard with the man's jaw. The hit barely seemed to faze his opponent however, and a moment later Drake grunted as Fayed landed a solid blow to the side of his head, followed a second later by a right hook that left his ears ringing.

Dazed, he staggered back as Fayed launched himself forward, tackling Drake around the waist like a football player and slamming him into a dumpster with bruising force. Fayed's dossier had listed his weight as 220 pounds, and every one of them was now being directed at Drake. The metal container shuddered under the powerful impact, bags of rubbish dislodged from their delicate balance to fall around the two men.

Drake had fought guys bigger and stronger than himself before, and it was never fun at the best of times. His training had taught him to use their size against them, keep his distance, capitalize on their lack of agility to wear them down. That was the theory, at least. The reality now was that Fayed was all over him, swarming in close so that Drake couldn't get away, couldn't use his superior speed to his advantage.

Now it was a slugging match, pure and simple. They were both hurting; it was just a question of who buckled first. He raised his elbow up and drove it into Fayed's back. The man grunted in pain, and Drake struck again with all the force he could summon. Adrenaline was coursing thick in his veins now, lending a desperate strength to his efforts, but the blows barely seemed to register. It was like trying to pound an anvil with his bare hands. Drake meanwhile was already feeling the effects of his crushing impact against the dumpster.

Fayed let go and pulled back to throw another punch so as to capitalise on his opponent's apparent lack of resillience. But just as he swung, Drake ducked aside to avoid the blow. The dumpster shuddered again as Fayed's fist slammed into the metal shell with bone-breaking force.

That was the moment. The tipping point when the momentum shifted from one fighter to the other, and the outcome of their contest became a foregone conclusion.

As Fayed backed off, clutching his injured hand, Drake seized him by the shoulder and gave him a knee to the chest that knocked the air from his lungs, followed by two vicious right hooks to the face. Shaken by the blows, his opponent staggered back and collapsed into a pile of garbage bags.

Drake coughed, tasting blood in his mouth. His clothes were soaked and torn, covered with mud and other less savoury substances that he preferred not to think about. He knew he'd regret this little tussle when he woke up tomorrow morning, but adrenaline was doing a good job of suppressing the pain for now. He was alive – the rest could be sorted out later.

'Hang in there, champ.' Reaching for his radio, he spat bloody phlegm on the ground, trying to get his breathing back under control. 'Target down.'

'Overwatch has eyes-on,' Frost confirmed. He couldn't see the drone hovering overhead, but presumably it wasn't far. 'Smile for the camera.'

Drake would smile once he was out of here with Fayed in tow. Removing a set of plasticuffs from his pocket, Drake knelt down beside his target and used them to secure the man's ankles together, followed by his wrists. Even if he woke up now, he wasn't going anywhere.

Hearing the sound of approaching footsteps, he looked up as McKnight emerged from the shadows, weapon up and ready.

'Jesus,' she said, taking in the unconscious man and Drake's dishevelled appearance. 'You okay?'

'Nothing I can't handle,' he replied, moving a short distance away to retrieve the weapon he'd dropped during the brief confrontation.

'Bullshit. This guy could have killed you.' McKnight gave him a disapproving look. 'I told you to wait for me.'

'And I told *you* I was going after him,' Drake shot back, an edge of irritation in his voice. 'Last time I checked, I'm in charge. Deal with it.'

'Guys, get a room,' Frost interjected over the radio net. 'All this tension's getting me horny.'

Glancing up, Drake at last spotted the drone hovering not ten feet above them. Its microphones were likely relaying their argument to the pilot.

'Piss off, Overwatch,' Drake ordered, giving the unmanned aircraft the finger. 'Get rid of that thing.'

'Copy that, One.' The amusement in her voice was obvious. 'Bringing the drone in.'

As the buzzing of the drone's engines receded, Drake retrieved a little mechanical device about the size of a ballpoint pen from a pouch in his jacket. Known as an autojet, it was a quick, easy and effective means of injecting the target with a preset dosage of Etorphine – a synthetic opioid between 1,000 and 3,000 times more potent than morphine. Even a small amount was enough to render an adult human unconscious for several hours, with the added advantage that it was easily countered by a compound called naloxone, allowing them to wake him up within a matter of minutes if need be.

Placing the head of the autojet against Fayed's neck, Drake had to do nothing more than depress the button at the other end to activate it. It was that simple. The last thing he needed was to be messing around with hypodermic syringes and risk sticking himself by accident, tearing an artery or snapping the needle at a critical moment.

There was a faint hiss as the autojet deployed its contents into the man's bloodstream. He was incapable of anything but the most feeble of movements, but Fayed's eyes were on Drake now, wide and frightened, as well they should be. Even in his fucked-up state of mind it would have dawned on him that his past misdeeds had caught up with him. No doubt he was now wondering what dark hole he was about to be dragged off to.

Drake avoided eye contact as he went about his work. Whatever his own thoughts on the matter, Fayed was a target to be secured, and nothing more.

And sure enough, within moments Fayed's recently opened eyes began to grow heavy once more. Drake kept a finger pressed against the carotid artery in his neck, monitoring his pulse as the drugs took hold and his consciousness faded.

'Target prepped for transport,' Drake reported over the radio. 'Units One and Three are exfilling now. ETA sixty seconds.'

'Two is in the stairwell, heading down,' Mason added.

'Copy that,' Drake replied, then turned to McKnight. The pain of his injuries was starting to kick in now, but he knew this was no time to stop and assess the damage. He could still walk and function, and that was enough.' Give me a hand with him, would you?'

She didn't protest. Despite their brief argument, both knew that cooperation wasn't just a matter of necessity at times like this; it was a matter of survival. However, the look in her eyes told him the matter would be revisited later.

Taking an arm each, they heaved the unconscious man to his feet and dragged him back down the alley towards the waiting van. If anybody in one of the adjacent apartments overlooking the alley had heard something unusual, they made no effort to challenge the two operatives. Either they had succeeded in a silent retrieval, or people in this part of the city had learned to mind their own business.

Drake was pretty sure he knew which one was true.

In any case, he had other issues to contend with. Carrying a heavily built man through a rubbish-strewn alleyway at night is no easy task, and Drake and McKnight were soon breathing hard, their arms and shoulders aching by the time they rounded the corner and found the truck parked before them.

Mason, having returned from Fayed's apartment, was already in the driver's seat. The rear doors were open, and Frost was waiting for them.

'Just had a report of a disturbance from one of the apartments,' she called out, a pair of headphones pressed against one ear, linked to a police scanner. 'Police are sending a unit to take a look.'

'ETA?' Drake asked, realizing they hadn't been quite as lucky as he'd hoped. Even in a place like this, the sound of breaking glass didn't pass unheeded.

'Four, five minutes tops.'

'Let's not be here when they arrive,' Drake said, heaving the unconscious man into the van's cargo area. As he finished securing the prisoner, Drake spotted a second man lying in an alcove nearby, apparently unconscious. 'Problems?' he asked, clambering in beside McKnight.

The woman glanced at him, flashing a knowing smile. 'Nothing I can't handle.'

As Drake slammed the doors shut, Mason started the engine up and eased the truck out of the alleyway, then onto the main road beyond. Within moments they were accelerating away from the scene of the lift, with no evidence of pursuit or follow-up.

'And that's the way we do it!' Frost said, pounding the steel panelled walls for emphasis. 'Screw the A-Team. We owned that one.'

Drake didn't quite share her jubilation. True, they had recovered their target alive and more or less unharmed, but it had come at a cost. Their op had almost been blown by the botched entry, not to mention the beating he'd taken subduing the man.

Fayed's dossier had described him as an administrative officer in the Libyan army – a pen-pusher, more used to doing battle with spreadsheets than armed combatants. Where the hell had he learned to fight like a seasoned field operative? And what had really brought him to Paris, of all places?

'Cole, you find any intel in his apartment?' he called out, wondering if there had been anything on site that might give them some clues about Fayed.

'Lots,' Mason replied. 'Laptops, cell phones, the works. It's all encrypted and password-protected, but it seems he was running some kind of op from that apartment. I've bagged it in the back there.'

Reaching into Mason's holdall, Drake retrieved a laptop computer that looked like it had been packed away in a hurry, the charging cable still hanging loose where Mason had ripped it out of the wall. Unfolding the device, he held down to the power button to boot it up. Sure enough, a password screen appeared right away.

Unwilling to risk triggering some kind of automated data wipe, he glanced at Frost. 'Keira, can you do anything with it?'

The young woman studied the computer for a few moments, then shook her head. 'Not here. I need a proper terminal to get down into the system registry.'

'Shit,' he concluded, closing it down. This sort of thing was the work of the rendition team they were soon to hand Fayed over to; it was a breach of protocol to even be messing with the evidence they'd collected.

Perhaps he would never know the truth about their mysterious captive, or perhaps he was just being paranoid. Shepherd teams were there to capture and bring back their targets, not to interrogate or question them. Once they dropped him off, he was gone for good.

Such was life.

Stripping off his soaked and dirty jacket, he reached into one of their equipment bags, retrieving a bottle of water and a first-aid kit. Taking a deep gulp to satiate the thirst that always seemed to follow operations like this, he followed it up with a couple of painkillers.

In truth, he would have preferred something stronger, but that would have to wait for now. They still had to deliver Fayed to his rendition flight.

'Relax, Ryan,' Frost said, sensing the lingering tension in him. 'Hard part's over.'

Drake wanted to believe that.

—

Marigny Air Base, situated in the Marne region about seventy miles east of Paris, had been laid down during the 1950s as a NATO base for fighter interceptors. According to Drake's briefing notes, it had been designed as a 'bare bones' facility with just enough infrastructure to keep the place ticking over in peacetime, ready to be quickly brought into action in the event of a Soviet invasion of western Europe.

Fortunately such an invasion had never happened, and by the 1980s the base had fallen into disuse. These days it was more of a wildlife sanctuary than a military stronghold, its 3,000 metre long runways beginning to crack and break up as weeds and grass slowly prevailed over poured concrete.

They were still serviceable enough to land aircraft, however, as evidenced by the Gulfstream jet parked at one end of the runway. Sleek and compact, it was visible only by the glow of instrument panels in the cockpit – everything else had been powered down to reduce its infrared profile.

'Almost there,' Mason called from up front. 'Time to wake up sleeping beauty.'

They had been monitoring Fayed's vitals during the hour-long drive from central Paris. Fortunately he had remained unconscious and stable the whole time, easing the pressure on his captors.

Now it was time to bring him round. The retrieval team waiting on the jet would want to verify that he was conscious and responsive when they took possession of him, and Drake felt the same way, mostly to cover his own arse. If Fayed died during the flight, at least he could rightly claim that he'd been alive and well when he handed the man over.

Removing an autojet filled with naloxone, McKnight pressed the device against Fayed's neck and hit the pneumatic plunger to trigger it. There was a faint hiss as the device deployed its potent cocktail of stimulants.

Meanwhile Drake had switched frequencies on his radio, selecting a channel agreed before the operation began. 'Boxer to ground team. Whirlwind. I say again, whirlwind.'

Whirlwind was their code word for a successful retrieval mission. It was also an invitation to respond with the appropriate confirmation word. If Drake didn't hear 'Hotel' in the next few seconds, he would order Mason to turn the van around and get them out of there as quickly as possible.

'Copy that, Boxer,' came the reply. 'Hotel. Repeat, Hotel.'

Drake relaxed, letting out a breath as Mason slowed them down and finally came to a halt a short distance from the plane, the engine idling.

A sudden commotion alerted them that Fayed had regained consciousness, and was well and truly making his presence known. He was yelling something, though the gag they'd placed in his mouth as a precaution made it impossible to discern the words.

'Got a screamer,' McKnight said, sounding remarkably calm as she fought to hold the struggling man down. Even with his feet and wrists bound, he was making it hard work.

'No shit,' Frost remarked, wrinkling her nose in distaste. 'You want to tase him again?'

She shook her head. Use of such weapons always carried an element of risk, and the last thing they needed was for him to go into cardiac arrest mere feet from his rendition flight.

Leaving them to it, Drake opened his door and stepped out into the cool morning air to meet with the retrieval team. This far from the city, there was little in the way of ambient noise save for the gentle chug of the truck's engine. Dawn was still a couple of hours away, but the sky in the east was gradually lightening, the twinkling stars giving way to the deep azure of predawn.

'Nice morning for it,' a voice remarked.

Drake directed his gaze toward the plane as the leader of the retrieval team moved forward to speak with him. He was short and stocky, probably in his early fifties, with thinning brown hair combed over the considerable dome of his skull. Combined with a pair of thin-framed glasses and a bushy handlebar moustache, the impression thus conveyed reminded Drake more of a bank manager than a case officer in command of a rendition flight. Then again, he knew from experience that it took a certain kind of man to apply a power drill to someone's kneecaps, then go home and sleep soundly at night. Presumably this guy was such a man.

'Name's Wilkins,' he said, offering a pudgy hand.

Drake shook it. 'Good to meet you, Wilkins.'

He saw a faint gleam as Wilkins smiled, perhaps amused that Drake had neglected to give his own name. 'By the sounds of things, you've got a live one for us,' he said, nodding towards the truck, where a couple of muted thumps resounded from within.

'We dosed him up with 10 cc's of Etorphine about an hour ago. Just brought him out of it,' Drake said, knowing it was important to explain what they'd shot Fayed up with.

Wilkins nodded, watching as Mason and McKnight half dragged, half shoved Fayed towards him. Even bound, he was still thrashing and kicking like the best of them. Frost followed behind, carrying a holdall laden with the intel that Mason had snatched from Fayed's apartment.

'Any injuries?'

Drake shook his head.

'Looks like you caught a shiner yourself,' Wilkins remarked, studying Drake's bruised and grazed face.

Drake shrugged. 'Like you said, he's a live one.'

'We'll keep that in mind if he gives us any shit,' Wilkins promised him. 'Otherwise, good work. We're done here, so get your team clear of the area.'

As he said this, two members of his team moved forward to grab Fayed; one tall, black and well built, the other short and wiry. Neither man spoke a word.

Handovers like this were always brief affairs, Drake knew. There was never any paperwork to sign, any agreements to be made, any official recognition of what had just happened. How could there be? Black flights like this were by their nature clandestine enterprises, with no paper-trails left to incriminate anyone.

Anyway, no doubt Wilkins and his team were anxious to be airborne and on their way before French police arrived to investigate the landing of a private jet at a supposedly deserted airfield. In that respect, Drake was in complete agreement. They'd be leaving as soon as they could get the truck turned around.

Already the Gulfstream's engines were spooling up, preparing for departure. The main hatch was open, permitting a glimpse into the private aircraft's interior.

That was when Drake caught sight of him. Another man was in there, seated in one of the big leather chairs that dotted the cabin. A man who had apparently preferred to hang back while the retrieval team handled the prisoner.

He was in his late thirties, Middle Eastern in appearance, with dark olive skin, a slender and angular face that emphasized his prominent nose, and receding hair cut short on top. He was wearing a grey suit with an open collar, but Drake sensed from his uncomfortable body language that that wasn't his usual attire.

'Where are you taking him?' Drake asked before he could stop himself.

He wasn't even sure why he'd asked that question. Perhaps it was the sight of the jet's mysterious passenger, or perhaps his previous encounter with Fayed in the alleyway had left a lingering doubt in his mind. Either way, it had happened before he could stop himself.

Wilkins stopped for a moment and glanced back at him, that same faint smile visible beneath the bushy moustache. 'Come on, Ryan. You know better than to ask that.'

Leaving those words to sink in, he turned away and resumed his walk toward the jet. 'Pack it up, gentlemen. We're out of here.'

In short order, Fayed was manhandled aboard, the outer hatch was pulled shut, and the Gulfstream's engines roared with increased power. As the aircraft began its taxi down the runway, McKnight approached Drake, who was standing in silence watching it go.

'What was that all about?'

Drake didn't take his eyes off the plane. 'Just a feeling.'

'Good or bad?'

He wished he could answer that one.

'Come on,' he said, turning towards the truck as the Gulfstream roared into the night sky, heading for an unknown destination. 'We've got our own flight to catch.'

Chapter 5

Six hours later, Drake found himself seated in a small, cramped briefing room, skim-reading the sparse operational report he'd compiled on the flight back from France. The walls that pressed in uncomfortably close around him were plain white plasterboard, the tables low-quality wood veneer, the floor dark linoleum. Everything in here was cheap and sparse and utilitarian.

The hard plastic chair on which he sat wasn't doing his bruised back any favours, though he tried to ignore the dull ache, concentrating instead on his work. Breckenridge had demanded a debriefing as soon as possible, which meant he wasn't willing to wait for the team to return to Langley.

In any case, there were no transatlantic flights available for several hours yet.

Instead they had made a short hop across the English Channel before landing at RAF Mildenhall, a military airfield located near the Suffolk coast. Officially it was an RAF station, but in reality most of it belonged to the US Air Force, home to the 100th Air Refuelling Wing and various other support elements. All told, there were over 16,000 American personnel living and working here.

And where the Air Force went, the Agency was sure to follow. The Shepherd team's unregistered flight had landed half an hour ago, its four passengers discreetly hustled away from the aircraft and into a waiting car which had ferried them to a remote administrative building on the edge of the base. And here they'd at last had a chance to draw breath and take stock of the situation.

'So that's what we have so far,' Drake concluded, bringing his debriefing to a close. 'We exfilled the area before law enforcement could arrive, and delivered the target for rendition as ordered.'

Silence filled the air for several seconds.

'Well, I guess it could have turned out worse,' Breckenridge's voice crackled through the speaker unit in the centre of the table. Even from the other side of the Atlantic, Drake could hear the scorn in his voice. 'It also could have turned out better. Your mission was to carry out a covert extraction, Drake, not to start a fist fight in the street.'

And that was about as close to a 'well done' as he was ever likely to get. Drake was grateful the room didn't have video-conference facilities, otherwise he wasn't sure he'd be able to hold back from saying what was really on his mind.

'It couldn't be avoided. He had an escape route in mind,' he said, his tone carefully neutral. 'Which brings me to another point. This guy wasn't just some admin officer; he had field training. He was ready and willing to fight in that alleyway.'

'I'm still waiting for that point,' Breckenridge prompted him.

Drake clenched his fists. 'My point is, this man wasn't just some rogue intelligence source on the run. What if he had a reason for being in Paris?'

'What if he did?' his boss asked. 'That's the rendition team's job to find out. Shepherds are there to deliver a package, not to unwrap it. You know the score.'

In that regard, at least, he was right. It wasn't Drake's job to question this sort of thing.

But that didn't mean he wasn't going to.

'We're also supposed to be briefed on the targets we've been assigned.'

'You were.'

'Were we?'

'I'm quite sure I don't know what you mean, Ryan.'

That was when Drake knew something was wrong.

Ryan. He never called him Ryan.

He leaned closer to the speaker unit. 'Then let me spell it out for you. We get called in at short notice to extract a rogue asset that even *you* could deal with, but instead we find ourselves up against a trained field operative who's expecting trouble, and who seems to be running some kind of op from his own apartment. You tell me, how are we supposed to do our jobs if we don't know what we're up against?'

'You do your job by following orders. Like all of us,' Breckenridge replied pointedly.

'Not all of us have to risk our lives to follow orders,' Drake reminded him, his tone making it clear who such criticism was aimed at.

'Stop it,' Breckenridge cut in, his voice hard and cold. 'If you're trying to get yourself brought up on a disciplinary for insubordination, you're going the right way about it. You were given an objective, and despite a few screw-ups along the way, you achieved it. This operation's over, so I'm going to do us both a favour and forget this conversation happened. Have I made myself clear?'

Drake leaned back in his chair, saying nothing.

'Good,' he said, taking Drake's silence for affirmation. 'Your flight back to Langley leaves in six hours. I suggest you be on it. Out.'

With that, the line dropped out, leaving Drake alone to contemplate what had just happened. It might have been easy to explain away the man's attitude as an attempt to cover up his own ignorance, or a simple belligerent desire to keep him in the dark, but Drake could tell there was something else at play. What it was, he didn't know, but he was starting to get an uneasy feeling about the operation.

As usual, however, Breckenridge had left him with no answers. And with Franklin out of action for the foreseeable future, he had precious few avenues to pursue.

He shifted position in his chair and stretched, the bruised and knotted muscles in his back aching with the movement. He was tired and hurting, and despite his irritation at Breckenridge he had neither the energy nor the inclination to pursue the matter further that night.

'Fuck,' he proclaimed, that single word neatly summing up his attitude to the events of the past couple of days. Tossing his report and hand-written notes into a file folder, he pushed himself away from the conference table and strode out of the briefing room, heading for the temporary sleeping quarters allocated to him.

Sleep was the last thing on his mind, however. The hip flask of whisky waiting in his holdall was at the forefront of his thoughts now.

No such luck. McKnight was lurking in the corridor, waiting to ambush him as he left the briefing room. She'd changed into fresh clothes now that the op was concluded, and judging by her slightly damp hair, she'd showered while he'd been giving his report.

There was no sign of Mason or Frost, though he could take a wild guess that they'd headed for the nearest mess hall in search of food. The only thing the two specialists enjoyed more than arguing was eating, and happily enough they could indulge both passions there.

'If it's not good news, I don't want to hear it,' he said without breaking stride. 'Consider yourself warned.'

'Your threats terrify me,' she remarked, falling into step beside him. 'And no, it's not good news. I wanted to talk to you about what happened in that alley.'

'So talk,' he prompted, still intent on reaching his room as quickly as possible. 'I'll listen. I'm good that way.'

'Don't bullshit me,' she snapped. 'I warned you about charging in alone.'

A passing Air Force corporal glanced away uncomfortably, trying to avoid what was clearly the beginning of a heated argument. Likely he'd been warned not to approach or interact with the Shepherd team members, but it was hard not to overhear them when they were bitching at each other in the middle of a corridor.

'That you did,' Drake acknowledged, brushing past the younger man. 'And I considered myself duly warned.'

'But you went ahead and did it anyway. Alone, like always. Your own way, like always. Same shit, different country.'

Drake could practically feel his hackles rising. 'Your point being?'

'When are you going to drop the lone-wolf routine and start trusting the rest of us? We're here to help you, but you won't let us in. Sooner or later that's going to ruin you.'

Drake halted outside his darkened room, shoved the door open and turned to face her. 'I'll start trusting them when they start living up to it. You were slow, Sam. You were in the wrong place at the wrong time, and you couldn't help me. That's not my problem.'

Even as he turned away to close the door on her, she shoved her foot out, barring it. 'You arrogant asshole,' she snapped. 'One of these days that's going to catch up with you.'

They were so close he could feel the warmth of her breath on his cheek, could see the tiny flecks of hazel in her green eyes, the faintly visible freckles across her

43

nose. Her full lips were parted slightly as she drew breath, her cheeks flushed, her pupils dilated in the dim light as she glared back at him.

It happened fast.

Before he was even aware of it, his mouth was on hers, hard and insistent, driven by the sudden, powerful need that had come over them both. He couldn't say whether it was the danger they had faced together in Paris, the lingering anger and frustration that had yet to find an outlet, or the fear of the uncertain future that lay ahead. He couldn't say, and nor did he care at that moment. Neither of them did.

Far from being shocked or surprised, Samantha returned his gesture in equal measure, pulling him close with eager, overwhelming desire as her body strove to meet with his. He could feel her arms around his neck, her fingers running through his hair as they backed into the room, Drake kicking the door closed behind him.

–

Heart pounding, a faint sheen of sweat glistening on her skin, Samantha let out a strangled moan as the rising tide of pleasure reached an unbearable peak within her and suddenly burst forth, engulfing her in wave after wave of glorious release.

She clutched at Drake as her muscles tightened, her fingers raking his back, feeling the warmth and the strength in him as his own pleasure came not long after. He thrust in and out of her a few more times before at last relaxing on top of her, utterly spent.

She couldn't say how long they lay together like that, their naked bodies entwined, breathing hard, hearts beating so close they were almost as one. She could hear the sound of the movement in the corridor outside, the droning hum of an air conditioner, the distant roar of a jet coming in to land outside. Normal sounds of people and activity that she'd heard most of her life, and that she always found somehow comforting.

At last he raised his head up to look at her, his green eyes shining in the dim light filtering in through the drawn blinds. It was dawn outside, grey and pale and indistinct.

He said nothing, and for that she was glad. This wasn't a moment for words. It was enough just to be alone together.

She saw a faint smile tug at the corner of his mouth. Was he pleased with himself? She supposed he had some right to be, if the tingling afterglow of his efforts was anything to go by.

'Something funny?' she asked, curious.

'Arrogant asshole,' he said, repeating her earlier insult. 'Nice choice of words. Not sure I deserved that one, though.'

In truth, their argument hadn't quite been the intense confrontation they'd made it out to be. That wasn't to say her grievances were entirely unfounded, but she wasn't quite as ready to quit his team as anyone who'd observed them might have believed. Still, appearances had to be kept up, as it were.

She grinned mischievously. 'No, you did. Someone has to keep you in line.'

'And you think you're up to the job?'

Leaning forward, he kissed her, light and playful. At the same moment his hand traced a path along her side, fingers just brushing the contours of a small firm breast. She let out an involuntary gasp as he squeezed a sensitive nipple, the feeling caught somewhere between pleasure and pain.

'Still think you can keep me in line?' he whispered in her ear, seemingly enjoying the reaction his touch had provoked.

'Well, that depends,' she sighed, closing her eyes for a moment to enjoy the pleasurable sensation. Then, deciding he'd had his fun for now, she reached down between his legs and grasped him, not hard enough to hurt, but enough to show that she could if she wanted to. 'What do you think now?'

Again she saw that smile. A silent acknowledgement that neither one was there to hold sway over the other. Then, just like that, he pulled away, rolled off her and reached for something in his canvas holdall lying beside the bed.

'Not losing your stamina, are you?' she teased, her smile playful as she watched him. She couldn't help but notice the play of tight corded muscle beneath his skin as he moved; the strong, wide shoulders and well-defined arms. As he turned around, her eyes followed the firm pectoral muscles downward as they gave way to a flat stomach and narrow waist. Drake was a well-made man in the prime of his life, his body hardened and tempered by years of training and experience.

But it was a body that bore the unforgiving marks of those experiences, from the faded silvery white lines of deep gashes, many of which had been sutured closed, to the distinctive circular mark of an old gunshot wound. As evidence of his more recent escapades, his back and right shoulder were deeply discoloured by heavy bruising, complimented by the red crust of cuts and grazes. Drake had taken more than his share of injuries in the course of his career, both in the Agency and before, and seeing it literally laid bare before her was a sobering reminder of just how many times he'd brushed with death.

He glanced at her with a wry smile. 'I was on my way here for a reason, you know. It wasn't all for show.'

Lifting a hip flask out of his holdall, he unscrewed the top, held it to his lips and took a drink. When he held it out to her, she accepted it and sipped the contents, savouring the powerful smoky, almost salty, flavour.

'Bowmore?' she said uncertainly, responding to his unspoken question.

'Ardbeg,' he corrected. 'Right island, wrong whisky.'

'Damn it.' She was slowly learning the different varieties of Scotch, though it was hard going and there were so many different brands – many of which were beyond her ability to pronounce – that she wondered if she'd ever get a handle on it. 'Give me a glass of chardonnay any day. Maybe one day I'll teach you fine wines as payback.'

'Good luck,' he snorted, taking another drink.

It was at that moment that she caught a twinge of pain in his face, perhaps caused by moving the wrong way at the wrong moment. He reached down, his hand instinctively covering the gunshot scar that marked the left side of his abdomen.

Unlike many of the others it was a fairly recent scar, no more than a year or two old. She hadn't been there when he'd earned it, but she knew how it had come about, and who had given it to him.

'It still hurts?' she asked quietly.

Drake shook his head, brushing it aside. 'Just a twinge every now and then. It's nothing.'

Rising up, she knelt behind him on the bed, encircling him with her arms and pressing her body against him. She could feel those same muscles she had only recently admired, as her hands traced a gentle path down his chest until she felt the slight dimpling of scar tissue.

And as close as she was, she felt him tense up when she touched it.

'Is that how it is when you think about her?' she asked. 'A twinge of pain every now and then? Something that comes and goes?'

Anya – the woman Drake had been sent to rescue from a Russian prison. The woman who had almost killed him, and had placed countless others in danger. The woman who Samantha knew haunted his dreams even now.

'Anya's gone,' he whispered. He reached up and took another pull on the whisky. 'Nothing's going to change that.'

She felt a stab of pain at this lie. They both knew Anya wasn't dead, that her apparently murder last year had been a carefully constructed ruse, but only one of them believed the other to be ignorant of this.

'Would *you* change it, if you could?'

She wanted to know, wanted to understand the hold that this woman had over him. What was it about her that had compelled him to risk everything more than once in the vain, forlorn hope of reuniting with her?

Would you do the same for me, Ryan? she caught herself wondering.

But before he could answer, the moment was interrupted by the buzz of his cell phone, still in the pocket of his jeans, which lay amongst a heap of discarded clothes – his and hers.

Shrugging out of her embrace, Drake snatched the phone up and studied the caller ID, his brow creasing in a frown. 'Sorry, I have to take this,' he said, rising to his feet and hitting the Accept Call button. 'Jessica, I wasn't expecting—'

He never got a chance to finish, his greeting interrupted by a rush of conversation on the other end of the line.

Samantha watched him in silence, studying his reactions as he listened intently to what was being said. She knew little of Drake's sister Jessica, having never met the woman personally. Drake himself wasn't inclined to talk much about his family, but she'd eventually discovered that Jessica had become caught up in the events of two years previously, taken hostage by agents of Cain as leverage to make Drake cooperate. Only the actions of Drake and Anya had saved her life.

She couldn't say for sure what kind of relationship he had with her now, but whatever it was, she sensed this wasn't a social call. She was delivering bad news.

'Jess, just calm down,' he said, his voice as tense as his posture. 'Tell me what happened.'

That was when she saw the change come over him. The concern and the tension left him then, replaced by something else. Something she'd so rarely seen in him – shock.

'When?' he asked, his voice low and soft. 'But how did you... ?'

He fell silent again, listening, trying to absorb what he was hearing.

'I see.' She saw the muscles in his throat tighten. 'Of course, I'll be there. Give me some time to sort things out here. We'll talk more soon. Okay... bye.'

'What is it?' Samantha asked as he killed the phone and sat down heavily on the bed, staring at the far wall and seeing nothing.

Slowly he reached up, held the hip flask to his mouth and took a long, deep pull. 'My mother,' he said, speaking the word as if it were unfamiliar to him. 'She's dead.'

Chapter 6

Gasping, heart pumping, ignoring the sting of sweat in his eyes and the ache in his muscles, Drake moved in against his opponent, ducked a clumsy right hook and responded with a sharp cross that sent the other fighter staggering back.

Sensing another spectacular knockout for which the talented and aggressive young fighter had become well known, the gathered crowd roared in excitement, rising to their feet as one to cheer him on.

Drake sensed it too. Their roaring and screaming filled his body, coursed through his veins, investing his body with renewed strength. Before the other fighter could recover, he rushed forward and drove a right hook into the man's flank, followed by an uppercut that landed flush to the jaw.

The other man was against the ropes now, gloves up, arms tight by his sides as the pummeling continued. Drake's hands ached with the jarring impacts of bone against flesh, his muscles burning from the exertion of maintaining the assault. His strength was waning, yet still the other fighter wouldn't go down. Still he remained defiantly on his feet.

What was wrong with him? He was beaten. More than that, he was completely outmatched. He'd been pitted against someone far younger, stronger and fitter than himself. Why not go just go down and call it a day? There was no shame in it after the pounding he'd taken, and he was at the end of his career anyway. Such stubborn defiance was just making it harder for both of them. Why?

Why?

He was drawing back his arm for another weary punch when the bell sounded, ending the round. To carry on would risk a points deduction, and he'd never had to resort to such underhand tactics before; he wasn't about to start now. And as much as he hated to admit it, the sheer effort of trying to knock the man down had left him physically drained. He needed some time to get his breath back, then he could renew the attack and finish him off in the next round.

Reluctantly he turned away from the old fighter and stalked back to his corner as the crowd roared approval.

–

Brecon Beacons National Park, Wales

'Shit,' Drake swore under his breath, bringing his rental car to a halt on the narrow country road. Overhead, the sun shone down brightly through scattered cloud,

48

illuminating a world of towering snow-covered mountain peaks, tiny fields ringed with hedgerows, and rolling woodland crowding in close to fast-flowing rivers. The kind of picture-postcard landscape that people travelled hundreds of miles to bike and walk through.

Perfect, apart from the irritating obstruction on the road up ahead. A shepherd was busy moving his flock of sheep along the road, probably transferring them from one field to another in search of better grazing. The herd, easily a hundred strong, were so tightly packed on the winding lane that their woollen coats seemed to merge together into a single undulating white mass.

The minutes ticked by with the car's engine idling as the elderly shepherd eased the flock along with no great sense of urgency, and Drake resisted the urge to glance at his wristwatch. They were deep in the Welsh mountains, and he had spent enough time here in the past to know that things happened at a different pace from the rest of the world. Patience wasn't just a virtue here, it was a necessity.

Unfortunately, patience was something that Drake was fast running out of. Today wasn't a day for patience.

Fuck it, he decided, throwing the car into reverse and performing a three-point turn – no easy feat on the narrow stone-walled road – before stamping on the accelerator and leaving the flock behind in a spray of mud and stone chips. His new route would take longer, but it felt good just to be moving.

As the fields and mountains slipped by outside his window, he reflected for a moment on how strange it felt to be back in this neck of the woods. After applying to join the Special Air Service nearly two decades ago, he'd been based out of RAF Hereford not more than a dozen miles from here. The arduous selection programme had seen him turned loose in these very mountains in the depths of winter as part of his escape-and-evasion training. Armed with little more than a moth-eaten greatcoat and boots that didn't fit properly, he and a few dozen other hopefuls had marched, run, swam and climbed for two days in rain, snow and mud to reach their objective. Less than half made it to the end.

He'd never forget one of the little challenges they'd been set along the way. Finding a rusted old car seemingly abandoned in the middle of the windswept moorland, they'd been instructed to open the vehicle's trunk and memorise as much as possible about the random assortment of items contained within. Two days later while being debriefed, the first question they'd been asked was the car's license-plate number.

That had pretty much set the tone for what the regiment expected of its candidates – be ready for anything.

Today, with temperatures in the high teens and a satnav unit to guide him, his journey was rather more comfortable than it had been back then. However, he couldn't say he was quite as excited about reaching his destination.

During the three-hour drive from RAF Mildenhall, he'd tried in some way to process the news that his sister had delivered in the early hours of the morning, that his mother had been found dead at an industrial site on the outskirts of Cardiff. It was as simple, and yet as inexplicable, as that – just a plain, stark fact. How she'd ended up there, what events had led up to it, even the cause of her death were as yet unknown.

He was hoping to learn more when he eventually rendezvoused with Jessica.

It took another twenty minutes, and another diversion, for him to reach what the car's satnav unit claimed was the address. He wouldn't have known – he'd never been to this place in his life.

The building that his mother had called home appeared to have been converted and modernized from some much older structure, possibly a barn or even a water mill of some kind. Big, square and built from the same uncompromising grey stone as everything else around here, it seemed to be as much a part of the landscape as the mountains themselves.

An unpaved, single-track road led up to the property, and Drake took care to ease the rental car along this makeshift roadway, trying to avoid the worst of the potholes. An old Land Rover Series III parked to one side of the house, its dark green paintwork splattered with mud, suggested that his Ford Mondeo wasn't the optimal vehicle for getting around this part of the world.

How the hell had his mother ended up way out here in the sticks? He remembered her as a passionate city dweller, enthralled by the fast pace of life in central London and the plentiful career opportunities it offered. Then again, how well had he ever truly known her? She'd been around little enough during his childhood, and for the past ten years he'd had no contact with her whatsoever. Perhaps she'd changed her priorities in her later years, or perhaps this was a side of her he'd just never experienced.

Pulling in beside the Land Rover, Drake killed the engine, closed his eyes for a moment and let out a breath, psyching himself up for what was coming.

His sister Jessica had arranged to meet him here, though he had no idea why. Certainly there were arrangements to be made, and the contents of the house would no doubt have to be sorted through and disposed of, but there was no need to start all of that yet.

Still, at least the choice of venue spared him from having to make uncomfortable conversation with her husband Mark. The two men had never really hit it off, even from the beginning, and the events of two years earlier had done little to spark up a friendship. The last time Drake had visited them, Mark had waited for an opportune moment, taken him quietly aside and explained in no uncertain terms that Drake wasn't welcome in his house, and it would be best for everyone if he stayed away.

Drake's initial impulse had been to break the arm that had been laid so patronizingly on his shoulder during this chummy conversation, but with some effort he'd reined it in. After all, the man's wife had been kidnapped and very nearly executed because of what Drake had become involved in. The fact that Drake himself had rescued her wasn't going to make that go away.

With that less-than-cheerful thought hovering over him, he pulled open the door and stepped outside. He was greeted by the scent of recently cut grass and wild flowers, the bubbling gush of a nearby stream, and the feel of sunlight streaming down through scattered cloud. It seemed absurd given the maelstrom that had so recently engulfed his already troubled life, but he could scarcely imagine a more tranquil scene than the one which greeted him at that moment.

He was just turning towards the house when he heard someone call out.

'Ryan!'

He barely had time to react before Jessica rushed across the driveway and threw her arms around him, pulling him tight and holding on as if her life depended on it. Drake did nothing but hold her in return, guessing that she didn't need words at that moment.

She wasn't crying when she finally pulled away, but her eyes were red.

'I knew you'd come, but I never expected to see you so soon,' she said, managing a weak grin. The kind of playful teasing that used to happen so easily between them. 'Let me guess – you could tell me but you'd have to kill me?'

'Nah, too much paperwork.' Drake decided not to mention the recent operation that had seen him return to the UK. 'Forgive the stupid question, but how are you holding up?'

She let out a breath, her shoulders sagging a little. She opened her mouth as if to speak, then seemed to think better of it and merely shook her head. There were fresh tears glistening in her eyes now.

'Why don't we go inside? I'll make you some tea,' Drake suggested, steering her towards the front door. He didn't really want a cup of tea, and he doubted she did either, but that was what normal people seemed to do at times like this. It was what he remembered his parents doing as a child when his grandfather had died, anyway.

She raised an eyebrow. 'I thought you lived on coffee now.'

'When in Rome,' Drake replied.

Ten minutes later, they were seated at the big rustic oak dining table in the kitchen, each nursing a cup of sugary tea. It had taken a while to find what he'd needed in the unfamiliar kitchen, but even he was capable of making a brew without too much difficulty.

It was a strange experience being there, seeing the new life his mother had built for herself, and the faint reminders of the old one that he still vaguely remembered. Most of the furniture and personal possessions in the house were new and unknown to him, but every so often he'd spot something he recognized; a table lamp that he'd knocked over with a football as a child, a rug bought during a family holiday in Tunisia, a globe that he'd spent hours staring at, dreaming of the far-flung places he would one day visit.

'It's stupid when I think about it,' Jessica said, staring into the steaming liquid in her cup.

Drake surveyed his sister. 'What is?'

'How I reacted when the police showed up at my door. You know what my first thought was? You – I was sure they were going to tell me something had happened to you. Some... mission they couldn't tell me the details of. It never occurred to me that Mum…' She trailed off for a moment, taking a gulp of her drink. 'Part of me still can't believe it, can't accept she's really gone.'

'What did they tell you, Jess?' Drake asked, feeling the time was right to seek answers to some of the questions that had haunted him for the past several hours. 'What happened to her?'

The young woman sighed. 'Not much. They told me the body had been found on some industrial site, lying in a pit of some kind. But…' She swallowed hard and closed her eyes. He could see her lip quivering, could almost feel the strain she was under, trying to keep her composure.

Rounding the table, Drake laid a hand on her shoulder. 'What is it?'

When she looked up at him and he saw the pain in her vivid green eyes, he could already sense what was coming. The circumstances of her death already pointed to one inescapable conclusion.

'They told me she'd been murdered,' his sister managed to say, before breaking down in sobs.

Everything changed in that instant. Drake sat down beside Jessica, sinking into the chair like a fighter dropping to the canvas after taking a haymaker punch, the world swimming and fading into darkness around him.

Murdered.

Not a death by accident or illness. Not the commonplace tragedy that families all over the world experienced every day; the kind that could be rationalized and understood and eventually accepted. Nothing like that.

Someone had killed his mother.

'Murdered,' he repeated, as if trying to grasp the word. 'How? Why?'

Jessica sniffed, wiping her nose. 'I… I don't know,' she said at last. 'They wouldn't tell me anything else. And when I tried phoning them, they keep saying they're not able to comment on it.'

'Christ, I'm so sorry, Jess,' Drake said, taking her hand. It felt cold in his, as if all the life had been drained out of her. The death of a family member was a tragedy, but a murder was something else altogether. 'I had no idea.'

It didn't take long for the darkness to recede from his mind, for the world to come back into focus as the disparate thoughts and emotions whirling through his head coalesced into a single, stark, utterly clear objective – to find the person who had killed her, and to make them pay for it.

–

Feeling the need to escape the house for a while, Jessica led him outside on a walk through the surrounding fields and narrow country lanes. And for a time they spoke little more of the killing, content merely to trade little pieces of news about their lives, to reconnect with each other after nearly a year spent apart.

Drake was content to let her do most of the talking, his thoughts lingering on other more pressing matters, but he knew this little slice of normality helped her and that was enough. In truth, it felt good to be out in the sun, walking through the peaceful countryside and talking about nothing at all.

But it couldn't last forever. He was eager to broach a subject that had weighed heavily on him since she'd first delivered the terrible news, though he'd held off during their walk, unsure how to bring it up.

'You're wondering how I knew about her,' Jessica said as the house loomed into view once more, perhaps guessing his train of thought. 'When she'd disappeared from our lives.'

The answer was as obvious as it was difficult to accept. 'She contacted you.'

His sister nodded slowly.

'How long?'

'Two years.'

Drake's heart sank. Two years she'd been part of Jessica's life. Two years during which his sister had reconnected with her, forged a new relationship, mended bridges. Two years she hadn't seen fit to share with him.

'Why didn't you tell me?'

He saw a blush creep into her face. 'She... asked me not to. *Told* me, actually.'

And that, Drake thought, pretty much summed it up. 'Did she ever say why?'

She sighed. 'It's complicated. As far as excuses go, I know it doesn't get much worse than that, but Mum was...' She trailed off, as if unable to find the words she needed. 'Well, there are things about her she didn't like to talk about. Things she didn't want either of us to know.'

Drake was starting to get an uneasy feeling in the pit of his stomach. It was the same sort of feeling he'd had during his phone call with Breckenridge during the night. 'What do you mean? What sort of things?'

At this, she picked up the pace, heading back down the driveway towards the house. 'Come with me. There's something I want to show you.'

With little choice, Drake followed her.

Situated to the rear of the house, and adjacent to the ivy-covered brick wall that encircled the garden, was a small garage. It was newer than the residence it served but constructed of the same grey stone and with the same slate roof, probably to satisfy some local conservation law. Unlocking the sturdy padlock holding the wooden doors closed, Jessica swung them open to reveal the building's interior.

For the most part, it was exactly what Drake had expected in a garage that was seldom used. Cobweb-ringed windows, musty-smelling air, old tins of paint stacked on rickety shelves, and a few rusted gardening tools near the back.

However, most of the internal space was occupied by a vehicle of some sort, hidden beneath a dust cover. From the general dimensions and contours, Drake guessed it to be a sports car of some kind.

His suspicions were proven right a moment later when Jessica took hold of the edge of the dust cover and whipped it off, raising a cloud of dust that forced them both back a step while it cleared. Only then was Drake at last able to see the car that had been hiding beneath, its chassis gleaming in the hazy light filtering in through the grimy windows.

'I don't believe it,' he gasped, stunned by what he was seeing.

It was a 1967 Austin-Healey 3,000 convertible. A British sports car that had long since been discontinued, the model had competed at countless racing events around the world, from Le Mans in France to Sebring in the USA. Just over 40,000 of them had been built, and they were still considered one of the best-looking cars ever produced.

Drake knew all of this, because his father had possessed an almost obsessive enthusiasm for classic cars, and this particular one had been his pride and joy. He'd bought it nearly derelict and painstakingly restored it to mint condition, even teaching his reluctant son a thing or two about engines along the way. Drake recognized the gunmetal-grey chassis immediately. This was the first car he'd driven after passing his test; one of the few times his father had allowed him to really push the machine to its limit.

He couldn't help himself. Taking a tentative step forward, he reached out and gently ran his fingers across the front wheel arch, noting the faint trail they left in the newly settled dust. He hadn't laid eyes on this car in over fifteen years, and certainly hadn't dreamed of ever finding it again.

He heard Jessica move close to stand beside him. 'The keys are in the glove box, in case you're wondering.'

'Where did you get this?' he asked, his voice hushed. 'I thought everything was sold off after Dad died.'

Parting with the car had been a heart-wrenching decision, but their father had left behind a trail of debts and unpaid bills when he died. And with neither of his children possessing much money at the time, there had been little choice but to sell off everything of value.

'It was. She bought it anonymously at auction,' Jessica explained. 'She kept it in storage all these years, just waiting.'

'For what?'

'For you. She knew it meant a lot to Dad, and to you as well, even if you wouldn't admit it. I think maybe she intended it as a peace offering, but... it never happened. She couldn't bring herself to do it. I can't say why. Maybe the time was never right, or maybe she was afraid.'

Drake closed his eyes, his hand resting on the bodywork clenching into a fist. He hoped she wasn't about to start waxing lyrical about what an amazing childhood they'd had, or how thoughtful and loving their parents had been, and how empty their lives were without them. He was sensitive to her grief in light of everything that had happened, but that sensitivity didn't extend to outright self-delusion.

'The time wasn't right,' he said, making no effort to hide his disdain. 'That's the story of my life where she was concerned.'

He regretted those words as soon as they'd passed his lips, but he couldn't stop them. Years of simmering anger and resentment, exacerbated by today's devastating news, had suddenly come to the fore, and there was no holding it back.

'Ryan, that's not what I meant,' Jessica protested, hurt and anger in his voice.

Drake whirled around to face her. 'It's the truth, though. Don't you get it? She was never interested in either of us, or Dad. If she had been, she would have shown up for his funeral, she would have helped us deal with all the shit that came with it. For once in her life she would have done *something* for us, she would have been there. But she wasn't. I suppose the time wasn't right,' he said, his words a mockery of her earlier statement. He gestured to the convertible. 'An old car isn't going to change that.'

Far from retorting in anger, Jessica regarded him sadly. But there was more than just sadness in her eyes. He saw disappointment there too – she had shown faith in him, expected more from him, and he'd let her down.

'She always loved you, Ryan.' He couldn't say for sure whether it was him she was trying to convince or herself.

'She loved her career more than she ever loved me, and she never forgave me for taking it away.' He let out a slow breath, mastering his conflicting emotions with some difficulty. 'We... *I* needed her fifteen years ago. Guess what? She wasn't there.'

Only now did he see the growing light of anger in his sister's eyes. Without warning her left hand whirled around, catching him a stinging slap across the cheek.

'And where were you when *I* needed you, Ryan?' she asked, trembling visibly with the effort to hold her emotions in check.

Drake let out a breath, smarting from the unexpected strike. 'What do you mean?'

'What do you think I mean?' she snapped. 'I was abducted practically from my own doorstep, hauled halfway around the world and almost killed right in front of you. Remember now?'

Of course he remembered. Never in his life would he forget a moment of it.

'We got you out,' he protested, though his argument lacked conviction. 'I brought you home—'

At this, Jessica let out a hard, bitter laugh. 'And you think it's that easy, do you? Just drop me back into my old life and I carry on like nothing ever happened? Well it did happen, Ryan. Something pretty fucking horrible happened. I almost made my two girls grow up without a mother. I watched men die right in front of me. You think you can just wash that sort of thing away? I needed you *here*. I needed you to help me make sense of all this, to deal with it, and guess what?' Taking a step closer, she stared him in the eye. '*You* weren't here.'

'I was trying to keep you safe.'

'Safe?' she repeated. 'I haven't felt safe since the day they took me. Every stranger I pass on the street, every car that drives past our house a little too slow, every time I hear footsteps behind me...'

She swallowed hard, closing her eyes and forcing the thoughts from her mind. When she opened them again, she appeared calmer, colder somehow. She surveyed him for a long moment, then shook her head as if he were a puzzle once easy to decipher but now impossible to solve.

'Maybe that's what really separates us, Ryan. You can do the things you do, live in the world you're in, and not let it get to you.' The bitter smile she gave him was almost one of sympathy. 'I'm not like you.'

With those chilling words still ringing in his ears, his sister turned and strode out of the garage. Moments later, he heard the Land Rover's big diesel engine cough and rumble into life.

Drake was moving immediately, abandoning the garage and rounding the front of the house. Already he could hear the crunch of gears as his sister fought with the unfamiliar gearbox.

'Jessica!' he called out, having to yell to be heard over the sound of the thirty-year-old engine. 'Jessica, wait!'

He was moving to get in front of the car and block her path, but never got the chance. Finally finding first, Jessica released the clutch and stamped on the accelerator, sending the powerful vehicle lurching forward in a spray of dirt and gravel chips. Within moments she had made it onto the road and was soon putting distance between herself and Drake, the Land Rover bouncing and wallowing through deep potholes.

For a moment Drake considered following her, but one glance at his rental car was enough to dissuade him. An underpowered suburban hatchback was no vehicle to take on a Land Rover on roads like these.

'Shit,' he said under his breath, watching as his sister was swallowed up by the pleasant fields, walls and hedgerows.

Chapter 7

Cardiff Royal Infirmary, Wales

Drake wasn't sure how to feel as he made his way along the cold, clinical white-washed corridor towards the hospital morgue. Everything that had happened over the past several hours seemed to have passed him by in a blur of fragmented images and memories.

He remembered composing a brief email to Breckenridge explaining that he wasn't going to be on the next flight to Langley due to a family emergency. He remembered donning civilian clothes and requisitioning a car for the drive off-base, exerting his authority as a Shepherd operative to bypass most of the red tape that would have kept him tied up for hours.

Most of all, he recalled McKnight, Frost and Mason's awkward but genuine attempts to console him, and their offer to accompany him here, the team rallying around their friend and leader in a time of crisis. He'd absently thanked them for their show of support while politely refusing their offer.

He didn't want them here for this.

Always doing things alone – that was what Samantha had said about him. Perhaps she'd been right, perhaps he still couldn't bring himself to truly let anyone in, but there were some things that were meant to be done alone.

He'd tried to prepare himself for what was coming, to sort through his own confused and conflicting feelings and focus on the practicalities of what needed to be done, just as he'd been trained to do in the course of his long and eventful career. Don't think about the things beyond your control; just focus on each step on the path, each challenge, each hurdle to overcome.

He was accompanied on his grim errand by the police sergeant who had been waiting to receive him upstairs. A stout, amiable-looking man with wiry red hair and a complexion that was almost as florid, he had greeted Drake with the clinical politeness of one well versed in dealing with grieving families. Drake had barely even registered the man's name when he'd introduced himself – only the tag on his jacket confirmed it now as Forbes.

A thousand questions were whirling through Drake's mind as he trudged down the corridor beside the sergeant, his feet like blocks of lead that he had to force himself to lift and place down, over and over, each step bringing him inexorably closer to his final destination. Questions that had no answers. Questions he'd never expected to find himself asking.

'It's just through here,' Forbes said, pushing open a set of double doors that led into the room beyond. Drake paused only a moment, taking a single breath, before following him. Straightaway he felt the drop in temperature as they ventured inside, the chill raising the hairs on the back of his neck.

He supposed another man might have felt anger, grief, sadness, loss or even regret at a moment like this. And yet, standing there in that chilly basement room with a row of cold-storage units stretching out in front of him, he didn't feel any such emotion – he just felt numb and empty.

One refrigerator unit about halfway along the row had already been opened in preparation for his arrival, its occupant still covered with a plastic sheet. The tag at the end of the sliding table read 'Freya Louise Shaw'.

Of course she had reverted to her maiden name, Drake thought. She had been calling herself that ever since the divorce two decades earlier, but seeing it written there somehow still felt like a slight, as if it had been done to erase even the memory of the family she'd once been such a reluctant part of.

'Here we are, Mr Drake,' Forbes said quietly, halting next to the table. He exhaled, his breath misting in the cool air as he searched for the right words. 'Family members often find the formal identification… upsetting. Do you need a moment before seeing her?'

Drake shook his head. This wasn't the first time he'd seen a dead body, and he doubted it would be the last. In any case, he'd waited ten years to see her; a few more seconds wasn't going to change anything.

Saying nothing further, the police sergeant gently reached out and pulled back the plastic sheet, folding it over so that it exposed her face and neck but kept her covered from the shoulders down. This done, he stepped back, giving Drake his first look at the woman who had once been his mother.

His first thought was that she had aged visibly since their last meeting. The once fine and barely noticeable lines that had traced a path around her mouth and eyes were deeper and more obvious now, her neatly cut hair streaked with grey. And yet there was no denying that she had once been an attractive woman; tall and slender, with dark hair, pale skin and vividly green eyes.

He'd often been told that both he and Jessica took their looks from their mother. He'd seen it in his sister, but never in himself. Not until now. Age, and perhaps the changes that were even now taking place after her death, had hardened the once soft and feminine features of her face, made them more definite and pronounced, somehow, so that he did at last see something of himself in Freya Louise Shaw.

His next thought was that she had kept herself in remarkably good condition for a woman of her age, though he supposed that wasn't entirely surprising. The Freya he remembered from his childhood had been a seemingly inexhaustible well of energy and vitality, always eating healthily and rarely indulging in alcohol. When she wasn't at work – which was rare enough – she was out running or biking, at a swim or a yoga class.

It wasn't until much later that he'd realized these excursions served a different purpose – an escape from the unhappy marriage she'd become trapped in.

Nonetheless, they had crystallized in his mind the image of someone who was almost indestructible, and that wasn't an easy impression to shift.

But in truth these thoughts were nothing more than observations prompted by the physical reality before him; superficial impressions that stirred no deeper feelings. He'd almost hoped that the sight of her would have provoked something in him; some long-buried emotion that would allow him to feel the grief of her death, the anger at the years of each other's lives they had missed out on, the sad knowledge that they would never get the chance to reconcile their bitter differences.

Instead he just felt empty.

Drake swallowed, forcing that thought aside, willing his mind to be cool and analytical as he surveyed the body, looking for evidence that might give him some clue as to her fate.

The signs of a recent struggle were plain to see even for untrained eyes. Her lower lip was split, and though she'd been cleaned up by the mortuary technicians, he could see the glistening sheen of blood in the cut flesh.

The left side of her face was darkened in places by bruising that was all the more obvious against the pale skin. He also saw some lacerations near her temple, almost hidden by her hairline, which were likely the result of a strike by a solid object.

Glancing further down, he saw her right hand partially exposed by the movement of the plastic sheet. He reached down, moving the cover aside far enough to reveal the hand and forearm.

Deep marks and bruising in a narrow band around the wrist, suggesting she'd been bound. Tied up, beaten and taken out to a lonely area of waste ground to be executed. And it most certainly was an execution. This had been no random act of violence by a low-level criminal, no opportunistic killing or a mugging gone wrong, but a targeted and planned execution carried out by a professional.

He could feel his heart beating faster as the image flashed through his mind, but once again pushed it away. He would deal with that later. Now wasn't the time.

'I was told she'd been murdered,' Drake said, his voice subdued as he looked down on her. 'What was the cause of death?'

'According to the pathologist's report, she was killed by a single gunshot wound to the chest,' he replied, his voice carrying the weary sympathy of someone called upon too many times to explain something that was inherently inexplicable. 'From what I understand, it was quick. The damage to the heart was extensive; she would have passed away within a matter of seconds. Like a light turning off.'

Like a light turning off, Drake repeated in his head. They'd said the same thing when his father passed away years earlier. Perhaps it was the kind of line they were taught to recite at times like this. After all, what could be more mundane, more quick and easy than a light turning off? Was that what the end of a human life boiled down to?

In any case, Forbes had misunderstood the motivation behind his question. He wasn't looking for comfort or reassurance, but information. He needed to know the facts behind her murder.

'Were there reports of a gunshot in the area?'

'I'm... not sure about that.'

Drake frowned. 'What about the bullet? Have your ballistics people done a workup on it?' Drake asked. 'I assume they've removed it already. Any idea of the calibre? Make and model of the weapon?'

When his question garnered no response, he turned to find the sergeant regarding him with a perplexed look.

'What line of work did you say you were in, Mr Drake?'

The muscles in Drake's jaw tensed for a moment or two before he forced calm back into his body. 'I'm trying to understand how and why my mother was murdered,' he said, managing to keep his tone even and controlled. 'If there were no reported gunshots, that means the killer probably used a silencer, which means they were connected enough to get their hands on one, and prepared enough to have it ready for the killing. If the bullet was a 9x18 mm, that could mean the weapon was of Russian origin. If it's a 9x19, it could be American, which might suggest an IRA link. There's a hundred other possibilities I don't have the time or the inclination to go into, but your answering questions about how she was killed will help me understand *who* killed her. And right now, I'd very much like to meet that person.'

There was a look in his vivid green eyes now that caused the police sergeant to stare at him. He didn't take a step backward – he was too good for that – but Drake could sense him shrinking away a little, trying to put distance between them without being obvious about it. He was afraid of this stranger asking questions he had no cause to be asking, and no amount of training and professionalism was going to hide that.

'So, what can you tell me about the murder weapon?' Drake repeated.

He refused to meet Drake's gaze. 'I'm afraid I don't have that information.'

'Then who does?'

Forbes shook his head. 'You don't understand. This case is out of our jurisdiction, Mr Drake. The police are just here to keep the body secure.'

Drake's eyes narrowed in suspicion. 'You're the police. Someone's been killed. Who else is supposed to deal with it?'

At this, Forbes glanced over his shoulder, as if checking that no one was eavesdropping on their conversation. 'Look, we're not supposed to talk about this, all right? I could be in trouble just for mentioning it, but...' He glanced down at the woman laid out on the mortuary table, then leaned in closer and lowered his voice. 'Not long after they brought the body in, a group of men showed up, told us they were taking over the investigation.'

Drake was liking this less with every passing moment. 'On whose authority?'

Forbes's complexion seemed, if possible, to have grown more red, in stark contrast to the body lying before him. 'I asked as much myself, and they wasted no time putting me in my place.' He let out a sigh, looking Drake right in the eye before going on. 'They were Section 6. If I'm right about you, then you... know what that means, don't you?'

Indeed he did. Military Intelligence Section 6, better known to the general public by its famous abbreviation MI6, was the United Kingdom's main foreign intelligence arm, charged with monitoring and countering any kind of threat to national security, from terrorism to rival nations, espionage, spying and anything in between. Working as he did for the Agency, he was well acquainted with their British counterparts.

The question he couldn't answer was why they were involved in a murder investigation.

'Did they give a reason?' he asked without much hope.

'No, and to be honest they didn't have to. These weren't the sort of chaps you start interrogating,' Forbes said, sounding almost defensive. 'I'm telling you this because you've lost someone close to you, and I think you deserve answers. If you want to find them, you're asking the wrong man. You'll have to take it up with them.'

Which was easier said than done. If MI6 had intervened in this case, it must have been because they suspected some kind of threat to national security. The nature and scope of that threat was of course a mystery to him, and finding the answers he sought was unlikely to be easy. If they were anything like the Agency, they could afford to stonewall him indefinitely if they felt like it, hiding behind an impenetrable veil of government legislation.

Fortunately, Drake was not a man without resources in that regard.

'If you'd like some time alone, please take as long as you need,' the sergeant said, moving back from the table to give Drake some space. In truth, he seemed eager to be out of there before he said anything to further endanger his career, and Drake couldn't blame him. 'I'll be outside.'

He shook his head. 'No. I've seen enough.'

Reaching out, he gently unfolded the cover and allowed it to fall back in place. And just like that, she was gone, as if she had never been there at all.

'I'm finished here.'

Returning outside a short time later, Drake powered up his cell phone and brought up the internet browser, doing a quick search for the British Foreign Office. It wasn't as if MI6 made their contact details publicly known, but like any government department they ultimately fell under the umbrella of one that was more accessible.

Finding the Foreign Office website, he selected the Contact Us page and dialled the first number on the list. He imagined he'd be transferred around more than a few times before he reached the man he was looking for, so he didn't particularly care where he started.

The line rang out for a good ten seconds before it was answered by an efficient, if slightly bored-sounding, switchboard operator.

'I need to speak to one of your department heads named David Faulkner as a matter of urgency,' Drake began, wasting no time on pleasantries. 'He works for Section 6. This concerns national security.'

'Sir, I'm afraid we can't transfer calls to specific employees. If you're calling to report a terrorist threat, you have to—'

'I'll speak to him, and him alone,' Drake cut in. He knew full well what their procedures were, just as he knew they were trained to route priority calls to departments normally inaccessible to the outside world if the situation called for it. 'If you won't transfer me, then trace this call and pass my details on to him. Tell him Ryan Drake wants to speak with him. He'll know who I am.'

Chapter 8

It was early evening, and the Red Lion Inn was already bustling with groups of people out for dinner, hikers from the nearby Beacons slaking their thirst, and locals just there to relax and shoot the breeze over a few pints. It seemed like a decent place to do any of those things in Drake's opinion, seated as he was at a corner table with a pint of lager. The public room was low-ceilinged and L-shaped, with a comfortable, well-worn feel to it. Even the deeply stained roof beams overhead looked like they were actually real, and not some tacky twenty-first century attempt replicate period charm.

An open fireplace at the far wall was smouldering away, the smell of wood smoke mingling with that of cooking food from the kitchen, the distinctive odour of draft beers, and the faint lingering aroma of tobacco – a legacy of the days when people were still allowed to smoke in pubs.

With his brief summons delivered to the good people at the Foreign Office, Drake had left the hospital and journeyed back to his mother's house, hoping to link up with Jessica again. No such luck; the house had been locked up when he'd arrived. He could only assume she'd returned to her home in central London, though she was still refusing to answer his calls.

However, her absence had at least afforded him an opportunity to inspect the house in a little more detail. Locked doors and windows had presented little obstacle for a man with his skill and training, and in short order he'd discretely made entry so he could search the place for some clue as to his mother's recent activities. He wasn't exactly proud of having broken into his own mother's home, but finding answers had been the overriding priority.

In the event, there was little to see on cursory examination. The paperwork and folders in her office had yielded little beyond household accounting and personal correspondence. Nothing remotely suspicious. Same deal with her laptop – no passwords, no encryption, and an internet history that held nothing more interesting than news sites, online shopping and banking.

The only point of interest had been the collection of Word documents on her hard drive, which he assumed to be journalistic pieces in keeping with her profession. He hadn't had time to peruse them all, but a random selection had revealed a heavy emphasis on Libya, particularly human-rights abuses by the Gaddafi regime, conspiracy theories about the dictator's collusion with the West and even his harbouring of international terrorists. Not much to go on, but it was a wrinkle worth noting, and something he'd keep in mind.

Anyway, he wasn't surprised by the lack of definitive evidence. Whatever secrets Freya Louise Shaw had harboured, he doubted she would have been foolish enough to leave them in such an insecure location.

Reluctantly he'd locked the place up and taken his leave, sensing he'd find little else of interest. Lacking the energy to travel into London tonight, he'd booked himself a room in the nearby village of Madley, intending to grab what rest he could and tackle his problems in the morning.

The much larger town of Hereford was just a couple of miles away and would have offered more options, but he was reluctant to visit any of his old haunts. The chances of bumping into a former comrade from the regiment were slim, but the last thing he wanted right now was to have to paste on a fake smile and reminisce about old times.

He'd done enough reflecting on the past already today. What concerned him now was the present.

Jessica was in trouble; there was no denying that. He hadn't expected her to just fall back happily into her old life after everything that had happened, but nonetheless he'd hoped that time and distance from him would help her regain a sense of normality. That was what he'd tried to tell himself – leave her alone, give her some time, don't remind her of what happened.

Everything will be all right eventually.

But it wasn't, and maybe it never would be. Perhaps he would have seen it if he'd looked a little closer, thought a little more about it, questioned her outward displays of positivity. Had her forced optimism been nothing but a mask to hide a growing problem? Had she been holding it together this long only for his sake?

And what of his mother? What secrets had Jessica hinted at that she'd been so reluctant to share with them? What the hell had she been involved in that had brought about such a sudden, violent end?

For now, he was left with a lot of questions and no answers.

Drake sighed and took a sip from his pint of Carling. Despite his troubled thoughts, he knew he wasn't going to achieve much more this day, nor did he want to. He was tired and run down after the events of the past few days, and in need of rest. A few more pints would probably grant him his wish, then he could try to pick up the pieces in the morning.

He was just laying the glass down when he became aware of it. That feeling you get when someone's eyes linger on you just a little too long, their gaze a little too intense.

Someone was watching him.

Without reacting, he fished his cell phone out of his pocket and held it up as if he were checking his emails or composing a text. Situated in a corner as he was, nobody could see the screen but him.

Instead he powered up the camera function. Staring at the screen with an expression of bland disinterest, he slowly moved the phone in his hand, panning it from left to right across the crowded public room.

At a table near him were a group of men in their seventies, probably locals judging by their clothes and demeanour, chatting amiably amongst themselves with not the slightest interest in what was going on around them.

At another table, a middle-aged couple picking at their dinner, an empty bottle of wine standing upside down in an ice bucket waiting to be replaced. Conservatively dressed, the woman looking slightly bored, the man looking slightly drunk. Neither one glanced at him.

Further back, a group of younger men in hiking clothes, celebrating the end of a long day's hill-walking with pints all round. They looked to be in good spirits, laughing and joking amongst themselves. One of them rose a little unsteadily and ambled up to the bar to order another round.

That was when Drake spotted him. A man standing on the far side of the bar beside some of the other patrons, nursing a glass of Coke. Mid forties, dark jacket that was easy to conceal a weapon inside, close-cropped hair and a serious, focussed demeanour that was out of sync with the atmosphere in the bar.

No, it wasn't just him, Drake realized then. The woman beside him, posing as his companion, was part of it too. She was younger, perhaps in her late thirties, slender of build, with long red hair, pale skin and sharp, hardened features that stopped somewhere short of attractive.

Another person might have glanced at the unremarkable pair and seen nothing out of the ordinary. Average height and build, neither ugly nor appealing, no distinguishing features to speak of. The sort of people one passed every day without ever seeing.

But for Drake, the thing that set alarm bells ringing was their eyes. The look, the intensity, the constant awareness of everything going on around them. He had come to know that look all too well.

This was no married couple out for a quiet drink – they were field operatives. They had been sent here to watch him, and perhaps more. But why? And by whom?

Focussing the camera phone on the two of them, Drake zoomed in enough to get a decent image of their faces and surreptitiously took a photo. He'd run the image through facial recognition later, try to discern their identity.

Now that he'd established he was being watched, the question was what to do about it. Trying to run was a bad move. For all he knew there could be more of them waiting outside, and he didn't have a weapon with him.

If this man and woman were part of a team sent to lift him, they were unlikely to do it in the middle of a crowded bar. But then, he couldn't stay here forever. The place would have to close sooner or later, and then he'd have no choice but to leave.

Alone he might have been, but it didn't have to stay that way. He could summon the rest of his team, currently encamped at RAF Mildenhall awaiting his return, but it would take them hours to get here. Anyway, he was reluctant to involve his companions in his own problems, particularly when he didn't yet understand the nature of the threat.

He was contemplating his next move when he spotted a third man entering the public room. A man who turned and made his way straight towards Drake's table, as if he'd known exactly where to find him.

And of course, he almost certainly did.

He was slightly below average height, but well dressed and well groomed, his expensive fitted suit emphasizing the trim figure beneath. He was, as Drake knew, easily in his fifties by now, yet there was scarcely a line on his face. His thick blonde hair showed not a strand of grey, though the lighting in the bar betrayed the tinge of artificial colouring, and as Drake looked closer he couldn't help but notice the unnatural pattern of hair plugs at his temples.

David Faulkner had always been a man of many interests – one of which, apparently, was himself.

'Hello, Ryan,' he said, smiling with pleasure as if he'd just been reunited with an old friend. 'Room for one more?'

Without waiting for a response, he helped himself to a seat at the small table, studying Drake for a long moment.

'You're looking well, old boy,' he remarked conversationally, his English accent as refined and precise as his clothes. An Old Etonian, raised on rugby pitches and country estates. 'Life in the States been treating you well?'

Drake's green eyes flashed at his light-hearted banter. 'That depends on your point of view, David.'

Spotting the new arrival, a waitress made her way through the maze of tables to take his drinks order.

'Give me a fresh orange juice, would you, dear?' Faulkner asked, flashing a charming smile at her. The kind of smile that came courtesy of dental bleaching. 'And another pint of whatever my good friend here is having.'

As the young woman headed off to the bar to fetch their drinks, Drake surveyed the older man across the table. 'Wasn't expecting a personal visit.'

'I can't sit down with an old friend for a quiet drink or two?' Faulkner affected a look of wounded pride. 'After you left such a charming message with the Foreign Office, it seemed only right that I drop by and say hello.'

'We were never friends,' Drake pointed out. 'You found me because you used MI6 resources to track me, which means you have something important to tell me.'

It was hardly professional to talk shop in a public place like this, but their table was located in a secluded corner where few could overhear, and the ambient noise was sufficient to prevent their words carrying far. Plus, Drake was feeling belligerent and was happy to blow off steam any way he could.

Faulkner was still smiling at him, but there was a little less warmth in his eyes now. 'You're right, of course,' he acknowledged. 'Firstly, I wanted to offer my condolences about your mother. I'm sorry for your loss, Ryan.'

Drake had to hand it to him, Faulkner was a good actor. If he didn't know the man better, he almost would have bought it. Then again, intelligence handlers like Faulkner made a living out of spinning bullshit and making others buy it.

66

'Did your two friends up by the bar come to offer their condolences as well?' Drake asked, nodding to the pair of field operatives.

He chuckled in amusement. 'Still sharp, I see. That's good. But really, I wouldn't trouble myself about them. They're quite charming, in their own way, and useful. Can't have too many friends – that's what I always say.'

'Depends on the friends,' Drake said, draining the remnants of his first pint. 'You know why I left that message for you, I assume?'

'I do.'

'Section 6 has taken over the murder investigation. Why? What are you trying to cover up?'

No sense beating around the bush. Drake's question was framed as directly as he could put it. Unfortunately, if he was expecting a similarly direct answer, he was to be disappointed.

Faulkner took a sip of his orange juice, taking his time before going on. True to his health-conscious nature, he rarely drank alcohol, and Drake doubted he'd be sampling the steak pie or burgers on the pub's evening menu.

'The answer concerns you as much as it does her.'

'What do you mean?' Drake asked. He had no desire to sit here and listen to this man speak in riddles.

'I mean, like any good piece of intelligence, it comes at a price. I can tell you what you want to know, but in return I want something from you.'

Drake didn't like where this conversation was heading one bit. 'What, exactly?'

'Let's start with what I know about you, Ryan,' Faulkner said. 'Firstly, I know things didn't work out well with Special Operations in Afghanistan.'

'That's interesting, considering you recommended me to them,' Drake observed pointedly. Faulkner was the British intelligence officer who had plucked him out of the regiment after his second tour in Afghanistan, recognized his potential and offered him a place in a 'special task force' he was helping put together with the Americans.

That had been seven years ago. A lot had changed since then.

'Do you want to know what else is interesting? I'm largely the reason you're not in a military prison right now, Ryan. Or worse.' He allowed that one to sink in for a moment or two. 'After that business with Operation Hydra, they were all set to drop you in the deepest, darkest hole they could find. I had to call in quite a few favours to stop them.'

Drake could feel himself tense up. Just the mention of Hydra had brought back memories of a time he'd much rather forget. Memories of a day that had changed the course of his life forever.

And it had all started with the man sitting opposite him.

'And of course you did that out of the goodness of your heart,' Drake remarked cynically. Faulkner had many qualities, but altruism wasn't one of them.

He shrugged, taking another sip of his orange juice while he studied Drake closely. 'It's a bit like buying a new hammer to tighten a screw. It might not be the right tool for the job at hand, but you keep it around because you know one day it'll come in useful.'

'Sorry, am I supposed to be the hammer or the screw?'

Faulkner chose to ignore the remark. 'The second thing I know is that things haven't been working out very well for you with our friends in Langley either. You've taken part in some rather... questionable ops lately, and made yourself some powerful enemies in the process. The kind of enemies that might soon be running America's whole intelligence show.'

Drake had nothing to say to this. Thus far Faulkner's assessment of his situation had been disconcertingly accurate.

It was time for Faulkner to play his trump card. 'Lastly, I know all of this has happened on account of one woman. Someone dangerous and angry enough to topple the house of cards that so many people have devoted their lives to building. Someone who could turn our world upside down if she were left unchecked.'

'You know a lot,' Drake admitted tersely.

At this, Faulkner shrugged and leaned back in his seat. 'We live in a big pond, but it's a pond all the same. Throw a big enough stone in, and sooner or later the ripples will reach even the farthest shore. And you've been throwing some pretty large stones around these past couple of years, Ryan my boy. People are starting to take notice.'

'Including you.'

'Including me.'

'So you've told me what you know. Now tell me what you want.'

The smile was back. 'As strange as it might sound, I want to help you.'

'While helping yourself, I assume?'

The smile broadened. 'I see no harm in a bit of... mutual assistance. Do you?'

'Depends on what you want assistance with.' Drake cocked an eyebrow. 'And more importantly, what you're offering.'

'We'll talk about what I want in a moment,' Faulkner promised. 'As for what I'm offering, that comes in two parts. The first part is protection for you and your family, for the rest of your lives. No more looking over your shoulder, no more waiting for that sword to fall. I can guarantee their safety, and yours. For good.'

'How?'

'That brings me to the second part.' Moving his drink aside, Faulkner folded his arms and leaned in close, staring Drake in the eyes. 'I'm going to help you take down Marcus Cain.'

Chapter 9

George Washington University Hospital, Virginia

Dan Franklin felt like he was submerged in the depths of a dark, murky pond, faintly able to discern sounds and movement on the surface yet unable to comprehend them. But he knew they were important somehow, knew he had to find a way to reach them.

Forcing his confused and muddled thoughts together behind a coherent purpose, he strove to move towards the sounds, to concentrate, to listen and feel again.

Open your eyes, Mr Franklin.

Open your eyes.

His eyes blinked open once, harsh light flooding his retinas for an instant before he closed them. But his mind was coming round now, his fragmented thoughts coalescing into a growing understanding of his situation.

Open your eyes.

This time he managed to raise his eyelids, though it took a great effort to keep them open. For a moment or two the world around him was a white, stark blur that he could make no sense of, but slowly the shapes resolved themselves into places and objects.

White walls, chairs, a table, a window. Beside him, the beeping of some machine. He inhaled, tasting dry conditioned air and the sharp odour of antiseptic.

'Hello, Mr Franklin,' a quiet, nasal voice said.

With great effort, Franklin turned his head towards the source of the voice.

A man was sitting beside his bed. An older man with a neatly trimmed beard and greying hair, his slender reading glasses perched on the bridge of a prominent nose as he made some notes on Franklin's chart.

Lewis Engelmann, an expert in spinal surgery at Washington University. The man who had operated on him. How long? Hours? Days?

'Can you hear me?' Engelmann asked.

Franklin swallowed, his throat thick, his tongue seemingly unwilling to respond to the commands from his brain. Unable to form the words, he settled for nodding.

'Good,' Engelmann concluded, nodding to himself. 'You're still feeling the effects of the anaesthesia. It should wear off over the next couple of hours. But it's a good sign that you came around so fast.'

'How... ?' Franklin mumbled. 'How... ?'

'How did it go?' Engelmann finished for him. 'Well, that's something we'll find out over the next few days. How do you feel right now? Any pain?'

Franklin frowned, concentrating hard. He was accustomed to the constant ache in his injured back, the pain of cramping muscles and damaged nerves. But now, at last, there was nothing. No pain, no sensation at all, in fact...

Oh God.

The beeping beside him was growing faster as his heart rate increased, fear charging through his confused mind. He could feel nothing below his chest, as if his body simply ended there. It was a curious, bizarre, terrifying notion.

'I... I can't feel...'

Engelmann nodded in understanding. 'It's all right, there's no need to panic. The swelling will have compressed your spinal column, probably pressing on the nerves. It's common to feel no sensation after surgery like this, especially with the anaesthetic still in your system. That's why I said we'll find out over the next few days how successful the operation was. With luck, the sensation should gradually return as the swelling eases.'

'What if... it doesn't?' Franklin managed to say.

The surgeon looked away, avoiding his desperate gaze.

'Get some rest, Mr Franklin,' he advised. 'We'll talk more later.'

Chapter 10

Drake eyed up Faulkner across the table. As with most things in life, he made it all seem so easy, so convenient, as if bringing down one of the most powerful men in the Agency were as simple as ordering groceries.

Drake on the other hand knew all too well what a daunting, dangerous, perhaps insurmountable challenge Cain posed. Two years of toil and struggle had done much to educate him about just what sort of opponent he was up against.

Nonetheless, he knew Faulkner wouldn't have made such a claim unless he had something to back it up with. That much, at least, he'd come to understand about the man – he wasn't one for bluffing.

'Keep talking,' he prompted.

'Yesterday you extracted a man from Paris on Agency orders. No doubt you'd been briefed that he was an intelligence source who had gone rogue and started selling secrets to the highest bidder. Don't ask how I know this, because you know I won't tell you. But suffice to say, that man wasn't what he appeared to be.'

Drake was starting to get the same feeling he'd had during his tense debriefing with Breckenridge. 'So what was he?'

'A victim of a very secret and very dirty agreement between the CIA and Libyan intelligence. An agreement brokered by Marcus Cain, no less.'

'What kind of agreement?'

'An exchange. It's simple, really. The Libyans have been harbouring al-Qaeda and Islamic State commanders for years, particularly since we pushed them out of Iraq. We know this, and they know that we know, but they also know we're not going to do a damn thing about it, because those commanders are their bargaining chip. We want them, and we're willing to pay for them. So, a deal was struck – they give us a few of our enemies, and in return we give them a few of theirs.'

Drake leaned forward. 'Who, exactly?'

'Enemies of the Libyan government. Well, enemies of Colonel Gaddafi, really,' he amended. 'And there are plenty of those nowadays, believe me, both real and imagined. Leaders of opposition groups, insurgents, revolutionaries, even journalists who speak out too loudly against the regime. Anyone who poses a threat to them. Anyone who might help start a popular uprising that could overthrow Gaddafi.'

Drake let out a breath, feeling like he'd been punched in the stomach. 'You're telling me we handed over an innocent man to be tortured and executed?'

Faulkner gave an unconcerned shrug. 'Innocence is a matter of perspective. From the Libyan's point of view, Fayed was an enemy trying to recruit foreign support for an armed insurgency. For the Americans, he was a commodity to be traded. For you, he was a mission-objective. As I say, perspective.'

Drake felt as if he was going to throw up. His career as a Shepherd team leader was supposed to have represented a fresh start; a change of direction in a life that had all too often been muddied by questionable decisions and disastrous outcomes. Certainly it was dangerous and at times exacted a high price, but their cause was still a righteous one – to find and recover people who needed help. Not now, it seemed.

'Not such an easy thing to accept, is it?' Faulkner asked, guessing his thoughts. 'You've been used, Ryan. Deal with it.'

Drake glanced up at him, anger simmering behind his vivid eyes. 'I'm still waiting to hear how my mother was involved in any of this.'

Faulkner regarded him for a long moment before going on. 'Section 6 have an interesting case-file on her, which I reviewed before this meeting.'

'MI6 was keeping tabs on her?' Drake asked.

Faulkner gave him a knowing look. 'We keep tabs on anyone with the brains and the will to hurt our interests overseas. As it turns out, Freya possessed plenty of both. From what I understand, she was politically active for most of her adult life, and particularly vocal in her opposition to Gaddafi's rule in Libya. She wrote a good number of articles online about it, in fact. Human-rights abuses, state-sponsored terrorism – all the usual stuff.'

He mentioned it in such an offhand way, as if it were a long-accepted fact of life that the West dealt with dangerous and unpredictable dictatorships who enslaved their own people.

'Anyway, it seems she'd built up quite a network of contacts within the Libyan expat community here in the UK, even became personally close to one or two of them.' He let that hang for a few moments without further comment. 'That was when things started to go wrong. One of her best sources was arrested and put on a rendition flight to Libya. You might say that put her on the warpath. She began actively working to expose the prisoner-exchange programme, trying to out the whole thing to anyone who would listen.'

Drake had a sinking feeling in the pit of his stomach. 'You're saying she was killed to keep her quiet.'

Faulkner sighed and nodded. 'From what the chaps at GCHQ deduced from her phone records, she was supposed to be meeting with a new source who claimed to have information that could expose the entire programme. That was two days ago. She travelled to meet with him, and... well, you know the rest.'

Drake's fists were clenched tight, the knuckles standing out hard and white against the skin. 'So who ordered the hit?'

For a moment, the horrific thought occurred to him that perhaps the Agency or MI6 themselves had arranged her death, though he doubted Faulkner would be here telling him about it if that were the case.

Reaching for his cell phone, Faulkner powered it up and turned it towards Drake. 'Do you recognize this man?'

Drake leaned in closer, studying the digital photograph displayed on screen. It was a long-range shot, clearly taken without the subject's knowledge, but straight-away the image sent a chill of recognition through him. Mid thirties, slim face with prominent cheekbones, long straight nose, olive skin, receding hairline...

Oh Christ.

'He was there,' Drake whispered, feeling like he was about to be sick. 'On the rendition flight from Paris. I saw him right there with the Agency retrieval team.'

It was almost unbelievable. Drake himself had unknowingly aided the very man who had ordered his mother's death.

'I'm not surprised,' Faulkner acknowledged. 'Apparently he likes to apply the personal touch when they hand over detainees.'

'Who is he?'

'His name's Tarek Sowan; a colonel in the Libyan intelligence service, and one of the main players in the prisoner-exchange programme. He's the one that Cain chose to reach out to when he first proposed the deal, he provides the list of names for rendition, he even helped the Agency choose locations for their black sites in Libya. There aren't many people who know more about the entire setup than our friend Sowan here.'

Drake was staring at the image intently, wondering at the mind, the soul that lurked behind that lean, unassuming face. This was a man who made a business out of torture, who specialised in inflicting pain and suffering. There was no way of knowing whether it was out of duty, out of pleasure, or perhaps a little of both.

'Whatever his qualities from an operational point of view, it seems patience and subtlety aren't amongst them,' Faulkner went on. 'When Sowan learned of your mother's efforts to expose the programme, he bypassed the Americans completely and ordered her assassination. Needless to say, we weren't too impressed when we found out a British citizen had been murdered on British soil on the orders of a foreign government. And so here we find ourselves, at a bit of a crossroads.'

Not as far as Drake was concerned. There was only one path that lay ahead for him – the one that led directly to Tarek Sowan.

'You can probably guess where this is going,' Faulkner went on. 'I'm prepared to give you information that can lead you to Sowan. If you were to find him and bring him to us for... debriefing –' He put a certain emphasis on the word that left Drake in no doubt that Sowan would receive a little of what he'd been dishing out over the years – 'then I'm quite sure he'd give us enough actionable intel to expose Cain to the world. Careers have ended for less than this, believe me.'

Two birds with one stone. A chance to take down Cain at a stroke, and more importantly to get his hands on the man who had ordered his mother's death. He had no idea how legit this offer was, but he knew one thing with absolute certainty: once they'd finished 'debriefing' Sowan, he belonged to Drake.

'You said information comes at a cost,' he reminded the British intelligence officer, wary of things that seemed too good to be true. 'What do you want in return?'

Faulkner couldn't hide his smile if he'd wanted to. 'You, Ryan – not to put too fine a point on it. Well, actually, you and your female friend.'

Drake's brows rose at this. 'Why?'

'Come, now. Neither of us are stupid, so let's not act like it,' Faulkner chided him. 'She used to be one of the Agency's top operatives. Even if she's been out in the cold for a few years, she probably knows more about their classified operations than we ever did. And from what I've read, she can still give most of our field operatives a run for their money.' He smiled and reached for his orange juice with a well-manicured hand. 'I'm not overly fond of football analogies, Ryan, but I know that if you want to play in the top division you've got to sign the best players. Well, that's one player I want for *my* team.'

'She's got a lot of red cards against her name,' Drake reminded him, sticking with the football analogy. 'They won't go away easily.'

'All of which are down to Cain. He's her enemy,' Faulkner countered. 'We remove one problem, and the other solves itself.'

He made it all seem ridiculously simple. Unfortunately the reality of Anya was anything but. Drake seriously doubted she would allow herself to be brought back into the fold after everything she'd endured, to go back to shovelling the same shit for different masters.

'You said yourself that she's dangerous and angry, and one of the best operatives they ever had. You really think you could control someone like her?'

Faulkner was looking right at him now. 'Not me, Ryan. You.'

'She doesn't answer to me.'

She didn't answer to anyone, for that matter.

'But she *does* trust you, and I'd be willing to bet she cares for you.' Faulkner was watching him intently as he said this. Drake said nothing in response to it, which told Faulkner what he needed to know. 'In my experience, that's more than enough to get people on side. So, picture this. She works with you, you work for me, and together we stop a lot of bad things from happening and make the world a nicer place. That's not such a bad deal, is it?'

Apart from the fact he'd be indebted to a man he trusted only a little more than Cain himself. He had no idea if Faulkner was being on the level with him, but the prospect of giving Anya over to such a man didn't sit well with him at all. Not to mention the fact that she'd likely never agree to it anyway.

However, Faulkner's proposition had stirred a different possibility in his mind. The possibility of achieving the same aim without ending up in the pocket of another dangerous and unpredictable master. Such a plan could leave him with powerful enemies on both sides of the Atlantic if it failed, but the potential rewards were considerable.

'I need some time to think about this,' he said truthfully. As much as he wanted to get to the bottom of his mother's death, making a rash decision based on emotion was a bad road to go down, particularly when David Faulkner was involved. One didn't make a deal with the devil without reading the small print first.

Draining his pint, he rose from the table and reached for his wallet.

'It's on me,' Faulkner said, standing up as well. Even drawn up to his full height, he was a couple of inches shorter than Drake, though he cared not a jot. Reaching into his pocket, he handed over a card with a phone number printed on it. 'And by all means, consider it. Give me a call when you've made up your mind. But don't take too long, Ryan. This window won't stay open forever.'

Drake took his meaning well enough.

–

A short while later, Drake once again found himself in his rental car, the headlights illuminating the winding country road that lay ahead. He kept an eye on his rear-view mirror, wary of pursuit by his two friends from the pub earlier, though so far he'd seen nothing.

One advantage of being out in the countryside like this was that it was difficult to shadow someone unseen, the lack of traffic and narrow, darkened roads making it impossible to navigate without headlights.

After excusing himself from the bar, he had retired to his room upstairs at the Red Lion just long enough to collect his things, before leaving the area at high speed. He doubted Faulkner would attempt to have him abducted or killed, but the fact that the man knew where he was staying was enough to prompt Drake to bail out.

He was unlikely to find a hotel or guest house at such a late hour, and the prospect of spending the night in his mother's vacant house miles from the nearest settlement was less than appealing, leaving him with little choice but to make the long drive back to RAF Mildenhall. It wasn't a prospect he relished after such a difficult day, but needs must. At least it was secure.

Swinging through a tight corner into a long straight section of road, he found his cell phone and dialled a number. It rang out for some time before it was finally answered.

'Ryan? That you?' Frost asked, having to practically shout to make herself heard. Loud music and voices blasted out through the car's Bluetooth system.

'Where the hell are you?' It was pretty obvious from the background noise that she was no longer on the base.

'A pub in... wait, where are we?' he heard her ask someone in the background. 'Cambridge. Yeah, that's it. I gotta say, I'm disappointed. I expected this place to be more like Hogwarts.'

'What the fuck are you doing in Cambridge?' he demanded. He'd been allowed off base because of the family emergency he'd faced, but the rest of his team were another matter. In fact, the only reason they weren't already on a flight back to Langley was because they'd successfully bullshitted Breckenridge into believing they hadn't had a proper mission debriefing from Drake.

However, it wasn't hard to guess what had happened from there. RAF bases weren't known for their vibrant night life, and since Frost had never been to the UK before, he imagined she'd snuck out and travelled to the nearest city to go exploring. The fact that her travels had led her to a pub or two wasn't surprising either.

'Give me a second,' she evaded. 'I can't hear shit right now.'

There was the rustling of fabric, and the sound of footsteps. A door opening, and more voices, then at last the background noise seemed to fade out.

'You okay?' she asked, able to speak normally now. 'Where are you?'

'On my way back,' he said, deciding not to bore her with the details.

She was silent for a moment. Normally the acid-tongued young woman wouldn't have hesitated to tear him a new one for interrupting what was clearly turning into a rowdy night out, but not this time. Like the rest of his teammates, she knew what had brought him back to Wales.

'You... want to talk about it?' she asked.

Drake almost smiled at the notion. Getting all deep and meaningful came about as naturally to her as cake-baking did to him, but it meant something that she was willing to listen. As it happened, though, he had another reason for calling.

'Relax, I'm not here to pour my heart out,' he assured her. 'I just need a favour.'

Her relief was palpable. 'Sure.'

'You sober enough to take this in?'

'Go fuck yourself.' Business as usual, he thought.

'I need a trace put on a UK cell phone.' Reaching into his pocket, he held up the business card that Faulkner had given him. His phone number was printed on it. 'Also, I'm going to text you an image of two people I saw tonight. Do me a favour and run them through the usual databases, see if they turn up anything.'

'You run into trouble out there?' she asked, suddenly wary.

'Not exactly, but I'd like to know who I'm dealing with. Can you do it?'

'Not from a sports bar in Cambridge,' she remarked cynically. 'But I can call in a few favours at Langley. Send it on to me and I'll see what I can do.'

Drake sighed and nodded. No matter what he asked of her, Frost never seemed to let him down. She might have grumbled and protested – at times vociferously – but she always came through for him. 'Thanks, Keira. I appreciate it.'

'Ryan, listen...' She trailed off, not knowing how to express what she wanted to say. 'I know I suck at this sort of thing, but... we're all here for you, okay? You need our help, we've got your back. All of us.'

He smiled. 'I know.'

Chapter 11

London, United Kingdom – 5 May

Jessica's home was a three-storey townhouse nestled in a fashionable residential street in Hammersmith. Just a few miles from the centre of London, it was a world away from the remote country homestead in which they'd met yesterday. Even at this early hour, the traffic was already making life miserable.

Since she'd refused to return any of his calls, Drake had thought it best to speak with her face to face. Doing so would likely mean having to deal with her husband Mark's disapproving looks and barbed remarks, but that was something he could tolerate. Right now, he had bridges to build and answers to get.

He was angry at himself for the way he'd acted yesterday, throwing a tantrum like a petulant child. There were bigger issues at play now, and he needed to deal with them. If he'd dealt with them properly in the first place, perhaps they wouldn't be in this mess now.

His phone was vibrating. Reaching out, he set the device to hands-free and then hit the Receive Call icon. Straightaway Frost's voice blared through the car's Bluetooth system.

'Ryan, you there?'

'Yeah, I'm driving right now. How's the head?'

'No idea what you mean,' she evaded.

Despite himself, he smiled a little. 'How did it go with the trace?'

'Not good,' the young woman admitted. 'The number you gave me belongs to an encrypted cell phone. High-level, government-issue stuff.'

'Can you break in?'

'Not without executive authorization. And I'm guessing you don't want to go down that road.'

'Shit,' Drake swore under his breath. 'How about the image I sent?'

'No better. Facial recognition turned up nothing on any of our databases. Whoever they are, they don't belong to us, and they're not criminals.'

Drake had suspected as much from a man like Faulkner, but it was irritating nonetheless. 'All right, Keira. Thanks for trying.'

'Thanks for getting me out of that pub last night. Don't tell anyone, but I was getting my ass kicked at pool.'

Drake grinned. 'Your secret's safe with me.'

Spotting a parking space just up ahead, he brought the Mondeo to a halt and sized it up. The space, sandwiched between a pair of compact urban hatchbacks, was scarcely longer than his car. Added to the fun was an indignant-looking sign overhead warning that these bays were for residents only. Still, parking spaces were as a rare as rocking-horse shit in this part of the world – this was his third trip around the block – so before he knew it he'd engaged reverse, twisted around in his seat, and was soon busy trying to squeeze the big car into the inadequate gap.

Once more he found himself contemplating his poor choice of rental car. From the rough potholed roads of the Welsh countryside to the dense urban sprawl of central London, he'd yet to find any scenario where it excelled.

Still, after a bit of swearing on his part and a near miss with the front wing, he finally managed to ease the car in. He was just straightening up when he noticed movement up ahead. someone emerging from one of the townhouses further down the street.

A woman. Jessica.

She was wearing a black hoodie and grey sweat pants, her dark hair tied back in a haphazard ponytail – a far cry for her usual stylishly dressed self. For a moment he wondered if she might be out for a morning run.

Drake was about to get out of the car and call to her, pleased that he'd caught her just as she was leaving and hopeful that they might speak alone, but one look at her was enough to make him pause.

She was upset. That much was obvious from her fast, agitated strides, the tension in her shoulders, the stubborn jut of her jaw. He'd come to know that expression well after more than a few quarrels as children and adults, and it hadn't changed.

A moment later, another figure emerged from the house. A man, tall and lanky, with dark wavy hair receding a little at the sides, his once boyish good looks starting to fade now that the big 4-0 was looming. He was dressed in a plain grey t-shirt and pyjama trousers, meaning he likely hadn't planned on going outside.

Striding after Jessica on his long legs, he reached out and tried to grab her arm, but she shrugged out of his grip and yelled something in his face. Drake couldn't make out the words from this distance, but he could see the anger flashing in her eyes, the clenched fists, the body readying itself to fight.

Turning around once more, she stomped off in the opposite direction, leaving her husband staring after her in dismay. He shouted one more parting remark, which she didn't react to, before turning and slinking back into the house.

Drake leaned back in his seat, unnerved by what he'd just seen. As much as Mark had given him a hard time in the past, and naturally Jessica had disapproved, Drake had always sensed the strong bond between them. As the cliché went, they weren't just husband and wife – they were friends, a unit, a team. They'd been comfortable around each other, easy-going in a way that few married couples were at that age. He'd never seen them so much as raise their voices at each other before, never mind descend into a full-blown argument in the street.

Unbuckling his seatbelt, Drake eased himself out of the car and started off in pursuit of his sister. She had already turned left at the end of the road and was out of his sight, but he had a fair idea where she was heading. He knew her well enough to know where she'd go to cool down after an argument.

He made a point of staying on the opposite side of the road as he passed their house. He didn't think Mark would observe every passer-by, but he was taking no chances. The last thing he wanted was to be waylaid by a man who clearly hated him, especially not until he knew the lay of the land.

Fortunately there was no movement from inside the house, no twitching curtains or shadows moving behind the front door, and Drake passed by without incident. In under thirty seconds he'd reached the end of the street and turned left, quickening his pace to catch up with Jessica.

He found her in the small public park about two blocks from her home, staring out across the grassy expanse where a group of kids was playing football beneath the leafy shade of towering oak trees. He couldn't see her expression from this angle, but he didn't have to be an expert in body language to tell she was still fuming.

Picking his way through the playground with its empty swings and metal slide that looked like it had seen better days, Drake approached his sister with caution, as if she were a volcano that could erupt at any moment.

'Remember when we used to do that?' he said quietly, as one of the kids managed to punt the football between the two piles of jackets they were using to represent goalposts.

Jessica whirled around at the sound of his voice, startled by his almost soundless approach. Old habits die hard. He'd become accustomed to moving quietly, and found it hard to shake even when he wasn't in the field.

'Ryan.' She let out an exasperated breath, struggling to regain her composure. 'What are you doing here?'

'You wouldn't return my calls. There wasn't much choice but to come here.' He moved forward to stand beside her as she turned her attention back to the park.

'How did you find me?'

He shrugged. 'Wasn't hard. I know you always come to places like this when you need to think. Or calm down.'

She took his meaning immediately and looked at him, a blush rising to her face. 'You saw it?'

Drake nodded. 'Just as I was pulling up.' He was silent for a few moments, watching as two of the kids nearby got into an argument over whether one of them had been offside. He only wished that was the biggest cause of tension in his own life. 'I know I'm not the greatest talker in the world, but I listen quite well.' He glanced sidelong at her. 'I'm listening now, Jess. If you want.'

He watched the muscles in her throat moving up and down as she swallowed, watched her close her eyes for a moment and bow her head, letting out a long slow breath.

'I'm leaving him.'

She opened her eyes then, and when she looked at him they were clear and focussed, betraying little hint of emotion.

'Mark. My husband. It's over, we're... done.'

Drake was stunned, as much by the cold, matter-of-fact way she'd delivered the news as the words themselves. It was as if she'd simply cut all emotional ties, isolated herself from the reality of what she was contemplating.

'You can't mean that.'

A faint, bittersweet smile. 'We've been living a lie, Ryan. These past two years. Doing all the right things, saying all the right things, pretending our life was just like it had been before, when it wasn't. It'll never be like it was. *I'll* never be like I was.'

Only now was Drake starting to understand the full extent of the damage that had been done. Jessica; his sister, the lifeline that kept him tethered to the real world while everything around him seemed to be falling apart, who somehow offered the hope that one day he too might find his way back into the light. She too was being broken apart by the dangerous, shadowy world he lived in.

He'd seen it happen to other people; other operatives who found it increasingly difficult to deal with 'normal life' when they weren't in the field. But never had he expected to see it in Jessica.

'There are people you can talk to,' he suggested, not knowing what else to say. 'You're not the first one to feel like this after... what happened.'

She sighed. 'I'm done talking. Mark and I... believe me, we've spent a lot of time talking about all of it. No amount of talking is going to change how I feel. It's better for both of us if we spend some time apart,' she said firmly. 'God knows, he's probably sick of me anyway.'

'What will you do?' Drake asked, not knowing what else to say. 'Where will you go?'

'Mum's place,' she said, nodding faintly as if to confirm the notion in her mind. 'For now at least. It's out in the open, away from other people... easier to defend.'

Drake felt a chill run through him at that moment. 'Defend?'

'I was a victim before, Ryan.' She turned to look at him again. 'Don't you see? When they came and snatched me right off the street, I didn't even see it coming. I was shocked, terrified, everything you can imagine. But something else happened as well. It was like a light turned on inside my head. I realized then that I'd been living in a bubble my whole life; a safe, stupid, complacent bubble. And when it was gone, it opened my eyes to the real world. Well, I'm not going to be a victim again. Not ever.'

Reaching behind her, she pulled up the hoodie just far enough for him to make out the distinctive shape of a pancake holster at the small of her back. He couldn't tell what make and model of gun was holstered in it, but he did see the gleam of a stainless-steel frame for a moment or two before she allowed the loose garment to fall back in place.

'Where the fuck did you get that?' Drake demanded immediately, shocked both that she'd somehow gotten her hands on an illegal weapon, and that she was stupid enough to be carrying in a public place.

This wasn't the States, where guns could be bought at the local Wal-Mart by anyone with a driver's license and a clean record. If she was caught with it here, she was fucked, and there would be nothing he could do about it.

Jessica sighed with impatience, like a teenager vexed by an overprotective parent. 'Mum gave it to me. Don't worry, I'm not going to blow my foot off or anything. She showed me how to use it, how to look after it. I'm actually a rather good shot, if you must know.'

Drake couldn't believe what he was hearing. Their own mother had given her daughter – a woman with two children of her own – an illegal firearm and showed her how to use it? What the hell was she thinking? More importantly, how had she gotten her hands on it in the first place?

'Fucking Christ, give me that thing,' he said, making to grab for it. Whatever good she thought she could do with it, she was sorely mistaken. The moment he got his hands on the weapon, he intended to leave this place and dispose of it in central London's biggest munitions dump – the river Thames.

But there was no way she was prepared to surrender the weapon, and she twisted aside out of his reach. Backing off a pace, she glared at him with her feet slightly apart, fists clenched and arms raised, ready to defend herself. Drake recognized the stance of a trained fighter right away.

Clearly shooting lessons hadn't been her only project in his absence.

'Don't even think about it,' she warned him.

Drake forced himself to relax, not to provoke her further. This situation needed to be defused right away. 'What are you going to do, Jess? Shoot me?'

His hard tone and harder stare seemed to cut through her anger. She exhaled, allowed her arms to drop a little, though she remained on guard.

'I won't get taken again,' she said, her voice filled with bitter resolve. 'I can't be that person again. Mum understood. That's why she agreed to help me.'

Drake shook his head in dismay. 'I don't understand. Mum was a fucking freelance writer. How was she even able to get a weapon for you?'

At this, Jessica bit her lip and glanced away uncomfortably. 'She told me not ask where she got it… said she would break off contact with me if I tried to find out. But she knew things, Ryan, and she showed me things. How to use weapons, how to protect myself, how to not be a victim. So I went along with it, I did what she wanted and I didn't ask questions. Because I needed her.' She sniffed and wiped her eye. 'I won't let myself be a burden again. You of all people should understand that.'

'Jesus, is that what you think?' he asked. 'You've never been a burden. Never.'

'They can get to you through me,' she countered, unmoved by his words. 'I'm your weakness. Don't you understand? As long as I'm vulnerable, so are you. I had to do something.'

Drake had no words. How could he make her understand the magnitude of what she was up against? How could he make her understand that his enemies didn't employ mere street thugs who would be easily deterred by a show of force? If they came for Jessica, it wouldn't matter what weapons she possessed, how many self-defence courses she'd attended, how well protected she thought she was. They would take her, or kill her, or whatever else they'd been sent to do, and there was nothing she could do to stop it.

'I understand what you're trying to do,' he said at last, taking a tentative step towards her. 'But listen to me, Jess. Really listen. I can protect you, keep you out of this fight, but you have to promise not to get involved. If you try to take these people on, if you go too far into their world or they begin to see you as a threat, I guarantee this will only end one way. So I'm asking you, please, forget whatever you're thinking before you get yourself killed.'

His sister said nothing for several moments. She just stood there staring at him, as if failing to comprehend what he'd said.

But she did understand it. That much soon became obvious as the shock gave way to anger and indignation. And something else. Disappointment. The same look of disappointment she'd given him yesterday.

'You understand, do you? If that were true, if you really did understand me, you'd never ask me to do that.'

'Jess—'

He reached out to her, but she batted his hand away.

'I thought I could rely on you. I thought you of all people would know what I was trying to do. Maybe I was wrong, about a lot of things. About you,' she said, her voice icy calm now. 'I'm going to walk away now. Don't follow me, don't try to stop me. I don't want to speak to you. I don't want or need your protection any more. I can take care of that myself.'

Her harsh, bitter warning thus delivered, she turned and strode away. Drake watched her go in silence, reluctant to let her leave but unwilling to risk another confrontation in such a public place.

So he did nothing. He just stood there and watched her leave, his mind consumed by the dark past harboured by his mother, and the even darker future that his sister seemed to be rushing headlong into.

As if echoing his own thoughts, a voice spoke up from behind him.

'She's walking a dangerous path. The kind you do not come back from.'

Drake knew that voice all too well. Whirling around, he found himself facing a tall, blonde-haired woman. She was dressed in jeans and a tan leather jacket, seated on one of the swings in the play park, idly allowing it to move back and forth with gentle movements of her legs.

He could scarcely have imagined a more uncharacteristic setting for someone like Anya than a children's play park.

'You were there the whole time,' Drake said, mystified that she'd somehow managed to approach unheard and unseen. That always seemed to be the way of it, he reflected.

'Close enough to hear what was said,' she confirmed.

He should have been angry at her for eavesdropping on such an intense, private conversation, but he knew there was no malice in her intentions. She had been curious – nothing more.

'She talks like she's going to war.'

Anya thought about that for a moment. 'Your sister has a right to be angry, and frightened,' she decided. 'But anger and fear are poor reasons for getting involved in someone else's fight. For her sake, make her understand that.'

Fine words, but they were undermined by her ignorance of the situation. Anya didn't know Jessica like he did, hadn't seen her grow into the capable, utterly determined woman she'd become. When she set her sights on something, she just kept going until she got it.

'I've interfered in her life before,' he reminded her. 'Everything I've done has made things worse.'

Anya's pale, intense blue eyes focussed on him. 'Then do better, Ryan.'

Drake wasn't amused, and it showed in his face. 'I presume you didn't come all the way here just to play Jeremy Kyle with me.'

Clearly the reference was lost on her.

'What do you want, Anya?' he asked instead, deciding to be blunt.

The look in her eyes softened a little. It wasn't exactly compassion, but it was about as close as someone like her was going to get. 'I know what happened to your mother,' she said, her voice unusually quiet and subdued. 'I'm sorry... for your loss.'

She might not have been good at talking about emotions – hers or anyone else's – but he sensed that her awkwardly delivered condolences were sincere nonetheless.

'We weren't close,' Drake said, feeling no need of her pity or her sympathies. 'And you didn't come to London just to tell me that.'

'I have... business here.' Anya, true to form, saw no reason to lie to him. As a general rule she despised liars, and rarely indulged in lying herself unless her survival depended on it. However, that didn't necessarily mean she was always forthcoming with information. Quite the opposite, in fact.

'What kind of business?'

She gave him a sharp look. 'The kind that doesn't concern you.'

'Remember that little talk we had last year?' he said, referring to their meeting in Washington DC after his return from Russia. 'The one where we promised to cooperate and not keep things from each other? Because generally when we're not upfront, it leads to a whole lot of pain and problems for one of us – usually me.'

Rising from the swing, Anya drew herself up to her full height – she was almost as tall as Drake himself in her heeled boots – and took a step towards him.

'I agreed to be truthful about anything that affects you, and I will abide by that. But if you expect me to tell you every detail of what I do and what I'm planning, you're very wrong. For both of our sakes, it's best that neither of us knows too much about the other.'

He should have expected as much. He and Anya had come to blows last year, both of their lives almost ended because of her refusal to explain the complex subterfuge in which she'd been involved. Since then, they had agreed that an element of mutual trust and good faith was needed if they were to take down Marcus Cain.

But that trust, it seemed, was slow in developing.

Those thoughts must have been plain to see on his face, because Anya let out a faint sigh before carrying on. 'I have made contact with a man living in this country; an expert in computers and technology. I will say no more about him, but if he can do what he promises, he may be able to discover who betrayed me to the Russians six years ago.'

Despite himself, he was intrigued by her revelation. 'Do you trust him?'

'I haven't made up my mind,' she answered, honest as always. 'But he has served me well in the past. Maybe he will again.'

Drake wasn't sure he understood the merits of her plan. Even if he was successful, Anya's mysterious contact could do little more than fill in gaps in her own history. Drake was less concerned about the past than he was about the future.

'Is this really worth it?' he asked. 'Worth the risk?'

The look in her pale blue eyes would have made another man step back a pace. 'I spent four years of my life in a Russian prison cell. Four years without speaking to another human being. Because of them, I forgot what it was like to walk on grass or feel wind and sun on my skin. I thought I would die without ever seeing the sky again. Yes, Ryan – it's worth it.'

He should have known better than to question that, having seen for himself the deplorable conditions she'd been forced to live in during her captivity. If it had been him, he knew he would have wanted to find those responsible as well.

But he had his own problems now.

'Well, then… I hope it works out for you,' he said, his tone stiff and formal. In light of his confrontation with Jessica, he'd already made up his mind what he was going to do. 'If you don't mind, I've got… business of my own to attend to.'

He had nothing else to say to her. Not now, at least. Perhaps later, if things worked out as he hoped they would, they would speak again.

Turning away, he made to leave the park.

'Think about what I said, Ryan,' she called after him. 'Your sister needs you now. Give her what she needs.'

I intend to, Drake thought as he fished out his cell phone. Faulkner's card was in his jacket pocket, slightly crumpled but still legible. By the time he'd left the park and crossed the road that bounded it, he'd punched in the number and was listening to it ring out.

Unsurprisingly, it didn't take long to be answered. 'Yes?'

Faulkner's phone manner was as smooth and polished as his appearance. Drake could almost imagine him running a hand through his perfectly coiffed hair as he spoke.

'It's Drake,' he said, in no mood for pleasantries. 'I'm in.'

'Glad to hear it, Ryan.'

You won't be when I'm through, Drake thought as he headed towards his rental car.

Chapter 12

Drake had seen a lot of strange things in the course of his career, a lot of surreal moments that would forever be imprinted on his memory. However, none of them quite measured up to the sight of his three Shepherd teammates sitting around a table in a traditional London pub. It was like seeing Arnold Schwarzenegger walk onto the set of *EastEnders* – his mind just couldn't reconcile it.

He'd chosen the Nag's Head as their meeting place for two reasons: it was right around the corner from Covent Garden station, and the name reminded him of his favourite TV show as a kid. In any case, the bar area was about half filled with patrons starting to drift in for the midday rush, their chatter providing enough ambient noise to make conversation easier. He'd also made sure to select a secluded booth near the back of the room where he and his companions could talk freely without fear of eavesdroppers.

'Okay, Ryan, spill it,' Frost said, unzipping her jacket and tossing it on the table before sliding into the booth. 'And it had better be good, because I've just spent the past hour sandwiched between a mom with the baby from hell, and a guy who made Jabba the Hutt look like Skeletor.'

He hadn't expected someone like Frost to take well to the intimate nature of the London Underground.

'Yeah, but at least leg room wasn't a problem for you,' Mason quipped, taking a sip of his pint. Drake had ordered a round of drinks from the bar before sitting down, hoping to placate his restless team mates. In Mason's case at least, it seemed to be working.

Still, the look that Frost shot him was almost enough to put him off his drink. The volatile young woman didn't take kindly to his jokes about her diminutive height at the best of times, and times were far from their best.

'Just be real thankful we weren't allowed to bring our sidearms with us, Cole,' she said, her tone dangerously cold. Then, turning her attention back to Drake, she added, 'I take it you didn't summon us to London to go sightseeing.'

'Not exactly, unless you're really into sand dunes,' Drake said.

A dark brow arched in silent question.

'I brought you all here because what I'm about to tell you isn't the sort of conversation to be had over the phone. In fact, if you value your careers then you should probably walk away now and pretend none of this ever happened.'

That was enough to get their attention, which was just as well because Drake had a lot to say. For the next few minutes, the group listened in silence while he related his encounter with Faulkner, the revelations about the man they had extracted from Paris, and the Libyan intelligence officer who had been lurking on the rendition flight.

'If what Faulkner says about him is true, this guy Sowan holds the key to bringing Cain down,' Drake concluded. 'He's in charge of the Libyan end of the extradition programme. He can tell us everything we need – names, dates, details of exchanges. If it came out that Cain had brokered a deal to extradite innocent civilians to Libya for interrogation and torture, it would be enough to fuck him over permanently.'

However, the one thing he'd been careful to leave out was Sowan's connection to his mother's death. It went against his nature to keep things from his teammates, but in this case he didn't want emotion clouding the issue. As far as the rest of the team were concerned, Sowan was a resource to be secured. That was all.

If only he could make himself believe it too.

Frost regarded him dubiously. 'That sounds great, but how do we get all this information from Sowan?'

The look in Drake's eyes told her everything she needed to know. She'd suspected that was why he'd called them all together, why he'd gone to such pains to explain the value of this man, but she had to ask the question. She had to know for sure that was what he was planning, what he was asking of them.

'Should have seen it coming.' Frost glanced down at the pint of bitter sitting untouched in front of her. 'You only buy me a drink when you want something.'

'He's a bad person who does worse things to others,' Drake said, knowing all too well how true that was. 'We'll do what we have to to get answers from him. As for the op itself, the only way we can get to Sowan is where he thinks he's safe – his home. We pull everything we can find on the place – blueprints, alarm systems, security measures – so we know exactly what we're up against, and how to beat it. We make entry in the middle of the night, take out the security, snatch Sowan and get him to a safe zone for extraction. Standard procedure. We've run a dozen ops just like this.'

'You can't be serious, Ryan,' McKnight protested. 'You're talking about launching an unsanctioned snatch-and-grab operation in a foreign country.'

He shrugged. 'Isn't that our day job?'

'Yeah, with unlimited logistical support, all the equipment and weapons we need, and the full backing of the Agency.' She was keeping her voice down with some difficulty. 'You might as well be talking about running a covert op out of your living room.'

'I didn't say it would be easy,' Drake admitted.

'You didn't say it would be suicidal either. That doesn't mean it's not.'

Mason however was taking a more pragmatic stance on the matter. 'Say for the sake of argument you do manage to get him out. What then? You plan to hand him over to the Brits and—'

'I'm not handing him over to anyone,' Drake interrupted.

'Excuse me?'

'Faulkner might be telling the truth, or he might be full of shit,' Drake explained. 'Either way, I'm not trusting him with Sowan's life, or mine. Once I get him out, he's going to tell me everything he knows, and I'll make the decision on whether it's enough to move against Cain.'

McKnight was watching him carefully. 'And what if he doesn't want to talk?'

When Drake looked at her, there was a light in his vivid green eyes that made her pause. 'He'll talk. Believe me.'

His implied threat wasn't lost on her.

'Is that who we are now, Ryan?'

'None of us are angels.' Least of all me, he thought. 'Right now, we are what we have to be. That's all there is to say about it.'

McKnight glanced at Mason, hoping for a show of support. 'You've usually got something to say for yourself, Cole. What about now?'

The big specialist chewed his lip and shrugged, perhaps recognizing that trying to change Drake's mind in matters like this was futility itself. 'If what Ryan learned about him is true, Sowan's done far worse in his life than what we're proposing. And we helped bring this guy another innocent victim. Can't say that sits well with me.'

'Me neither. But we know dick-all about this guy, apart from what Ryan's new best friend told him. We sure as hell aren't fit to judge him for crimes he might not have committed.' McKnight shook her head in exasperation. 'What you're suggesting isn't much different from what you're accusing Sowan of.'

'Are you finished?' Drake asked, his stare challenging. 'Because I didn't bring you here for a lesson in morality, Sam.'

McKnight said nothing for several moments, clearly weighing up her next words carefully. 'Could we have a few minutes?' she finally said, glancing at Frost and Mason.

'Stay where you are, both of you,' Drake countered. 'You're not going anywhere.'

'*Could we have a few minutes?*' McKnight repeated, putting emphasis on every word. She didn't look at either of them, keeping her eyes fixed on the man sitting opposite her.

Mason glanced at his younger companion, eager to escape what seemed like a rapidly brewing confrontation. 'Pretty sure I saw a Burger King about two blocks away,' he suggested, rising from the seat. 'Little taste of home.'

Frost was quick to take the hint, and reached for her jacket with some reluctance. Unlike Mason, she relished a good fight and was disappointed to miss this one. 'Fine, but you're buying.'

Drake had the good grace to wait until his two companions were out of earshot before speaking his mind. 'What's going on, Sam?'

'I could ask the same thing,' the woman countered. 'Have you got a death-wish or something? This plan of yours is just giving Cain exactly what he wants – an excuse to take you down.'

'You're assuming it's going to fail.'

'You're assuming it won't.'

'That's the spirit,' he remarked sarcastically, taking a sip of his pint.

'Don't be a smartass. You and I both know there are about a million ways this could go wrong—'

He'd heard enough of this. 'This is what we do, Sam. This is what we *have* to do to survive. If you're afraid to take risks, then run home and hide under the bed.'

McKnight stared at him for a long moment. 'Is that you talking, or Anya?'

He felt himself flush. 'This has got nothing to do with Anya.'

'Bullshit. It's got everything to do with her. She's the reason we're in this mess in the first place. She's the reason you put your life on the line time and time again, the reason we have to watch you tearing yourself apart, and for what? You think she'll be grateful for this? You think you're anything but a means to an end, a disposable asset, for her?'

Drake slammed his pint down with such force that he half expected the glass to shatter. Mercifully it remained intact, though his outburst attracted more than a few curious glances from the other patrons.

Far from being daunted by his open display of aggression, McKnight regarded him with something akin to pity. 'What are you going to do, Ryan? Hit me? Is that what *she* would do?'

Drake let out a breath, his anger dissipating in the face of her cold accusation. Straightaway he regretted his outburst, and most of all the fact it had been directed at Samantha. Worse still, she didn't truly understand why Sowan meant so much to him.

'Look, you've been through a tough time lately. I know you're hurting, even if you won't admit it,' she went on, her tone softening a little. 'I'm sorry for what's happened, I really am. But please take a second to think about this. You're risking everything on a crap-shoot.' She shook her head. 'I've seen guys double down on a losing streak before, thinking they're going to turn it all around. Believe me, it didn't work for them and it won't work for you now. I'm asking you not to go for this, Ryan. Please.'

Even Drake was taken aback by the sheer emotion behind her plea, the compassion and sadness in her eyes. There was no denying that what he was proposing was a move born from desperation, that there were a hundred different ways for it to go wrong, and that the odds weren't in his favour. But he had faced bad odds before and come out on top. All he needed was for it to play out one more time for him.

'It's not just about me now,' he said, letting out a sigh as he thought about the weapon that Jessica now carried with her at all times, the dangerous path she was walking. 'My sister... Jessica. She's not safe any more, Sam. This world you and I live in, all this shit that I tried to keep her away from, it's pulling her in. She's started carrying a weapon, training like she's going to war. I can't keep her out of it. And if I don't do something to stop it soon, it'll be too late.'

'Then help her, Ryan,' she implored him. 'But not like this. She doesn't need you on the other side of the world trying to fight impossible battles. She needs you with her now. Just be there.'

'It's not enough,' Drake said. 'I can't protect her all the time. And if Cain decides to come for her, it won't matter if I'm there or not. I won't be able to stop him.' He shook his head. 'One way or another, this has to end.'

McKnight said nothing to this, though it was obvious from the look in her eyes that she wasn't unmoved by his revelation.

'I know this is going to be dangerous,' he admitted. 'It always is. But we're running out of time and I can't see a better option. I have to do this.'

Her shoulders slumped a little, and she let out a faint sigh of resignation. 'You won't change your mind.'

Drake shook his head.

The woman swallowed and looked at him, raising her chin a little. 'Then I'm in, too.'

'You said yourself how dangerous it was,' he reminded her.

'It is. But you stand a better chance with someone watching your back.'

'Couldn't have put it better myself,' another voice chipped in from behind him.

Turning around, Drake watched Frost's head pop up from the booth next to theirs, with Mason close by. They couldn't have come back in through the bar area or he would have seen them in his peripheral vision. They must have circled around the side of the building and made their way in through the kitchen, whose door lay directly behind him, though he had no idea how they had bluffed their way past the staff. Such things didn't seem to faze his companions however.

'You listened in,' he said, not sure whether to be amused or angry at their resourcefulness.

Mason shrugged apologetically. 'I never would have heard the end of it if Keira had missed that. How's your beer, by the way?'

Drake said nothing, though he could feel a blush rising to his face as Mason and Frost slipped back into their booth. His confrontation with McKnight was something he'd rather none of them had witnessed.

'You're probably concocting some noble speech in your head right now about how we don't owe you anything, how you can't ask us to go through with this and that you'd never forgive yourself if something happened to one of us, so let me save your breath,' Mason advised him. 'The fact is, you're right. We *don't* owe you anything. We *could* walk away right now and not have to feel guilty about it. But we all know we're not going to do that. We've stuck with you this far because we *want* to, because we're a team and we know you'd do the same for us. And whether you like it or not, we're all involved in this. We've all been part of it since the beginning. That being the case, let's finish it once and for all, and put that son of a bitch out of business.'

'What he said,' Frost added, flashing one of her grins that fell somewhere between mockery and fierce, enduring loyalty.

89

Drake looked at each of them in turn. His team, his friends, his family as much as any blood relative, each willing to risk everything for him one more time. Never could he have asked for a finer group of people to stand by his side.

'All right,' he said at last, knowing they wouldn't be swayed from their course any more than he would. 'Let's get started.'

Chapter 13

Washington DC, Virginia

Deputy CIA Director Marcus Cain was in the back seat of his Chrysler 300, en route to Langley for his morning briefing. Not that he needed it – the laptop laid out next to him had been logged into the Agency's secure network before he'd taken his first sip of morning coffee, and he'd already made a host of phone calls with department heads and station chiefs all across the globe.

Up front, the driver kept his eyes studiously fixed on the road ahead, a radio comms piece trailing from his ear allowing him to stay in constant contact with a second vehicle trailing about a hundred yards back. In it were three additional field agents, all highly trained, heavily armed and hand-picked by Cain himself. The kind of men who didn't come from the Agency's own pool of field operatives, but who belonged to a far more select group. The kind of men who had already proven themselves on the battlefields of Iraq and Afghanistan, and other more exotic places that their government would never admit to.

He travelled virtually everywhere with a full security detail these days, officially because his status as a high-ranking member of the US intelligence community made him a target for everybody from terrorist organizations to foreign govern-ments. That was the official cover, but Cain knew the real reason.

Anya – once his protégé, his most successful asset, his greatest achievement. Now his most bitter and dangerous enemy.

She was out there somewhere at this very moment, planning, preparing, waiting for her chance to strike. In the past two years she had killed virtually everyone else that had stood between them, settling a few old scores along the way, and now she was out to settle one more.

And she might succeed. Cain was under no illusions about his own invincibility, or the infallibility of his mind. He was intelligent, cunning, gifted with the ability to perceive the deeper motivations in almost any action, able to wield some of the most powerful resources on the face of the earth and protected by multiple layers of security, but in the end he was still only a man. And as Anya had demonstrated with typical ruthless efficiency, all men could be killed.

But he possessed an advantage that Anya did not – knowledge. Anya, forever the soldier, so used to fighting the enemies she saw on the battlefield, still failed to understand that the true enemy was the one she couldn't see. That had been her undoing before, and it would be again.

'Listen to me, Quinn. We've been chasing our tails for the past six months, and we're nowhere. Our drones can't help us unless we know what to point them at. Our human intel has been useless, outdated or plain bullshit right from the start. Well, that stops now. The Pakistanis are the key to this. They always have been,' he said, speaking calmly and carefully into his secure satellite phone. Conversations with CIA station chiefs halfway around the world were no time to risk being misunderstood. 'If we don't have them onside, we'll never get to his inner circle.'

'I understand, but you know we can't lean too hard on them. They barely tolerate us as it is, and they'd never give up actionable intel to one of our own. Not willingly, at least.'

Cain hadn't missed the implication in that last sentence. Hayden Quinn was a good man, a reliable and ambitious case officer who Cain had seen fit to promote to station chief, overseeing all Agency operations in Pakistan. His appointment had been part of a gradual reshuffling of senior personnel that Cain had begun almost as soon as he'd been promoted to Deputy Director, making sure that key posts were occupied by competent people loyal to him.

He intended to put the seal on his promotion to full Director with a victory in the War on Terror. The kind of victory the American people had been waiting eight long years for, that even Anya with all her guile and cunning had been unable to give him. The kind of victory that would ensure his elevation to the highest levels of power and influence.

'That's a card we can only play once. And we'd have to be sure it was the right time,' he acknowledged. 'And the right man.'

The prospect of kidnapping and torturing foreign intelligence operatives didn't trouble him if it yielded the results he needed, but if it failed then they'd be left with nowhere to go.

'Send me everything you've got on their senior personnel,' he said at last. 'I want to review them all before we do anything. All we need is a way in – there's always a way in.'

'Of course, sir.'

Their conversation was interrupted when a call came through to Cain's private cell phone. There weren't many people in the world who knew that number, so when it rang, it was advisable to pick up.

Ending his satellite phone call with Quinn, he fished his cell from his pocket and checked the caller ID. Sure enough, this was one call he couldn't afford to ignore.

Taking a moment to marshal his thoughts and his composure, he hit the Receive Call icon. 'Yes?'

'Marcus, always good to speak with you again. I trust I'm not disturbing you?'

The voice on the other end was warm, pleasant, almost friendly. An old acquaintance calling to touch base after a period of absence.

But Cain knew the man that voice belonged to, knew all too well that the warmth, the pleasant demeanour, the friendly tone was nothing but a veneer, a facade to hide the cold darkness that lurked beneath.

The man to whom he was speaking was but one of many, carefully selected for their individual skills, experience, insight and influence; there to help guide and direct the collective whole. He was one of many, but he was the man to whom Marcus Cain, the Deputy Director of the CIA, answered.

'Of course not,' Cain assured him. 'What can I do for you?'

'I think you know why I'm calling, Marcus.' The tone had become a little less pleasant, a little less friendly now. 'We've lost one of our assets – a key one, with information that could compromise us. There's a concern amongst the group that we need to hold Antonia back.'

Cain could feel himself tensing up, knowing that what occurred during this call could make or break his plans. Antonia was one of the biggest initiatives the group had undertaken in the past several years, and much of it was because of him. But he couldn't do it alone. As with everything, the group's collective decision was the absolute final authority.

Just as this man's influence could help steer them in one direction, so others could move it a very different way. He knew there were naysayers, those with more to lose and less to gain, who hadn't been in favour of the plan, but he had to prevail. He had to convince them to move forward despite the risks.

'We both know that any delay now would kill our chances of success. We can't afford to stop; not when we're this close. You know we won't get another opportunity like this.'

That much at least was true. The conditions for success now were as good as they were ever likely to get. Launching their initiative earlier would have incurred too much resistance, while waiting much longer would mean losing their chance, and their potential gains. One way or another, it had to be now.

Silence; thoughtful, tense and unpredictable.

'I do,' the caller conceded. 'But not everyone feels the same way. If I was able to offer them some… reassurances, it would go a long way towards settling a few nerves.'

Cain knew exactly what he was asking for. He wanted Cain himself to vouch for this plan, to put his own reputation on the line, to take the hit if it went wrong.

'I've got some of my best people working on it right now,' he said truthfully. 'They're reliable. They'll make sure things go as they're supposed to.'

Silence again. Cain knew his contact as well as anyone could know such a man, and had come to understand at least some of what drove him. He was cold and ruthless as any in the group, but paradoxically he was also a risk-taker, inclined to lean towards plans that offered a greater reward in a shorter time.

All he could do now was hope that he was ready to take one more risk.

'As you say,' he decided. 'I'll forward your thoughts on to the others. It was good to speak with you again, Marcus. We'll have to meet up some time.'

'Looking forward to it,' Cain lied. Meeting with this man in person was even more fraught than their phone calls, but it was a necessary evil. Just like so many other things he'd done over the years.

With that final remark, the man hung up, leaving Cain alone with his thoughts.

Chapter 14

Brecon Beacons National Park, Wales

With their objective decided, the first order of business for Drake and his team had been to find somewhere they could formulate a plan to make it happen. A pub in Covent Garden might have sufficed for their initial discussion, but clandestine research and detailed mission-planning required something a little more secluded.

And as it happened, Drake knew just the place.

'Christ, I'll be wiping cow shit off my boots for a week,' Frost said, glancing around the living room with thinly veiled distaste. The Welsh countryside came about as naturally to her as flower arranging and evening dresses.

'It's sheep shit, not cow shit,' Mason corrected her.

'Like it matters.'

McKnight looked around, perhaps reflecting on her earlier remarks in the pub. 'Well, this is a first. We literally are running an op out of your living room.'

'It's a roof over our heads, and its miles from anywhere. Anyone tries to spy on us, and we'll know about it,' Drake pointed out. 'Keira, get set up. We have a lot of work to do.'

Frost began to unpack her laptop and various other pieces of equipment in preparation for the task ahead.

If Mason was amused by Drake's mild reproach, it was to be short-lived. 'I want someone on stag at all times today. Two-hour shifts, full perimeter sweep. Cole, you're up first.'

Mason, already settled into the couch, gave him a disapproving look. 'Why me?'

'Because you're not doing anything useful,' was his simple answer.

'Yeah? And what are you planning to do?'

Drake fished a cell phone out of his pocket; a cheap burner phone he'd purchased the previous day. 'Contact an old friend.'

He wasn't looking forward to this one. The man he was about to ask for help had once been a specialist in covert extractions, starting with Eastern Europe during the Cold War before moving on to Africa and the Middle East in later years. He'd since transitioned into the Agency and become a Shepherd team-leader himself, but Drake knew he still had access to a decent network of contacts.

He was about the only person Drake could think of who could get him what he needed at short notice and outside the Agency's umbrella. Unfortunately, whether or not he would agree to help was another matter. The two of them had a chequered history to say the least.

The phone rang out for a good ten seconds, which wasn't surprising. It was early morning in DC, and from what Drake knew of the man, he didn't take kindly to unexpected contacts like this.

'Who the fuck is this?' a gruff voice demanded, carrying a hint of a German accent. 'How did you get this number?'

Drake might have smiled if the success of the entire operation didn't rest on this man's cooperation. Jonas Dietrich had never been one for pleasantries.

'Jonas, it's Ryan.'

'Ryan?' He paused for a moment. 'What do *you* want, man?'

'It's business.'

At this, Dietrich snorted in amusement. 'Really? Well, I've got enough business to keep me occupied. Don't call me again.'

'Don't hang up,' Drake implored him.

'Why shouldn't I?'

'Once an asshole, always an asshole,' Frost remarked as she waited for her laptop to power up.

She'd said it loud enough to carry down the line; a fact that wasn't lost on Dietrich. 'Who was that?'

Drake glared at Frost. 'It's Keira; she's here with me,' he explained, keeping his voice remarkably calm given the circumstances. 'She says hi.'

'Tell her to piss off. And she still owes me for that beer,' Dietrich shot back. He seemed to be the only person on earth whose temper matched Frost's. 'You planning some kind of reunion, Ryan? Well, if you're thinking about rescuing any more insane bitches from Russian prisons, count me out. Once was enough.'

Dietrich had been part of the team that Drake had led into a Siberian prison to recover Anya from captivity. His motives for going along had been dubious at best, but in the end he'd proven himself a valuable, if reluctant, ally.

Drake closed his eyes and let out a weary sigh. 'It's an open line, Jonas.'

He was unpopular enough in Russia after the events of last year. The last thing he needed was for even more serious transgressions to come to light.

'Like I care,' Dietrich shot back. 'We both know you're calling me on a burner. Nobody's listening in, but if you're worried about it, I'll save you the trouble and hang up now.'

'I need your help,' Drake cut in, adopting a harder tone now. 'And you're going to give it to me.'

Silence greeted him for a few seconds. 'This had better be good. And I mean Oscar-winning good, not Golden Globe good. If you're going to give me some speech about how you helped me out of that prison after I got shot, that I owe you my life or something like that, I'll be very disappointed. You lost that advantage when I risked my career and my life to get you out of Iraq. As far as I'm concerned, we're even.'

'Maybe in your mind we are, but not as far as Marcus Cain's concerned. Guilty by association, Jonas. You're a liability now. The only reason you're still alive is because of the deal Franklin cut with him, but Franklin's out of action now and there's no telling when he's coming back. You're running out of time just the same as us. If you won't help us, then for fuck's sake help yourself and give me what I need.'

His words were met with stony silence. In Drake's mind, this could play out one of two ways – either Dietrich would agree to his request, or he would slam the phone down and never speak to him again. He honestly couldn't say for sure which way it would go.

'All right,' he said at last. 'What do you want?'

It was all Drake could do to keep from letting out a sigh of relief. 'We're planning a little holiday in Libya and we need some support, no questions asked.'

'Off the books?'

'Of course.'

'What kind of support?'

'Logistics. Ground transport, weapons, ammo and breaching equipment. Standard package for a covert extraction.'

'How many in your team?'

'Four, plus one guest.'

'When do you need it?'

'At most, two days from now. Maybe less.'

Dietrich sucked air through his teeth, like a builder about to give a bad quote. 'That won't be easy. Guys who work at short notice are expensive, and they'll want half in advance.'

'Fine.' There wasn't much else he could say to that. However this played out, he suspected he'd be a lot poorer by the time it was over. 'But your contacts need to be reliable, and so does the gear. I can't have someone who cuts and runs at the last minute.'

Dietrich thought on that for a moment or two. 'I might know a guy,' he finally conceded. 'I'll make some calls.'

With that, the line went dead.

'That sounded… interesting. Do you think he'll come through for us?' McKnight asked, as Drake laid the phone down on the kitchen counter top.

'Hard to say,' he admitted. 'But he'll try. That's the best we can hope for right now.'

In any case, he had another call to make. If this was to play out the way he hoped, they would need transport in and out of Libya. Arranging it at short notice would mean calling in a few favours, but at least he had someone in mind.

Chapter 15

Despite her earlier complaints, Frost threw herself into her task of digging up intel for their hastily planned operation with the kind of ruthless dedication that Drake had come to expect from her. Casting her net far and wide into the digital ocean of the internet, she soon began to unearth all kinds of information about the luxury two-storey villa on the outskirts of Tripoli that Tarek Sowan called home.

Everything from original construction blueprints, to planning applications for major remodelling, to purchase orders for alarm systems and security cameras; all of it fell victim to her relentless online forays, to be downloaded and sorted through on her laptop.

For Drake, this part was almost as crucial as the execution of the op itself. The generally held theory amongst the Shepherd teams was that 5 per cent more effort at the planning stage usually meant 50 per cent less chance of being killed later, and he wasn't inclined to dispute that. To the best of his knowledge, no operation had ever failed on account of having too much intel.

Armed with everything Frost could throw at them, Drake and Mason went to work piecing together a detailed picture of the target building. Trained in house assaults and well-versed in the difficulties that could easily derail such operations, they knew exactly what to look for. Years of experience allowed them to quickly assimilate the information they were given, to understand the systems of protection that surrounded Sowan, and most importantly devise a plan for how to defeat them.

At about mid-afternoon, they were alerted by a shout from Frost, who was standing watch outside. 'Vehicle coming in.'

Drake tensed up immediately, preparing to hide the computers and printed maps and documents that now lay strewn across the kitchen table. 'Make and model?'

'Sports car, dark green. Hell if I know the make.'

It didn't matter to Drake. She'd just told him what he'd been hoping to hear. 'It's all right. The driver's a friend.'

'An Anya kind of friend, or a real friend?'

'The kind of friend that's going to get us in and out of Libya.'

Taking a welcome break from the arduous planning session, Drake made his way outside just as an E-type Jaguar came screeching to a halt on the gravel driveway, its British racing-green paintwork splattered with mud after a bumpy journey down winding single-track roads, probably at high speed, knowing the owner.

Drake had encountered a lot of people in the course of his career as a Shepherd operative – some good, some bad, some infuriating to work with and others that he considered valuable friends. And some, like the owner of the car now sitting just a few feet from the front door, were genuinely unique.

He'd first met Vanil Chandra during an extraction mission from a muddy improvised airfield in Kosovo several years earlier. The weather had been terrible, the landing strip questionable to say the least, and the threat of enemy ground-fire from renegade Yugoslav units in the area ever-present.

Drake, wet and exhausted after an eight-mile slog through mountainous forest, had been bracing himself for the worst – a radio call from the pilot of their extraction flight warning that it was impossible to land in such conditions, and that regrettably they were on their own. It wouldn't have been the first time such a thing had happened to him, though given the large number of hostile units tasked with hunting his team, he'd suspected it might well be the last.

Then he'd heard it – the distinctive buzz of twin turboprop engines somewhere in the dense clouds overhead. To his everlasting amazement, a twin-engined transport plane had suddenly dropped from the low-lying cloud-deck like an old dive bomber from the war, tearing in just above the treetops before setting down hard on the improvised landing strip. Drake had actually seen it bounce twice before settling down and taxiing to a halt less than fifty feet away.

Running forward to express his thanks and disbelief that the pilot had executed such a dangerous manoeuvre, he'd found himself confronted by a relaxed and smiling Asian man with neatly cut hair and the kind of clean-cut good looks of that belonged in a menswear catalogue. Grinning at Drake, he'd gestured to the rear hatch and, with an impeccable English accent, remarked, 'Grab yourself a seat, old boy. Weather's a tad unpleasant today, but we'll soon be out of it.'

And that had been his introduction to Vanil Chandra, a freelance pilot who ran his own business hauling cargo – legal and otherwise – and who did occasional work for the Agency, usually in places where most rational men were unwilling to fly. His success wasn't so much down to the skill he possessed behind the stick, but rather because he seemed entirely unfamiliar with the concept of fear. Bad weather, bad terrain, even the possibility of being shot down didn't seem to trouble him.

Drake had always thought that the man had simply been born half a century too late. He would have been quite at home in the cockpit of a Spitfire.

Killing the engine, Chandra stepped out onto the gravel drive, drawing himself up to his full six-foot-three-inch height. By now in his late-forties, he still possessed the rangy build and sprightly energy of men half his age. Combined with lean, finely chiselled features and a mane of dark hair that was just starting to show flecks of grey at the temples, he cut a striking figure that few people failed to notice.

Spotting Drake, he flashed the infectious grin that hadn't changed since the day they met in Kosovo, and strode forward to greet him.

'Ryan, good to see you again, my friend!' he beamed, grasping Drake's hand in a strong handshake. 'How the devil are you?'

'Could be worse,' Drake acknowledged. Could be a hell of a lot better too, but there was no sense starting the meeting on a downer.

'My apologies for running a little late. Damned sheep-farmers held me up.'

Drake made a face, recalling his own experiences getting here. 'You get used to them, mate. Thanks for coming at short notice, though. I appreciate it.'

Chandra shrugged. 'Of course.' He leaned a little closer, his tone conspiratorial. 'To be honest, it was an excuse to get away from the lady for the afternoon.'

Drake decided not to pry too much into that. Being a wealthy, good-looking man who flew aircraft all over the world for a living, it wasn't hard for Chandra to attract female attention, and he was more than happy to capitalize on that fact. Bizarrely, he always referred to his latest girlfriend as 'the lady', rather than using her actual name, possibly because there was more than one and he didn't want to risk being caught out. Or maybe he himself had trouble keeping track.

'So tell me, what are you planning that you need my help with?' Chandra asked, growing a little more serious now that they were talking business. 'I assume you didn't invite me round for a chat and a cup of tea, though I wouldn't refuse the latter.'

'I can sort out both those things for you,' Drake assured him. 'Come inside and I'll introduce you to everyone.'

Normally introducing a newcomer to the rest of the team was a tense, awkward business, with Drake constantly on edge that one side would say or do something to offend the other. In this case, however, Chandra did most of the work himself, making his way from person to person and greeting them with an enthusiastic handshake and his characteristic beaming smile. Drake couldn't help noticing that he paid particular attention to McKnight, perhaps recognizing that Frost was a little too young and volatile to reciprocate, and hid a flash of annoyance that she seemed pleased by his casual flirtation.

'Before you steal my entire team away, why don't we go over what we need from you?' he suggested, his tone making it clear the time for socializing was over.

Chandra made a show of his disappointment. 'Excuse me, Samantha. Duty calls,' he said, giving her a wink before crossing the room to join Drake by the kitchen table. 'Fine people you associate with, Ryan.'

'They are. And I'd hate to think I was leading them on a one-way trip,' Drake added. 'That's where I need you.'

Chandra raised a dark eyebrow. 'How can I refuse an offer like that? Do tell.'

This he did. Leaving out the background and motivation behind the operation, Drake outlined his intention to lead his team into Libya no later than forty-eight hours from now, capture a high-ranking member of their intelligence agency in his home and covertly spirit him from the country to a safe location for interrogation.

'This is an unsanctioned operation,' he added, recognizing the need to be honest with Chandra before they went any further. 'The Agency doesn't know about this. In fact, almost everyone who does is in this house right now. We can't expect any support from outside.'

'This is nothing new,' Chandra remarked with a wry smile. 'But tell me, what has this man done to earn such attention from you? Is this personal?'

Drake knew he had to tread carefully with this one. 'If what I know about him is true, he deserves whatever he gets.' However this panned out, he'd make sure Sowan ended up in either a concrete cell or a wooden box. 'But this isn't about revenge, if that's what you mean. This man might hold the key to stopping a whole lot of wrong before it happens. I can't say much beyond that, but it's very important I get to him and find out what he knows. For that, I need your help.'

'I'd expected as much,' Chandra confirmed. 'You need extraction from Libya.'

'Two questions. Can it be done, and will you do it?'

The veteran pilot inhaled slowly, his usual bonhomie having vanished now as he contemplated what was being asked. 'I won't be able to enter their airspace without being detected, I can tell you that much. It would have to be done legally. I would need a flight plan that takes me to Tripoli, plus entry visas, which means I need a reason for being there, which usually means a few bribes to the right people. But in theory, I could make a short landing on the homeward leg, maybe plead mechanical problems.'

'Where?' Drake prompted.

Studying a map of the target area, he indicated a spot to the east of the city. 'As I recall, there's a small private airfield right around here. It shuts down at night, but a resourceful chap like you should be able to find a way in and set up some improvised lights.' He glanced up at Drake. 'That's the theory, at least. The timing would have to be rather spot-on, since their air-traffic controllers would know something was wrong if I started circling the field waiting for you.'

'But if we could make it happen, it could work.'

Chandra chewed his lip for a moment, deep in thought. 'It could.'

The next question was obvious enough, but it had to be asked all the same. 'So putting theory into practice, will you do it?'

He regarded Drake for a long moment. 'My fee would be twenty thousand, to cover fuel costs, paperwork, bribes and... well, unforeseen hazards. Half payable in advance, the other half on completion. Sorry to be rather mercenary about this, old boy, but it's the business we deal in now. I'll file the flight plan, get myself and my plane to Tripoli, and make sure I'm over the airfield at the agreed hour. The rest is up to your good self, I'm afraid. If you're not there in time, I'll have no choice but to head home without you. How does that sound?'

Hiring men like Chandra was a somewhat different prospect when a government agency wasn't underwriting the pay check, Drake reflected. He hadn't expected Chandra to risk his life for nothing, and it wasn't as if he was in a position to negotiate on price, but neither did he have £20,000 in disposable income just lying around. Especially not when he still had to purchase weapons, equipment, and pay off the man hired by Dietrich to provide ground transport.

'I don't have that much,' he said, bracing himself for the worst.

Chandra gave an apologetic shrug and pushed himself away from the table. 'Then I wish you the best of luck, my friend.'

'Wait,' Drake implored him. 'I can't pay you in cash. But... I can offer something else.'

Chandra regarded him sceptically. 'What might that be?'

He hesitated a moment, knowing the line he was about to cross and hating himself for it. But he could see no alternative. 'Follow me.'

For the second time in the past couple of days, Drake found himself in the little secluded garage set back from the main house. Undoing the padlock that was the only modest nod to security, Drake swung the double doors open to reveal the meticulously preserved vehicle hidden within.

The moment Chandra laid eyes on Drake's father's sports car, he let out a low whistle of approval. Ever the classic-car enthusiast, there was no question that such a machine would make an impact on him.

'An Austin-Healey 3,000,' he said, his voice sounding almost reverent. 'This is a Mark 1, if I'm not mistaken. They made fewer than three thousand of this model. There can't be more than a few hundred still in existence, and even fewer in such good condition.'

'Worth about twenty grand on the open market, wouldn't you say?' Drake prompted him.

Chandra immediately grasped what he was suggesting. Stepping inside the old building, he did a slow circuit of the car, even reaching out to run a hand along the gunmetal-grey paintwork. 'Does it still run?'

'Bet your arse it runs. My dad restored it himself,' Drake informed him, surprised at the pang of sadness and longing that it evoked.

'This belonged to your father?' Chandra glanced up at him, giving him a dubious look. 'I don't mean to lecture you, old boy, but are you sure this is what you want? Something like this is... irreplaceable.'

'He gave it to me, now I'm offering it to you.' Drake tried for a dismissive shrug, but didn't quite manage it. 'Anyway, I'm not much of a car enthusiast. You'll probably treat it better than me.'

Chandra let out a slow breath, nodding faintly in acceptance. 'It's your choice.' He held out his hand. 'If this is what you're offering, then we have a deal.'

Drake shook it, trying to silence the accusing voices in his mind. 'Done.'

–

For the next couple of hours, Drake worked virtually nonstop at his makeshift base of operations, alternately seeking advice, recommendations and opinions from the four other people in the house, each of whom had their part to play and their own areas of expertise. And gradually, a plan began to take shape.

By eight o'clock that evening, with the high straggling clouds tinged orange and long shadows stretching out across the garden outside, all was ready. Taking a sip from his fourth cup of coffee since arriving at the house, Drake called together his team to review the plan that he'd managed to hammer together.

'All right, time's not on our side, so I'll get right down to it.'

On the table in front of him was a satellite image of Tripoli downloaded courtesy of Google Maps, for lack of a more sophisticated source of data. The image depicted a dense sprawl of urban streets and residential areas, laid out in a rough grid pattern that would be familiar to his American companions.

'As best we can tell, Sowan beds down each night here.' He indicated one particular building that had been circled in red pen. 'It's a walled compound in the Gargaresh district, on the west side of the city. Apparently it's an affluent neighbourhood, so it's popular with high-ranking government and military types.'

'In short, one mistake and we'll have half the Libyan army on our asses,' Frost remarked.

Drake wasn't about to argue with her less-than-optimistic appraisal of the situation. Likely there were a lot of security operatives in that district, there to protect the most vital elements of the government while they slept.

'That's why we're going to do this right, first time. No fuck-ups, no mistakes,' he said, giving her a hard look. She didn't say anything further, so Drake turned his attention back to the map. 'So, phase one – insertion. Considering the resources available and the target area we're aiming for, an airborne drop is out of the question. There's too much chance of being spotted, and if we miss our target we'd be caught in the centre of a busy city. Covert border crossings are out too because it would take too long to scout out a route, which leaves us with the sea.'

Referring to an expanded satellite map of the Libyan capital, Drake circled an area of rugged coastline some distance to the west of the city.

'We expect heavy security around the commercial port and waterfront districts, but this stretch of coastline to the west should be quiet enough for us to get ashore undetected.'

'Yeah, but get ashore in what, exactly?' McKnight asked.

'By Zodiac. Chandra has agreed to get us as far as Malta by plane. From there, it's 190 nautical miles to Tripoli. A fast boat can cover that distance in under four hours. We leave at sunset, and we arrive in the early hours of the morning.'

Zodiacs had been used for decades by military and special-forces units for missions just like this. Difficult to spot at night, capable of transporting half a dozen men plus equipment, and able to outrun just about anything else on the water, they were ideal for covert insertions. Drake had ridden in the powerful, semi-inflatable craft plenty of times, and he knew that one outfitted with extra fuel canisters could easily make such a journey.

'Okay, so once we're ashore, what then?' Frost asked.

'The main coastal road is only a few hundred yards from the beach. We lay up there, wait for the vehicle that Dietrich's contact will supply. That brings us to phase two – neutralizing security.' He glanced up at his companion, indicating for him to carry on with the briefing. 'Cole?'

'If Sowan follows the typical pattern for high-level intelligence officials, he'll have a security detail of between three and five men guarding his house – one coordinating, the others walking the perimeter,' he explained. 'There are also security cameras monitoring all approaches to the house, meaning nobody can get close without being seen.'

'Could be inside too,' Frost pointed out.

'Unlikely.'

'Why?'

Mason glanced at her. 'It's a secured compound, but it's also his home. Would you really want someone watching while you take a dump in the middle of the night?'

She had no answer for that, leaving Mason free to continue. 'Based on the blueprints we've seen, the security system is linked back to Libyan intelligence headquarters by shielded fibre-optic landlines, meaning even if we take out the guards on site, there'd be a second pair of eyes watching us.'

McKnight pursed her lips, staring at the printed plan of the house and its walled grounds. 'So how do we get in?'

'The fibre-optic network should work against us, but actually it's our ticket in,' Drake explained. 'We know exactly where the cables are buried, which means we can access it. We dig one up, patch into their system, and use it to take control. A few minutes of looped camera footage should be enough to create the illusion that everything's normal.'

Frost was starting to see where he was going with this. 'Buying us time to get inside.'

'Exactly,' Drake agreed. 'Once we have control, we shut down the cameras, then move in to take out the security operatives before they can raise the alarm. Signal jammers should be enough to disrupt their radios, giving us a window to take them down. After that, it's a straight-up house assault. We move in, secure Sowan and get him of there with a minimum of fuss.'

'So how do we get out of the country?'

'That's where Chandra comes in,' Drake said, gesturing to the pilot who had been observing in silence thus far. He pointed to another area circled on the map. 'There's a small private airstrip about twenty miles out in the desert. He'll meet us there.'

'I'll land in Tripoli at about the same time you make landfall, posing as a commercial cargo flight,' Chandra explained, taking up the narrative. 'I'll need to refuel at that point anyway. Once you give me the code word *Tempest* via text message, I'll take off and head east for the private airstrip. But keep in mind that I can't land the bloody thing in pitch darkness, so you'll need to find a way of turning on the runway lights. Assuming you do, I'll land, pick you all up and we'll be out of Libyan airspace before anyone is the wiser.'

'It's not perfect, but it's what we've got,' Drake concluded, glancing up at his companions. 'Thoughts?'

This was a crucial moment in any operation, from the military to the Agency to this informal gathering. Everyone now had the chance to provide their insights, voice their objections or concerns about the plan, regardless of rank or any other consideration. At such a time, everyone involved was an equal, because they all had the same to lose. Drake had seen more than one operational plan torn to shreds or abandoned altogether because of problems that only came to light at this stage.

McKnight chewed her lip. 'A lot of moving parts, Ryan,' she warned. 'Any one of them fails, and the whole op's a bust.'

Drake nodded, his brow wrinkled in a frown. Single points of failure were the bane of operational planners, and there were all too many of them here. Normally they would have backups in place, additional resources they could call upon, but here there was nothing. Just Drake and his three teammates attempting a complex snatch-and-grab operation that a group twice as large and with far more resources would struggle to accomplish.

'And we're toast,' Frost added, quite unnecessarily.

'If you've got anything better, now's the time,' Mason prompted her.

For once, she said nothing.

'Will you be able to do what we need from you?' Drake asked her, wondering if her reluctance was due to a specific concern. 'The fibre-optic lines, the cameras, the security systems. If there's something you're worried about, be honest.'

He expected nothing less than honesty from her, but it never hurt to reiterate it. The worst thing anyone could do at a time like this was make promises they couldn't deliver on, for fear of being the naysayer of the group. If there was some insurmountable technical problem preventing them from going through with it, he'd rather know now.

The young woman mulled it over for a few moments. 'If the system's set up the way I think it is, then yeah, I can do it.'

Satisfied, Drake turned his eyes on McKnight. 'Sam? The same goes for you.'

'Can it work?' McKnight asked, staring right back at Drake. 'You know these kind of ops better than any of us, so no bullshit. Do you think we can pull this off, Ryan?'

'It's a gamble,' he conceded. 'There are a lot of ways this plan can go wrong, but in the end it's not about the plan. The plan's only as good as the team following it, and there's nobody better at this than the people standing around me right now.' He looked down at the map once more. 'If anyone wants to pull out, then this goes no further. I won't think less of you.'

Nobody said a word.

Drake let out a sigh and nodded. 'All right, then. It's a go.'

Chapter 16

That wasn't the end of it, of course. The 'go' decision might have been made, but there were still innumerable details to be pored over, countless minor problems and challenges to be resolved before the plan could be considered ready for action. The devil really was in the detail when it came to things like this, and there was simply no substitute for care and attention.

As the sun dipped below the horizon and darkness descended on the fields and woodlands outside, Drake and the others worked long into the night, testing and refining and searching for flaws they might have missed first time around.

At last, with the clocks rapidly approaching midnight, they could do no more and finally called a halt to their work, each of them mentally and physically exhausted from their efforts. Still, their reward was a plan of action which was about as complete and comprehensive as it could be, given the circumstances, and one that just might allow them to get what they needed without being killed in the process.

By the time the clock struck midnight, most of the group had drifted off to bed. But mindful of the need to safeguard the secrecy of their clandestine operation, Drake volunteered to take the first watch, partly because he knew his companions needed the rest more than he did, but mostly because he had too many things on his mind to surrender to sleep.

The success or failure of their plan rested on each and every one of them. If one failed in their designated task, all failed. And yet, for all that, he was still their leader. The ultimate responsibility rested with him. He was the one who had made this happen, not because he'd been ordered to do it, not because the mission had been handed to him via the Agency's complex bureaucracy, but because he'd made the conscious decision to go ahead with it.

If one of his companions didn't make it home, the blame rested solely on his shoulders.

Thus he found himself in the living room with a glass in hand, listening to the pop and hiss as a couple of small logs burned low in the open fire, the modest blaze helping to keep the room warm as the temperature fell outside. As it turned out, his mother hadn't been much of a whisky drinker, but he'd found a bottle of vodka on the sideboard. One small glass – not enough to impair his judgement, but enough to take the edge off and perhaps allow him to get his head down for a few hours later.

He felt bad for helping himself to her drink, and even worse for commandeering her home as a makeshift base of operations, but he told himself it was only for one night. Anyway, temperamental and difficult his teammates might have been at times, but they each came from a military background and had likely been well disciplined at cleaning up after themselves. When his sister returned here, she would find the place exactly as she'd left it.

Drake took a sip of the vodka as he sat on the couch, idly spinning the antique globe that had so fascinated him as a child, watching countries and continents whirl past in the blink of an eye. A world of possibilities and adventure that had once stretched out before him, just waiting to be discovered.

How things changed, he thought as he took another drink. The potent liquor burned his throat on the way down, and carried on burning as it settled reluctantly on his stomach. The world had shrunk, and the adventure hadn't turned out quite the way he'd hoped.

'If you're looking for Libya, you might be there a while,' McKnight said from the doorway. 'Doesn't exist. Actually, neither do Tunisia, Iraq or Iran.'

Drake glanced around and smiled at her. Half the countries depicted on the antique globe had ceased to exist, or their borders had been radically altered. 'Old map.'

'Old memories, I think.'

He said nothing to that.

Crossing the room softly on bare feet, she sat down on the edge of the couch and nodded to the drink in his hand. 'Be a shame to leave you drinking alone.'

Drake took the hint, and headed to the sideboard to pour her a glass. 'Take it you couldn't sleep either?'

'Pretty much.'

'I was always the same before a big operation,' he said, splashing a measure into one of the crystal glasses. 'Nervous, restless, wishing I could just get it over with. The waiting was the hardest part.'

'And now?' she asked, nodding in thanks as he handed her the glass.

He thought about it for a moment. 'Not much has changed.'

McKnight smiled and took a drink, holding his gaze as she tipped the glass back.

'It's good,' she remarked.

'It should be. Knowing Freya, it probably came all the way from Moscow.'

'Big drinker?'

Drake swirled the clear liquid around his glass before taking a gulp, grimacing a little as it went down. 'Big traveller.'

McKnight eyed him curiously. She hadn't missed his unhappy tone, and incorrectly assumed her question had stirred up the grief of his recent loss. 'I'm sorry, Ryan. I didn't mean to push.'

'You didn't,' he assured her. 'And don't worry. I'm not about to put away a few more of these and break down in front of you. It wasn't that kind of relationship.'

'So what was it? If you don't mind my asking.'

That wasn't an easy question to answer, because as the past couple of days had demonstrated, he didn't know half as much about his mother as he'd once thought.

What he did know, or what he'd been told more times than he needed to hear, was that he'd been born just as her career as a freelance writer was taking off after years of toiling away in obscurity, her newfound success at last offering her the chance to travel the world in search of new stories.

It was no easy thing to do that with a newborn baby, and even less so to find the time to write about it. Just like that, all those opportunities for exploration and adventure and excitement had been suddenly pushed aside, replaced by the mundane slog of caring for a screaming, demanding, draining new life.

Neither she nor his father had ever said anything explicitly, of course, but Drake had always sensed the lingering resentment she felt towards him. It had been there in every exasperated look, every frustrated sigh, every longing glance at the antique globe now sitting just feet away from him. She'd always been a little less patient with him, a little less understanding, a little harder to please.

As if being born at the wrong time had been his fault.

It had been different with Jessica, of course – she had been a conscious decision. Perhaps resigned to the fact they'd started their family earlier than planned, his parents had made the best of a bad job and had their second child just a couple of years after him.

Getting it out of the way all at once, as his father had so aptly put it. That was certainly the way Drake had always been made to feel. Something to get out of the way as quickly as possible, to be tolerated and endured, and then eventually escaped from.

'We… didn't talk much,' he said at last. 'And I think that suited both of us just fine.'

'But you must feel something, being here,' she said quietly, reaching out and touching his hand. 'Seeing all these reminders of her.'

'I do,' he admitted. 'But it's something I'll deal with later, when we've done what we have to. Until then, I can't let it in.'

He took another drink and looked away, staring into the flames in brooding silence, and for a time neither of them said anything more.

'Just answer me one thing,' she said quietly. 'Is this worth it? Everything we're doing, everything we're risking. Tell me it's worth it, Ryan.'

Drake glanced at the globe again, trying to recall the feeling of wonder it had once evoked in him. Instead, all he could see was his mother kneeling at the edge of a shallow pit, her hands bound behind her back, unable to resist as her killer levelled a weapon at her chest and pulled the trigger. Whatever his relationship with her had been, he knew that image would haunt his every waking moment.

Until he'd found the man responsible.

Drake looked at her then, his green eyes reflecting the glow of the fire. 'To punish him for what he did, to take away everything he took from us, to make him suffer like we have. Yeah, it's worth it,' he said with utter conviction. 'It's worth all of it.'

The woman stared at him in silence, taken aback by the determination in his eyes, the sheer force of will behind his words. There was nothing she could say to that. Drake was a man set on his course, and nothing and nobody could stop him.

Nobody except her.

'Get some sleep,' he said quietly after a time. 'Tomorrow's going to be a long day, for all of us.'

She didn't doubt it for a second.

Excusing herself from Drake's company some time later, McKnight crept outside, fished her cell phone from her pocket and typed in a number from memory, glancing over her shoulder once or twice to check no one was watching her.

Taking a breath, she paused for a moment as if debating with herself one last time, then hit the Call button. There was a click, then a faint buzz as the encrypted line was connected.

'What do you have for me, Samantha?' a familiar voice asked.

'It's on,' she said quietly. 'We leave for Libya tomorrow.'

'Excellent. And I can expect the operational details soon, right?'

McKnight's jaw tightened. She hated every moment of this. 'I'll send them to you when I can, but it's not easy. If they suspect me, it's over.'

Silence for a moment or two. 'Not losing your nerve, are you?'

'You brought me in to do a job. Let me do it, my way.'

She heard a faint chuckle of amusement on the other end. 'Well, the kitten has claws, I see. Just be careful where you point them, Samantha. Wouldn't want to see all your hard work be for nothing.' Marcus Cain let that threat hang in the air for a moment. 'Keep me updated. Out.'

With that, the line went dead.

Part II

Extraction

Responding to Libyan requests to hand over opposition leader Abu Abdullah al-Sadiq for rendition, a CIA case offer wrote, 'We are committed to developing this relationship for the benefit of both our services.'

Chapter 17

Whatever his shortcomings on a personal level, Dietrich had certainly delivered the goods when it came to support for this operation.

The man himself had been waiting for Drake and his team as they disembarked Chandra's aircraft at Malta International, grunting a terse greeting before shepherding them into a waiting car. From there, it had been a short journey to a secluded waterfront warehouse in the midst of the bustling Malta Freeport on the south side of the island. It hadn't taken long to get there; the entire island stretched little more than ten miles from east to west, and the airport sat barely a mile from the harbour area.

A rocky, arid spit of land in the southern Mediterranean covering just 120 square miles, Malta's geographic position as an air and naval base had given it an inherent strategic and political value that far outstripped its modest size. A succession of naval powers had conquered and fought to hold the small island over the centuries, from the Romans to the Spanish, French and British, before it had finally found independence in 1964. These days it was a major hub for commercial and cruise ships rather than warships of old, and Drake had certainly seen plenty of both as they arrived at their destination.

The warehouse now serving as the staging point for tonight's clandestine operation had come courtesy of Dietrich's contacts, as had the inflatable Zodiac resting on a trailer in the centre of the big open workshop, its powerful outboard motor almost as large as a car engine and certainly more powerful. Apparently it had been 'borrowed' from a local diving school, and was expected to be returned in the same condition it had been given.

Drake however was less interested in watercraft than he was in the equipment laid out on the collapsible workbench in front of him.

A set of four Browning L9A1 automatic pistols complete with attachable silencers was perhaps the most important aspect of their gear for this mission. The weapons were standard issue in the British military, plus a few dozen other countries, and were basically just modified versions of a design that dated back to the 1930s. Old they might have been, but they were tried and true, and hopefully enough to see the group out of trouble if it came down to it.

Normally a Shepherd team would have gone in with heavier firepower to back them up if things went sour, but as Dietrich had explained without a word of apology, this was the best he could manage at short notice. In any case, stealth and surprise were their best weapons tonight. The aim was to get in and out discretely, not to get drawn into a pitched battle they could never hope to win. The silenced Brownings would have to do.

Drake had personally field stripped and reassembled each of the four weapons, checking for flaws or – more tellingly – intentional sabotage. However, after spending nearly an hour working on them, he was obliged to admit they were all in good order. He'd even test fired a couple of rounds from each to verify the ammunition was fit for purpose.

Their other weapons for this job were far less precise than the Brownings, and intended to be used only if things went decidedly off-plan. Eight grenades – four smoke and four stun – were laid out in a row beside the handguns. Each member of the group was to be issued with one of each, giving them all a degree of much-needed tactical flexibility.

The Marine Corps motto that "Every Marine is a rifleman first" was, as far as Drake was concerned, just as applicable to Shepherd operatives. No matter what their trade, specialty or mission role, each member of his team was expected to be able to fight their way out of trouble if the need arose. For that reason, he wanted them as well armed as possible.

Stun grenades, known as flashbangs for the noise and light they produced, were non-lethal weapons designed to temporarily blind and deafen a target, making them invaluable for house assaults like this. Of course, the noise would certainly alert anyone within half a mile if they were used, but there was no telling whether they might need them.

Likewise, smoke grenades were intended to produce a dense cloud of chemically induced smoke. If they were forced to use the flashbangs for whatever reason, they might well need the smoke grenades to cover their escape.

Next to the weapons were their tactical radios – encrypted transmitter units fitted with discrete ear buds that would allow the team to communicate on a secure network without fear of electronic eavesdropping.

The flipside of that particular coin was the pair of signal jammers that they would use to disrupt radio communications amongst the guards patrolling Sowan's compound. Resembling walkie-talkies with several antennas of various lengths protruding from one end, they were designed to broadcast static noise on all known frequencies, jamming everything from short-range radios to television sets to cell-phone coverage. Their area of effect was limited, and it would mean the team's own radios would be similarly nullified while the jammers were active, but with luck it would buy them the time they needed to make entry.

He would rather have used their own gear for something like this, but there hadn't been time to source the equipment they needed in the UK, and doing so might have set off alarm bells with police and government agencies. In any case, Frost had done a thorough check on each unit to ensure it was in good order.

Further along the bench lay an assortment of different tools and gear that would be split amongst the team, from flashlights to spare batteries, plastic cable ties, duct tape, knives, ropes, lock picks, signal flares, about $500 worth of Libyan money and some basic medical kits. He didn't expect or hope to use all of it, particularly the last item on the list, but it never hurt to keep the bases covered. Despite all their careful planning, there was no way to predict what might happen once they were on site. As the saying so rightly went, it was better to have it and not need it, than vice versa.

'We don't offer warranties on this stuff, if that's what you're thinking.'

Drake turned to face Dietrich, who had wandered over to check on his progress. A tall, dark-haired German in his late forties, Jonas Dietrich possessed the grim, unsmiling countenance and cynical personality of a man perpetually pissed off with life. Strange, Drake had always thought, because he seemed to have lived something of a charmed existence.

He'd started out his career with the West German intelligence service back in the 1980s, running operations in Eastern Europe against the Soviets. He'd been responsible for helping a number of high-value targets to defect to the West, willingly or otherwise, but with the Cold War winding down he'd moved to America and soon been snapped up by the Agency.

On the surface he'd seemed like an intelligent, meticulous Shepherd team leader with a flair for creativity, but by the time Drake had encountered him he'd become arrogant, overconfident and hopelessly addicted to heroin. One of Drake's first acts had been to arrange Dietrich's demotion to specialist, which hadn't exactly done their working relationship any favours.

He'd straightened himself out since then and regained his former position as a team leader, but as far as Drake could see, his personality still needed some work.

'No worries, mate. If they don't work when we need them, we won't be around to ask for a refund,' Drake remarked, lifting one of the Brownings and pulling back the slide to check the action again. 'Sure you don't want to join us, see firsthand how it goes?'

Dietrich gave him a sour look. 'Don't hold your breath. The last time we worked together, I took a round through the leg and almost got killed.'

'You also got promoted to team leader,' Drake reminded him. 'Not a bad trade.'

'Why do you think I'm here?' He gave a rare smile that looked quite out of place, and soon faded as his manner turned serious again. 'You know, it's a strange thing seeing everyone together again.'

Drake glanced at him. 'Never thought of you as the nostalgic type.'

'I'm not, but it does seem like history repeating, and not in a good way. How many times are you going to risk your life for Anya before your luck runs out?'

Drake laid the weapon back down on the table. 'I'm not doing this for her.'

He wasn't willing to say more than that. If Dietrich only knew his real reason for going through with this, he might not have been so willing to help them.

'Very heroic, Ryan.'

'None of us are trying to be heroes tonight,' Drake assured him. 'I'd settle for getting everyone through this in one piece.'

Dietrich said nothing to this, though his silence told its own story. 'Our Zodiac pilot says we'll be ready to get underway in sixty minutes,' he said instead, concentrating on more practical matters. 'Consider that a warning to get your shit together. He's not likely to wait around too long.'

Though most of them could operate the Zodiac at a push, they had no first-hand experience of the waters off the Libyan coast where they intended to make landfall. Arriving in sufficient time to complete their objective before sunrise while taking into account tides and currents was no easy task.

For this reason, Dietrich had recruited a pilot for their clandestine trip tonight – an ex-Navy man who had been living and sailing in this neck of the woods for the past twenty years. Apparently he was 'reliable', which was Dietrich's way of saying he was no stranger to illicit journeys of questionable legality, and therefore wouldn't ask any questions.

'Tell him we'll be ready,' Drake said.

At this, Dietrich chuckled in amusement. 'More balls than brains, as usual. Well, it seems to have worked for you so far. Maybe it'll be enough tonight.'

With that less-than-encouraging remark, he turned and strode away, lighting up a cigarette as he went. Once he was well out of earshot, Frost ventured over to speak with Drake.

'Guy still gives me the creeps,' she remarked, casting a dark glance after him. 'I don't care what anyone says. He's bad news.'

Drake chewed his lip. 'He's what we've got.' Turning his attention back to matters at hand, he gestured to the equipment laid out on the table. 'Run a check of the radios and the jammers.'

'I already tested them,' she protested.

'Test them again.'

He was already heading for the doorway leading to the quay outside.

'Where are you going?'

'To get some air,' he called over his shoulder. 'I'll be back in five, and I want those checks finished.'

'Yes, sir,' Frost called out mockingly, then added in a quieter tone, 'Asshole.'

'I heard that.'

'You were supposed to.'

It was a warm, balmy evening in the southern Mediterranean as Drake emerged onto the waterfront quay that fronted the warehouse. The sun had just dipped below the horizon, its dying rays casting a final spectacular display of fire on the canvas of clouds overhead. A faint breeze sighed through the palm trees that fringed the waterfront, carrying with it the tangy scent of the ocean, and the rather less palatable odour of diesel fumes from the nearby Malta Freeport.

He watched as a massive bulk cargo hauler, its decks piled high with bus-sized storage containers that resembled so many multi-coloured Lego bricks from this distance, eased out of its mooring. Its passage was assisted by teams of small but powerful tugboats, water frothing at their sterns as they laboured to keep the immense vessel on course.

Taking a breath, Drake reached into his pocket for his cell phone, then held it for a moment, silently debating the wisdom of this decision. It was certainly a breach of operational security to be making a private call on the very eve of their mission, but at the back of his mind lurked the telling possibility that he might not get another chance.

He'd dialled the familiar number almost without thinking. Whatever else happened, he had to at least try to make amends.

The phone rang out for some time, causing him to question whether or not she'd even answer his call, before it suddenly went silent.

'What is it, Ryan?' Jessica asked impatiently. 'I thought I told you not to contact me.'

Drake winced inwardly at her scathing words. 'I know. I know, Jess. I just…'

He sighed, looking out across the glittering waves to the distant horizon. Somewhere out there, far beyond his sight, lay the Libyan coast. And the man who had ordered his mother's death.

'What is it?' she prompted him. 'Whatever you have to say, say it and get it over with.'

'Look, I don't have much time. I had to go away, just for a couple of days.'

'Go away? Go where, Ryan?' The anger was still there, but there was something else beneath it now. 'Christ, please tell me you're not working. Not for *them*. Not now.'

'It's not for them,' he assured her. 'Believe me, it's not. I can't go into the details, but if things work out the way I hope… well, you might be able to throw that gun away, after all.'

Silence greeted him. Tense, fraught, anguished silence.

'If not, I wanted you to know that… you were right.' He swallowed, raising his chin a little as a faint breeze blew across his exposed skin. 'I should have been there for you, Jess. I told myself I was doing the right thing, that I was fighting the good fight, but really I was running away from it. I should have been there for you, and I'm sorry I wasn't. I know that doesn't change anything, but… I at least wanted to be honest with you for once. I wanted you to know I'm sorry, and… I love you.'

'Ryan, don't—'

'Take care of yourself,' he whispered, ending the call. He'd powered down the phone before she could call him back, unwilling to listen to any attempt to dissuade him from his plan. He was set on his course now, and one way or another had to see it through.

It was a shitty thing to do – just another item to add to the list of his mistakes over the past couple of years – but if everything went wrong tonight and he didn't come home, at least his last words to her wouldn't have been spoken in anger.

Drawing what comfort he could from that, Drake slipped the phone into his pocket and headed back inside to continue his work.

–

An hour later, and Drake and his team were geared up and ready. The Zodiac boat had already been rolled into the water and detached from its trailer, ready for its passengers to embark. The pilot was waiting behind the wheel, engines idling, with Dietrich beside him. He would accompany them as far as the Libyan coast, then make the return journey with the boat to Malta.

Whatever plans and preparations they could make had been made. From this moment on, the success or failure of their mission tonight would depend on quick thinking, improvisation and no small measure of luck. The first two they could certainly count on. As for the third, that was as always beyond their control.

'All right, guys. Gather round for a minute, would you?' Drake said, beckoning his team to join him in the centre of the room.

As they closed in around him, he looked at them each in turn. All were dressed in black for the night operation, webbing covering their torsos and equipment packs slung over their shoulders, silenced weapons holstered and ready. Each wore the same look of focussed, tense resolve. They were prepared, both physically and mentally, for what lay ahead, and were eager to get started.

'Thank you. For this, for everything. I owe you a debt I can't begin to repay,' he said, his voice quiet, almost reverent. 'We go in tonight as a team, just like we always have. We watch out for each other, we trust each other, we listen to each other, and we come home the same way. Together, as a team.' He paused a moment. 'Everyone ready?'

He was met by a round of resolute, determined nods.

This was the moment – the last chance to call it off, to back down and abandon the dangerous mission that could see one or all of them killed. Drake wouldn't have thought less of them if they had. But they didn't, just as he'd known they wouldn't. They faced it down, and not one of them flinched.

'All right. Let's get it done.'

Chapter 18

Fifteen years earlier

Drake winced as his fist connected with the other fighter's torso again, pain radiating out from the damaged joints in his hand like ripples in a pond. At last, like a mighty tree surrendering to the relentless blows of a woodsman's axe, his opponent buckled under the blow. His legs gave way beneath him and he went down on one knee, bloodied and bruised, gasping for breath.

'Stay down, for fuck sake!' Drake yelled, his voice almost drowned out by a mixture of cheers and boos echoing from the crowd all around. A couple of rounds earlier they had applauded his every move.

He'd been a popular fighter right from the start; young, energetic and aggressive, eager to take the fight to his opponents and rarely backing down. Virtually all his fights had ended with dramatic early knockouts. He was met with cheers every time he stepped into the ring, and he loved it.

But now he sensed the shift in their collective consciousness; the admiration and respect turning to frustration and outright hostility. In their eyes, he was taunting the older fighter, humiliating him, beating him to the verge of a knockdown but refusing to finish him for good.

They couldn't have been further from the truth. He wanted this to end as much as they did. He had no interest in humiliating the man. And more than that, he was hurting. His increasingly desperate efforts to knock his adversary out were wearing down his stamina, his endless flurries of heavy punches taking their inexorable toll on his hands.

'You've done enough. It's over! Stay down!' he screamed.

The older man looked up at him, breathing hard, blood dripping from a cut above his eye and another on his cheek. Then his jaw clenched, he planted his feet firmly on the ground and forced himself to his feet.

The crowd cheered their approval for the tough, resilient underdog, and Drake's heart sank.

–

Drake glanced down at his right hand, slowly clenching and unclenching it, feeling the familiar ache in the damaged joints. The old injury rarely troubled him, except sometimes when the weather was cold or damp. Then he felt it; a silent reminder of a very different sort of battle he'd fought a lifetime ago.

He reached up, wiping the stinging salt water from his eyes as another blast of spray arced over the Zodiac's prow to strike him full in the face. It had started out as a small but inevitable annoyance when they'd first cleared Malta Freeport and the craft's pilot had throttled up to full power, sending them hurtling across the sea towards the distant, unseen coast of North Africa. Now, three hours later, the combination of unceasing wind and occasional random soakings were wearing on his nerves.

It wasn't the only discomfort he had to endure. His legs and back were aching from holding the same position for so long as the black inflatable craft powered its way through the rolling waves of the southern Mediterranean, its five passengers crouched down on the semi-rigid deck in stoic, uncomfortable silence.

In reality the weather conditions were mercifully good tonight, with little wind and only a light swell to contend with. But their vessel was small and moving at high speed, and thus every gently rolling wave felt like a mountain of iron beneath them, pitching and bumping the small craft with endless impacts that were taking a slow but inexorable toll on its reluctant crew.

Behind him, manning the wheel, was their pilot, a gruff, grizzled man of at least sixty years who answered to the name Hoyes and nothing else. Drake knew little about the man, save what Dietrich had told him; that he'd once been an officer in the Royal Navy before taking early retirement and settling into a far more profitable business ferrying 'cargo' around the Med.

Sporting a short greying beard and the kind of craggy, weathered features that could only come from a life of exposure to salt and sea, he stood as tall and unmovable as a statue at the helm. Spray and wind seemed not to trouble him in the slightest as he adjusted their course or tweaked the throttle controls. Whatever his dubious past, he seemed to know his business when it came to boats, and that was enough for now.

Drake glanced at his watch, knowing he wouldn't like what he saw. Three hours and forty minutes since departing Malta. Under normal circumstances they should have been ashore already, but the sighting of a large commercial vessel directly across their path about an hour into the journey had forced Hoyes to alter his course eastward, adding precious time to their already tight schedule. Time was one resource they couldn't afford to waste.

But it was more than just the minor delay that had stirred his unease. Despite himself, Drake couldn't shake the feeling that somehow it was an ill omen. He wasn't given to superstition when it came to things like this, but neither could he deny the evidence of past experiences.

He'd been on his share of operations where an early problem or setback invariably meant further difficulties ahead; for whatever reason, nothing seemed to go right afterwards. Whether it was genuinely down to something as intangible as luck, or whether an early blow to a group's collective morale affected its decision-making ability, he couldn't rightly say. All he knew was that if an op got off to a smooth start, the rest seemed to fall into place.

Feeling a hand tap his shoulder, he turned and leaned close to Frost so he could hear her speak over the roar of the outboard motor and the tearing wind around them.

'Remember when I said I'd never parachute into another mission as long as I lived?' she prompted, grimacing as they hit another wave that jarred their bones. 'I take it back.'

Trying to hide his misgivings, Drake grinned at her. No sense in bringing his comrades down. 'I'll keep that in mind.'

No sooner had he said this than the ever-present roar of the big outboard motor began to drop away as Hoyes eased off the throttle.

'I see lights,' he called out. 'Port beam. On your ten o'clock.'

Drake twisted around once more. Sure enough, he could faintly make out the glimmer of electric lights against the darkness of the horizon maybe fifteen miles distant.

That was Tripoli, where their target Tarek Sowan was – hopefully – tucked up in bed and fast asleep. With no idea what was coming for him.

Ahead of them lay the darkness of the Libyan coast. According to their limited intel, the stretch of coastline where they were to make landfall was uninhabited, save for an oil and gas complex several miles to the west. It was about the only viable location in easy range of their target.

'What do you think about our landing place?' Mason asked.

At this, Hoyes offered a far from reassuring shrug. 'We'll know if they start shooting at us, won't we, son?'

With the engine running at half speed to reduce noise, the Zodiac crept in towards the coast. At first the stretch of coast ahead of them remained invisible, shrouded in the darkness, but gradually they caught occasional flashes of car headlights moving by on the Libyan Coastal Highway that ran the length of the country.

At last Drake spotted the coast itself; rugged and inhospitable, with rocky headlands and narrow beaches giving way to steep slopes and weathered cliffs. Few trees grew in what was clearly an arid, desert landscape, meaning the group would be afforded little cover as they made their way ashore.

About 400 yards offshore, the engine powered back and finally shut down altogether. Compared to the constant mechanical roar that had been their companion for the past four hours, the silence that followed was deafening in its totality.

'Right lads, this is as far as we go under power,' Hoyes said, nodding to the set of oars lashed to the deck. 'You're younger than me. Time to put that energy to good use.'

He certainly wasn't going to lend a hand. Instead the oars were unfolded and quickly put to work by Drake and Mason. Noise carries a long way over water at night, so the final leg of their journey would have to be completed by old-fashioned hard work.

As they bent to their task, Frost and McKnight took up position in the bow, silenced weapons out and ready. Likewise, Hoyes stood on constant alert, ready to drop the engine back into the water and power the craft out of the area if anything looked amiss. For obvious reasons, small-arms fire was deadly to inflatable boats like theirs.

However, despite their precautions, they saw no sign of activity as the rocky coastline crept closer. No lights were directed their way, no sudden eruption of weapons fire. The land ahead was mercifully, eerily quiet.

'We're close,' McKnight whispered, her voice partly obscured by the steady crash of breaking surf. 'Twenty yards out.'

Both men were sweating, their arms and shoulders starting to burn with the exertion when they finally felt the hull bottom grate against a rocky shore.

The two female operatives up front wasted no time, leaping down into the knee-high water and peeling off left and right, taking up position to cover their two companions as they prepared to disembark. There was about ten metres between them; close enough that they could communicate easily, but far enough that a single grenade or burst of fire couldn't take them both down.

Mason went next, weighed down with both Frost's equipment pack and his own. Since Frost and McKnight were first out, they needed to move fast and unencumbered. They would redistribute their gear once they were all ashore.

Snatching up McKnight's pack, Drake paused for a moment at the bow and gave their pilot a nod of gratitude, then turned his attention to Dietrich.

'Thanks, mate. For the help,' he said quickly.

Dietrich reached out and shook his hand. 'Good luck, Ryan. My man should be waiting for you near the road. Now get your ass ashore.'

Leaping down from the vessel's prow, he felt his boots come down hard on loose pebbles as water splashed around his knees. Straightaway he was moving up the shore, fighting his way out of the water that would inevitably slow him down.

Dropping down on one knee, he laid McKnight's pack in front of him and drew his automatic. Already the Zodiac was moving away, both Dietrich and Hoyes lending their arms to the oars to get clear of the coastline.

For the next twenty seconds or so, Drake said and did nothing; just sat there listening and waiting, allowing his senses to tune into his new environment. His eyes were by now well adjusted to the darkness, allowing him at least a partial view of the rocky cliffs and slopes ahead of them. He could sense nothing out of the ordinary.

Reaching up for the little radio transmitter fixed to his throat, he switched on the unit and spoke a quiet command. 'All units, move up.'

Rising to his feet, he advanced up the beach at a steady, ground-covering pace. There was no need to run, since they weren't in immediate danger. Running over rough ground in the dark expended needless energy they might need later, and was also a quick way to fall and break an ankle. The latter would spell death for their chances of success.

Clearing the beach, Drake halted in the shadow of a big rectangular boulder that seemed to have tumbled down the slope in years gone by. By unspoken consent, the rest of the group converged on his position.

'Everyone good?' he asked. The golden rule on missions like this was that nobody ever played the strong, silent hero. If someone had a problem, they were expected to make the group aware of it right away so it could be dealt with.

'Good to go,' Frost replied as she shouldered her pack.

Ignoring her remark, Mason pointed up the slope. 'There's a draw over there to the right. It's a little exposed, but it's probably the easiest way up.'

Drake followed his line of sight, spotting a path that wound its way up through the tangled brush and boulders. 'All right. Five-metre spread. Cole, on point. Sam, Keira, behind me. Move.'

Mason, a former army Ranger with years of reconnaissance experience, was an ideal choice for scouting ahead. He also seemed to have a nose for trouble. Whether it was particularly keen senses or just natural intuition, Drake didn't really care. But it would serve them well tonight.

With Mason leading the way, the group advanced up the slope, heading for the high ground overlooking the cove. There was no talking as they picked their way over rocks and around bushes that could snag on clothes and make additional noise they didn't need right now. If someone had something to call out, they would. Otherwise they remained silent.

Nearing the crest of the slope, Mason suddenly held up his hand, gesturing for them to halt. Straightaway they froze, watching him closely for further information. There was no thought of challenging him. The man on point was, in effect, the leader of the group until relieved of that duty. Any instructions he gave were obeyed without question.

The general rule in situations like this, when the point man had seen something the others couldn't, was to do exactly what he did. Thus, when Mason lowered himself into a crouching position, the others did likewise.

Drake watched as Mason held up a clenched fist, moving it slowly from side to side as if he were holding an imaginary steering wheel. He'd spotted a vehicle.

Next he held up a single finger pointing skyward. One target in sight.

Lastly he ran a hand down his chin as if stroking a beard. One target, male.

Drake could feel his heart beating faster. It certainly sounded like the man Dietrich had arranged to meet them, but there was no telling for sure until they made contact.

Careful to avoid disturbing any loose rocks, Drake crept forward until he was close enough to whisper in Mason's ear.

'One vehicle, one man?' he whispered, wanting to ensure he'd understood his companion.

'Yeah. Two o'clock, about thirty yards,' Mason confirmed. 'Think he was having a smoke.'

Deciding to chance a look, Drake edged up over the crest and directed his gaze where Mason had indicated. Sure enough, he could make out the dark square bulk of a van silhouetted against the night sky. And beside it, a figure stood hunched over. Judging by the height and general build, it was indeed a man, and he was cradling something in his hands. Drake saw the distinctive red glow of burning tobacco as he took a draw on a cigarette.

The whole movement took less than two seconds. It was time enough to get what he needed. Ducking back down, he turned to his companion.

'What do you think?' Mason asked.

There was only one way to find out if this was the man sent to help them.

'I'll circle around him to make contact,' he decided. If the van driver proved to be less than friendly, at least he wouldn't know which direction to look for the rest of the team. 'Cover me, and be ready to pull back in a hurry.'

With luck, their friends in the Zodiac wouldn't have left the area just yet. There was a good chance they could summon Hoyes back for an emergency extraction if the shit hit the fan.

'Copy that.'

Wary of making undue noise but increasingly aware of their limited time, Drake crept along the edge of the slope, keeping just out of sight as he moved through the shadows. The Browning automatic was a solid, comforting weight in his right hand. He knew it wouldn't offer much protection if this turned into a shooting match, but it was an awful lot better than nothing.

Judging that he'd covered about thirty yards, Drake reached up and hit the radio transmitter at his throat. 'Set.'

'Copy,' came Mason's tense reply.

Taking a breath and focussing his awareness, Drake rose to his feet, gripping the weapon tight. The truck was straight ahead, maybe ten yards away, and the owner was beside it, standing near the driver's side door. His back was to Drake.

Raising the silenced automatic, Drake took a step towards him.

'You're late,' an old, raspy voice remarked with the kind of casual irritation one might ascribe to a delayed train.

The stub of a cigarette was thrown on the ground, and the man turned slowly, unhurriedly, to face him. He looked just as he sounded; old, worn and hardened by a life neither short nor easy. Five foot ten, with the spare, angular frame of a man used to both hardship and physical toil, he seemed almost lost in the drab, stained juba and waistcoat that he wore. A scraggly grey beard trailed down from a gaunt, deeply lined face.

He eyed Drake's weapon without a trace of concern. Drake suspected it wasn't the first time this man had had a gun pointed at him.

'You are Ryan, yes?' he asked. For some reason he pronounced the name Ree-ann.

'That's right.'

'I am Aarif. Jonas sent me.'

'Are you alone, Aarif?' Drake asked.

'Are *you*?' he echoed. 'I was told there would be four of you. Where is the rest of your team?'

'Around,' Drake said, unwilling to give him more than that. 'You didn't answer my question.'

Aarif smiled, revealing a set of teeth that looked like they hadn't seen a toothbrush in a very long time. 'A man like you is wise to be cautious, but do not confuse caution with fear, Ryan. I am not your enemy, and you are not my friend. I was sent to bring you and three others to Tripoli, and this I will do, but not at gunpoint.'

He shrugged. 'Or… you could kill me right now and take your chances. But then, you do not know which roads to take, which checkpoints to avoid, which soldiers to bribe.'

Drake lowered the weapon, feeling somehow like a child being scolded by an impatient teacher.

'Better,' Aarif decided, his tone softening just a little. 'To answer your question, yes, I came alone. My instructions were to deliver you to the Gargaresh district in central Tripoli. Jonas said you were very specific about the location?'

'Yeah.'

'It will not be easy. There are many embassies and government employees living in that area – security is tight.'

'That's what we're paying you for,' Drake pointed out.

Again he saw that crooked smile. 'Jonas said you would say that. But lucky for you, I know a way in. Getting out will be your own business, of course.' Turning away, he hauled open the door of his dilapidated van. Old hinges creaked with the effort. 'If you are a shepherd as Jonas says, now would be the time to gather your flock.'

Without waiting for a reply, he turned the ignition, coaxing the tired engine back into life. It was plain he was going to leave shortly, with or without Drake and the others.

Holstering the weapon, Drake reached up and hit the transmitter at his throat. 'All units on me now. Good to go.'

Within moments, Mason, Frost and McKnight had emerged from cover and were hurrying towards him, weapons up and ready.

'In the back, all of you,' Aarif called out over the rumble of the engine. Like its owner, it sounded rough, tired and in need of serious attention. 'The door is unlocked.'

'This ought to be good,' Frost mumbled, heaving the rear door open. A dark, rubbish-strewn cargo compartment awaited her.

Within moments, the remainder of the team had piled in after her. Aarif gunned the engine, swinging the van around in a wide arc to head back towards the coastal road before Drake had even closed the door.

They were on their way to Tripoli.

Chapter 19

Situated on a rocky spur of land at the edge of the vast and largely uninhabited Sahara Desert, the ancient capital of Libya had a long history stretching back nearly 3,000 years, to when it had been established as a trading port by the Phoenicians. Since then it had been fought over and ruled by everyone from the Greeks to the Romans, the Ottomans and the Italians, and finally by one Muammar Muhammad Abu Minyar al-Gaddafi.

Colonel Gaddafi had been the sole leader of the country since coming to power by military coup in 1969. In the four decades since then, the fickle and unpredictable leader had charted a meandering course between advancing the cause of Islamic Socialism, stirring up border conflicts with Egypt and Chad, financing and supporting foreign militants and terrorist groups, sabre-rattling against America and occasionally torturing and executing anyone who posed a threat to his stranglehold on power.

He was generally seen as a loose cannon by most of the power brokers in Washington and London, particularly since he'd been implicated in blowing up a US airliner over Scotland back in the 1980s. A loose cannon he might have been, but he was also sitting on some of the largest crude-oil reserves outside of Saudi Arabia, making him the kind of pain the Western world was prepared to endure.

For now.

With this newfound spirit of cooperation in mind, UN sanctions on Libya had been lifted back in 2003, and foreign investment had promptly flooded the country. Decades of isolation and economic decline had been reversed, and nowhere had these effects been more profound than the city that Drake and his companions now found themselves in.

Everywhere Drake looked he saw building sites – the steel and concrete skeletons of hotels, office blocks, skyscrapers and shopping complexes rising into the night sky. Even at this late hour, sleek late-model saloons and SUVs cruised by on the brightly lit main drag, many carrying foreign executives home after a night out on the company's dollar. The ancient city was being dragged rapidly into the twenty-first century, its headlong rush fuelled almost entirely by oil.

'It is impressive, yes?' Aarif said over his shoulder, speaking to Drake through the small ventilation grate joining the driver's cab to the cargo compartment. 'There is much money in Libya these days. Like America, but less fat people.'

'I'll take your word for that,' Drake said. He was more interested in Libyan intelligence officers than fast-food chains. 'How long 'til we get there?'

'Three, maybe four minutes.' Tapping a cigarette from his packet, Aarif lit one up and took a slow, thoughtful drag, then held it up to Drake. 'Smoke?'

Drake shook his head.

'Clean living. Good for you, Ryan. You will live longer, yes?' He chuckled at his own joke. 'Me? I don't worry. If God wants me dead, it will happen. If not, it won't.'

Drake wasn't so sure about the clean-living part. There were other vices apart from smoking. 'How long have you been doing this?' he asked instead.

'Helping people like yourself? Not for a long time. I was… retired when Jonas contacted me. But I owed him a favour, so here I am. After tonight, I consider my debt repaid. And that is good.'

Drake frowned, intrigued by his statement. 'How do you two know each other?'

'It is, like you say, a long story. One I do not wish to share with a man I barely know.'

Before he could say anything further, Aarif tensed up, having spotted something on the road up ahead. A couple of military-patterned vehicles were parked on either side of the road, with several armed men in uniform milling around between them.

'Checkpoint ahead,' he warned. 'Stay down. Do and say nothing until we are clear. Understand?'

He did. That didn't mean he liked the idea of waiting in silent darkness, wondering if they were about to be caught by Libyan security services before they'd even reached the house. 'Will they search the van?'

'Depends how well they have been paid this month,' Aarif admitted. 'Now be still!'

Reaching behind him, he pulled the little grate closed, plunging Drake and the others into darkness.

'What the fuck's going on out there?' Frost asked, glancing up from her hand-held satellite-navigation unit as they began to slow down.

'Checkpoint. Kill the GPS, and the radios. No lights, no sound,' Drake said quietly, lowering himself onto the steel deck.

'Got it,' Frost mumbled, powering down the unit she had been using to monitor their progress.

The van slowed before finally coming to a stop, engine idling and exhaust venting steam and fumes. Straining to hear, Drake detected the murmur of voices outside. They didn't sound raised or angry, but rather seemed to be conversing casually in Arabic.

Drake was far from fluent in the language, but he'd assimilated enough over the past couple of years to understand the basic flow of the conversation. Aarif seemed to be trying to bluff his way past, remarkably using the same delivery-driver bullshit that Drake and his team had employed four days earlier in Paris. The only question was whether the guards would buy it.

The seconds crawled by with no discernible change in the situation outside. Then an answer of sorts came a moment later when the metal interior of the van resounded with a loud, reverberating thump as something hammered against it. The effect was not unlike being inside a steel drum while someone laid into it with a baseball bat, and Drake and his companions instinctively flinched at the sound.

The sudden noise was accompanied by an angry shout, almost certainly from Aarif. Several voices were then speaking all at once, louder and distinctly agitated now. It was difficult for Drake to follow the confused clamour of different voices, but he caught a few angry curses and a remark about having to follow orders.

With the grate closed and no windows fitted to the cargo compartment, the darkness inside the van was absolute. Drake couldn't even see the hand in front of his face, but dared not risk even the smallest light in case some unseen hole in the chassis alerted the soldiers outside.

Instead he reached down, gripped the butt of the Browning automatic and gently eased it from the holster, thumbing the safety to the off position. The faint scraping and metallic clicks around him told him that the rest of the team were doing likewise, preparing to defend themselves by unspoken mutual consent.

The thin metal walls of the van would offer no protection if the men outside decided to open fire on the vehicle. He hadn't gotten a good look before the grate was slammed shut, but Drake was willing to bet they were armed with AK-47s or some derivative. The powerful assault rifles could punch through the vehicle's skin like damp paper, tearing through anyone unlucky enough to be caught in their bullets' path with equal ease.

For a moment, Drake considered the option of making the first move. If they were quick, they could throw the doors open and come out shooting, hoping to kill or injure as many of their enemy as possible before making a break for it. From there, they would hijack one of the many civilian vehicles that were still cruising the main highway, and use it to try to get back to the coast. As with most operations thrown into disarray by an unexpected problem, they would have little choice but to improvise a way out.

The sound of raised voices was almost equal to the pounding of Drake's heart as adrenaline flooded his bloodstream, urging him to either fight or make a run for it. Simply sitting there in deathly silence with armed men just feet away was enough to strain even the nerves of experienced operatives, yet nobody made a sound. Disciplined and professional, they wouldn't do a thing unless Drake ordered it.

But he didn't, partly because he knew their chances of survival would be slim, but mostly because it felt like the wrong call. The only thing worse than being caught off guard was to snatch defeat from the jaws of victory by panicking at a crucial moment. There were times to cut one's losses and make a break for it, and times to stick it out and see if the situation might yet right itself. Drake's instincts told him this was the latter.

Sure enough, something must have been said to calm the tense situation outside, because soon the voices began to quieten, returning to something like normal volume. At one point, Drake could have sworn he even heard a brief snort that might have been laughter.

And then, just like that, he heard the faint thump of a hand against the driver's door up front. The engine rattled back into life as Aarif gave it some gas, and they were on their way once more.

It was another twenty seconds or so before the grate slid open.

'I don't know if they were well paid this month,' the driver announced over his shoulder, taking a draw of his cigarette. 'But they are a lot wealthier after tonight.'

Now off the main drag and into the maze of small roads and tight junctions that characterized many of the residential quarters of Tripoli, Aarif led them on a winding route that took them in a generally south-westerly direction, through what appeared to be a fairly affluent area by Libyan standards. Most of the houses here were two- or even three-storey affairs, surrounded by walled gardens and imposing security gates that were probably sufficient to deter most opportunistic thieves.

According to the sporadic research Drake had been able to conduct before leaving the UK, this was where the rich dentists, company directors, foreign investors and generally well-to-do people of Libya based themselves. It was like the North African equivalent of Kensington.

'This is it, just up ahead,' Drake said, indicating an area of waste ground in the midst of this suburban splendour that seemed to be in the midst of being cleared for new developments. Most likely an old or neglected building had been bulldozed away, ready for some new apartment complex to be erected in its place.

Pulling off the main road as instructed, Aarif switched off the lights and manoeuvred the van between heaps of weed-clogged rubble that were all that remained of the previous building. Satisfied that it was more or less hidden from view, he switched off the engine and twisted around in his seat to regard Drake and the others.

'This is as far as I go, Ryan,' he announced. 'The rest is up to you. The van is yours if you want it.'

'What about you?' Drake asked.

'Do not worry about me.'

It was at this moment that Aarif did something quite unexpected. Reaching up, he tugged at the grey scraggly beard sprouting from his face, pulling until the glue holding it in place came loose and it separated, taking much of the fake wrinkled and sallow skin with it. The teeth, yellowed and crooked, were next to go, followed by the unkempt mane of grey hair partially hidden beneath a tatty woollen cap. Last of all, he pulled his juba robe over his head and tossed it on the passenger seat, revealing a Libyan army uniform beneath.

The overall transformation was startling, even to one like Drake, well versed in the art of disguise. In less than a minute, their driver had gone from a wizened, gaunt and careworn man in his sixties, to a relaxed and confident army officer in the prime of his life.

'As I said, this is not the first time I have done this, but it may be the last,' Aarif said, his voice suddenly much younger, stronger and smoother than it had been before. He smiled, revealing a set of straight white teeth. 'Good luck to you, Ryan.'

With that, he pulled open the driver's door and vanished into the night.

'Fuck me,' Drake whispered.

'Where'd he go?' Mason asked, unable to see what Drake had just witnessed.

Blinking, Drake returned to himself and glanced at his watch. Time was not on their side. They would have to hurry if they were to get what they needed and be out of here by sunrise.

'He's gone, like we need to be,' he said, moving to the rear door and unlatching it. 'Keira, get your gear and be ready to move. Time to do your thing.'

Easing the rear door open, with the Browning at the ready, he found himself facing out into a stretch of dusty, barren ground interspersed with tangled brush and mounds of broken concrete and masonry. The area was barely lit by the dim glow of street lights some distance away.

'Spread out, cover the area and be ready to move,' Drake ordered. Straightaway McKnight and Mason were out the door, fanning out to secure the immediate area around the van.

'Got a fix,' Frost reported, studying the handheld GPS unit in her lap. 'Looks like we're right on the money.'

Drake nodded. 'You know what to do. Move.'

Chapter 20

Creeping forward between the mounds of rubble and dry, desiccated bushes that marked the boundary of the area currently being redeveloped, Keira Frost was a barely noticeable shadow slipping through the darkness. Moving with nimble grace despite the heavy equipment pack weighing down on her, she edged forward, a silenced automatic in one hand and a Magellan satellite navigation unit in the other.

She had turned the screen illumination down to its lowest setting to avoid giving away her position, but even then it seemed to her eyes like a shining beacon in the darkness that surrounded her. The sooner she could dispense with it, the better.

At last the Magellan emitted a single muted beep to let her know she had reached her destination. The unit, designed to be used by aviators and round-the-world yachtsmen, was accurate to within a few metres, so she was fairly confident she was where she needed to be. Crouching down and pushing the unit into a pouch at her waist, Frost slipped her heavy pack off and laid it on the ground before her. The next piece of equipment she needed wasn't quite as sophisticated as the Magellan, but was just as vital to her task – a long metal rod with a battery pack and a simple gauge readout at one end, and a circular magnetometer at the other.

She'd picked up the commercial metal detector from a hunting and fishing store in London just before departing the UK, selecting the most expensive one she could find in the hopes that its performance would justify the price tag.

The air was hot and humid despite the late hour, raising a sheen of perspiration that coalesced into tiny droplets and trickled down her face. Pushing a lock of damp hair out of her eyes and doing her best to ignore the discomfort, she fired up the metal detector and went to work scanning the ground. There was no real science to this sort of thing; one simply had to establish a grid and work through it line by line, like a farmer ploughing a field.

'Come on, baby. Find me a target.'

She hadn't covered more than a dozen paces before the magnetometer sprang into life. She had disabled the speaker lest it emit a high-pitched wail that would draw any curious civilians within a hundred yards to her position, but she was able to make out the sudden spike on the simple inbuilt measurement gauge.

Clearly the unit had found something metallic, but that was hardly conclusive in a location like this. Far from celebrating, Frost continued to move the detector back and forth, trying to establish a pattern. She couldn't afford to waste time digging up a tin can or a vestige of some demolished building.

However, the signal remained strong and constant, and it didn't take her long to figure out the general placement and orientation of the buried object. As far as she could tell, it matched precisely what she was looking for.

Dismantling the metal detector, she retrieved her next tool from the pack – a simple flat-bladed shovel – and went to work.

For once she was glad of their desert location. Had this operation been mounted in a cold country, the ground could well have been frozen and impossible to dig. Likewise, waterlogged ground would have left her trying to excavate a sea of mud, making her task infinitely more difficult. As it was, the dry rocky soil made for difficult going as the blade kept catching on stones, and with nothing to bind it together the dirt tended to fall off the shovel before she could properly excavate it.

Still, after digging down about two feet, she felt the blade make contact with something hard and unyielding. Wiping a hand across her dusty, sweat-stained brow, she knelt down in the small hole and used her hands to scrape away the remaining dirt, exposing a thick black cable buried in the ground.

'Gotcha.'

Sowan's home a couple of hundred yards away might have been a tightly controlled compound with its own formidable security measures, but such a place had infrastructure and support needs like any other. Power, water, gas, and above all, communications.

Some covert online snooping on her part had confirmed that the facility used a DSN (defence switched network) line to communicate with the outside world. In theory it was a secure hard-line data system that allowed stations all over the country to exchange information, make phone calls, send emails and perform countless other tasks that a high-level intelligence officer might require. It also allowed the men responsible for protecting Sowan's safety to keep an eye on the feeds from the security cameras positioned around his home, meaning that even if the guards on site were neutralized, someone would still be watching.

It was impressive on paper, but the fundamental elements of the system were no more complex than a regular telephone network. They even used standard L-carrier coaxial cables buried in the ground to transmit their data, mostly relying on the fact that the cables were laid in secret and unmarked to keep them safe.

However, for someone with illegal access to construction reports and engineering blueprints, they were all too easy to find.

Satisfied that she'd found what she needed, Frost carefully removed an electrical toolkit from her pack. Running her hands through her damp hair to get loose strands out of her eyes, she wiped them against her trouser leg to remove the worst of the dirt, then set to work.

It took about two minutes to cut through the data cable's rubber insulation, expose the copper core and connect a wireless data transmitter to it. This done, she scooped some of the loose dirt back into the hole to cover everything except the transmitter's antenna, rendering her handiwork almost invisible amidst the jumbled stones and other debris that littered the site. Retreating a short distance, she hunkered down in a shallow depression near the berm of bulldozed dirt that fringed the perimeter of the site, then powered up her laptop computer. It took another two minutes to connect remotely to the half-buried transmitter nearby.

With the connection established, her laptop automatically scanned the various channels and electronic signals coursing through the wire, linking them into its own data-management program, which then separated and decoded them into something usable.

Six minutes after unearthing the cable, and Frost now had access the house's electronic security systems. She could even tap into the video feeds from the security cameras, giving her a near-total picture of what was going on within Sowan's compound. Unbeknownst to the men guarding him, the system in which they placed so much faith had just been turned against them.

Even as she scanned each video feed, taking in everything she could discern about the layout and security setup, she began recording footage from the cameras directly onto her laptop. When she turned out the lights, she would switch to this recorded video, making it appear to anyone else watching that all was normal.

Reaching up for the radio microphone at her throat, Frost hit the transmit button. 'This is Overwatch. We're in,' she reported, her voice low and calm. 'I have eyes on three armed Tangos in the compound. Two walking the perimeter counter-clockwise, one in a guard hut by the main gate.'

She would much rather have been alongside the rest of the group as they prepared to make entry, but the signal jammers they were about to employ would render her computer just as useless as the radios and other gear inside the compound, and she needed it to maintain the facade that everything was normal. So for now, she had little choice but to remain crouched down in her dusty hole in the ground, waiting for the rest of the team to begin the assault.

'Copy that,' came Drake's crackly reply. 'Monarch has eyes on the compound. Moving in sixty seconds. Stand by to cut the feeds. Over.'

Monarch was Drake's radio codename for the duration of the operation. Mason was to be known as *Cameo*, and McKnight was *Envoy*. None of their chosen call-signs meant much on the face of it; they were simply a means of identifying each other without resorting to actual names. The only stipulation about such things was that they had to be short and easy to say, and more important easy to differentiate even over a bad radio signal.

'Understood. Good luck, Monarch.'

Considering he was about to venture alone into a heavily defended compound in one of the most secure districts of a foreign city, where the smallest mistake could see this entire house of cards collapse, she had a feeling he'd need all the luck he could get.

They all would.

Chapter 21

A hot night.

Hot, damp and humid; the air still and stifling.

Outside, the chirp of cicadas and other night insects echoed through the warm darkness; a strange nocturnal music of changing rhythm and intensity. A dog barked somewhere off in the distance, and a car drove by on the tarmac road that ran outside the entrance courtyard, the old engine rough and unrefined.

Tarek Sowan lay sprawled on the bed, chest rising and falling as he slept. But it was a troubled sleep that brought little rest. The covers were thrown in a tangled mess by his feet. It was too hot to sleep with them on. Overhead, a ceiling fan rotated slowly on its fixture, the low hum of the motor serving as a constant backdrop to the familiar sounds of a neighbourhood at night.

A faint breeze, imperceptible but for the slight stirring of the curtains it provoked, sighed through the room, carrying with it the scent of sea air and concrete and freshly cut grass.

Sowan stirred, shifted position slightly and reached out, feeling the familiar warmth of his wife's body beside him, and relaxed a little.

–

In the walled courtyard down below, a wooden guard post had been built beside the main gate, its roof offering some protection from occasional bad weather – if not from the heat – for its lone occupant.

With his chair tilted back and his boots resting on the desk, he stared listlessly at the trio of security monitors facing him. In total, half a dozen cameras covered every approach to the walled compound, making it virtually impossible for anyone to get in unnoticed.

And if they did somehow manage to get past this first line of defence, he and two other armed tactical agents were on hand to deal with them.

As a high-ranking member of the country's Mukhabarat el-Jamahiriya, also known as the National Intelligence Service, Tarek Sowan had almost certainly made enemies both at home and abroad in his time. Plenty of people would like to see him, and perhaps the government he served, taken out.

Despite the monotony of night shifts, protecting this man while he slept was a duty that he and his comrades took as seriously as a heart attack. After all, the Mukhabarat didn't look kindly upon failure. If Sowan were killed or abducted, the blame would fall squarely on those charged with protecting him.

He glanced up as one of his fellow operatives strolled past the hut, his uniform neatly pressed, hand resting lightly on the automatic holstered at his hip. The two men exchanged nods, silently acknowledging each other, and their mutual boredom. This late at night, they had exhausted most topics of conversation anyway. All that was left was to patiently endure the next three hours until shift-changeover.

He was just settling back in his chair when suddenly the three monitors blinked and went out, displaying only blue test screens to indicate they were receiving no signal.

He frowned, more irritated than concerned at this stage. The compound had recently been upgraded with a new suite of cameras, and they were still chasing down occasional glitches in the system. The fact that all of them had gone down simultaneously suggested it was a fault with the receiver in the guard hut.

Still, there were procedures to follow. For all he knew, this might have been a test of his own diligence and decision-making. The Mukhabarat were just as paranoid about their own employees as they were about the population they were charged with 'protecting'. Any hint of incompetence or dereliction of duty was punished with ruthless dedication.

Not only were the feeds from the security cameras routed to his guard hut, but they were also relayed to the Mukhabarat headquarters building a couple of miles away. Whatever he saw, they saw. Or didn't see, in this case. They would be expecting a situation report.

Letting out a vexed sigh, he reached for the radio handset mounted on his desk and keyed the transmit button. 'Post 18 here. Possible camera fault. Please advise. Over.'

His report met with no response, save for an unusually loud static buzz that rang in his ears. Poor atmospherics? Unlikely, since the weather seemed calm and fair tonight.

'Repeat, this is post 18 reporting camera faults and loss of signal. Please respond. Over.'

No reply. The crackle and buzz of electronic distortion continued.

His irritation at the unexpected fault was now tempered with a growing undercurrent of unease. Problems with the cameras he could put down to simple technical glitches, but loss of radio contact was less easy to explain.

Switching frequency to the personal headsets used by his fellow guards, he hit transmit again. 'All units, we've lost camera signal. Any activity outside?'

Again there was no response.

He frowned, checked the frequency and keyed the radio again. 'All units, report in.'

Nothing. It was as if his two comrades had ceased to exist.

'What the—?'

He was just rising to his feet when suddenly a figure moved in front of the open window, seeming to appear from nowhere. He saw a blur of movement, something pointed at him, and then suddenly his world was on fire.

He went down, jerking and shaking violently as thousands of volts surged through his body, utterly incapable of reaching up to remove the two little metal prongs embedded in his chest. By the time the agony ceased, he was curled up in a foetal position, muscles still trembling and breath coming in laboured gasps.

He was powerless to resist as his hands were pulled behind his back and secured in place with a pair of plastic cable ties, followed a moment later by his ankles. He tried to let out a warning cry as a gag was tied around his mouth, but all he could manage was a strangled groan. And throughout the whole ordeal, he never once saw the face of his masked attacker.

With the guard neutralized, Drake crouched down in the shadows cast by the wooden shed that served as a guard hut. The black balaclava was hot and clung uncomfortably to his face as his body temperature rose steadily from both the exertion and the tension of the moment, but he ignored it. Concealment was more important than comfort now.

He remained crouched in the shadows, a silent and deadly presence, his senses painfully alert to the slightest noise as he surveyed the compound. His finger was on the trigger of the silenced Browning, ready to bring the weapon to bear the instant he spotted a threat.

Apart from the two-storey villa that dominated the central area, most of the compound was given over to the storage and movement of vehicles. A wide gravel turning space encircled a stone fountain in front of the villa, while a double garage stood against the wall on the far side. He had no idea what was inside, but from the general affluence of his home, Drake was willing to bet that Sowan's cars reflected his status as a high-ranking government employee.

Framing the driveway were stretches of short, coarse grass that were likely as close to a lawn as one could get in such a hot, arid country. Fruit trees and decorative shrubs were growing near the compound walls; all of it looked well ordered and maintained, probably by professional gardeners. Faulkner would have been quite at home here.

Radio communication with his fellow team members was impossible as long as the signal jammer carried on his belt kit was still transmitting. The deceptively innocuous little devices had disrupted their enemy's communications, buying them the time and the confusion they'd needed to make entry to the compound, but the door swung both ways. Their enemies couldn't talk to each other, but neither could they.

He had no way of knowing whether Mason and McKnight had succeeded in taking down the other two guards, though he imagined their failure would be announced promptly enough by the crackle of gunfire. For now, all he could do was trust in their abilities.

They had agreed in advance that the signal blackout would last sixty seconds. Sixty seconds to scale the nine-foot wall, drop down on the other side, take out three armed men and prepare to assault the house. Glancing at his watch, he counted down the time remaining like a starving man waiting to eat.

Five, four, three, two, one...

Switching off the signal jammer, Drake reached up and touched his transmit button.

'Monarch. Guardhouse secure,' he said, his voice low. The tactical microphone was picking up the vibrations in his throat rather than the sounds coming out of his mouth, so no matter what was going on around him there was never a need to raise his voice. 'Sitrep.'

'Cameo. Tango down,' came Mason's voice in reply. Calm, controlled, focussed. 'No further contacts.'

'Envoy, Tango down. Standing by.'

'Overwatch. Alarm system disabled.' Normally acerbic and volatile in daily life, Frost was a model of self-control at critical moments like this. 'You're clear to move.'

'Copy that,' Drake replied, letting out a silent breath of relief. 'Overwatch, move in and cover our exit. Envoy, Cameo, on me. Rendezvous at the main entrance. Move.'

'On it.'

'Envoy and Cameo are en route.'

Rising to his feet and keeping his weapon up and ready, Drake rushed across the turning circle, passing the stone fountain in the centre, the gentle splash of falling water a strange counterpoint to the hard crunch of boots on gravel and the loud, urgent pounding of his heart.

The next phase was the most critical of all – apprehending their target.

–

Sowan stirred again, his unconscious mind alerted that something had changed, some tiny shift in the nature of his surroundings that might be important, that might constitute a danger. His dark lashes flickered for a moment, held still, then parted.

For several seconds he lay there, mind caught somewhere between sleep and wakefulness, wondering what had disturbed him. His eyes scanned the shadows of the room, looking for anything out of the ordinary. There was nothing obvious that he could see, and yet his instincts told him to be alert.

Then, he heard something – a muted thump from somewhere deep in the house. Against the background of insects and the tinkle of water in the fountain outside it was almost indistinguishable, but his hearing was particularly sensitive to such disturbances.

Something was happening, he realized, and that realization soon drove away the last vestiges of sleep. In the course of his life, he had learned that the ability to wake quickly, and to trust his instincts when they told him something was wrong, often meant the difference between life and death.

Now was such a time.

Easing himself out of bed without disturbing the sleeping woman beside him, he reached into the bedside drawer and felt his fingers close around the cold metal grip of a Beretta pistol. He drew back the slide a fraction of an inch, just enough to see the faint glimmer of the brass shell casing in the breach.

Now armed, he rose from the bed and crept across the room, his body taut and ready. Eyes by now accustomed to the darkness, he advanced into the hallway, keeping the pistol low. The only sounds he could hear were the faint tread of his bare feet on the carpet, and the beating of his own heart, strong and steady despite his growing unease.

Fear was useful in itself. Fear kept you alert, kept you focussed. But fear unchecked could lead to panic, and panic got you killed.

Another tiny shift in air pressure sighed past him, carrying with it the scent of fresh-cut grass and flowers outside. An open window? An open door?

The first room on his left was the study. Gripping the pistol in sweating hands, he paused outside the door for a moment before opening it. Within stood his writing desk, cluttered with papers and documents, and his computer still humming away on standby. Nothing out of place.

He repeated the same process in the spare bedroom and bathroom, clearing each room as he had been trained to do as an infantryman in the Libyan army so long ago. Old lessons, perhaps, but ones which had never left him.

In short order, the first floor was secure.

As he reached the end of the corridor, he moved down the stairs to the ground floor. The stairs were old and wooden, and a daunting task to negotiate without making noise, but he knew the loud spots and his feet sought the best path almost by themselves.

As he emerged into the main reception hall, the front door came into view. It was standing ajar, open just a few inches, the warm night air seeping in.

He felt a tiny bead of sweat forming at his temple. Someone was in here. How the hell had they been able to get past the guards outside, and defeat that lock without triggering the alarm? This building was supposed to be impregnable.

He was just turning towards the alarm unit when a voice spoke up; a man's voice, hard and commanding. 'Don't move.'

Fear charged through him. He froze, glanced down at the pistol, wondering whether the intruder knew he was armed. Maybe, if he was quick…

'Forget it,' the voice warned. 'You'll just die.'

Sure enough, he felt something cold and metallic jammed against the back of his head. The barrel of a weapon.

'Drop the gun. Now. Drop it!'

With little option but to comply, Sowan laid the gun down on the floor at his feet. Straightaway his attacker kicked it away. The weapon skittered and slid across the tiled floor, coming to rest in one corner of the reception hall.

'Turn around, hands behind your head.'

Sowan turned slowly to face the man who might very well have been sent here to kill him. However, before he could even take in the man's appearance, he blinked and squinted as a bright flashlight was shone right in his face.

Carefully examining the bewildered and dishevelled-looking man standing before him, Drake concluded immediately that he was the same man he'd seen on the flight out of Paris.

'On your knees. Now.'

Again Sowan complied, knowing better than to resist an armed man who had the drop on him. He had overcome his initial shock at the sudden encounter, and his mind had quickly rallied, going into threat-assessment mode.

The man had spoken in English, which meant he knew or suspected that Sowan also understood the language. His own knowledge of national accents wasn't perfect, but he detected a British lilt to his attacker's voice.

'If you are here to abduct me, you won't get out of Tripoli alive,' he warned, keeping his voice calm and controlled. Showing fear would only empower the man. 'We have troops everywhere. You should leave now while you still can, my friend.'

'Shut the fuck up,' Drake said, keeping him covered while Mason moved forward and yanked his hands behind his back, securing them with a pair of cable ties.

With Sowan restrained, Drake gestured to his two comrades who had made entry with him. 'Secure the upper level. I've got this one.'

Straight away they were moving to ascend the stairs, weapons out and ready.

It was at this moment that Sowan, having calculated his captor's intentions, as well as how far they were prepared to go to achieve them, made a split-second decision and acted upon it.

'Laila! Run!' he shouted in Arabic at the top of his voice.

He wasn't able to shout any further warnings, as the butt of a pistol slammed into his temple like a hammer. Stars exploded across his eyes as the force of the impact knocked him sideways, and he collapsed in a heap with his blood staining the pristine tiled floor.

Nonetheless, the damage had been done.

In the bedroom upstairs, Laila Sowan awoke with a start, her mind roused from sleep to immediate, painful alertness at the sudden cry of her husband's voice. She didn't know what danger had befallen him, but at that moment it didn't matter. There was only one reason he would have commanded her to run – an intruder was in the house.

That being the case, there was only one course of action. They had rehearsed for this terrible possibility many times at his urging, despite her misplaced belief that it could never happen. They had practised it until she was quite certain she could have performed the steps in her sleep.

She was moving almost without thinking, throwing the covers aside and leaping from the bed even as the sound of booted feet echoed up the stairs. The room was in near-total darkness, but that didn't matter. She knew where she was going.

Heart pounding with the sudden, frantic surge of adrenaline that was more powerful than any drug, she tore across the room to the simple closet door opposite.

But this was no simple closet. Beyond the flimsy wooden door lay a room perhaps eight feet square, its interior starkly utilitarian compared to the tasteful comfort of the rest of their home. Its walls were uncompromising whitewashed concrete reinforced with steel, the immensely strong structure designed to protect the occupant from any intruder.

It had always seemed so unnecessary to her – a panic room in a house that was already well protected. It was the sort of pointless frivolity that American celebrities might indulge in; another means of bolstering their already inflated egos by pretending people were so obsessed with them that they might actually try to break into their homes. But Tarek had insisted on it for reasons that had nothing whatsoever to do with vanity. Only now did she understand why.

They were almost upon her. She could hear them sprinting down the corridor towards the bedroom, shouting to each other as they sought their target, their flashlight beams bouncing crazily across the walls and floor.

Rushing into the foreboding-looking room, she turned and reached out for the emergency-close button to seal the reinforced steel door.

At the same moment, Mason and McKnight charged into the bedroom, flash-lights and weapons sweeping left and right. It was McKnight who spotted the blur of movement out of the corner of her eye, saw a woman in a nightdress disappear into a smaller room off to their left. A room whose lights blinked on when she reached out and stabbed a button against the wall.

It took only a heartbeat to realize what was happening; a heartbeat during which the panic room's reinforced steel door began to roll shut, propelled forward by powerful electric motors that wouldn't stop until it was sealed and locked.

If she was allowed to seal herself away in there, there would be no way to get her out. Even worse, she could conceivably call for help, since the room was almost certainly fitted with some kind of communications gear.

Reacting on instinct, McKnight braced her foot against a wooden chair set in front of the small dressing table she was standing beside, and kicked it towards the doorway with all the strength she could summon. Her aim was good, her timing near flawless. The chair slid across the polished wood floor and caught in the gap between door and frame. There was a crunch as wood splintered and gave way, and the door's relentless momentum faltered. It shuddered forward another couple of inches, breaking apart the chair's frame, its powerful motors whining as they tried to force their way through the obstruction.

The chair had been reduced to a crushed, broken mass of wood by the door's relentless pressure, but even this great power couldn't obliterate it entirely. A gap almost a foot wide prevented it from locking in place.

Realizing what was going on, Laila kicked desperately at the obstruction, trying to force it clear. Her bare feet lacked both the strength and the support for such a task, and she let out a cry as splintered wood sank into her flesh.

'Panic room!' McKnight cried in warning. 'Get her before we lose her!'

Mason needed no prompting. Already he was moving forward with his weapon up and levelled at the woman's head.

'Open the door!' he yelled. 'Open it now or I'll fire!'

He had a shot. He could take it, put her down for good and eliminate the chance that she might warn others. But doing so would mean killing an unarmed woman.

The answer came all too quickly. Ducking aside behind the door, Laila desperately grabbed for the weapon that was kept on a shelf running along one wall. It was a Smith & Wesson revolver, its six chambers loaded with armour-piercing rounds. Tarek had once explained to her that weapons which used magazines couldn't be left loaded for long because the constant tension would weaken the magazine springs, causing them to misfire. Revolvers, on the other hand, could be kept almost indefinitely, ready to be used at any time.

Hefting the weapon in a clumsy grip, she aimed it towards the gap in the door just as she saw a figure appear, and squeezed off a round.

Quick reactions and his assailant's poor aim were about the only things that saved Mason from taking a round full in the chest. Twisting aside just as the woman opened fire, he was in time to see the round bury itself in the wall beside him.

The echoing crack of the shot reverberated around the room, loud as thunder, followed immediately by a second.

–

Downstairs, Drake winced at the distinctive sound of gunfire, torn between concern for the safety of his two operatives and the horrible, sickening realization that their cover had just been blown. Every house in the neighbourhood would have heard that shot. People would be pulling themselves out of bed, startled and befuddled by the noise. Some might dismiss it, or be too slow-witted and indecisive to react in time, but others would be trained and prepared for such things. Even now, men would be shouting orders into phones and radios, vectoring in police and security units.

Their time here was rapidly running out.

Reaching up, he pressed his radio transmitter. 'Envoy, Cameo, report now.'

–

Keira Frost was sweating and out of breath by the time she reached the compound, having run several hundred yards through backstreets and alleyways to get here from the construction site. Her balaclava clung uncomfortably to her face, the coarse fabric irritating her skin, though she resisted the urge to peel it off as she approached Sowan's residence.

The compound was surrounded by a nine-foot-high perimeter wall made of solid brick. There was only one way in or out: a wrought-iron gate secured with an electronic combination lock.

Normally such a security measure would have presented a formidable obstacle, but fortunately Frost had already trawled the building's security system and discovered the pass code for the gate.

Pausing only a moment by the gate, she punched the code into the little numeric keypad mounted on a steel plinth that was obviously designed to be used by drivers pulling up to the main entrance. A light on the keypad blinked green, there was a click as the lock disengaged, and with a smooth hum the gates swung open.

She was just crossing the threshold when she heard the distinctive crackle of gunfire from within the building. It was somewhat muted by the villa's structure, suggesting the shots had been fired from deep inside, but the noise was unmistakable. And since her companions were armed with silenced weapons, it could only mean one thing.

She was moving right away, darting across the open courtyard to the villa's main entrance. Her pack weighed heavily on her back, the straps biting into her shoulders, but she couldn't care less. Her teammates could be in trouble; getting to them was all that mattered.

With her weapon drawn, she pushed through the front door, emerging into a wide, plush entrance hall that reminded her more of a hotel lobby than a private residence. If this was how Libyan intelligence operatives lived, she couldn't help thinking she was working for the wrong agency.

As she'd hoped, Drake was there, standing guard over an unconscious figure lying curled on the floor. Spotting someone making entrance, Drake raised his weapon and trained it on her instinctively, but relaxed a little when he recognized his teammate.

'You trying to get yourself shot?' he growled. 'Announce it when you're coming in.'

'Sue me. What's going on up there?'

He shook his head, having already decided what to do next. 'Stay here, and don't take your eyes off that fucker for a second.

Without waiting for a reply, he left her and sprinted up the stairs.

–

'Shit! She's armed. Go loud!' Mason called out, realizing that stealth was no longer a factor in this equation. The priority was getting to the woman and neutralizing her as quickly as possible.

Reaching into his jacket, he produced a small cylindrical device, olive green in colour, with a simple pin-fuse at one end.

'Flashbang!' he shouted, yanking the pin and hurling the stun grenade in through the gap.

Within the room, Laila winced as waves of pain travelled up her arm. The kickback from the little weapon had been deceptively powerful – far more than she'd expected, and her shots had gone wide as a result. The report of the gunshot in such a confined space had been even worse, the deafening crackle leaving her ears ringing.

She almost didn't notice the little green can that was thrown in through the gap, bouncing off the wall with a metallic clang before landing on the ground a few feet away. Even if she'd been trained to anticipate such a move, it was unlikely she would have had time to do anything about it.

She was just turning to glance at the unexpected object when suddenly there was a flash, a boom that wiped out whatever hearing remained to her, and her world was engulfed in pain and darkness.

Blinded and disoriented by the grenade's concussive effects, she stumbled back against the wall, accidentally squeezing off another shot as her finger tightened involuntarily on the trigger before falling to her knees. Tears were streaming from her eyes, as if to clear the veil of iridescent light that had overwhelmed her pupils.

Outside, Mason wasted no time in taking advantage of his target's vulnerability. She might be down for now, but the grenade's effects wouldn't last forever.

'Tango down!' he shouted, leaning in far enough to survey the room. He could see the downed target, but the gap in the door was too narrow for him to fit through. 'Fuck, I can't get in.'

'Move, move!' McKnight called out, practically shoving him aside as she attacked the gap. Smaller and lighter than her companion, she was their best chance of getting inside. It was unfortunate that Frost was too far away to assist them, since the diminutive specialist could almost certainly have slipped through the gap with ease.

Moving shoulder-first, McKnight forced herself in, stepping over the mangled remains of the chair that was the only thing stopping the door from crushing her to death. As if to emphasize that unpleasant prospect, she felt the debris give another fraction of an inch, the massive steel door straining against her with bone-breaking force.

'Come on, goddamn it!' she gasped, exerting all her strength. Door and frame pressed against her body, desperately trying to trap her in their deadly grip, but somehow the chair held them back, and with a sudden release of pressure, she fell through to the other side.

The woman was moaning and looking around, blinded and deafened by the grenade, but perhaps aware on some level that there was another person in the room with her. She started to raise the gun, but McKnight quickly yanked it from her grip before she could do any more damage.

Finding the automatic-door control mounted in the wall above, McKnight hit the release button. There was a single beep, and just like that the door retracted back into the frame, allowing Mason to finally make entry.

'A fucking grenade?' she hissed, furious with him. If people in the houses nearby hadn't been sufficiently alerted by the gunshots, the detonation of a flashbang would certainly have finished the job.

Mason glared back at her. His face was obscured by the mask, but the anger in his eyes was plain to see. 'You got a better idea?'

McKnight said nothing to this. Now wasn't the time to be bickering.

'Screw it. Help me get her up,' she said instead, heaving the injured woman to her feet.

Carrying the stunned target between them, they dragged her through the bedroom and out into the corridor beyond. As they emerged, they promptly ran into Drake who was coming from the opposite direction.

'You all right?' he asked, his concern for their safety overriding any other considerations at that moment.

'Hundred per cent,' McKnight assured him.

'What the fuck happened?' he hissed, concern quickly giving way to anger now that he knew they were unharmed. 'We're compromised.'

'The house has a panic room. She almost made it inside.'

'Had to flash her,' Mason added with an apologetic shrug.

Drake thought to say more on the matter, but quickly silenced such a notion. There were more important things to deal with now.

Instead he focussed on the woman they were dragging between them, presumably Sowan's wife. She was wearing a nightgown that was partially torn by her previous struggles. It was hard to tell from the angle and poor lighting conditions, but he guessed her age as late thirties. Long raven-black hair hung in a dishevelled mass around her face, while blood from numerous cuts – no doubt a by-product of the grenade – glistened in the wan light of their flashlights.

'Talk to me, Monarch,' he heard Frost call over the radio, the tension in her voice obvious. 'It's getting real lonely down here.'

'Monarch,' Drake replied, knowing all too well how she must be feeling. 'Tango down. All units green. We're evaccing now. Any activity outside?'

'No, but their comms net is going ape-shit. My guess is we've got a couple of minutes at best before they bring down holy hell on this place.'

Drake had reached a similar conclusion already. Private security in the nearby houses didn't concern him – they'd be interested only in safeguarding their own clients – but Libyan police and field teams from the Mukhabarat were almost certainly being vectored in right now. It was only a matter of time before they locked this place down.

'Copy that. Get ready to move. As soon as we're downstairs, get outside and cover the main gate. Call out if you see anything.'

'What about the van?'

Drake considered it only for a moment. The van that had brought them here was slow and unreliable, completely unsuited to the kind of fast exit they now needed. But if his hunch was right, the solution to that problem might well be close at hand.

It had better be, otherwise they were royally fucked.

'It's too far away. Just cover our exit. We're coming down now.'

'Copy that. Overwatch, out.'

Leaving Frost to it, Drake turned to McKnight. If anyone could secure them the means of escape they needed, she could. 'The garage outside.'

He didn't have to say anything more. 'On it.'

As the woman darted off down the corridor, Drake hooked an arm under Sowan's wife and together with Mason carried her down to the main hallway.

'I'm sorry, Ryan. I had to make the call,' Mason said as they descended the stairs, supporting the woman with some difficulty. The anguish in his voice made it plain he blamed himself for what was happening.

Drake shook his head. He understood why the man was so cut up – nobody wanted to be the one who let the team down. Mason in particular had only recently returned to active field-duty after a lengthy period of convalescence, and no doubt still felt he had to prove himself. But Drake had known Cole Mason long enough to trust the man's decisions at times like this.

'It happens, mate. We'll deal with it.'

Mason said nothing.

–

As McKnight had expected, the door to the big double garage outside was securely locked. She had neither a key nor the time to search for one, but a single round from her silenced automatic was enough to solve that particular problem.

Hauling the door up and over, she found herself facing into a large, well-ordered garage whose exacting attention to detail reminded her of a military barracks. A small workshop had been set up in one corner, racks of tools and spare parts neatly stacked on the workbench.

And in the centre of the open space, gleaming black and spotless in the wan light filtering in from outside, was the big, imposing form of a Toyota Land Cruiser. The kind of powerful four-wheel drive that was favoured by CIA and FBI field teams back home for its rugged practicality and ability to blend in with civilian traffic.

Wasting no time, she hurried towards it and went to work.

–

Sowan was lying where Drake had left him, hands and feet bound with cable ties, moaning softly into the gag that had been placed in his mouth. There was an ugly dark bruise near his temple, and a little blood had seeped from a gash just above his hairline to pool on the white tiles beneath him, but the injury was unlikely to be life-threatening. Drake had deliberately checked his force, but even so it was a relief to see him beginning to stir. Knocking people unconscious was far from an exact science, and the last thing he needed was for Sowan to die from a cerebral haemorrhage before they could interrogate him.

Death would come later, when he'd given them everything there was to give.

Setting the woman down beside her husband, Drake went to work restraining her in similar fashion. She'd caused enough trouble already; he wasn't taking any chances.

'We taking her with us?' Mason asked, watching him.

'We might need her,' he said, without meeting his friend's gaze.

He hadn't explicitly acknowledged it yet, but in some part of his mind he knew that the man's wife might be useful in getting him to talk if he wasn't feeling cooperative. After all, he had risked his life to warn her of their presence. Everyone had their weakness, and she might well be his.

'I saw Sowan's office upstairs,' he said, concentrating instead on matters at hand. 'Gather any intel you can carry. Phones, computers, anything we can use later.'

As Mason hurried back up the stairs, Drake's earpiece buzzed with an incoming transmission. 'All units, Overwatch. We've got company inbound.'

Drake crept over to the front door, drawing his automatic once more. Easing the door open, he surveyed the open space beyond. There was no sign of activity save for Frost crouched in the shadows near the main gate, but he did hear something carrying towards him on the night breeze. A distant wail, rising and falling slowly in pitch.

Police sirens.

–

It had been a while since McKnight had been obliged to hotwire a car, but it was a skill that was taught to all Shepherd operatives as part of their selection process. After all, operating without support in hostile environments, there was no telling what means they might have to resort to in order to escape pursuit.

Lying on her back in the driver's foot well, the door sill digging uncomfortably into the small of her back, she unsheathed her field knife and used it to pry open the access panel at the base of the steering column. Inside were neatly bound bundles of wires of various colours, two of which needed to be severed and manually spliced together to complete the car's ignition circuit, causing the engine to start. It was a difficult and complex task at the best of times, not helped by the desperate urgency of the situation.

Having come from a career in explosive-ordnance disposal, McKnight was no stranger to working with delicate electronics under pressure, but even she couldn't quite keep a tremble out of her hands as she worked her way through the wires, searching for the ones she needed.

'Goddamn luxury cars,' she said under her breath, cursing the multitude of pointless extra features that added to the complexity of the vehicle's electrical system. If this had been a twenty-year-old Ford Escort, she could have had it up and running in under ten seconds.

As if to add to her problems, her radio unit crackled to life. 'Envoy, what's the situation on that car?'

'Working on it,' she replied through gritted teeth, selecting one wire that looked like it might be part of the ignition circuit, and using her knife to sever it.

'We've got police units inbound.'

'How long?'

'About thirty seconds.'

McKnight let out a muttered curse as she touched the exposed wire, a jolt of electricity surging up her arm. At least she'd found the power source, she thought with dry humour.

'How long do you need, Envoy?' he pressed.

'About thirty seconds,' she said, somehow managing to keep her voice calm. 'Envoy, out.'

—

Crouched by the main gate, her diminutive form barely noticeable, Frost surveyed the street beyond, gripping the automatic in sweating hands as she awaited the inevitable flashing lights of police cruisers.

She had no idea what they would do if they found themselves cornered by local law-enforcement. Shepherd teams were amongst the elite of the Agency's field operatives, and the four people in her group tonight were, between them, capable of causing serious problems for anyone looking to take them on. But they were still only four people, lightly armed and with few resources to call upon. They had come here to make a quick, surgical strike, not to conduct a fighting withdrawal against heavy resistance.

As if to add fuel to the fire, she was alerted by the glow of windows lighting up on the opposite side of the street. Curtains parted, revealing a man in a dressing gown with wiry black hair sticking up all angles, peering down short-sightedly into the street. Further along, an elderly woman was surveying the scene with the kind of dour disapproval one might reserve for a dog owner who doesn't pick after their pet when it takes a shit.

Keeping a tight grip of her weapon, she carefully reached up and pressed the radio microphone at her throat.

'Overwatch,' she whispered. 'I've got activity in the residential buildings on my twelve o'clock. Looks like local civvies. We're totally exposed out here, they can see right into the compound.'

'Copy that, Overwatch.'

'Hate to sound like a broken record, but can we leave now?' she urged him.

'We're working on it,' was Drake's only reply.

'This is turning into a cluster-fuck, Monarch.' Frost gritted her teeth and cursed under her breath. 'Recommend we ditch the targets and exfil on foot.'

They certainly couldn't carry Sowan and his wife out, but if they left now there was a good chance they could slip into the same maze of alleyways and side streets she had used to get here. Abandoning their objective to save their own asses was a shitty thing to contemplate at the best of times, but occasionally it had to happen. Sticking to the mission regardless of the danger didn't mean much if you weren't alive to reflect upon your courage.

'Envoy, what's the status on that car?' Drake demanded.

'I'm close, Monarch,' McKnight replied, no doubt unwilling to make promises she couldn't keep. Nonetheless, the tension in her voice was near breaking point. 'Give me a little more time.'

'We don't have any.' Taking Drake's lack of protest as serious contemplation of her plan, Frost pressed harder. 'We can get out, but we have to go now, Monarch. Either we leave them behind or we all die here. Make the call, for Christ's sake.'

Not far away, Drake looked over at Sowan, who was beginning to show signs of regaining consciousness. The man they had travelled thousands of miles to find, who they had risked their lives to recover, was lying mere feet away from him. The secrets he held might just be enough to turn everything around, put right everything that had gone so wrong over the past couple of years, ensure the safety of his friends, and most of all his sister.

On the other hand, he might very well represent a lost cause, the relentless pursuit of which was carrying Drake and his team to their deaths.

Frost was right to suggest bailing out; he didn't blame her for saying what was on everyone's mind as the seconds ticked by and the net closed around them. They could leave Sowan and his wife behind now and make a run for it. Resourceful and highly trained, they might well escape Tripoli and, through luck and skill, make it out of Libya as well. But even if they did, what then?

It would mean a return in failure. A return to watching his back at every moment, to seeing Jessica fall slowly and inexorably into the murky world that had snared him, to waking up every morning wondering if today was when the axe would at last fall.

Their situation would be no better than before. In fact, it might well be even worse. There was no telling if Cain had learned of this endeavour and guessed their intentions. If so, his retribution would be swift and final.

'I need an answer, Monarch,' Frost pressed. 'Make the call.'

That was when it happened, when everything else seemed to recede into darkness and in his mind's eye, he saw her. He saw his mother kneeling on the edge of that pit, hands bound, body bruised and cut, taking her final breath before the fatal shot.

Reaching for his transmitter, Drake hit the pressel at his throat. 'The answer's no. We're not leaving without him.'

McKnight had asked him yesterday if it was worth it, if this man was worth the risk. For Drake in that instant, getting his hands on Sowan was worth any risk.

His decision was met with several moments of strained, deadly silence. Then, as if in answer, he heard the distinctive throaty rumble as an engine roared into life outside.

'Envoy's good to go,' McKnight replied, sounding remarkably calm, given their perilous situation.

Drake clenched his fists, resisting the urge to cry out in relief. For now, at least, they were still in with a shot. Somehow, they might just be able to pull this off.

'Good work, Envoy. Bring it around to the front door. We're coming out.' Already he was reaching down to haul Sowan to his feet. 'Cameo, grab whatever you've got and rendezvous with us now.'

'Roger. Cameo's en route.'

Reaching up, Drake pressed his transmitter once more. 'All units, we're coming out.'

–

Outside by the main gate, Frost glanced around as a black Toyota SUV rumbled out of the parking garage. The windows were partially blacked out for privacy, but she could just make out McKnight behind the wheel as she manoeuvred the big vehicle around to the front door of the villa.

But her jubilation at seeing their escape vehicle finally moving was short-lived. Seconds later, Frost's worst fears were realized when a pair of red-and-white police cruisers came screaming around a street intersection about a hundred yards away, lights flashing and sirens wailing.

'All units, we've got company,' she hissed, reaching into her webbing and withdrawing both the smoke grenade and the flashbang she'd been issued with. 'Local PD. Two cruisers coming in from the east. Looks like four hostiles, maybe more.'

She laid each grenade by her feet, keeping them within easy reach as she raised her silenced automatic.

–

'Copy that, Overwatch.' Drake glanced at Mason, who had just returned from upstairs. His pack looked a little bigger and heavier now that he'd stuffed it with anything useful he could find in Sowan's office, and he was breathing harder after his exertions. 'Take Sowan. I've got his wife.'

Nodding, Mason grabbed the still-dazed captive and dragged him forcibly towards the door, shoving it open with his shoulder. The SUV was parked right outside as instructed, engine rumbling, tailgate open to provide access to the trunk.

Descending a couple of steps from the front door with his captive in tow, Mason circled to the rear of the vehicle and forced the bound man inside.

–

The police cruisers were slowing as they approached the compound, doubtless on the lookout for signs of trouble. It wouldn't be immediately obvious from street level that Sowan's home was currently the scene of an armed kidnapping, so the police would be taking their time, assessing the situation, making sure they didn't blunder right into the middle of a shootout.

If they followed the standard practice of law-enforcement agencies, they would take up flanking positions at either end of the street, forming an armed cordon that it would be difficult to break out of without taking heavy fire.

The only way to prevent, or at least delay, this was to strike first.

Raising her silenced automatic, Frost took aim at the closest vehicle.

'Contact,' she said calmly, squeezing off the first round. The weapon kicked back sharply, the recoil jarring her wrist as the silencer thudded heavily, a brass shell casing flying out to ping off the wall beside her.

The police cruiser's windshield was made of toughened glass designed to protect the occupants from thrown missiles and other debris, but the impact of a high-velocity round was still enough to break through and leave a spider web of cracks radiating out from the fist-sized hole. This impact was followed a moment later by a second shot that caused even more damage, showering the occupants with fragments of broken glass.

Adjusting her aim, Frost targeted the second cruiser in similar fashion and opened fire, putting a couple of rounds in the windshield before shifting her attention to the front wheels. Two more shots pinged off the chassis before the third found its mark, shredding the rubber tyre and disabling the vehicle.

The effect of her fire was dramatic. Straightaway both drivers jammed on their brakes, bringing the cruisers to a shuddering, skidding halt. The second driver had the presence of mind to throw his cruiser into reverse and started to back up, bumping and grinding on a flat tyre that rapidly disintegrated under the strain.

With one cruiser in retreat, Frost focussed her attention on the second, this time putting a round through the wing mirror that blasted it apart in a hail of glass and plastic. Another shot shattered the side window.

That was enough for the driver to get the message. Engine roaring, wheels kicking up dust and smoke from burning rubber, the cruiser backed up in full retreat.

Taking advantage of the confusion and panic, Frost reached down for the smoke grenade at her feet, yanked the pin free and leaned out far enough to hurl it down the street. Moments later, there was a flash, a loud pop and suddenly the street was engulfed in a cloud of blinding white smoke. Frost could just make out the glow of blue lights through the haze.

She had done what she could. Rising to her feet, she ejected the spent magazine from her weapon and retreated towards the SUV parked by the front door. Even as she approached, she could see Mason shoving their prisoner into the vehicle's trunk.

'We're out of time,' she called out, slipping a fresh magazine into her sidearm. 'We need to go now!'

–

In the villa's entrance hall, Drake could hear the commotion outside. Police were on the scene, and unless they wanted to spend the rest of their days alongside the man they'd abducted from Paris, they needed to be out of here now.

Grabbing Sowan's wife by the wrist, he pulled the woman to her feet and steered her towards the front door. Straightaway she tried to break and run, forcing him to hold her by both arms while she kicked and bucked, screaming into the gag. Her feet lashed out, catching him painfully in the shins a couple of times in what he was sure was a calculated act of reprisal for what he was putting her through.

Struggling to control her, he paused by an arched doorway leading into what he presumed was a living room. Expensive-looking furniture dotted the room, while thick curtains hung from the windows. Plenty of material that would burn well enough.

Reaching into his webbing, he fished out his flashbang grenade, pulled the pin and hurled the little device against the far wall.

He was just shoving his way through the front door when it detonated, blasting out the living room windows, the concussive boom leaving his ears ringing.

Straightaway he smelled ammonium from the chemical reaction, accompanied by the distinctive smell of burning fabric. In addition to light and sound, flashbangs produce a lot of heat, usually setting fire to anything combustible in the vicinity. Given the quantity of fuel in that room, Drake was counting on it turning the house into a blazing inferno within a matter of minutes.

With luck, police and fire units would have to divert their attention to tackling the burning building, perhaps buying them enough time to get clear of the area.

Practically lifting the woman off her feet, Drake carried her towards the SUV that was now waiting just outside, tailgate open, engine idling. McKnight was seated behind the wheel, her face masked just like his own. But for a moment they made eye contact as he approached, and Drake recognized her unspoken relief at seeing him again.

Ignoring the kicks that were still raining against him, Drake lifted his captive over the edge of the sill and dumped her unceremoniously into the trunk beside her husband. She landed hard, clearly not expecting it, and unable to brace herself with her arms bound. He heard a grunt of pain, and what would certainly have been a stream of curses had she not been gagged.

With their cargo deposited, Drake slammed the trunk shut and rounded the vehicle, pulling open the passenger door beside McKnight. On the street outside, the wail of police sirens continued, accompanied by shouts and panicked orders.

'Let's go, for fuck's sake!' Frost shouted from the back.

Holstering his weapon, Drake hoisted himself up into the seat and pulled the door shut behind him with a resounding clang.

'We're clear. Go! Go!'

McKnight needed no further prompting and stamped on the accelerator, kicking up a spray of stone-chips and dust as they hurtled towards the open gate. Behind them, smoke and flames were beginning to issue from the shattered windows on the villa's lower floor, the flashbang having done its work well.

Ahead of them lay an impenetrable wall of white smoke, the result of Frost's handiwork.

'Don't stop! Gun it!' Drake commanded. To slow down now could be fatal.

Flooring the accelerator, McKnight took them straight into the smoke screen that now filled the street, throwing the wheel hard left to avoid barrelling into the houses opposite. She was operating by instinct and memory rather than sight, but they served her well all the same.

After a few heart-stopping seconds, the smoke vanished, revealing an open road ahead of them. McKnight wasted no time in taking advantage of their newfound freedom, hitting the gas once more to put as much distance as possible between themselves and the scene of the kidnapping.

'Jesus Christ, that was close,' Mason breathed, peeling off his mask.

Drake said nothing. They might have cleared the immediate crime scene, but whether they made it out of the country remained to be seen.

Chapter 22

Tripoli International Airport

The business-class lounge was almost empty at such a late hour, save for a scattering of frazzled-looking international travellers nursing drinks while they waited for their flights to be called. With the ambient music turned down low and the lights dimmed, there was a pleasant, mellow atmosphere about the lounge. Nobody was in much of a rush to do anything or be anywhere; they were content to share the space in comfortable silence.

Seated at one end of the bar, Vanil Chandra took a leisurely sip of his coffee; served black with no sugar, as it should be. Adding milk to good coffee was uncouth and insulting to the flavour.

He glanced at the woman sitting on the stool next to him. A flight attendant – he recognized the British Airways uniform well enough – no more than thirty years old, blonde-haired and petite, with the kind of delicate, elfin facial features that were quite unusual in Brits. The name tag on her uniform said Suzanne.

She was staffing a long-haul flight from Heathrow, currently on layover with the rest of her crew. And like himself, she had nothing but time to kill until her next flight departed. Seeing no sense in passing up an opportunity for pleasant company, Chandra had struck up a conversation with her almost immediately. After all, they both flew around the world for a living. It wasn't hard to find common ground.

'You know, it is a true crime that you have never visited Rome. A stunning city, magnificent architecture,' he said with a regretful shake of his head. 'A woman as beautiful as you would be quite at home there.'

She laughed; an entirely pleasant sound to his ears.

'Does that line work on all the flight attendants you meet?'

'That would be telling,' he admitted. 'But it seems to be going down well so far.'

She had the good grace to blush a little at his praise, though he was quite certain that, like most pretty girls, she was aware of her good looks. 'To answer your question, though, I've not had the chance to visit. Work is… well, demanding. It takes me to lots of places I don't particularly want to go, and not many places I do.'

Chandra smiled. 'My plane is five minutes from here.'

'Tempting,' but I make it a rule never to accept rides from strangers.' Despite her playful refusal, the look in her eyes suggested she wasn't unreceptive to his attention.

'Then we should get to know each other a little better,' he said. 'I know this truly wonderful seafood restaurant, right in the shadow of the Pantheon...'

Before he could renew the offensive in earnest, he paused, feeling the vibration of his cell phone. Fishing it from his jacket pocket, he swiped a finger across the screen to unlock it. A text message was waiting for him. A single word printed on screen.

Tempest

Chandra let out a faint sigh of relief. Flirtation aside, he knew he'd just about outstayed his welcome here. Any longer, and he would have been forced to return to his aircraft or scrub his flight plan and risk hours of delays while he waited for a new one to be approved.

Slipping the phone back into his pocket, Chandra glanced at the flight attendant and gave her an apologetic smile. 'Suzanne, it has been a pleasure being in your company tonight, but I'm afraid duty calls.'

The young woman pouted. 'Now, that's just rude, leaving a lady all alone. I'll have no one to keep me company now.'

'My employer isn't one for lateness, I'm afraid,' Chandra said, draining the last of his coffee. He laid down enough money to cover both their bar tabs. 'Nice enough chap, I suppose, but always making a fuss over nothing.'

-

'I'm seeing blue lights up ahead!' McKnight warned. Sure enough, the flashing lights of another police cruiser were coming into view about half a mile away. 'They must know this car's stolen by now. You think they're moving to intercept?'

'I doubt it,' Drake lied. 'We're in a black SUV. We passed half a dozen of these on the way into Tripoli. They can't know it's us.' He pointed to an intersection up ahead. 'Take a right at the next junction. Get us off the main drag.'

In truth, he had no idea how quickly the Libyan police would react to an armed kidnapping. He was banking on the fact that the smoke grenades combined with the fire rapidly taking hold of Sowan's house had diverted their attention for now, but it was quite possible they wouldn't take the bait.

He was far more worried that Libyan intelligence had woken up to what was going on. Police they could handle, but the Mukhabarat were another matter entirely.

'Found the tracker!' Frost said, leaning in between the two front seats. Working under pressure, she had forcefully dismantled part of the car's central console to access the inbuilt GPS tracking device.

'Kill it.'

A single sharp blow with the butt of her knife was enough to destroy the device. It was possible that others had been fitted in places they couldn't access, but there wasn't much they could do about that right now.

'Cole, give us a position,' Drake called out. In their rush to escape the immediate vicinity of the raid, they had cut through unfamiliar side streets and slip roads, rapidly losing all sense of orientation. For all he knew, they could be heading entirely the wrong direction now. 'I need an ETA.'

Mason, sitting in the back, was poring over the screen of his handheld GPS, trying to plot a course to the private airfield where they were to rendezvous with Chandra. Frost had powered down the device during the raid to save the battery, and he'd only just managed to restarted it and get a satellite fix.

'Looks like we need to bear south-east from—'

Reaching the junction, McKnight swung the wheel hard right, barely taking her foot off the gas. Tyres squealed in protest and the traction-control warning blinked on the dashboard, accompanied by muffled cries from their two captives in the trunk.

'Jesus fuck!' Frost shouted, having been slammed against the door by the sudden change in momentum. 'You trying to get us killed?'

'Trying to get us the hell out of here.' McKnight's knuckles were white on the wheel, her jaw clamped tight. Like the rest of them, she had peeled off her balaclava as soon as they'd cleared the area, but her face was still flushed and damp with perspiration.

As soon as they'd turned at the junction, she spotted an alleyway to her left and turned into it, killing the lights and the engine.

Twisting around in his seat, Drake watched as the blue flashing lights of the police car shot past the junction, carrying on as if nothing had happened. Darkness and distance must have masked them sufficiently so as not to attract attention.

'We're good,' he said.

Firing up the engine once more, McKnight backed out of the alley and onto the main road, giving it some serious gas to put them on their way again.

'Ease down, Sam,' he warned, trying to sound calmer than he felt. They were in an SUV, not a high-performance racing car. If McKnight lost control and rolled their only ride, their escape was over before it had even begun.

'I'm fine. But I'd love to know which direction I'm meant to be heading,' she replied tersely.

Drake nodded. 'Cole, get me that position.'

'On it. I've got a route now.' Leaning forward, Mason handed him the GPS.

Drake studied the screen. According to the inbuilt journey calculator, they were about fifteen miles from their destination. The good news was that they were now heading in more or less the right direction. The bad news was that, even taking the optimal route by road, they'd still need more than twenty minutes journey time.

'This is going to be tight,' he said quietly. Chandra had made it plain that he wouldn't wait for them if they were late, and Drake believed him. They needed to be there in time to light up the runway so he could land safely. If not, they could kiss goodbye to their ride home.

In the trunk, Sowan and his wife had apparently regained consciousness, and were well and truly making that fact known. The vehicle resounded with the muted thumps of feet against chassis, accompanied by strained cries and groans. The chances of them breaking out were non-existent, but the noise was quickly wearing on the team's already frayed nerves.

'Deal with them,' Drake instructed, unable to reach them from the front seat.

Twisting around, Frost folded down the centre armrest and yanked open the little access door leading to the trunk. Before anyone could stop her, she had drawn her weapon and shoved it in through the gap until it made contact with human flesh.

'Shut the fuck up back there or I swear to God I'll kneecap both of you,' she hissed, pressing the barrel of the weapon in harder.

Whether they both understood her or not, a loaded gun has a tendency to cross most language barriers. The shouting and banging subsided almost immediately.

Letting out a breath to calm herself, Frost holstered the weapon, closed up the access door and turned back around, meeting Drake and Mason's eyes with a faint smile of amusement.

'Better?' she asked.

Neither man said anything.

Chapter 23

Sitting in the cockpit of his private aircraft with the engines turning over, Chandra watched as the Turkish Airways 737 ahead of him rocketed off down the runway, jet turbines roaring and trailing blue flames. The nose went first, followed a few seconds later by the rear wheels as the heavy beast of an aircraft lumbered into the night sky.

Next to that, Chandra's own twin-prop Beechcraft C-12 cargo transport seemed like a toy. But it was a toy on which four people's lives might well depend tonight.

With that thought hanging over him, he keyed his radio to the control-tower frequency and hit transmit. 'Tripoli tower, this is Golf-Zulu-Six-Eight-Two. I'm in final position. Requesting clearance for takeoff.'

A moment later, his headset crackled with a tinny voice in response. 'Understood, Six-Eight-Two. You're cleared for takeoff.'

Gripping the throttle controls, he increased power to both engines, feeling the vibrations through the airframe as their output rose to meet his demands. A final check of his instruments confirmed the plane was functioning normally in all respects. Satisfied, Chandra released the brakes, allowing the aircraft to ease forward, slowly and tentatively taking its place at the runway threshold.

Pausing a few moments to make sure the nose was lined up with the centre line, Chandra let out a breath and checked his radio to make sure he wasn't transmitting.

'I hope you are ready for this, Ryan,' he whispered, throttling up to full power.

The Beechcraft C-12 might have been an old propeller-driven workhorse dating back thirty years or so, but there was plenty of life still left in her. He felt the familiar lurch in the pit of his stomach as the plane surged forwards, quickly gathering pace as the engines roared with power, twin propellers clawing the night air. Off to his left, the bright lights of the terminal building flitted by, moving faster with every passing moment.

The nose seemed to rise up almost of its own accord as the lift generated by the wings drove it skyward. Checking that his ground speed was sufficient to lift off without stalling, Chandra eased back the stick. There was a bump, and then suddenly his passage seemed to smooth out. He was airborne.

This was it; no going back now. Now that he was aloft, he would be tracked by the Libyan air-traffic-control network, his course and speed carefully monitored by both military and civilian radar. Any deviation from his official flight plan would be met with a stern interrogation over the radio, most likely followed by a military interception if he failed to respond or comply immediately.

In short, he was committed to his course now. All he could do was hope that Drake and the others were waiting for him when he arrived.

–

With over a million residents and stretching nearly twenty miles from its western tip to its eastern suburbs, Tripoli was by far the largest and most populous city in Libya. However it was a long and straggling sort of place, with most of its population crowding in close to the shores of the Mediterranean. Rarely did it extend more than a few miles inland.

Heading almost due south at well over the speed limit, Drake and his companions soon found the densely packed urban streets giving way to wider suburban sprawl, and finally to scattered villages and settlements interspersed with irrigated fields. The road-quality declined noticeably once they were away from the main highways, pristine asphalt gradually deteriorating into rough potholed tarmac that felt like driving over a dried riverbed.

The only consolation was the almost total absence of other vehicles, particularly police cruisers. McKnight wasted no time in taking advantage of this, pushing the engine hard. The speedometer crept up to 70 mph, which was about as fast as any of them would risk driving on a rough road in the dead of night.

Reaching into the pack that was now by his feet, Drake removed a plastic bottle of water and downed a mouthful. He couldn't say what it was about operations like this, whether it was the ambient temperature or the tension and nervous energy that caused them all to overheat, but by the time it was over he was always possessed by a ravenous thirst. And judging by the way Frost and Mason were attacking their own water canteens, he wasn't the only one.

Taking another gulp, he held the bottle out to McKnight, who was happy to accept it. 'Thanks,' she said, gulping it down. 'I'd prefer a beer, though.'

'When we get out of here, I'll buy you a case.'

Sparing him a momentary glance, she offered a playful smile. 'I'll hold you to that.'

He knew deep down that it was too soon to start celebrating. No operation was over until you were on that flight home, but despite himself, Drake couldn't help feeling good about their work tonight. Despite numerous problems and a few close calls during the house-assault, they had overcome the challenges like they always did – together, as a team. They were on the home stretch now. A few more miles, and they would reunite with Chandra, bearing their prize away with them.

Then, when they had reached the safety of a remote house in a neutral country, they would find out what exactly what Sowan knew. But that was a concern for tomorrow. Tonight, they could be content with the knowledge that they had succeeded.

'I hate to shit on this feel-good vibe, but we've got a problem,' Frost said from the back seat, breaking his momentary spell of optimism. 'A big one.'

Twisting around in his seat, Drake frowned at her. 'Talk to me.'

'I've been watching the GPS. We're falling behind, Ryan. At this rate we're going to miss our window.'

'That's impossible,' Mason countered. 'We worked out the route in advance. Timings, roads, everything.'

'But we're not following the route,' the young woman explained. 'We're all over the place. Half the roads on our maps don't even exist.'

Drake winced inwardly, realizing now that he'd underestimated the difficulties of traversing such a haphazard and primitive road network. Despite McKnight's best efforts to keep them on course, the winding roads and awkward junctions, many of which didn't exist on the unit's inbuilt map, kept forcing them to make detours and sudden turns. They were wasting time, taking a long and indirect route towards the airfield where they were soon to rendezvous with Chandra.

'Shit, she's right,' Mason said. 'We're not making up the time.'

McKnight shook her head. 'If we go much faster, we'll drive right off the road. What do you want me to do, Ryan?'

Drake chewed his lip as he considered their situation. The road they were currently barrelling down seemed to run between a pair of fields, probably irrigated as there certainly wasn't enough rainwater in this part of the world to sustain crops. This was remote farmland, even the scattered shanty-town settlements that clustered around the city having petered out.

He glanced at the GPS, as if searching for answers. Sure enough, the road was gradually curving away towards the north-east, carrying them further away from their destination. At this rate they could spend all night trying to negotiate the spider's web of farm tracks that crisscrossed the region.

'This car's an off-roader, right?' he said, deciding to go with the only idea that had come to mind. It wasn't exactly elegant, but desperate times called for desperate measures.

McKnight glanced at him, saying nothing.

'It's time we went off road.'

If McKnight was harbouring any reservations about his plan, she gave no voice to them. Instead she reached up for her seatbelt, pulled it across and carefully locked it in place. Drake did likewise.

'Get strapped in,' he warned his two teammates in the back. 'This could get rough.'

'Fuck,' Frost said under her breath, fumbling with her own belt. 'And I was having a ball until now.'

There was nothing they could do about their two unwilling passengers in the trunk, except hope that they emerged at their destination with nothing more than a few bruises and a bad attitude.

Giving McKnight a nod, Drake braced himself as she swung the wheel over. Straightaway they veered right, leaving the potholed road in a spray of dust and stones before rolling down a shallow embankment and into the field beyond.

The SUV resounded with an almost painfully loud bang as they hit the ground at high speed, suspension and shock absorbers strained to their limit by the impact. Nonetheless, the engine was still running and the wheels clawed at the rutted ground, forcing them onwards.

Whatever crops they were growing here presented no obstacle to the Toyota's relentless momentum, parting like the sea before an ocean liner and flattening beneath their wheels.

'Don't turn, just take us straight there,' Drake ordered, keeping his eye on the GPS as the distance to destination slowly crept down. He had to raise his voice to be heard over the rumble of uneven ground beneath them.

'Good thing this isn't a rental,' Mason remarked as the big SUV rumbled through a deep hole in the ground, taking the abuse like a pro rally car. Likely this little jaunt would put the car's undercarriage out of commission, not that it mattered as long as they made their destination.

As it turned out, the field was bordered by another road about half a mile distant. Reluctantly obeying Drake's instructions, McKnight took them straight up and over it, barely slowing down. She did her best to ignore the protesting groans and bangs coming from beneath the car as they landed hard on the other side. Broken shock absorbers wouldn't prove fatal, but if they snapped an axle or a tracking rod, it was game over.

Nonetheless, somehow the sturdy car held together, carrying them across a couple of miles of rough open ground that didn't seem to be used for much of anything. Even the lights of the city had faded into the distance, the only illumination provided by the vehicle's dipped headlights.

Ahead of them lay a sparse, bleak landscape of dusty scrub, stony plains and rocky outcroppings that McKnight was obliged to desperately weave her way through. The car might have been an all-terrain vehicle, but even it couldn't hope to traverse the walls of sandblasted rock that confronted them.

In the midst of this, Drake cocked his head, listening intently to the faint, crackly voice that was filtering through his radio earpiece.

'... Monarch. Repeat... in, Monarch.' The signal was fading in and out, occasionally overwhelmed by scrambled static. 'Am... borne, approaching... field.'

Drake's heartbeat stepped up a gear. It was Chandra radioing them that he was on approach, though presumably he was right at the edge of transmitting range. 'Eagle, this is Monarch. Say again your last.'

'Monarch, this is Eagle. Do you copy now?'

'Go, Eagle.'

'Am airborne and en route. ETA is less than five minutes. Are you in position?'

'We're close,' Drake replied. According to the GPS, they were less than a mile from their destination.

'Then I suggest you hurry, Monarch. Because I'm staring out into a whole lot of darkness at the moment. I can't land without lights, and I can't circle around for another pass. I'm flying as slow as I can without stalling, but if you're not there when I pass by, I must leave you.'

'Understood, Eagle. We're on it.' Clenching his fists, Drake looked at McKnight. 'We need to be there now, Sam. Whatever it takes.'

McKnight's arms were aching from constantly wrestling with the wheel, her eyes stinging with sweat, and her nerves as shredded as their tyres would be if she failed to spot one of the countless rocky spars that studded their path. It was like driving through a minefield blindfolded.

It was then that she spotted it. Standing directly across their path, easily ten feet high and stretching as far as she could see in the beams cast by the car's headlights. A metal chainlink fence, supported by steel posts driven into the ground at ten-metre intervals.

'Got a perimeter fence ahead,' she warned.

Drake gritted his teeth. There was no time to go around. 'Go through it. Hold on, everyone!'

Closing her eyes, McKnight stamped on the gas, propelling them towards the imposing-looking barrier.

The impact wasn't what she'd expected. She felt a moment of resistance as the fence flexed under the pressure, metal links straining to hold it back, then suddenly there was a horrible wrenching, popping sound as it gave way, and the resistance vanished. A heartbeat later, the broken remains of the fence impacted the windshield, cracking the glass, before tearing across the roof and chassis. The scream of rending metal made her wince, but still she kept her foot on the gas, praying for them to power through it.

A moment later, it was over. The obstacle was behind them. She opened her eyes, hardly believing they'd made it. The ground was considerably smoother now that they'd entered the grounds of the airfield itself, though she had no idea where they were in relation to the field's facilities.

'I don't see a runway,' she said, searching the dusty ground for a sign of tarmac.

Drake shook his head. 'I think this *is* the runway.'

The airfield was, in reality, little more than a stretch of level ground that had been fenced off and cleared of rocks and other obstructions. Drake had no idea why they'd bothered to erect a fence around a dirt landing strip when there seemed to be little here worth protecting. Perhaps the government here had intended to pave the runway and built a more substantial facility, but hadn't gotten around to it yet.

It wasn't going to be a fun landing for Chandra, but then, that was what he was being paid for. Anyway, Drake had seen him set down on worse.

Spotting a cluster of small buildings up ahead that he assumed were related to the operation of the airfield, Drake pointed to the nearest one. 'This looks good. Stop by the closest building.'

Bringing the battle-scarred SUV to a halt, McKnight let out a sigh and slumped back in her seat, too drained to do anything else for the next few moments. Drake meanwhile leapt right out of the passenger side, sweeping the area with his weapon. It all seemed quiet.

There were three structures in total. One was a refuelling tank that looked like it hadn't been used in some time, its paintwork scoured away by years of sand and wind. The other two were roughly equal in size, made from corrugated-metal sheeting probably fixed to a steel framework beneath. There was no obvious indication as to their purpose, no signs or words scrawled on them, but they were far too small to be aircraft hangars.

Nonetheless, he still held out some hope that one of them might contain controls for the field lights, a generator or something similar.

'Cole, cover our backs. Keira, on me,' he ordered, as he advanced on the closest building, his boots crunching on the rocky ground.

Frost was right behind him, similarly armed. 'On your six.'

Pointing to the second structure, Drake closed in on the nearest one. There was only one door, also made of corrugated metal. There was no lock that he could see.

Unhooking a flashlight from his belt, Drake halted for a moment, checked that his Browning was ready to fire, then reached out and pulled the door open.

Even without the flashlight, the purpose of this small structure became apparent the moment he opened the door and the stench of human excrement wafted out. Struggling not to gag, he flicked the flashlight on and allowed its beam to play briefly across the walls and floor. As he'd suspected, the toilet was nothing more than a hole in the ground, with a set of wooden planks placed around the outside to help the user balance while they went about their business.

He supposed even pilots had to relieve themselves from time to time, though he couldn't imagine what kind of urgency would compel him to venture any further into that place.

Nothing useful in there. Gratefully allowing the door to swing closed, he killed the flashlight and backed off just as Frost trotted over to join him.

'You okay?' she asked, noting his pallid complexion. 'You look like me after too many shots of tequila.'

'Fine,' he lied. 'It's clear in there. Anything in the other one?'

She shook her head. 'Just old tools and junk. No lights, no power. This place doesn't have shit for us, Ryan.'

As if sensing their difficulties, Chandra radioed in once more. 'Monarch, this is Eagle. I'm inbound, closing in fast. I need those lights now.'

They were wasting time. Whether or not this airfield even had landing lights was irrelevant now. They had no time to investigate the matter further.

'We're working on it, Eagle,' Drake replied, striding back towards the SUV.

'Then whatever you are going to do, I suggest you do it soon. My instruments are telling me I'm almost on top of you.'

'Copy that, Eagle. Stand by.' Clicking off his radio, he called ahead to Mason. 'Cole, get your pack. We need your signal flares.'

Mason, covering the area around the vehicle, caught on immediately. 'On it!'

'Keira, you too,' Drake instructed the young specialist. 'Get your arse down to the west end of the runway. Cole, you take the east. I'll cover the centre.'

It wasn't going to be much of a landing grid for Chandra, but it was the best they could manage with the resources at hand. Hopefully it would be enough.

'Jesus, Ryan. Why do I have to do all the running?' Frost protested as she withdrew the signal flares from her pack.

'Because you're fast,' he admitted. Despite her short stature, she was as quick and nimble as an athlete. 'And it'll shut you up for a while.'

She shot him a hard look. 'One of these days we're going to have a falling-out.'

Before Drake could respond, McKnight threw open her door and jumped down from the SUV. 'Give me the flares, Keira,' she said, holding out her hand. 'I'll take care of it.'

'I need you here to cover Sowan,' Drake said.

'Sowan's locked in the trunk. He's going nowhere.' Her eyes flashed in silent challenge. 'What's the matter? Don't trust me?'

'That's not what I meant.'

They both knew the real reason he didn't want her to go, and it had nothing to do with trust. He didn't want her out there alone, separated from the group where he couldn't protect her. They knew this, just as they knew his sentiment was as dangerous as it was unfounded. There was no room for favouritism or protectiveness in situations like this.

'Good. Then you won't have a problem with this.' Without waiting for a reply, she snatched the flares out of Frost's hand. 'Stay on comms. I'll let you know when I'm in position.'

Giving him a wink, the woman turned and sprinted off into the darkness. Mason, flashing a wry grin of amusement at Drake, likewise took off in the other direction, with two flares tucked into his webbing, clutching his silenced automatic.

'Fuck,' Drake said through gritted teeth.

'You guys *really* need to get a room,' Frost remarked sagely.

'Piss off,' Drake replied, shoving two flares down the front of his webbing.

Frost said nothing, though her smirk was hard to miss.

'Cover Sowan,' he instructed her. 'The last thing we need is some arsehole stealing the car with him in it.'

The young woman drew her weapon. 'Be a hell of a story, though.'

Before Drake could reply, Mason called out over the radio, 'Cameo's in position.'

'Copy that, Cameo. Envoy, how's it looking?'

'Almost there,' came McKnight's breathless reply. 'I see an earth berm up ahead.'

Sending out a silent prayer for this to work, Drake hit his transmit button. 'All right, light them up.'

Mason's flares ignited first, twin points of red light suddenly appearing in the darkness about a hundred yards off to the east. Drake watched as the flares separated, one dropping to the ground as Mason laid it down, followed by the other a short distance away.

With one end of the runway marked out, Drake turned his attention to the other. McKnight had already ignited one flare and dropped it in the corner of the landing strip, and as Drake watched he saw the other burst into life.

With the four corners now illuminated, he sprinted out into the runway, moving westward until he'd reached what felt like midway between the two sets of flares. Reaching down for the first device, he pulled the safety pin designed to prevent it triggering by accident, then twisted sharply on the plastic trigger at the base.

There was a flash, and suddenly his world was engulfed in red light and acrid chemical smoke as the incandescent contents ignited. Dropping it on the edge of the dirt landing-strip, he hurried over to the other side and triggered his second flare in similar fashion.

Coughing and turning away from the intense light that was destroying his night vision, Drake keyed his radio again. 'Eagle, this is Monarch. The field is lit. Look for the red lights. Do you copy?'

'Roger. I see them, Monarch. Not much of a landing pattern, but it will do. Coming in on approach now. Stand by.'

Drake closed his eyes for a moment, allowing the relief of the moment to flood through him before turning his thoughts back to the task at hand.

'Copy that, Eagle.' Already he had turned and was sprinting back towards the SUV. 'Cameo, Envoy, on me. Overwatch, get the cargo prepped for transport.'

'With pleasure, Monarch,' Frost replied.

–

About a mile to the west, Chandra eased the aircraft into a gentle left turn, aligning his nose with the meagre landing strip laid out for him. Checking his airspeed was sufficient to compensate for the increased drag, he reached out and flicked the landing-gear switch. There was a loud hum as the gear extended and locked in place.

He was grateful that the weather was favourable tonight, otherwise such a landing would have been unfeasible even for the likes of him. He was quite content to take risks, but even he recognized there was a line between bravery and suicide.

As he'd anticipated, his change in course and altitude hadn't gone unnoticed by Libyan air-traffic control.

'Flight Golf-Zulu-Six-Eight-Two, this is Tripoli Tower. Please return to heading zero eight zero, flight level fifteen. Acknowledge.' There was agitation in the man's voice that was plain even over the radio. He was probably tired and unhappy at pulling the night shift, and certainly didn't need some cowboy private-aircraft pilot ruining his night.

Adopting his most apologetic tone, Chandra hit his transmit button. 'This is Six-Eight-Two. Copy that, Tripoli Tower. One of my ailerons keeps locking up; think one of the control lines might be jamming. I'm landing to inspect it. Over.'

'Six-Eight-Two, recommend you circle around and return to Tripoli.'

'Don't think I can make that turn, Tripoli. Not on one aileron. Over.'

'Six-Eight-Two, are you declaring an emergency?' The mild irritation was gone now, replaced by genuine concern for a pilot in trouble.

'Not at this stage, Tripoli. I still have control. Over.'

'Roger, Six-Eight-Two. Stay on comms.'

Chandra smiled as he eased the twin-engine aircraft in for final approach. It was almost too easy.

–

Frost was waiting when Drake returned to the SUV. She had already popped the trunk and hauled Sowan out, and was busy doing the same to his wife. Standing with his ankles now untied to make him easier to transport but with hands still bound behind his back, Sowan made no move to either advance or retreat, knowing full well that Frost would take him down before he'd made it five yards.

Nonetheless, he looked remarkably calm and composed given his dire circumstances. The man was no stranger to fear, it seemed. Standing in a t-shirt and pyjama bottoms, with his hands bound behind his back, he glared openly at Drake as he approached.

The gag prevented him from saying much, but it was clear from the look in his eyes that he recognized his captor and was far from pleased by this turn of events.

Eyeball me all you want, you bastard, Drake thought to himself. We'll have plenty of time to talk later.

'I'm on your six, Keira,' Drake called out, in case she heard him approaching and mistook him for an enemy. Then, seeing that she was having difficulty with the second prisoner, he added, 'You need help?'

'No way. I'm having the time of my life,' Frost replied with heavy sarcasm.

Sowan might have been inclined to bide his time and wait for a more opportune moment to resist, but his wife clearly didn't share this attitude. She was kicking and thrashing in the trunk of the SUV, screaming into the gag and lashing out at Frost every time the Shepherd operative tried to pull her out.

'Stop fighting me, you stupid bitch!' Frost shouted, to little effect. Finally tiring of the stalemate, she drew her silenced pistol and pressed it hard against the woman's forehead. Staring her in the eyes, she said in a cold, emotionless voice, 'We need your husband. We don't need *you*. Give me an excuse to pull this trigger, please.'

Whether she understood the threat or not, the weapon was enough to quieten her struggles. Ceasing resistance, she allowed herself to be helped out of the trunk and led over to stand beside her husband.

'Very diplomatic,' Drake said quietly as Frost backed off, covering the two captives with her weapon.

Frost shrugged. 'Once you find common ground, it's easy to make friends.' She waved her weapon at their female prisoner. 'Isn't that right?'

She could say nothing in response, but the hostility in her eyes was obvious.

'You sure you want to take her with us?' Frost asked. 'She could cause problems later. Maybe we should leave her here.'

He shook his head as he gathered up their equipment packs, laying them on the ground by his feet. All of it, particularly the intel gathered by Mason from Sowan's office, would be going with them. 'We might need her if he doesn't talk.'

Frost said nothing to that.

Laying down the last pack, Drake hesitated, listening carefully to a faint noise carrying to him on the night breeze. A low drone like a swarm of bees, coming from the west, growing louder as it closed in.

Aircraft engines.

Moving towards Sowan, Drake reached out and removed his gag, staring the Libyan in the eye for a few seconds. 'Still think we won't make it out of Libya?'

'Who are you?' the man demanded. 'What do you want with me?'

'What do I want with you?' He lowered his voice, moving a step closer with his fist clenched. He could feel his hands trembling with barely suppressed rage now that he and Sowan were mere inches apart. 'I want to hear everything you have to say about Freya Louise Shaw. And you're going to tell me, you piece of shit. By the time I'm done with you, you'll be begging to tell me everything you know.'

The eyes staring back at him betrayed no trace of recognition, though his dark brows drew together in a frown. 'What are you talking about?'

The bastard was trying to play him, Drake realized. They'd see just how ignorant he was once Drake had some time alone with him.

'Don't worry, we'll have plenty of time to talk about it, you and I.' Glancing away, Drake touched his radio transmitter. 'Cameo, Envoy. Last orders at the bar. Our taxi's almost here.'

Mason, already on his way back, answered his instruction verbally rather than via the radio net. 'Music to my ears, buddy,' he called out, emerging from the darkness at the western end of the landing strip. He was breathing hard after running nearly the full length of the runway twice, but otherwise seemed in good shape.

The sound of engines was growing louder by the second. Glancing up, Drake could see the flashing recognition lights on the wingtips of Chandra's plane as it approached, settling in lower as he prepared to land.

'Where's Sam?' Frost asked, looking around.

–

Nearby, Chandra was concentrating intently on his difficult task as he reduced engine power, keeping the nose slightly elevated while he brought the aircraft in for landing. With only limited visual cues provided by the signal flares, he was relying mostly on instrumentation to gauge the rate of his descent.

Speed, 120 knots; altitude, sixty feet. Fifty feet. Flaps extended, reduce power. Angle the nose up a little more.

Altitude, forty feet. Perfect approach.

Such was his concentration on the task at hand, he didn't see the tiny bloom of a muzzle flash off in the distance, and certainly didn't hear the sound of the shot. Only a second or two later did he feel the effects.

There was a loud crunch as something impacted the aircraft, followed an instant later by an explosion of shattered glass as a portion of the canopy blasted inwards, showering him with tiny fragments. He had no time to contemplate this however as something slammed into his chest with such force that he was jerked back violently into his seat.

His first thought, stupid as it might have been, was that he'd collided with something in mid-air, some unseen obstruction across his path, perhaps even a flock of birds.

Looking down, he felt a fleeting sense of disbelief at the sight of blood pumping from the entrance wound in his chest. Even as shock started to cloud his judgement, he simply couldn't understand how this had come to be.

He didn't even register the next shot as it whizzed in through the shattered canopy, striking him in the head.

–

On the ground, Drake, Mason and Frost watched in horrified fascination as the aircraft suddenly yawed sideways, the port wing dipping low towards the ground as the nose angled downwards. With no one at the stick to correct the terminal dive, the airspeed increased rapidly as gravity took hold.

The twin-engine plane impacted the ground at about 140 knots, the port wing crumpling immediately under the impact and digging into the dirt landing strip, causing the fuselage to swing around in a violent arc. The port engine, still turning under half power, disintegrated in a deadly hail of flying wreckage as its highly stressed machinery tore itself apart.

The nose hit next, the entire forward section crumpling under the impact, as if it were made of cardboard. Even if Chandra had still been alive, no one could have survived such a crash.

Propelled by its considerable momentum, the remainder of the plane cartwheeled across the runway, scattering dirt and debris in its wake, and destroying the starboard wing and propeller in the process.

'Jesus Christ!' Frost gasped, horrified by what she was witnessing.

Drake's shock was no less. He was watching a good friend die right in front of his eyes, his aircraft consumed in a storm of dirt and smoke and flying metal. But even in the terrible moment of loss, he still had the presence of mind to realize the danger they were in.

'Cover!' he yelled, grabbing Sowan and pulling him to the ground as flying debris began to rain down around them, one piece passing dangerously close, to shatter one of the car's side windows.

Mason tackled Sowan's wife, partially shielding her with his own body, while Frost threw herself behind their car to escape the shower of wreckage. Fortunately they were far enough away that only the lighter pieces of debris reached them, most of it too small to cause serious injury.

A sudden flare of orange light told them the fuel tanks had finally ruptured and ignited, their burning contents spraying across the open ground. Even from a hundred yards away, they could feel the heat of the blaze.

Letting out a breath as the sounds of the crash faded, Drake slowly picked himself up, surveying what was left of Chandra's plane in shocked, uncomprehending silence, his eyes already starting to water as oily black smoke from the burning aviation fuel drifted towards them. There was little in the field of burning wreckage that resembled a plane now, and certainly no chance of survival for the pilot.

He was gone, as was their means of escape.

'What were you saying about getting out of the country?' Sowan asked, still lying where Drake had tackled him to the ground.

But Drake wasn't thinking about such things. Another, even more terrible thought had occurred to him as he took in the scene of devastation laid out before him. The plane had come down right where Samantha had been standing.

Heart pounding, he reached up and pressed his radio transmitter. 'Monarch to Envoy. Come in.'

His request was met with nothing but the pop and crackle of static.

Each second that passed was like a knife driven deeper into his heart. 'Envoy. Respond.'

'What the fuck happened?' Mason asked, coughing as the acrid smoke stung his throat. 'What happened to our plane?'

Drake had no answer for him. Indeed, even if he had, he wouldn't have had time to voice it. 'Stay here,' he ordered, drawing his weapon. 'I'm going after Sam.'

Drake was turning away when Mason rushed to catch up, grabbing his arm and spinning him around. 'Are you out of your mind, Ryan? It's suicide to go out there.'

'Get the fuck off me!' Drake snarled, yanking his arm free. 'She could be hurt. I have to find her.'

Before Mason could utter a reply, someone else spoke up for him. Someone Drake had hoped never to see again.

'Ryan, you disappoint me. Letting emotion cloud your judgement.'

Whirling around, Drake was just in time to see Faulkner emerging like a demon from the drifting smoke, lit crimson by the red glow of the nearby flames.

He was smiling that same knowing, mocking smile Drake had come to fear. The smile of a man who knows exactly what his opponents will do long before they do it. The smile of a winner.

'Good to see you again, old boy.'

Chapter 24

Despite his shock at the plane crash and Faulkner's sudden arrival, Drake's training and instincts as a field operative were still with him. Operating on instinct, he dropped to one knee beside the pile of equipment packs and levelled his weapon at his opponent. Frost and Mason reacted in kind, taking up positions on either side of him, with Mason keeping Sowan and his wife covered.

Far from being unnerved by the weapons pointed his way, Faulkner merely shook his head. 'I wouldn't, if I were you. Be a shame if things got out of hand.'

'Got targets left and right,' Mason hissed. 'They're flanking us.'

Sure enough, several of Faulkner's men were moving to outflank them, all armed with MP5 submachine guns. Formidable weapons that were devastating in close-range engagements like this, and more than capable of wiping out Drake and his team in a hail of 9 mm automatic fire.

Drake counted five of them, plus Faulkner himself. Six against three. Submachine guns against pistols. Bad odds by anyone's standards.

'That's far enough, Faulkner!' he warned, making sure he had the man's head in his sights. 'Or you'll be the first to go.'

'I think we've made our point, lads,' Faulkner said, signalling for his men to halt where they were. 'No sense in aggravating things. Not when we can resolve this like adults.'

'What do you want?' Drake demanded.

'You're smart enough. I think you can guess,' Faulkner replied, nodding to Sowan. 'He's standing about five yards from you.'

'We already agreed to bring him to you.'

The British operative chuckled. 'Ryan, please, don't take me for a fool. I knew the moment I handed you this job that you had no intention of honouring our deal. Predictable as always, and just as easy to control.'

Only now did Drake see how Faulkner had manipulated him, getting them to do his dirty work, to recover the man he himself wanted to get his hands on. He'd played them, and Drake, blinded by grief and his thirst for revenge, had walked right into it.

Faulkner let out a breath, focussing on Sowan once more. 'I'll make this simple. You put your gun down and give me Sowan, and we each go our separate ways with a minimum of aggravation.'

'Bullshit. The minute we lower our guns, he'll kill us all,' Frost countered.

'Your young friend is mistaken. I mean what I say.'

Drake's eyes narrowed. 'Give me one reason to believe that.'

Faulkner shrugged. 'It's a matter of priorities, Ryan. My priority is to recover Tarek here, preferably without losing men in the process. Your priority is to get out of Libya alive. At least, it should be. So I ask you now, which means more to you? The mission, or your... friends?'

'Ryan, what are we doing?' Frost whispered, unable to hide the fear in her voice. They were surrounded by a group with superior firepower. It didn't take a genius to recognize that their position was untenable.

Faulkner glanced at his watch, impatient with the delay. 'I'm sure that crash will have been reported by now. Libyan police and army units are probably on their way as we speak. I don't know about you, but I'd prefer to be gone by the time they arrive, so I'm going to make this very simple. I'll count to three, then my men start shooting. One...'

'Go to hell,' Mason snarled, eyes blazing with impotent anger.

'You're outnumbered and surrounded, Ryan. If you don't see sense, this is only going to end one way.' His lips were parted in a malicious smile. 'Two...'

'I have a shot,' Frost whispered. 'I can take him.'

It was a valiant sentiment, but even if they took down Faulkner, the rest of his group would hose them down with automatic fire before they could get a second shot off. As Faulkner himself had observed, they were outnumbered and surrounded. To fight would be suicidal.

'Three...'

Around them, Faulkner's men were tensing up, gripping their weapons tighter and preparing for the inevitable recoil when they opened up on full automatic.

It was at that moment that Drake acted. A wild gamble, driven by desperation and gut instinct. Swinging his weapon around, he took his sights off Faulkner and brought it to bear on Sowan.

'Wait!' Faulkner called out, raising his hand. Around them, his men held their positions, weapons trained on Drake. 'What do you think you're doing, Ryan?'

He was trying to convey the impression of amusement at Drake's sudden change of tactics, but Drake could see beneath the confident, arrogant facade. He'd rattled his adversary by threatening the one thing that was truly important to him. That told him what he needed to know.

'Lower the guns or he dies right now,' Drake warned.

'Not going to happen, I'm afraid.'

Drake's vivid green eyes glimmered in the crimson glow of the flames. 'You want him alive. You engineered this whole thing, came all the way to Libya to get him alive, which means you can't afford to go home without him. Now lower your fucking guns, or I put a bullet through his head right now.'

Faulkner flashed a thin, cold smile, but nonetheless glanced at his companions and gave a curt nod. With that, they lowered their guns a little, fingers relaxing on triggers. They could still bring their weapons to bear at a moment's notice, but they no longer had the drop on Drake and the others.

'So what are we to do now?' Faulkner asked. 'Keep this little stand-off going until the Libyans arrive to arrest us?'

'Everything comes at a price. That's what you told me.'

The British intelligence officer cocked his head curiously. 'And what might that price be?'

Drake exhaled, knowing this was the last card he had left to play. 'Let my friends go. Once they're out of here, I'll give you Sowan. Not before.'

'Ryan, what the fuck?' Frost hissed. 'We're not leaving you here.' She had no more wish to die than he did, but if it came down to it she'd rather go down fighting than watch her friend sacrifice his own life for them.

'It's all right, Keira,' Drake promised her, wishing there was more he could say. This might well be the last time they spoke. 'I've got this. You and Cole get out of here.'

No way was he letting Faulkner get his hands on Sowan alive. As soon as they were clear of the area, Drake fully intended to execute his hostage. It would likely be his final act, but if so, it wasn't a bad way to go.

'Still playing the hero, Ryan,' Faulkner said mockingly. 'I think you underestimated yourself the night we spoke.'

That was when heard it. A noise, distinct against the background of burning wreckage and the shifting night breeze that stirred up loose sand across the open space. A faint metallic ping that Drake well recognized from his years of training and military experience, that his keen analytical mind was able to categorize and insert into a possible chain of events which instantly set his heart racing.

'No,' he said, staring at his adversary through the drifting smoke as he readied himself to act. 'You're the one who underestimated me.'

It was at this moment that Faulkner began to react. Either he'd heard or seen something that had tipped him off, or he'd sensed from Drake's expression and body language that something was about to happen. Whatever the reason, he opened his mouth to shout out something – a warning, a command to fire, Drake couldn't tell.

Nor did he care.

At the same instant he saw something fly through the air towards them, hurled into their midst from an unseen source. Something small, cylindrical in shape, its metal surface glinting briefly in the firelight.

Something that confirmed Drake's wild, fervent hope that she was still alive.

In the half-second before he closed his eyes and turned away, he saw Faulkner likewise change direction and throw himself aside, seeking to shield himself from the detonation.

The flashbang grenade exploded before it had even hit the ground, igniting in mid-air about fifteen feet away from Drake. Even with his eyes closed, Drake saw the lightning-like flash that seemed to burn right through the thin skin of his eyelids, trying to sear its indelible mark on his retinas.

He might have been partially protected from the flash, but the thunderous boom almost knocked him off his feet. As it was, he dropped to his knees to steady himself. He felt like an artillery piece had just gone off right by his head, and desperately tried to fight back the sudden sense of vertigo that threatened to overwhelm him. The effects of the grenade could damage the inner ear, disturbing a victim's sense of balance and orientation.

But if he was so afflicted, the others would be too. And they hadn't been expecting it. He'd bought himself an opening. A small opening, perhaps, but a crucial one. What happened in the next few seconds would likely determine whether they all lived or died.

As he brought his weapon up, he could barely hear his own voice screaming out a warning to his friends. 'Keira, Cole! Get down!'

Opening his eyes, Drake took a rough aim at Faulkner and opened fire. The disorientation caused by the blast had similarly affected his ability to aim, and the first shot went wide, as did the second, allowing his adversary to disappear behind one of the corrugated steel sheds they had encountered on arrival.

Realizing he'd missed his chance, Drake shifted his aim to the nearest member of Faulkner's strike team. The man had been caught off guard by the blast, and had dropped to one knee to present a smaller target while he frantically tried to clear his vision.

Without hesitation, Drake pulled the trigger a third time. This time his shot found its mark, slamming into his target's left shoulder and spinning him around with the force of the impact. Rising to his feet, Drake carried on firing even as the man went down, determined not to let him return the favour. There was no finesse, no strategy to what he was doing – there was no time for such things now. He simply had to put as many rounds on target as possible and hope that it was enough.

Out of the corner of his eye he saw Frost open fire on another of Faulkner's men, who instinctively squeezed off a burst from his own weapon in response, the thunder of automatic gunfire splitting the air around them. He had no idea if Frost was scoring any hits or if it was simply covering fire to keep their heads down, but he was glad of it all the same.

By the time he'd risen up on unsteady legs, the weapon in his hand was no longer firing, but his target was no longer moving either.

'Ryan!'

His head snapped left, and through smoke and blurred vision he saw a figure emerge from the darkness, hurrying towards him with a weapon in hand. A woman.

'Sam!' he cried out, hardly believing what he was seeing.

She was coughing, her face smeared with dirt and soot, her eyes streaming in the oily smoke, but she was alive. Relief flooded through him at the sight of her, where only moments earlier he'd felt nothing but the sickening grief of her loss.

Gripping him by the straps on his webbing, she pulled him close and stared into his eyes. 'We have to get out of here!' she shouted, her voice sounding dull and distant in his ringing ears.

In that, he was in complete agreement. He had no idea how she'd survived the crash, how she'd understood that Faulkner had ambushed them and set up her own improvised rescue, but he knew there was no time to question her about it now. Survival was the priority, for all of them.

Nodding, he turned towards the vehicle that had brought them here. 'Cole, Keira, get in the car! Move!'

Outgunned and surrounded, this was one fight they could never hope to win. The only option was to bail out, fast.

Stumbling across the dusty ground back to the SUV, Drake and McKnight almost collided with Mason, who was forcing their two captives back into the car at gunpoint.

'Where's Keira?' he yelled, his eyes wet with tears that had left tracks down his soot-covered cheeks. Like the others, he'd been caught unprepared and temporarily blinded by the grenade blast.

'She's coming,' Drake said, ejecting the spent magazine from his weapon. 'Get them inside!'

McKnight went in first, taking up position in the rear seats. With no time to open the trunk, Mason simply shoved his two captives in behind her and slammed the door closed. It didn't take her long to turn her weapon on both of them, in case they harboured any thoughts of escape.

Drake meanwhile had circled around to the driver's door. He was about to clamber in when he spotted movement in his peripheral vision, and glanced up in time to see one of Faulkner's men emerge from behind the steel shithouse. He saw the barrel of the MP5 come up towards him, saw the man lock eyes with him as he squeezed the trigger.

Drake's reaction was one born from years of experience in firefights like this, and a practical understanding of the weapon he was up against. The MP5 was a compact little submachine gun, ideal for close-range combat because of its light weight and ability to spit out a high rate of fairly accurate fire. But the cost of its small size was its relative lack of stopping power. Its 9mm rounds struggled against even light body armour. If he was right about the level of paranoia of its owner, the Toyota came with more extras than just air conditioning.

Throwing himself to the ground, he allowed the SUV's door to absorb the initial burst of automatic fire as he brought his own weapon to bear. The distinctive scream of projectiles whanging off the metal bodywork was complemented a moment later by the dull thump of Drake's silenced weapon as he took aim at the man's centre mass and opened fire.

His aim was improving as the grenade effects wore off, and the first two rounds found their target, slamming into his chest with enough kinetic energy to send him staggering backwards. His finger tightened reflexively on the trigger as he fell, sending another burst of automatic fire sputtering skywards.

Rather than collapsing in a heap however, he managed to regain his balance enough to throw himself behind the shed for cover. He was almost certainly wearing body armour, and while Drake's shots were unlikely to do any lasting damage, they might have bought a few precious seconds to make their escape.

Scrambling to his feet, Drake paused just for a second to stare at the string of penny-sized holes that had been punched in the SUV's door panel. It seemed that he'd been wrong about the car. Either Faulkner's men were using armour-piercing rounds, or the vehicle wasn't as well protected as he'd thought.

Fumbling for the ignition key, he turned it over once and felt rather than heard the engine rumble back into life. He had no idea what kind of shape the Toyota was in after the punishing drive from Tripoli, but the engine still had some fight in it at least.

Having deposited his charges in the back seat, Mason circled around to the front and hauled open the passenger door, practically throwing himself inside. This car would become a bullet-magnet within seconds, and as they'd just learned, it offered little protection against small-arms fire.

'Where's Keira?' Drake called out.

'She's pinned down, man.' Mason pointed out to the open space near where the grenade had detonated.

Drake turned towards it. Sure enough, Frost was crouched behind the empty refuelling tank for cover, having become cut off from the rest of the group. She was still snapping off the occasional round from her Browning, but her slow rate of fire warned him she was almost out of ammunition. Her enemies meanwhile had her covered with automatic weapons, and it would only be a matter of seconds before they finished her off.

Mason's reaction was immediate, concern for his teammate overriding any thoughts for his own safety. 'Cover me. I'm going after her.'

'Forget it. Get in,' Drake ordered him.

Mason stared at him in disbelief. 'We can't just—'

'Shut up and get in!' Drake shouted, throwing the SUV into gear.

Nearby, Frost took aim and sent a single round whizzing off towards her target, hearing the distinctive *ping* as it ricocheted off the steel shed he was hiding behind. Her fire had kept them at bay thus far, but that would only last as long as her ammunition.

The Hollywood myths of people standing in open ground firing from the hip, or charging toward their enemies en masse heedless of the danger, were pure nonsense. As she'd long since learned, most firefights quickly devolved into a cat-and-mouse game, with both sides staying under cover and trying to either outgun or outflank the other. Nobody was going to risk getting killed in a suicidal charge, or by exposing themselves needlessly. Numbers and firepower were usually the deciding factors, and Faulkner's men had more of both.

As if to echo this, the response to her single shot was a long sustained burst of fire that howled off the metal framework around her. She was thankful this airfield was more or less disused, and that the fuel tank above her was empty, otherwise this exchange would have been brief indeed.

Smoke from the burning aircraft would help to keep her hidden and perhaps buy her a few more seconds, but the advantage worked both ways. She'd be less able to see her enemies as they closed in to finish her, like wolves circling their wounded prey.

Her one consolation was the sudden roar of a vehicle engine off to her left, still dimly heard since her ears were ringing from the grenade blast. Her distraction, however dearly paid for, had at least bought Drake and the others time to make good their escape.

She tried to hold onto that thought as she leaned out and sent another round whizzing out through the gathering darkness towards her enemies. The slide on her weapon flew back and locked in place to expose an empty breech. She was out. The only thing left to do was get her head down and run, hoping she could slip away into the darkness.

However, no sooner had she picked herself up to flee than the roaring engine grew suddenly louder and, with a squeal of brakes and a spray of dust, the big SUV came to a shuddering halt mere feet away. The vehicle now stood between her and Faulkner's men, blocking their line of sight.

The passenger door flew open, propelled by a kick from inside, to reveal Cole Mason, his clothes covered in dust and his eyes streaming from the recent grenade detonation. 'Get the fuck in!' he yelled.

She didn't have to be told twice, scrambling to her feet and leaping up into the vehicle. With nowhere else to go, she ended up sprawled uncomfortably on top of him.

'She's in. Go! Punch it!' Mason cried, fumbling to close the door behind her.

Wasting no time, Drake floored the accelerator. The big engine rumbled with power, wheels skidding on the dark packed dirt before finding purchase and lurching forward.

Gunfire traced through the air around them, pattering off the bodywork and shattering windows that showered the occupants with broken glass. There was a muffled cry from the back seat, though it was barely audible amidst the chatter of weapons fire and the roar of the labouring engine.

'Stay down!' Drake warned, keeping his foot pressed firmly on the gas and hoping there was nothing ahead of them that the Toyota couldn't overcome. There was no thought of manoeuvring for the best escape route at that moment; their only defence was distance.

Rocketing across the runway, they soon found themselves in the rougher ground on the far side. Rocks and sharp stones hammered the vehicle's underside while sudden dips and bumps strained the already battered suspension, but somehow it kept going. Somehow the engine continued to drag them onwards, wheels chewing up the uneven ground, until the incoming fire started to slacken off and the only sounds they could hear were the rumble of the engine and the whistle of wind through bullet holes in the windshield.

Heart pounding, breath still coming in shallow gasps, Drake chanced to raise his head above the level of the dashboard. He stole a glance in his rear-view mirror, mercifully seeing no sign of pursuit.

'Everyone all right?' he asked, hardly believing they'd made it out alive. How long they would stay that way in a foreign country with no support and no immediate means of escape was another matter, but for now their priority was simply to get out of the area.

'Hundred per cent,' Frost replied, oblivious to the blood dripping down her cheek where a shard of glass had cut her.

'Slightly crushed,' was Mason's response. With no other space to occupy in the passenger seat, Frost had resorted to dumping herself unceremoniously on his lap. However, his attempt at humour earned him a slap across the face that seemed to lie somewhere between affection and irritation.

McKnight however, seated behind them, was in no mood for jokes.

'Ryan, we've got a problem here,' she said, her voice quiet and urgent. 'Sowan's been hit.'

Chapter 25

As the SUV receded into the distance, David Faulkner turned his face skyward, closed his eyes and slowly exhaled through his nose, forcing calm into his body once more. To be sure, anger had its place in the great tapestry of human emotion. Anger endowed one with the strength and the will to do things that others might balk at, to commit acts of violence that would shock people who considered themselves normal. It was a vital weapon in the armoury of any operative like himself.

But anger alone was destructive and short-sighted, and this wasn't the time for it. Now was the time for cold hard decision making, starting with his own team.

Two of his men were crouched down beside one of their comrades, who had been severely injured during the brief fire fight. Colin Maxwell, the man Faulkner had entrusted with keeping their hostage under control, was lying on his back in the dirt, blood from several gunshot wounds pooling beneath him. Close-range shots that must have retained enough power to penetrate his body armour.

He was breathing hard and fast, teeth gritted against the pain, unable to keep from moaning as the lifeblood flowed out of him.

'Well?' Faulkner asked impatiently.

Samuel Tarver, the team medic, glanced up from his vain attempts to stop the bleeding. 'Three gunshots to the torso. He's alive, but he won't be for long unless we get him to a hospital.'

Faulkner let out a disappointed sigh. Maxwell was a good man; an army veteran who had served everywhere from the Falklands to Iraq in his long career. He'd worked for Faulkner for a number of years and never let him down in any appreciable way, until today.

It would be a shame to lose him.

Taking a step forward, he looked Maxwell hard in the eye. The old veteran stared right back at him, perhaps sensing what was coming. But like a good soldier, he didn't flinch, didn't plead or beg. Perhaps because he wasn't able to speak, but Faulkner preferred to attribute it to quiet courage.

'Sorry, Colin,' Faulkner said quietly, drawing his pistol. One shot to the head was enough to put Maxwell out of his misery.

Ignoring the horrified stares of the two men who only seconds earlier had been fighting to save his life, Faulkner holstered his weapon.

'Right, that's that taken care of,' he said, relieved that the matter was resolved. Death wasn't such a bad thing really, but drawn-out deaths were just tiresome. 'Sam, bring the car around, would you? We'd better be on our way before the police get here.'

Hesitating a moment, Tarver thought better of whatever objection he'd been about to voice, and hurried off to retrieve their own vehicle.

The fourth member of Faulkner's men had jogged over to investigate the gunshot, having secured the perimeter in the wake of the fight. Peter Boone, a tough and wily little Glaswegian whose spare frame and craggy face betrayed a hard-as-nails character and a bluntly grim outlook on life. He surveyed Maxwell's dead body without comment or emotion. Indeed, it was hard to know what, if any, kind of soul lurked behind his solemn grey eyes.

'What about Drake and the others? If they get away with Sowan, we're fucked.'

Faulkner fixed him with a baleful glare. Most other men would have wilted under such a gaze, but Boone was one of the few who seemed to have no sense of fear. Faulkner still couldn't decide if he respected or resented that.

'Then we'd best make sure they don't,' he said calmly. 'Hadn't we, Peter?'

Boone straightened up a little. 'What do you want us to do?'

The key, as always, was to apply a little logic to the problem, to take what he already knew, carefully consider its implications and use it to arrive at a rational conclusion.

A row of canvas backpacks were lying on the ground nearby. Presumably Drake had intended to take them on the aircraft that had been due to pick them up, but instead they'd been abandoned during the chaotic fire fight. Intrigued, Faulkner walked over and knelt down to inspect their contents.

Wary of booby traps, he took his time opening the first one. Tools, electronic equipment, water, food, even a Magellan satnav unit were all stowed away inside. Faulkner smiled faintly at the realization that his adversaries had, in their haste to escape, likely abandoned most of their vital gear.

Drake was now stranded in a hostile country with no immediate means of escape and few resources to call upon. He was driving a car which, in addition to being registered as stolen, was now sporting more bullet holes than a road sign in Alabama. By the time the sun came up – which according to his watch was in less than two hours – Drake would have no choice but to ditch the incriminating vehicle or risk immediate police pursuit.

A group of foreigners with two hostages in tow wouldn't get far on foot, especially not with temperatures likely to hit the high thirties by midday. With this in mind, Drake's first priority would be to find somewhere he could switch vehicles, regroup and plan his next move.

Drake might have been well trained at escape and evasion, but so was Faulkner, and he'd been playing this game a lot longer than his adversary. It wouldn't take Drake long to realize there was only one feasible course of action left to him now. One dangerous gamble that might offer a way out.

And Faulkner would be ready for him.

–

'Talk to me, Sam,' Drake called out, trying to make out what was happening in the back seat while keeping his eyes on the rough terrain ahead.

Behind him, McKnight was bent over Sowan, working quickly to assess the damage.

'He's taken a round in the leg. Must have punched right through the door.'

Drake winced inwardly. As he'd feared, their ride had offered little protection against the hail of gunfire that had been directed their way in the final few moments of the battle. It was a miracle none of them had been killed outright.

Gripping the material of Sowan's trouser leg, McKnight yanked hard, tearing it apart to expose a gory entrance wound in his left thigh. Blood was pumping out of the torn flesh in time to his rapid pulse.

'Shit, he's shot up pretty bad. Looks like arterial bleeding,' she said, applying pressure to try to staunch the flow of blood. Sowan, his hands still bound, cried out in pain and arched his back as if trying to fight her off.

'How bad is it?' Frost asked, twisting around to look.

McKnight fixed her with a blazing look. 'His blood's pumping onto the floor instead of around his body, so I guess it's pretty bad, Keira.'

Normally the temperamental young specialist wouldn't have tolerated such an outburst, but even Frost knew when to back off.

'Can you stop it?' Drake asked.

'Not unless I can clamp the artery, and I'm not even sure I can do that. I need a med kit, now.'

In the front seat, Drake looked to Mason for assistance. The specialist shook his head gravely. 'Had to ditch our packs at the airfield. There was no time to retrieve them.'

'Fuck,' Drake said under his breath. No packs meant no equipment, no medical supplies, no spare ammunition or even navigational aids. They literally had nothing but the clothes on their backs.

'Check the glove box,' he said, hoping for a lucky break. 'See if there's a first-aid kit.'

Popping open the little compartment in front of her, Frost rummaged through the contents. After tossing aside a road map, some ownership documents and a couple of user manuals that looked like they'd never been opened, she shook her head.

'I got nothing.'

'He needs a trauma surgeon, not a band aid and a sticky plaster, Ryan,' McKnight warned as the car bumped through a deep depression, prompting an agonized groan from the injured man.

'Just do what you can.'

'You mean sit here and watch him bleed to death?' she asked, fumbling to undo her belt. 'Because that's what's going to happen if we don't get him to a hospital in the next fifteen minutes.'

Sowan's wife was screaming into her gag, probably going into shock at the sight of her husband's blood everywhere. Drake ignored her. There were bigger problems to deal with.

'People ask questions in hospitals, Sam.'

'And I don't think there are too many doctors on call in this neck of the woods,' Mason added, gesturing to the inky blackness outside.

Wrapping her belt around Sowan's thigh a few inches above the injury, she cinched it up as tight as she could manage, prompting another groan of pain. Sowan was squirming and kicking, trying to get away from her, perhaps thinking she was doing more harm than good.

'Don't struggle,' McKnight warned him. 'I'm trying to save your life.'

Painful it might have been, but her makeshift tourniquet had nonetheless slowed the bleeding. She had bought him time, but not much.

Glancing out her shattered window, Frost spotted something off to the left. 'I see lights, on our ten o'clock.'

Following her line of sight, Drake saw them too. A small cluster of electric lights in the sea of darkness that surrounded them; possibly a village or other small settlement. Whatever it was, it had to be reasonably well supplied to have electricity, which might also mean a medical clinic or doctor's surgery. At the very least they had to have basic medical supplies.

'Can't be more than a couple of clicks away,' Frost added.

Mason looked at the leader of their team. Drake was staring fixedly ahead, gripping the wheel tightly. It was obvious what was on his mind. 'Faulkner will be coming after us.'

'I know.'

'We've got nothing to defend ourselves with.'

'I know.'

'If we stop now, we'd be painting a target on our heads.'

'And if we don't stop, Sowan's as good as dead,' Frost reminded him. 'That what you want, Cole?'

At this, Mason shrugged. 'Better him than us.'

'Then all this was a waste of time. We came all this way, risked our lives, lost a man for nothing. That's fucking bullshit.'

'You know what else is bullshit? Dying in some desert shithole trying to save a man who'd just as soon kill us all and piss on our graves. I say we ditch him and get our asses over the border to Tunisia tonight.'

'So we just keep driving and hope for the best?' the young woman shot back. 'For Christ's sake, use your head! Even if we get away, we still lose. Faulkner will hunt us down no matter where go.'

'So let him. I'd rather fight on my own terms.'

Drake had remained silent thus far, rapidly turning over the various risks and possibilities in his mind. Each argument had its merits, but there was no denying the pragmatic reality of Mason's plan. They were driving a stolen car in a hostile country, with a high-ranking government official and his wife held hostage. Not only was Faulkner hunting them, but so was the Libyan government. Every minute they spent here increased the chances of being caught by one side or the other.

On the other hand, they were less than a hundred miles from the Tunisian border. They could cut Sowan loose right now, make a dash westward and with luck be out of Libya before first light. It would mean leaving with nothing to show for their efforts tonight, but they would at least have escaped with their lives.

But as Frost had so rightly pointed out, what then? Clearly Faulkner was a man with considerable resources at his disposal, and the will to use deadly force to get what he wanted. Drake knew he had no hope of fighting a war on two fronts. One way or another Faulkner had to be dealt with, and somehow Sowan was the key to that.

It was obvious the man wasn't what Faulkner had claimed him to be, but he was important, perhaps even dangerous. Faulkner had orchestrated this whole thing, had manipulated Drake and his team into coming here, had even risked his own life to get his hands on Tarek Sowan.

Why?

One thing was for sure – they would never learn the truth if Sowan bled to death in the back seat of their car. If they wanted to learn the secrets that Faulkner was so determined to protect, their captive had to live.

'We need Sowan alive if we want to get out of this. We're going for it,' Drake decided, swinging the wheel over and charting a path straight towards the distant settlement.

'Goddamn it,' Mason swore under his breath, though he was wise enough not to protest Drake's decision. Arguing at this point would achieve little except to fragment the group further.

'Check your weapons and ammo,' Drake said. He didn't know what kind of reception they could expect, but it was unlikely to be friendly.

'That won't take long,' Frost observed. Between the escape from Tripoli and the fight at the airfield, the group had expended most of their limited ammunition.

They were certainly in no shape to fight another battle, but with luck they wouldn't have to. When dealing with civilians, the mere display of a weapon was often enough to silence thoughts of resistance.

'Just get it done,' Drake said as they bumped and jolted their way towards the small settlement. 'When we go in, it has to be fast and hard. Keira and I will secure the house. Cole, you cover Sam. As soon as the place is secure, bring Sowan inside. Everyone understand?'

He was met by a round of affirmatives.

'How's he doing?' Drake asked over his shoulder.

'Pulse is dropping,' McKnight replied, her hands and forearms stained crimson. Sowan was still moaning in pain, but his movements were growing sluggish, his eyes heavy. 'We need to stop this bleeding, now, Ryan.'

He said nothing to that, concentrating instead on getting them to their destination as quickly as possible.

It almost came as a shock when the rough stony ground beneath their wheels suddenly gave way to asphalt as they intersected a main road. Guessing that it ran close to the settlement nearby, Drake swung them left onto the narrow roadway and stomped on the accelerator. The surface beneath them was roughly finished and in poor repair, yet after jolting and rolling across miles of open country it felt as if they were driving on air.

As he'd hoped, after half a mile a junction split off to the right, apparently an access road for the settlement. Drake went right for it, leaving a cloud of dust and stones in his wake as the SUV rumbled along the last few hundred yards.

Off to his left, rows of bushes or small trees flitted by in the darkness, all laid out in neat regularly spaced lines that clearly weren't natural in origin. It took him a moment to realize they were driving through a fruit orchard. This was an agricultural area.

The small cluster of buildings that served the orchard appeared to be laid out at the southern end, all well illuminated by electric lights. The biggest of them was, he assumed, a barn or warehouse for storing produce and equipment, but the others looked more like conventional dwellings for the people who worked here.

Approaching to within a hundred yards of the farm complex, Drake eased off the throttle and took the engine out of gear, allowing the SUV to coast along the flat ground with little more than the crunch of its tyres betraying its approach.

'This is it,' he called out. 'Get ready to move.'

The farm buildings were arranged in a rough semicircle, all facing into an open space in the centre where vehicles could turn or park. Only one of them looked like a residential building, however. A single-storey brick structure with a tiled roof, shuttered windows and an arched portico leading to the main entrance, it looked unusually grand and elaborate for such a rural location.

The weathered and pitted walls suggested this building had been around for quite a while, and the quality of the workmanship told Drake it wasn't a product of one of the Gaddafi government's haphazard construction programmes. Likely it was some holdover from the days of colonial rule, when the Italians had owned the country and the nearby orchard had produced olives or figs.

Allowing the SUV to coast almost up to the front door, Drake stomped on the brakes to bring them to a halt.

Frost was moving before they'd even stopped, throwing open her door and leaping down with her weapon already drawn. Drake went out a moment later, feeling his boots make contact with hard-packed dirt that had been rendered like stone by the passage of countless vehicles over the years.

Pausing just for a moment, he cocked his head to listen in on his surroundings. The sound of an engine of some kind was coming from the warehouse nearby, though the steady chugging reminded him less of a vehicle and more of a portable generator. That probably explained where the electricity was coming from, in a region where most houses didn't even have running water.

Gaddafi had once boasted to the world that nobody had to pay electricity bills in Libya because it was free for all citizens to use. Whether or not that pledge had come true Drake had no idea, but it was probably made easier to achieve when the majority of houses weren't even connected to the grid. With oil and petrol being dirt-cheap here, it was easier for farms like this to run their own generators twenty-four hours a day.

Still, power generation was the last thing on his mind as he headed for the portico, with Frost on his left side and slightly behind to cover him. Both operatives had their weapons up and ready, though with roughly half a magazine apiece they'd have to rely more on intimidation than firepower.

Their arrival hadn't gone unnoticed. Even as they closed in on the arched portico, they heard the rasp of a bolt being drawn, and suddenly the front door swung open to reveal what Drake assumed was the owner of the plantation.

A big bear of a man in his late sixties, he sported a halo of bushy grey hair and a face so deeply lined and tanned that it reminded Drake of a worn leather couch. He was wearing stained work trousers, sandals and a crumpled grey shirt that struggled to contain his voluminous stomach.

Of greater interest than his appearance however was the double-barrelled shotgun he was clutching in his meaty hands. A break-action, over-and-under job whose wooden stock was so darkened by years of use that it resembled its owner's face, the shotgun looked like it belonged in a museum rather than a farmhouse.

Old it might have been, but it was more than enough to make a mess of anyone caught within twenty yards if it went off. Drake suspected the trusty old gun had been used in the past to see off trespassers and potential thieves, and wondered if this farm always had someone standing watch at night. It would explain why the lights were on at such an hour.

Spotting the two operatives heading towards his home, the man started to raise the weapon, an angry shout already forming on his lips. Drake, blessed with faster reflexes and a smaller and lighter automatic, easily beat him to the punch.

'Drop it!' he ordered, keeping the man's forehead in his sights. 'Drop the gun now!'

Even if he didn't speak English, he got the message without much trouble. His dark eyes swept from one operative to the other, taking in the silenced gun barrels now pointed his way. Recognizing that this was one intrusion he wasn't going to see off with a few shouts and a warning shot in the air, he lowered the old gun and laid it down on the stone floor at his feet.

Drake was on him immediately, turning him forcibly around and marching him back inside with the silenced automatic pressed into his back, using his considerable bulk as a human shield.

'Let's go, mate. Inside,' he said in the man's ear. 'Cooperate and we won't hurt you.'

The farmer growled something in response which Drake suspected was less than complimentary, not that he could blame him. He felt shitty for invading an innocent man's home in the middle of the night and holding him at gunpoint, but there wasn't much alternative. Desperate times and all that.

'Anyone else live here?' he asked in fragmented Arabic. 'Anyone with you?'

'This is my house,' was the only reply he received.

Venturing in through the arched doorway, Drake found himself in a wide entrance hallway with white walls and a tiled floor. Ahead lay the kitchen, with a solid wooden table in the centre. To the left, another arch led through to a living room. Drake spared it a momentary glance, taking in the patterned rugs, worn furniture and boxy-looking TV in one corner. Pretty unremarkable for a moderately prosperous home in this part of the world, save for one detail. A PlayStation games console was sitting on top of the television, its controllers hanging down the side by their power cables.

Straightaway alarm bells started ringing in Drake's head. Somehow this 60-year-old farmer didn't strike him as hardened videogame player.

'Keira, go right. Eyes on,' he said, his voice low and commanding as he pointed to a closed door. 'Check your fire. Could be kids in the house.'

'On it.'

The farmer was getting more agitated now as they moved deeper into his home, his voice growing louder and more aggressive with each passing moment. It must have been obvious to him by now that they were neither common thieves nor the dreaded Libyan state police.

'Shut up,' Drake hissed, jabbing the silencer hard into his fleshy back. He didn't want to panic him, but he needed the man to take him seriously.

Far from being cowed by this display of force, however, the threat of violence only seemed to stoke the fire of his anger. Swinging around to face Drake, he jabbed a thick finger at him and continued spouting off in Arabic, his face twisted in hatred. Drake caught the liberal use of Allah along with some other less pious words, and doubted the man was pronouncing a blessing on him.

Before he could respond, however, his attention was distracted by a commotion to his right. Just as Frost was reaching for the door leading deeper into the house, it had suddenly swung open to reveal a pair of men in their early twenties. They were both tall and gangly, and bore enough of a resemblance to the farmer that they had to be related.

Judging by their bleary eyes and dishevelled hair, they'd been woken by the noise in the hallway and had come through to investigate. One, perhaps sensing trouble, had had the presence of mind to bring a knife with him. It looked like more of a utensil than a weapon, but a knife was still a knife, and Drake had enough injures to contend with tonight.

The sight of his father being held at gunpoint was more than enough to drive away the last vestiges of sleep for the young man. Quickly taking in the scene, he let out a cry and lunged at Frost with the blade.

Frost, to her credit, reacted to the unexpected encounter like the professional operative she was. Ducking aside to avoid the vicious swipe, she lashed out with a kick to the stomach that doubled him over, finishing it with an elbow to the back of his neck that sent him crashing to the floor.

Even as this was happening, the second youth started towards her. He was unarmed and looked more frightened than angry, but if his brother's life was in danger he wasn't about to stand and do nothing.

Raising her weapon, Frost took aim and put a round through the wall less than a foot from his head, the high-powered projectile blasting a gaping hole in the plasterwork. That shot across the bow was enough to halt his stride.

'Back off! Both of you!' she shouted, gesturing with the still-smoking barrel of her gun for them to move into the hallway where she could cover them.

It was at this moment, while Drake was momentarily distracted, that the farmer decided to act, making a sudden grab for his gun. It was a gutsy move for a civilian, and against a different opponent it might well have worked, but not today.

Sidestepping the clumsy move, Drake retaliated with a hook to the side of his face that jerked his head around, staggering him. A kick to the back of the leg dropped him to his knees, allowing Drake to step back a pace and cover him with the weapon once more.

'Don't try that again,' he warned in the man's own language, then glanced over at Frost. 'Bring the kids over here, and secure the rest of the house.'

He saw a father and his two sons, but what about the mother? His recent experiences in Sowan's house warned him against the dangers of leaving loose ends untied.

Shoving the young men into the centre of the hallway where Drake could keep all three residents covered, Frost turned and darted off through the open doorway.

'Down on your knees, both of you,' Drake said, indicating for them to get down.

Reluctantly the youths complied. One of them, the one who had thought to use the knife against Frost, glowered at him and spat a muttered curse, only for his brother to hush him. Drake said nothing, hoping that silence would allow the more sensible of the two to prevail.

Much to his relief, Frost soon returned from her sweep of the house. 'We're clear. Nobody else is home.'

Drake nodded. Thank fuck for that. Reaching up, he touched his radio transmitter. 'The house is secure. Bring them in.'

'Copy that,' Mason replied over the radio net.

'What do you want to do with *them*?' Frost asked, nodding to their three new captives. 'At this rate we're going to need a fucking minibus.'

'Tie them up and secure them in the living room for now,' he decided. 'Someone will find them once we're out of here.'

The young woman glanced at him. 'They'll call the police.'

Drake shrugged. 'Let them. We'll be long gone by the time they get word out.'

They'd be sure to destroy any phones or radios in the house before leaving, hopefully buying enough time to get clear of the area.

Behind him, the front door flew open and Mason appeared, supporting a heavily bleeding Sowan on his arm.

'Anyway, we've got bigger problems right now,' Drake added, watching the arrival.

While Frost went to work on the farmer and his sons, Drake hurried over to Mason and helped him carry Sowan through to the kitchen, leaving a trail of blood on the tiled floor as they went. The big dining table he'd spotted earlier was cluttered with dishes, cups and cutlery – the remains of last night's dinner – but one swipe of Drake's arm was enough to send it all crashing to the floor, creating enough space for them to work.

Laying the injured man on the table, Drake stepped back, allowing McKnight access to him. Reaching behind him, she cut the bindings at his wrists. Even if he was foolish enough to make a break for it, he wouldn't make it more than ten paces on that leg.

Leaning over him, she looked him hard in the eye, hoping to see a response. His pupils were dilated, his eyes unfocussed as he teetered on the verge of unconsciousness.

'I'm going to help you now,' she said, speaking slow and clear. 'It'll hurt, but the less you fight me, the easier it'll be. Nod if you understand.'

For a moment she saw a flicker of recognition, of understanding, in the dimming eyes. He nodded; a slight but purposeful acceptance of what had to happen.

His wife too had been brought into the kitchen, rather than risk leaving her alone outside. Even bound and gagged she could still cause problems. At least here they could ensure she didn't try to run.

Escape however seemed to be the last thing on her mind. She was backed up against the kitchen worktop, staring at her husband and the bloody gunshot wound that was slowly killing him.

'Cole, look around, see if you can find a med kit,' Drake said, surveying the small, cluttered kitchen. They were on a farm, after all. With plenty of heavy machinery at work, the possibility of injury was never far away – surely such a place would keep basic medical equipment on hand. 'Keira, how are you doing?'

'Party central here,' she called through. 'What about Sowan?'

Drake looked over at the injured man just as McKnight loosened the tourniquet for a few moments, allowing blood to flow through his leg. If she didn't, the tissue would die off and become infected. There was no point in treating his gunshot wound only for him to die later of gangrene. However, the result of her effort was a renewed surge of bleeding from the open wound.

Glancing up, McKnight met his gaze, the look in her eyes telling him everything he needed to know before she'd spoken a word. 'We're losing him, Ryan. I can't stop the bleeding.'

It was at this moment that something happened. Something even Drake hadn't expected.

Sowan's wife had not been idle since they'd brought her into the kitchen, neither overcome with grief nor paralysed by fear. Instead she had backed up against the cluttered kitchen worktop, managed to grasp a small cooking knife with her bound hands, and had used it to quickly saw through the plastic cable ties securing her wrists. With her hands suddenly freed, she reached up and tore the gag from her mouth.

Spotting the movement and realizing that she'd somehow managed to free herself, Drake drew his weapon. If she intended to attack one of his teammates with the kitchen knife, he wouldn't hesitate to drop her.

'Drop the knife,' he warned. 'It's not worth dying for.'

Straightaway the knife clattered to the floor, though he got the impression it was because it had served its purpose rather than because his threat carried much weight. And far from expressing anger or dismay at having her desperate plan thwarted, the woman merely aimed a disdainful glance his way.

'If you want to shoot me, then do it. I am not afraid of you,' she challenged him, speaking nearly flawless English that carried only a faint accent. 'But you will be killing the only person who can save this man's life.'

Drake frowned, surprised both by the fact she spoke English, and by the grim warning she'd just issued. 'What do you mean?'

'I am a surgeon, *Ryan*.' She practically spat his name. 'This man has a laceration of the profunda femoris artery, and since I don't see an exit wound, it seems likely the bullet is still inside. He needs surgery to remove it, an immediate arterial clamp and repair of the artery if he is to live. If any of you think you can do this, then please go ahead. Otherwise get out of my way and let me save him.'

Her dark eyes swept across each of her captors, burning with anger and barely suppressed hatred.

'He won't last much longer, Ryan,' McKnight warned, tightening the tourniquet once more in a desperate effort to conserve whatever blood remained to him.

Drake still had his weapon levelled at Sowan's wife. 'How do I know you won't kill him?'

If she felt they were fighting to save his life simply to torture him to death later, she might well kill him to spare him the suffering.

'He is my husband. I am going to help save his life.' She took a step forward, her eyes locked with his. 'As I said, if you want to stop me, then do it now. Otherwise stand aside.'

She took another step forward, and another, until the silencer was pressing into her chest. Still she wouldn't back down.

For Drake the choice, stark and unforgiving though it might have been, was clear. Kill her and watch Sowan bleed to death, or let her live and risk killing him anyway.

Hell of a decision.

'If you kill him, you die next,' he promised.

She didn't flinch for a moment. 'If killing is all you understand, then so be it.'

Saying nothing further, Drake lowered the weapon and reluctantly moved aside, allowing her access to the patient.

She wasted no time taking charge of the situation, quickly checking his pulse and papillary response. 'I need boiled water, a sharp knife, a pair of pliers and any medical equipment you can find. Bring the owner of this house in here, if you haven't killed him already,' she added with a scornful look.

'Keira, bring the old man through,' Drake called out.

In short order, the farmer was escorted through to the kitchen at gunpoint. He surveyed the scene before him; the injured man, the bloodstained table and the woman in a nightgown working frantically to help him.

Straightaway she started talking in Arabic, speaking her questions in a low, quiet, efficient tone so as to convey her needs as quickly as possible. The farmer glanced at Drake and the others suspiciously, perhaps unwilling to help them even if an innocent man's life was at stake, though a more forceful prompting at last elicited a response.

'He says there is a first-aid kit in the barn outside, just to the right of the main door,' she translated. 'Bring it here now.'

'Cole,' Drake ordered.

Mason nodded. 'On it.'

McKnight had already set a pot of water on the gas cooker, and was working the controls to start it boiling.

Sowan's wife wasn't finished yet however. 'I need pliers, tweezers, anything that can grasp a small object. Find something.'

It was Drake's turn to start looking. The small kitchen was cluttered with objects and items of all shapes and sizes, from the usual crockery, cutlery and frying pans, to food and spices, to tools like screwdrivers and wire cutters, and even dismantled electrical goods. There was no real order or system to it; it had just been dumped wherever was convenient at the time. It reminded him of his kitchen back home.

That being the case, what he needed was The Drawer. Every kitchen in the world had one. It was the place where everything useful seemed to end up sooner or later, from spare batteries to light bulbs, instruction manuals, keys and pretty much everything else that didn't have a logical storage place.

Rifling through the old-fashioned kitchen units, it took him three attempts to find what he was looking for. In this case, The Drawer was home to a small box of shells for the shotgun, electrical wiring, nuts and bolts and screws of various sizes, and mercifully a pair of needle-nose pliers.

'Got them,' he said, turning towards Sowan's wife.

She inspected them for a moment before apparently deciding they were suitable. 'Throw them in the boiling water. They must be sterile.'

With the pot on the cooker now steaming and just starting to bubble, Drake dumped the pliers in. As far as field operations went, this was undoubtedly one of the most improvised jobs he'd witnessed.

At that moment, Mason came running back into the kitchen, breathless and clutching a small green first-aid box.

'Here,' he said, practically tearing it open, and dumping the contents on the table.

Amongst the sterilized dressings, rubber gloves and alcoholic wipes, Sowan's wife spied a little suture kit and held it up. 'This will have to do,' she decided, quickly pulling on the gloves. 'Give me the pliers, and get ready to hold him down.'

A severed artery was rather like a burst hosepipe; as long as there was water flowing through it, it would continue to leak until some way was found to clamp it shut.

There was no great technicality to what she had to do next. Her first objective was to find the bullet and extract it. Once it was out, she needed to find the damaged artery and use the pliers to clamp it shut. It wasn't a permanent solution by any means, but it would stop the blood loss and allow them to stabilize his condition. If it worked.

Sowan had been hovering on the verge of unconsciousness since they'd laid him on the table, but the moment his wife pulled apart the wound and pushed the pliers inside, he kicked and thrashed, crying out in agony and threatening to fall right off the table.

'Hold him!' she commanded, having to raise her voice to be heard.

Mason and Drake gripped him by the shoulders while McKnight took his legs, exerting no small amount of force to keep him pinned down. For a dying man suffering from severe blood loss, he was still capable of putting up quite a fight, pain and adrenaline lending frantic strength to his efforts.

The combined force of three operatives was enough to keep him still, allowing the surgeon to go about her work. Nonetheless, her task was far from easy. Working in dim light, with the most basic medical equipment imaginable and with her unsedated patient screaming and thrashing against her, she bent close, jaw clenched tight as she focussed utterly on her task.

'He'll go into shock if we keep this up,' Drake warned, wondering how much Sowan's already weakened heart could withstand.

'I feel the bullet,' she said, manipulating the pliers with infinite care. 'I almost have it.'

'Then pull it out, for Christ's sake,' Mason implored her. Listening to a man screaming in agony was enough to try even the staunchest nerves.

'It is close to the artery.' She didn't look up, but if she did then Drake was certain her eyes would be filled with unrestrained fury. 'If I do this wrong, it will sever completely and he will die within seconds. So be silent.'

Unable to do anything but hold the patient down and trust to her skill, Drake watched as she moved the pliers a fraction of an inch deeper, ignoring the chaos and noise around her. There was something oddly calming about this woman, as if her inner focus and quiet confidence somehow radiated from her and affected those nearby.

He watched as her fingers drew together, tightening their grip on the pliers' handle. And then in a smooth, graceful motion, she withdrew them. The motion was accompanied by an agonized scream from Sowan, though it soon faded out as his consciousness waned – pain and blood-loss at last causing him to faint.

A quick check of his pulse confirmed he was still alive. Sure enough, a bloody 9mm slug, its head flattened by its violent passage through metal and human flesh, was clenched between the jaws of the pliers.

For a moment, Sowan's wife's eyes met with Drake's. 'I daresay you know more about these than I do,' she acknowledged. 'Is this all of it, or could there be more still in the wound?'

Drake held out his hand and she dropped the slug into it. He turned it over, studying the shape, size, weight and general contours of the round. It wasn't unknown for bullets to fragment on impact, particularly when striking hard surfaces like a car chassis, but luckily this one seemed to have remained intact.

'This is all of it,' he confirmed.

She nodded, satisfied. 'Then I can start to undo some of this damage.'

Working with both speed and great care, she was able to use the pliers once more to press down on the damaged artery, exerting just enough force to stop the flow of blood without damaging the arterial walls. Her task was made a great deal easier with Sowan unconscious and no longer fighting and crying out, allowing her to pull the wound apart far enough to inspect the damage. Drake had found a working flashlight amongst the kitchen paraphernalia, and was holding it overhead to assist her.

'I see it,' she said quietly. The artery itself was visible as a pale pink tube about the thickness of a drinking straw. A hole perhaps a centimetre in length had been torn in it by the passage of the bullet. 'Fortunately it hasn't been completely severed. Hand me the suture kit.'

Reaching over, Drake placed it carefully in her hands, making sure she didn't drop it. Checking the little needle was properly threaded, the surgeon leaned forward and began the first delicate stitch along the edge of the tear.

'Where did you learn English?' he couldn't help asking. Sowan's command of English made sense. After all, the man worked in the intelligence sector, and much of his dealings were apparently with English-speaking operatives. His wife however was another matter.

'I studied ophthalmology at Johns Hopkins for two years.'

That explained it. This woman had studied in Baltimore, barely forty miles from his own home in DC. He might have passed her on the street and never known it.

'Have you done many operations like this?'

'You mean removing a bullet from my own husband?' she asked without looking up from her task. 'I can't say I have.'

'That wasn't what I meant.'

'I know what you meant,' she said. 'I'm an eye surgeon, not a battlefield doctor. I specialise in cataract removals and corneal transplants. Elective surgeries in well-equipped operating theatres. You might say I'm quite outside my area of expertise at the moment.'

Drake stared at her in amazement as she threaded another loop with infinite care. He couldn't believe how calm, how focussed and composed she was, considering she was fighting to save the life of a man she loved, using tools and resources that where wholly inadequate for the task.

'But compared to the human eye, this is really quite simple,' she went on. 'Like fixing burst pipes.'

'If you say so,' he said, not sure he shared that assessment. Like everyone in the team, he'd been trained in battlefield medicine, but what she was doing now far surpassed his basic skills. 'You know, we were never properly introduced.'

'What? You mean you came all this way for us, and you never troubled yourself to learn my name?' she scoffed with grim humour. 'I am disappointed, *Ryan*.'

'We didn't come for you.'

'No, you didn't. You came for my husband. Which begs the question of what will happen to him once I've finished. Clearly you need him alive, which means you want him for something. Assuming he survives long enough to serve your purpose, what then? Do he and I just… "disappear"? That's the word people like you use, isn't it? So much easier, so much more clean and clinical than *murder*. Maybe it even helps you sleep better at night.'

'Yeah, and how do you suppose your husband sleeps at night?' Frost asked derisively. Sitting on the kitchen counter in the corner of the room, she had been watching the operation in sullen, brooding silence until now.

The cut above her eye had been cleaned and bound with some adhesive sutures from the first-aid kit, not that it had done much to improve her mood. 'Hate to break this to you, but he ain't no fucking boy scout either.'

'Go outside, get some air,' Drake advised her, not wishing to antagonize the one person who had the power of life and death over their target.

'There's air in here.'

Drake fixed her with a hard glare. 'Don't make me ask again. Go outside and walk the perimeter. Stay on comms.'

Snorting in disgust, Frost eased herself down off the countertop, surveyed the injured man for a long moment, then finally left the room, muttering to herself.

'What did she mean about Tarek?' the surgeon asked.

Drake hesitated. Was it possible she didn't know what her husband did for a living? he wondered. Did she really have no idea that the man she was fighting to save had likely overseen the torture and execution of countless men and women whose only crime had been their opposition to the government of this country? That he might well have ordered the death of Drake's own mother?

'She's angry. Angry people lash out.' It wasn't entirely untrue either. 'But my team aren't in the business of murder.'

That much was true at least. He couldn't say the same of himself however.

'You will forgive me if I don't take you at your word, Ryan.'

She had completed the third tiny loop of suture, and now prepared to pull the stitches together to close the wound. Using a pair of tweezers from the suture kit, she gripped the end of the thread and pulled the loop slowly together, the pressure causing the hole to close up. With that task accomplished, all that remained was to tie the ends off and find out if her repair had been a success.

'Also, you didn't answer my question. What do you intend to do with us?'

Drake let out a breath. It wasn't an easy question to answer, because what happened to them depended greatly on what Sowan was able to tell Drake and the others – if he lived that long.

'I came here for answers,' he said. 'The kind only your husband can give me. But right now, I'm not the one you need to be worrying about.'

This prompted a raised eyebrow. 'Your friends back at the airfield?'

He nodded. 'Your survival depends on ours. If they find us, they'll kill us. All of us.'

'Why?' she asked. 'What is Tarek's life worth to them?'

Truly that was the question. 'That's what I'm hoping to find out.'

With her makeshift repairs completed, she reached over and slowly released the pressure on the pliers, allowing blood to flow through the damaged artery once more. Mercifully, the sutures appeared to hold. At least there was no sudden rush of arterial blood like before.

She nodded, satisfied with her work. 'I think it should hold. For now, at least.'

With the artery stabilized, the hard part was over. It was a fairly simple task to stitch up and bandage the wound, which she again insisted on doing herself. Only when a clean field dressing was firmly bound around his leg did the woman at last allow herself to relax.

'Keep a close eye on him,' she advised. 'If his blood pressure drops suddenly, it could be a sign the sutures have failed.'

Drake didn't need to be told about keeping him under observation. He intended to have someone on permanent watch around Sowan until the man regained consciousness.

'If you don't mind, I would like to wash up.' She was still wearing the surgical gloves, her arms and nightgown smeared with blood, her hair tangled and dishevelled.

'Of course.' Reaching up, Drake keyed his radio. 'Monarch to Cameo. Any activity outside?'

'Nothing here, Monarch. It's all quiet.'

'Good. Get in here and keep an eye on the target.'

It didn't take long for Mason to return to the kitchen. With Sowan now under watch, Drake escorted his wife down the hallway to a wash room that apparently served all the residents of the house.

'I need to keep the door open,' he said apologetically. The chances of her clambering through the small ventilation window and making a break for it were slim, but it was a risk he wasn't prepared to take at this point. 'Take as long as you need.'

She didn't seem to be paying attention now, her uncanny focus and stern composure having at last deserted her. Leaning over the sink, she started a tap running and fumbled to remove the surgical gloves, finally tearing them off and dropping them on the floor at her feet.

Holding her hands under the running water, she watched as the blood swirled around the sink, fading and dissipating yet never truly disappearing. She reached up and began to wipe it from her arms, slowly at first but soon growing faster and more agitated, as if the sight of it now disgusted her. It was then that Drake noticed her hands were shaking, her breath coming in short, frantic gasps.

Only now did he understand her apparent lack of emotion earlier. At the time he'd attributed it to a naturally cold and detached personality, or perhaps a marriage that had long since lost its intimacy. Now he saw her detachment for what it was – a facade, a professional defence-mechanism born out of necessity.

She had put aside her own feelings while she did what she had to do to save the man's life. Only now that he was out of danger could she finally let those defences drop. Only now could she allow herself to feel the pain, the shock, the agony at what she had seen and done tonight, and what had been done to her.

Reaching into his webbing, Drake held something out to her. 'Here. Take this.'

His words seemed to rouse her slightly from her shock, and she turned her head slowly to look at him, frowning in confusion at the hip flask in his hand.

'It'll help,' he assured her. 'Trust me.'

He was expecting an argument from her. She seemed like the sort to question and fight against everything, but not this time. This time she reached out, snatched the flask and held it to her lips, gulping down a mouthful of the potent liquor.

Like most staunchly Islamic countries, Libya's official line was that the sale and consumption of alcohol were strictly forbidden. Then again, just because something was against the law didn't mean it didn't happen. Libya had had more exposure to Western culture than many countries in this part of the world in recent years, and Drake knew from experience that the degree of adherence to Islamic law varied from neighbourhood to neighbourhood, even house to house.

She stifled a cough as the whisky seared a blazing path down her throat, though she made no attempt to spit it out. In fact, she took another gulp almost immediately, a deeper one this time.

'Take it easy,' Drake said, reaching out and gently lowering the flask before she consumed too much. 'It's to settle your nerves, not knock you out.'

'All things considered, I would settle for the latter tonight.'

You and me both, Drake thought.

She looked at the hipflask again and wrinkled her nose in distaste. 'What is that damn stuff, anyway?'

'Sixteen-year-old single malt. Good for what ails you.'

'It tastes awful.'

Drake couldn't help but feel a twinge of disappointment at that.

'Well, it's what we've got.' Since he'd opened it, he saw no harm partaking in a little himself. It was a welcome relief after the night's events. 'And I'd say you've earned it.'

She said nothing to this, though when she went back to washing herself it was with somewhat more control and composure. In due course she had cleaned most of the blood off her exposed skin, run her fingers through her long raven black hair to work the worst of the tangles out, and finally splashed some water on her face.

'We'll find some clean clothes for you,' Drake said. A bloodstained nightgown wasn't going to serve her well from this point forward, though he didn't hold out much hope of finding anything suitable in a farmhouse shared by three men.

'Laila,' she said at last, drying her face with a towel. 'My name is Laila.'

Drake was about to say something in return, to offer some expression of thanks for everything she had done tonight, to apologize for what they'd been forced to put her through, but she cut him off immediately.

'But if you think this changes anything, you're mistaken. I told you simply so that you would know the person whose life you destroyed tonight.' She looked at him, and he saw a light burning behind her eyes that was enough to put a chill through even him. 'Personally, I hope you and your team die and go to hell before the sun rises on another day.'

Drake said nothing to that. Instead he took another gulp from the hipflask and led her back through to the kitchen. They had far bigger problems to deal with tonight.

Chapter 26

'Quite a mess,' Adnan Mousa remarked, gesturing to the pile of smoking wreckage that had once been an aircraft. It had been a raging inferno when the first police units had arrived at the private airfield about twenty minutes earlier, and emergency crews were still working to damp it down in case it flared up once again. 'I doubt we'll get much out of the pilot.'

His comrade, a short and bull-like man named Bishr Kubar, didn't smile at Mousa's grim joke. Then again, he didn't smile at much of anything. *Bishr*; now there was one of life's little ironies. The name meant 'joy' in Arabic, though the man seemed to find little in this world that was joyful.

Then again neither he nor his comrades had much reason to smile tonight. Tarek Sowan, one of their organization's high-level intelligence officers, had been abducted from his supposedly secure home just hours earlier. The guards, the cameras, the layers of security designed to protect him, had all counted for naught.

Understandably, alarm bells were ringing throughout the Mukhabarat. They wanted answers. They wanted their man back. They wanted to know how this had happened, who was responsible, and most of all they wanted the perpetrators caught and punished in the harshest way imaginable.

It had therefore come as little surprise to Bishr Kubar that he'd been chosen to head up the investigation, for he was well aware of his own reputation for ruthlessly pursuing objectives and brutally removing of any obstacle unwise enough to stand in his path. His was a reputation earned long before he joined the Mukhabarat.

'We have the tail number,' Kubar said impatiently. The aircraft might have been charred and burned in the crash, but the lettering on the tail section was still legible. 'What do we know about this plane?'

Mousa consulted the notes he'd scribbled down after a phone call with Libyan air-traffic control only minutes earlier. 'It's registered to a private air cargo firm operating out of the United Kingdom, landed at Tripoli International earlier tonight for refuelling. According to the flight plan, they were heading onwards to Cairo, but about ten minutes after takeoff the pilot radioed in with control problems, said he was going to land to check it out. Then they lost contact.'

A faint breeze sighed across the runway, carrying the stench of aviation fuel and burned rubber. Grimacing in distaste, Kubar reached into his pocket for a pack of cigarettes and lit one up.

'It's a fake,' he decided after taking a deep pull on the cigarette. 'This was no normal cargo run. It was their means of escape.'

Normally the crash landing of a small aircraft at an isolated runway would have held little interest for Kubar – such things could and did happen from time to time – but coming as it had less than an hour after Sowan's abduction, the connection was hard to miss.

Coincidences were for fools, as far as he was concerned. Every action was a reaction to something else, and in this case the crash was a reaction to the kidnapping. What he still needed to understand was the chain of events leading up to it.

'But who exactly are "they"?' Mousa asked rhetorically. (The man was irritatingly fond of stating the obvious when genuine insights failed him.)

Still, the question nonetheless remained unanswered. Certainly there were plenty of agencies capable of staging such an audacious raid. The Americans, the British, the Israelis, even the Russians had the expertise and the resources to make it happen.

The members of Sowan's household security detail had been of little help, offering only fragmented and contradictory reports of large numbers of masked operatives storming the compound and overwhelming them with advanced weapons. Kubar knew bullshit when he heard it, and it was all over their self-serving testimonies. Doubtless they were wary of allegations of incompetence resulting from the loss of their charge, and were trying to protect themselves by exaggerating the size and strength of their enemies.

But despite their bluster and claims of defeat in the face of impossible odds, there was likely a grain of truth hidden away somewhere. Clearly Sowan's abductors had sufficient technical expertise to bypass the building's complex security system, as well as the training to take down three armed men without raising the alarm. Local police had even reported the use of smoke and stun grenades to cover their escape.

All of this led him to the irrefutable conclusion that this was far more than some petty revenge attack by rebel tribesmen or any kind of criminal undertaking. Instead, they were dealing with an elite, dangerous and highly organized special forces group who had come here with a specific objective, and a plan to achieve it. Indeed, the only thing that seemed to have gone wrong for them tonight was the loss of the aircraft intended to carry them and their captives to safety.

Ignoring his comrade's remarks, Kubar took another pull on his cigarette as he weighed up what was at stake. They couldn't afford to lose Sowan. Aside from his value as an asset and the damage he could do if forced to talk, his capture was a massive blow to the Mukhabarat's prestige and integrity.

Kubar was no fool. He understood better than most that the winds of change were blowing in Libya. Its people were weary and resentful after four decades of Gaddafi's rule, and growing increasingly vociferous in their opposition. Power and prestige were no longer effective tools of suppression – only fear mattered. And the Mukhabarat was the instrument of that fear; the all-seeing and all-knowing eyes and ears of the government. The terrifying men in blacked-out cars who came knocking in the middle of the night.

If word got out that one of their own had been taken from his very home, that they could be hurt just as they hurt others, that fear and power would vanish. Like blood in the water, it wouldn't take long for the sharks to start circling.

'I want military and police checkpoints on all major roads within fifty miles,' he said. 'Increased border patrols and searches of all ships leaving our ports. Any cars driven by Westerners are to be stopped and thoroughly searched.'

Mousa looked at him. 'You know that will make a lot of rich men very unhappy.'

The look Kubar gave him in return made it plain that such concerns were the last thing on his mind. Taking a final draw on his cigarette, he flicked it to the ground and stamped it out with his shoe.

But as he did so, he felt his heel come down on something. Something hard and round, that rolled a little with the motion of his foot.

Frowning, Kubar knelt down and reached for it, grasping it delicately between his thumb and forefinger as he held it up for a closer look.

'And get our ballistics teams on this,' he added, staring intently at the brass shell casing in his hand. 'I want to know where our friends came from.'

No matter what it took, he would get to the truth. He always did.

Chapter 27

With Sowan and Laila under guard and no activity reported outside, a brief period of relative calm had descended on the farmhouse. It was a welcome reprieve from the near constant pressure the team had been under since making landfall on that rocky stretch of coastline near Tripoli. It felt like a lifetime ago now.

Venturing outside with a steaming cup of tea in his hands, Drake found himself surrounded by the chirp and click of night insects, punctuated by occasional birdsong as the world began to rouse itself for the start of a new day. With less than an hour until first light, they would have to decide on a course of action soon, he knew.

McKnight was sitting on the stone porch, keeping an eye on the approach road. She was armed with a silenced Browning and had removed the magazine to count out the remaining rounds.

There weren't many.

'Here,' he said quietly, holding the cup out to her.

The woman glanced up from her work, seemingly distracted by her own thoughts, then shook her head. 'I don't need it.'

'You've been on the clock all night, Sam. I don't need you passing out on me.'

Letting out a resigned sigh, she grabbed the cup and gulped down a mouthful before turning her attention back to reloading the magazine.

'I never got the chance to say it before,' Drake began, staring out into the darkness beyond the floodlit farm compound. 'But thank you, for what you did back at the airfield. I doubt any of us would be here now if it wasn't for you. You saved the entire team, Sam.'

Her eyes were turned downward, focussing on her task as she thumbed each round into the magazine, but to his surprise he saw a flicker of pain behind them, as if his words had touched a raw nerve.

'When Chandra's plane came down, I...' Drake trailed off, replaying that terrible moment when he'd first seen the stricken aircraft plough into the ground, felt the heat of the fireball and the gut-wrenching realization that Samantha's life could have been ended in that instant, the fear and anger and desperation that it had provoked in him. He'd known then that he would have torn Faulkner apart with his bare hands to protect her, would have traded places with her in a heartbeat if it would spare her life.

And that frightened him more than anything else that had happened tonight. To be a leader, to get his team through this, he had to be willing to put each of them in danger. They knew it, they accepted it. But what if he couldn't? What if he was afraid to risk Samantha's life, and his hesitation put the others at greater risk?

'I thought I'd lost you,' he said at last. 'I thought that was it. And right then, I didn't care about Sowan or Cain or anything else. If I lost you, it would kill me, Sam.'

'Maybe it would be better if you did,' she said in a sad, forlorn voice.

Drake frowned, struck by the change that had come over her. 'What do you mean?'

She sighed, her shoulders sagging. 'I mean, doing what we do, maybe we shouldn't get too close, trust each other too much. It's safer... for both of us.'

Drake winced. McKnight had been sullen and withdrawn since Laila had taken over with the injured man, though he hadn't understood why. He'd sensed this kind of sentiment might rise to the surface sooner or later. It often did when things went wrong and people were given time to reflect on their actions, to question their decisions and second guess themselves. But this was one line of thought that needed to be shut down right now.

Reaching out, Drake laid a hand on her shoulder. 'Sam, look at me. Look at me.'

Reluctantly she dragged her gaze upward, making eye contact.

'You're part of this team now, whether you want it or not. We need you.' He lowered his voice, speaking in barely a whisper. '*I* need you.'

Suddenly she jumped to her feet and strode off several paces across the porch, arms folded across her chest. The tension in her muscles was obvious, her body filled with nervous energy that it couldn't get rid of.

'You don't need me, Ryan. You make your own way – you always did. That's why we're here,' she said, keeping her back to him. 'And look where it got us. Chandra's dead. Our way out's gone, and we're being hunted by the man who sent you here in the first place.' She shook her head. 'There are no happy endings for people like us. We both know that.'

Drake had heard enough of this. Rising to his feet, he walked right towards her, gripped her by the arm and spun her around to face him.

'I didn't come all this way to lose, Sam,' he said, his tone hard and flat as he fixed her with a piercing stare.

'And what are you prepared to give up to win?' she asked. 'I heard what you said to Faulkner at the airfield. You were ready to kill yourself rather than hand Sowan over. Victory at any cost. Where's it going to end, Ryan?'

Before either of them could say anything further, they were interrupted by the sound of the main door opening behind them. Both of them turned to see Frost standing in the arched doorway. The young woman took in their troubled expressions, their sudden look of discomfort and embarrassment at her arrival.

'I miss something?' she asked.

Drake released his hold of McKnight's arm. 'What is it, Keira?'

'You might want to get in here. Sowan's awake.'

Drake let out a breath. The man he'd risked so much to get his hands on was conscious at last. Now perhaps he'd get some answers.

He glanced at McKnight, who gestured towards the house. 'Go. I'll keep watch.'

Nodding, Drake paused for a moment, wishing there was something else he could say to her, some reassurance he could give. There was nothing. Words counted for little now. All that mattered were results.

Reluctantly he followed Frost inside, leaving the woman alone with her thoughts.

–

Sowan was indeed awake, struggling to rise from the kitchen table, with Mason attempting to hold him down. Laila too was on hand, speaking in Arabic and trying to calm her husband.

The moment Drake entered the room, however, the man's struggles eased. His dark eyes focussed on his captor, edged with pain but clear and alert once more.

'I know you,' he said after a long pause.

'No, you don't.'

'I saw you at the airfield near Paris,' Sowan countered. 'You work for the Agency.'

Drake said nothing to that. Instead he allowed the image of Freya Shaw lying cold and dead on a mortuary table to linger in his mind. His grip on his weapon tightened until he could feel the wooden checkering press into his flesh.

Sowan tilted his head, his gaze shrewd and assessing. 'I was going to ask if David Faulkner sent you to kill me, but since he apparently tried to kill you as well, that seems unlikely. So the question is what exactly you want with me.'

'I want answers. Lots of them,' Drake said at last. 'And you're going to give them to me. We're going to talk about Faulkner. You're going to tell me how you know him, and why he wants to get his hands on you. But first you're going to tell me about Freya Louise Shaw. You're going to tell me why you ordered her murder.'

'I know nothing of the woman you mentioned.' Sowan's thin lips parted in a smile. 'As for Faulkner, I could tell you a great deal, but I won't. Not unless I have assurances that my wife and I will be released.'

Drake was well and truly finished with such games. Drawing his Browning, he allowed the silencer to rest on the edge of the table with a heavy *thunk*.

'The only thing you need to be *assured* about is that your life – your *lives* – are entirely in my hands. I could kill both of you right now, burn this house to the ground and be out of the country before anyone figures out what happened. The only reason I didn't let you bleed to death in the back of our car is because you know something that might be useful.'

'That was my car, actually,' Sowan pointed out.

Drake ignored his attempt to rile him. 'You're going to tell me what I want to know, Tarek. You're going to tell me, and then I'm going to decide whether it's worth keeping you alive.'

'And if I don't, what will you do? Shoot me?' The lean, wiry man shrugged his narrow shoulders. 'If you think death frightens me, you are truly in the wrong business.'

'Not your death.' Drake allowed the barrel of his weapon to angle towards Laila. 'Cole, put her arm on the table. Now.'

Moving forward, Mason grabbed Laila's right arm and twisted it behind her back, eliciting a cry of pain and anger. Smaller, lighter and nowhere near his match in strength, she was powerless to resist as he forced her to turn around, pressing her hand down hard on the table.

'What are you doing?' Sowan demanded, some of his calm confidence deserting him as he watched Drake draw a knife from his webbing, drawing the blade slowly across the edge of the sheath so he could hear the distinctive metallic rasp.

'You were unconscious while she was working to save your life, Tarek. Shame, really. What she was able to do, the skill and the control of those surgeon's hands, it was impressive.' Circling around behind her, he laid the edge of the blade against her wrist. 'Be a shame to lose them.'

'Ryan, don't do this,' Laila protested, trying in vain to break free of Mason's grip. 'God will not forgive you if you do this.'

Drake met her gaze without compassion. He had little left in him at that moment. 'I'm already going to hell, remember?'

Laila was speaking now in Arabic, her words fast and urgent, but Sowan hushed her. He was keeping his cool, but it didn't look quite as effortless as before. Drake had found a chink in his armour.

'I have played this game many times myself,' he said, staring Drake in the eye without flinching. 'It takes a certain kind of man to do something like that, believe me. You're not the sort.'

Outwardly he appeared unconcerned, as if he knew exactly what Drake was capable of and was happy to call his bluff on something the man would never do. But Drake saw it. He saw the tiny bead of sweat roll down the side of Sowan's face, the twitch at the corner of his mouth, the slight movement of his Adam's apple as he fought the urge to swallow.

Drake stared right back at him, but there was something in his eye now that none of the others had ever seen. A hardness, an edge of cruelty and malice that had long lain dormant within him. A shadow of the man he'd once been, now taking form once more.

'Only one way to find out.'

'You will *not*!' Tarek said, raising his voice for the first time.

'Tell me about Freya!' Drake yelled back. 'Why did you order her death?'

Frost, who had until now held her tongue, now glanced uncertainly at Mason. 'Ryan, where's this coming from? What makes you think he knows anything?'

Drake wasn't listening to her. He was in his own world now. He hadn't intended to let it out, hadn't wanted to open that door in his mind, but it was there. It was open, and there was no closing it now.

'Let her go!' Sowan shouted.

'Look at him, man. He doesn't know anything,' Mason protested, though he maintained his grip on the woman.

'Fuck this,' Drake decided. 'You had your chance.'

With that, he pressed the blade in, slicing downward. Like carving up a roast.

Laila let out a scream. Not a cry of pain. The nerves in her arm wouldn't have transferred the full import of what was happening to her brain yet. It was a scream of fear. She didn't need to feel the pain of what was happening; she knew well enough as the knife bit in and blood welled up from severed flesh.

'Stop!' Sowan cried out. 'Stop, please!'

Drake paused in his grisly work, glancing up at him. What he said in the next few seconds would decide Laila's fate.

'I'll tell you everything I know,' the man said through gritted teeth. 'I'll talk.'

Slowly Drake withdrew the blade, the edge stained red with Laila's blood. Fortunately he'd stopped before it had done any real damage. A minor skin-deep slice had been enough to get the reaction he'd wanted.

He let out a breath and clenched his fists, trying to keep them from trembling, trying to regain his composure.

'Why did you kill her?' he demanded once he trusted himself to speak.

Sowan shook his head, his shoulders slumped in defeat. The pain and weariness of his ordeal tonight seemed to weigh more heavily on him now.

'I know nothing of this woman you mentioned,' he said at last.

Drake drew his knife once more.

'Wait!' Sowan implored him, staring pleadingly into his eyes. 'I swear to you, I have never heard the name Freya Shaw, and I have ordered no killings of women. If Faulkner has told you otherwise, then I suggest you ask him the same questions you asked me. But nothing you say or do can make me admit to her death, because I know nothing.'

Drake stared right back at him, trying to pierce the veil of those dark eyes, to discern what secrets lay hidden beneath. For his own part, much as he wished it were different, he could detect no hint of deception in them, no attempt to lie or conceal anything.

He was telling the truth. He hadn't ordered Freya's death.

Raising the knife in a sudden explosive outpouring of anger, Drake brought the weapon down with all the force he could command. There was a thump, the table shook beneath the impact, and Sowan found himself staring at the blade impaled in the wooden surface, still quivering from the force of the blow.

Drake closed his eyes for a moment and lowered his head, gripping the edge of the table for support. He could feel his breath coming in short, shuddering gasps, his heart pounding in his chest.

Faulkner had played him, killing his mother as bait to lure Drake out. To get him to agree to such a foolishly dangerous mission into Libya. To recover the man now seated just feet away from him.

Why?

Raising his head up, he looked at his prisoner once more, forcing back the grief and anger with difficulty. He'd made enough mistakes letting emotion rule over logic; he could afford no more. 'Let's start with what you *can* tell me. How do you know Faulkner?'

Sowan swallowed hard, looking genuinely frightened by the display of brute force and aggression. 'He is one of our main contacts with British intelligence.'

'Contact for what?'

'Prisoner renditions.'

Drake was starting to get a sinking feeling in the pit of his stomach. 'Keep talking.'

'Two years ago, Faulkner approached us with a deal. We give him a list of Libyan exiles and dissidents taking refuge in the West, and he would hand them over to us without question. In return, we would give him the location of Islamic State commanders in Libya and north Africa, and allow the CIA to set up black sites in our country where they could be interrogated.'

Drake closed his eyes and clenched his fists as the full magnitude of his own folly was at last revealed to him. Faulkner hadn't just lied to him about Cain being the driving force behind this dirty international arrangement, he'd used it as a smokescreen to cover his own involvement.

'So if you two have been in bed together for the past two years, why the fuck did Faulkner send us here to kidnap you?' Mason demanded, visibly angry at the realization they had risked their lives tonight for nothing.

'Because…' He trailed off, unwilling to continue.

'Now's not the time to hold out on me, Tarek.'

Sowan glared at him. 'Because we have not lived up to our end of the agreement.'

Drake frowned. 'What do you mean?'

A sigh. 'We have given them only scraps from our table. Snatches of information, rumours, perhaps a few low-level commanders that were expendable anyway. Our government has been trying to play both sides of the War on Terror – supporting Islamic State with one hand, and America with the other.'

'Why?' Mason challenged him.

Sowan looked at him with contempt. 'Is it not obvious? Money, of course. The Americans have channelled billions of dollars in aid and development funds into Libya in the past few years, lifted sanctions, made it possible to start exporting oil again. We are prospering like never before. As for Islamic State, they believe we are still championing the Jihad against the West by giving them shelter here. Instead of invading like they did in Iraq, they hold back because they see us as allies. In some ways, the plan had merit.'

'Except Faulkner realized what you were doing.'

Sowan chewed his lip, but nodded. 'Since we have given them nothing useful, I suppose Faulkner decided to take matters into his own hands. Likely he wanted to interrogate one of our officers to find out how much we really knew.'

It didn't take much imagination to guess what would have happened to Sowan if they'd handed him over. Faulkner would have made sure the man gave him every scrap of information the Mukhabarat possessed, right before he put a bullet in his head.

'What about the man we lifted in Paris?' Drake asked, still seeking to understand how that particular piece fitted into the puzzle. 'Who was he really, and what did you want with him?'

At this, Sowan shook his head. 'I don't know.' Seeing Drake's dubious look, he added, 'And I mean that. He was not listed on any of our intelligence dossiers.'

Drake wasn't buying that. 'So why the hell were you there for the extraction?'

'The orders came from my commanding officer. He said Fayed was a high-value target, that he had to be recovered at all costs along with any intel in his possession. So we made the arrangements, and you delivered him.'

Once more Drake remembered the laptop he'd tried to access on the journey to the airfield near Paris, and the encryption that had prevented its use. Somehow he sensed that Fayed played a bigger part in this than any of them realized. That man, and the intel they'd recovered from his apartment, were part of something.

'So what did you learn from him?'

If Fayed was as important as he believed, the Libyans would have wasted no time interrogating him. Surely they must have learned something by now.

'I don't know,' Sowan admitted.

'We're hearing that a lot from you,' Mason said, bristling with anger. 'I smell bullshit.'

Sowan glared at him. 'It is the truth. I was not present for his debriefing; I was just there to make sure he arrived on schedule. If you or Faulkner kidnapped me because you believe I have some insight into this man, you're very much mistaken.'

'Faulkner wants to get his hands on you,' Drake pointed out. 'He won't stop until that happens.'

'And you?' Sowan asked with a gleam of hope in his eye. 'What do you want?'

His answer was blunt and honest. 'To get out of this fucking mess alive.'

Sowan smiled in grim amusement. 'Then it seems we are not so different, after all.'

'Don't compare us to yourself, you piece of shit,' Frost said, eyes brimming with hatred as she surveyed the bloodied and injured man lying before her. 'We're nothing like you.'

'Really? How so?'

'For a start we don't imprison and torture innocent people,' Mason chipped in.

'Neither do I. My job is to seek out and capture enemies of my state.'

'There's a party line if ever I heard one,' Frost snorted derisively. 'You mean people who have the guts to speak up against Gaddafi?'

'I mean people who blow up hospitals and crowded marketplaces. People who kidnap and murder government ministers. People who want to incite a civil war that would cost thousands of lives and tear this country apart. Those are *my* enemies,' he said, his dark eyes flashing with anger. 'And Gaddafi is no more my friend than you are, but he is probably the only thing holding Libya together and keeping Islamic State from taking over. So I do what I must, and serve him.'

'And collect a nice fat pay cheque for your troubles,' Frost added. 'We saw your house, dude. It's enough to make Kim Kardashian jealous.'

'Actually, the house belonged to my wife's family,' Sowan corrected her. 'My pay cheque is not so fat as yours, I suspect. And while we are talking about arrest and torture, have you not imprisoned the innocent civilians who run this farm? Did you not abduct my wife and me from our own home? Did you not threaten to torture and kill her?' He shook his head and chuckled in amusement. 'Perhaps my mind is not clear, but remind me again what makes us so different?'

'Our lives were at stake. We did what we had to do,' Mason said, though his words lacked conviction. He was savvy enough to sense he'd been backed into a corner.

'We all do what we must to survive,' Sowan agreed. 'Like learning to work with our enemies for the greater good.'

Frost however was unmoved by his sentiments. 'Pass me the fucking Oscar, because you're in the wrong business, pal.' She shook her head and turned her eyes on Drake. 'We'll get nothing useful from this asshole. Cole was right – I say we cut him loose and take on Faulkner ourselves.'

'Your foul-mouthed friend is wrong,' Sowan promised. 'I have spoken the truth.'

If he was hinting at some kind of alliance against Faulkner to save his own arse, Drake suspected he was in for a disappointment. The whole 'enemy of my enemy' philosophy didn't hold up too well when you'd taken a man hostage and threatened to mutilate his wife. Sowan would kill him in a heartbeat if he thought he could get away with it.

'Can you prove any of this?' Drake asked, turning over possibilities in his head. 'Your deal with Faulkner, the black sites, all of it.'

Sowan chewed his lip for a moment, finally shaking his head. 'Not from here. All of the files and communications are in my office.'

'Which is where, exactly?'

Sowan exhaled slowly, preparing to deliver bad news. 'Mukhabarat headquarters in Tripoli.'

Chapter 28

It took about ten minutes for Drake to consider everything he'd heard and decide on a course of action. Desperate and dangerous it might have been, but it was the only way he could think of getting them all out of this alive. However, convincing his teammates of the merits of his plan was far more difficult.

'You can't be fucking serious,' Mason said, shaking his head vehemently at the mere thought of what Drake was proposing. 'It's insane. You might as well paint a target on our heads and ask the Libyans to pull the trigger.'

'Sowan has enough evidence to put Faulkner away for life,' Drake pointed out.

'If he doesn't kill us for fun first,' his friend countered. He jerked a finger towards the kitchen where Sowan, still weak from loss of blood, was being cared for by his wife. Frost was keeping an eye on both of them. 'You know how this game works. That man is a professional spook – he'll say and do anything to gain our trust, then he'll fuck us over, the first chance he gets. I know I would.'

'I don't think he's like that,' Drake countered. When Sowan had spoken of reluctantly doing his job out of duty and desire to hold his country together, he'd sensed the man was telling the truth. And as much as it pained him to admit it, he knew now he'd been wrong about Sowan ordering his mother's death. 'He knows we're not the real enemy.'

Even if he was lying about the two groups having common cause against Faulkner, Drake now had leverage over him that they both knew he couldn't ignore.

'You broke into his house and abducted him in the middle of the night, almost got him killed, and threatened to mutilate his wife right in front of his eyes. Christ, if that's not enough to earn a grudge, I don't know what is.' Mason sighed and shook his head once more. 'This is suicide, Ryan. Let it go.'

Realizing he would get no support from Mason, Drake turned his attention to McKnight, who had remained largely silent until now. 'Sam, what about you?'

Her troubled eyes turned to meet his. 'It's hard to say, Ryan. It depends on why you're really going after Faulkner.'

'What do you mean?'

'You know exactly what I mean,' she countered. 'You never told any of us that you thought Sowan was behind your mother's death. You told us this was about bringing down Cain and protecting your sister.'

'It is.'

She cocked an eyebrow. 'Is it? Or is this really a revenge trip for you? Sure, you might have used Sowan for information, but tell me you didn't plan on killing him once he'd served your purpose.'

If he were to tell her that, it would be a lie. So he said nothing.

'That's what I thought. You lied to us, Ryan,' she hissed, keeping her voice down with difficulty. 'You used us to get to him. Is that what we are to you?'

Drake was all too aware of the folly of his actions, his questionable decision not to make his companions aware of what he knew, but hearing it laid out like that in such blunt, accusatory terms made it even harder to bear.

'Take it easy, Sam,' Mason cautioned her.

Drake held up a hand. 'It's all right, Cole. She has a right to ask. You all do.' He sighed and glanced away for a moment. 'You're right, Sam. I did know, and I chose to keep it from you. I wanted you all focussed on the mission, not on me. I thought we could get through this, and I'd... deal with him later. But I was wrong about that. I should have trusted you all, and I'm sorry I didn't.' He looked right at Samantha. 'I won't make that mistake again.'

McKnight stared back at him for a long moment, her thoughts hard to gauge. She was angry with him – that much was obvious – and she had a right to be. But beyond that, it he couldn't tell what she was thinking.

'You asked for my opinion on your plan,' she finally acknowledged. 'My opinion is we're pretty much screwed right now, Ryan.'

Drake said nothing. It was an honest, if blunt, answer.

Taking his silence as a prompt to elaborate, she obliged. 'Either we run, try to get out of Libya and probably get caught in the process. And even if we do make it out, we'll have Faulkner hunting us down. Or... we go with your plan, which also has a good potential to get us all captured and killed. But on the very slight chance that it works, it might just give us what we need to take the son of a bitch out.' She shrugged, apparently resigned to their grim prospects. 'Like I say, we're screwed, and our chances of success either way are piss poor. But I'd rather go with the option that at least offers a way out of the shit we're in.'

It was hard to argue with her assessment of the situation, or the merits of what he was proposing. At least he counted this as a vote in his favour.

'Just say for a moment this plan actually works,' Mason went on. 'What do we do with your new best buddy in there when this is all over?'

Drake had been pondering the same question. 'He has a story to tell, so let him tell it. I'm sure there are plenty of people who'll listen.'

If they could get him out of the country, it wouldn't be hard for a man of Sowan's resourcefulness to find people in the Western media willing to hear what he had to say. And if nothing else, it might shed some light on the dirty deals being done between the Agency and the Libyans, and the innocent people suffering because of it.

Drake was under no illusions that this action would turn him into a saint or some kind of moral crusader. He'd seen and done things in his life that there was no coming back from, but perhaps just this once he could do something good. Perhaps he could undo some of the damage that had been done.

And deep down, the fact that at least one man had died because of Drake's own actions weighed more heavily on him than he cared to admit.

'And there are plenty of people who'll kill to shut him up,' Mason countered.

Drake shrugged. 'Like you said, he's a professional spook. He knows how to play the game, and survive it.'

'Doesn't he just,' Mason said under his breath.

Sensing that his companions were onboard, albeit reluctantly, Drake glanced at McKnight. 'All right. Sam, get yourself back outside and do a sweep of the perimeter. Cole, keep an eye on the civvies. I'm going to have a little chat with our friend.'

Returning to the kitchen that now resembled a bloody, chaotic field hospital, Drake found their prisoner sitting on a chair carried through from the living room, his injured leg propped up on a stool. He was clutching a cup of hot, sugary tea that Laila had ordered him to drink, knowing how urgently his body needed to replace the fluid it had lost. He was still pale and weak, but his eyes were clear and focussed when he looked up at Drake.

'I would stand up to greet you, but...' He gestured to his injured leg.

Ignoring his attempt at humour, Drake knelt down beside him and looked the man hard in the eye. 'Listen to me now, Tarek. I'm going to ask some simple questions, and I want simple and honest answers. If I could get you inside your headquarters building, could you retrieve the intel we recovered in Paris?'

A flicker of a smile. Faint, but visible all the same. 'Yes.'

'And you could get it to us on the outside without being caught?'

'It would not be easy, but it is possible.'

'And you wouldn't think about betraying us, would you? Because a man like you would be sensible enough to know we'd keep your wife as insurance while all this is going on. And if you were stupid enough to tell anyone the truth, you'd also know that we'd make good on our threat from earlier.'

Sowan's grip on his cup tightened. 'I would do nothing less in your situation,' he said in terse acknowledgement. 'In any case, who would I tell? My superiors could be involved in this cover-up as well. A lot depends on their relationship with the British and Americans.'

'Fair enough,' Drake conceded.

'It does beg the question, of course, what becomes of me once this is over?' Sowan went on. 'If I make good on our agreement, what do I get in return?'

'Firstly, you get Faulkner off your back,' Drake pointed out. 'He might have failed with us, but sooner or later he'll send someone more reliable to kill you, and we won't be able to stop him.'

'And secondly?'

'When this is over, we'll get you to a country where you can disappear. The rest is up to you. It's not much, but it's the only deal I'm offering, and it's a hell of a lot better than the alternative.' He glanced at his watch. 'Time's not on our side, so I need to know right now, are you in or out?'

As Drake had said, it was the only offer Sowan was likely to get, and the Libyan was smart enough to appreciate that fact. But that didn't mean he would be easily swayed.

'What guarantee do I have that you'll keep your word?'

'None. But I can guarantee that if you're no use to us, we'll leave you here for Faulkner to deal with.' There was no sense in lying, since the man would easily see through any false assurances he might make. 'In or out? Decide now.'

Sowan stared back at him in silence; the tense, fraught seconds stretching out between them. Finally he gave a single, gruff nod of assent.

With the matter decided, Drake called through to the rest of his team. 'All right, everyone. Get your shit together, we move out in five minutes. We'll be travelling on open roads, so ditch the webbing and combat gear. Civilians clothes only, even if you have to use what's here. Oh, and Cole?'

'Yeah?'

'Gather as much water as you can. We might need it.'

'On it.'

Glancing at Laila, Drake added, 'Get him ready to move.'

'The wound must be stabilized. I would advise against it,' she warned.

'I'm sure you would.' Reaching for his radio, he put a call through to McKnight outside. 'Envoy, come in.'

'Go, Monarch.'

'There's a pickup truck in the barn outside. Bring it round to the front door. We're leaving in five Mikes.'

'Wilco. Envoy's en route.'

As the rest of the group set about packing up what little gear they had, Sowan spoke up once more. 'How exactly do you plan to get me inside?

With a certain amount of skill, and a great deal of luck, he thought. 'You do your part,' he said instead. 'Let us worry about the rest.'

Accustomed as they were to leaving places at short notice, it didn't take the team long to get ready. Obeying Drake's instruction, they removed their webbing and any articles of clothing that would identify them as soldiers or paramilitary operatives, replacing them with anything they could pilfer from the wardrobes of the house owners. In practice this mainly meant faded jeans, loose shirts and scuffed work boots.

They certainly wouldn't win any fashion awards once they were finished, but on casual inspection they would at least pass muster as civilians. With this task accomplished, they gathered together what little gear and supplies they were taking with them, and piled it into the back of the pickup truck that McKnight had brought around to the front door.

An old-model Ford with a covered rear bed, its battered and sand-scoured bodywork looked like it had seen better days. Still, the engine sounded like it had been better cared for, and McKnight had confirmed that it drove well, so it would serve for now. In any case, it was a far better option than the bullet-riddled Toyota SUV they'd arrived in.

Before leaving it behind, McKnight had made sure to pull out and destroy all the fuses, rendering the engine inoperable in case the farmer and his sons thought to use it to drive to the nearest police station.

To this end, they had also disconnected the landline, scavenged up all the cell phones they could find and thoroughly smashed them. They didn't imagine it would take long for the family to escape their bonds once they were left unguarded, but they did need at least some time to get clear of the area before the alarm was raised.

Standing in the living-room doorway looking at the three bound and gagged captives, Drake couldn't help feeling bad for them. Not only had they been broken into, taken hostage and had their kitchen turned into an operating theatre, but they'd also had most of their valuables stolen or destroyed. A shit night by anyone's standards.

With that thought fresh in his mind, he removed some of the emergency money they'd brought along for this operation and laid it on the floor by his feet. The farmer stared at him, his eyes holding a mixture of confusion and simmering hatred. Drake couldn't blame him either way.

'I apologize for this,' he said in Arabic as he backed out of the room.

With their gear stowed and the vehicle waiting, the last task was to get their injured prisoner out of the house. With Mason and Drake supporting him on either side, Sowan gingerly limped down the hallway and out through the main door. He didn't cry out or even moan in pain, but Drake could feel his muscles tense up every time he put weight on the injured leg.

Nonetheless, he made it to the rear of the pickup without incident, and with a final heave, Mason and Drake lifted him inside. Laila went in behind, now dressed in a pair of faded jeans, t-shirt and work jacket scavenged from the farmhouse, all of which were too big for her. Mason clambered in after her to keep watch on them both.

'What the hell are you bringing that thing for?' Drake asked as Frost approached with the farmer's double-barrelled shotgun slung over one shoulder, as if she were about to indulge in a spot of duck hunting. 'Skeet shooting isn't exactly what we've got in mind.'

The young woman shrugged. 'It's a gun, isn't it? And we're short on firepower.' She hefted the bulky weapon, testing the balance. 'Anyway, I kinda like it. Might take it home when this is all over.'

Drake merely shook his head. If they found themselves in the midst of another firefight, he doubted an antique shotgun was going to tip the balance in their favour. Still, he was well aware how futile it was to argue with her in matters like this.

'Just get your arse inside,' he said, gesturing into the pickup's rear bed.

With Frost in, he closed the tailgate and circled around to the front, where McKnight had moved over to the passenger seat and wrapped a length of patterned cloth around her face and head to form a keffiyeh, the traditional headdress usually worn by men and women in this part of the world. In this case, her decision was influenced less by fashion or local custom, and more by the need to disguise her ethnicity when they would almost certainly be seen by other drivers out on the road.

She'd been thoughtful enough to provide a second keffiyeh for Drake, who in turn wrapped it around his face. In truth, he'd worn garments like this many times before on desert operations during his time in the SAS, where they were usually referred to as *shemags*. They might look a little outlandish, but they were invaluable in hot, dry climates where sand and dust were constant problems. The Americans hadn't been so keen on them, as he recalled, perhaps seeing them as clothing of the enemy, but they'd soon changed their attitude when heatstroke started afflicting their troops.

'Ever get the feeling this day's going from bad to worse?' McKnight asked as he finished securing the head garment.

'All the time,' Drake said, starting the vehicle up.

Part III

Intervention

A thirty-nine page dossier recovered in Tripoli in 2011 contained detailed questions prepared by British intelligence services for use on opponents of the Gaddafi regime.

Chapter 29

'Who's in charge here?' Bishr Kubar demanded, sweeping into the farmhouse like a force of nature, and scattering police officers and forensics technicians before him. Even if he hadn't already identified himself as an officer in Libya's much-feared Mukhabarat, his bullish attitude and the dangerous glimmer in his eyes would have been enough to give even hardened field operatives pause for thought.

For the past few hours he'd been busy overseeing the fruitless manhunt, attempting to comb thousands of square miles of land for a trace of Sowan's abductors. Until half an hour ago he'd turned up nothing but false alarms and dead ends. Then, not long after sunrise, the call had come through. A call from the local police reporting that the owner of a small fig orchard and his family had been taken prisoner by a group of armed attackers.

It was just the break he'd been waiting for.

Hearing the disturbance, one police officer dared to step forward. 'I am, sir. Sergeant Maghur.'

Tall, skinny, and with the youthful, almost boyish face of one who hadn't yet seen thirty years. Still a kid, Kubar thought derisively. He could scarcely remember being young.

'What do you have to report, Sergeant Maghur?'

'One of our patrols was sweeping the area when they found a four-wheel-drive Toyota matching the one reported stolen in Tripoli. When they moved inside to investigate, they found the house owner and his two sons bound and gagged. There was no sign of the people who did it to them.'

Kubar had seen the bullet-riddled vehicle still parked outside. 'What can he tell us about the group who attacked him?'

'According to his testimony, there were four of them, all armed and dressed in dark military-patterned clothes. Two men and two women. He says they were foreigners.'

Kubar arched an eyebrow. 'Israeli? American?'

He knew the Israelis made use of women in some of their more exotic special-forces units, and they certainly had no love of the Libyan government after Gaddafi had openly called for the annihilation of Israel, but such connections meant little at this stage. What interested him were verifiable facts.

'He couldn't say for sure, but he thinks they spoke English amongst themselves. They also had two hostages with them – a man and a woman dressed in night clothes.'

Almost certainly Tarek Sowan and his wife Laila, he thought, awoken in the middle of the night and taken from their home. At least he knew they'd made it this far alive.

'The man was injured, bleeding from a leg wound,' Maghur went on. 'He says they operated on him in the kitchen. He and his sons could hear the screaming, and we found blood and improvised medical equipment in there.'

Kubar was intrigued. It certainly tied in with the evidence of a firefight at the airfield, though the aggressors and the reasons for it remained a mystery. Presumably Sowan had been injured in the crossfire, and had required medical attention.

'I want to speak to the owner,' he decided, knowing he needed to know more beyond the bare facts. What he wanted were nuances, details, the things that dry police reports omitted.

The farmer, going by the name Umar Jalloud, was sitting in the centre of his threadbare couch, the old piece of furniture sagging visibly under his considerable weight. His back was hunched, his massive shoulders slumped as he stared down at the carpet, trying to ignore the police and security personnel tearing apart his home in search of clues.

'Mr Jalloud,' Kubar said, standing before him. 'I'd like to ask you some questions about what happened.'

Jalloud looked up at him wearily. Approaching seventy years of age, he was possessed of the kind of robust good health that prosperous farmers tended to enjoy, yet the years seemed to weigh more heavily on him after last night.

'I've already told your people everything I know,' he protested. It was clear he was tired, pissed off and in no mood for answering more questions. 'I don't know what else you want from me.'

'Only the truth,' Kubar said, keeping his tone calm and even. 'You can either give it to me here, or I can take you back to Mukhabarat headquarters for a more… thorough debriefing. Which would you prefer?'

He saw the muscles in the man's fleshy neck move up and down as he swallowed, saw the sudden edge of fear in his eyes. Like every citizen in Libya, he knew of the Mukhabarat all too well. He'd heard the stories of men and women being hauled off to the infamous Abu Salim prison in the middle of the night, never to be seen or heard from again.

'I'll do my best,' he said at last.

'Good.' Finding a nearby chair, Kubar pulled it across the room so that it was directly facing Jalloud, then settled himself down and took out his pen and notebook. He didn't rush. He was slow and methodical about it, making it plain that he controlled the tempo of the conversation. He had long ago learned that one projected power by one's actions and demeanour, not the badge one carried or the organization one represented.

'You said there were four attackers,' he began, once he was good and ready. 'Two men and two women.'

'Yes.'

'Did you get a look at any of them? Could you describe them to me?'

It was an obvious question, but perhaps worth a try anyway.

'They were wearing masks. Only their eyes were visible.'

'What about weapons? Did you see what they were carrying?'

'Pistols of some kind. I don't know the make, but they had silencers on the ends.'

'I see. Nothing bigger? No rifles or other such weapons?'

He shook his head. 'Not that I know of.'

That was good news as far as Kubar was concerned. The less firepower this group had at their disposal, the easier they would be to take down when he eventually caught them. And he *would* catch them; of that he was certain.

Kubar was nothing if not tenacious. The son of an impoverished Bedouin family, he'd been born into a life of hardship and grinding, ceaseless struggle amidst the endless dunes of the Sahara Desert. His parents, belonging to a generation that had grown up before the Libyan Revolution, were barely-literate nomads who had lacked the ambition, the education and most crucially the intelligence to strive for anything better. Their short and difficult lives had come to an abrupt end when a dispute with a neighbouring tribe had flared into violence, as such things inevitably did.

Only their 10-year-old son survived the attack, wandering alone in the desert until an army patrol had picked him up, dehydrated and close to death. That was when he'd resolved to put his former life behind him, to become an educated and intelligent man; part of the new generation helping to free Libya from the shackles of ignorance and primitive tribal bickering. That path had been neither short nor easy, but he'd stuck to it with the ferocious determination that would one day become his greatest asset.

'When they made entry to your house, how were they acting?'

The farmer blinked. 'What do you mean?'

'I mean, were they angry and aggressive, or cold and under control?'

He thought about that for a moment. 'Calm and controlled, I suppose, like professionals who had done such things before. At least to begin with. Later I heard a lot of shouting and arguments between them and their hostages.'

That certainly fit with his assessment of the situation so far. A team of professionals under pressure, trying to improvise a new escape plan after watching their old one literally go down in flames, and debating their next course of action.

'Do you know what they were arguing about?'

He shook his head. 'I don't speak English.'

'Was there anything recognizable? Any place names or words that kept coming up?'

Even a man with no grasp of a language might still glean something from an overheard conversation, particularly among a group trying to secure another means of escape from the country. Even a reference to a town or landmark might provide invaluable clues to their intentions.

Jalloud was silent for some time, replaying the snatches of overheard conversation in his mind. Kubar made no further attempt to prompt him, knowing he needed to be given time to arrive at the information – or not – by himself.

'There was one thing,' he said at last. 'A name, I think. I heard them say it several times. Faulkner.' He shook his head, the meaning lost on him. 'I can't say for sure if it was a place, a man or just a thing, but they seemed very focussed on it.'

That was enough for Kubar. He'd already noted the name down.

'Thank you for your cooperation,' he said, his tone stiff and formal. He'd never been good at expressing gratitude to anyone, because he'd rarely had cause to do it in his life.

'There is something else,' Jalloud blurted out, just as Kubar was turning to leave. Reaching into his pocket, he produced a roll of Libyan dinars and tentatively held them out. Judging by the size of the roll, it represented a couple of months' earnings for a man like Jalloud. 'Before they left in my truck, the leader of the group laid this money on the floor. He apologized to me in Arabic, then he left..'

Kubar frowned, surprised by this bizarre revelation about the attackers. Nonetheless, it was something else to keep in mind. Nodding acknowledgement, he excused himself.

'Wait. Do I have to hand these back?' Jalloud called after him.

'Keep them,' Kubar said over his shoulder. He already had everything he needed from this man. 'Put them to good use.'

Leaving the farmer to contemplate how he'd spend his newfound windfall, Kubar returned outside. His colleague Adnan Mousa was surveying the bullet-riddled Toyota that had been abandoned near the front door to the villa.

'Get anything interesting from him?' he asked.

'Possibly.' Kubar reached for a pair of sunglasses in his suit jacket and slipped them on. The sun was just rising above the horizon, but it was already shaping up to be a hot day. 'The leader of this team we're hunting – he is a puzzle to me.'

'Why?'

'He's willing to risk his life to abduct a man from a heavily secured building in the heart of our capital, yet he leaves the security guards alive when it would have been in his interests to execute them. He breaks into this farm, steals clothes and a vehicle, yet again spares the lives of potential witnesses. He even leaves money by way of compensation.' He shook his head. 'I don't understand this man.'

And that worried him most of all. Usually his adversary's intentions were obvious enough to his keen mind; a logical objective giving rise to understandable, if ruthless and deadly, actions. But in this case, no consistent pattern of behaviour was emerging. All he saw were contradictions.

'Perhaps he's a pacifist,' Mousa remarked with a wry smile.

Kubar didn't dignify that with an answer. Instead he turned to more practical matters. 'Do me a favour and run the name Faulkner through our records. Let me know if it turns up anything.'

'Of course. What are you expecting?'

Kubar was deep in thought as his dark eyes surveyed the arid, scorched landscape that rolled off toward the horizon.

'I don't know yet, but it may be the key to understanding all of this.'

Chapter 30

The mood in the truck's rear cargo area was tense and brooding as the vehicle bumped and jolted across the rough, barren terrain far to the south of Tripoli, with Drake opting to avoid all but the most rudimentary of roads now that the sun was up. They had so far encountered no police or military checkpoints, and indeed hadn't seen another vehicle of any sort for nearly an hour.

The temperature was rising quickly now that the sun was up. Even with wind gusting in through the open rear door, the air was hot and stifling, raising a sheen of perspiration on Frost and Mason, who were charged with guarding the two prisoners.

They were well and truly in the badlands now. The scattered farms and primitive settlements that had ringed the capital city had long since given way to wide open expanses of dusty basins, sand-scoured hills and ancient dried-up river channels. There were no trees, no grass, no bushes save for a few skeletal patches of scrub growing in some of the more sheltered valleys. Only the most hardy of life forms could scratch out an existence in such a bleak place.

'Goddamn wasteland,' Mason said, surveying the bleak landscape as he took a gulp of water. They had filled as many containers as they could before departing the farm, but even so it wouldn't take long to exhaust their reserves.

This wasn't like a normal escape-and-evasion situation, where the group could live off the land if necessary while they made good their escape. In this case, there was no land to live off. They wouldn't last more than a couple of days out here.

As Mason was contemplating this, he noticed Sowan's eyes on him. The Libyan was watching him from the other side of the truck's flatbed.

'I grew up in an area not unlike this,' Sowan remarked. 'A small town named Jalu near the border with Egypt. Not much except desert in all directions, and a small oasis to the north. My father worked the irrigation fields there, growing tomatoes and dates.' He smiled at the memory. 'As a boy, I used to grow so bored of his talk about tomato plantations, I promised myself I would leave Jalu as soon as I was old enough. I imagined myself living a life of adventure and excitement, as far away from tomato growing as possible.' He glanced down sheepishly at his heavily bandaged leg stretched out across the deck. 'Now I wonder if perhaps I made a mistake.'

Mason said nothing as he took another sip of water. His own father had served in the Marine Corps most of his adult life, so his particular apple hadn't fallen far from the tree.

'May I?' Sowan asked, holding out his hands. They'd been secured together with cable ties in case he still harboured some mad desire to go for one of their weapons.

Sowan was no good to them if he died of thirst. Mason reluctantly passed the plastic water bottle over. Accepting it gratefully, Sowan handed it to his wife, who gulped down a few mouthfuls.

'Thank you,' he said, nodding.

'Doesn't mean we're friends now,' Frost reminded him. 'We just don't want you to die yet. Be inconvenient.'

He shrugged, unperturbed by her implied threat. 'Even enemies may show each other respect and compassion. It is a lesson we Libyans learned centuries ago; the need to win the peace after you have won the war.' He eyed Frost for a long moment. 'Perhaps your country would do well to remember it.'

Far from rising to his barbed remark, the young woman merely smiled back at him, though there was no warmth in it. 'I'll keep that in mind at your war-crimes trial.'

'Will you be taking the stand with me?' he asked. 'After all, you played a part in this when you delivered an innocent man into my custody.'

'We didn't know who you were.'

'Or you didn't care,' he shot back. 'Plausible deniability is something your agency is quite fond of, I understand. Intentional ignorance is perhaps a more accurate term in this case. You knew nothing because you chose not to ask any questions. Do you think that absolves you of blame? Do you think a jury would see it that way?'

He was pressing her because he knew she was no threat to him. Drake was the one in charge of this group; none of his subordinates would act without his say-so. As much as she might ache to put another bullet in him, they all knew she wouldn't.

Frost was wise enough to realize it as well. Rather than engage in further debate with a man who seemed quite proficient at twisting words to suit his needs, she merely stared back at him, saying nothing, but the hostility was tangible.

The uncomfortable deadlock was finally broken when the pickup eased to a stop on the lea side of a low hill. Shutting down the engine, Drake stepped out and circled around to the rear gate, the keffiyeh now hanging loose around his neck.

'We're here. Get her out,' he instructed.

This was where the group had agreed to part ways, with Frost and Mason remaining behind to guard Laila, while Drake and McKnight continued on to their destination with Sowan. It went against their better judgement to split the team up, but it was necessary if their plan was to succeed.

Mason moved forward to help Laila up, but the woman batted his hand away. 'I can manage myself,' she warned, a dangerous glint in her eyes. 'Just give us a moment, would you?'

Mason glanced at Drake, who nodded just a little.

Reaching up, Sowan gently ran a hand down his wife's face, staring into her eyes. Those deep, compassionate, intelligent eyes so often filled with laughter and joy. But not now. Now he saw only fear and sadness reflected in their depths.

'Be brave, but be careful,' he said quietly in Arabic. 'Don't give them a reason to harm you.'

'And you. Give them what they want, Tarek,' she warned, perhaps sensing he was planning something else. She grasped his hand and squeezed hard. 'I don't care about the rest. You're all that matters. Do you understand?'

Swallowing, the man nodded. 'We'll be together again. I promise.'

With these parting words, Laila turned away and leapt down from the truck, declining any offer of assistance.

She found that they were parked at the base of a low, gently rolling hill, its summit crowned by a tumble of ancient ruins now reduced to little more than sand-scoured walls and piles of crumbled bricks. She had no idea what period the structure belonged to, or even what shape it had originally taken, but its prominent position on the hill suggested it might once have had a military purpose.

With their hostage out of the vehicle, Mason turned his attention to the stockpile of water and other essential supplies they would need to survive in this world of relentless sun and searing heat, stacking their limited cache on the ground near the truck.

Frost also emerged from the truck's bed, still clutching the shotgun she'd taken from the farm earlier in the day. Neither she nor Mason were happy about being left behind on babysitting duty while their companions risked their lives, but they knew further debate with Drake was futile. His mind was made up. All that remained was to see it through.

As Mason finished unloading the essential supplies, Drake surveyed the land around them. There wasn't much to see. The terrain was hilly and uneven, wind-scoured slopes and sandy plains fading off into a dusty, indeterminate horizon, all bathed in the relentless glare of the fiery orb overhead. Just looking at this landscape was enough to make his eyes water.

According to the road map they'd stolen from the Toyota before abandoning it, they were at the western end of the Nafusa mountain range, not more than a dozen miles from the Tunisian border. This was pretty much the end of the line as far as civilization was concerned. To the south lay the vast, empty expanse of the Sahara Desert. Hundreds of miles of sand dunes and searing heat where almost nothing could survive.

'The border's not far from here,' Drake said quietly, turning his attention back to his two companions as they prepared to part ways. 'We'll do everything we can to make this work, but if we're not back by dawn, we're not coming back. Get yourselves across into Tunisia. *Don't* wait for us. Understand?'

Neither of them said a word.

'I need to hear you say it,' Drake pressed, well aware of the thoughts they were harbouring. The prospect of leaving teammates behind didn't sit well with either of them.

'We've got it,' Mason reluctantly assured him. 'We'll do what we have to do.'

Drake nodded, satisfied that he'd impressed the importance of this matter on them. He needed to know they would follow through on what could very well prove to be his final order, as hard as it might be for them. He needed to know that if the mission failed, at least two of his friends would get out of Libya alive.

'Just make sure it doesn't come to that, okay?' He offered a weak grin. 'Keira will never let me hear the end of it otherwise.'

'You can bet your ass I won't,' she promised.

Mason held out a hand to him. 'Good luck, Ryan.'

Drake clasped his hand tight. It was a simple enough gesture, but it meant a lot to him at that moment.

'Try not to screw this up,' Frost added, looking at Drake for a long moment as if considering her next move. Then, without warning she reached out and hugged him, gripping him tight in a fierce embrace that was quite at odds with her diminutive size. Her cheeks were flushed from more than just the heat when she finally let go and backed away. Despite himself, Drake couldn't help but smile. It was as close to an emotional outpouring as he was likely to get from her.

'I'll do my best,' he promised. Then, realizing that time was off the essence, he gestured to the nearby ruins. 'Now get your arses up there and find cover.'

Frost hesitated a moment before shouldering the shotgun, hoisting a plastic container or water onto her back and starting the slow trek to the top of the hill. Mason and Laila followed not far behind, each carrying their own water supplies.

Drake lingered a few seconds longer, watching their progress in silence and trying to ignore the gloomy sense of finality that had settled on him, before returning to the pickup truck. McKnight had taken up position in the rear bed, keeping watch over Sowan.

'Good to go?' Drake asked.

The woman nodded, though her eyes were on the rest of their group as they made their way up the hill. She didn't like this any more than he did.

Sensing her misgivings, Drake laid a hand on her shoulder. 'We'll see them again.'

She nodded again, saying nothing.

Knowing they could afford to wait no longer, Drake returned to the driver's cab and fired up the engine. Never had he felt more alone as the bleached ruins receded into the distance behind them.

In the back, Samantha McKnight was harbouring similar thoughts, though for entirely different reasons. The more time she spent with this group, the more she saw and felt the bonds of trust, respect and friendship that bound them together, the more she felt like an outsider. The more she hated who and what she was, and what she would be called upon to do.

They might have trusted her, might have respected her and even considered her a friend, but they were wrong. She deserved none of those things from them.

Part of her actually wished they had found her out, that they might uncover her secret and exile her from the group forever. At least that would make it easier to bear. At least she wouldn't have to stand by and watch while Cain tore them apart, while he destroyed everything Drake had fought so hard to protect. At least she wouldn't have to live with the knowledge that their pain and suffering was down to her betrayal.

'He means something to you, yes?'

McKnight blinked, disturbed from her dark thoughts. Glancing over, she found Sowan observing her with a shrewd, knowing look.

'What?' she asked, taken aback by the question.

His gaze flicked to the driver's cab in front. 'I saw the way you looked at each other, the way you stand a little closer, the way his touch lingered on you just a moment too long. Small things, perhaps, but it is the small things that give us away.'

'You see a lot,' she evaded.

He smiled, sensing from the subtle tension in her body that he was right. 'It is my job to learn things about people, and I have learned a lot about you, Samantha. That is your name, I assume? We weren't introduced, but he called you Sam before.'

'My name's not important.'

'Of course it is. How can we be expected to work together if we don't even know each other's names?'

'We're not working together,' she corrected him. 'We're not friends, we're not partners and we're not allies. You're cooperating to keep your wife alive, so don't pretend this is about anything except survival for both of you. I know you'd kill us all if you had the chance.'

'Would I?' he repeated, tilting his head a little. 'How much do you really know about me, beyond your own assumptions and what you have been told by others?'

'I know enough.'

'Enough to do what? Judge me? Condemn me?' He leaned a little closer, his expression almost conspiratorial. 'Kill me?'

There was no answer she could give to such a question, so she said nothing. Instead she glowered at him from the other side of the compartment, her grip slowly tightening on the haft of her knife.

'It's about giving,' he went on. 'This job, this world that you and I live in. Giving up parts of yourself. The parts that shrink away from hurting others, that tell you it is wrong to kill and maim, the parts that are weak.'

'I don't live in the same world as you,' she countered, offended by the implication. 'I'm nothing like you.'

'And yet here we are together. Me the prisoner, and you the captor. Your role requires you to guard me, threaten my wife and me with harm if I don't cooperate, perhaps even kill me if it comes to it. And I believe you would do it if you had to. Would you do it out of malice or spite? No, of course not. Our actions are dictated by something far more powerful – logic. It is what binds us, what drives us, and what frees us.'

He licked his thin lips, as if savouring the moment.

'Logic allows me to torture a helpless man almost to death, to threaten his family with execution, and feel no shame in it. Logic lets me do this, because I know his suffering will save the lives of dozens, if not hundreds of innocent people who deserve life more than him. Giving up one life to save many more. It is a logical exchange; nothing more, nothing less.'

He glanced to the front of the vehicle once more, to the driver that neither could see, but both knew was there.

'But emotion... that's when things become dangerous. Emotion can undo all the hard-won work of logic. When you feel such an... attachment to another person, both of you are at risk, whether you know it or not. Each becomes a liability, a weakness to the other. You should learn to guard those emotions better, Samantha, because one day they will be your undoing.'

She'd heard enough. In that moment, the guilt and self-loathing that had been simmering away inside her suddenly erupted in a burst of anger and violent action.

Pushing herself off the thin metal-panelled wall, she launched herself across the narrow space, drawing her knife in the same motion. In a heartbeat, she had the blade pressed against Sowan's throat, her face mere inches from his as she stared hard into his eyes. Her muscles were trembling, her heart pounding with barely suppressed fury.

The dark eyes staring back at her showed little fear; only surprise at the vehemence of her reaction. 'As I said, emotion is our undoing.'

'Stop it,' she hissed. 'I'm not here to play your goddamn games.'

'You could kill me, Samantha,' he acknowledged. 'Right now. I'm unarmed, I can't stop you. You could probably even make up a story that I tried to escape. But ask yourself why you want to kill me so badly at this moment. Is it logic or emotion that controls you?'

She let out a breath, her grip on the knife relaxing a little. She couldn't believe how easily he had manipulated her.

'You talk a lot,' she said, forcing each word out through clenched teeth as she slowly backed away to her place on the other side of the vehicle. 'One day that'll be your undoing.' He shrugged, his faint smile making it plain he'd scored a point, exposed a chink in her armour that he might exploit later if he chose.

'Perhaps,' he acknowledged. 'But I doubt you will be there to see it.'

Chapter 31

Drake made sure he took a slow, winding route to their destination, wanting to confuse Sowan's sense of direction in case the man thought to betray the location where they'd left the remainder of the group behind.

Nonetheless, an hour or so of bumpy cross-country driving brought them to the small town of Nalut, a straggling settlement nestled in a winding river valley just ten miles from the Tunisian border. It was here that the next stage of their plan was to begin.

Bringing the pickup truck to a halt in the shadow of a rocky outcrop on the outskirts of town, Drake circled around to the rear of the vehicle to confer with his captive.

'Any trouble?' he asked, noticing McKnight's unhappy expression right away.

'No.' She stared across the open space at the injured man. 'No trouble.'

He could tell she was hiding something, but now wasn't the time to pursue such questions. It was time to focus on the task at hand.

'Get in the front, and be ready to move,' he instructed.

She was more than happy to oblige, leaping down from the rear gate with graceful ease and striding to the passenger door.

With McKnight gone, Drake pulled himself up and hunkered down before Sowan, staring him hard in the eye. They had outlined their plan to him already, and Drake didn't doubt that the shrewd and intelligent operative would have easily memorized every detail, but he needed to be sure.

'You know what's about to happen?'

Sowan met his gaze evenly. If he was nervous or apprehensive about what was coming, he gave little sign of it. 'I do.'

'You know the story we gave you?'

He nodded.

'Repeat it to me.'

He did, flawlessly. If nothing else, the man's memory was formidable.

'Once you have the information we need, call me on the number I gave you. We'll be there to pick you up and get you out of the country.'

Sowan said nothing to this, but it was clear he understood what was expected of him.

'We'll be close by at all times. You won't see us, but we'll be there,' Drake promised him. 'If you come through for us, we'll come through for you. We'll get you and your wife to safety and do what we can to help you start over. But if you try to fuck us, if you tell anyone about our deal, if you bring company to the exchange or we suspect you've been followed, all bets are off. You'll never see Laila again. If we're captured or compromised, she dies regardless. Do you understand?'

Playing a role like this reminded him uncomfortably of his own experiences when a ruthless enemy had taken his sister hostage and used her to manipulate Drake, but their situation was desperate. In lieu of trust, fear would have to suffice.

'Perfectly,' Sowan assured him.

Drake nodded, satisfied. 'I have to gag and bag you now.'

'Of course,' the older man agreed, no doubt seeing the necessity of it if their plan was to succeed. 'But before you do, answer me one thing.'

Drake paused, looking at him.

'What was this all really for?' he asked, for once betraying genuine bafflement. 'I've been turning it over in my mind all morning, but still I can't understand what you expected to get out of me. Who was Freya Shaw?'

Drake chewed his lip for a moment, contemplating whether it was even worth the explanation, whether Sowan could possibly understand the desperate situation that had prompted his mission here.

Perhaps it was, he judged.

'She was my mother.'

'Faulkner told you that I killed her, yes?'

When Drake looked at him, the full extent of his anger and guilt was plain for Sowan to see. It wasn't just anger at Faulkner, though there was plenty of that to go around. If he was really looking for someone to be furious with, he needed only to look in the mirror. He'd been impulsive and short-sighted, his eagerness to take revenge for Freya's murder overriding the caution and scepticism that would have warned him something was wrong.

He could have seen what was coming, but he'd chosen not to. And now they were all paying the price for it.

Sowan let out a faint sigh and nodded, acknowledging the unpleasant reality of his situation. 'I'm sorry for your loss,' he admitted. 'But if it means anything, it will be my pleasure to help you destroy Faulkner.'

Saying nothing further, he placed the gag in Sowan's mouth, then slipped a simple black hood over his head and helped him down so that he was lying flat on the truck's steel deck. A final length of sack cloth laid on top was enough to disguise his form to casual observation.

'Can you breathe all right?' Drake asked, to which he received a nod of affirmation. 'All right, brace yourself as best you can. This might get bumpy.'

Slamming the tailgate closed, Drake slipped his keffiyeh back on and returned to the driver's cab, clambering into the seat. McKnight was waiting for him, similarly attired.

Saying nothing, he reached over and squeezed her hand before firing up the engine once more and easing them away from their brief hiding place. Their destination, the town of Nalut, lay just over a mile away.

–

Being a traffic policeman in a busy border town like Nalut was a hot, stressful, dangerous job at the best of times, and today was no exception. Many of the roads in the ancient settlement were little more than dirt tracks, their basic layout unchanged in millennia. Remnants of an age where the horse and cart was the predominant mode of transport.

Directing the relentless flow of cars, buses, vans, trucks and motorbikes through such a crowded and inefficient road system, surrounded by dust and heat and choking engine fumes, was enough to try any man's nerves.

Salim Osman shook his head in dismay at the angry horn blasts resounding at a busy intersection nearby, where a cattle truck laden with goats had tried to turn left and found itself without enough space to make it. The driver's attempts to back up only served to enrage the impatient drivers behind him, and the hapless traffic cop on duty was powerless to stop the ensuing war of horns.

Well, at least it wasn't his problem right now, he thought as he took a sip of his soft drink. He was seated at a street cafe near the main drag, taking a well-earned respite from the ceaseless work. Soon enough he'd be obliged to return to the fray, but for the next ten minutes or so his time was his own.

And yet, even though he was technically off duty, he couldn't help observing the flow of vehicles on the road opposite. He'd been doing this job close to twenty years, and it was as ingrained in him as the dust that coated his uniform at the end of each weary day.

His eye was drawn to a beat-up looking Ford pickup truck approaching from the east. A rugged, workmanlike vehicle little different from so many others used by local farmers and labourers, it was interesting not because of its appearance, but because of its two passengers.

They were both wearing the traditional keffiyeh, which largely hid their facial features, but it was clear to him that neither of them were Libyan. They were Westerners, the pale skin around their eyes betraying their ethnic origins.

What were Westerners doing here? Certainly they appeared more often in Libya these days on business, and occasionally as tourists, but those individuals were invariably rich and spoiled. They had people to drive them around, people to watch over them, probably people to wipe their asses for them. They certainly didn't resort to driving battered old pickup trucks.

Caught as they were in the ebb and flow of traffic caused by the chaos at the intersection, they were obliged to slow and finally stop quite close to him, affording Osman a good view of the driver. The traffic cop looked at him curiously, even making eye contact for a moment, though the man quickly glanced away, as if uncomfortable to be under such scrutiny.

He saw the passenger exchange a worried glance with the driver, saw the fabric of their keffiyehs move as they spoke to one another. They were worried about something. Perhaps the traffic. Perhaps the road. Perhaps him.

Osman couldn't quite define the moment he realized something was wrong about this truck. He couldn't explain how he knew. If he'd been a fan of American cop shows, he might have attributed it to a hunch; a kind of sixth-sense feeling born from years of experience and knowledge.

Whatever the reason, his drink and his rest break were quickly forgotten as he rose to his feet, taking a step towards the vehicle.

That was when the driver reacted. Throwing the truck into reverse, he stamped on the accelerator, causing the big vehicle to lurch backwards suddenly. It made it about five yards before slamming into the front fender of an old hatchback stopped behind, but the movement bought sufficient manoeuvring room for the driver to swing the wheel over, engage first gear and stamp down hard on the gas.

'You! Stop!' Osman shouted, running to catch up. Other people were watching now, alerted by the shouting and the horn blasts and the screech of skidding tires, but none of them would step in. They wanted no part of this.

To his credit, the driver made it about halfway down the road towards the next junction before a crowded bus swung into his path, forcing him to turn hard right to avoid a head-on collision. His wild evasive move caused the balding tires to lose purchase on the dusty road surface, and before he could regain control the pickup barrelled straight into a telephone pole.

There was a loud bang, the crunch of buckling metal and the tinkle of broken glass as the truck's front bumper and engine block absorbed most of the impact. There was going to be no driving away from this one – the pickup came to a halt immediately against the unyielding barrier.

Osman was running flat-out towards it now, dodging in between cars that had come to a halt to watch the drama unfolded. As he neared the wrecked vehicle, steam now billowing from the shattered radiator, he was just in time to see the driver throw open his door and jump down.

'Stop, right now!' Osman commanded, drawing his riot baton. Traffic police weren't commonly issued with firearms, a failing he'd had cause to lament on more than a few occasions.

Before he could say another word, the driver had turned and darted off, vanishing into a service alley that ran between a pair of breeze-block shop units. His view was momentarily obscured by another truck that had edged forward, trying to clear the area around the crash. By the time Osman circled around it and reached the crippled truck, both the driver and his passenger were long gone.

Osman swore under his breath as he eyed their escape route. Much as he would have liked to give chase, he was keenly aware that he was only one man against two potential adversaries. And since he was on the wrong side of fifty, his chances of catching up with them were far slimmer than his expanding waistline.

In any case, before he could consider the matter further, he was alerted by a muted thump coming from within the truck. Frowning, he pulled open the driver's door and peered into the cab, finding no sign of any other passengers.

The thump was repeated; the distinctive clang of something hammering against the metal chassis, and this time accompanied by the low moan of a human voice.

Gripping the baton tight in sweating hands, Osman crept to the rear of the vehicle, from where the noises seemed to be emanating. He took a breath, reached out and undid the latch holding the tailgate shut, allowing it to fall open with a resounding clang.

Only then did he see the bound and hooded figure lying prone on the steel deck, writhing and kicking in a desperate bid for help.

'My God,' Osman breathed, realizing then that he was dealing with something far bigger than a mere traffic accident.

—

Drake and McKnight didn't stop running until they were nearly a mile from the scene of the crash. After sprinting down the service alley and vaulting a chain-link fence at the end, they had carried on at full speed down a minor side road, ignoring the bark of angry dogs and the curious glances of the old women busy hanging laundry and gossiping in a nearby courtyard.

They were careful to stay away from the bustling main thoroughfares as they made good their escape, preferring to move quickly and quietly through the maze of back alleys and narrow streets that seemed to honeycomb the area.

Nalut's architecture seemed to be a bizarre and entirely incoherent mix of the ancient and the modern, with no discernible pattern or logic to the placement of either. One moment they could be darting beneath the shadow of a Roman-era archway, the next they found themselves skirting around a roughly finished breezeblock garage. Millennia of changing architecture and technology had risen and fallen here, been rebuilt and replaced, then built on again.

Only when they emerged from a side street onto one of the main roads running through the city did they finally slow down and adopt a more casual walking pace, doing their best to get their breathing back under control in the stifling hot air. Drake reached out and took McKnight's hand, pulling the woman a little closer as they walked together along the busy pavement.

Libya might have been fairly progressive as far as North African countries went, but it remained a staunchly Islamic society. Women seen in public without a male escort were frowned upon and liable to attract entirely the wrong sort of attention, so Drake would have to act as her chaperone for the time being.

'You think it'll work?' she asked quietly as they brushed past a group of young men with buzz-cut hair and AC Milan football shirts. A couple of them gave the two Westerners a curious glance as they passed.

'Hard to say,' Drake admitted, painfully alert for any sign of police or military activity in the area. 'But I think he'll keep to our agreement.'

'Assuming you didn't kill him in the crash. That was a hell of a piece of driving, Ryan,' she said, squeezing his hand harder than was necessary. Airbags were unheard of when that truck had been built, and the crash had left both of them with bruising across their chests and shoulders. They could only imagine how Sowan, unrestrained in the truck's flatbed, had fared.

'It's not an exact science,' he reminded her. 'Anyway, it had to look real.'

The distinctive wail of a police siren caused them both to tense up. Glancing ahead, Drake was just able to make out the distinctive flash of blue lights as a police cruiser roared along the main road towards them, traffic parting like water before it.

'Shit,' he said under his breath.

The most obvious course of action was to simply act normal and hope to tough it out. Undoubtedly the police were responding to the crashed truck just a couple of blocks away, and perhaps they'd even been advised about the bound man in the back, but it was unlikely they would be switched-on enough to start searching for the two fugitives. There was a good chance they would just drive right by.

But what if they didn't? What if the sight of two Westerners was enough to pique their interest, causing them to stop and question them? With no ID and no good reason for being here, they would be hard pressed to bluff their way out of such a situation.

The other option was to run. Both still had their silenced weapons, though they were careful to keep them hidden from sight. They could use them as a last resort, but he was far from optimistic about their chances of fighting their way out of a situation like this.

It was at this moment that McKnight took the initiative, pulling him towards a shop front that faced directly out onto the street. As far as he could tell, it seemed to sell everything from cell phones, to food and drink, to rotating displays of cheap sunglasses that could be found on just about any street anywhere in the world.

'Oh, honey!' she gushed, adopting her best gee-whiz tone as she selected a pair of shades and tried them on. 'Would you buy me these? I left mine back at the hotel, and this sun's killing my eyes. Please?'

Drake forced an indulgent smile, keeping his back to the road as the police cruiser sped past, completely ignoring them. 'How could I refuse you?'

'We both know you never could.' Beaming with happiness, she pulled him close and hugged him. The simple gesture of a loving wife towards her husband. But as she held him, she whispered a warning in his ear, 'We might have company.'

That was enough to undo his short-lived sense of relief. Drake was on alert already after their narrow escape from the scene of the crash, his situation awareness about as good as it could be, but even he didn't have eyes in the back of his head.

'Where?'

'On your six, other side of the street,' she explained. 'One male, early fifties, greying beard. Big guy with a tribal cloak. He's looking away right now, but he had eyes-on.'

'Government?'

'Don't think so. It's hard to tell, but he looks Caucasian.'

'One of Faulkner's men?' If so, they were in real trouble.

'Maybe,' she allowed. 'Could just be a curious civilian. He's turning away now.'

Letting go of her, Drake glanced around to survey the street, feigning a look of casual disinterest as he scanned the thronging pedestrians. Men with greying beards weren't exactly in short supply in this neck of the woods, but sure enough he caught a brief glimpse of a big man walking away from them, his large frame hidden beneath a sandy-coloured cloak, before his view was obscured by slow-moving traffic.

It was hard to tell much about him from such a brief encounter, and certainly impossible to discern his intentions. With luck, McKnight's relative lack of experience of situations like this was making her overcautious, mistaking curiosity for something more sinister. At least, he hoped so.

In either case, their next course of action was the same. 'Let's get you these sunglasses,' he said, raising his voice to normal volume as he led her into the shop.

Their mysterious observer would have to wait.

In the end, they came away with a pair of shades each, plus some bottled water and a couple of energy bars whose brand Drake didn't recognize. Neither of them was in the mood for eating, but they knew they needed to keep their energy up. And after driving all morning in the scorching heat, not to mention their sprint through the back alleys of Nalut, they were certainly ready for the water.

Emerging from the shop with his eyes obscured behind the cheap polarized lenses, Drake scanned the far side of the street for their new friend. As far as he could see, there was nobody amongst the mass of pedestrians that fitted the bill.

'Any sign of him?' he asked, leading her down the street once more. She'd gotten a better look at the man than he had – maybe he'd missed something.

'He's gone,' she said, glancing around while feigning only casual interest. Despite her act, there was a tension in her shoulders that she couldn't hide. 'I guess it was nothing.'

Both operatives remained wary as they made their way northward, away from the distant wail of police sirens attending the accident. For now, at least, all they could do was wait and see whether Sowan made good on their agreement.

Chapter 32

Nalut Hospital, Tripoli

A relatively new facility, the 300-bed Nalut Hospital served not only the town that gave it its name, but the entire western district of over 100,000 people. It was here that the injured passenger of the crashed pickup truck was brought after being discovered by the startled traffic police. It was here that he was interviewed by law-enforcement officials, where his identity was confirmed and his incredible story began to emerge.

And it was here, a couple of hours after his discovery, that Bishr Kubar stormed in after a high-speed drive from Tripoli, flanked by a pair of Mukhabarat field operatives.

He was oblivious to the hostile looks of some of the patients, and even the doctors. The Nalut district was well known for the anti-government sentiments amongst its predominantly Berber population, and there had been a simmering undercurrent of unrest here for some time. This very hospital had been built by the Gaddafi regime as part of efforts to appease the disgruntled populace.

So far, at least, the gesture seemed to have failed.

'He was battered and bruised and suffering from a gunshot wound to the leg when they picked him up,' his colleague Adnan Mousa said, struggling to keep up with Kubar's energetic stride as they made their way to the room where Sowan was being treated. 'Looks like his captors did some basic surgery to patch him up.'

That tied in with the testimony of the farmer he'd spoken with earlier, Kubar thought. 'Any sign of them?'

'None so far. According to the report, they panicked when they were caught in traffic and a local traffic cop spotted them. They tried to make a run for it, then bailed out after they ran the pickup into a telegraph pole.'

'What were they doing in Nalut in the first place?' Kubar asked without breaking stride. It didn't make sense. Why head for such a densely populated settlement and risk discovery when their vehicle was capable of handling off-road terrain?

'Police reported the truck was almost out of petrol,' Mousa explained. 'I'd guess they were planning to refuel before crossing the border.'

Kubar clenched his jaw, unhappy at the news. Something about this wasn't right. What Mousa was describing were the actions of desperate amateurs, not the driven and committed group of professionals who had snatched Sowan from his home in the middle of the night.

'By the way, your search on the name Faulkner turned up something,' Mousa went on. 'Apparently there is a David Faulkner on our files.'

'Who is he?'

'A British intelligence-liaison officer, working with us and the Americans as part of a joint operation against Islamic terrorist networks.'

That was enough to make him break stride. Coming to a halt, he turned to face his partner. 'And where is this Faulkner now?'

'We don't know,' Mousa admitted. 'We tried contacting his office in London, but they say he's on compassionate leave at the moment. Death of a close friend, apparently.'

Kubar wasn't buying that for a moment. In fact, he was beginning to wonder what exactly they had stumbled upon. If the Brits really were behind this operation to snatch one of their top officers, it could destroy the uneasy alliance that had prevailed between their intelligence agencies for the past several years. The newfound spirit of cooperation between Libya and the West could unravel within a matter of weeks, and what then? Were they to become the next Iraq or Afghanistan?

But if the British were involved, what were they hoping to achieve by such an action? And was it really as simple as a snatch-and-grab operation? He found it hard to believe that British intelligence would be so sloppy as to leave a trail of clues pointing to their involvement all across Libya, not to mention allowing their target to fall back into enemy hands.

One way or another, he needed to get some answers on this, and there was only one man who could give him what he needed.

Sowan himself was being treated in a private room away from the main wards. Without bothering to knock, Kubar threw open the door and strode in, startling the young Korean doctor who had been examining the patient. Due to a lack of trained doctors in the region, many of the staff here came from overseas – Indians, Pakistanis, even Filipinos.

'May I speak with the patient?' he asked, feigning politeness. He'd always had an inherent dislike of medical professionals, and found it hard to hide his discomfort now.

The doctor, a short and wiry man with a mane of jet black hair, adjusted his glasses before glancing at Sowan. 'I was just finishing up my examination,' he said in halting Arabic.

'Finish it later,' Kubar advised him in a tone that made it plain the matter wasn't open for debate.

Hesitating a moment, the doctor considered the merits of further protest, then reluctantly nodded acceptance. Snatching up his clipboard of notes, he turned and scurried out of the room.

'I see you haven't lost your bedside manner, Bishr,' Sowan remarked with dry humour as the door closed. Though hardly close friends, the two men had worked together long enough in the same agency to have had dealings in the past. Sowan was well aware of the stories about Kubar's taciturn and abrasive personality.

Kubar surveyed the patient candidly. Though battered and bruised by his ordeal, he was sitting upright in bed without assistance, dressed in a clean surgical gown and with his injuries tended to.

'How are you feeling?' he asked, more because it was expected than because he was concerned for the man's wellbeing.

'You mean, apart from being kidnapped in the middle of the night, shot and driven into a telephone pole? Just fine, thank you.' Sowan remarked. 'But that's not what concerns me right now. What about my wife? Where is Laila?'

Kubar sighed and shook his head. 'We're working on it. We'll do everything we can. That much I promise you.'

The injured man said nothing to this, merely clenched his fists and closed his eyes for a moment to keep his composure. Perhaps he'd expected as much.

'About the kidnapping,' Kubar began, pulling a chair over beside the bed. It squeaked on the brand new linoleum floor. 'We've been trying to piece together what happened, who did this to you and why.'

'Any luck?'

'I was hoping you could help with that,' Kubar admitted. 'Can you tell us anything about the group who took you? Nationality, names, anything?'

Sowan was silent for a time, perhaps trying to make sense of the jumbled thoughts in his mind. 'They spoke English. Beyond that, I know nothing of where they came from.'

'Did they give any indication of what they wanted? Question you on anything?'

He shook his head. 'They seemed interested only in getting me out of the country.'

Kubar frowned. 'And the bullet wound? Can you tell me what happened at the airfield?'

Sowan's gaze darkened. 'I can't say for sure. Laila and I were being held in the car. I heard a plane coming in to land, then it crashed nearby and all of a sudden there was gunfire everywhere. The group retreated to the car and drove away. That's when I was hit.'

Which told Kubar absolutely nothing he didn't know already. 'Do you have any idea who ambushed them?'

Again Sowan shook his head. 'I was blindfolded. I saw nothing.'

'So they took you to a nearby farm to treat your wound,' Kubar went on, an edge of impatience and frustration in his voice now. 'The owner says there was a lot of shouting. Can you tell me anything of what was said?'

'I'm ashamed to say I blacked out from pain and blood-loss,' his comrade admitted. 'By the time I awoke, we were on our way again.'

'And Laila was still with you at this point?'

'I think so. I could feel her on the floor beside me.'

'So when did you last see her?'

Sowan's brows were knitted together in a frown. 'It must have been a couple of hours before the crash. We stopped, they took her out. Then it was just me. I... don't know what happened to her after that.'

It didn't take a genius to see where his dark thoughts were heading. Nonetheless, Kubar was far from impressed by his story. If his testimony was to be believed, Sowan had seen, heard and learned nothing of value during his captivity. Either his captors had proven more diligent and careful than their hasty abandonment in Nalut would suggest, or something else was going on.

'I understand.' Kubar leaned a little closer, speaking quietly so that only the two of them could hear his words. 'Is there… anything else I should know? If there's something about your kidnapping you were afraid to tell anyone, anything at all, you know you can trust me with it. I can help you, but I must have the truth. Give me that, and I will do the rest.'

Sowan was staring right into his eyes now, and for the next few seconds, neither man said a word. For a moment, Kubar could have sworn he was about to say something. He sensed him teetering on the brink, his mind poised perfectly between two opposing desires.

Just a moment, and then it passed.

'I have told you all I can,' Sowan said.

'Of course. Thank you.' Realizing he would get little more from the man, Kubar made to stand up, only to think better of it. 'Oh, just one other thing. Does the name Faulkner mean anything to you?'

That was when he saw it. That flicker of recognition in his eyes, the momentary glimmer of panic and surprise before his mask of composure reasserted itself. The tell of a poker player caught bluffing.

'Faulkner?' he said, repeating the word as if it were unfamiliar. 'No. No, I don't think so. Why do you ask?'

'Oh, just something that came up in our investigation,' Kubar said, rising from his chair. 'Probably nothing. Try to get some rest, Tarek. We'll talk more later.'

Leaving the patient, he returned to the corridor outside, where Mousa was waiting for him. 'Well?' the younger man asked expectantly.

Kubar reached for the packet of cigarettes in his pocket, then thought better of it when he spotted the angry red No Smoking signs overhead.

'Get some transport organized,' he said. 'I want him back in Tripoli before sunset.'

Sowan was hiding something; of that he was certain. And once he got the man back to Mukhabarat headquarters in Tripoli, he would find out exactly what he was keeping from them.

Chapter 33

Shielding his hands against the harsh glare of the sun now rising to its zenith in a sky devoid of clouds, Mason surveyed the shimmering, bleached landscape surrounding their hilltop refuge. There wasn't much to see.

Rocky escarpments and withered, inhospitable uplands lay to the north, forming a range of low mountains that marched in grim procession eastward. To the south stretched a vast sea of sand dunes that seemed to carry on forever, their tops slowly eroding under the burning-hot wind that sighed across the arid, shimmering desert.

Nothing in every direction. No sign of humanity at all, save for the bleached ruins in which they found themselves. They might have been on the edge of the world for all he knew.

'Jesus,' he breathed, captivated and perhaps a little intimidated by the harsh, stark, unforgiving land. It was almost a mystery to him why any people would try to carve out an existence in such a place.

With no activity in their vicinity all morning, Mason felt secure enough to interrupt his vigil and return to the shade for some water. His eyes were dry and sore after staring at the desert for so long, and his throat was parched.

The interior of the building was a mess. Whatever roof had once been supported by these walls had long since collapsed, leaving a veritable maze of broken archways, fallen pillars and crumbled masonry in its wake. It was here that the other two members of his group had set up their meagre camp.

Frost was sitting on her heels in one corner, keeping to the shade as much as possible. She had drawn her field knife from its sheath, and was idly running the edge across a piece of stone to sharpen it. It helped to pass the time, and perhaps take her mind off their two companions who might be risking their lives at this very moment.

Laila, their captive, was sitting with her back against the wall. Her eyes were closed and her legs crossed, almost as if she were meditating. Unlike her captors, the heat didn't seem to trouble her. Indeed, it was hard to know if she was even awake.

'Ain't much to look at, huh?' Frost remarked without glancing up from her task. 'Let me guess – sand and lots of it.'

He gave a wry smile. 'Give me Russia any day. That was a vacation next to this.'

'No argument here.' The young woman paused for a moment, thinking. 'Afghanistan, now there was a country. Hot as hell, but at least there was stuff to look at. Mountains, valleys, rivers, even trees and grass.'

Mason said nothing to that, because he knew she was referring to something he hadn't been part of. He'd been sidelined for nearly two years after taking a round to the shoulder during their mission to retrieve Anya from a high-security prison in the icy wastes of Siberia. Little could he have imagined then the chain of events that ill-fated adventure would unleash.

'Keegan liked it there, I think,' she continued. 'It was his kind of country. Wide open spaces, no people around. Son of a bitch probably thought he was John Wayne out on the frontier.'

The young woman had an oddly wistful look in her eyes when she spoke of their former teammate, killed during a mission in Afghanistan the previous year. It wasn't often that she indulged in nostalgia, but then, he supposed they hadn't had many opportunities to talk like this.

Mason eased himself down onto a massive block of masonry that had probably once formed part on an archway, picked up his plastic bottle of water and took a drink.

'Still miss him, huh?'

He had felt the loss of a trusted comrade keenly himself, but it wasn't the same. He hadn't come to know Keegan the way Frost had.

She drew the knife edge slowly along the stone, the rasp of metal an eerie counterpoint to the sighing wind beyond the walls. 'This the part where I say he was like a father to me, that he looked out for me and that… it feels like I lost part of myself when he died?'

'This is the part where you be honest.'

She shrugged, clearly uncomfortable talking about such personal matters, and for a time it seemed like she wasn't going to speak at all. 'Well, he drank too much, couldn't cook for shit and he was definitely one of the most sexist guys I ever met, but… he was still a better man than my real dad. And I miss him.' She chewed her lip and looked down. 'I guess that counts for something.'

'Yeah.' He smiled, a little amused and strangely touched by her characteristically honest eulogy for a fallen friend. 'Yeah, I guess it does.'

Seeking to change the subject, she laid the knife down, snatched up a plastic bottle of water and tossed it to Laila, who opened her eyes and glared at the young woman as it landed in her lap.

'Drink,' Frost commanded.

'Why?'

'Because it's our job to keep you alive. I sure didn't ask for it, but it's ours anyway, and I'm not going to let our friends down because you were too stubborn to keep yourself hydrated.'

'I'm not thirsty.' No doubt considering the matter settled, she closed her eyes once more and resumed her meditation.

Frost however was in no mood to let the matter rest. 'Okay, if that's how you want to play it, I'll make this real simple. Drink the fucking water, or we'll hold you down and force it down your throat. Your choice.'

The older woman let out a slow, weary sigh. 'God deliver us from Americans. Does every other word that comes from your mouth have to be a curse?'

Mason watched the smile spread across Frost's face. It wasn't a smile of pleasure or satisfaction, but rather anticipation of a good fight – something she seemed to enjoy a great deal.

'It's called freedom of speech. I don't suppose you're too familiar with that.'

Laila regarded her as one might regard a bothersome fly to be swatted. 'If you mean freedom to act as uncouth idiots, then you have used your rights with great enthusiasm.' Grabbing the bottle of water, she hurled it away in disgust. 'And if this is the best you can muster, the rest of your so-called "team" have probably been captured or killed already.'

Frost said and did nothing for a few moments, as if she were weighing up the situation and carefully considering her next action. She didn't look angry. She was past that stage now, which worried Mason far more. Now she was making a calculated choice about what she could get away with doing to their captive.

Then, just like that, she seemed to reach a decision. With a single, rapid movement she leapt to her feet, fists already clenched, muscles taut in preparation for what seemed likely to turn into a physical confrontation.

At the same moment, however, Mason raised his hand and hissed a single word of command. 'Quiet.'

Angry and resentful she might have been, but Frost was still aware enough to know the danger they were all in. If Mason had appealed for silence, it had to be for a reason. Straightaway she froze, saying nothing, her eyes on him.

Her look said it all – what have you heard?

Straining to listen over the mournful sigh of the desert wind and the faint hiss of billions of grains of constantly shifting sand, Mason waited, tense and silent, hoping against hope that what he'd heard had simply been in his mind. A trick played by the wind and the heat and his own imagination.

Seconds passed, strained and anxious, as he waited. Nothing save for the background noise. He let out a breath slowly, wondering if it had been a false alarm.

Then he heard it. The distant braying of an animal of some kind, accompanied by the clang of a bell. It was coming from somewhere off to the south.

His eyes locked with Frost's, that one look communicating everything they were both thinking in that moment.

Contact.

Straightaway he made a gesture with his hand, pointing two fingers to his eyes, then to Laila. *Watch her – I'm going to check it out.*

Drawing his silenced weapon, Mason loped over to the south side of the ruined building and backed up against the wall, next to a gaping hole that might once have been the frame of a window.

While Frost kept an eye on the prisoner, Mason took a breath, then edged around the hole just enough to glimpse the desert beyond their temporary sanctuary.

As with his previous stint on lookout duty, there was little to see. The vast empty expanse of sand and weathered rock seemed to stretch off into infinity. No other buildings, no vehicles, no people.

He squinted as the hot breeze carried with it tiny grains of windblown sand that peppered his skin and eyes. The horizon seemed to shimmer and fade in and out, as if it possessed only a tenuous foothold in reality and might dissolve out of existence at any moment. The silenced weapon was a leaden weight in his sweating hands as he watched and waited.

There!

A shape emerging from a small valley to the south-west. A single animal, long-legged and heavily furred, with the distinctive humped back of a dromedary camel. And perched on top was a single human rider.

He was clothed in the loose flowing robes typical of the indigenous peoples of this region, his head and face largely obscured by a keffiyeh. Most likely he was a Bedouin or a Tuareg, one of the nomadic tribesmen who inhabited the desert in this area.

He might not have belonged to the Libyan military or government, but he was far from unprotected. Even from this range Mason could make out the long knife sheathed at his waist, as well as the distinctive long barrel of a rifle slung across his back.

Perhaps 200 yards distant, he seemed to be heading towards their hilltop refuge at an unhurried pace, allowing his mount to choose its own speed and course. But he was undoubtedly coming their way.

'Shit,' Mason mumbled as he ducked back behind cover, cursing their bad luck at having run into this isolated traveller.

Knowing that Frost would be anxiously awaiting his report, he looked over at her and held his fingers to his eyes, then raised a single finger. *I see one man.*

Next he raised his hand with his thumb outstretched and his index finger pointed skyward. *One man armed with a rifle.*

She nodded understanding.

Leaving his vantage point, Mason hurried over to join her, keeping his head down.

'One tango on camelback,' he whispered. 'He's heading towards us.'

'Fuck,' the young woman hissed. 'Military?'

'Don't think so, unless the Libyan army's added camels to their ranks. Looks like a civvy to me.'

'We can't let him see us,' she warned him.

'I know.'

'If he reports us to the authorities, it's game over.'

'I know.' His tone was sharper than he'd intended, because he knew exactly what she was suggesting. If this new arrival spotted them, he couldn't be allowed to leave this place alive.

'Then you know what we have to do.' She was looking right at him now, needing to know if he was prepared to go all the way.

It wouldn't be the first time that operations like this had incurred such 'collateral damage'. It wasn't something anyone liked to talk about or even think about too much, but it was an ugly reality of their profession that every operative had to face up to sooner or later.

The rule they lived by was simple, hard and uncompromising – the mission came first. Always.

'I don't like it any more than you do, but it's him or us. *We* have to do something.' Sensing his reluctance, she shook her head and drew her automatic. 'Screw it. I'll take care of it.'

'No,' Mason cut in. Something about the distant figure continued to play on his mind, and only then did he realize why. 'He's travelling light. I saw no tent, not many supplies.'

'So what?'

'So he can't have gone far from his tribe. If he doesn't return home, he'll be missed. They'll come looking for him.'

One man with a rifle was a problem. An armed mob of angry tribesmen baying for revenge was something none of them would survive.

'We're in the desert. Maybe he doesn't need a tent,' she countered. 'He could live in a cave, for all we know.'

'You want to take that chance?'

'So what do you suggest?' she pressed him.

He chewed his lip for a moment, considering their limited options. 'We hide. With luck he'll be on his way before we know it.'

'And if he isn't?'

Mason eyed her hard. 'Then *I'll* take care of it,' he promised. 'Gather up our gear. No tracks. Hurry.'

Frost looked at him a moment longer, perhaps thinking to press her case, but reluctantly obeyed. There was no clear chain of command here as far as the two of them were concerned. They were equals, which meant neither had the final say in any decision making. But perhaps some part of her hoped to escape this without bloodshed, despite the risks.

Saying nothing, she turned away and quickly gathered together the water containers and their other limited supplies. As she did this, Mason turned his attention to Laila.

'I have to gag you and tie your hands for now,' he explained, speaking quietly and calmly. One scream from her was all it would take to alert the approaching tribesman, and that would force their hand. 'Don't make a sound, and everything will be fine.'

'I wouldn't count on that,' the woman said, though she held out her hands and allowed him to bind her wrists.

With their captive secure and their gear gathered up, the small group retreated to the north-eastern end of the building, where an alcove had once opened out into a small antechamber of some kind. It wasn't much, but it was as isolated and secluded a spot as they were likely to find. Assuming they remained quiet, nothing less than a full search of the building from end to end would uncover them.

Mason was just settling into the shadowy recess when Frost suddenly let out a gasp. 'Oh Christ.'

'What?' he demanded, angered by the noise made by her outburst.

For perhaps the first time since he'd known her, the young woman looked genuinely frightened. Not because of the danger they were in, but because she'd realized she had made a mistake. 'I left my knife out there. Shit!'

Mason felt his heart sink. The knife that she had been so methodically sharpening when he'd returned from his vigil outside. She had laid it down on the sand to throw the bottle of water to Laila, and must have forgotten it in their haste to relocate. He remembered the exact spot where it lay.

'I'll get it,' she said, making to get up.

No sooner had she begun to rise than a shadow appeared in the building's ruined entrance. Gripping the young specialist to hold her back, Mason watched as the tribesman dismounted his camel and leapt nimbly down from the beast, landing easily on the sandy ground.

Reaching behind him, he unwound his rifle from its strap and just stood there for several seconds, watching and listening. The weapon in his hands was an ancient Karabiner 98 – a German bolt-action rifle dating back to the 1930s. Old it might have been, but it was also one of the best long-range rifles ever made. With a proper sight, they were lethally accurate at up to 1,000 yards, and still occasionally popped up in conflicts all over the globe.

The wooden stock was scuffed and worn by decades of use, but the barrel and action still seemed to be in good order. They'd seen service in this part of the world during the Second World War, so it was possible some of them had fallen into local hands and been passed down through generations.

Apparently satisfied that the building was unoccupied, the tribesman laid his rifle against a collapsed pillar, then lowered himself to the ground and began to unwind the keffiyeh from his head, revealing a mane of long dark hair falling almost to his shoulders.

Mason glanced at Frost, leaned in close to whisper in her ear. 'Stay here. Cover Laila.'

Her eyes were wide, and she opened her mouth to protest, likely to the effect that she should be the one to do it, but he was already up and moving before she could stop him.

Now left alone with her captive, Frost gripped her Browning automatic and turned it on Laila, flicking the safety catch to the off position. If the worst came to the worst and they were compromise, she wouldn't hesitate to pull the trigger.

Slipping from the shadowy annex, Mason crept forward, keeping low and tracing a careful path through the maze of ruins before him. He knew that Frost had been seated against the west wall of the building, and that she had lain her knife at her feet; therefore it was off to the right of the new arrival.

There was a chance he might not see it, particularly if windblown sand had begun to cover the gleaming blade, but even a cursory investigation of that area would likely yield it up. Mason had to get to it before then.

Moving with infinite care and patience, he crept forward inch by inch. His profession as a Shepherd operative naturally required the ability to move with stealth, but for him those skills dated back even further. He'd been an Army Ranger before joining the Agency, part of a recon force specializing in operations behind enemy lines. He'd learned long ago the value of silence.

He could see the tribesman now through a gap in the ruins. Having removed a water canteen from his belt, he poured a measure into a small bowl on the ground before him. Then, to Mason's surprise, he bent forward and began to wash his face.

Strange that someone would waste such a precious resource for washing, he thought. Still, he cared less about the man's personal hygiene than he did about avoiding the prospect of killing him.

On he went, moving forward step by step. The sun, now past its zenith, beat down on him with merciless intensity. Beads of sweat dripped from his brow and into his eyes, but he ignored the stinging discomfort as he rounded a collapsed archway, closing in on his target.

The silenced automatic was in his right hand; a round chambered and the safety disengaged. If the worst came to the worst, he could bring it to bear and drop his target in a heartbeat. From this range he could scarcely miss.

Almost there. Forcing himself to keep his breathing under control, he rounded the same block of fallen masonry he'd been sitting on earlier, catching his first glimpse of the small open space beyond.

Shit.

The knife was there all right, exactly where Frost had left it; the finely machined blade gleaming in the harsh sunlight. The sand showed no signs of covering it any time soon, and likely the only reason their visitor hadn't spotted it was because his line of sight was partially blocked by the same pillar his rifle was resting against.

But worst of all, Mason knew in that moment there was no way for him to reach the weapon without being spotted. A gap of at least six feet without a trace of cover stood in his way. Even if he wasn't looking in that direction, the tribesman would spot the movement out of the corner of his eye.

Shit. Shit. Shit.

He glanced down at the weapon in his hands, the inevitable thought surfacing that it might be the only course of action left. He had tried. He'd come as far as he could, risked exposure to spare this man's life, but he could go no further.

Frost had been right about one thing; it was him or them.

He looked at the target once more. The nomad had finished washing his face and had turned his attention to his hands and arms. A slight turn of his head allowed Mason to catch a glimpse of his face in profile. A youthful face, the jawline showing only a darkening of stubble around the chin and upper lip.

Just a kid. No more than sixteen.

He was going to kill a kid.

As he watched, the young man removed his boots and began to bathe his feet with the remaining water.

It was only then that his seemingly inexplicable actions at last coalesced into a logical chain of events, leading up to a simple but profound conclusion. He wasn't washing out of a desire for personal cleanliness. He was purifying himself in preparation for Zuhr – the Islamic prayer offered up just after midday. If what Mason understood of the Islamic faith was correct, this might just give him the opportunity he needed.

Sure enough, the young man unrolled a small prayer mat from amongst his gear and laid it on the sandy ground, facing east towards Mecca.

Then, with great care, he stood before it, raised his hands up with his palms facing outward, then crossed them in front of his chest and began to pray.

Mason knew this was his chance. If this man was dedicated enough to pray out here alone with nobody watching over him, his mind and his senses would likely be focussed solely on his task. And for now at least he was facing away from the knife.

Taking a breath to psyche himself up, Mason moved out from behind cover and crossed the dozen paces to the fallen knife, keeping his target covered at all times with the automatic.

Reaching down without taking his eyes off the praying man, he felt around on the burning sand until his fingers brushed the edge of the blade. Sweat was pouring down his face, his throat was dry and his heart was pounding. At any moment he expected the young man to whirl around, catch sight of him and snatch up the rifle.

Gripping the blade, Mason lifted it from its resting place and began to back away, raising and planting each boot with infinite care. All the while the young man continued to recite the *salat*, oblivious to the danger lurking mere feet away from him.

Mason was gasping for breath when he finally lowered himself behind the substantial cover of a ruined wall, the nervous tension and anticipation held in check through sheer willpower at last making itself felt.

The prayer lasted another couple of minutes, after which the young man carefully rolled up his mat and stowed it away, along with the bowl and water canteen. Surveying the ruined interior of the building one last time, he picked up his old bolt-action rifle, turned away and mounted his camel once more to continue on his journey.

Only when Mason was certain that both beast and rider had receded into the distance did he allow himself to relax a little.

Rising from his hiding place, he was just in time to see Frost emerge from the alcove with the automatic still in hand.

'Jesus Christ, that was close,' she said quietly.

Mason tossed the knife to the ground at her feet, angry that her oversight had almost forced them to kill an innocent man.

'Take better care of it next time.'

Chapter 34

Sitting in silent contemplation, Tarek Sowan stared out the window of the third-floor office, watching the shadows growing across the homes and office blocks of central Tripoli as the sun began its long descent towards the western horizon.

His bandaged leg was throbbing with pain as the medication administered at the hospital in Nalut gradually wore off, though he paid it little heed. His mind was elsewhere, pondering all of the things that could so easily go wrong with his hastily conceived plan, all of the ways he could get himself and his wife killed today.

Seated opposite him was his superior officer, Hussein Jibril, carefully reading his debriefing file. A big man who always looked in need of a shave, Jibril projected an air of benign indifference in most matters, usually allowing others to take the initiative. It was a ploy, of course, intended to weed out those who took him for a fool, but an effective one all the same. Jibril was a good man who had fostered Sowan's career and personally recommended him for his current position.

Standing behind him was a far less welcome addition to the meeting. Bishr Kubar, the bulldog, was a silent and glowering presence. It was clear the man harboured suspicions about him, as well he might given the vague story he'd spun during his hospital debriefing. But there was nothing he could do about Kubar for now.

All that mattered was Jibril.

'Well, not much of a report,' the big intelligence chief remarked as he removed his reading glasses and looked up from the modest document. 'It seems we don't have a lot to go on, Tarek.'

For his part, Sowan made an apologetic face. 'I wish I could remember more, but they were good at what they did. I saw and heard very little the whole time I was with them – they made sure of it.'

'So it would seem. And you have no idea what they wanted with you?'

Sowan shook his head.

His boss sighed and leaned back, his chair creaking slightly under his ample weight. 'It's bad, Tarek. It looks bad for us when we can't even protect one of our own officers. These people march into our homes in the middle of the night, breeze through our security like it doesn't exist, and take what they want.' His air of genial indifference was gone now, revealing the wounded pride of an officer whose own competence had been called into question by recent events. 'This can't go unanswered. We must find who did this, no matter how long it takes.'

Sowan said nothing to this, though he felt his stomach churn at the thought of what he was about to do.

'I'd like to go over the debriefing again, compare your story with the other witnesses,' Kubar interjected. Then, wary of openly questioning the integrity of a fellow officer, he added, 'Perhaps it may help you remember things you didn't consider before.'

'I've considered everything, Bishr,' Sowan said, giving him a harsh look. 'It's all there in the report.'

'And if it isn't?' he replied. 'If there is some detail you overlooked? Something that may be the key to finding these people, finding Laila? Is that not worth a little more of your time, now, while it can still make a difference?'

Kubar as always was like a dog with a bone. He sensed something was wrong, and there was no way he would let it go until he got to the truth. Sooner or later he would find it; that much was clear. But Sowan didn't need to stall him forever.

Just long enough.

'As you say.' Stifling a yawn, he reached up and rubbed his eyes, feigning exhaustion. It required little acting talent after everything he'd been through. 'We can go over it again, if you think it will help.'

Jibril was quick to pick up on the fatigue in his voice. 'How long has it been since you got any sleep?'

Sowan looked at him ruefully. 'A while. A long while actually.'

'I thought as much. What you need right now is rest. You're no good to us exhausted and not thinking clearly. Get some sleep.' He gave Kubar a pointed look. 'Tomorrow Bishr can ask his questions.'

Kubar, for his part, was wise enough to stifle further protests. He might have been tenacious, but he wasn't stupid. Pressing the matter would only antagonize Jibril and increase his sympathy for Sowan. However, his dark expression made it clear he was far from pleased at having his investigation suspended with questions still unanswered.

Sowan gave a pained smile. 'I have nowhere to go.'

By all accounts, fire had largely gutted his home before local emergency crews could get it under control. His house, and likely all of his possessions, were gone. Just another thing he had Ryan Drake to thank for.

At this, Jibril nodded understanding. 'We have sleeping quarters at Bab al-Azizia barracks. Not much in terms of comfort, but at least it's secure. Even these bastards can't get through an entire army division. I'll have a couple of our agents waiting downstairs to drive you there.'

'Thank you,' Sowan said, rising from his chair with difficulty with the aid of a walking stick. His injured leg burned with pain, though he kept his face composed through stubborn willpower. 'If you don't mind, I'd like to freshen up first.'

'Of course.' Rounding his desk, Jibril shook hands with him. 'If it means anything, I'm sorry about Laila. We'll do everything we can to get her back.'

I'm doing everything I need to, Sowan thought as he nodded in gratitude, then excused himself from the office. Only when he was in the corridor beyond did he allow himself to start breathing normally again.

His heart was pounding as he limped down the hallway as fast as his injury would allow, knowing time was short. They would be expecting him in the parking lot downstairs, and if he delayed too long they would come looking.

He had only a limited window in which to act. He had to make it count.

Chapter 35

Drake slumped down in his corner, aching, lathered in sweat, gasping for breath. It was the end of the ninth round; there was only one more, and he was quite simply exhausted. The crowd was roaring and cheering, hundreds of voices baying for blood. They were watching the fight of their lives, and they were loving every moment of the drama now unfolding in the ring.

His corner-men went to work on his battered body straightaway, trying to control the bleeding cut over his left eye, and applying a cold compress to his bruised ribs.

'How you feeling, lad?' Jack, his trainer, asked. He was a short, stocky man, about seventy years old, with wavy grey hair and an expressive, deeply lined face that had always reminded Drake of a bulldog.

'How do you think I'm feeling?' he gasped. 'I'm fucking hurting.'

At least two of his knuckles were broken. He could feel the pain radiating out from the damaged joint, coursing in waves up his arm. He was breaking himself on a complete nobody.

'Aye? Well, so is he.'

Drake glanced over Jack's shoulder at his opponent. He was arguing with his trainer. The man was shouting and pleading with him to throw in the towel, but he was shaking his head, pushing aside the pleas and the protests.

Defiant to the end.

'Then why isn't he beaten?' Drake demanded, anger and frustration welling up inside. 'This was supposed to be a fucking walkover, Jack! What's wrong with him?'

The old man leaned in close, his ugly bulldog face only inches away. 'He's fighting for pride. Don't you understand? That's all he's got left.'

Drake had made a serious mistake with this fight. His opponent had once been a decent contender, but now he was old and past his prime, regarded as nothing but a stepping stone in his career. Anticipating an easy victory, Drake had done little training for the fight, and his lack of preparation was telling.

'He's making me look bad. What am I supposed to do?' he asked, at a loss.

'Fucking knock him out!' Jack yelled. 'Nobody else can do it for you. You have to stop him!'

'Ten seconds!' the timekeeper yelled to be heard over the crowd.

'It's you and him now, son. Forget the crowd, forget me, forget everything else. None of that matters. All that matters is the next three minutes. He wants this as much as you, so you have to take it away from him. Now get stuck in and finish it! Do it now!'

Taking a deep breath, Drake rose up on weary legs to start his last round.

Drake was crouched on the roof of a residential apartment building, overlooking the main road leading to the headquarters of the Libyan intelligence service. It had been easy enough for a man with his skills to sneak up here unseen, quietly disabling the lock on the fire door that led out from the building's central stairwell, and wedging it shut behind him.

Nobody else was coming up here without him knowing – he could be sure of that.

From his vantage point, he could just about make out the yellow-painted three-storey office complex that housed this country's most feared secret police force, its facade partially screened by trees, though it was impossible to get closer without risking detection.

From what he could discern, the HQ building itself was set within a large walled compound complete with vehicle checkpoints, guard posts and barbed-wire entanglements. Formidable enough security measures at the best of times, but it was the ones hidden from sight that were of greater concern. More than likely that compound contained enough armed operatives to see off all but the most determined assaults.

Not only that, but in his clandestine journey across town Drake had spied several men that were almost certainly plain-clothed agents. He'd been in the business long enough to recognize fellow operatives when he saw them, and though they didn't exactly announce their presence, it was clear they were there to keep an eye on the local population.

And he knew why.

It might have trying to join the good-boys club in recent years, but the Gaddafi regime was far more fearful of its own people than it was of foreign invaders. As it should have been. One didn't maintain an iron grip on power for nearly four decades through popular approval, but rather through fear and intimidation. With near total control over the media, and a culture of surveillance and distrust permeating every aspect of Libyan life, any hint of dissent or talk of rebellion was swiftly and ruthlessly put down.

In short, no one, Shepherd team or otherwise, was getting into that compound unless they were granted access. And he'd allowed Sowan, the one man who held the key to his salvation, to waltz right into that impregnable fortress. If he didn't feel like coming out, there was absolutely nothing Drake or his team could do about it.

Not for the first time, he found himself questioning the wisdom of his hastily conceived plan. It was a move born from desperation, and that was a poor motive for any course of action.

'Monarch, this is Envoy. How's your copy?' McKnight signalled via his radio earpiece. The tactical radios were discreet enough to wear without much fear of discovery, particularly with the keffiyeh to cover most of his face.

Well aware of the danger of travelling together, they had agreed to part company for the time being, with Drake taking up position as close to the headquarters building as possible. McKnight meanwhile was stationed at a coffee house about a quarter of a mile away, seemingly a popular destination for tourists. Either way, at least it allowed her to blend in easier.

'Good copy, Envoy,' he replied. 'No activity. What's your situation?'

'Well, the coffee's pretty good here. But I've had some fat Italian guy creeping on me for the past twenty minutes. Think he's taking a leak right now.'

Drake couldn't help but smile. Her report didn't exactly conform to radio discipline, but he didn't mind. Their radios were operating on an encrypted frequency, so nobody else could listen in on the conversation. It was just the two of them.

'Sorry to hear that.'

'Don't be. I plan to take him up on his offer if this thing goes south.'

This time he actually chuckled in amusement. For a few precious seconds he allowed himself to forget their precarious situation, forget the danger and the paranoia and the fear that had driven them since all this had begun. They had been under near-constant pressure since their arrival in Libya, and as much as they were trained to deal with such things, it was a relief to step back from it just for a moment.

'We'll get through this,' he said quietly, his voice carrying a more serious tone now. 'I promise.'

'I know.' She lapsed into silence then, but he could sense she had more to say. Something that had been preying on her mind. 'Ryan, I—'

'Wait,' he interrupted. 'Don't... don't say anything, Sam. Just for a few seconds.'

Closing his eyes, he exhaled slowly, the drone of traffic and people and music and the countless other sounds of the bustling city fading into the background of his consciousness as the seconds stretched out. He could feel the warmth of the setting sun on his face, the faint breeze sighing in from the Mediterranean.

McKnight might not have been on that rooftop with him in person, but she was connected to him all the same. He imagined her there beside him, the scent of her, the warmth of her skin next to his, the feel of her breath on his cheek.

Just for a moment.

'There's something I need to ask you,' she said, breaking the spell.

'Yeah?'

'Back at that farm, when you had Laila hostage. Those things you threatened to do to her... Would you really have gone through with it?'

Drake was glad then of the distance between them. Glad she couldn't see the look in his eyes. Glad she couldn't know what was in his mind, and his heart.

'It didn't come down to that,' he said quietly. 'I knew Sowan would break.'

'But if he hadn't,' she pressed him. 'What then?'

Drake could feel the muscles in his throat tightening, because she was asking a question he'd avoided himself until now.

You're afraid, a voice in his head said accusingly. Is it because you know the answer and you're afraid to admit it, or because you don't, and that scares you even more? Do you really want her to know what kind of man you once were, and could still be? Or are you scared that man isn't as deeply buried as you thought?

'You and the others are my priority. I'll do whatever it takes to keep you safe, Sam.' He sighed and looked up to the evening sky, wondering how many times those same words had been used to justify horrific, deplorable acts. 'Whatever it takes.'

Silence greeted him. It wasn't the answer she'd sought, wasn't the reassurance she needed, but she was smart enough to know it was the best he could truthfully offer.

'There are people nearby. I have to go,' the woman said, her voice somehow more remote, more detached and businesslike. She was back in work-mode now. 'Signal when you have something.'

'I will.'

–

Easing the door open, Sowan slipped inside and quickly pulled it closed behind him, letting out a breath. He was alone, for the time being at least.

The familiar, mundane office in which he now found himself was an absurd contrast to the frantic, desperate events of the past twenty-four hours that had seen the rest of his life turned upside down.

Even he had to admit there was a certain comfort in the familiarity of it all – the cheap wood-veneer desk with coffee rings all over, the obligatory framed picture of Colonel Gaddafi hung on the wall, the stack of papers awaiting his attention and the antique letter-opener resting on top. A gift from his father-in-law when he'd been promoted to his current position.

None of that was important now, however. What he cared about was the computer occupying the centre of the desk. That was where he'd find the information he needed. That was what might well mean the difference between life and death, for him and for Laila.

Limping over to the other side of the desk, he eased himself gratefully into the worn office chair, reached out and switched on the machine. A low hum permeated the small office as cooling fans whirred into life.

As he waited for the machine to boot up, he glanced at the desk again, his gaze lingering on the framed picture that had occupied this office almost as long as he had.

It was a photograph, taken several years ago on a beach far to the east of Tripoli, well away from buildings and cars and noise and disruption. A photograph of Laila. Momentarily distracted, she hadn't even realized he was taking her picture. It truly was a moment frozen in time. A moment for which he was forever grateful.

Normally he hated taking pictures. The formality of it, the awkwardness, as if human beings were mannequins to be posed and positioned with no will of their own. But not that time. That time he'd caught her in a perfect moment, sitting on the pristine white sand, knees drawn up to her chest, staring out across the waves in silent contemplation.

It was her eyes that had so captivated him. The look in them was one of such great wonder and wistfulness, that even years later he still found himself moved by it. He'd always wondered what she had been thinking at that moment, but in all these years had never brought himself to ask. In truth, he didn't really want to know.

Some things were better left unknown.

The computer was ready. Logging into the secure network with his own credentials, he called up the main file directory and inputted a single search term – Minos.

Minos was the codename under which the prisoner-exchange project had operated. Perhaps given the subject matter, its moniker had been assigned with a certain dash of ironic humour, for Minos was a figure in ancient Greek mythology who forced the king of Athens to choose men and women to send to his twisted, winding labyrinth, never to return.

As the directory opened up, Sowan found himself confronted with multiple sub-folders dedicated to every aspect of the programme, from prisoner dossiers to logistical arrangements for their incarceration, debriefings about their capture, interrogation reports, networks of aliases and additional contacts.

Everything within this directory had been carefully saved and catalogued, and not for simple reasons of posterity. One never knew when a seemingly innocent piece of administrative data could prove to be a useful tool, or weapon, if the need arose.

Eager to download what he needed and get the hell out before he was missed, Sowan selected the main prisoner-transfer list and opened it up.

No files found.

'What?' he gasped, trying again.

No files found.

Trying to convince himself it was merely a fluke, an oversight, an error, he opened a different directory, this one filled with time-logged communications between Libyan intelligence and their Western counterparts.

No files found.

With mounting desperation, Sowan opened another file, and another, seeking an exception, only to meet with the same chilling result every time.

The entire Minos directory had been deleted.

Letting out a pained sigh, Sowan held his head in his hands as the full magnitude of his discovery sank in. Someone within the Mukhabarat was trying to erase all record of the project. Someone with administrative-level authority. Who? Why?

That was when it happened. A click from the door. The click of a lock being disengaged, moving parts working, a handle being turned.

Glancing up from the screen, Sowan watched as the door swung open to reveal his superior, his friend, his mentor. Hussein Jibril, the Director of the Mukhabarat.

Chapter 36

For a few moments, both men remained frozen in place, just staring at each other without saying a word.

'Tarek,' Jibril said, finally breaking the silence. 'What are you doing here?'

Sowan's mind was racing, composing and discarding half a dozen excuses and explanations in the space of a few seconds. Thinking fast, Sowan reached for the framed photo of Laila and held it up. 'A keepsake,' he said, allowing the sorrow and worry to show in his eyes. 'It's the only one I have left now.'

'Ah, of course,' Jibril said, nodding. 'I can't imagine how you must be feeling. You must be losing your mind with worry.'

'I am,' Sowan admitted truthfully.

The computer was still humming away. Cocking his head curiously, Jibril folded his arms. 'What's that for? I thought you'd be eager to get out of here for a while.'

I bet you did, Sowan thought.

Someone with administrative-level privileges trying to erase all evidence of Project Minos. Including perhaps the men involved in it.

'I've been thinking,' he began.

'About what, exactly?'

'About the men who kidnapped me. Why they did it, what they were looking for. I had a hunch, so I came here and did some digging.'

'Why didn't you say something?'

'Because I didn't know who I could trust,' Sowan said, allowing some emotion to creep into his voice. A man wrestling with the difficult and dangerous notion that his comrades might not be who he thought they were. 'I didn't want to say anything until I had proof.'

'And do you?' Jibril prompted, taking a step closer. 'Have proof?'

Sowan gestured to the computer screen. 'Take a look for yourself.'

Curious, Jibril rounded the desk and leaned in closer to take a look at the screen, while Sowan rose from his chair and stepped back to give him some room.

The timing was perfect. Reaching out, Sowan seized up the letter opener resting atop his stack of unread mail. Jibril began to look up, alerted by the sudden movement, but a backhanded strike with Sowan's free hand sent him reeling, stumbling over the chair that Sowan had deliberately placed behind him.

The stunned man tumbled to the floor with a loud, fleshy thump, letting out a grunt of pain and surprise. Sowan was on him in a moment, the point of the letter opener pressed into the skin just beneath his right eye. It was hardly a formidable weapon, but used in such a vulnerable spot it was more than enough to blind or even kill him.

'Make a sound, and you'll be dead before you finish your first word,' Sowan hissed, the righteous anger now burning inside him enough to temporarily override the pain of his injured leg. 'Nod if you understand.'

Swallowing back his fear, Jibril nodded.

'What have you done with the Minos files?' he demanded.

Jibril's eyes were wide. 'Tarek, I don't know what you think—'

'Don't lie to me!' Sowan snarled, pressing the blade in harder. Hard enough to draw blood. 'I know you're part of this. After everything that's happened, there's no way you should have let me walk free after my debriefing. Any intelligence officer would have known I could have been compromised, but not you. You wanted me to leave this place, take a ride with your security detail. Where? Out to the desert where you could kill me?'

Jibril said nothing to this, and that hurt far worse than any injury. It was the pain of knowing he was right, that a man he trusted was ready to have him killed.

'Why, Hussein?' he pleaded. 'Why are you doing this to me?'

'You don't understand. It's not me who made this happen.'

'Who, then?'

His friend's fleshy throat moved as he swallowed. 'The Americans. They demanded you in exchange for one of their own, said they would break our alliance if we didn't hand you over.'

'What do you mean?'

Jibril gave a weary, resigned sigh. 'The man you brought back from Paris. He wasn't an Islamic terrorist. He was CIA.'

That was when everything changed. That was when the world seemed to fall apart around him. Sowan felt like a knife had just been plunged into his stomach. Fayed, the terrorist accused of trying to organize an armed insurgency in Libya, was in fact working for their supposed 'allies'?

The only man who could answer his questions was right in front of him. 'What the hell do you mean he was CIA? What was he doing there?'

'Faulkner. He tipped us off that the Americans were preparing to move against us, channelling weapons and money to opposition groups in the western provinces. The deal they cut was nothing but a delaying tactic to hide their true intentions. They're planning to start a coup here, Tarek. He gave us the name of one of their key weapons suppliers, told us where and how to find him, so we did. We put you in charge of capturing him, only the Americans found out what we were doing, traced the rendition order back to you. They must have sent a team in to capture you. When that failed, they demanded that we put you on a rendition flight to the United States. We deleted all references to Faulkner's intel on our systems as a precaution.'

'And you just agreed to it?' he managed to say, stunned by what he was hearing. 'Why?'

'To buy time. The man you captured was one of the key elements of the coup attempt. He knew everything – names, bank-account numbers, the time and place of transactions, even the routes they were using to smuggle weapons into the country. All of it was stored on his computers, but their contents were encrypted. We needed time to break in, decipher it all. Until then, we had to keep the Americans on side.'

'On side?' Sowan repeated, incredulous. 'The men you knew were plotting our downfall? How did you ever expect to keep them on our side?'

'Use your head, Tarek. We both know the situation in our country. Half the western provinces are on the verge of open rebellion, there are more attacks and demonstrations with every passing month. We can kill and imprison as many rebels and dissidents as we want, but in the end it will make no difference. The tide is turning against us, and sooner or later we are all going to be washed away by it. Unless we have allies who will help us, protect us when the time comes. Allies who owe us a favour, because we uncovered their plans but chose not to act against them.'

Sowan felt like he was about to throw up. This man that he trusted, believed in, who was supposed to be leading the fight to hold Libya together, was openly admitting defeat. Worse, he was virtually sanctioning a foreign-backed revolution to save his own skin.

'You're talking about standing by and allowing them to start a civil war? Letting them tear our country apart? '

'I'm talking about survival. That's all it comes down to in the end.'

Sowan let out a breath, shock and disbelief vying with a growing sense of disgust and hatred towards the man cowering beneath him. Survival, he thought with grim resignation. Saving his own fat ass at the cost of hundreds, maybe thousands of lives. Was such a man really worthy of survival?

Did Sowan himself deserve to live, knowing he'd played a part in this terrible chain of events that might well destroy his country? What might he do now that the evidence he'd planned to use against Faulkner was gone? Stand impotently by and watch the tragic events unfold? Run away and hide, hoping that history never caught up with him?

No, he thought, a fire of defiance kindling inside him.

He wouldn't stand by and do nothing.

'The intel you recovered from the American. Where is it?'

Jibril's eyes lit up, perhaps guessing what he was thinking. 'Tarek, you can't—'

Withdrawing the letter opener, Sowan raised it up and plunged it suddenly into Jibril's left hand, feeling the spongy resistance as the slender blade passed through his flesh, followed by the jarring impact as it buried itself in the floorboards beneath.

He was able to clamp a hand over Jibril's mouth, muffling his scream sufficiently that no one in the corridor outside was likely to hear.

'Tell me what I want to know,' he whispered in the man's ear. 'Or the blade goes somewhere far more… personal next time.'

It was a good few seconds before Jibril had calmed down enough for Sowan to remove his hand. When he did, the man was breathing hard, his teeth clenched against the pain.

'Where is it?' Sowan repeated.

'Evidence room,' he spat. 'Locker… G43. But you can't get to it, even if you try. You need high-level security clearance just to get in.'

'You mean this?' Reaching down, Sowan yanked Jibril's access key card off the pin holding it to his shirt. 'I'll take my chances.'

With some difficulty he rose to his feet. Adrenaline was coursing through his veins, and doing a good job of suppressing the pain in his injured leg for now. Jibril, with one hand still pinned to the ground and a noticeable pool of blood seeping out beneath, was forced to remain where he was.

'You hate me,' he said, seeing the look in his former friend's eyes. 'You hate what I am, what I've done. The compromises I've made, the people I've chosen to side with. Maybe you have a right to, but that doesn't mean I regret it.'

'I know,' Sowan said sadly, reaching for the walking stick he'd been using since his discharge from hospital. 'And that's what hurts the most, Hussein.'

A swift, hard blow to the face was enough to slam Jibril's head back against the floor. There was fleshy thump, and Jibril let out a grunt of pain and surprise in the fleeting moments before his consciousness faded away.

Dropping the stick, Sowan knelt down beside him once more. With trembling hands he quickly searched the unconscious man, helping himself to Jibril's cell phone and car keys, shoving the keys in his pocket alongside the security card.

The cell phone was his first priority. Swiping a finger across the screen to unlock it, he punched in a number from memory and hit the dial icon.

As he'd expected, it didn't take Drake long to answer.

'What's your situation?' he asked, his voice low and deceptively calm.

'The files are gone,' Sowan replied, a little out of breath as he pocketed the car keys. 'The director was part of this. He ordered them deleted before I could get to them.'

Sowan could only imagine what was going through Drake's mind. 'Then we're finished.'

'Maybe not. The CIA are planning a coup in Libya, sending weapons and equipment to anti-government rebels in our western desert. If they succeed, the country will fall into civil war. Tens of thousands will die.'

Silence for several moments. 'You're sure of this?'

'The director himself confessed to me.'

'Jesus Christ,' Drake breathed.

'That is what this was all about; protecting that operation, and the man you captured in Paris was the cornerstone of the whole thing.'

'So where is he now?'

'Dead,' was Sowan's blunt response.

'You mean executed.'

'I mean dead. He killed himself in his cell the night we brought him in, took his own life rather than give up the rest of his conspirators.'

'Shit,' Drake growled. 'Then we've got nothing to go on.'

'Maybe not. The laptop he had with him was heavily encrypted, which means it likely holds something of great value,' Sowan went on. 'Our experts have not been able to break into it yet, but if we can get to it and decrypt it—'

'We can stop this thing before it even begins,' Drake finished for him.

'I can get to it, but I don't have much time. I've been discovered. Hussein Jibril, the director, he found me. I had to take him down, but it won't be long before people realize he's missing.'

'Did the man have car keys on him?'

'Yes.'

'Do you know what kind of car he drives?'

'I think so.' He vaguely recalled seeing Jibril entering a silver Lexus in the past. 'The parking lot is downstairs, in the basement.'

'Then you need to get out of there,' Drake said. His voice was still calm and controlled, but there was an edge to it now. The commanding tone of a man used to giving orders and making decisions under pressure.

'Not without that computer.' Sowan's tone was equally firm.

Another pause. 'Can you make it?'

'For all our sakes, I hope so.'

'Fuck,' Drake said under his breath, realizing there was no way he could stop Sowan going through with his hastily conceived plan. 'Then you'd better get moving.'

'On my way.'

Powering down the computer, Sowan dragged himself to his feet, wincing in pain as damaged flesh and muscle protested. Injured, tired and afraid he might be, but he was here, and nobody else could help him now.

Even if this desperate plan somehow succeeded, he would certainly have no future in Libya. He would be a traitor, an outcast; shunned and despised for his betrayal and hunted by agents of the very organization he had worked so hard to serve. Assuming he made it out of the country, he didn't doubt his ability to disappear and remain hidden from them for as long as he had to. After all, he had played that game from the other side and knew all the tricks his people employed.

But such a life of running and hiding, forever watching his back and keeping his guard up was a failure, a defeat. A humiliating end to a life and career that could have been so much more. He'd once imagined himself as a protector, a bastion of peace and order striving to hold back the tides of chaos and bloodshed that threatened to engulf his country. A good man fighting a good cause.

But there were no good men in this world. He saw that now well enough, and felt nothing but shame for his part in this disgusting abuse of power. His only hope now was to prevent more innocent lives being lost.

One way or another, he had to see this through himself.

Leaving Jibril sprawled on the floor, he paused for a moment at the door, listening for activity in the corridor beyond. Satisfied that the coast was clear, he retreated from the room, pulling the door shut behind him and locking it.

With luck, it would buy him enough time to do what he had to.

–

On a rooftop several blocks away, Drake moved the phone away from his ear and instead hit the radio transmitter at his throat.

'Monarch to Envoy.'

'Go, Monarch.'

'We've got a problem,' he said, speaking fast and urgently. 'Sowan may be compromised. We'll need to make a quick exit. Ditch your position and converge on me.'

Straightaway her voice stepped up a gear. 'Wilco, Monarch. Envoy is en route now.'

Drake's heart was beating fast as he abandoned his rooftop observation post, making his way to the emergency fire escape. If this went wrong, both he and McKnight would need to be able to leave the area quickly.

'Copy that. Stay on the net, Envoy. Monarch is moving to street level.'

As he removed the wedges holding the door shut and ventured into the darkened stairwell beyond, Drake sent a silent prayer that their erstwhile prisoner made it out of that compound alive. He could do nothing to help until Sowan was clear of those walls.

Until then, it all depended on him.

–

Taking a breath, Sowan reached out and swiped Jibril's access card through the security reader beside the door. There was a moment of tense silence, then mercifully a green light appeared on the reader, followed by a buzz as the door's electronic locks disengaged.

Sowan couldn't get into the storage vault on the other side fast enough. As the door closed behind him, automatic lights sensed his presence and blinked into life, illuminating the room for the first time.

Even now, the scale of the place took him by surprise. Resembling a warehouse rather than a secure archive facility, the room was a good thirty yards long and half as wide, crammed to the ceiling with row after row of metal shelves, each laden with cardboard boxes of every shape and size imaginable. Within them, painstakingly archived and catalogued, were the evidence containers of every active operation currently undertaken by the Mukhabarat.

The air here was cool and dry, the climate monitored night and day to ensure the delicate paper documents didn't decay. It had the feeling of a tomb, which wasn't inappropriate considering many of the documents and pieces of evidence dealt with death in its countless forms. Everything from kidnapping and torture to execution and assassination was archived here. A world of secrets that only his agency's most trusted members were allowed free access to.

But he didn't need the world today. Just one laptop computer.

Focussing on that goal, he strode forward through the labyrinth as fast as his injury would allow, ignoring the countless shelves he passed along the way, and the secrets they contained. After fifty yards he reached Section G and turned left, seeking container number 43.

He was close now. He could feel it.

His heart sank when he stopped at the section he needed, staring upward in dismay. The container he needed was on the top shelf.

'Damn it,' he said under his breath.

Grabbing a movable ladder that had been fixed into rollers at the base, he slid it along until he'd reached the correct area, took a breath to prepare himself, and struggled up the steps. Every step was agony, forcing damaged muscle to bunch and contract as he pulled himself upward. He was sweating visibly by the time he made it to the top, having to clutch at the ladder with trembling hands to steady himself.

'How's it going in there?' Drake asked over the phone line.

'Ask me in a few moments,' Sowan replied tersely, reaching out for the box occupying position forty-three and flipping the lid off. He held his breath as he reached inside, gripping the plastic evidence bag to pull it out.

His fears vanished the moment he saw the distinctive outline of the laptop, nestled within the sealed plastic container.

'I have it,' he said, letting out the breath he hadn't realized he'd been holding.

Drake's reaction was immediate. 'Thank Christ. Now get your arse out of there.'

He didn't have to be told twice, clambering down the ladder with only one arm to grip the railing, while cradling the precious computer with the other. In under a minute he'd rifled through a couple of other evidence boxes until he'd found a canvas rucksack, dumped out its contents and placed the laptop carefully inside, then slung it over one shoulder.

He was ready, he'd found what he needed. His only task now was to get it to safety.

Chapter 37

Great Falls National Park, Virginia

Marcus Cain disliked being summoned anywhere at the best of times. As deputy director of the CIA, there were few people on this earth who had either the official authority or the personal power to demand his presence. Unfortunately, the man now walking beside him on the quiet woodland trail possessed more than enough of both to force his compliance.

So here he was, out in the woods ten miles from central DC in Fairfax County. It was a cool, damp, misty afternoon in Virginia, the sky visible as an unbroken sheet of grey through the dripping tree canopy overhead. The air smelled of moss and wet earth, the ground still coated with a remnants of last season's dead leaves that clung to his expensive shoes as he walked.

He'd never cared too much for the outdoors. His busy work schedule permitted little time for vacations, and even if that hadn't been the case, he doubted he would have chosen to spend his time somewhere like this. But his lone companion today liked to meet here, liked the silence of the empty woodlands and the privacy they permitted. He knew each of the trails that wound their way through the area, so here they met.

'I'm hearing worrying things from Libya,' he began, stepping over a fallen branch as the two men walked side by side, their trail taking them close to fast-flowing river swollen by recent rains. 'Abductions of senior personnel, police shootouts, plane crashes at private airfields. Their security services are on high alert; they suspect something's wrong. So I have to ask, what exactly is going on out there?'

Richard Starke wasn't a big or imposing man, didn't project an aura of charisma or authority like so many others in positions of power. In fact, his manner and appearance reminded Cain of a history professor – pensive and thoughtful, conservative in both his words and his actions. A man who spoke less than he listened, who rarely roused himself to displays of anger, who functioned best alone with his own thoughts.

But Starke was no history professor, and his quiet demeanour masked a ferociously intelligent mind backed by a capacious memory, a deep understanding of the world he helped to shape and direct, and an iron will to make his objectives happen.

Cain would have expected nothing less from the director of the National Security Agency, America's premier source of signals intelligence, charged with

255

monitoring global communications for potential threats, espionage, listening in on rival nations and just about anything else their government might need. Very little escaped his knowledge, in particular the events currently playing out half a world away in Libya.

'There have been some problems. We're handling it,' Cain assured him. He'd known this was going to be a difficult conversation.

Starke glanced at him, his grey eyes giving away nothing at all. Even Anya would have been hard pressed to discern the man's thoughts and motivations. But Cain was in no doubt that Starke was assessing him, regarding him with that same cool, calculating, analytical mind, perhaps judging whether he was worthy of the position to which he'd been elevated.

'You know, I like you, Marcus,' he said at length. 'You're smart, capable and creative. You see things your predecessor didn't. That's why I vouched for you, put my own reputation at stake to bring you into the group.'

And there lay the heart of this discussion. The group, as it was known to those who were truly part of it, though it had no true name even amongst its most senior and trusted members. For others, those on the outside, or foolish enough to believe they understood its nature and purpose, it was known by many names: the section, the circle, even the faction.

Each was as true and as false as the other, for that was the very nature of the group; a twisting serpentine force of baseless lies and formless shadows. Deceit and subterfuge were its modus operandi, misdirection its greatest weapon.

The irony was that this most secretive of organizations made no effort to hide it existence. Indeed, its members had actively encouraged speculation over the years, with careful leaks of misinformation, expertly fabricated trails of breadcrumbs for those willing to follow. And people had followed – they always did. The rumours, claims and counter-claims had slowly blended fact with fiction, truth with lies, eventually becoming so thoroughly seeded into popular culture that normal people had long since dismissed them as ghost stories and wild conspiracy theories.

Secrecy wasn't their veil. Apathy and ignorance was what kept them hidden in plain sight.

But for all their misdirection, the group was very real.

To their allies they represented a shifting entity of uncertain identity and active deceit, coupled with undeniable strength, unknowable goals and unproven loyalty – a dangerous combination that bred mistrust and paranoia. To their enemies they were a true nightmare; a foe that could strike from any direction, that seemed to thwart any stratagem and strike at weakness no matter how well hidden.

'That's not a privilege; it's not a reward or a token of respect. It's a responsibility, perhaps the greatest and most terrible responsibility anyone could ever wish for. You wanted a seat at the big table – this is how you have to earn it. In short, this is one responsibility you do not wish to take lightly, Marcus. The group doesn't reward failure with second chances.'

'Have I ever let you down?' Cain asked frankly. 'In all the years we've known each other, have I ever given you reason to doubt me?'

Starke raised his eyebrows in a gesture that might have been grudging acknowledgement.

'The risk of failure is growing,' he observed with clinical detachment. 'If we're
discovered—'

'We're handling this,' Cain repeated, driving home the point with absolute
conviction. 'Antonia is on schedule, just as we discussed. In a few days, we'll be
in a position to change the balance of power across the entire region. Millions of
lives will be changed forever. Isn't that worth the risk? Isn't that what the group
exists to do?'

Starke had stopped walking, had turned to look at him, regarding him with
those depthless, unknowable grey eyes. Those eyes that gave away nothing. Cain
met those eyes without reservation, without fear. Fear could destroy men like him.

'We'll see,' Starke conceded, turning away to resume his walk.

Chapter 38

Most of the cars in the facility were stored in an underground parking lot, regularly patrolled by security teams armed with handguns and sniffer dogs, in case one of the cars was carrying something more sinister than a speeding ticket.

Usually the parking lot was accessed via a pair of elevators at the west and east ends of the building, but these were heavily used by overweight analysts who couldn't be bothered making their own way between floors. Sowan had no desire to encounter such people now, or indeed one of the operatives Jibril had assigned to escort him off the premises. For all he knew, they could be looking for him already.

Instead he sought out the nearest stairwell and made his way down, taking the steps as fast as his injured leg would allow. Every movement sent lightning bolts of pain shooting upward from his thigh, but he clutched at the railings for support and forced his way through the pain. Pain could be dealt with later, when he was far away from this place.

'Where are you now?' Drake asked.

'In the stairwell, heading down.'

'Good. Take it slow and steady. Don't run.'

'Easy for you to say,' Sowan grunted, anger flaring up for a moment. 'You are not here.'

'I know. But I'm close. Once you're outside, I can help you.'

Suddenly he froze, alerted by the click of shoes on the steps further down. Pulse hammering in his ears, Sowan leaned out over the railing to view the stairs below, and sure enough spotted a man in a grey suit making his way up. He was big and burly, the light reflecting off the top of his shaven head, but crucially he wasn't rushing up as if he was moving to intercept a wanted fugitive. Rather, he seemed to be taking the steps at his own pace.

Realizing there was little option but to bluff his way past, Sowan quickened his pace, forcing himself to walk straight and steady despite the pain. Rounding a corner, he found himself approaching the man in the grey suit.

He barely looked up at Sowan, his attention instead focussed on the cell phone in his hands as he typed out a text message.

'I don't care if you have to work on this all night,' Sowan growled into his phone in Arabic, using it to block the man's view of his face as they passed each other.

'Those reports were supposed to be in two days ago, and I'm not going to take the blame for your mistakes.'

The other man had clearly heard such things many times before, and gave a pained look as he passed by.

Letting out a breath, Sowan quickly covered the last flight, grateful beyond words when he reached the base of the stairs.

Like most of the rest of the building, the doors at the bottom which opened out into the parking lot were controlled by key card access. Removing Jibril's card from his pocket, he swiped it through the reader. There was a crisp beep, and a buzz as the door's magnetic locks disengaged.

He was out.

The parking lot beyond occupied most of the building's subterranean footprint, easily a hundred yards across and almost the same in length. Brightly lit by harsh electric strip lighting suspended from the concrete ceiling, the parking lot offered few places to hide save for the occasional support pillar. His only saving grace was that the place was less than half full at such a late hour, making it easier to find Jibril's car.

Like most intelligence agencies, the Mukhabarat never stopped no matter what time of day or night it was, but its employees were still only human. Unless there was a major incident, the building operated with minimal staff overnight.

'Keep your eyes open for security cameras,' Drake advised. 'Try to use the phone to block their view of you. And don't run. Running draws attention.'

'Any other insights?' Sowan asked with unveiled sarcasm as he made his way down the rows of parked vehicles, trying to look like he knew where he was going. There were plenty of silver cars here, many of which conformed to the same basic size and shape of Jibril's vehicle.

He had the key fob in his hand, and every so often gave it an experimental press to see if any of the nearby cars responded. So far nothing.

He was about half way down the row when the echo of voices drew his attention to the right, where a two-man security team had just appeared from behind the elevator bank. One of the guards glanced his way, giving a disinterested nod of acknowledgement.

Sowan nodded back, trying to look equally disinterested. Just another tired and stressed analyst making his way home at the end of a long day. At least he looked the part, unshaven and dishevelled as he was.

Pressing the key fob again, he carried on with his seemingly fruitless quest.

'I can't find it,' he said, his quiet tone belying the mounting sense of urgency he felt. 'There's a security team here. They're watching me.'

'Just keep looking,' Drake said. What else was he going to say? Give up and turn yourself in? 'It's no big deal. People forget where they park all the time.'

Chancing a look at the security team, he saw the same guard glance his way again. There was a hint of curiosity in his gaze now. Sowan wasn't acting like the other drivers he was so used to seeing.

'They sense something is wrong,' he said, feeling himself tense up involuntarily. He knew that tension would manifest in his body language – something the guards were trained to look for.

'Listen to me,' Drake said, cutting in. 'When I was a kid, I stole a video game from a shop in Brixton.'

Such was Sowan's dismay at his bizarre change in subject that he actually forgot about his dangerous situation for a few moments. 'What are you talking about?'

'Listen, this is important. Keep walking and listen. I was eight years old, probably in with the wrong crowd. You know the story. Anyway, I wanted to impress my mates, so we agreed to each steal something from a shop on Brixton High Street. I chose a Game Boy game, because I thought it was more impressive than anything they took. So I walked down the aisle calm as you like, swiped it and stuffed it in my jacket and turned to leave. That's when it hit me. I couldn't do it. I felt like everyone in the world was watching me. All I had to do was walk out the main door, but every step was like walking through treacle.'

Sowan was so perplexed by his story that he passed right by the security team on the other side of the parking lot, scarcely noticing them as he went.

'That's when I realized the secret to getting out of these places. Act like a dickhead. Act like you're pissed off at the world, like you own the place, like nobody's got a right to get in your way. Act like you couldn't give a shit what anyone else thinks of you, because you've got no time for them. So I did. And I walked.'

Sowan paused, alerted by the distinctive *whup-whup* of a car's central-locking system disengaging. Glancing left, he finally spotted Jibril's silver Lexus LS parked in the far corner of the lot, and made straight for it.

Practically collapsing in the driver's seat, he closed his eyes and let out a sigh of relief. 'I'm in,' he said, hardly believing it was true.

'Good man. See? Act like a dickhead. Works every time.'

'Did it work for you?' he couldn't help but ask.

'Nope. The security guards nailed me before I'd gotten ten yards from the store. Makes a good story, though.'

Sowan shook his head as he turned the ignition over and fired up the engine.

Chapter 39

Hussein Jibril was in darkness. All around him was a void, sheer and absolute. A world without light or colour, sound or shape.

Then vaguely he became aware of a sound. Not a voice as such, but the shadowy resonance of a voice somewhere off in the distance, like the after-echo of footsteps in a great empty mosque.

He heard it again, closer now, louder and more distinct. Concentrating his thoughts, he focussed in on the voice as the discordant sounds slowly merged together to form words. A name. His name.

'Hussein! Hussein, can you hear me?'

The dark void around him was lightening now, the empty shapelessness of it giving way to a world of sound and sensation.

'Hussein! Wake up.'

With great effort he forced the darkness back, fighting and railing against it, pushing his mind towards the world beyond. The world in which it belonged.

Blinking his eyes open, he found himself staring into the grim, unshaven face of Bishr Kubar. Stoic and serious at the best of times, he looked even more so now. His dark eyes betrayed anger, confusion and an edge of concern, which only lifted slightly when Jibril showed signs of consciousness.

'What happened to you? Who did this?'

'How... how long was I out?' Jibril asked, fumbling to find the right words. His normally sharp mind was dull and sluggish, and just making his mouth form the right sounds required a great effort.

Trying to sit up, he grimaced as the world swam and lurched in and out of focus, the blood pounded in his ears and waves of pain radiated from inside his skull like the pealing of a bell. Reaching up, he touched his forehead. His fingers came away slick with blood.

'Who did this to you?' Kubar repeated.

In a flash, memories of those last few moments before darkness engulfed his world exploded through his mind once more.

'It was... Tarek,' he said, swallowing down the rising tide of nausea. He reached down and patted his pockets, feeling for the objects that were supposed to be there but weren't. 'He knocked me out, took my phone... and my key card.'

Kubar was moving before Jibril had even finished speaking, abandoning the injured man to reach for his cell phone. He was barely able to hold his wrath in check as he punched in a number and waited for it to connect.

What a fool he'd been! He'd suspected something was wrong the moment he learned of Sowan's rescue in such deceptively easy fashion. Too easy for the professionals hired to abduct him. It was a play, designed to get him back inside the Mukhabarat, though to what end he had no idea. Only Sowan himself could tell them.

And he *would* tell them. Kubar would make sure of it personally.

At last someone picked up, and Kubar wasted no time on pleasantries. 'Security? This is Bishr Kubar. The director has been attacked and his key card stolen by Tarek Sowan. I repeat, Director Jibril's key card has been compromised. Cancel his security clearance, lock down the building and arrest Sowan right away. Move!'

–

A wide, tree-lined central avenue led away from the main office complex, heading towards the security gate on the perimeter. With bushes and lawns on either side of the road, it was a deceptively pleasant environment considering the compound's sinister purpose, though Sowan understood the reasoning well enough. The greenery had been put in place for practical rather than aesthetic reasons, helping to screen activity within the compound from prying eyes in the city beyond its walls.

Seated behind the wheel of Jibril's car, Sowan turned onto this avenue and gave it some gas. It took all his self control not to floor it towards the compound's exit, as excitement and elation at his approaching freedom vied with the growing threat that it could all come to a crashing halt. Every second that passed carried him further away from the office complex behind, but also increased the chances that someone would raise the alarm.

But he was close now. All that remained was to bluff his way through the security checkpoint at the main gate, and then he could escape into the city beyond. He was almost certain that he could persuade or intimidate the guards on the gate into letting him pass, even if he didn't have the correct paperwork. After all, he had served here for a number of years and was well known to most of them.

They would let him go. He would make this work.

'Listen to me, Ryan,' he said, speaking into the phone that he now had wedged against his shoulder. 'I was wrong about Faulkner's involvement. It went even deeper than I thought.'

'What do you mean?'

'The man you extracted from Paris; he was an American operative. Part of a plan to stage a coup, overthrow the government. Faulkner betrayed him to us, but the Americans found out and demanded my life in return. I think he is trying to play both sides against each other for his own gain.'

'That doesn't make any sense,' Drake argued. 'Recovering him was an Agency-led operation. If the man from Paris was CIA, it would have been red-flagged before we even left Langley.'

'Then perhaps he was not CIA,' Sowan suggested. 'Perhaps this was a private venture. Another group that your Agency wasn't aware of.'

Whatever the case, the answers they needed lay in the laptop resting on the passenger seat beside him. Getting it to safety and deciphering its contents might well prove to be the only way out of this, both for himself and for Drake.

His thoughts were intruded upon as the main gate rolled into view. A pair of armoured security booths stood on either side of the road, with lowered barriers and a concrete chicane built to control the flow of traffic. Watch towers stood guard over the approach road, ready to take down anyone trying to approach without authorization.

Through the barriers and the concrete roadblocks, Sowan could just glimpse the buildings and streets and fast-flowing traffic of central Tripoli. Barely fifty yards away; so agonizingly close. All that stood between him and freedom was the trio of armed soldiers pulling guard duty, the leader of whom waved him down as he approached.

'I have to go,' he said, slipping the phone into his pocket.

–

This was it. Having emerged onto street level just a couple of blocks away, Drake was afforded a close enough view of the formidable security checkpoint to make out the vehicle that had just slowed to a stop.

He was too far away to see Sowan's face without binoculars, but he knew it was him. The man, and the evidence he had recovered, were little more than a hundred yards away.

His radio earpiece crackled into life. 'Monarch, do you have eyes-on?'

'Affirmative, Envoy. I have him in sight,' he replied, surreptitiously touching his radio transmitter. 'He's stopped at the main gate.'

'Copy that,' came McKnight's reply, the strain in her voice evident now that the time had come. 'What's your position?'

'I'm on an intersection two blocks to the north-east, beside an outdoor cafe.'

'I don't like it.'

'What's to like?' he bit back. 'We're committed now. We have to see it through.'

'You're too close,' she warned him. 'They have agents all over this area. Back off before they spot you, Monarch.'

'I told him I'd be here.'

'And he knows that. He could be using this to draw us in.' He heard an exhalation of breath. 'If he screws us, we're totally exposed here.'

Drake clenched his fists, windblown dust stinging his eyes as he strained to watch events play out, so agonizingly close but so terribly far. The silenced automatic was a cold, heavy weight pressing against his back, hidden beneath his sweat-stained shirt.

In this deadly game of deception, he had nothing left to go on but his intuition. His choice was simple – fold and run, or stick it out and risk everything on this last gamble. Whether his intuition was right or wrong depended on what happened in the next few seconds.

'Stick to the plan,' he said quietly. 'He won't let us down.'

Forcing calm into his mind and body, Sowan rolled down his window as the officer in charge of the checkpoint came forward to speak with him.

'Evening, sir,' the guard said, nodding in greeting. 'Can I see your ID?'

A young man, probably no more than thirty years old, clean-shaven, tall and in good shape. The kind of man the Mukhabarat liked to have standing at their checkpoints for the rest of the country to see.

Sowan recognized him as a Corporal Ibrahim, and recalled that he'd always been fairly laid back and friendly compared to some of the men who stood this post. The kind of man who might be willing to overlook a few irregularities for a trusted employee.

Perhaps.

Reaching into pocket, he handed over Jibril's security pass. As he'd expected, it didn't take Ibrahim long to spot the problem.

'I'm sorry, sir. This doesn't seem to be your card.'

Sowan made a face – the pained expression of a man about to make an uncomfortable confession. 'I know. I lost my own card when I lost my house last night.'

Ibrahim's eyes opened wider as his words sank in. Like most of his comrades, he had seen the news broadcasts about the attack on a house in central Tripoli the night before; the images of the burned-out shell of the building and the reports of gunfire and car chases during the raid. There had been plenty of speculation that terrorists from Egypt or Chad or even the disgruntled Berber population in the west of the country were responsible, but few solid facts.

The details had been kept as a closely guarded secret, even within the Mukhabarat. The revelation that one of their own had been the victim of this attack was enough to leave the young corporal stunned.

'I–I'm sorry. I wasn't told.'

'I was hoping to take a look at the damage myself, see if anything could be salvaged,' Sowan went on with grim resignation, capitalizing on the guard's reaction. 'Hussein was good enough to lend me his car and his badge for an hour or so. I know it's not protocol, but it would mean a lot to me if I could go.'

Ibrahim swallowed, clearly torn. What Sowan was suggesting was a breach of regulations, and if he was found out then it could mean serious repercussions for all of them. But Tarek Sowan had served the agency for some time, was well respected and trusted. Aside from that, the man had lost everything. He deserved a little compassion.

'No more than an hour?' he asked, uncertain.

Sowan nodded. Ibrahim couldn't see, but his grip on the steering wheel was so tight that his hands hurt.

'All right. I'll swipe you out,' Ibrahim said, sliding the card through an electronic reader inside the guard hut.

Sowan let out a breath, his heart surging with elation. He'd made it! He was in the clear!

But instead of handing the card back and raising the barrier, Ibrahim frowned, staring at his computer screen with a deep frown creasing his brow. His eyes flicked to Sowan, briefly perplexed, but filled with a growing wariness.

That was when Sowan knew. Something was wrong.

He'd been discovered.

Perhaps someone had found Jibril and realized his ID card had been stolen, or perhaps the man himself had recovered enough to raise the alarm. Whatever the reason, the result was the same. In the office complex behind them, Sowan heard the distinctive wail of alarms blaring out as the complex went into lockdown.

Turning his attention back to the car and its driver, Ibrahim reached for the sidearm holstered at his waist, training and discipline rapidly winning out over compassion and familiarity. 'Sir, I'm afraid I'll have to ask you to step out of the car.'

Sowan wasn't about to wait around for Ibrahim to detain him. Stamping down on the accelerator, he gripped the wheel tight as the car rocketed forwards, breaking through the lowered barrier with such force that it left a spider's web of cracks across the windshield.

Behind him, he could hear Ibrahim and the other guards on the gate shouting out, commanding him to stop. Sowan ignored them. He was committed now, with nothing left to lose and his future hanging by a thread; to stop would be suicide.

Swinging the wheel hard left, he forced the car through the concrete chicane, wheels skidding and clawing at the dusty road surface as the vehicle's traction control fought to stop it spinning out. Behind, he heard the distinctive crackle of gunfire, and ducked down as the rear windshield exploded in a shower of glass fragments.

Frightening it might have been, but the fire being directed his way was still panicked and uncoordinated, and unlikely to stop him. All he cared about now was putting distance between himself and the compound before they could organize a pursuit.

Like most facilities of its sort, the majority of its security measures were focussed outward to prevent people getting in, not to keep supposedly trustworthy employees from getting out.

Rocketing down the main approach road at full speed, Sowan swung the car right into the busy main drag beyond, narrowly avoiding a collision with a crowded bus that was heading in the opposite direction. He gritted his teeth and wrestled with the wheel, bringing the fishtailing car back under control and ignoring the angry horn-blasts left in his wake.

–

Drake watched in disbelief as the Lexus roared away from the vehicle checkpoint, taking small-arms fire along the way before barrelling straight into the main drag beyond. In a matter of seconds Sowan had swung hard right, merged with the busy traffic and disappeared from Drake's view, though the horn blasts and hard-revving engines announced his progress just as effectively.

Either Sowan had bottled it and panicked, or he'd sensed the game was up and was trying to make good his escape before they could box him in. Whatever the reason, he had played his last hand now. A police chase through the centre of Tripoli could only end one way.

All that remained now was to try to salvage something from this mess.

'Fuck, he's going for it!' Drake spoke quickly into his radio, shoving his way through the crowds that had stopped to rubberneck as the drama unfolded. 'He's been compromised.'

'Are we blown too?' McKnight asked immediately.

'Can't tell. Hang back – I'm in pursuit now.'

–

Sowan's heart was pounding, adrenaline rushing through his veins as he desperately weaved the big Lexus through the obstacle course of cars lying before him, taking ridiculous chances on narrow gaps, and losing a wing mirror to a near miss.

The highway traffic was a mixture of ultra-modern 4x4 cruisers (a sure sign of a driver who had profited from the relaxing of the oil embargo), luxury sedans and clapped out old vans and hatchbacks held together by nothing more than the sheer willpower of their drivers. But old or new, all of them were caked brown with dust, and all of their owners seemed to be angry at him.

Shoving his hand into his pocket, he grasped the cell phone that he'd hidden during his approach to the vehicle checkpoint.

'Ryan. Can you hear me?'

'I'm here. What the fuck's going on?' Drake demanded.

'I'm sorry. The alarm was raised, I had to do something,' he gasped, swinging the Lexus through a gap between a modern sedan and a rusted pickup truck, stamping on the accelerator to power through an intersection up ahead. 'They're closing in on me.'

'No shit,' Drake countered. Sowan could hear him breathing harder as he sprinted through the crowded streets, trying to get a look at the chase. 'You need to ditch the car.'

'No!' Fleeing on foot was out of the question. Simply walking unaided required a great effort with his injured leg.

'Listen to me! Use your head,' Drake implored him. 'You're in a stolen car – they know the make and model, and they *will* find you. You're drawing more attention to yourself with every block you cover. Find a quiet alleyway nearby, slow down and for Christ's sake get out. Stay on the phone and I'll come and find you.'

Sowan knew he was talking sense, even if he didn't want to hear it. Approaching the intersection, he eased off the gas, allowing the Lexus to slow down a little. Already his mind was racing ahead, thinking of possible locations to ditch the vehicle.

Only one came to mind.

'There is a market nearby. There are many back streets we can—'

His sentence was cut short as ten tonnes of articulated truck slammed into the left side of the Lexus, crumpling the chassis and shattering windows. The big vehicle was hurled across the road by the force of the impact like a toy flung by a petulant child. Sowan didn't even have time to react as the car rolled over and over, showering him with broken glass and debris.

Then suddenly there was a loud shuddering bang, an explosion of white light, and he knew no more.

Chapter 40

Left behind by Sowan's frantic rush to get clear of the area, Drake didn't see the crash as it happened, but he did hear the crunch of the impact, the tinkle of shattering glass and the tearing roar as an engine at high revs was suddenly broken apart.

The moment he heard the unmistakable sound of metal impacting with metal, Drake felt his blood run cold. Straightaway he knew that the short-lived escape attempt had come to a violent, jarring halt.

Rounding a corner, he was just in time to see the silver Lexus come to rest on its roof, lying in a crumpled heap on the sidewalk.

'Oh fuck.'

–

Sowan's mind drifted back from the verge of unconsciousness, alerted by the distant sound of voices. Something was happening, he knew. Something important.

With great effort he forced his eyes open, and found to his surprise that the world was upside down. Beyond the shattered windshield, he could see the intersection where he'd been hit, the line of commercial buildings stretching out on either side, the rough potholed road now above him. Dry windblown grit whipped in through the broken windows, peppering his face and eyes.

He'd been hit, he realized then. He remembered trying to speed through the intersection, ignoring the flow of traffic in the hope of making it past unscathed. He remembered the sudden appearance of headlights from his left, and the terrible, explosive impact that followed.

The vehicle must have come to rest on its roof. Still strapped into his seat, he was inverted. How foolish he must have looked to anyone observing him, some part of his mind reflected.

He wasn't sure if he was hurt or not. He wasn't in much pain, but everything felt hazy and disconnected, his reactions deadened as if he was intoxicated. He was vaguely aware of something warm and wet dripping across his face, and smelled the distinctive odour of petrol.

Something was lying on the roof next to him. A simple canvas rucksack, the material frayed and worn in places, but bulked out by the shape of something hard and square inside. The laptop. The information he'd risked everything to retrieve.

Reaching out, he grasped one of the straps and pulled it towards him, dragging it through broken glass and pieces of shattered plastic. If he could just get out of here with it...

The sound of more voices nearby caught his attention, raised and angry. He could hear boots scuffling on the tarmac outside.

'Hurry, get it open! Get him out of there!'

–

Drake arrived just in time to watch Sowan's arrest. Moments after the crash, a military-patterned jeep – no doubt dispatched from the compound Sowan had just fled – had come screeching to a halt next to the wrecked vehicle.

He couldn't be sure of the make, but it looked like a Kozlik; a rugged little Soviet-era jeep that had been in service since the 1970s. It made sense, since most of Libya's outdated military equipment had come from the USSR.

'They've got him,' Drake hissed into his radio, watching as a pair of armed soldiers worked to lever the driver's-side door open. More would surely be here imminently. 'Monarch has eyes on two tangos.'

'It's over. Break off, Monarch.' The concern in her voice was obvious even over the radio net. 'You can't help him now.'

Bollocks he couldn't. No way was he letting Sowan get himself killed when they'd risked so much to get him here. And in any case, one way or another, Drake was leaving with that laptop.

'Stand by, Envoy,' he instructed, reaching behind his back.

–

Suddenly the vehicle's chassis resounded with a dull metallic thud. A crunching, grinding noise was coming from the passenger door. Someone was hammering and levering it with something, trying to wrench it open.

'Careful, no sparks! I smell gas.'

It was then that Sowan spotted a pair of combat boots outside, scuffed and dirty but unmistakably of military origin. This was no group of concerned citizens attempting to rescue an injured man from a wrecked car, but armed soldiers dispatched to bring him in.

And they were going to get him. There was nothing he could do to stop it as the lock finally gave way and the partially buckled door was hauled open from outside.

A pair of thick, burly arms appeared through the gap, followed a moment later by an unshaven, angry face that focussed immediately on him. The hands reached out and unlatched his seatbelt, causing him to fall headfirst onto the roof.

Dazed and with stars and blobs of light dancing across his vision, Sowan was powerless to resist as they grasped him by the shirt and hauled him out through the buckled doorway, dragging the rucksack behind. Through fogged eyes, he could see locals gathering to watch the spectacle unfold. Nobody came forward to offer assistance, and nobody protested his rough treatment at the hands of the pair of soldiers who had apprehended him. They were wise enough not to intervene.

Nearby, the truck that had destroyed his car was still sitting at the intersection, its forward cab crumpled by the impact while steam billowed from the punctured radiator. The Lexus itself had fared no better. Its chassis was buckled and twisted, one whole side caved in as if it had been slammed by a giant fist. Its snapped axles jutted outward like shattered rib bones.

This was it, he realized, as the larger of the two men dragged him towards a military jeep parked beside the wrecked car. They were going to haul him right back to Mukhabarat headquarters, where he would be tortured and interrogated until he told them everything they wanted to know. Then, if he was lucky, he would be executed.

He had failed. His desperate, hastily conceived final gamble had been his undoing. More than that, he had broken his promise to Laila. There would be no joyful reunion for the two of them, no living out the remainder of their days in anonymity, no chance to find peace together.

It was at that moment, when the awful reality of what the remainder of his short life held for him was beginning to sink in, that everything changed.

There was a muted thump, a dull wet crunch, and the man dragging him towards the jeep suddenly released his hold and collapsed to the ground, his legs simply giving way beneath him as if the mind controlling them had ceased to function. Sowan felt something warm and wet splash his face, and twisted around in time to see the man fall in a crumpled heap, blood pooling around what remained of his skull.

His comrade had seen it as well, and instinctively turned to face this new and unexpected menace, his mouth already opening to shout out a warning. He never got a chance to say whatever he'd intended. A silenced round tore through his neck, destroying his windpipe. He went down, clawing at what remained of his throat while his blood painted the dusty ground.

This sudden and unexpected act of violence wasn't lost on the small crowd of onlookers, who cried out in alarm and began to run, scattering in all directions. Many had witnessed attacks like this before, and had no wish to become caught in the crossfire.

In disbelief, Sowan looked up as a man emerged from the chaos all around and sprinted straight towards him. A white man armed with a silenced handgun.

'Can you walk?' Drake asked, crouching down beside him with his weapon clutched in a white-knuckle grip.

Such was his shock at Drake's sudden arrival that Sowan couldn't even piece together a coherent response. All he could manage was a nod.

'We need to get off this street, now!'

With that, Drake hooked one arm beneath Sowan's and hauled the man to his feet, ignoring the cry of pain. Sowan could feel warm blood trickling down his leg and guessed the stitching around the gunshot wound had come away, though there was nothing he could do about it for now. All he could do was force himself onwards, clutching the rucksack as tight as Drake held his weapon, and hope that the artery itself wasn't ruptured again.

With the injured man in hand, Drake turned towards the wrecked Lexus. The fuel tank had ruptured during the crash, leaving a stream of petrol pooling around the upturned vehicle.

Leveling his weapon at the wreck, Drake snapped off a couple of shots at the buckled chassis, focussing his fire near the ground. The first and second rounds punched straight through, but the third ricocheted off the steel frame, producing a little shower of sparks that settled on the petrol-soaked pavement.

There was no need to watch what happened next. Turning away just as the first flames began to leap up, creeping towards the broken fuel tank, Drake practically dragged Sowan towards a nearby clothing shop that fronted out onto the street.

Shoving their way in through the front door, the two men hurried past racks of jeans, jackets and t-shirts of all shapes and sizes, heading for the rear of the store. Tinny pop music that Sowan didn't recognize was playing from a pair of domestic speakers crudely screwed to the walls above the counter; a strange contrast to the chaos outside.

The owner, a young man in a black shirt that looked far more expensive than the merchandize he was selling, caught sight of them right away. Deciding he wanted no part of whatever trouble they were involved in, he jerked his arm towards the street and started to shout out a warning to leave. However, the sight of a silenced pistol aimed at his head was enough to persuade him otherwise.

'Where's the back door?' Drake demanded in Arabic. 'The back door!'

The young man stared blankly at him for a moment or two, before pointing with a trembling hand to a curtained-off area behind the counter.

At the same moment, the flames which had been licking at the wrecked car at last reached the fuel tank and ignited its contents. There was a bright orange flash which illuminated the interior of the shop, the mannequins and clothing racks painting ghastly shadows across the walls, followed by a thunderous boom that shattered the store's windows and left Drake's ears ringing.

Glancing around, both men could see the fireball which had engulfed the car illuminating the night sky. The flames had reached almost to the front of the store, making access from the street impossible. For now at least, nobody could pursue them that way.

With the store owner now cowering behind the counter and clutching his ears, Drake pressed forward, shoving the curtain aside with the barrel of this automatic, to reveal what presumably served as the shop's store room. Racks and cardboard boxes of extra stock were piled everywhere, some reaching almost to the ceiling. As promised, a fire door with a simple bar lock was set into the brick wall at the back.

'Let's go. Move,' Drake said, leading Sowan towards it. A single swift kick was enough to send it flying open, allowing them to hurry out into the service alley running behind the line of shops.

As they did so, Drake's radio earpiece crackled into life.

'Monarch, what the hell is going on?' McKnight demanded over the radio net. 'I assume that explosion was you?'

'Had to cover our escape,' Drake replied, hurrying onwards. 'I have Sowan, and the laptop.'

He heard a muffled curse, and guessed she wasn't pleased by his reckless actions. 'I hope they were worth it, because you've brought the whole goddamn Libyan army down on this place.'

'Then it's time to make a sharp exit.' Now that they had what they needed, he didn't intend to spend a minute longer in Libya than he had to. 'We're in a service alley heading east from the crash site. Rendezvous with us at the far end.'

From what he could tell, the alleyway ran for another hundred yards or so before opening out onto a main street beyond.

'Copy that.'

'And we need a vehicle,' Drake went on. 'They'll lock down this entire area within minutes. You hearing this, Envoy?'

'A vehicle. Sure, why not?' she replied, her sarcasm obvious. 'Envoy's on it. Stand by.'

With that, the radio clicked off.

—

'Goddamn you, Ryan,' McKnight hissed, backing into an alleyway that ran between two residential buildings.

This evening was rapidly going from bad to worse, to disastrous. Shepherd teams were supposed to operate covertly, moving unseen and ideally completing their clandestine objectives without anyone even knowing they were there. What was unfolding around them now was about as far removed from their modus operandi as it was possible to be.

But she couldn't change it, couldn't undo what had already been done. All she could do now was try to stop them all getting killed.

Reaching up, she gripped the seam of the loose shirt she'd been wearing and yanked hard, tearing it roughly apart at the shoulder. This done, she unsheathed her field knife and drew the tip of the blade across the exposed skin. She felt the sting as the wickedly sharp blade bit into her flesh, followed by the warm upwelling of blood that quickly began to trickle down her exposed skin.

Her improvised blade job certainly wouldn't pass close inspection, but from a distance in poor lighting conditions, it might be enough to convince people that she was seriously hurt. A victim of the explosion nearby in need of help.

Checking that the handgun was still within easy reach, she took a deep breath and rushed out of the alleyway, staggering onto the road beyond while clutching her bloodied shoulder.

'Help!' she cried, doing her best to look like a panic-stricken bomb victim. 'Someone help me!'

The first driver she encountered was having none of it, and immediately swung his car into the oncoming lane to avoid her, honking his horn as he sped past at high revs. However, her second encounter proved to be more fruitful, mainly because traffic in the opposite lane was heavier and she had positioned herself in such a way as to be virtually unavoidable.

Hearing a screech of brakes, she watched as a pair of headlights came shuddering to a halt mere feet away. She couldn't tell the make and model yet, but judging by the low profile and throaty engine sound, it seemed to be some kind of sports car. Not exactly the unobtrusive vehicle she'd hoped for, but beggars couldn't be choosers. Clutching her bleeding shoulder, she staggered around to the driver's door just as it swung open and he stepped out to meet her.

'Oh, God!' she gasped, hoping to get as close to him as possible. 'Thank you! I need to get to a hospital. Please!'

She could see the driver more clearly now that she was out of the glare of the headlights. As she'd expected given his choice of ride, he was a young man in his early twenties, not very tall but broad and bulky like he'd been hitting the gym hard. She could see the bulge of overdeveloped pectorals and biceps beneath his tight-fitting t-shirt. The sort of man who could prove to be a handful if she didn't deal with him quickly.

'American?' he grunted, sounding more aggressive than surprised. It was hard to tell if he understood anything she'd said, but it didn't really matter now. She had him where she needed him.

The moment had come. Reaching behind her, she gripped the butt of the automatic and yanked it from her jeans, swinging it around and jamming the barrel of the silencer under his chin.

'Get away from the car. Move!' she hissed, all trace of fear and panic having vanished from her now. She was staring right into his eyes, daring him to make a move.

No way was he going to try it – she knew that within a second or two. Shock at finding himself the victim of a carjacking quickly gave way to the instinct for self-preservation, and he raised his hands to show he was unarmed. He might not have understood the words, but he got the gist of what she wanted.

Taking a step backward, he moved away from the driver's door, allowing her to slip into his place. McKnight in turn allowed him to back away, though she kept him covered with the silenced weapon.

'Get the fuck out of here,' she said, gesturing with the gun. 'Go now!'

He didn't need to be told twice, turning and fleeing down the sidewalk while yelling abuse at her the whole way. She imagined he would hail the first police officer he could find, but that didn't matter right now. She intended to be long gone by then.

Ducking inside, she slipped into the driver's seat and slammed the door shut.

–

'Come on, you lazy bastard. Almost there,' Drake said, having to exert more effort to keep Sowan plodding forward. A combination of exertion, pain and blood-loss was slowing him down, and there was nothing Drake could do for him until they were safely out of here. For now at least there was no choice but to tough it out.

'I can't believe Jibril would do this to me,' Sowan said, lost in his own world now. 'Betray a man he's known for ten years, hand me over to the Americans without a second thought.'

'He fucked you over. Believe me, it happens more than you think,' Drake assured him, his weapon sweeping the shadows ahead. 'Let's concentrate on getting out of here so you can return the favour.'

'Why did you come back for me?' Sowan asked suddenly.

Drake couldn't blame him for being curious. If he'd been in the man's position, he would have felt much the same way. Unfortunately for Sowan, he wasn't. He'd risked his life and the lives of his friends to get this far – he needed to know it hadn't been for nothing.

'Don't get all misty-eyed. I needed the laptop,' he said, quick to silence any notion that his actions were motivated by honour or loyalty.' That's all.'

'You could have taken the bag and left me behind.'

Drake shrugged, saying nothing.

Taking his silence for what it was, Sowan glanced at him. 'If I didn't know better, I would say—'

His sentence was interrupted suddenly by a heavy crunch as something slammed into his chest with such force that he was knocked backwards, out of Drake's grasp, landing in a sprawl nearby. A cloud of red was already painting the dusty ground beneath him.

Drake reacted immediately, his mind switching gears into survival mode in the blink of an eye. Throwing himself aside before the shooter could turn their attention to him, he landed behind an overflowing steel dumpster, pushed up against the rear wall of one of the commercial units which backed onto the alleyway. He hadn't heard the shot, which meant they must have fired from some distance away, probably from an elevated position that provided a good field of fire over the alleyway.

Backing up against the dumpster, he let out a silent curse of anger and frustration and anguish all mingled together. Had the Libyan intelligence service caught up with them? Was it the military? The police? He had no idea. All he knew was that a sniper with some kind of high-powered rifle was covering the area, and until they were removed from play, he was pinned down.

Gripping his automatic tight, he glanced over at the man he had risked so much to rescue. Sowan was lying on his back near the far side of the alleyway, still moving feebly as if to rise, though one look at him was enough to confirm to Drake that these were his last moments. The gunshot wound in the centre of his chest was oozing a steady stream of frothy blood from his punctured lungs, and there was likely to be an even larger exit wound at the back.

'Don't move, Tarek,' Drake hissed. 'I'm coming to get you.'

Slowly his head turned until he made eye contact with Drake. The damage done by that sniper round had robbed him of the ability to speak, but it didn't matter now. The look in his eyes said everything – he was dying, and he knew it. To attempt a rescue now would be futile.

'I'm sorry,' Drake whispered, knowing how pathetic a sentiment it was. But it was all he could offer the dying man.

The rucksack was lying beside him, dropped where he fell. With a trembling hand Sowan reached out, gripped it by one of the straps and hurled it across the alleyway in a final desperate exercise of strength, managing to get it within feet of Drake's position. Then with a final shuddering gasp, he lay still.

He was gone.

Drake allowed himself to feel only a fleeting moment of regret for the man's death, knowing grief was an emotion he could ill afford at that moment. Survival was the priority now, and even that hung in the balance.

His gaze rested on the rucksack that Sowan had tried to throw to him in his final moments, lying so tantalizingly close yet so maddeningly far. If he lost it now, then everything they had risked their lives for had been for nothing.

Lying several feet away in open ground, it was impossible to reach without exposing himself to the sniper's fire.

'Shit,' he hissed. Reaching up, he gripped the metal arm fixed into the side of the dumpster designed to help load it into garbage trucks, and, summoning up all the strength he possessed, began to drag the heavy unit towards the rucksack. The bulky container was fully laden and difficult to handle, but the rollers fixed to the bottom provided just enough mobility to allow him to shift it. Slowly, inch by inch, it began to move.

Drake felt the impact of another shot reverberate through the frame, and suddenly the movement ceased as the dumpster tilted slightly, one corner now resting against the ground. It took him a moment to realize the sniper had just shot away one of the wheels.

That was when he acted. Taking a breath, he launched himself forward, managing to close his fingers around one of the bag's shoulder straps before yanking it towards him as he scrambled back behind cover.

He was just backing up against cover when a second round tore through the thin metal sheeting of the dumpster, exploding out the other side dangerously close and forcing Drake to duck down low as pieces of discarded trash fell around him.

It was then that he felt an odd chill run through him, as if an icy hand had been laid on his skin, and realized with a vague sense of disconnection that something warm and wet was flowing down his arm. The round hadn't missed him, he knew then.

'You know, I rather expected I'd find you in a place like this, Ryan,' a voice called out from the mouth of the alleyway. A smooth, polished voice carrying an unmistakably English accent. 'Amongst the trash of the world.'

Drake closed his eyes for a moment as the realization sank in. It wasn't the Libyan police, the military or their feared intelligence service that were shooting at him. It was Faulkner who had tracked him down. Somehow he'd anticipated this move, had predicted that Drake would try to use Sowan to gather evidence against him.

And Drake had walked right into his trap.

Chapter 41

Bishr Kubar was pacing the room like a caged lion, bristling with anger that had yet to find an outlet. The building's security centre was a big room populated by more than a dozen staff members on permanent duty. With computer terminals every-where and most of one whole wall given over to flat-screen monitors displaying security-camera footage from all around the compound, it was a busy place at the best of times.

Tonight, with a security breach at the main gate and an operation underway to track down the escaped fugitive, the place was in virtual chaos. Security operatives were directing rapid streams of instructions into phones and radio sets, signals technicians hurried back and forth between stations, and overseers attempted to coordinate the whole operation.

Several computer screens were displaying footage of Jibril's stolen vehicle, now turned on its roof and engulfed in flames.

'Someone talk to me,' he growled, furious that Sowan had managed to escape the compound and was now apparently roaming free in the city beyond. 'What's happening out there?'

One of the overseers was the first to step up. 'We're still getting reports in, but it looks like the suspect's car was involved in a crash at an intersection. Two of our field operatives tried to pull him from the wreckage, but they were taken out by a second man who carried him away. It looks like he torched the vehicle to cover their escape.'

So the man who had been pulling Sowan's strings had decided to reveal himself. 'Where are they now?'

'We're vectoring in all available ground units.'

That wasn't his question. 'Lock down the entire area, now. Nobody gets in or out.'

'We're trying, but it takes time. There are hundreds of civilians in—'

'Do I look like I care?' Kubar shouted. 'Just get it done!'

–

'Shame about Tarek there. The man had potential,' Faulkner went on. 'His problem was that he was too damned honest. This isn't a game for men like him. But *you*, on the other hand… you could make a career out of lying to people, Ryan. Tell me, what line did you spin to get him to cooperate? I'll get you and your wife to a safe place? We can take down the evil David Faulkner together?'

277

Drake cursed under his breath as he pressed a hand against the torn flesh of his left arm. The bone didn't seem to be broken, and he could still feel and move the fingers, which was a good sign. If the round had severed nerves or shattered the bone, that entire limb would have been out of action.

'I'm wondering why you're wasting time talking to me when you should be running and hiding,' he replied, reaching down to unscrew the silencer from the barrel of his weapon. 'I know what you've been doing here. I know you're playing the Americans against the Libyans, selling secrets to every man and his dog, trying to be everyone's friend at once. I wonder how both sides will feel when they find out the truth?'

At this, he caught a low chuckle of amusement. 'What makes you think they will? Come on, we both know you're not getting out of this alley. You've done well to get here, but this is as far as you go. Just give me the laptop and we can call this one a draw.'

With the silencer free, Drake placed it in his pocket and raised the automatic. There was a reason Faulkner was talking at such length, and it wasn't for the sake of dramatic tension. He was stalling, keeping Drake occupied while his men moved into position. He would want to finish this quickly, before the Libyans could form a cordon around the area.

Hearing the faint crunch of boots on the sandy ground, he leaned out just far enough to catch sight of one of Faulkner's men advancing down the alley towards him, keeping close to the wall and using the dumpsters as cover. They were closing in to finish him off, using the sniper to keep him pinned down while they moved in for the kill.

Gripping the automatic, Drake pointed it down the alleyway and pulled the trigger. There was a thunderous crack as the round exited the barrel, followed quickly by two more. If any of the Libyan operatives in the area were in doubt about where he'd fled to, he had just announced his presence about as loudly as possible.

The answering volley of silenced submachine gun and sniper fire slammed into the dumpster, practically tearing the metal shell apart and forcing Drake to flatten himself against the ground as the barrage continued. Pinned down and low on ammunition, there was little he could do to stop what was coming.

–

'We may have him!' the overseer called out, a radio headset pressed against one ear. 'Reports of gunfire coming from an alleyway in the vicinity of the car crash.'

Kubar was up and moving before the man had even finished speaking. Getting in close, he stared him hard in the eye. 'Scramble every unit you have in the area right now. Do *not* let this man escape. Do you understand?'

The look of fear in the overseer's eyes told Kubar that his orders, and the threat that came with them, were well understood.

At the entrance to the alleyway, Faulkner clenched his fists as the furious gun battle continued. This was taking too long, was too loud and obtrusive. The Libyans would have heard the unmistakable sound of gunfire and would be vectoring units to the scene at that very moment.

Reaching up, he touched his radio, managing to keep his voice a lot calmer than he felt when he spoke. 'Caitlin, do you have a shot?'

Caitlin Macguire was one of the best snipers he'd ever encountered. A veteran of the Ulster Volunteer Force in Northern Ireland, she'd been responsible for assassinating half a dozen IRA members before she'd turned thirty, plus one of her own men suspected of turning traitor. The Troubles might have simmered down since then, but Faulkner had found use for her. Time and again she had proven herself a ruthless and efficient killer, and she was sitting on a rooftop with a silenced sniper rifle barely two hundred yards away.

'If I had, do you not think I'd take it?' It took a brave man indeed to interrupt her during her work. 'Little bastard's dug in tight, so he is.'

No matter, Faulkner thought. He had another surprise for Drake. And if he was right, they should be in position any time now.

–

It was part instinct and part intuition born from years of experience that prompted Drake to look up. In urban combat like this, where streets and alleys could easily be turned into kill-zones, holding the high ground was vital, and Faulkner possessed both the manpower and the initiative to take it.

Glancing up to the residential blocks overlooking the alleyway, he spotted a figure sprinting just above the edge of the rooftop, their movement silhouetted against the electric lighting behind. A second shooter moving to outflank him while he was occupied with the first target in the alleyway below.

Raising his automatic and taking careful aim, he exhaled slowly, allowing the tension to leave the muscles in his arms and shoulders for a few precious moments, trying to forget the pain of torn flesh. The key to accurate shooting was not to tense up, not to anticipate the shot and the recoil but just to go with them when they happened.

It was the same lesson that had been drilled into him countless times when he'd been a young infantry soldier on the shooting range. Don't think about the shot. Just pull the trigger.

Relax. Aim. Fire.

The Browning kicked back against his wrist as he loosed the first shot, followed immediately by a second. Two shots, followed by a click as the hammer came down on an empty chamber. He heard a muffled cry up above, and suddenly the figure stumbled and disappeared from sight.

In response, the operative in the alleyway opened fire again, snapping off short bursts that slammed into the dumpster and ricocheted off the ground, keeping Drake pinned down while he advanced, manoeuvring for a shot.

Drake glanced down at the weapon in his hands. The slide had flown back to reveal an empty breech. Out of ammunition, there was nothing more he could do as his enemy closed in to finish him.

Nothing except save the one person who didn't deserve to be here.

Reaching up, he hit his radio transmitter. 'Sam, get out of here,' he whispered. 'We're blown. Get clear now.'

There was no response. In that instant, Drake felt his blood run cold. Had she been captured? Had she fallen prey to the same sniper that had taken out Sowan? Had another innocent life been lost because of him?

These were the last thoughts to enter his head as Faulkner's hit man rounded the dumpster, weapon raised and finger on the trigger. Pinned down by the sniper, there was nowhere for Drake to run, no place left to hide, nothing to fall back on. He saw a trace of a smile as the man swung the barrel of his submachine gun towards him.

This was it.

At that moment, the alleyway was suddenly filled with the throaty roar of a car engine at high revs, and Drake's would-be killer was illuminated with dazzling intensity by a pair of headlights.

He started to turn towards the source of the light, instinctively bringing the weapon around to counter this possible new threat, but never got the chance to act. In a terrifying blur of movement and the sickening thump of flesh meeting with fast moving metal, he was thrown up into the air, rolling clear over the windshield of the car that had barrelled into him, landing in a heap near the far wall.

Drake stared in disbelief as the car came to a screeching halt a few meters beyond. An old-model Toyota Celica; the kind of thing he used to see cruising along his local high street as a kid, its once-red paintwork faded by years of exposure to sun and windblown sand. The front brakes were now fully engaged, but the rear wheels continued to spin and skid on the dusty ground, kicking up clouds of dust and sand that enveloped the alleyway in a matter of seconds.

A smoke screen.

'Ryan! Get in, for Christ's sake!' he heard McKnight yell.

Drake didn't hesitate, didn't stop to question how she'd found him or the risk she was taking by being here. Sniper or no sniper, this was his only chance to get out.

Abandoning his position, he sprinted towards the vehicle with the rucksack clutched against his chest. With the passenger door already open for him, he threw himself inside just as the chassis resounded with the first impact of a high-powered sniper round. Though temporarily blinded by the dust kicked up by their arrival, the shooter was firing indiscriminately into the cloud, trying to kill the driver or disable the car.

'Go! Go!' Drake yelled, slamming the door closed. 'Drive!'

McKnight wasted no time, releasing the brakes and stomping on the accelerator just as another round shattered the rear window before embedding itself in the floor.

Drake could do little more than cling on for dear life as the walls of the alleyway sped by in a blur, the engine roaring as she pushed it to redline. The car might have been old and neglected, but its engine still had some horsepower lurking beneath the hood, and she was determined to use every ounce of it now.

Reaching the end of the alleyway, she swung the wheel hard over, turning left onto a main road so sharply that the car pitched dangerously sideways, two wheels threatening to leave the ground. Wrestling the wayward vehicle back under control with difficulty, she straightened their course and gunned the accelerator once more.

In a matter of seconds, they were clear.

–

Faulkner watched in silence as the car disappeared down the alley in a cloud of dust and tyre smoke, his jaw clenched tight, his face impassive. Only the look of barely concealed fury in his eyes betrayed his true emotions.

He had taken a great risk to come to Tripoli, believing he could intercept Drake and take out Sowan before they could cause further damage. His gamble had only partially paid off. Drake was as lucky as he was tenacious; a dangerous combination that had twice saved his life.

So absorbed was he in these thoughts that he was only vaguely aware of the sound of footsteps approaching from behind, the thump of boots on pavement, the click of weapons being raised.

Suddenly a voice yelled an instruction in Arabic. 'Hands up! Get your hands up now!'

Faulkner let out a faint sigh of exasperation. Another mess that needed to be cleaned up, he thought as he raised his hands and turned around to face his would-be captors.

A Libyan security detail – three operatives dressed in plain clothes, armed with a mixture of semi-automatics and submachine guns, all of which were trained on him.

'Down on your knees!' the leader of the group shouted. His companion was already reaching for his radio to report in on the situation. 'Down!'

'I'm sorry,' Faulkner responded, his Arabic smooth and polished after years of practice. 'If it means anything to you, I would have rather avoided this.'

The leader of the group frowned, then took a step towards him with his weapon raised. He never got a chance to take another. The high-powered sniper round that slammed into the back of his head dropped him like a stone, followed quickly by a second shot that took out his companion with the radio.

The third man was just turning towards the source of the shots when he too fell victim to Macguire's lethal sniper fire, falling to the ground in a jerking, quivering heap.

Faulkner spared them scarcely a glance as he strode away from the scene, reaching for his concealed radio. 'All units, pack it up. We're leaving.'

This situation was escalating beyond his ability to contain it. Sowan was dead at least, but as long as Drake remained alive he was a threat. A threat that had to be dealt with quickly if his work here was to survive.

Too much depended on this for it to fail now.

Chapter 42

They were clear.

After coming so close to disaster, neither Drake nor McKnight could quite bring themselves to believe it. At any moment they expected to find a convoy of Libyan army vehicles barring their path, or to catch the blue lights of police vehicles in their rear-view mirror. Neither thing happened, yet still the woman wouldn't ease off, keeping her foot planted firmly on the accelerator while banking left and right to avoid slower moving traffic.

Turning right at the next junction, McKnight spotted a quieter street up ahead and went for it, block-changing into fourth gear and stomping on the gas once more. The engine roared like a wild animal in response, rough and unrefined after years of abuse, but still with enough fight left in it to send them hurtling onwards.

'You all right?' she asked, unable to take her eyes off the road for fear of losing control of the fast-moving vehicle.

'I'm fine,' Drake mumbled. He barely felt the pain in his arm now, though he was vaguely aware that blood was dripping down his arm and staining the seat. Now that he was out of danger, for the moment at least, his mind was able to think beyond the bare essentials of survival, to begin to process what had just happened.

She glanced at the torn, bloodstained fabric of his shirt. 'You're bleeding.'

'I said I'm fine!' he snapped, struggling with the impotent rage that welled up inside.

They could have left the country already, could have made it to safety with Sowan and his wife in tow. But he had made the decision to come back here, to risk his life and the lives of everyone else on the foolish hope that they could somehow make all of this right. And another good man was dead because of it.

He'd been wrong about Sowan – he knew that now. Before he'd seen a ruthless, cold-hearted man who cared nothing for human lives or the suffering his work caused, but now he saw him for what he was. A good man in a bad place, who had tried to make the best of his situation.

And who had died for it.

'Faulkner was ready for us. He knew exactly what we were planning.'

He closed his eyes for a moment, trying to hold it back, trying to keep it under control. It was a futile effort.

'Fuck!' he snarled, slamming his fist into the dashboard.

'Stop it!' McKnight called out. 'He's gone, Ryan! I know it's a shitty thing to face up to, but you need to deal with it now. I need you thinking clearly.'

Drake said nothing to this. She was right, of course. Losing control now wasn't going to help anyone. But that didn't make him feel any less guilty for what had happened, or less angry at himself for failing to prevent it.

'I know what you're feeling. I know, but this wasn't your fault,' she carried on, quieter now. Her gaze lingered for a moment on the rucksack lying at his feet. 'Sowan found what we need. Now we have to make it count.'

Drake let out a breath, forcing those dark thoughts aside, forcing his mind to focus on the situation at hand and everything that had to happen for them to survive this night. Samantha was right. He could play the blame game later when circumstances permitted it, but for now the priority was reuniting with their friends and getting the fuck out of Libya for good.

Unzipping the rucksack, he reached inside and pulled the laptop out. Its casing was cracked and dented, damage likely sustained during the car crash, but he knew all that mattered was the hard drive. As long as that was intact, they still had a shot.

'We need to head south-west from here, away from the city,' he said, glancing around for landmarks that could aid navigation. He pointed to a road sign for Alzintan, which he remembered as belonging to the same mountainous region as Nalut. 'There. Take the next slip road.'

This she did, swinging them off the city street and onto a larger cross-country highway heading in a generally southern direction out into the desert. Easing off the gas a little, she merged with the other late-night traffic, hoping that the relative darkness would disguise the broken rear windscreen and bullet holes in the chassis.

Sooner or later they would have to ditch the highway or risk running into a police or military checkpoint, but for now the primary goal was to put some distance between themselves and the scene of the desperate gun battle.

With a relative period of calm now upon them, they lapsed into silence, each harbouring their own thoughts as the lights of oncoming traffic flitted past.

'Thank you,' Drake said quietly, breaking the silence.

She frowned. 'For what?'

'For coming back. I never got the chance to say it before, but you risked your life for me.' He looked over at her, reached out and laid a hand on her arm. 'I'd be dead if it wasn't for you, Sam.'

'What was I going to do? Leave you behind?' she said, feigning a wry smile. 'Keira would never let me hear the end of it.'

'Really? I thought she'd be glad to see the back of me.'

'You'd be surprised.'

She was trying to make light of it, but he sensed how much this meant to her, and why. Her appointment to their team had coincided with the loss of one of their own in Afghanistan, and though she had worked hard to fit in and prove herself, she still acted as if she were somehow an outsider. But nothing could be further from the truth, either for his comrades, or for Drake himself.

'Look, I know it hasn't been easy for you. Fitting in, feeling like you're being judged against someone you never really knew. But I need you to know that none of that matters. It never did. You're part of this team now, Sam. We're here for you… *I'm* here for you, no matter what.'

He saw the muscles in her throat moving as she swallowed, saw her fingers tighten on the wheel. Her attention was still focussed on the road ahead, but there was something in her eyes, some hidden pain that his words had somehow exposed. She pressed down a little harder on the accelerator, causing their speed to creep up.

'Take it easy,' Drake advised her, wary of overtaxing the car's ageing and neglected engine. Already it sounded like it hadn't seen the inside of a garage in a very long time. 'This car's a heap. It's not going to take much more.'

Reluctantly she eased off, though the tension remained in her. 'I don't want to let you down, Ryan,' she said at last. 'I don't want you to be disappointed in me.'

'You won't,' he promised her. 'You never could.'

Samantha said nothing to that, concentrating instead on driving.

Chapter 43

Oblivious to the forensic specialists and security personnel swarming all around him, Kubar stared down at the lifeless body of Tarek Sowan. This man had once been one of the Libyan intelligence service's rising stars; bright, intelligent and ambitious. Now he was lying sprawled on the dusty ground of a Tripoli back alley, his blood staining the sand.

Whatever he'd hoped to achieve through his desperate escape from Mukhabarat headquarters, it had ended abruptly here with a high-range rifle bullet to the chest. What had happened to bring him to this? How had this inconceivable chain of events played out? Who had killed him and why? And where were they now?

As always, he had more answers than questions.

'He was killed by a long-range shot from an elevated position. Ballistics should be able to give us the calibre of weapon shortly,' Mousa reported, his voice devoid of its usual wry humour. This was no time for jokes. Traitor or not, one of their own was lying dead, as were several other good men dispatched to take him into custody.

'A sniper,' Kubar concluded. 'The same one who took out our field team?'

'Most likely. Their wounds are consistent with sniper kills.'

Kubar rubbed his eyes, fatigue weighing heavily on him at that moment. 'It doesn't make any sense. Sowan flees our compound, crashes his car, and a mystery man appears to save him from capture. They run here, Sowan ends up dead and the other man vanishes.' He glanced over at one of the metal dumpsters that littered the alleyway, its metal frame shredded by multiple bullet holes. 'What the hell happened here?'

'The evidence of a firefight is obvious. We found plenty of 9mm shell casings scattered around,' Mousa went on. 'As well as blood that doesn't seem to belong to Sowan.'

Just like at the airfield, he mused. Both times they'd found evidence of a sudden, brutal confrontation between two different groups, with Sowan apparently caught in the middle. Why were they fighting over him? Was he working for one group, both, or neither? Had he been an active participant, or an unwilling accomplice to whatever scheme they had concocted?

Kubar let out a slow, weary breath. 'Strings.'

'Excuse me?'

'Tarek Sowan was a puppet,' he concluded grimly. 'The man who dragged him away from the crash scene was the one pulling his strings.'

'Whoever he is, he was able to coerce one of our operatives into betraying his own people, infiltrating the most secure compound in our country, and waltzing right out before we could stop him. Not to mention killing every man who stood in his way.' Mousa shook his head, simply unable to comprehend how all their efforts thus far had ended in failure. 'We may as well be fighting a ghost.'

'Ghosts can disappear. Men can't,' Kubar reminded him with a sharp look. 'He's out there somewhere, and it's our job to find him. What else do we know?'

'We have a report from a local civilian of a carjacking at the same time as the attack. The perpetrator was a Caucasian woman, standing in the road pretending to be injured. When he stopped to investigate, she pulled a gun and stole his car.'

Kubar frowned. Another piece of misdirection, or the desperate actions of a group trying to escape something they hadn't anticipated? 'Make and model?'

'A red Toyota sports car. I've already forwarded the license plate and vehicle description to police and military units.'

'Good.'

'If they are as smart as they seem to be, they'll ditch the car soon enough,' Mousa warned him.

'Maybe, maybe not. Either way, it's worth a try.'

'There's something else.' Mousa paused. A strained, uncomfortable pause as he sought a good way to deliver bad news. 'We checked the key card access logs back at headquarters. Sowan didn't just go to the parking lot after stealing Director Jibril's access card.'

Kubar looked up from the body, turning his attention to his comrade. 'Well spit it out, damn you. Where else did he go?'

'The evidence vault.'

Kubar clenched his fists, struggling to hold his emotions in check. The evidence vault. One of the most secure rooms in the entire compound, where the Mukhabarat's most deadly secrets were kept, where even he was unable to venture without an armed escort.

He could practically feel his blood pressure rising by the second, and with it a growing headache, but he no longer cared. At last he understood what Sowan had been looking for, and the danger it represented if he found it.

'I want them found,' he said, his voice icy calm. 'No matter what it takes. Do you understand? We find them, and we make them answer for this.'

His colleague knew better than to question him.

—

They hadn't gone far before it became obvious that McKnight's high speed escape through the streets of Tripoli hadn't done their ageing vehicle many favours. Their speed had begun to drop off noticeably despite her attempts to coax more power from it, and the engine's note had become less of a throaty growl and more the shuddering rumble of metal grinding against metal.

The final straw came when Drake glanced out the broken rear window and spotted clouds of white smoke billowing from their twin exhaust.

'We need to stop,' he decided, nodding to the engine temperature gauge, which was now close to maxing out. Already he suspected the cause of their problems, but he needed to see for himself how bad it was.

Spotting a low sand berm up ahead, McKnight turned off the minor road they'd been following for the past fifteen minutes and pulled to a halt on the far side, more or less shielding them from view of passing cars.

Stepping out into the slightly cooler night air, Drake paused for a moment to survey their surroundings in case anyone happened to be around. There wasn't much to see save for undulating dunes stretching off into the darkness. Deciding the area was more or less safe, he circled around to the front of the vehicle and popped the hood.

The resultant cloud of steam billowing from the engine compartment, accompanied by the faint hiss of high-pressure water escaping through a narrow gap in the engine block, was enough to confirm his suspicions.

McKnight too had approached to survey the damage. 'Tell me we're not screwed.'

'I could, but I'd be lying,' he said, leaning over to get a better look. 'We've blown the cylinder-head gasket.'

With the gasket designed to separate the various fluids vital to the engine now compromised, water from the cooling system was leaking into the combustion chamber. The engine was literally burning up its own coolant as it ran, reducing its power output drastically and causing steam to billow from the exhaust.

'Anything we can do?'

Drake surveyed the stricken engine, his expression grave. Then, removing his shirt, he wrapped it around his right hand to form a crude glove, reached out and unscrewed the water filler cap. The sudden eruption of steam and boiling water that followed was enough to make both of them back off a few paces.

'That'll keep the pressure down, hopefully buy us some time,' Drake explained, tossing the plastic cap away. He didn't add that without any additional water to top up the coolant reservoir, there was nothing they could do to stop the engine eventually running dry and seizing up.

'So what's the plan?'

'We go cross-country from here. We can't afford to stay on the roads any longer – not in this condition. Anyway, the terrain looks flat enough to drive on.'

He would rather have tackled such a journey in a Land Rover, or one of the Toyota Hiluxes that seemed to be ubiquitous in this part of the world, but beggars couldn't be choosers.

He glanced up at the night sky, trying to take his bearings. With little light pollution and no clouds in such a dry desert environment, his view of the star constellations was almost perfect. It didn't take long to pick out Ursa Major, followed by Ursa Minor, and finally in the extreme northern hemisphere, Polaris – the North Star.

'It's got to be a hundred miles to the rendezvous,' McKnight said dubiously. 'Can we make it that far?'

Drake said nothing to this as he glanced at his watch. They had perhaps six hours until sunrise. Six hours to find Frost and Mason, and get the hell out of this country.

'Get in,' he said, slamming the hood shut. 'I'll drive.'

After some persuasion, the car shuddered reluctantly back into life. Trying to keep the engine revs low so as not to stress the failing machinery, Drake eased them away from their temporary hiding place and back onto the road, leaving a cloud of steam in their wake.

Six hours to cover a hundred miles of rough and hostile terrain in a 20-year-old sports car on its last legs, with few weapons to defend themselves.

Nothing like a challenge.

Chapter 44

Sitting with his back against a crumbling sandstone wall, Cole Mason was in a sombre mood as he surveyed the rolling desert that disappeared off into the night, like a dark and stormy sea frozen in time.

All throughout the afternoon they had maintained a constant vigil on the desert surrounding their hilltop refuge, wary of being caught off guard by another passing traveller. Having no knowledge of this area, it was hard to understand whether these ruins held any special significance for the local tribesmen, perhaps acting as a landmark or even holy ground, or whether the encounter had been nothing more than random chance.

Whatever the reason, Mason knew it was almost time to move. Drake had specifically warned that if they hadn't heard from him, they were to pull out and get themselves across the border to Tunisia before dawn. He hated the thought of abandoning his two teammates, but as Drake had rightly pointed out, if he hadn't made contact by now then the chances were he never would.

'Goddamn it,' he said under his breath, rising to his feet and returning to the interior of the ruined building.

Frost was waiting for him, her dark expression making it clear she knew why he was there, and what he wanted to say.

'Forget it, Cole,' she warned, pre-empting him. 'We're not going anywhere.'

'I don't like it any more than you do. But Ryan ordered us—'

'Fuck his orders.' She rose to her feet, fists clenched. 'I don't go in for that noble self-sacrificing bullshit any more than you do. He could still make it.'

'Yeah, he could.' Mason's voice was quiet, even gentle. He knew that shouting at her was a waste of time. She had to be persuaded to see sense. 'But he gave us those orders for a reason. If we're still here at dawn, we won't be able to move until tomorrow night. Our water won't last three people that long.'

Being captured or even killed was one thing. Dying slowly of thirst out here in the burning sun was quite another.

'So we cut the number of mouths to feed,' the young woman said, glancing at Laila.

Mason let out a sigh. If the worst came to the worst and they were forced to leave Libya without Drake and McKnight, they would cut Laila loose once they reached a friendly country. She might not have much of a future to look forward to with no home and no husband, but at least she'd have her life. He wasn't about to execute an innocent civilian now, when he'd risked discovery to avoid doing so earlier.

'That's not who we are,' he said, staring into her eyes. 'You know that.'

Frost held his gaze for a moment, then seemed to waver as the import of her hasty suggestion sank in. She swallowed, looking away uncomfortably. 'What are you suggesting?'

'We get ourselves close to the border, then we wait and listen out on the radio. If we still haven't heard from Ryan by dawn, then we go.' It wasn't much of a window, but it was the best he could offer. 'Fair enough?'

Frost chewed her lip, which she always seemed to do when she was unhappy. Then, seeming to reach a decision, she reached down and picked up the shotgun that had been resting against a fallen pillar beside her.

'I'm not giving up on him,' she mumbled, unwilling to look him in the eye.

That was about as close to an agreement as he was likely to get, but it was enough. Mason reached out and laid a comforting hand on her shoulder, knowing there was nothing he could say or do that would make them feel better about what was happening.

But just as he was about to speak, he was alerted by a noise over by the north wall. The scuffling of footsteps on the sand, followed by the faint metallic clink of a weapon being readied.

His head snapped around, and straightaway he caught sight of a figure rising up from the shadows like a ghost, having approached unseen and unheard.

'Contact,' he hissed, reaching for his automatic.

Frost too went for her weapon, dropping to her knees to present as small a target as possible as she brought the shotgun to bear.

'You not move!' a voice shouted from behind, warning her that a second attacker had them covered.

Even as she began to turn towards this new threat, she spotted a third man crouched in the rubble on the east side of the building. A man dressed in traditional Bedouin desert clothes, armed with a long-barrelled rifle. A man who had prayed at this very spot earlier in the day.

In a matter of seconds they were cornered and surrounded, covered from three different directions at once. They had fucked up by letting that young man escape earlier, she realized then. The tribesman who they had believed ignorant of their presence had obviously seen something and quietly left to report it, coming back later with reinforcements.

They should have killed him when they'd had the chance.

To start shooting now would be suicidal; she knew that right away. The shotgun was effective at little more than fifty yards, and could fire only two shells at a time before it had to be reloaded. Mason too was low on ammunition for his silenced automatic, leaving them at a heavy disadvantage in both numbers and firepower.

Still, she wasn't afraid to fight, and if it came down to it she would rather die on her feet than rot away in a Libyan jail for the rest of her life. She glanced at Mason, wondering if he was of like mind.

'Wouldn't try it, if I were you,' a voice warned them. A voice that certainly didn't belong to this country. 'Put down your guns and raise your hands.'

Frost let out a startled breath. She knew that voice.

Hearing footsteps on the sand by the south wall, she turned in time to see a man emerge from the growing shadows. A man dressed in desert camouflage gear, with a cloak wrapped around his body and a khaki-coloured keffiyeh covering much of his face.

An AK-74 assault rifle, its barrel and stock painted yellow-brown to help it blend in against the desert background, was up at his shoulder, covering them. She knew all too well that a single sustained burst would be enough to wipe them all out.

Reaching up with his free hand, he unwound the keffiyeh and allowed it to fall away, revealing the face beneath.

Frost felt her blood run cold as her worst fears were confirmed.

'Oh fuck.'

Chapter 45

'Envoy to all units, acknowledge,' McKnight said, speaking quietly into her radio as their car bumped and rumbled across the open desert. 'Repeat, all units acknowledge this transmission.'

'You're wasting your time,' Drake warned her, steering the Toyota around a dune that would almost certainly have bogged them down had he tried to tackle it head-on. 'We're still too far out.'

They had been driving cross-country for the best part of two hours. With the headlights turned off to hide their presence and the slowly deteriorating engine running at low revs, Drake had rarely been able to achieve more than 30 mph as the difficult terrain required constant attention. It had been a wearying task, to say the least, not helped by the constant threat of pursuit or interception.

Nonetheless, the miles had slowly crept by beneath their wheels – ten, twenty, thirty. According to the odometer they had covered more than sixty miles, with about forty still to go. Forty miles. Still beyond the range of their compact tactical radios.

'The atmospherics seem pretty good tonight. Figured it was worth a shot,' McKnight replied. 'If only we had a bigger antenna.'

Drake glanced around. 'I'll let you know if I see any.'

They had encountered virtually no signs of human habitation in the past two hours, save for a line of crooked fence posts without anything to link them together. McKnight had spotted the recognition lights of a small aircraft off to the south some time earlier, possibly a chopper judging by the low airspeed. The distant sighting had forced them to halt their progress and kill the engine, waiting in tense silence to see if the mystery aircraft came any closer.

Mercifully, the lights had faded off towards the east before disappearing over the horizon. If the Libyans were indeed conducting a search for the stolen vehicle, they had over 700,000 square miles of desert to cover. A daunting task to say the least.

McKnight smiled a little at his remark, though her demeanour soon turned more serious. 'How are we doing?'

'Well, oil pressure is almost zero, oil temperature is off the gauge, and engine temperature's right behind it. Oh, and we're running low on fuel.' He gave her a sidelong look of mock disapproval. 'You picked a winner here, Sam.'

'Screw you,' she retorted, though she could sense the intended humour in his remark. 'It's not like people were lining up to give me their cars. I had to pretend to be dying for this guy to stop.'

'I thought you could charm your way into one.'

'I'm not that charming.'

He shrugged. 'I don't know. You have your moments.'

The woman looked at him, torn between surprise and amusement at his unexpectedly playful attitude. 'Seriously? Are you flirting with me right now?'

'Wouldn't dream of it.'

'Yeah, sure you wouldn't.' She grinned, warming to the game that seemed to have developed between them. It certainly beat staring out into the darkness in tense silence, wondering what lay out there. 'Anyway, I can't blame you. It's a pretty common reaction.'

'To what?'

'To being here, doing what we do,' she explained. 'Happens all the time to soldiers after a battle. The danger, the adrenaline, the rush of being so close to death and making it out alive. The rational part of your brain eases off the gas and the primitive side takes over. Pretty soon all you can think about is doing what you're designed to do.'

'That being?'

'Screw, of course.'

So taken aback was he by her blunt sentiment and matter-of-fact delivery that he couldn't help laughing. 'Well, there's a chat-up line if ever I heard one.'

'No shame in admitting it,' McKnight said, her tone one of playful consolation. 'It's human nature; might as well be honest about it. Look at me and tell me you're not feeling that way now.'

Drake opted not to rise to that particular challenge, partly because he needed to concentrate on the difficult task of negotiating the rough terrain they were driving through, but mostly because he knew she was right.

'Thought so.' She leaned back in her seat with a smirk on her face, placing her feet up on the dashboard as she surveyed the great expanse of desert beyond the windshield. 'So do you want to pull over and go for it on the hood?'

Drake couldn't say exactly why he started laughing. Maybe it was the tension and stress of the past couple of days that had finally found a means of release, or the knowledge that they were at last on their way out of this country which had brought them nothing but danger and death since their arrival, or maybe just because it felt good to be here with Samantha, to hear the sound of her voice, to know she was with him.

Whatever the reason, he just couldn't help himself. And before long, she was laughing along with him. Because she understood as well as he that they both needed it.

However, their amusement was short-lived. A sudden bang and crunch up front told them something mechanical had just come apart, and within moments the steering wheel went slack in Drake's hands. Turning it left or right seemed to make no difference at all. No longer answering to the wheel, the car slewed off to the right, following the slight downward contours of the land before coming to a grinding, shuddering halt.

'What was that?' McKnight asked, her smile gone now. 'We lose power?'

Drake shook his head. The engine, though rough and clearly not in a good way, was nonetheless still running. The problem didn't lie there. It was as if something had become caught in the car's axle.

Opening his door, he stepped outside and picked his way around to the front to inspect the damage.

'Shit,' he said under his breath. Both front wheels were pointing in different directions. 'We've snapped a tracking rod.'

A vital component of the steering system, the tracking rod was there to keep the front steering wheels pointing in the same direction. If it failed, the car simply couldn't move.

'Any ideas?' McKnight prompted.

'Not without a full workshop and a new rod.' Drake looked at his watch, doing a rough calculation based on time and distance. 'We've got about four hours 'til sunrise. We can make it, if we move fast.'

The woman eyed him dubiously. 'Thirty miles in four hours. That's a hell of a walk, Ryan.'

There was no need to add that if they were caught out in the desert after sunrise, they'd be unlikely to survive the day without water.

'Then we'd better get moving,' Drake said, rallying his flagging strength for the task ahead. Every moment they spent here talking was a moment wasted.

Chapter 46

Keira Frost knew this man. This man standing before her with an assault rifle levelled at her chest, who had tracked and cornered her out here like a wild animal, who might very well kill her at any moment.

Certainly he looked different from the last time they'd met. He had aged visibly; his hair grown out, his face marked by lines that hadn't been there before, his jaw partially hidden by a greying beard. But for all the changes brought about by time and circumstance, it was unmistakably the same man she'd met during their mission in Afghanistan last year.

The man who had presented himself as Drake's old friend; someone to be trusted, someone they could rely on. The man whose betrayal had cost the lives of several Agency operatives. Including her friend John Keegan.

'Cunningham,' she said, practically spitting the name out in disgust. 'You fucking piece of shit.'

She had no idea what inexplicable chain of events had brought him to this part of the world at this time, whether he had been sent to hunt them by the Libyans, whether he was working for Cain or Faulkner or some other group entirely, or whether this whole encounter was nothing more than terrible coincidence.

She didn't know, and nor did she care. He was here, and so was she.

'Drop the weapon,' he repeated, speaking in the same broad Scottish accent she remembered so well. 'I won't say it again.'

Frost glanced down at the shotgun in her hands. A heavy, old-fashioned weapon, difficult to handle and poorly suited to her small frame. Certainly no use for what she had in mind.

Releasing her grip, she allowed the gun to drop to the sandy ground at her feet. A heartbeat later her hand went for the knife at her waist, yanking it from the sheath even as she launched herself towards him.

She heard a cry of warning off to her left, thought that perhaps it might have been Mason pleading with her not to do it. Cole Mason; a good man who didn't deserve to die in this shithole at the ass end of nowhere. She pushed that thought from her mind the moment it entered. She couldn't think about that now, couldn't think about anything except closing to within knife-range of her target.

She wanted Cunningham. If he really had been sent here to kill her and the others, she wouldn't go down without a fight. Even if it cost her her life, she would take that bastard down with her.

He had the drop on her; she knew that, even as she closed in on him, the knife clutched tight in a death grip. Her unexpected attack might have caught him by surprise and bought her a moment or two, but such an advantage was short-lived. He was still armed with an automatic weapon capable of wiping out all three of them with a single devastating burst, and certainly wouldn't hesitate to use it.

At any moment she expected to see the distinctive muzzle flare as the first round was fired, and to feel the crushing impact as it tore into her unprotected body. She didn't care. Images of Keegan lying dead amidst the shattered ruins of an abandoned farm in Afghanistan assailed her mind, just as they had done every night for the past year.

And yet, to her disbelief, he didn't fire. Instead she saw him cast the weapon aside as if he had no need for it, and raised his hands to defend himself. She almost smiled at the realization that he intended to fight her hand to hand. The arrogant bastard actually thought he could take her in a fair fight.

She would show him. This fight would be anything but fair.

Planting her foot on a fallen block of masonry, she leapt towards him with the knife held high, ready to plunge it down into his chest. Then, even as he prepared to duck aside to avoid the plunging blade, she suddenly reversed her grip on the knife. Landing with nimble grace on the sandy ground, she allowed her momentum to carry her downward, before springing back and thrusting the knife upwards into his abdomen.

A stomach wound. One of the slowest and most painful ways to die, she thought with a momentary glimmer of satisfaction. Acids from the ruptured stomach walls filling his abdominal cavity, burning and destroying the torn flesh even as he bled out. This far from civilization, he'd never get to a doctor in time.

But her deadly strike never found its mark. Even as she thrust the blade upwards to meet him, he suddenly twisted aside with a speed that belied both his size and his age, causing the knife thrust to miss by mere inches.

Surprised by his quick reflexes but unwilling to give him a chance to recover, she jumped back to her feet and launched herself at him again with renewed frenzy, swiping the blade around to catch him in the neck. A quick death, perhaps, and certainly better than he deserved, but a death all the same.

Yet even as the knife arced in towards its target, it came to a sudden, jarring halt as he clamped a hand around her knife-arm mid-swing, in a painful, bruising grip. Keira Frost was well versed in fighting, was nimble and agile and capable of sudden, explosive bursts of strength and aggression that had surprised more than a few enemies over the years. But there was a different kind of power that only came with sheer size and muscle mass, and those were two things in which she could never hope to equal her opponent.

Before she could even attempt to free her arm from his grip, she felt herself lifted bodily off the ground and tossed aside like a rag doll. She did her best to roll with it and absorb the impact, but the unyielding wall that slammed into her back was enough to knock the wind and the fight out of her. She felt like her entire ribcage had been crushed as she slumped to the ground, coughing and struggling to draw breath.

She looked up in time to see Cunningham looming over her; a massive and terrifying presence about to finish the job he'd started. She saw him crouch down to pick up the knife that had slipped from her grasp when she hit the wall.

Killing her with her own weapon.

'Do it!' she cried, though the injury had robbed her voice of much of its strength. She glared up at him defiantly despite the pain that now wracked her body. 'Finish it, you... fucking coward!'

But far from using the knife to end the brief fight, he instead threw it aside in disgust. 'If I wanted to kill you, you'd be dead already,' he snarled. 'Anyway, we've got a lot to talk about.'

Of all the reactions she had expected, this wasn't one of them. Frost looked at the knife lying a short distance away, then back up at him, wondering if this was some attempt to goad her into action. She was quick to suppress any thoughts of renewing her attack, however. He'd fought her off with ease once already, and she was barely capable of standing in her present condition.

He knew that as well. Why then had he spared her life?

'Who the hell are you?' Mason asked, having witnessed the brief confrontation with horrified but impotent fascination, unable to intervene lest the two men covering him open fire. 'What do you want with us?'

Cunningham glanced at him for a moment, regarding him as one might regard a piece of dog shit stuck to one's heel. 'Shut it, big man. I know her; I don't know you. That means I don't give a fuck if you live or die. Understand?'

Mason said nothing to that, though the simmering anger in his eyes made his thoughts on this man plain.

With that matter settled, Cunningham glanced at one of the two Bedouin men accompanying him – the same young man that Mason had come so close to killing earlier – and spoke a quiet command in Arabic. Lowering his weapon, the man hurried over to Laila, produced a cell phone from a pocket in his robes and held it up in front of her, comparing her face with the one displayed on the screen.

A simple nod from him was enough to confirm that it was a match. They had, apparently, found who they were looking for.

Kneeling down beside Frost, who was only now starting to drag herself up from the sandy ground, Cunningham surveyed the injured woman without compassion. 'I'm going to ask some direct questions and I want direct answers, aye? So let's get started. Where's Ryan?'

'Go fuck yourself,' Frost replied, coughing again. 'That direct enough for you?'

'That's the girl I remember,' he said, smiling in amusement at her words. 'I always said that mouth of yours would get you in trouble.'

In response, she reared back and spat bloody phlegm at his feet. 'If you're going to shoot me anyway, shut up and get it over with, you Scottish prick. I'm not telling you shit.'

Cunningham exhaled slowly, thinking the matter over. 'The funny thing is, I believe you,' he acknowledged at last. 'Lots of people talk tough when they've got their backs against the wall, but it's just piss and vinegar when you get right down to it. But *you*... you've got that fire in your belly. You'd rather die than tell me what I want to know, which means you're protecting something. Or someone.' His gaze travelled to Mason, who was holding his ground a short distance away. 'Let's find out, shall we?'

Without saying another word, he reached for an automatic holstered on the left side of his chest and trained it on Mason, flicking off the safety catch with the same movement.

'No!' the young woman cried out.

'I don't know him, remember?' Cunningham prompted her. 'So I don't have to care if he dies. It's all on you.'

'Don't give this asshole a word,' Mason urged her, glaring at Cunningham.

'You know the drill, Frost. I'll give you to the count of three,' their captor warned her. 'A bit old-fashioned, but it does the trick. One...'

She could see his finger tightening on the trigger. Considering he was already responsible for killing several Agency personnel, she didn't doubt he would happily add another to that list.

'Two...'

Her gaze flicked to Mason, knowing these could be his final moments. She'd already lost one good friend to Cunningham. She couldn't bear to lose another, couldn't allow him to die for this, but neither could she betray Drake and McKnight. To tell Cunningham anything might well seal their fate. The agony of indecision and conflicting emotions was plain to see in her eyes.

That was when she saw it. The faint nod of acknowledgement, of under-standing. Mason knew what she was feeling, and accepted that neither of them would betray their companions to this man. Even at the cost of their own lives.

'Three—'

'Wait!' another voice called out.

Surprised, Cunningham turned toward Laila, who had taken a step toward him with her arms raised to show that she was unarmed.

'Killing these people will do little to help your cause,' she carried on. 'If you wish to know what has brought them here, I will tell you.'

Cunningham lowered the weapon, though he didn't holster it. What he did with it would depend on the answers she gave him in the next few minutes.

'See that, Frost?' he said, glancing at the young woman lying on the ground before him. 'We're all out to help each other here. All it takes is a bit of negotiating.' He turned his attention back to Laila. 'So, enlighten me.'

Chapter 47

'So Faulkner's playing the Agency and the Libyans against each other? Doesn't make any goddamn sense to me. If the man we recovered from Paris was part of an Agency black op, we would have known about it. Why would they let us render one of their own men?' McKnight said, a little out of breath after maintaining their brisk pace for the past several hours.

Both she and Drake were physically fit and well conditioned to environments like this, and their progress westward had been surprisingly swift, helped no doubt by the relatively cool temperature overnight.

That would change soon, however, as the sky in the east gradually lightened with the coming dawn. Normally travellers welcomed the start of a new day, but not this time. This time it would mean merciless, unending heat, burning rays that would sear their skin and tear the moisture from their throats, and winds that could whip the drifting sand up into storms intense enough to blot out the sun.

Already they could feel the temperature starting to rise.

'I don't know,' Drake admitted. Sowan's revelations about the chain of events that had led them to Libya had been a bombshell, but he sensed the picture was still incomplete. Some vital element still eluded them. 'The only logical explanation is that the Agency didn't know who this guy was really working for.'

'That's not making me feel better.'

'Me neither.'

For some reason, his conversation with Charles Hunt at Arlington resurfaced in his mind, particularly the man's cryptic warning about the enemies Drake faced.

The real power in this country doesn't lie in buildings that give guided tours, or men who have to answer to oversight committees or voter groups. The real decision makers are the ones you can't see, that you don't know about because that's exactly how they choose to make it.

'Maybe there's something else at work here,' he mused. 'Some covert group we haven't seen before.'

'They must be pretty damn good at staying hidden, if they have the resources and the intelligence assets to overthrow a military dictatorship without anybody even knowing they exist.' She shook her head. 'I'm not buying it.'

'And I'm not selling it, but it fits with what we know.' He adjusted the straps of his rucksack, feeling the solid weight of the laptop shifting a little inside. 'We get this bloody thing to Keira, maybe she can give us some answers about our new friends.'

In that at least, McKnight seemed to be in agreement, and said nothing further on the matter. 'By the way, you never did tell me how you and Faulkner know each other.'

'When I left the Regiment, he made contact with me, said he knew about a new unit being formed for special work in Afghanistan,' Drake said, reluctant to go into too much detail. His exit from the SAS hadn't exactly been a happy time in his life. 'He said they needed... men like me.'

'What did he mean by that?'

Drake didn't say anything for a time.

'I've done things in my life that I'm not proud of, Sam. Some of those things I deserved to be punished for. But that unit... they wanted men like me, they *rewarded* men like me. Men who were ready to be more than just soldiers. That's what he meant.'

'And that's what you became?' she asked, a little uncertain now. She was opening a door she might not be able to close again. 'More than just a soldier?'

He shrugged. 'I was what I needed to be. Let's leave it at that.'

They both paused for a moment as the first shafts of sunlight broke over the eastern horizon, bathing the world before them in a bright orange glow and causing their own shadows to stretch out far ahead.

McKnight cast an apprehensive glance at the ball of fire rising slowly and inexorably into the sky.

'We need to hurry,' Drake said quietly, urging her forward.

Chapter 48

David Faulkner was in a foul mood as his convoy of two SUVs headed south away from Tripoli at high speed. They had already encountered two military roadblocks on their journey, hastily set up in the wake of the shootout near the Mukhabarat headquarters, but fortunately the team's diplomatic credentials had been enough to get them through without incident.

Talk about fixing the barn door after the horses had bolted, he thought with mild irritation. The horses in question were now on the loose somewhere in Libya, and he had no idea where they'd gone. Satellite tracking might have allowed him to trace their movements from the scene of the shootout in the alleyway, but calling upon such a resource would draw undue attention to his venture here. And attention was something to be avoided at all costs.

Up until now, Drake had been entirely predictable in both his decisions and his actions. Bold and audacious perhaps, but predictable all the same. Now the game had changed. Drake had lost the very thing he believed he needed most. What he would do next was hard to predict.

So for now Faulkner was left with no option but to wait, monitoring Libyan police and military transmissions for any mention of Drake and his companions.

Waiting. At a time when countless lives, including his own, depended on the outcome of this venture, he was sitting on his hands doing nothing.

Suppressing a sigh of frustration, he took a sip from his glass of orange juice. The car's air conditioning was working overtime to keep the interior of the vehicle cool and comfortable, protecting the occupants from the nightmarish desert heat outside, but just being in this godforsaken country was enough to make him feel dirty. He couldn't wait to leave once his mission here was completed.

Sitting opposite him was the pale, almost waiflike figure of Caitlin Macguire, her expression sullen and brooding as she stared out at the desert through the car's tinted windows. Perhaps she was pondering the implications of their failure last night, or perhaps she was simply annoyed that a target of hers had escaped. It was hard to know what was going on behind those steely blue eyes of hers, whether she truly appreciated what was at stake.

As if in response to these dark thoughts, he felt the cell phone in his pocket vibrating. Setting his drink down, he fished the phone out and glanced at the screen, feeling a chill run through him when he saw that the caller ID was blocked. Few people knew his number, and even fewer were able to call while masking their identity.

'Yes,' he began, managing to keep his tone flat and composed.

'You have an update for me?' The voice that spoke was American. Soft and surprisingly pleasant to listen to, but laced with a harder undertone of command now. The caller was accustomed to making decisions that could end lives, and it showed.

'Sowan is dead,' Faulkner reported, deciding to open with the one piece of good news he could supply. 'He can't compromise us now.'

A pause. 'And Drake? The information you were sent to retrieve?'

'We're working on that.'

A longer pause. Faulkner winced inwardly, bracing himself for what was coming.

'You're *working on that*?' he repeated. 'Maybe I didn't make myself clear. Anger-management; losing ten pounds in time for summer; building a new fence around your front lawn. Those are things that you *work on*. This is something that you *do*, David. You were brought in to *do* something for us – not to work on it, not to try your best, not to give it a shot, but to get it done. But you're not getting it done. You're failing, and every failure is piling up on the ones that came before it. Every failure is bringing us closer to losing everything we've been working for. That is not something you need to *work on*, David. That is something you need to *fix right now*.'

Faulkner swallowed hard. The AC vents were still blasting icy cold air at him, yet he could feel beads of sweat trickling down the side of his face. 'It's not over yet.'

'No, it's not. Not for us. But it will be for you if you don't get this done,' he promised, his grim warning delivered with the absolute conviction of a man who had pronounced such a sentence many times before. 'So I'll make this very simple. Find Drake, find the information... or we'll find you, David. No matter where you go, no matter what you do, no matter how long it takes, you know we'll find you. And you know what we'll do after that.'

With that, the line went dead.

Closing his eyes for a moment, Faulkner laid the phone down, reached for his drink and took another sip, though he couldn't quite keep his hands from trembling.

'What the fuck was that about?' Macguire asked, her voice betraying an edge of concern for perhaps the first time.

Faulkner didn't answer. He had far more important matters to concern himself with now.

Chapter 49

The next couple of hours were a grim, monotonous march across largely featureless terrain, marked only by their gradually slowing pace under the wilting sun. With no visual landmarks to mark their progress or take a bearing, accurate navigation could only be accomplished with a compass.

Had time been less critical, they would have found a place to rest up for the day, conserving their strength while they waited for the relative cool of night to push onward. In this case however, they simply couldn't afford to wait. The only option was to keep going and hope they were able to rendezvous with the rest of their group before they succumbed to heat and dehydration.

'Breaking rocks in the... hot sun,' Drake mumbled as he trudged wearily onwards, having a hard time forming the words. His tongue felt like it was glued to the roof of his mouth. 'I fought... the law and the law won.'

He had taken to singing, or as close to it as he could manage under the circumstances, to maintain his sense of time and progression.

Having operated in hot countries many times before, he was well aware of the dangers that came with loss of water in the body. The symptoms usually started after losing just 2 per cent of the body's water, increased heart- and respiration-rate being the first noticeable signs, as the body tried to compensate for decreasing blood pressure.

At around 5 per cent water-loss, headaches, nausea and impaired judgement began to make themselves felt. By 10 per cent, vision loss and delirium set in. And if they lost more than 15 per cent, multiple organ-failure and death were the most likely outcomes.

These unpleasant thoughts were interrupted by a hiss from McKnight, who was several paces ahead of him. Glancing up, Drake saw her standing tense and alert with one fist raised; a signal to halt.

She had spotted something.

Her silent warning thus given, she lowered herself down on one knee, drawing her weapon at the same time. Drake did likewise, crawling forward until he was close enough to whisper in her ear.

'What you got?'

'One vehicle on our eleven o'clock, about a hundred yards out,' she replied. 'Looked like it was parked between a couple of dunes.'

Drake's heart rate stepped up a gear. 'Just one?'

'Yeah.'

'Military?'

'Couldn't tell for sure, but it was definitely a four-wheel drive. I didn't see any hostiles. Could be a lookout position.' She looked at him. 'We could try to box around it.'

Drake paused for a moment, considering their situation. A lone vehicle wouldn't have ventured this far from civilization without good reason. It could well be part of a search operation mounted by the Libyan government. If so, they had very nearly blundered right into an ambush. Only McKnight's sharp eyes had saved them.

They could indeed try to work their way around this unexpected obstacle, but the landscape here was largely flat and provided little cover. They would have to venture far indeed to slip by unseen, and that would waste precious time and effort. Not to mention the chance they might encounter another vehicle forming some kind of search grid.

The alternative was just as risky, but also had the potential to solve their current problems at a stroke.

'We go for it,' he decided. 'Split up and converge from different directions, take out the crew and steal the car. Then we find the others and get the fuck over the border.'

As far as plans went it was neither sophisticated nor foolproof, but it was the only one that came to mind. There were only two of them, lightly armed and already feeling the effects of their long march. There was a good chance they might find themselves both outnumbered and outgunned, but Drake had faith in their abilities – they had taken on larger forces before and prevailed. And the element of surprise might just tip the scales in their favour.

'I like that plan.'

'You circle around to the north, I'll come at them from the south and we'll meet in the middle. We go in hard and fast, try to take them alive if they look like civilians. Otherwise, we put them down.'

McKnight nodded. She knew as well as he did what was at stake here. If anyone onboard that vehicle managed to send out a call for help, they were fucked.

'Stay on comms and call out if you see anything. Oh, and try not to shoot me when we move in.'

She flashed a wry smile. 'Any more remarks like that, and I just might.'

With that, she turned away and hurried northward, bent so low that she was soon a barely noticeable shape flitting between the dunes. Drake likewise took off in the other direction, trying to choose a path that provided at least some cover for him. Taller and larger than McKnight, he was a more prominent target.

The Browning automatic was clutched tight in his hand. He'd expended his own supply of ammunition during the ambush in Tripoli, but McKnight had shared out her remaining rounds between the two weapons, giving them five shots apiece.

Not much of an arsenal with which to take on an unknown number of hostiles, but better than nothing. He would be sure to make each shot count if it came to it.

The hot sun continued to beat down on him as he worked his way forward, the heat and exertion raising beads of sweat that trickled down his back, causing his dusty shirt to stick to his skin.

Sure enough, he could make out the distinctive boxy frame of an old-style 4x4 over the tops of the dunes as he moved into position. Its paintwork seemed to have been scoured bare over the years so that it was difficult to tell what colour the vehicle had once been, but Drake thought he saw faint camouflage markings.

'Envoy's in position,' McKnight reported over the radio net. 'No sign of hostiles. What's your sitrep?'

Damn, that was fast, he thought. Picking up the pace, he hit his radio transmitter. 'Almost there. Ten seconds.'

'Move your ass. I'm exposed here.'

Coming to a halt at what he guessed was the southern edge of the depression around the vehicle, Drake took a couple of deep breaths, drawing the hot dusty air into his lungs to try to prepare himself for what was coming next. They were both tired and weakened, but they had to see this through. They couldn't afford to waver now.

'Monarch's in position,' he called in. 'Move in three, two, one... Go!'

Rising to his feet from behind the scant cover offered by a low drifting dune, Drake advanced quickly towards the vehicle with his weapon raised. About a hundred yards away, he spotted McKnight doing the same thing.

'Monarch has no targets,' he warned, wondering if this might be a trap.

It didn't make any sense. No driver, no guards, no passengers taking a piss nearby. Not even footprints. Nothing but drifting sand and the sigh of the wind.

He was almost there now. The jeep that had been partially hidden behind a dune at last came into view, allowing Drake and McKnight their first proper look at it.

Straightaway he felt his heart sink.

Now he understood why they'd encountered no resistance on their way in. Coming to a halt, he lowered his weapon and grimly surveyed the blasted shell of a Libyan army jeep, its forward wheels destroyed by some kind of explosives, most likely a mine or IED. Whatever remained had long since been stripped of useful parts, so that only the broken chassis was left; a silent memorial to the crew that had likely perished in the explosion.

He had no idea which conflict or even which decade this forgotten battlefield belonged to. Libya had seen plenty of armed clashes over the years, both inside and outside its borders. This could have happened last month or last century.

McKnight walked towards him, her shoulders slumped in defeat. Reaching down, she picked up a twisted piece of metal that had once been the steering wheel, holding it a moment or two before hurling it away in disgust.

'Goddamn it,' she said, closing her eyes for a moment.

He understood how she felt. Things like this happened sometimes. Mistaken identities, fleeting glimpses on which one suddenly had to make life or death decisions. Not every call was the right one.

'Nothing for us here,' he said quietly, resigned to the grim march that lay ahead. 'Let's go, Sam.'

–

Mukhabarat headquarters, Tripoli

Seated at his desk in his cramped office, Bishr Kubar sighed and rubbed his eyes, struggling to focus on the computer screen in front of him. He was no stranger to fatigue, yet even he couldn't keep working without sleep indefinitely. He'd been awake for nearly forty-eight hours now, and was growing increasingly aware of the effect it was having on him.

He reached for the cup of coffee beside him and took a mouthful, realizing vaguely that it was long cold. He could feel his eyes closing almost of their own volition, as if his mind no longer had any say in the matter.

He found his thoughts wandering like a ship without a tiller, drifting between vague and disconnected memories. One moment he was a young boy fighting with his older brother near a river, the next he was a grown man surveying the scene of carnage in the wake of a car bomb in central Tripoli.

He pictured his brother as a young man now, still tall and gangly but beginning to show the strength and maturity of manhood. Old enough to join his father as they went off to settle a grievance with a neighbouring tribe.

Old enough to get himself killed.

The dreamlike trance was shattered by a knock at the door. Without waiting for a reply, Mousa rushed into his office, flushed and perspiring.

'We may have something,' he announced triumphantly.

Kubar stared at him. 'What?'

'Aerial reconnaissance just picked up a red sports car abandoned in the desert south-west of the city. No sign of the driver. They may have switched vehicles or struck out on foot.'

That was enough to jar him awake, his heart surging as a fresh wave of energy rushed through his tired body. South-west. Heading towards the border with Tunisia, back towards the remote mountain region near Nalut which had always been so difficult to patrol.

'Get me a bearing on that car,' he ordered, jumping to his feet. 'Vector in ground units. I want to know why it was abandoned. And mobilize every unit we have in the area.'

No way was he letting them get across the border alive.

Chapter 50

Pressing on, Drake began to notice the character of the land changing, the flat dune plains giving way to rocky slopes and rugged foothills. They were in the Nafusa Mountains, a range of craggy hills running roughly from east to west, with the coastal plains to the north and the Sahara to the south. In several places, steep canyons and ancient dried-up river valleys bisected their path, forcing them to veer off course to find a way around.

It was wearying work that served only to lower their spirits, but Drake knew there was little to be done now except get their heads down and power through it. He'd been on more than his share of forced marches in his life, particularly during the arduous selection process for the SAS. Some of those had pushed him close to breaking point, but then that had been the whole idea.

Drake hadn't been the fittest member of his selection group by any measure. He hadn't been the biggest or the strongest, but he did possess one quality that had stood him in good stead amongst his comrades – he had been utterly determined to prevail. He'd seen guys who could have given Olympic athletes a run for their money fall behind and drop out, not because they were physically broken but because they simply couldn't hack it any longer. The lesson had been stark and clear; in a situation where every man was pushed to the point of exhaustion, it was their mental rather than physical reserves that made the difference.

So it was now.

'And to think, I used to get... pissed off when they made us march through rain and snow,' Drake gasped, managing a dry laugh. The mere thought of bleak windswept moorland and driving rain sounded like heaven to him at that moment. 'Give me the Brecon Beacons any day.'

There was no response from his companion. Turning around, Drake was surprised to see McKnight some distance behind. She was slowing down, her head low, shoulders hunched over, plodding forward on leaden feet.

'Shit,' he said, backtracking to intercept her. Even this small diversion from his course left him with a pang of regret, knowing he'd have to retread the same ground again, but there was no question of going back. She came first.

'Sam,' he called out as he approached.

At last she looked up at him. Her face and arms were already red from exposure, and coated with a fine dusting of sand. Her eyes were focussed on him, but there was a heaviness to them, a sense of great fatigue.

'I'm fine, don't wait for me,' she said, waving him off.

It was a brave gesture, but totally counterproductive. Nobody wanted to be the weak link in the chain, but the moment people started pretending they were fine when they weren't, things went wrong. Drake had seen it happen too many times to let it happen now.

'I'm running on empty,' he said, deciding to give her an opening. It wasn't exactly a lie either. 'Why don't we rest for a few minutes, yeah?'

Either she saw his offer for what it was and decided to let it go, or she was simply too tired to care. Whatever the case, she sank to the ground and lay there with her back against a low boulder, its contours scoured smooth by long years of exposure to wind and sand.

Drake sat down beside her, trying to observe her surreptitiously. She was breathing fast and shallow, as if her lungs were struggling to suck in enough oxygen. With a naturally fair complexion, she was already burned by the sun, despite covering up as much as possible, and that was only going to get worse as the day wore on.

She was staring out across the desert, perhaps contemplating whether it would be the last thing she ever saw. The look of sad, reluctant acceptance in her eyes made his heart ache, particularly since there was nothing he could do about it.

'You ever think about getting out?' she asked suddenly.

Drake blinked, his slowing thoughts shifting back to the present with some difficulty. 'From the Agency?'

'From everything,' she corrected. Twisting around, she looked at him with frank honesty. 'Just pack up and leave it all behind for good. No more Agency, no more Cain, no more Anya. No more risking your life for other people's bullshit agendas. That's not such a bad thing, is it?'

'And what would I do?' he asked, taken aback by the unexpected emotion in her plea.

'Live, Ryan. You'd get to live.' She sighed and leaned back against the boulder, staring up at the flawless blue sky. 'Find a house on some remote island, somewhere even Cain couldn't reach you. Live a simple life, do normal things. Forget all of this ever happened.'

A simple life. Normal things. It had been so long since Drake's life had been anything close to normal, he'd almost forgotten what it could feel like. The very prospect of it, of no longer living with a sword above his head, of waking up each morning without a care in the world, seemed like an impossible dream – something to hope for, to strive for but never to reach.

Even if he did take up her suggestion and walked away, it wouldn't last. He knew that as surely as he knew the sun would rise in the morning. There was no place on this earth that Marcus Cain couldn't reach him, given time.

'It's not just about me now,' he said quietly. 'Even if I walked away, there are others he'd use to get to me. Including you.' He shook his head. 'I can't walk away from that.'

He hadn't said it, but there was another reason he couldn't go, another person he couldn't leave behind. He hadn't say it, but there was no need. From the look of pain and sadness in her eyes, McKnight sensed what he was thinking.

'Sometimes I think you're in the wrong business, Ryan,' she said. 'You're too good a man for this.'

Drake frowned, wondering just how wrong she was about him. But before he could say anything else, the woman took a deep breath and rose unsteadily to her feet once more.

'I'm ready,' she said at length, her voice heavy with fatigue. 'Let's go.'

–

The sun waxed and their strength waned as they continued the relentless, gruelling march. The wind began to pick up, lifting and scattering sand in blinding clouds that blasted exposed skin and reduced visibility.

An hour crawled by, and there was no longer even the pretence of maintaining awareness of their surroundings. Half blinded by fatigue and windblown grit, they stumbled along, heads down, seeing nothing but the ground at their feet.

'Monarch to all units,' Drake spoke into his radio, barely managing to croak the words out. 'Can anyone hear me?'

The only response was the pop and hiss of static. He couldn't tell if the silence was down to their being too far away, or the sandstorms causing interference, or if, worst of all, nobody was around to answer.

He could barely feel the ache in his injured arm now. Dry, crusted blood coated his skin, sticking to his clothes, while the improvised field dressing threatened to come away. At another time he might have worried about infection and even blood loss, but those were the least of his concerns now.

His reactions were slowing, his thoughts growing muddled. Not long ago he had become convinced that they had somehow turned around and were heading in the wrong direction. It had taken him a good five minutes of slow, painful, methodical thinking to work out that he'd been wrong.

It couldn't be much further to the rendezvous, he tried to tell himself. Assuming they were still making two or three miles an hour, they should be close…

But how long had they been walking? He couldn't remember. It felt like a lifetime now. Maybe it was further than he thought.

How fast had they been going? He didn't even know that. There were no landmarks, no signposts, nothing to gauge their progress. He thought it should have been possible to work it out, but it was so much effort just to get the gears of his mind turning.

'All units, this is—'

So preoccupied was he with retaining his tenuous grip on his mental faculties that he didn't even see the cliff edge until his right boot went over the edge and disappeared into nothingness. Teetering forward off balance, Drake at last snapped back into awareness as the yawning drop opened up beneath him.

Swaying like a drunkard, he stumbled backwards, scrambling away from the edge and almost knocking over McKnight, who was still trudging on with weary, relentless determination.

'Sam, we can't go that way,' he warned her. 'It's a sheer drop.'

She didn't look up, didn't even acknowledge him. There was a vacant, uncomprehending look in her eyes.

He reached out and grasped her arm. 'Sam! Focus on me.'

With what seemed like a great effort, she turned to look at him, and some vague spark of recognition seemed to kindle behind her eyes. 'Ryan?' she said, as if seeing him for the first time.

'That's right. It's Ryan.'

'What's wrong?'

They had stumbled across a wadi – an ancient dried-up river bed that had once carved a deep channel through the mountainous region in which they found themselves. Millennia ago, this might have been a fast-flowing river, but now it was little more than a deep rocky canyon with steep walls on both sides.

For fit and experienced climbers, such a natural obstacle would have presented little more than a temporary inconvenience, but in their weakened state it might as well have been a mile-deep canyon. Even if they could somehow clamber down this side to reach the valley floor, neither of them possessed the strength or energy to make it up the far bank.

They would have to detour around it, try to find a shallow crossing point.

'The way ahead's blocked,' he explained, pointing to the sheer drop that lay just a few yards in front of them. 'We have to go around.'

Lifting her gaze, McKnight stared out across the wadi, taking in the wide expanse of ancient sediment below and the imposing rock walls in the distance.

That was it for her. Her shoulders sagged, her legs seemed to give way and with a faint, defeated sob she sank to her knees. Her expression was one of absolute, crushing despair.

'Sam, we can't stay here,' he warned, kneeling down and pulling her close so that her face was only a few inches from his. 'You have to get up. Do you understand? You have to get up now!'

'I can't,' she whispered, shaking her head. 'I can't go any further.'

He couldn't afford to let such thoughts take hold. He had to get her up and moving now, or she would never leave this place. 'Yes, you can! You can, Sam! You've been a pain in my arse this whole time, you're not going to fucking give up on me now! Not when there's still breath in your lungs, now get up.' Reaching out, he gripped her shoulders hard. 'Get up now!'

She looked at him again, her eyes more alert now. He saw a flicker of anger and defiance in them. Good – anger was better than blind indifference. Anger could mean the difference between living and dying.

Planting one foot in front of her, she pushed herself upward from the ground, muscles trembling, teeth gritted with the effort. And for a moment, it seemed like she might regain her footing.

A moment, and then it was gone. The brief fire of strength died away, and she slumped back onto the dusty earth.

She was finished. She'd given it everything she had, but the sight of the impassable natural barrier before them had finally broken her will. Now she had nothing left to give.

He should have seen this coming, he thought in a moment of bitter self-recrimination. He shouldn't have pushed her so hard, forced her to keep going when she was already beyond her limits. He should have stopped her from coming here in the first place.

Drake looked away for a moment, unable to face her. She was going to die here.

'No,' he said, the thought of losing her kindling a spark of defiance in him. 'Not here.'

He was deathly tired and hurting, but desperation drove him on. Shoving one hand beneath her legs and the other across her shoulders, Drake took a deep breath and tensed up, trying to force more blood into his weary muscles.

'Come on, then. Off we go.'

Then, with every ounce of strength left in his body, he lifted her up off the ground, staggered for a moment, then rallied his last reserves of flagging energy and started to walk. Too weary to protest, she merely clung to him.

Samantha was of average height for a woman, with the trim, compact build that came from regular aerobic exercise. She probably weighed no more than 130 pounds. An easy weight for him to manage under normal circumstances.

But not today.

Every step he took was agony. His chest heaved, his heart pounded and his vision grew hazy, yet still he battled on, one laboured footstep after another. Their pace had slowed to a pathetic crawl as he stumbled along near the edge of the wadi in a vain search for a crossing point, hoping against hope that there was still a way out of this.

He couldn't rightly say how long he managed to carry her, how much ground he covered, because all such concepts had ceased to mean anything to him. His grip on the woman in his arms was growing weaker. His arms trembled with the effort of holding her.

'Not... far now,' he gasped, trying to focus his eyes on the ground ahead.

Plodding along as he was, at the limits of his endurance, it was only a matter of time until something finally brought him down. He felt his foot come down awkwardly on a rounded stone, felt it slip out from beneath him, felt his tenuous balance start to fail him.

With a breathless cry, he pitched forward, his desperate grip on Samantha slipping so that she tumbled to the ground in a dusty heap beside him, letting out an agonized groan as her weakened body absorbed the rough impact.

'No more,' she rasped, tears carving glistening tracks down her sand-covered cheeks, her voice raw with overwhelming fatigue and emotion. 'No more, Ryan. Please.'

Drake stared at her, at the young woman who had willingly faced so many challenges with him. So much had happened in the short time they had known each other, he almost couldn't remember life without her.

She was as exhausted as he was, her skin reddened by long exposure to the sun and marked by grime, sweat and dust. Her face was drawn and sunken, her normally thick dark hair hanging limp. Only her eyes still held some vestige of life, though they were filled with the same grief and defeat that he imagined she saw in him.

'It's okay. We'll rest here... for a while,' he managed to say between gasping breaths, trying to find something, anything that might offer some comfort. 'We'll feel better once... we've rested.'

The look in the woman's eyes made it obvious that such reassurance was as unnecessary as it was untrue. She managed a faint, bittersweet smile. 'You always were... a bad liar.'

Drake clasped her hand tight, unable to do anything else except be there with her.

'Listen to me, Ryan.' She reached up and touched his face, her hand trembling with the effort. 'You did... your best. You don't... have to pretend anymore.'

Drake swallowed. At least, he would have done if there had been any moisture left in his throat. 'It's not over yet.'

'Not for you,' she said, halting a moment before going on. 'Will you... do something for me?'

Drake leaned a little closer. 'Of course.'

Her eyes were locked with his, burning with fierce, desperate resolve. 'Leave me here. Go on without me.'

He felt the breath catch in his throat. 'What?'

'I'm done... I'm finished.' Her tone was one of quiet, resigned acceptance. She had fought her battle and lost. 'You might... still make it. But not... with me.'

Drake's reaction was immediate and instinctive, his mind utterly rejecting the notion. 'Fuck that. I'm not leaving you behind. Never.'

He tried to pull away, but she clung on to his tattered shirt, her grip surprisingly strong given her dire condition. 'Listen to me. Listen!' she pleaded. 'We both... know I won't make it. You can't carry me, but... you still have... some strength left. Go on alone. Find... Keira and Cole. Get... out of Libya.'

'Sam, there's no way—'

'Don't argue with me!' she cried, pulling him closer. 'This has... to happen! You know it does. I'm dying... Ryan. You can't change... that now. Killing yourself... won't save me.' At this, she choked back a sob, gritting her teeth to keep her composure. 'Take... the computer. Get it to Keira. Don't... let this be for nothing. Please.'

It was heartbreaking to see her like this, watching her fade away in front of him and knowing there was nothing he could do to prevent it.

'And leave you to die here?' he asked, shaking his head vehemently as he imagined the pain and delirium she would experience as her body shut down and her vital organs failed. 'No. I won't. I... I couldn't live with it.'

The woman let out a breath, her eyes still locked with his. 'I'm... not asking you to.' She raised her chin a little, readying herself as she reached for the automatic pushed down the back of her trousers. 'I'll take care... of it. All you need to do... is walk away.'

Oh Christ, he thought as she held the weapon up. She was serious. She meant to do it. She meant to end her own life.

He could have stopped her, could have snatched the weapon and tossed it away. But he didn't. He didn't stop her, because he knew deep down that she was right. Unable to go any further and with no hope of rescue, what was the point in prolonging the agony? How much longer could they last anyway? An hour? Two?

McKnight likely had less even than that.

She was right. He couldn't help her, couldn't get her out of this. He might well die soon enough as well, but he would make it a little further without her. It was a terrible thought to entertain, but that didn't make it any less true.

'I won't leave you.'

'Go, Ryan,' she implored him, holding the weapon in trembling hands. 'You don't... need to see this.'

Almost without being aware of it, he'd reached for the pistol and taken it gently from her hands. Struggling to make his fingers work, he disengaged the safety and pulled back the slide to make sure a round was chambered. He heard the ping of a brass casing being ejected.

'You don't have to do this alone,' he promised her.

She saw what he was doing, guessing his intentions. She didn't resist.

Gripping the weapon in one hand, Drake pulled her close, feeling the rapid beat of her heart, then rested his forehead against hers and closed his eyes as he raised the weapon.

'I'm here, Sam,' he whispered, his finger tightening on the trigger. 'I'm here with you.'

It remained there, trembling, straining, a mere fraction of an inch from firing. Drake clenched his jaw tight, willing himself to finish it, to do what had to be done. One pull, and it was over. He would spare her the pain of death that was encroaching by the second.

'It's all right,' he heard her say, her hand squeezing a little tighter. 'I'm ready.'

He had done all he could, had given it his all. But it wasn't enough. She'd been right – there was no happy ending for people like them.

Do it, a voice in his mind implored him. Pull the trigger, you coward. Do it now!

No!

With an agonized cry, he threw the weapon aside, off the edge of the wadi. He couldn't even hear the weapon clattering off the rocks below.

He couldn't do it. He *wouldn't* do it. Even if it was the right thing to do, even if it would spare them both the suffering of death by dehydration, he wouldn't just lay down and give up. Even now the will to live, to keep fighting and clawing for survival no matter what the odds, was too strong.

'I can't kill you,' he whispered, shaking his head. 'I'm sorry, Sam. I can't do it.'

She looked up at him then. He didn't see anger or disappointment in her eyes. All he saw was sadness.

'I understand,' she whispered. 'You're a good man, Ryan. Better than this.'

That was when it happened. Raising herself up from the ground with a final desperate effort, she managed to get her feet beneath her, and for a moment he wondered if his refusal to pull the trigger had kindled some hidden spark of determination, had tapped into some unknown reserve of inner strength.

He watched as she turned and stumbled away from him, moving on unsteady legs towards the edge of the wadi, and only then did he realize what she was planning. She was about to do the one thing he couldn't.

'Sam! No!' he screamed as she pitched forward and disappeared over the edge.

Scrambling forward, he fell by the edge of cliff, staring down at the woman lying in a dusty heap far below at the base of the slope. Too far for him to reach without suffering the same fate. She was gone.

She was gone.

Drake was no longer capable of crying. His body had no tears left in it, but he could feel them stinging his eyes as he looked down at her. The woman he had fought so hard to save, and who had sacrificed herself to give him a fighting chance.

Overwhelmed with grief and shock, Drake bowed his head and closed his eyes as sobs shook his body.

Chapter 51

The next hour was the hardest of Drake's life as he trudged wearily onwards, withered by sun and heat and blasted by windblown sand. At first he'd followed the course of the wadi, trying to find some way down to get to Samantha, determined to recover her body, but as time wore on and his grieving mind wandered, he began to lose all sense of what he was doing and where he was going.

The world seemed to have shrunk around him to the point that simply staying awake became his sole focus. It reminded him of being a kid watching a movie late at night, feeling his eyes starting to droop, then realizing what was happening and pulling himself back from the brink, only for it to start again a few moments later.

But despite his best efforts, it was a battle he was slowly losing. His mental and physical reserves were all but spent, his mind teetering on the brink.

It was then, at the moment of greatest need, that he at last saw something at the crest of a hill up ahead. A shape, vague and indistinct, half hidden by drifting sand. It wasn't a rock or a hill or a dune. Its lines were straight, deliberate and rectangular. It was man-made.

His eyes opened wider as the realization finally hit him. It was the ruined building where Mason and Frost were waiting!

'What?' he gasped, hardly believing what he was seeing.

Somehow his wandering path must have carried him to the right place. Somehow, through some bizarre quirk of luck or fate, his salvation was now less than a hundred yards away. All he had to do now was get to it.

Sand and burning wind whipped into his face, blasting his already exposed skin, but he kept his eyes fixed on the ruined building in the distance. It was the centre of his world now. All his thoughts, all his willpower, all his hopes were focussed on getting there.

The ground beneath him was rocky and uneven, sloping gradually uphill towards the structure. He knew that if he fell, he wouldn't get up again.

This was it. This was his last chance.

An unknown time passed as he laboured on. Minutes? Hours? He didn't know. He felt like he had been walking his whole life.

The building crept closer, now tantalizingly near. He felt like he could reach out and touch it.

He looked down at the ground before him, his vision swimming in and out of focus as he stumbled on, all his thoughts now directed towards making each laboured step. Left foot. Right foot. Left foot. Right foot.

Almost there. He had to be.

Left foot. Right foot.

Bone-dry air seared his throat with every breath as his overtaxed lungs fought in vain to draw in more oxygen. Adrenaline and desperate, stubborn resolve was all that kept him going now.

Left foot.

Right foot.

This had to be it now. Chancing his luck, Drake looked up, expecting the ruined archway that led inside to be yawning wide before him.

'No...' he mumbled breathlessly, staring in disbelief at the empty, barren slope before him. It was gone. The building that had looked so immediately familiar to him had vanished. How was that possible? How?!

It had been a lie, he realized in some dim, half-understood part of his mind. A mirage. A trick played by his exhausted and delirious brain. There was no building, no ruins, no hope of salvation. There never had been.

The realization that his final hope was nothing but a fantasy was all it took to crush his last vestiges of strength. Letting out an anguished, futile cry, he fell to his knees.

'It was here,' he whispered, his eyes stinging with tears that wouldn't come. 'I saw it. It... was here.'

This was it, he knew now. After all the risks, all the danger and threats and adversaries he had faced since this all began, he was going to die a miserable death of thirst here on this lonely hilltop in the middle of nowhere. He couldn't help wondering whether Marcus Cain would feel relieved or cheated when he eventually learned of the ignominious end that had befallen him.

'Ryan.'

Drake froze, his mind jerked back into awareness by the sound of a voice, faint and distant yet strangely immediate. He reached up and touched his radio earpiece, wondering for a heart-stopping moment if it was picking up a distant transmission.

'Ryan, look at me.'

A whisper, barely heard, like a distant voice carried on the wind. Although not from his radio, it seemed to be around and inside him all at the same time. He looked around, screwing up his eyes to focus his failing vision as he sought the source of the voice.

That was when he saw her, standing before him, as real and solid as the ground beneath his feet. McKnight, strong and healthy once more.

'Sam,' he rasped, almost choking the word out through cracked lips.

Somehow she must have survived the fall. Someone must have found her, given her water and clean clothes. Mason and Frost! They must have disobeyed his order and come looking for them.

His heart swelled at the thought of his two companions, always loyal but rarely obedient. He imagined Frost berating him for keeping them waiting, and Mason watching the drama unfold with his broad, infectious grin.

And most of all, he felt tears of joy and relief stinging his reddened eyes at the sight of the woman before him. The woman he'd fought so hard to protect, who he thought he'd lost forever.

'I thought you were gone. I thought... you died.'

Kneeling down beside him, Samantha reached out and gently caressed his cheek, her eyes filled with compassion and understanding.

'Shh, it's all right,' she said soothingly. 'I'm here, Ryan. It's going to be okay now.'

Drake closed his eyes for a moment as relief washed over him. 'Keira? Cole?'

'They're just beyond the ridge,' she confirmed. 'They had a hell of a time finding me. You won't believe what they've been through.'

He couldn't help but laugh. 'I'm sure... they'll tell me all about it.'

'They will,' she promised. 'But you have to get up now. You have to get to them.'

With great effort, Drake opened his eyes and looked up. The slope on which he had collapsed was part of a low ridge running more or less directly across his path, strewn with rocks and sand and small boulders. He hadn't made it to the top, lacking the energy or the will to go any further when the futility of his efforts was at last revealed to him.

'Come on, Ryan,' Samantha said, her voice gentle and encouraging as she took his arm to help him. 'Time to get up. Get up now.'

Drake took a breath, his throat parched, his eyes dry and gritty, searching deep inside for some final reserve of energy. She was right. He could do this. He could make it.

Managing to get his boot planted firmly, he heaved himself up from the ground. His vision swam for a moment and he staggered sideways, clutching at the rocky ground for support. His knuckles grazed the rough stone, cutting the skin and causing vivid red blood to well up. He didn't notice the pain. He was beyond that now.

Tired, bruised and battered, the two fighters emerged from their corners for the last round. One was younger, stronger and fitter, but not as confident as he'd once been. This hadn't been the walkover that he'd expected. It had been a hard, brutal slog, and it was telling.

The other fighter was older, battered and bleeding, chest heaving as he gulped for air. But he remained defiantly on his feet, his jaw set with determination as he moved forward to meet his opponent.

Somehow Drake fought back the darkness that seemed to be encroaching on his mind. Somehow he forced his leaden feet to move as he shuffled up the hill, struggling to keep his balance as dizziness threatened to pitch him over.

'You're close, Ryan,' Samantha coaxed him, staying by his side every step. 'Just a little further.'

He had to make it. He knew it with a certainty that defied reason. Somehow he had to find the strength to keep going.

The ground was sloping uphill, strewn with rocks that had tumbled or been blown down from above in years past. His foot caught and he fell with bruising force, rocky ground rushing up to envelop him in a crushing embrace.

Ducking beneath a clumsy, tired punch, the older fighter moved in close, drew back his fist and slammed it into his opponent's ribs with enough force to bruise flesh and crack bones. The younger man grunted in pain and fell to his knees as the old fighter moved in to press home his advantage.

'Get up, Ryan. You have to get up,' Samantha urged him.

'I can't… I've got nothing left.'

'Yes, you do!' she said, her voice stronger and more forceful now. 'You didn't give up on me, I'm not giving up on you now. So don't you dare quit on me! Get on your feet and move! Nothing else matters now. Get up!'

Coughing and gasping, Drake clutched at the ground, fighting to rise to his feet once more. He lost himself then, lost all sense of orientation and direction. All he knew was that he had to keep moving forward.

That was all that mattered now.

'Don't you dare give up,' she warned him. 'You're going to make it, Ryan. I know you are.'

He clambered around a weathered boulder, leaning heavily on the burning hot surface, and with great effort took a stumbling, hesitant step forwards. Every step for him was a grim battle that he was increasingly struggling to fight, but still he clawed and fought his way up the slope, drawing deep on his last reserves of strength in a desperate effort to reach the summit.

Drawing deep, the younger fighter rose up and lashed out at his opponent, landing stinging lefts and rights that reopened old cuts. Bright red blood spotted the canvas beneath them.

The older man waded forward, weathering the blows like the old warrior he was. He'd been hurt many times in his career, and he wasn't afraid any more. This was the last fight of his life.

'Ten more feet, Ryan. Don't you dare quit on me! You don't get to quit until I say so!'

Now down on his hands and knees, the breath rasping in his throat, the vision fading from his eyes, Drake fought his way up inch by agonizing inch.

'Five more feet. Keep going!'

The old man drew back his arm to deliver the final blow, the haymaker that would end it. Even through the pain, the exhaustion, the blood and the sweat, his eyes were alight in the moment of victory.

But his attempt to land a final, crushing knockout had left him vulnerable, the moment of his triumph exposing an opening that his younger opponent exploited. Damaged bone and sinew clashed with bruised flesh one last time as the crowd's roars drowned out all else.

Letting out a final, exhausted groan, Drake collapsed at the crest of the ridge, his face resting on the burning sand, his fingers still clawing feebly at the ground.

Through gritty, blurred eyes, he stared out at the rocky undulating landscape that lay beyond, seeing almost nothing.

'I… made it. I made it. Where… are they, Sam?' he pleaded.

There was no answer. She was gone.

But before he could speak again, he saw something; a darker shape amongst the blasted rocks and sandy hills.

A shape that was moving towards him.

He heard a shout. A voice. A human voice calling out something, but it was so far away he couldn't make it out. The world seemed to be closing in around him, details swallowed up and sounds drowned out by the pounding blood in his ears.

Unable to fight it any longer, Drake's exhausted mind finally surrendered to the darkness that was so eager to swallow him.

Part IV

Retribution

Following the overthrow of the Gaddafi regime in 2011, files recovered from the headquarters of the Libyan intelligence service in Tripoli indicated that the US and UK governments handed over dozens of opponents of the Libyan regime for interrogation and torture. Neither country has officially commented on these claims.

Chapter 52

Samantha McKnight's body lay curled up in foetal position at the base of the rocky slope it had rolled down after she'd thrown herself off the cliff above. Silent, unmoving, already coated with a fine layer of drifting sand that would eventually cover it completely.

To any casual observer she would have seemed long dead.

But it was not so. A tiny spark of life still burned within her. Her chest rose and fell in shallow, rapid breaths, her hand twitched, and her eyes slowly fluttered open.

Just for a moment, she was at peace. There was no sound, no sensation. All she was aware of was the sandy ground around her and the flawless blue sky overhead.

Then, in an instant, her memory returned. And with it came the pain.

It hit with such force, flowing up and down her body like a tide, that she almost passed out again. Vaguely she remembered the fall from the cliff above, the jarring impacts as she tumbled down the slope, rocks and stones hammering her body from every angle, then at last an explosion of darkness that had claimed her.

But it hadn't killed her. Not yet at least.

She almost smiled at the irony. Couldn't even do *that* right.

Not that it mattered much now. She might have avoided a quick death from the fall, but the desert itself would likely finish her soon enough.

At least Drake was gone, and that thought was some comfort to her as her mind drifted towards unconsciousness again. She closed her eyes, grateful for the chance to rest at last. It felt so good to rest…

Then she heard it. A sound, low and rough. The rhythmic puttering of an engine, the rattle of a metal vehicle bumping over rough ground, the creak of old axles.

It was growing louder. Too weary to move her head, Samantha could only wait, listening with curious detachment as the vehicle approached. Perhaps they wouldn't even see her. Perhaps they'd drive on by and leave her to her fate.

A sudden shout, the squeal of brakes, and the engine noise died away.

Only then did she see the pair of scuffed boots come stomping across the rocky ground towards her, the crunch of gravel just audible beneath the continued shouting.

They stopped beside her, and Samantha felt strong hands grip her by the shirt, rolling her over onto her back. She saw a dark face silhouetted against the burning sun overhead before she finally lost consciousness again.

Chapter 53

Drake gasped in shock, his mind jerked suddenly and painfully back to awareness by a chilling deluge of water. Blinking his eyes open, he looked around, trying to make sense of his surroundings.

All around him was darkness. Not the absolute darkness of a hood pulled over his head or bindings covering his eyes, but rather the deep shadows of night. How was it suddenly night? Where was he?

Slowly details began to resolve themselves as his vision cleared. He saw rock walls and a ceiling, rough and irregular – an interior space shaped not by man, but by nature. A cave. A cave lit by the flickering orange glow of a small fire somewhere nearby.

He could hear voices; several of them, their words blending together into a confused and jumbled drone that echoed off the cave walls. He tried to focus, tried to separate them and discern individual words, but his mind couldn't comply with his demands.

Then suddenly he saw a face above him. A woman's face, dark-skinned and framed by long black hair that fell all around him, blotting out much of his surroundings. A pair of piercing eyes were focussed on his own; hostility mingled with vague, professional concern.

Only then did a single voice emerge from the others, fighting its way through the fog of his brain to reach him. 'Ryan? Ryan, can you hear me?'

He recognized this woman who was now so focussed on him. A name slowly drifted from the dark recesses of his mind.

'Laila?' he croaked, struggling just to form the word.

'That's right. It's Laila. Ryan, tell me what happened in Tripoli. Where is Tarek?'

Tarek. That was another name he recognized, yet he couldn't say why. He felt as if his mind was a vast darkened room, and he possessed only a dim light with which to explore its depths. Concentrating, he tried to piece together the fragmented images and thoughts that seemed to swirl around with no clear pattern linking them.

Tarek. Laila…

He saw himself running through a darkened alley at night, supporting an injured man in his arms. He saw another man swinging a weapon towards him, then suddenly he disappeared in a storm of metal as a car drove straight into him. He saw himself struggling through the desert, sand and heat blasting him, trying to reach a woman who had collapsed to the ground in an exhausted heap.

And then, just like that, the fragmented and confused thoughts, images and memories suddenly coalesced into a single whole once more. His bleary eyes snapped open and he reached out, grasping Laila's arm, his grip strong and urgent despite his exhausted state.

'Sam!' he called out, the blood pounding in his ears. 'She was... with me. Where is she? Where!'

Her dark brows drew together in a frown. 'We found no one with you. They searched the area. It was just you.'

Drake released his grip, memories of Samantha staggering towards the cliff edge replaying like camera flashes in his mind. He saw her pitch forward, saw her disappear into the void beyond. And last of all, he saw her broken and lifeless body lying at the base of the slope.

'What about the others?' he asked weakly. 'Keira, Cole...'

'Listen to me, this is important,' she pressed on, desperate for answers. 'What happened to Tarek? Where is he?'

Drake's heart sank. Once again he saw Sowan lying on his back in that alleyway, foamy blood leaking from the bullet wound in his chest as he stared back at Drake, knowing he was dying. Knowing his promise to return to Laila would never be fulfilled.

'I'm sorry,' he said, looking up at the woman who had entrusted her husband's safety to his care. 'I couldn't get to him. I couldn't... help him.'

Lying so close to her, he was able to watch in agonizing detail as her mask of tight control and composure crumbled before his eyes. He watched as she reached up and held a hand to cover her mouth, watched as she bowed her head and tears began to fall, her shoulders moving up and down as she sobbed.

Then suddenly she looked up at him again, the grief and sorrow twisting and magnifying into hate and anger. Her right hand drew back and then arced down towards him, and his world was jarred sideways by the blow.

'You were supposed to protect him!' she yelled, her tear-streaked eyes burning with rage as she struck him again. 'He trusted you to bring him back. You used him, you bastard!'

Weakened and pinned down, there was nothing Drake could do to defend himself as the blows rained in, frenzied and driven by raw emotion rather than a cold desire to kill or injure. Still, they were doing damage all the same, and he knew that if the attack continued unabated there was a fair chance she might beat him to death before she realized what she was doing.

But as it turned out, she didn't get the chance. Another figure, big and imposing, suddenly intervened in the one-sided fight, grasping her arm just as she was reaching back to deliver another stinging blow. Exercising a strength that far outmatched her own, Drake's unexpected saviour shoved her backwards with such force that she was almost knocked off her feet. As it was, she had to scramble to regain her footing.

'Enough,' a gruff, accented voice decided. 'I didnae save the man just to watch you beat him tae death.'

Drake felt a chill run through him at the sound of that voice, even as the rational part of his mind cautioned him that such a notion was almost impossible. It couldn't be the man he thought it was. It just couldn't.

'My husband is dead because of him!' Laila shouted, jerking a finger towards Drake. She was trembling visibly with fury. 'He must answer for this.'

'Aye,' the voice agreed. 'He will. But first he'll answer tae me.'

With that, he turned around to regard the man lying on the floor of the cave, bruised and battered and exhausted. The moment Drake caught sight of his face, took in the familiar – if aged – features of the man he'd once considered both a friend and a mentor, he knew his suspicions had been proven horribly correct.

'Matt,' he managed to say.

The last time he'd seen Matt Cunningham had been nearly a year earlier, in the aftermath of a desperate gun battle in Afghanistan that had left one of his team dead and two others injured. The same night that Cunningham himself had tried to kill him.

Drake had promised to make him answer for his betrayal that night, if ever their paths crossed again. Apparently someone up there possessed a sense of humour, because now that they'd encountered each other again, Drake was in no condition to make him answer for anything.

Ignoring Drake for the moment, Cunningham directed a stream of Arabic to a young man dressed in Bedouin desert clothes standing nearby. Straightaway the youth moved forward and took Laila by the arm, escorting her gently but firmly deeper into the cave. The glow of another fire caused the two figures to cast grotesque shadows on the uneven walls.

'Useful, that one,' Cunningham remarked, watching her go. 'Her being a doctor and all. She's one of the reasons you're still above ground. Well, in a manner of speaking, at least,' he added, glancing up at the rocky roof. 'By my reckoning, that's twice I've saved your life now, son.'

Drake could scarcely imagine a more unlikely saviour, or a more unwelcome one. 'How did you find me?'

'I saw you in Nalut,' Mason explained. 'You and the lass from Afghanistan. Didn't take long to figure out something was up.'

Drake closed his eyes, replaying McKnight's earlier warning in his mind. A Western man with a greying beard, watching them from the other side of the road, only to vanish a short time later. It had been easy enough to dismiss at the time, but never could he have imagined that it was this man.

'So you followed us out here?' he asked.

'Not exactly. The young lad you saw there; Iskaw's his name. He ran into the rest of your team earlier today, rushed here and told me about it. So we came to question them. As it turned out, Laila there was the most cooperative of the bunch. She told us you'd planned to meet up with the others, so I sent the boys out to search for you. Lucky I did. You were about as close to death as I've seen any man. Even I had my doubts if you'd make it.'

325

Drake ignored that part. He didn't need Cunningham to tell him how close he'd come. 'What did you do with them?' he demanded, wondering if he was cold and ruthless enough to have disposed of them once he'd learned what he needed.

'The team comes first, eh? I expected as much,' Cunningham said, his tone half mocking. 'Aye, they're alive, before you go fretting about them.'

He leaned in a little closer, taking in Drake's dishevelled appearance. His expression made it plain he didn't like what he saw. 'You look like shit,' he decided. Reaching behind him, he unscrewed the lid from a water bottle and thrust it at Drake. 'Here, drink this. You need it.'

Drake eyed the water bottle warily, saying and doing nothing for several seconds. Being dragged unconscious to this place was one thing, but willingly accepting help from a man who'd tried to kill him the last time they'd met was quite another. Nevertheless Drake was now all too aware of the ravenous thirst that had seized him.

Knowing Drake well enough to guess his thoughts, the older man smiled in amusement. 'There's a lot of good reasons to die. Pride's not one of them, mate.'

Reluctantly Drake snatched the bottle out of Cunningham's hands, held it to his lips and drank. The water was warm and tasted faintly of chemicals – likely purification tablets – but to a man who had come close to dying from thirst just hours earlier, it felt like vintage champagne at that moment.

It was all he could do to control himself enough to keep from gulping it down in one go, though he knew that that would do more harm than good. It had to be taken slowly at first, sipped in small doses so that his shrunken stomach could adapt to the sudden influx of hydration.

'How's the head?'

'Like you care,' Drake fired back.

Cunningham eyed him with disapproval. 'If I didn't care, I wouldn't have sent the boys out looking for you. And I definitely wouldn't have wasted my afternoon dragging your sorry arse all the way here, just to have you dirty my beautiful home.' As he said this, he spread his arm out in a grand gesture to encompass the small cave.

'You live here?'

'Aye, from time to time. It's cheaper than the Hilton, and a handy place when I'm doing business in the area.'

Drake frowned. 'What kind of business?'

Cunningham reached into his pocket, found a packet of cigarettes and fished one out, lighting up and taking a draw before he spoke. 'I was a wee bit short on job prospects when I left Afghanistan last year. And my boss wasnae around to give me a reference, if you catch my drift.'

He certainly did. Richard Carpenter, the head of the private military company that Cunningham had worked for, had been assassinated by Anya after trying to have Drake's entire team murdered. Not long after, his double-dealings with an Afghan warlord had been exposed to the world, resulting in the dissolution of what remained of his company.

'Your boss was a lying, murdering piece of shit. He killed good people for money.'

'No argument here.' Cunningham shrugged, as if that were enough to put the matter to bed. 'Anyway, I went freelance, taking work where I could get it. Turns out I'm good at finding people – especially the kind who don't want to be found.'

It all seemed to fall into place then.

'You're a bounty hunter,' Drake said, his voice carrying an undertone of disdain.

There were lots of men like him in places like this nowadays. Iraq in particular had been swarming with freelancers during Drake's tour there, all hoping to claim the lucrative bounties placed on the heads of former regime members by the CIA. Most had been unemployed ex-military types looking for a quick payday, others mere wannabes out to make a name for themselves, while a few had been true hardcore mercenaries in the strongest sense of the word. Men who had fought and killed all across the globe, wherever the tides of war and fortune took them.

Those belonging to the latter category were some of the most genuinely frightening men Drake had ever encountered.

'No need to say it like that, mate. A man's got to work,' Cunningham reminded him. 'Anyway, you should be thankful I got into this business. You're the reason I came to Libya in the first place.'

'Me?'

'Aye, you. Kidnapping one of the Mukhabarat's best and brightest in the middle of the night, from his own home no less. Not a bad job you pulled there, if you don't mind me saying. Shame it all went tits up from there. But you can bet the Libyans weren't so impressed. They put a price on your head – a very hefty one actually – plus a bonus for returning Tarek Sowan alive. Looks like I won't be collecting that.'

It didn't take a genius to see where he was going with this. Cunningham's inexplicable concern for his welfare made a lot more sense now. 'So what now? You turn me and the others in, collect your bounty and fuck off?'

'That's one way this could play out.'

'Is there another?'

'That depends on you, Ryan.' Cunningham took another draw on his cigarette. 'What's on the laptop?'

Drake looked away, saying nothing. He had made the mistake of trusting this man with his secrets once already; he had no desire to do so again.

'Playing the strong, silent type isn't going to help you here, son. You kidnap a senior Libyan official, then let him go free, then travel *back* to Tripoli before ending up way out here with an encrypted computer. That's a pretty strange chain of events, even for you. So my question is, why?'

'What are you going to do? Kill me like you tried to in Afghanistan?' Drake challenged him, his green eyes flashing in the firelight.

'I don't expect you to trust me,' he conceded. 'Or forgive me.'

'Good, because I don't plan on doing either of those things.'

For a moment, he actually saw a flicker of pain in the older man, as if his words had genuinely hurt him.

'I made mistakes, Ryan. Aye, none of us can say we haven't. But I made mine, I admit it, and there's not a day goes by that I don't regret what happened.' Taking one last draw on the cigarette, he flicked it into the campfire and leaned in a little closer. 'You might hate me. You might even wish me dead. Christ knows, I wouldnae blame you. But I'm probably the only person in this country who *doesn't* want to kill you right now, so maybe you should think twice before you burn that bridge. Like I said, there are a lot of good reasons to die, but pride isnae one of them.'

Drake stared back at him in tense silence. He might have been sincere, or every word out of his mouth might have been a lie. After everything that had happened, Drake no longer trusted himself to tell the difference.

'You wouldn't believe me if I told you,' he evaded.

'Try me.'

He sighed and took another gulp of water. 'I was hired to bring Sowan in,' he admitted at last. 'The deal went sour, we had to improvise.'

'Hired by who?'

'A man named Faulkner. A spook with British intelligence.'

At this, Cunningham's eye opened wider. 'Faulkner? David Faulkner?'

'You know him?'

'Jesus, everybody in the Regiment knew him. Well, everyone who was around back in the day. It was long before your time, I suppose.'

Before his time. Fifteen years separated the two men. A lot could, and apparently did, happen in those ten years.

'What do you know about him?'

'A lot. He was around during the Troubles back in the eighties, when things were getting really out of hand, running undercover ops against our friends in the IRA. And boy, did he run them. Aye, he was all polite and gentlemanly on the surface, but underneath he was something else altogether. Liked to get very hands-on during the interrogations, if you know what I mean. And he *enjoyed* it. I've seen lots of men do it over the years, but not many that actually enjoyed what they did. He scared the shit out of most of us, so we avoided him as much as we could. Everyone did. That was something else he enjoyed – the fear.'

Drake let out a breath. He wasn't exactly surprised by what he'd heard, given his encounters with Faulkner over the past couple of days. But it didn't do much for his morale to know exactly what kind of man he was up against. A sadistic, intelligent and ruthless killer, with considerable resources at his disposal.

'In short, Faulkner's a man you should be very fucking afraid of. What on earth made you decide to work for a man like him?'

There was little to lose now by telling him the truth. Cunningham was already well acquainted with the sword hanging over Drake's head, having been told the whole sorry tale during their short-lived reunion in Afghanistan the previous year.

'Someone murdered my mother,' he said at length. 'Faulkner offered me answers, and like a fucking idiot I went for it. He was playing us... playing *me* all along, running some kind of black op to hand prisoners over to the Libyans in exchange for intel.'

Cunningham shook his head in dismay. 'So why go back to Tripoli?'

'Evidence. The Libyans kept everything to do with the project on file. Phone calls, emails, prisoner dossiers – enough to fuck him over, put him in jail for the rest of his life. Sowan went in to recover it, but his own people turned against him. They deleted all evidence of the op.'

'So what's on the laptop?'

Drake sighed and looked down. 'The Americans have been smuggling weapons and equipment to resistance groups over the border. They're building an army to topple Gaddafi.'

'Jesus,' Cunningham breathed. 'That's a disaster waiting to happen. The country would tear itself apart.'

He wasn't inclined to dispute that assertion. 'Faulkner found one of their key operatives and handed him over to the Libyans. Looks like he's trying to derail their coup to protect his own interests. The details might well be on that laptop, but nobody's managed to break into it yet.'

'So now you're caught between a rock and a hard place, aye? An entire country hunting you, the Agency trying to silence you, and a fucking lunatic out to kill you.'

Drake said nothing to this disconcertingly frank summary of his situation. 'Now you know why we were here. The question is, what happens now?'

'You mean, am I going to hand you over to the Libyans? Let them torture and execute you so I can earn a few extra quid?' Cunningham allowed that notion to hang in the air for a few seconds, as if he himself had yet to decide the matter. 'We were friends once, Ryan. You might have forgotten that, but I haven't. So here's what I'm thinking. We're a few miles from the border; the boys can escort you over before dawn, get you into Tunisia and let you be on your way. I'll take the woman and return her to the Libyans, maybe even claim a small reward at the same time. The rest is up to you.'

Drake was genuinely surprised by what he'd just heard. After everything that had happened between them, the tumultuous events of the previous year and the animosity that had developed since that day, Cunningham was still prepared to help him.

That being said, not everything about his plan sat well with Drake.

'Laila's been through enough,' he countered. 'If you hand her back to the Libyans, she could end up in a prison cell or a coffin.'

The older man shrugged. 'Aye, and I suppose you could offer her something better? They might grill her on what happened, but at the end of the day she's an innocent caught up in this. They'd realize that sooner or later.' He leaned a little closer. 'What's your answer, Ryan?'

'Do I have a choice?'

'Nope. You can consider this your get-out-of-jail-free card. You only get one, and this is yours – there won't be another,' Cunningham warned him. 'Oh, and you're welcome.'

'I'd like to see the rest of my team,' Drake said, not sure what else to say.

'Aye. Thought you might.' Rising to his feet, Cunningham held out a hand to help him up, which Drake refused.

Attempting to get up on his own, however, he soon regretted this show of stubborn defiance as his vision blurred and the familiar pounding headache made itself felt again. Clutching at the rock wall for support, Drake fought to control the rising tide of nausea and somehow managed to drag himself to his feet.

Saying nothing to this, Cunningham simply gestured to the low passageway that seemed to lead into a larger chamber beyond.

'After you, old son.'

Chapter 54

Mukhabarat headquarters, Tripoli

It was just past nine o'clock in the evening, with darkness descending on the city of Tripoli, when the news Bishr Kubar had been waiting for finally came through.

'We have one of them!' one of the communications technicians called out across the crowded operations room.

Pushing himself away from the map he'd been poring over, Kubar strode across the room to speak with him.

'Talk to me,' he growled, fatigue and frustration working together to leave his temper even shorter than usual. 'Give me details.'

'One of our roving patrols came across a Western woman out in the foothills of the Nafusa Mountains. She was dehydrated and close to death, and apparently alone.'

Kubar frowned, well aware that the reports of last night's shooting specifically mentioned a man leaving the area. 'Was she carrying anything with her? A laptop computer?'

The young technician's face paled. 'There was no word on personal possessions, but their report was filtered through three layers of military communications,' he explained. 'They may have neglected to mention it.'

The muscles across Kubar's shoulders tightened. 'What's her current status?'

'She's alive. They're transporting her to the nearest military command point for questioning.'

He nodded. 'Find out where that is. I want to be there when they bring her in.'

–

Pain.

Noise and jolting movement.

The smell of petrol and old leather and cigarette smoke. The feel of rough metal against her cheek. The pressure of plasticuffs biting into the flesh of her wrists.

With her mind lingering on the edge of consciousness, McKnight struggled to process any information beyond simple physical sensations. She opened her eyes with some effort and looked around, the world swimming into bleary focus.

She was in a vehicle of some kind. Military, simple and functional. Bare exposed metal, worn seats, dirty windows. The rough growl of an engine, accompanied by the strained groan as the suspension bore them across another patch of rough ground.

Beyond the windows, darkness illuminated only by the twin beams of headlights. Night had fallen on the desert. She wasn't sad about that – she'd seen enough sun to last her a lifetime.

She tried to move a little, and felt something tug painfully at the skin of her left arm. Looking down, she saw an IV line snaking out to a bag of some kind of liquid suspended from the vehicle's roof. Intravenous fluids. They had given her basic medical treatment, patched her up, bringing her back from the brink of death.

Already she could feel her mind growing sharper, her thinking clearer as her body recovered from the debilitating effects of dehydration. And with that heightened awareness came a greater appreciation of the pain she was in.

Somehow she had survived her leap from the cliff top and her tumble down the rough rock-strewn slope beyond, but the fall had nonetheless left its mark on her. Her entire body ached with the pain of deep bruising, not to mention the countless sharp stones that had torn her clothes and the flesh beneath. Every inhalation brought with it a stab of pain, suggesting she'd cracked or even broken several ribs.

Yet for all that, she was alive. Somehow she had clung on long enough to be rescued, though perhaps rescue was the wrong word.

She looked around, taking in her fellow passengers.

There were three of them – two up front, and a third in the back with her. All male. All dressed in military fatigues. It didn't take long to reach the inevitable conclusion.

She'd been found by the Libyan army.

Oh Christ.

'Where are you taking me?' she asked before she could stop herself.

A sharp blow delivered to her injured ribs prompted an agonized cry, and was sufficient to silence further questions.

'You not speak!' her fellow passenger commanded in halting English. 'We ask question. Where is the other one?'

Ryan, she thought, with a mixture of hope and fear. With luck, he'd made it out of the area before they'd found her. But even for a man as resilient as him, the chances of survival in such an inhospitable place were almost nil. What strange irony would have saved her life and condemned his?

Samantha gave no answer to this question, which only antagonized her interrogator further. 'You answer now!'

She looked him in the eye. He was a small man, lean and wiry, his combat helmet removed to expose the balding dome of his head.

'I'm not telling you jack shit,' she replied in a calm voice. 'If you fixed me up with this IV drip, it means you're keeping me alive so you can bring me in for interrogation. That means it's not your job to ask questions. You're just a grunt, an errand boy. So you might as well shut up and make this ride easier for both of us, because I've got nothing to say to you, asshole.'

That was when she saw the change come over him, saw his eyes open wide, saw his mouth twist in anger, saw him ball up his fist to deliver another agonizing blow. She didn't care. If she was lucky, the stupid bastard might actually draw a weapon and kill her.

It was at this moment that the passenger up front, presumably the man in charge of this small patrol, barked an order at her new best friend. She couldn't tell what he said exactly, but it might have meant something because the man froze immediately, glancing uncertainly from Samantha to his comrade, then reluctantly lowering his arm.

Twisting around in his seat, the patrol's leader eyed her with something akin to amusement. 'I know what you are doing,' he informed her. 'Soon you wish I had let him kill—'

His sentence was abruptly cut short by an explosion of glass as a fist-sized hole suddenly appeared in the jeep's windshield. There was a wet popping sound, and McKnight felt something warm coating her face as the driver slumped forward against the wheel, his blood covering the dashboard and side window.

Uncontrolled, the jeep veered off whatever minor road it had been following before rolling to a stop.

McKnight had no idea what was happening, but even she had the presence of mind to throw herself down, flattening against the rear seat.

Her two companions weren't so lucky. The man up front reached for a rifle resting in his footwell, only to jerk violently as a volley of rounds tore through his body. She heard only a faint sigh, as if of disappointment, as he slid sideways in his chair.

Last to react was her friend in the rear seat. Recognizing that the jeep was a lost cause, he threw open his door and practically fell out into the darkness, trying to make a run for it. A trio of dull thuds followed by an agonized cry told her he hadn't made it far.

She was alone now, she realized. Alone in the back seat of the jeep, weakened and injured, her hands bound.

She could do little but watch as a figure emerged from the darkness, walking towards her with the casual self-confidence of a man in control of everything around him.

In the crimson light cast by the dashboard instruments, McKnight was able to make out a distinguished middle-aged face, a mane of neatly combed blonde hair, a charming smile betrayed by cold, calculating eyes.

'Hello, Samantha,' Faulkner said. 'Good to meet you at last.'

Chapter 55

The short, winding passage was perhaps an inch higher than Drake's head at its apex, but he ducked down a little anyway as he passed through. His head was killing him already without adding a concussion to his list of injuries.

Emerging into the chamber beyond, Drake's first impression was of a large bubble formed inside the rock, roughly oval in shape with the far end being somewhat wider than the entrance. The floor, probably once sloping downward towards the centre, was covered by a deep layer of sand that had been blown in and deposited here over millennia, forming a rough floor space about five metres wide and eight in length. A single fire burned in the centre of this improvised living space, providing enough light for him to make out the cave's inhabitants.

The first thing he saw were the two Bedouin men standing guard at the entrance; one armed with an AK assault rifle and the other with an ancient bolt-action weapon that looked older than both of them combined. Drake couldn't help but notice the long narrow scar that snaked down the right side of his face, starting at his ear and tapering down to the edge of his mouth. But far from being a disfigurement, the scar lent him a rakish look, reminding Drake of a swashbuckling adventurer from some old pirate movie.

Facial scars notwithstanding, both men were fairly representative of the people who had somehow found a way to survive in this most inhospitable of environments – tall, lean and tough, possessing a wiry, sinewy strength that was far more useful here than any bulked-up musculature. And they bore enough of a resemblance to each other that they had to be either brothers or close cousins – a suspicion that was borne out a moment later as Cunningham introduced him.

'Ryan, meet the boys,' he began, gesturing to the bigger one first. 'This is Amaha. The one with the scar is his wee brother, Iskaw. They're Tuaregs and dinnae speak much English, so I wouldnae worry about introducing yourself.'

'Where did you find them?' he asked, perplexed how an out-of-work mercenary had hooked up with such an unlikely crew.

Cunningham shrugged. 'Long story, mate. The short version is that they stirred up trouble with another tribe. Iskaw there even got into a knife fight with the chief's son. That's why he's so pretty now. Got himself banished to avoid a tribal feud.'

Drake nodded, understanding all too well why such a drastic measure had been taken. Rivalry and distrust were endemic amongst the nomadic tribes in areas like this. Grudges were rarely forgotten or forgiven, and even petty disagreements could escalate into full-scale blood feuds that pulled in several other tribes and needlessly cost many lives. Severe punishments were the only way to maintain some measure of order and satisfy honour that had been slighted.

'Anyway, his brother decided to go with him, and they struck out on their own,' Cunningham carried on. 'Lucky for them, they had the good fortune to run into me about six months ago. I've been training them ever since. Sharp as tacks, both of them. A little too much bravado at times, but they're good lads. And Iskaw there can shoot better than either of us ever could.'

Drake wasn't so sure an encounter with Cunningham could be considered good fortune. Still, it was plain even to him that the man meant what he said about the two Tuaregs, taking an almost fatherly pride in their accomplishments.

Switching to Arabic, Cunningham spoke a few words to the two guards, who moved aside to allow Drake entry to the larger chamber beyond.

'Ryan! About goddamn time!' a female voice called out, speaking with a distinctly Boston accent that could only belong to Keira Frost.

Sure enough, the young woman rounded the fire and strode towards him. Her face was bruised and grazed in places from what had clearly been some kind of physical confrontation, but otherwise she appeared to be in good health.

The Tuareg guards tensed up when Frost made her move towards Drake, but a nod from Cunningham prompted them to stand down.

The young woman's strength certainly hadn't failed her as she threw herself at him, grabbing him in a fierce embrace that was equal parts relief and defiant protectiveness. It took him a moment to realize her hands were bound at the wrists with thick cordage, no doubt to keep her under control, and that she'd hooked them around his neck as she clung to him. Mason, who moved into view behind her, was likewise restrained.

'Ow! Take it easy, I'm still delicate,' he protested, though the relief in his voice was obvious, as was the strength of his own embrace in return.

'Goddamn it. I thought we'd lost you,' Frost whispered in his ear. Only now, in the relative safety of this place, could she finally acknowledge how close they'd come to never seeing each other again.

'No such luck,' Drake replied, feigning dry humour yet unable to hide the emotion in his voice. 'I'll be around to piss you off for a while yet.'

Reluctantly he eased out of her embrace and took a step back to regard his two friends. They were stranded thousands of miles from home in a hostile country whose government wanted them captured, hunted by a desperate man who wanted them dead, and imprisoned by a former enemy of dubious motives. But they were all together. That at least was something.

'Samantha?' Mason asked, though the look in his eyes suggested he knew the answer already.

Drake swallowed hard and shook his head.

His companion closed his eyes for a moment. 'I'm so sorry, Ryan.'

'It's not your fault. Nothing could have been done,' Drake said, knowing he couldn't let himself think about it now. Not here, not in front of everyone.

'What… what happened out there?' Frost asked. Her eyes were glistening, though she was able to hold it together, likely because she didn't want to show weakness in front of their captors.

Drake let out a breath. 'It was quick. Let's leave it at that for now.'

She was wise enough not to press him further.

'Sorry about the ropes,' Cunningham interjected, nodding to their bound hands. 'But they didn't exactly give us a warm welcome.'

Drake wasn't surprised. Frost had been captured, imprisoned and brutally interrogated as a result of Cunningham's betrayal last year, not to mention losing a close friend and comrade in the ensuing battle. He didn't doubt she would have happily torn his throat out if she'd had the chance.

'Untie them,' he ordered.

'Aye? So the wee banshee there can go in for round two?' Cunningham shook his head. 'I dinnae think so, mate.'

'Nobody's going to attack you,' Drake assured him, giving Frost a pointed look. 'Not now. Not after what happened today.'

The young woman cocked a dark brow, her relief at Drake's return now soured by distrust. 'Did I miss something, Ryan? This Scottish prick's the reason Keegan came home from Afghanistan in a fucking box.'

'He's also the reason I'm not dead,' Drake reminded her.

'So, what? You guys are best friends again?' she challenged him, eyes flashing with anger. 'That how this works?'

'The way this works is that we don't fuck with him, and he doesn't kill us all. So nobody's going to do anything stupid right now.' Gripping her arm, he pulled her close and spoke quietly in her ear. 'He'll answer for Keegan. But not today. *Not today.*'

The young woman stared back at him, the conflicting emotions of the moment clearly evident in her pale-blue eyes. Nonetheless, even she understood the necessity of cooperation, and reluctantly gave a nod.

With the matter settled, albeit with difficulty, Drake glanced at Cunningham. 'Let them go. You'll have no trouble from us.'

Cunningham studied him for a long moment before finally speaking a command to Iskaw, who lowered his weapon and drew a knife from his belt to cut their bonds. Drake couldn't help noticing that it was one of the military-issue blades given to his team by Faulkner.

Frost noticed it as well, and wasted no time speaking up as Iskaw severed the ropes at her wrists. 'I'll have that back now.'

Whether he understood the actual words was debatable, but clearly the intent wasn't lost on him. He smiled in amusement before sheathing the blade once more.

The young woman took a step towards him, but Drake was quick to intervene before she did something they all ended up regretting.

'Pick your battles, Keira.'

Frost hesitated a moment, then looked past him to the young Tuareg hunter, who seemed greatly amused by her defiant spirit. 'Keep smiling, asshole. I'll be taking that knife home with me.' Then, composing herself once more, she turned her attention back to Drake. 'Tell us what happened in Tripoli. How screwed are we?'

The look in Drake's eyes said it all. 'You'd better sit down for this one.'

She did, as did Mason. They listened in tense silence while Drake laid it all out – Sowan's arrival at Mukhabarat headquarters, the deletion of the evidence against Faulkner, the unexpected discovery that had forced him to improvise an escape, the desperate flight through the streets of Tripoli and the sudden, deadly ambush by Faulkner's men.

'They were ready for us,' he concluded. 'He knew what we were planning.'

'That son of a bitch,' Frost snarled, angrily tossing a stick onto the fire. 'The fucker's toying with us. He knows every move we make before we even know ourselves.'

Mason however had taken a more pragmatic view. 'He knows that we're going to do because he knows *you*, Ryan. You said yourself that he recruited you, probably studied you. He knows how you think. The question is, what are we going to do about it?'

'Well, that depends on what Keira can dig out of that laptop.' Drake didn't add that if she found nothing of use, they were pretty much out of options. Instead he turned to Cunningham. 'Where is it?'

The older man retreated to the far end of the cave, returning presently with the computer hooked under one arm. Hesitating a moment, he held it out to Frost, who snatched it out of his hand, laid it carefully on a low boulder and opened it up.

First impressions weren't good. The screen was marked by an obvious crack extending all the way across, and her initial attempts to power it up met with failure.

'I need tools. A screwdriver, pliers, whatever you've got,' she said, holding a hand out like a surgeon waiting for a vital implement.

It was Cunningham who came to her aid, much as she hated to accept his assistance, handing over an old and very well used Leatherman multi-tool. Unfolding a Philips-head screwdriver from the tool, Frost went to work on the laptop, removing the screws that held the outer casing together.

As the last one came undone, she managed to pry the plastic casing free and tossed it aside, exposing the machine's inner workings.

It didn't take long to see where the problem lay. The battery must have been damaged in the crash, allowing its acidic contents to leak into the delicate circuitry surrounding it. Already they could see the corrosive effects discolouring and warping the components the acid had come into contact with.

'Well, that ain't good,' the technical specialist said under her breath, pulling the battery free and tossing it aside. Letting out a vexed sigh, she looked up at the others. 'The motherboard's screwed. We're not going to be getting much out of this thing.'

Drake closed his eyes, the headache returning with greater force in that moment. 'What about the hard drive? Has it been destroyed?'

Working quickly, she unscrewed the metal casing which housed the laptop's memory unit. Situated on the opposite side from the damaged battery, it appeared to be untouched by the leaking acid.

'I don't think so,' she concluded after careful inspection. 'But it's useless unless I can hook it up to another machine. And there aren't many of them in this neck of the woods.'

'It was all for nothing, then,' Laila said from a dark corner of the cave, her voice raw with grief and laced with disgust at Drake. 'All of it. Tarek's life, his sacrifice. *You* failed him, just as you failed all of us. But still you live, Ryan Drake. Somehow you survive. It would have been a mercy on us all if the desert had taken you.'

Frost, never one to take an insult well at the best of times, rounded on her. 'Why don't you shut the—'

'Keira! Stop it,' Drake cautioned her, holding up a hand in an appeal for silence. 'She's right. I *did* fail.'

Frost, caught off guard by his frank admission, stared at him in silence. So did Mason, and even Cunningham.

'I failed all of you,' Drake repeated, raising his chin a little as he faced up to his personal mistakes. 'You followed me here. You supported me and you risked your lives for me, because I convinced you it was the right thing to do. But I was doing it for all the wrong reasons. I came here for revenge, to punish the man who took someone from me. But I was wrong. I gambled with other people's lives, with your lives, and... a good man is dead because of that. And Sowan *was* a good man,' he said, looking straight at Laila now. 'I was wrong about him, too. He trusted me. He gave his life to try to put things right, he deserved a lot better than what he got. I failed you both, and I failed Sam. And Chandra. All of them are gone because of me.'

There it was. His confession. His admission of guilt, for all the difference it made. He'd fucked up, and now he had to live with it. It might be hard for him, but it would be infinitely harder for Laila.

She said nothing. She had no words left for him, but he did see something in the flickering light of the nearby fire. He saw tears glistening in her eyes before she turned away, retreating into herself.

'So what do we do now?' Frost asked.

'Faulkner took a risk appearing in Tripoli like that. He came close, even killed Sowan, but he exposed himself at the same time. Because he was afraid – afraid of what we'd find. Afraid of what's on that hard drive.' Drake was staring into the flames as he spoke. 'I say we find out why. We get it out of the country, and we release its contents to anyone willing to listen.'

Drake looked up at Laila then, the red and orange flames reflecting in his eyes. There was only one thing left on his mind now.

'Then we destroy the bastard.'

Chapter 56

McKnight winced as the hood was yanked off her head, bright electric light flooding her eyes. Squinting, and trying to ignore the headache that still pulsed through her head like the steady beating of a drum, she glanced around, trying to take in as much detail of her surroundings as possible. There was no way of knowing when the hood might be thrown back on.

The source of illumination seemed to be a floodlight of some kind; the sort of temporary device that workmen would set up in underground tunnels while they went about their tasks. Its beam was directed straight at her, obviously intended to disorient her and make it difficult to tell what was going on.

In that respect at least, it was working. Her limited field of vision was enough to tell her she was in an enclosed room. It's dimensions were hard to judge, but it appeared to be both long and wide, and probably industrial in origin given the corrugated-steel walls on either side and the rough floorboards beneath her feet. A warehouse or factory perhaps.

But whatever the room's original purpose, the place seemed to be disused as far as she could tell. There was no machinery in view, no storage crates, no furniture save for a single wooden stool facing her. The air smelled of dust and sawdust and old engine oil.

Movement was impossible. Her wrists and ankles had been securely fastened to the chair she was now seated on, and she didn't doubt there were armed guards watching her in any case. In short, she wasn't going anywhere unless her captor allowed it.

Having removed her hood, the man in question now stepped into her line of sight, moving with the slow, deliberate ease of one who knows time is on his side. Pausing for a moment to wipe a layer of dust from the stool, Faulkner settled himself on it and regarded McKnight in silent, careful deliberation.

Needless to say, she did the same.

This was the first time she'd seen David Faulkner up close and she had to admit, his appearance was very much in line with what she knew of his personality.

Impeccably dressed in a neatly ironed white shirt and khaki-coloured trousers, he looked like he'd stepped out of lunch at an expensive country club. Everything from his watch to his shoes were designer brands.

She assumed him to be in his fifties, though his face had a strangely ageless quality about it, his forehead smooth and unlined, probably courtesy of a few shots of botox. Even his neatly coiffed blonde hair looked fake, either plugs or a toupee.

Only his eyes gave him away as something more than a rich middle-aged businessman preoccupied with his own vanity. Those eyes were fixed on her now, cold and cunning and assessing.

'Hello, Samantha,' he began, the words pouring out as smooth as velvet. 'I know this must seem like rather a moot point now, but it's occurred to me that we've never been properly introduced. My name's David. It's a pleasure to meet you.'

McKnight said nothing. She had no desire to converse with this man.

'You're probably wondering why I brought you here, why I went to all the trouble of liberating you from your Libyan army friends,' he went on. 'I was hoping we might sit down together and have a little chat... before things move forward. I always make a point of giving people a chance to be open and honest with me, perhaps save us all a bit of...' He glanced away for a moment and let out a faint sigh. 'Unpleasantness. After all, we're both reasonable people. There's no reason we can't converse in a reasonable way.'

She closed her eyes, the headache and pain of her numerous injuries seeming to return with greater intensity now. 'Look, asshole, I'm tired and I'm hurting and I'm really not in the mood to listen to all this crap. Let's save us all some time and get down to it. I know you're going to threaten me with all kinds of torture, maybe break out the hacksaws and blowtorches or whatever else you've got in mind. But the fact is you're wasting your time. You want to know where Ryan is? I can't tell you, because I don't have a goddamn clue. He could be on a flight home, or dead by now for all I know. He left me to die out in the desert, because I asked him to. I was unconscious when the Libyans found me, and God knows how long I'd been lying there. So do what you have to do, but drop the Bond villain routine. It's enough to make me throw up, if I actually had anything in my stomach.'

Far from being angered by her outburst, Faulkner merely smiled in amusement. 'Actually Samantha, I don't need to trouble myself with hacksaws or blowtorches in this case. The fact is, I believe you. I don't think you know where Ryan is, or even if he's still alive, so I'm not going to waste my time torturing you.'

At this, McKnight frowned in confusion. Of all the reactions she'd expected from him, this hadn't been one of them.

'I don't need you to help me find him.' Reaching into his pocket, Faulkner held up a cell phone. 'If I'm right, he'll find me.'

–

With their course of action decided, they had only to wait for the right time to put their plan into action. At Cunningham's recommendation, the group would remain in the cave until the following evening, giving them time to rest and recover a little strength before attempting the border crossing to Tunisia under cover of darkness. This mountain hideout was, according to him, about as remote and safe a place as it was possible to find anywhere on earth.

Thus, there was little to do for now except wait. Frost and Mason had chosen to occupy themselves with checking their limited supply of weapons and ammunition, trading insults and sarcastic remarks to keep their spirits up while they worked.

It was a habit they fell into more easily as time passed, dealing with tension and danger through mockery and dark humour as if by mutual consent. Perhaps it helped take their minds off the loss of one of their own, or perhaps it was enough simply to have someone around who understood.

Whatever the reason, it worked for them.

'Ow! Goddamn this thing,' Frost mumbled as the hacksaw blade slipped from her grasp for the third time, grazing her knuckles.

She was working to remove both the wooden stock and the lengthy barrel from the antique shotgun she'd stolen from the farmhouse the previous night, turning the gun into a bank robber's dream. It was a shame to ruin such a fine weapon, but its sheer size and weight made it impractical for transport or concealment.

Normally it was a simple enough procedure to modify a shotgun in this way, requiring just a few minutes in a decent workshop. Unfortunately the only tool at her disposal was an old hacksaw borrowed from Cunningham's limited cache of equipment. The blade had seen better days, and the handle had partially snapped off, leaving only an awkward metal stub to grasp. Severing the hardened steel barrel was an arduous task, and made no better by Mason's unsympathetic attitude.

'Hey, I'd have thought you had plenty practice doing that sort of thing,' he remarked with a wicked grin, watching as she resumed the rhythmic up-and-down sawing motion.

It took little imagination to guess what he was alluding to. 'Fucking pervert,' she hissed. 'Maybe I'll test this thing on you when I'm done.'

Mason winked at her. 'Good luck. You'd do more damage if you threw it at me.'

'Keep talking,' she mumbled. 'I'll remember this next time you need me to get your laptop working again.'

As the woman carried on with her difficult task, she became aware that Mason wasn't her only observer. Glancing up, she noticed both of the young Tuareg hunters watching her from the other side of the cave. One – she thought it might have been the older one, Amaha – was seated at an improvised comms station that looked to have been built from scratch out of frequency scanners and old military radios. He didn't seem to be transmitting anything, but rather passively listening in on other people's broadcasts.

Keeping one half of his radio headset pressed to his ear, he elbowed his younger sibling in the ribs and leaned closer, whispering something in his ear that brought amused chuckles to both men.

'Something funny, ladies?' she demanded, staring right at them.

Amaha spoke back to her in Arabic, struggling not to laugh.

'I'm sorry, I can't hear you. Why don't you come a little closer and say it?' she suggested loudly, tensing up a little in anticipation of a good scrap. They might not speak the same language, but she had a feeling she could teach him a little respect all the same.

'He says you work like you talk – fast and loud,' Cunningham explained to her. Leaning against the rocky wall nearby, he'd been smoking a cigarette in meditative silence until now. 'He wonders if you do everything the same way.'

Both young men were laughing now. Frost glanced at them, chewing her lip as she considered whether or not the hacksaw would work more effectively on human flesh than the antique gun.

Sensing her dangerous change in demeanour, Cunningham added, 'High spirits, lass. Wouldn't let it get to you.'

Frost spared him only a brief glance, not trusting herself to look at him for too long lest the memory of what he'd done override common sense. She had promised Drake not to cause trouble here, and she would abide by that, despite her better judgement.

'If I were you, I wouldn't let *me* get to *them*.'

With nothing more to say on the matter, she turned her attention back to the gun and started sawing once more. She was almost through the barrel when she heard the soft thump of boots on the sand nearby, and looked up to see the younger of the two Tuaregs, the one with the scar, approaching. She vaguely remembered his name as Iskaw.

'Boy, I'm really not in the mood for shits and giggles,' she warned him. Casual – albeit irritating – banter was one thing, but harassment was quite another. Promise or no promise, she'd have no problem putting the hurt on this man if he overstepped his bounds.

To her surprise, however, he hunkered down on the ground in front of her, his expression oddly serious now. 'I not laugh,' he said in broken, heavily accented English. 'I want… make sorry. You not… feel bad, we laugh.'

This at least prompted a raised eyebrow. 'Thought you couldn't speak English?'

Iskaw shrugged. 'I learn little, listen better than speak. *Wali* teach.'

'*Wali?*' she repeated. 'Who's that?'

The young man gestured to Cunningham, who was still sitting with his back to the wall. '*Wali* is name for him. Means… guardian, and friend.'

Frost couldn't help but smile at the irony. Matt Cunningham was many things, but guardian and friend didn't exactly spring to mind when she thought of him. 'Let me ask you something. Do you know who *Wali* really is? Where he came from, why he's in your country?'

She half expected Cunningham to intervene, to silence her and break up the conversation lest she expose him for who he was. To her surprise, however, he did no such thing. But she could feel his eyes on her even from the other side of the cave, listening and waiting to see what happened.

The Tuareg hunter nodded solemnly. 'He tell. He make mistake, do bad things for bad people. He tell good men die because of this.'

Frost sniffed and looked down at the gun in her hands. 'That's right. Good men die because of this. My friend died because of this.'

She heard a faint sigh from him. 'I not know *Wali* before. Good man, bad man… it is past. But I know now. I know he save me, give me shelter, teach me.

My… family force me out. He is stranger, but he help me. For this, I owe him a debt.'

Perhaps his relationship to Cunningham wasn't so incongruous after all, she thought with grudging recognition. There was a certain symmetry to their respective situations – one lonely outcast meeting another. 'So what are you now? His servant?'

'His friend,' Iskaw corrected her. 'Until my debt is paid.'

Remarkable that one so young should place so much value on honour and responsibility, Frost realized. It was of course misplaced, stupid, and as likely to get him killed as it was to repay whatever debt he imagined he owed, but she couldn't help feeling a touch of respect for him all the same.

'While we're talking about repaying debts, I should probably point out that you still owe me one knife,' she reminded him, switching to a topic she was more comfortable with. 'Feel free to give it back any time.'

Iskaw's hand went to the blade sheathed at his waist, though he made no move to draw it or return it to her. 'Not debt. You owe us your life.'

'And you owe us yours,' she pointed out helpfully. 'Go figure.'

'Why is this?'

'When you first showed up at our meeting spot alone, we could have killed you right there and then. It would've been the sensible thing to do, but we let you live. We're nice like that. The point is, you owe your life to us. You wouldn't be breathing if we hadn't held back.'

He was smiling now, seemingly enjoying their verbal sparring session. 'I knew you there. If you attack, you not live long.'

'Don't flatter yourself, pal. In the great scheme of things, you're not exactly John Rambo.' It was perhaps a universal truth that no matter where one was in the world, adolescent boys always suffered from that most debilitating condition – the chronically inflated ego. 'Anyway, if you knew we were there, why did you lay your weapon down to pray?'

'Allah protects,' he said, speaking in a flat, matter-of-fact tone, as if it were a well-established rule known by all. 'If He wills me to live, I live. If not, I die.' He flashed a wry grin. 'It seem safer to keep Him happy.'

'Suit yourself,' she said dismissively. Frost was about as religious as she was sensitive. 'Personally, I'd rather stick with body armour and common sense. Oh, and for the record, I argued in favour of killing you. Just thought you should know.'

At this, Iskaw chuckled to himself, reached into his cloak and unbuckled a second knife that he'd kept hidden until now. Held in a simple leather sheath that was scuffed and faded with age, it looked to be some kind of traditional hunting knife, clearly having seen many years of use. To Frost's surprise, he held the weapon out to her.

'You take,' he said.

Curious but wary, the young woman reached out and took it. The handle was made of a single piece of carved wood, so darkened by age and years of handling that it was impossible to tell what kind of tree it originated from. Grasping it, she pulled the weapon free of its sheath to inspect it.

The blade itself was slightly curved and shorter than her own knife, perhaps five inches in length, and narrowed considerably from having its edge repeatedly sharpened. Plain and unadorned with decoration, and clearly fashioned by hand, the weapon had a rough-and-ready feel about it that appealed to her. It wasn't some ornate piece of ceremonial garb, but a hunter's knife designed to do one thing only – kill.

'Why would you give me this?' she asked, failing to understand why he would favour her factory-assembled knife over this. It was old but certainly still service-able, and she presumed it had been inherited from a family member or friend. Did it mean nothing to him?

'Knife bring me trouble,' he explained, reaching up and tracing the scar along the side of his face. 'Bad memory. Better it move on.'

'Great. So I get the cursed blade, huh?' she remarked sarcastically. 'You gonna give me Sauron's ring next?'

If he understood the reference, he gave no hint of it.

'Luck change for you, maybe,' he suggested. 'And it make us even. No debt. No fight.'

Frost said nothing to this, strangely moved by the gesture but unwilling to show it. Instead she sheathed the blade once more and made to fasten the leather scabbard around her waist, only to find that the strap wasn't long enough to encircle her.

Frowning, she remarked, 'Either I'm putting on weight, or this strap's broken.'

'Not waist,' he corrected. 'Arm.'

Taking the knife from her, he fixed the leather straps around her left forearm, with the haft of the knife terminating at her wrist. Worn in such a fashion, it could be concealed easily beneath a long shirt or robe.

'Better,' he decided, his hand resting for a moment on her arm.

'Thanks,' Frost said, glancing away uncomfortably.

Sensing he'd done what he set out to do, Iskaw lingered a moment longer, then rose to his feet and returned to the other side of the cave.

'Got an admirer there, I think,' Mason whispered, grinning in amusement.

'Fuck off,' Frost replied, though she didn't look up for fear of revealing the blush that had risen to her face.

–

Not everyone desired such banter and camaraderie at that moment however. Drake had retreated to the cave entrance where he now sat perched on a boulder, staring out across the vast mountainous desert. It would be sunrise in a few hours, but for now the landscape was still cloaked in near-total darkness.

And with no lights obscuring his vision, he was able to look up to a breathtak-ingly clear night sky, countless thousands of tiny stars glimmering hard and remote in the vast inky darkness. Even the great galactic sweep of the Milky Way was easily distinguished, stunning in its raw celestial beauty.

But the view was lost on him in that moment. His thoughts were turned inward, to the woman who had given her life to save his. Even now he could scarcely process the reality that Samantha was gone.

Over and over he replayed the same image of her at the edge of that cliff, teetering for a moment on the brink before disappearing into the abyss beyond. What had she thought about in those final moments before impact? What had motivated her to make such a sacrifice, to lay down her own life to save his?

And she had saved it. Deep down he knew he would have stayed with her until she had eventually succumbed to dehydration, and by then it would have been too late. He never would have made that last desperate slog to reunite with the rest of the group. And the laptop he'd carried, that so many others had died for, would have disappeared with him, its secrets forever lost amongst the drifting sands of the Sahara.

Perhaps now they had a chance to put right some of the wrongs done by men like Faulkner. Perhaps they could make him answer for his crimes.

But Samantha would still be dead.

Was it worth it? That was what she'd asked him the night he'd committed to this insane venture, the last chance he might have had to back out. Drake, full of self-confidence and driven by an overwhelming desire for revenge, had answered without hesitation.

Now he knew better. Nothing was worth losing her for.

Nothing.

'Thought I'd find you out here, mate.'

Drake glanced around as Cunningham eased himself down onto a rock nearby. For a moment or two he just sat there in silence, staring up at the stars stretching from horizon to horizon.

'Beautiful, isn't it?' he said, his voice hushed, as if this were a place of reverence where talking was frowned upon. 'Almost enough to make you forget everything that's happening.'

'Almost,' Drake agreed sadly.

'You know, when I was a kid and I was pissed off or worried about something, or I just wanted to be alone, I used to go outside on nights like this and just... look up at it all. Forget everything else. Always made it easier to think and make sense of things somehow, because I felt like I could leave it all behind. For a while.' He looked at Drake then, taking in his wistful, pensive expression. 'You're thinking about her, aye?'

Drake nodded, saying nothing.

'Aye, we've both lost people under our command. Never gets any easier, does it?'

'It's not the same.'

'How's that?'

Drake let out his breath slowly. 'This wasn't some mission that was handed to us. This was my idea. I made all of this happen. Her death's on my conscience – no one else's.'

'And did you force her to come along?' Cunningham asked. 'Did you order her?'

Again Drake said nothing. There was no need.

'Then stop sitting on all the guilt,' the older man advised him. 'McKnight was a big girl; she knew what she was getting into. She came anyway, and she didn't make it back. That's a shitty fact, but it's the way these things play out sometimes. It's what happens next that's important now. You can either sit here and feel sorry for yourself, or you can make sure she didn't die for nothing.' He shrugged. 'Your choice.'

Drake snorted with grim humour. 'Life advice from a man who lives in a cave in the desert. Brilliant.'

Cunningham flashed a wry smile. The kind Drake hadn't seen for a very long time. 'Aye, but it's a nice cave.'

Before Drake could reply to this, however, the moment was interrupted by Frost, who had come running out from the cave entrance. Her face was flushed, her breathing coming in gasps that had little to do with the short run outside.

'Ryan, you'd better get in here,' she advised. 'You'll want to hear this.'

Chapter 57

Returning to the rocky bubble inside the mountainside, Drake found the rest of the group clustered around the improvised comms station that had been set up against the far wall. Amaha, the older of the two Tuareg hunters, was manning, listening intently to his radio headset.

'What the hell is all this?' Drake asked.

'A radio scanner,' Cunningham explained quickly. 'Made from stolen comms gear, plus a little magic I cooked up myself. It lets us listen in on Libyan military transmissions, until they change their encryption codes at least. How do you think I was able to keep track of your little adventures here?'

Moving forward, he spoke in hushed Arabic to Amaha, no doubt requesting a report on what he was hearing. Drake couldn't make out what the young man said in response, but it was enough to prompt Cunningham to take over with the headphones.

Curious at what had provoked such an urgent request for their presence, Drake watched his former friend's expression carefully. His brows were knitted together in a frown as he worked hard to listen in on the rapid stream of Arabic, but slowly the look in his eyes changed from intense concentration to one of confusion, shock, and finally growing awareness.

'I don't believe it,' he gasped.

'What, man?' Mason demanded, eager for news.

Reaching up, Cunningham removed his headset and looked at Drake. 'She's alive,' he said quietly. 'McKnight's alive.'

–

Mukhabarat headquarters, Tripoli

'What do you mean you've lost contact with them?' Kubar demanded, crushing his empty paper coffee cup in his meaty hand and tossing it aside. 'What's the problem?'

The communications specialist seemed to wilt beneath the fire of his wrath. 'The patrol that was transporting the prisoner never made it to their forward operating base. The army have tried raising them over the radio, but there's been no reply.'

Kubar closed his eyes, clenching his fists so hard that it hurt. This wasn't happening. This couldn't be happening now.

'How long ago was this?'

'About an hour, sir. It took time for it to filter through to us.'

The army doing its usual sterling job of keeping them in the loop, he thought. Now they were an intelligence agency without intelligence. When this was over, he intended to have a little chat with some of the military officers involved in this affair.

'So what are they doing about it?'

The young man swallowed. 'They have vectored in a pair of helicopters to search along the known transit route. Based on the last time they checked in, they're hoping...' He trailed off, head cocked to the side as he listened to an incoming report over his headset.

Kubar waited, holding in check his rising impatience. 'Well? What is it?'

The technician had paled visibly by now. Glancing up his superior, he spoke in a quiet, hesitant voice. 'They found the jeep, sir. All three members of the patrol are dead. There's no sign of the prisoner.'

–

Such was his utter shock at the news, Drake actually took a step backward as if Cunningham's words had landed like a physical blow. At the same moment, his mind was a whirl of impossible questions.

Alive. That single word was enough to shatter his world.

How could it be true? He'd seen her fall. He'd looked down at her lifeless body. How could she have survived that? Even if the fall hadn't killed her, the desert must have claimed her. How could she be alive now?

'What can you tell me?' he asked, somehow managing to keep his voice calm and steady.

'A Libyan army patrol picked her up,' Cunningham said. 'Near death from dehydration, but alive.'

'Jesus Christ,' Mason gasped.

Drake practically fell to the floor, his head in his hands. He felt like the world was swirling and spinning around him.

'They were bringing her in for questioning, only they never made it back. When a search team found the patrol, they were all dead and she was gone. Looks like they'd been hit hard and fast by someone who knew what they were looking for.'

Frost, putting the pieces together, spat out a single word. 'Faulkner.'

Faulkner. The man must have been listening in on Libyan communications, just like them. He'd known where to find the patrol, who they were transporting, how to catch them off guard. How to take what he needed.

'But what does he want with Sam?' Mason asked.

'Us,' Drake said without looking up. 'He wants us.'

Guessing what he was thinking, Frost knelt down beside him and laid a tentative hand on his shoulder. 'Ryan, there was no way you could have known...'

Shrugging out of her attempt to console him, Drake fixed Cunningham with a hard look. 'Do you have a phone I could use?'

Cunningham frowned. 'Excuse me?'

'A mobile phone,' Drake explained quickly. 'I know you've got one hidden away here. You need it for talking to your employers. Well, I need to use it. Now.'

'Ryan, that's not—'

Reaching behind his back, Drake drew his automatic and levelled it at the man's chest. In response, both Tuaregs jumped back, reaching for their own weapons, only for Cunningham to stop them with a raised hand.

'It's all right, boys,' he said, eyeing Drake hard. 'Ryan here's not going to do anything stupid. Are you, Ryan?'

'Give me the phone, Matt,' Drake commanded, flicking the safety off. 'I won't ask again.'

For a moment or two, Cunningham said and did nothing. Then, reaching slowly into his robes, he removed the distinctive bulky frame of a satellite phone and held it out to Drake.

'Think carefully before you use that, mate,' he advised. 'Faulkner believes you're dead. Maybe you should let him.'

Saying nothing, Drake snatched the phone from his grasp, turned away and punched in a number. A number he'd memorized ever since the man had handed Drake his business card. A number he never imagined he'd be calling again.

He hesitated only a moment before hitting the call button.

As he'd expected, it didn't ring for long.

'Yes?' Faulkner began, smooth and efficient as always.

'It's me.'

'Ah, Ryan. Good of you to call. I was expecting to hear from you sooner or later.' His voice carried the faint excitement of a man making contact with an old friend. 'You and I need to have a little chat, I think.'

'Let me speak to her,' Drake demanded.

'Straight to business, as always. You really should work on your social skills, you know. I always find it helps grease the wheels in situations like this. Still, never mind. You deserve a little reassurance, I suppose.'

The line went quiet for a moment or two, and he heard muffled voices in the background, at least one of which was Faulkner's.

Then, suddenly, a new voice came on the line.

'Ryan?'

The sound of Samantha's voice was like a knife driven into his heart, all of his hopes and fears made real at the same instant. There could be no denying it now. She was alive.

And he had abandoned her.

'Sam...' He trailed off, not knowing what to say, what he could possibly offer that would undo the damage he'd caused.

'Ryan, I'm sorry,' she called out, raising her voice to be heard as the phone was withdrawn. 'Don't come for—'

349

Her voice was abruptly silenced, replaced a moment later by Faulkner's. 'I think you can see where this is leading, Ryan,' he went on. 'I have something you want, you have something I want.'

'If you hurt her—'

'I'm a reasonable man,' Faulkner interrupted. 'I don't see why we can't deal with each other in a reasonable manner. Give me what I want, and I'll give you Samantha, alive and unharmed. Doesn't that sound reasonable to you?'

'How do I know you'll keep your word?'

At this, his adversary chuckled in amusement. 'You don't, just like I don't know if you'll keep yours. That's why these little games are so endlessly fascinating. Like poker, don't you think? It all comes down to the players involved.'

Drake let out a breath. 'When and where do you want to do this?'

'That's more like it, old chap,' Faulkner taunted. 'Dehiba, just over the Tunisian border at noon. The ruins overlooking the central square. Think you can make it there?'

'I'll find it,' Drake assured him.

'I'm sure you will. And I'm sure I don't need to warn you against bringing anything except the laptop.'

Indeed he didn't. 'I'll come alone.'

'Good man. In the meantime, get yourself some rest. It's going to be a long day.'

With that, he hung up.

Lowering the phone, Drake closed his eyes and tilted his head back, letting out a breath that he hadn't even realized he'd been holding.

'Matt, can we make it to Dehiba by noon tomorrow?' he asked, his eyes still closed.

'Aye.'

'You can't be serious,' Mason said, breaking the tense silence that had descended on the room. 'He'll kill you *and* Sam the second he gets what he wants.'

'He's got one of our own,' Frost challenged him. 'What do you suggest?'

'Take him on,' was Mason's gruff answer. 'Find the son of a bitch and kill him, like we should have done all along.'

'Yeah, and how do you plan to do that? We don't even know where he is,' the young woman pointed out. 'He's been ahead of us every step of the way. If he's as smart as everyone thinks he is, he'd have all the bases covered.'

'But he doesn't know where we are right now, either.' Mason looked Drake in the eye. 'Maybe we should use that.'

'You're suggesting we walk away from this one?' Frost prompted.

'You want a war you can't win? Fine, good luck to you. I say we get the fuck out of the country and regroup before we take him on again. At least that way we get to fight him on our own terms.'

'And let that slimy son of a bitch get away? Who's to say he doesn't have connections in the Agency?' Frost hit back. 'And what about Sam? You planning to write her off too? Well, screw that, because I'm getting her back. We don't leave our people behind.'

It was at this moment that Drake, who had remained silent until now, finally spoke up.

'Nobody's leaving her behind, but we're not going to lose any more people. You two are going to get out of the country as quickly as you can,' he said, his tone hard and final. 'I started this thing, and I'm going to finish it. Alone.'

It didn't take Frost long to make her thoughts on the matter plain. 'Well, I can't live with that.'

'Neither can I,' Mason agreed. 'This is no time for going it alone.'

'I didn't ask you if you could live with it,' Drake reminded her. 'Too many people have died already because of what I did.' He shook his head. 'I won't lose any more.'

'Then don't!' she implored him. 'Think, for Christ's sake. You can beat this guy, Ryan. You're better than him. He's been ahead of you this whole time because he knows you, he knows how you think, so change that. Do something he *doesn't* expect.'

Drake turned away, leaning his hands against the wall of the cave.

Something Faulkner didn't expect. How was he supposed to change his entire way of thinking, undo an entire lifetime of lessons and decisions and experience? What was he missing?

It was at that moment that a McKnight's words drifted back into his mind. Their argument at the RAF base back in England, where she had admonished him for trying to take all the risks himself.

'But you went ahead and did it anyway. Alone, like always. Your own way, like always. Same shit, different country.'

Drake could practically feel his hackles rising. 'Your point being?'

'When are you going to drop the lone-wolf routine and start trusting the rest of us? We're here to help you, but you won't let us in. Sooner or later that's going to ruin you.'

That was when it came to him. She'd been right, he realized now.

She'd seen that failing in his character, even if he couldn't. He might have cooperated with his teammates, directed their actions, but he'd never truly let them in.

Until now.

'I know what I have to do,' he said, looking up.

Chapter 58

By the time the new day dawned, the group were already well on their way, having crossed the unmarked border into Tunisia via one of the isolated trails that was well known to Cunningham and his Tuareg guides. Cresting a low rise, the straggling procession halted as the sun crept above the eastern horizon, its first rays illuminating the small town of Dehiba on the wide, flat plains below.

A modest settlement of perhaps 5,000 inhabitants, it certainly didn't look like much from their distant vantage point – just a collection of stone buildings clustered around what looked like a busy central plaza, with residential neighbourhoods sprawling outward in gridlike streets. It could have been any small town in the American Midwest, such was its lack of distinguishing features.

Drake knew little about this place, except that its location marked the convergence of several major roads that crisscrossed the desert. It was, according to Cunningham, the only major population centre within fifty miles, and it was on the Tunisian side of the border. That second point buoyed his spirits a little. Though he knew he was no safer here than he had been the previous day, it felt good to leave Libya behind.

'The main square's at the base of that hill,' Cunningham said, handing him a pair of binoculars and pointing to a low rounded hilltop near the centre of town that, strangely, didn't appear to have been built on.

Looking closer through the magnified lenses, Drake spotted some low brick walls and the stumps of several pillars poking from the dusty ground like broken teeth. No doubt an archaeological leftover from more ancient times, to be preserved rather than built over.

Sure enough, beyond this hill Drake could make out the town's main square. Most of the roads seemed to radiate out from it like the spokes on a wheel, and even from this distance he could see the haze kicked up by dust and engine fumes. A busy place, with plenty of civilian traffic into which a man could blend and disappear. That was the hope, at least.

'Yeah, I see it,' he confirmed. 'Should be able to get there in time.'

He might not have been familiar with the layout of the town, but his guide certainly was. Cunningham had, by his own admission, used this place as a stopping-off point many times before crossing over the border into Libya under cover of darkness.

With his course decided, Drake turned to regard the unlikely group of companions who had made the journey with him. Several of them he owed his life to, some of them he was still decidedly unsure of, and one of them bore his deepest regrets and sympathies. Nonetheless, they had all made the journey here with him in their own ways, each somehow aiding him and bringing him closer to his final destination.

But it was here that he was to part company with them, much as they might have protested, much as he might have regretted it. This final confrontation was something that had to be faced alone. In any case, his friends had another task to perform; one that was far more vital.

'You sure you want to do this?' Mason asked, still trying to dissuade him even now. 'He could just kill you on sight, you know.'

Drake nodded. His plan was a gamble – no doubt about it, but Frost had been right in her assessment of Faulkner last night. He'd been one step ahead of Drake all this time because he knew how the man thought, how he acted, how he dealt with threats. The only way to beat him was to change the way he thought, to do the one thing Faulkner didn't expect.

'I know,' he admitted. 'But I have to try.'

Frost, who had been quiet until now, moved a step closer, staring up into his eyes. 'I know this makes me sound like a pussy, but promise me you'll be careful out there. It… well, it would be nice if you didn't get yourself killed over this.'

Unable to help himself, Drake smiled at her. 'I'll do my best.'

Reaching out, she pulled Drake close, holding him in a tight, longing embrace. She knew what was coming; there was no avoiding it, but she wanted this moment before they parted ways. And so did he.

'You'd better get moving,' Cunningham advised when the pair at last released one another. 'It's further than it looks.'

Drake nodded, taking a breath and steeling himself for what lay ahead. Taking one last look at his companions, he turned and began his march towards Dehiba.

–

Dehiba, Tunisia – 10 May

Drake took a breath, the scorching dry air searing his throat, tiny grains of wind-blown sand stinging his eyes. Overhead, the sun beat down mercilessly from a cloudless sky, raising beads of sweat on his already burned and reddened skin.

Around him, locals and small groups of tourists moved back and forth through the crowded central square, paying little attention to the Westerner in dishevelled clothes leaning against the wall beside a small cafe. Perhaps the cuts and bruises marked him out as someone to studiously avoid, or perhaps the dangerous flicker in his eyes was what really kept them away. Whatever the reason, the ebb and flow of humanity seemed to part around him like a river slipping past an implacable boulder.

Glancing up, Drake turned his gaze towards the low hilltop about half a mile away overlooking the bustling town centre, where the weathered and tumbled walls of the ancient settlement still rose up against the pristine blue sky, heavy stone blocks jutting from the parched earth.

That was the place where it was supposed to happen; the place where the tumultuous events of the past week would reach their final, deadly conclusion. Everything he had fought for, everything he had sacrificed, every compromise he had made… it had all led him here.

He would live or die by what happened today.

His pulse was pounding strong and urgent in his ears, almost drowning out the tinny ring of the cell phone as he held it against his head. The man he was trying to reach would be wary of calls like this. He wouldn't answer readily, might not answer at all in fact. Either way, there was nothing he could do to change it.

All he could do was wait, and hope.

And just like that, the ringing stopped. He was connected.

'So you're still alive, Ryan,' a voice remarked on the other end of the line. A smooth, confident, controlled voice. Not the voice of a man whose own future hung in the balance just as much as Drake's. 'And you're late. Didn't I make it clear what was at stake?'

'You did,' Drake replied, his eyes scanning the crowds around him. 'I have what you want.'

'Then I suggest you bring it to me, so we can finish our business.'

Drake knew this was the moment of choice. His last chance to back out.

'No,' he said, speaking with calm finality.

There was a pause. A moment of confusion and doubt; a chink in the armour momentarily exposed. 'Excuse me?'

'We both know I'm dead the second I hand it over. You'd never let me live after everything I've seen, everything I know.' He was committed now. There was no going back – the only choice was to move forward. 'So I suggest you remember this moment, because this is as close as you're ever going to get to what you want.'

To his credit, his adversary remained surprisingly composed in the wake of this blatant act of defiance. A different man might have railed against him, shouted down the line about how foolish Drake's actions were and how he would surely be punished for them.

But this man was another sort.

'Ryan, maybe you've forgotten the reason we're in this position,' the calm, pleasant voice went on. 'If you need reminding, I'm quite prepared to leave behind a piece of her at our meeting place. And believe me, it'll be a piece she'll miss.'

Drake closed his eyes for a moment, swallowing down the fear and horror at what he was hearing, because he knew well enough that this was a threat his adversary was quite prepared to make good on. A sadist who took pleasure in inflicting suffering on others.

'You won't do that,' he replied, sounding more confident than he felt.

'Really? Enlighten me.'

'I'm offering you something better.'

'And what would that be?'

'There are three ways this could go. First, you kill her, I release the files across the internet, then I turn all my attention to hunting you down. Believe me, I'm good at finding people, and I'm prepared to devote every waking moment of my life to finding you. And when I do, anything you do to her will be nothing but a happy memory compared to what I do to you. Second, you kill me before I can get to you. The files have been uploaded to an automatic email server, and without me to stop it, everything you've worked to cover up gets released within two hours of my death.' He allowed that prospect to hang there for a moment or two. 'Either way, you lose.'

'As do you, Ryan,' he reminded him.

'There's more at stake here than you and me. We both know what you're really playing for. Are you ready to give all that up, watch it fall down around you?'

There was a pause. A gambler weighing the risks against the potential rewards. 'I presume there's a third option?'

Drake took another breath of the sandy, stifling air. 'You give her back to me, unharmed. I agree not to interfere with your plans or tell anyone what we found, you agree not to come looking for me, and everyone walks away. It's that simple.'

'Very heroic of you,' he remarked with dour humour.

'I'm no hero. Never was,' Drake said, truly meaning it. 'And this isn't my war. I just want it to end.'

This was it. He had said and done everything he could. The rest depended on the man on the other end of the line.

And then he heard it. Not some vicious curse, not a growl of anger or even a muttered promise that he would pay for this one day.

What Drake heard instead was a low chuckle of amusement. The laugh of a man finally springing a trap that had been long in the making.

'Come now, Ryan. We both know this can only end one way.' He paused a moment, allowing his words to sink in. 'Look down.'

Glancing down, Drake saw something on his stained and crumpled shirt. A splash of red light that hadn't been there before. The glow of a laser sight.

'Wouldn't run if I were you. You're covered from two different directions, and my friends are just itching to pull those triggers.'

They had found him. Somehow they had tracked him here, predicted this move, known exactly what he was going to do. And now they had him out in the open, the time had come to spring their trap.

No sooner had this thought crossed his mind than a black SUV pulled up nearby. The rear doors flew open and a pair of men leapt out. Men Drake had encountered before. Men who had tried to kill him more than once over the past few days, and who wouldn't hesitate to do so now if they were given the order. Their hands were on weapons hidden just inside their jackets, ready to draw down on him if he so much as twitched.

'Like I said, Ryan,' the voice on the line said, filled with the confidence of a man in total control of the situation. 'This can only end one way.'

Drake lowered the phone as the retrieval team closed in on him.

–

'Come on, Keira. We need this now,' Mason said, pacing anxiously back and forth the cramped workshop. Shelves laden with spare hard drives, cooling fans, power supplies, circuit boards, memory sticks and countless other pieces of electronic hardware crowded in around them, giving the already small room a claustrophobic air.

The owner of the computer repair shop had granted them use of his workshop after a little persuasion – and bribery – on Cunningham's part, though he was keeping a wary eye on the small group of foreigners from the shop entrance.

'I'm working as fast as I can,' the young woman bit back, her eyes never leaving the computer she was hunched over. The hard drive they had salvage from Sowan's laptop had been crudely wired into it, allowing her to inspect its contents. 'It's locked down by some kind of custom encryption scheme I've never seen before. More sophisticated than anything the Agency uses.'

'Can you break it?' Mason asked.

'Nope. Whoever designed this was really fucking paranoid about security,' she acknowledged, throwing her hands up. 'The second I try to copy the drive or make a brute-force attack, it'll delete the entire thing. Nobody's getting into this without the decryption software.'

Mason let out a frustrated sigh. 'Goddamn it. Ryan's depending on us.'

It was at this moment that Cunningham felt the buzz of his satellite phone in his pocket. Turning away from the others, he opened it up to read the incoming message.

It was from Iskaw, observing events in the central square about a mile away. His brief missive explained that Drake had been picked up and driven away by Faulkner's men.

Right on schedule, Cunningham thought, turning his attention back to the two specialists.

Chapter 59

Drake blinked as the hood was yanked off his head, harsh light flooding his eyes and giving him his first view of his surroundings since being marched in here from the car outside. He glanced around, trying to take in as much as of his environment as possible.

He was in a room of some kind, long and wide, with rough wooden floors and corrugated steel walls. A factory or warehouse of some kind, he assumed. He knew he was on an upper floor, because he'd been dragged up at least one flight of stairs to get here.

Light filtered in through dirty windows set at intervals along the walls, and in the high ceiling overhead. He guessed the place had fallen into disuse, since he saw no machinery, storage boxes or office equipment anywhere in the vicinity.

However, he could hear the drone of traffic and the occasional car horn outside, which meant he was still somewhere in Dehiba. The car ride here hadn't lasted more than a couple of minutes through the busy town streets.

As for his purpose here, that much at least was obvious. Killing him in full view of hundreds of people would have been inconvenient. Faulkner wanted somewhere private and secluded to go about his work.

As if in response to these dark thoughts, the man himself sauntered into view, carrying a single wooden chair not unlike the one Drake was currently tied to. As always, he appeared well rested and well groomed, not a hair out of place or a hint of fatigue in his eyes. Dressed in a white cotton shirt, khaki-coloured trousers and a light jacket, he looked like a high flying businessman taking a few days out of his busy schedule for some rest and relaxation.

Setting the chair down front of Drake, he surveyed his prisoner with a welcoming smile.

'Mind if I take a seat, Ryan?' he asked. 'Damned heat's more than a man can stand.'

Without waiting for a reply, he sat down and made himself comfortable, then produced a handkerchief from his pocket and dabbed at his forehead.

Glancing over Drake's shoulder, he nodded to someone out of sight. 'Could I have something cold, please?'

Within moments, another man strode into view with a plastic bottle of water, handing it to Faulkner as if he were a waiter at a high-class restaurant. Unscrewing the top, Faulkner took a careful, almost dainty sip. Drake resisted the urge to lick his parched, cracked lips.

'Well, here we are again, Ryan,' he remarked, once he was satisfied. 'Catching up over a few quiet drinks. Brings it all to a close rather nicely, don't you think?'

All the while his eyes were on Drake, scrutinizing every move he made from across the short distance that separated them; every twitch of a muscle, every glance, every movement of his arms and legs. A master poker-player sizing up his opponent, trying to get a feel for what kind of man he was up against.

Drake stared right back at him, his vivid green eyes filled with absolute hatred. This was the man who had killed Chandra, who had killed Sowan, who had taken McKnight hostage and tried to have his entire team murdered. This was the man responsible for handing over countless men to be tortured and executed by the Libyans, all for his own personal gain.

Did he even care? Did the slightest flicker of remorse and humanity still burn beneath that polished exterior, or was it all just business to him?

'You're wondering how I found you,' he observed. 'How I knew where you'd be when you took such pains to disappear, drop off the grid, or whatever those idiots in the CIA call it these days. Don't worry, we'll get to that part in good time. But for now, I'm more interested in the information our friend Tarek passed on to you.'

'I bet you are,' Drake agreed. 'We can't have the ugly truth getting out, can we?'

'And whose version of the truth might that be?' Faulkner asked. 'Yours? Sowan's? Do you even know what this is all about, or are you just making uneducated guesses based on what you'd *like* to believe?'

'I'd like to believe you're in a world of shit right now,' Drake said truthfully. 'That's why you're talking to me instead of having me killed. You found me; there's no getting around that. You could kill me any time you want, but we both know you won't.'

Faulkner said nothing. He just sat there watching Drake while he raised the bottle to his lips and took a drink.

'You're afraid of what'll happen if you pull that trigger. Sorry, I mean order someone else to pull the trigger, because we both know you don't like getting your hands dirty. You're afraid of what will happen if I'm not around to stop all that embarrassing evidence from getting out. You brought me here to negotiate because you knew there was no other way to get what you want, but you needed to do it from a position of strength. So congratulations, you've found me. But it doesn't change the fact that I have what you want, and there's only one way you're going to get it – my way.'

–

Caitlin Macguire was crouched virtually motionless on the rooftop of the disused factory overlooking downtown Dehiba, her M110 semiautomatic sniper rifle resting on its collapsible bipod at the edge of the roof.

Having long ago honed her mind and body to ignore the discomfort that often went hand-in-hand with the profession of sniping, she was oblivious to the burning heat, the intense glare and the windblown dust that irritated her skin with every passing moment. All her attention was focussed on the street below as she shifted her sights from target to target, her keen eyes scanning every passing civilian through the rifle's magnified scope.

Situated near a busy thoroughfare as they were, there was a constant stream of civilians moving in both directions, many with their heads and faces covered. Any one of them could be a hostile, requiring constant observation and threat-assessment.

It was a difficult, frustrating task for any sniper, but one that she wouldn't allow herself to fail at. After all, she'd made a living out of killing men trained to evade people just like her, and over the years had grown extremely proficient at it. She had no intention of ruining that fine track record today.

In any case, they had Drake now. Once Faulkner got what he needed out of the man, they could get out of here and leave this fucking desert behind.

Her radio earpiece crackled with an incoming transmission. 'There's too many civilian targets. It's a fucking mess down there.'

That was Sam Tarver; another member of their team posted in a second sniping position on the rooftop of an apartment building not far away. Between them they could cover pretty much the entire area; at least in theory. The reality was that they were becoming overwhelmed with the hustle and bustle of a busy town, and the strain was taking its toll on her comrade.

Without breaking concentration, Macguire reached out and touched the transmit button that she'd fixed to the rifle's fore-grip.

'Stay focussed on the main approach,' she instructed. With Tarver being the weaker of the two snipers, it made sense to give him a stationary target. 'I've got the side streets.'

'Let's just kill this arsehole and get the fuck out of here,' Tarver growled.

'We're almost finished here.' Macguire made a quick mental note of Tarver's position, lest she was forced to turn her rifle on him. It wouldn't be the first time she had taken such an extreme measure. 'Don't lose your nerve now.'

Whatever his reply to this curt instruction, he had the good grace to turn off his radio first. Lucky for him, she thought, as she focussed her sights on another target.

–

'I'm annoyed with you, Ryan,' Faulkner said after considering Drake's words. 'You've caused me a lot of aggravation over the past few days, wasted my time and forced me to do things I'd sincerely hoped to avoid. And for what? What have you really achieved with all of this nonsense?'

'For starters, I've exposed you for what you are.'

'Really?' Faulkner looked intrigued. 'And what exactly do you think I am?'

'The polite version is that you're a lying, murdering, manipulative piece of shit. You handed innocent men over to the Libyans to be tortured and executed. You betrayed an Agency operation, and God knows how many men died for that. And you did it all for what? Another step up the ladder? Another commendation to mount on your office wall?' Drake shook his head, still mystified at the man's motivation. 'Is that enough, or should I keep going?'

Far from being angry with his scathing assessment, Faulkner merely chuckled in amusement. 'You actually think this is about me, don't you?' He reached for his bottle of water, taking a drink to settle himself. 'All of this… everything we've done here, everything we've sacrificed, and you think it was about *me* going after a *promotion*?'

Drake said nothing, even managed to keep his expression carefully composed as the older man tried to taunt him. And yet, there was no denying that his words had exposed a doubt; something that had been lurking in the back of Drake's mind since Sowan had first revealed the truth to him. The one question his subconscious had been asking him again and again without answer – what if I'm missing something?

'That's your problem in a nutshell, Ryan. You see the obvious, but the bigger picture is lost on you.' Faulkner shook his head as if in disappointment. 'It's a shame you didn't keep to our agreement. You might actually have opened your eyes.'

'And what would I have seen?' Drake challenged him, his voice betraying just a hint of doubt now.

He saw a flicker of a smile. The smile of a man who had at last witnessed his opponent make a misstep. 'The group I represent… well, let's say they exist a little beyond the almighty CIA. Their reach and their goals are broader than any one agency, because unlike you, they see the bigger picture. Military, industrial, political, economic… it's all part of one big tapestry to them. And right now, they have their eyes on Libya. They know the Gaddafi government will fall sooner or later – all they're doing is speeding up the process. They've been channelling weapons and equipment to certain factions in the country for some time now, so that when the time comes, we know the right side will win. Our side.'

'You mean warlords.'

He shrugged. 'One man's warlord is another man's freedom fighter. History is the only judge, and we're the ones who write history.'

'For what?'

'Why does one ever show interest in these hot, unstable, miserable little countries? Oil, old boy.' He said it as if it were an obvious fact that Drake should have picked up on long ago. 'By conservative estimates, there are nearly 50 billion barrels of it beneath the Libyan desert. Enough to make anyone with a controlling stake embarrassingly rich. For example, people who backed the future leaders of Libya in their bid for power.'

'Money,' Drake spat. 'You're doing this all for money?'

Again that smile. 'Still not seeing the bigger picture. Like I said, money is just one part of a larger whole. Libyan oil will be enough to keep the wheels turning in America for the rest of the century, and reduce their dependence on Russian and Persian Gulf reserves. With Gaddafi no longer around to shield them, Islamic

State will have nowhere left to run, and we can kill them all. Everybody wins, really.'

'Except everyone who's going to die in the war you start.'

Faulkner's eyes betrayed neither regret nor remorse. Far from it, Drake saw only triumph in them. He had found Drake's weakness, had exposed a chink in the armour, and now he was ready to deal the finishing blow.

'Sorry, Ryan, but that ship's sailed. The war's coming no matter what any of us do. You were right about one thing, though,' he conceded. 'This is the part where I show you just how easy you were to manipulate.'

Reaching into his jacket pocket for a radio, he spoke a short, quiet command. 'Would you bring her in, please?'

Drake could hear footsteps moving behind, slow and deliberate, the squeak and bump of wheels moving across the rough floorboards. His bonds made it impossible to turn around, but soon it didn't matter. Soon the man in question strode into view, bringing with him the woman he'd risked everything for.

His first sight was of the prisoner, strapped to an office chair much like himself. A woman, her skin reddened by exposure to the desert sun, cut and bruised in countless places, her dark hair hanging limp and dirty. A strip of duct tape across her mouth prevented her speaking.

But she was alive. Her eyes were locked with his, the intensity of that single look conveying more than mere words. He well understood the grief and despair she was feeling at seeing him thus imprisoned, because he felt exactly the same thing at seeing her.

Reassured at least that McKnight was alive, Drake looked up at her captor. It was a man he had twice placed his trust in, to his great cost.

'I'm sorry, mate,' Matt Cunningham said, circling around in front of him. 'I didn't want it to come to this.'

Drake watched him through narrowed eyes, his hands curling into fists as he strained against the ropes. 'You fucking—'

'Language, Ryan. No need to make a scene,' Faulkner chided him. 'Not that I don't sympathize, of course. Nothing quite compares to that sinking feeling when you put your trust in someone and they let you down. Believe me, I know.'

'How did you... ?' he trailed off, seemingly unable to go on.

'How did we turn him?' Faulkner finished for him. 'Well, every man has his price. Money, power, influence... whatever. In his case, it was something more fundamental.'

'Amnesty,' Cunningham explained, his voice edged with sadness and regret. 'They offered me immunity from prosecution after Afghanistan. No more looking over my shoulder, no more waiting for the axe to fall. There aren't many second chances going around these days, son. You know I couldn't turn it down.'

Indeed he did. Cunningham was, if nothing else, a survivor.

'Don't feel too bad, Ryan,' Faulkner said. 'We've both played the deception game in our own way, but I've been playing it a lot longer than you.'

Drake looked up, staring right at his former friend. 'I hope it was worth it, Matt.'

'I'm sure it was,' Faulkner answered for him. 'On the subject of which, do you have something for me, Mr Cunningham?'

Reaching into his webbing, Cunningham produced a wrapped package and handed it carefully to his master. Smiling like a child on Christmas day, Faulkner undid the wrapping, exposing the hard drive taken from Sowan's computer. The hard drive that had been recovered at such great cost.

'And the others?' he asked with only mild curiosity, as if enquiring after a distant acquaintance.

'On the way now,' Cunningham confirmed. 'One of my boys is bringing them in.'

Drake closed his eyes and bowed his head as the words sank in; a man crushed and utterly defeated by a superior opponent

–

Perched on a rooftop high above the street cafe, Sam Tarver leaned in a little closer to his rifle, keeping the sights focussed on the approach road to the abandoned factory. He was sweating profusely from a combination of stifling heat, burning sunlight and growing tension; all of which were wearing on his nerves.

Two of his comrades, Regan and Palmer, were watching the gate, with more available as backup inside the building itself. A lot of guns were guarding Faulkner and his prisoners, yet still Tarver could feel the tension building by the moment. This was taking too long, leaving them too exposed. They needed to finish it and get out *now*.

Glancing past the gate and the two armed bodyguards protecting it, Tarver absently watched a pedestrian hobbling along the road past the factory. An old woman in dirty clothing, bent with age and leaning heavily on a staff as she shuffled along the pavement, her face and head covered by a tattered old keffiyeh. Another beggar, perhaps looking to scrounge up enough money to survive until the next day. The small town was littered with them.

If he was to put a round through her head, he'd probably be doing her a favour.

No sooner had this thought flashed through his mind than he felt the heat of the sun abate for a moment as a shadow fell across him. Glancing up from the weapon, he was just starting to turn when suddenly strong hands gripped his head and yanked it back so hard that he let out an involuntary gasp of pain and shock.

This was silenced a second later when a wickedly sharp blade bit into his exposed throat, severing the windpipe with a couple of terrible sawlike thrusts.

Unable to cry out, he could manage only a terrible gurgling groan as he fell to the ground, clutching at his mangled throat. His last sight as his vision faded was of a young man in Arab desert clothes picking up his sniper rifle and taking his position, oblivious to the man he'd just murdered.

'So much trouble for such a simple thing,' Faulkner mused, turning it over in his hand. 'You'll understand if I confirm the contents before you go on your way?'

'Of course,' Cunningham acknowledged.

A single radio call from Faulkner, and a third man entered the room, armed with a laptop computer. A lean, spare-looking man with thinning blonde hair tied back in a limp ponytail, his eyes hidden behind darkened glasses. Setting the computer on an upturned oil drum, he retrieved the hard drive from Faulkner and connected it up, waiting a few seconds while his laptop recognized it.

'Looks good so far,' he said after a few moments, bent over the screen. 'Running decryption now.'

'Take your time,' Faulkner said, helping himself to another sip of water. His eyes met with Drake and he smiled, confident and in control as always. The strategist, the planner, the enemy. The winner of their game. 'No rush, after all.'

But Drake wasn't hearing him now. All his attention was focussed on Samantha. She was staring right back at him, her eyes pleading for understanding, for forgiveness. She didn't need to speak for him to understand her thoughts.

I'm so sorry, Ryan. I never knew this would happen. I didn't want you to give up your life for me.

Faulkner too could sense the unspoken sentiments. Moving close to her, he reached up and gently brushed her cheek with his hand. His touch provoked a shudder within her, which seemed to amuse him greatly.

'You know, I would have happily taken any one of you hostage,' he admitted. 'But I wanted her. There's something so much more... intimate about having a woman at gunpoint, don't you think, Ryan? I mean, if I was to do something like this...'

Reaching for the weapon holstered inside his jacket back, he drew it, and levelled it at McKnight's head.

'No!' Drake cried out as he pulled the trigger.

But there was no thunderous crack as the round discharged, no sickening moment of impact, no spray of blood and brain matter as it cleaved its way through her head. Instead there was a dull click as the round hit an empty chamber. McKnight let out a strangled gasp, flinching instinctively at the sound.

'You see what I mean?' Faulkner said, smirking in amusement as he withdrew a magazine from his pocket and inserted it in the weapon, pulling back the slide to chamber the first round.

'Only a woman can provoke that kind of reaction. The fear in their eyes, the sound of their breath coming faster, the feel of their heart beating so fast and urgent,' he whispered as he traced the barrel of his gun down the side of her face, her neck, her breasts. 'It's... primal, arousing. Maybe it stirs up that protective instinct, gets the blood pumping just a little more, eh?'

'Fuck you,' Drake spat, staring back at him with absolute hatred.

Far from being offended or angered, Faulkner seemed to relish the emotions his words had stirred up. 'Let's not get ahead of ourselves.'

With that, he holstered the weapon for the time being, removed his cell phone and began composing a text message, perhaps reporting to his handlers that the situation was now firmly in hand. No doubt he was envisioning the praise that was soon to be heaped on him.

Drake said nothing further as the hot sun continued to beat down on them through the dirty windows, as traffic rumbled by outside and distant horn-blasts sounded. A tiny bead of sweat ran down between his shoulder blades, trickling down his back. His heart was beating hard and fast, his muscles tightening in anticipation.

'You know, it's a shame,' he remarked, staring across at his nemesis.

Faulkner glanced up, disturbed from his work.

'Despite all of this. Despite all the killing and the double-crosses and the secret agendas, there's one thing neither of us can get away from.'

'Really? And what might that be?'

Drake smiled. 'You dress like an absolute wanker.'

Shaking his head, Faulkner drained the last of his water and set the bottle carefully down on the floor beside him. 'You disappoint me, Ryan,' he said, rising from his chair. 'I was hoping we could have resolved this like civilized men.'

'That's not what I think of when I look at you.'

At this, Faulkner smiled coldly. 'Stubbornness must run in your family. It's funny; Freya was just like you.'

Chapter 60

In that instant, everything around Drake seemed to fade into darkness. Every danger, every consideration, every plan and contingency and measure that he'd tried to encompass within his mind simply ceased to exist.

All he could see was the image of his mother laid out on a mortuary table a lifetime ago, her greying hair combed back to reveal an aged face once so familiar, now cold and pale.

And beside it, the simple and blandly efficient name-tag – Freya Louise Shaw.

'What did you say?' he whispered.

Faulkner could barely contain his malicious glee as he sprung his final trap. 'Oh, I'm sorry. I forget you're still playing catch-up. Never did get around to telling you the truth about dear old Mum, did I? Then again, neither did she.'

'What truth?'

Faulkner looked him hard in the eye. 'Didn't you ever wonder why she was so preoccupied with her work? Always coming home late, running off at the last minute, all those urgent trips overseas? Didn't you ever stop to question what she did that was so important?'

Drake felt like the world was spinning around him. He closed his eyes, having to swallow hard to keep even a shred of his composure. Again and again he saw images, camera-flashes of his mother tensing up every time the phone rang, saw her retreating into another room to take the call, saw the focus and intensity in her expression as she left. Again and again he pictured her departing suddenly on 'business', gone for days at a time with little or no explanation.

He'd sensed, on some childish level, the growing rift her preoccupation was creating between his parents, the strain it was putting on the entire family. And he felt again his own resentment and jealousy that she valued her stupid, unimportant job more than her own children.

Only now did he begin to perceive another explanation. Only now did the jumbled pieces of the puzzle begin to reorder themselves, forming a terrible, chilling conclusion that was at once inconceivable yet impossible to ignore.

'It's not possible,' he gasped, willing it not to be true. 'It can't be.'

'Can't it? Or is that what you'd rather believe?'

'She was… one of us?'

The mere thought of it was ludicrous. How could she possibly have kept such a secret without her own family knowing? And yet, at the same moment he realized that he himself had once maintained much the same deception. He himself had told the same lies, lived the same secret life.

Faulkner chuckled in amusement. 'Think bigger, Ryan. Like I said, you see the obvious, but the subtleties are lost on you. Freya was part of something far more important than one country's intelligence service. She was part of the group that I represent, because like me she saw and believed in the bigger picture. She even pulled some strings to help keep you and your sister safe for the past couple of years. Just in case you thought you'd made it this far on charm and good looks.' He leaned in closer, his tone conspiratorial. 'You honestly didn't know?'

Drake said nothing, which prompted a laugh of sheer delight.

'Ryan, it's almost poetic. Two generations of the same family, living the same lie. One day they'll write songs about you.'

'What happened to her?' Drake asked, finally mastering his thoughts enough to speak. 'You killed her?'

Faulkner sighed with what seemed to be a touch of regret. 'Every asset has their day, I'm afraid. She had hers, but… she did have one last role to play. She brought you to me. I suppose I should be thankful for that.'

It took only a heartbeat for the full import of his words to sink in. A terrible, agonizing moment as the full extent of Faulkner's treachery was at last revealed.

Drake's heart was beating so fast and loud that it almost seemed to drown out everything else around him. All of it; the burning sun overhead, the noise and smell of traffic, Faulkner standing by so close… All of it seemed to be drowned out by the pounding of blood in his ears.

The world seemed to tremble and shiver around him as the truth sank in. Everything he'd come to believe was a lie. The ground upon which he'd built his life had given way.

'Don't feel too bad, Ryan,' Faulkner advised him, his voice barely audible above the pounding of Drake's heart. 'From what I'm told, she put up quite a fight.'

Chapter 61

Tom Regan reached up, drawing a dusty sleeve across his sweating brow. The heat of the midday sun was unbearable, beating down on him with an almost physical intensity. The weapon holstered in his jacket was a leaden weight that seemed to be dragging him down towards the ground.

The sooner they were out of here, the better.

His thoughts were interrupted by a low, guttural voice a short distance away. His head snapped around, and he found himself staring at a bent, gnarled old woman in loose tribal clothing that looked so stained and dusty that it was practically one with the desert landscape. Another beggar; one of many in this godforsaken shithole.

She saw a white man in reasonably good clothes and took him for an easy payday.

'No money. Piss off,' he warned, waving her away, but she ignored him, moving forwards with one hand outstretched.

'Shoot the stupid bitch,' his comrade Raymond Palmer snorted, looking away in disgust.

Regan had no time for this. Reaching into his jacket, his hands closed around the butt of his automatic. He was loath to shoot someone in public, but with luck, the mere display of a weapon would be enough to make her fuck off.

'I told you to—'

Even as he spoke, the woman suddenly straightened up, drew a silenced weapon from her loose robes and levelled it at his head. Such was the speed and fluid grace of her transformation, he didn't even have time to react as her finger tightened on the trigger.

There was a muted flash, an explosion of white light, and then he knew no more.

His companion turned towards the source of the noise, but he was too late to react. A second shot went in through his temple, blowing out the back of his skull.

Even as he slumped to the ground, Keira Frost reached for her radio. 'Gate secure. Roll in.'

–

The moment was suddenly broken by a shout from Ponytail. The very words that Drake had been waiting for.

'We're in,' he reported. 'Everything's intact.'

He was just turning towards the others when suddenly a far larger man rushed at him, grabbing his head by the ponytail. Before he could even think to fight back, powerful muscles forced his head down, slamming it into the edge of the oil drum with bone-shattering force.

Even as he let out a muffled, shuddering groan, his attacker grasped at him, yanking away the weapon he kept in a shoulder holster on the left side of his chest.

Faulkner, focussed momentarily on Drake, took half a second longer than usual to realize something was wrong. Half a second before he reached into his suit jacket for his weapon, already turning towards the source of the disturbance.

Half a second too late.

'Don't even think about it,' Cunningham warned, covering Faulkner with Ponytail's weapon. 'Lay the gun on the floor, then get down on your knees.'

Savvy as he was, Faulkner could tell right away that resistance would be suicidal. Lifting his gun out with his thumb and forefinger, he laid it on the ground and slid it towards Cunningham, who immediately snatched it up and hurried towards Drake.

'How are you doing, mate?' he asked quietly, undoing the knots that held him down.

Drake said nothing as the bonds slipped away. Instead he rose to his feet slowly, rubbing his wrists to get some circulation going again, and approached his erstwhile captor. Faulkner was on his knees, hands behind his head, staring up at Drake with something akin to respect.

'Bravo, Ryan,' he said, smirking in amusement. 'I didn't know you had it in you.'

'Gun,' Drake said, holding out one hand to his companion.

Cunningham was happy to oblige, laying Faulkner's weapon in his grip. 'The safety's off, there's one in the pipe.'

'Untie Sam,' Drake said quietly, not taking his eyes off Faulkner for a moment.

'Aye.' Hurrying over to the woman, Cunningham drew a knife from his waist and made short work of the plasticuffs holding her arms and legs secure. 'You all right, lass?'

Such was her disbelief at this sudden turn of events, McKnight could only nod.

Cunningham flashed a brief smile. 'Hang in there. We'll get you out.'

'Hard drive,' Drake prompted, well aware of how short they were on time.

Leaving the erstwhile hostage to sort herself out, Cunningham turned his attention to the laptop, his eyes quickly scanning the screen. 'Jesus, this is a fucking gold mine. Contacts, delivery times, everything; their whole operation's on here.'

'Never mind, just pack it up. We're taking it with us.'

'Got it,' he confirmed, folding up the laptop and drawing his weapon to cover Faulkner.

At the same moment, another voice spoke up.

'Ryan.'

Taking his eye off his enemy, Drake spun around to find himself face to face with the woman he'd risked everything to save. Much like himself, she looked exhausted and dishevelled, her clothes stained with dirt and sweat, her skin red with sunburn, but she was alive and on her feet all the same. The same defiant will to keep going that had kept them both alive in the desert had pulled her through the hours following her rescue when her life still balanced on a knife edge, and even her time in Faulkner's grip.

Unable to summon up the words, Drake reached out and pulled her tight against him, as if to reassure himself she was real and solid and alive. The thought of what might have happened was like a knife twisting in his guts, and he held her even tighter in response, tears stinging his eyes.

'It was all a lie, wasn't it? To get your hands on that intel,' Faulkner said, watching them in disgust.

'Couldn't have decrypted it without you,' Cunningham said over his shoulder.

Faulkner's eyes were on Drake. 'So what now, Ryan? Are you going to shoot me? Kill the only man who knows the truth about your mother?'

Letting go of McKnight, Drake turned towards him, his grip tightening on the weapon. Then, suddenly, he swung it in a wide arc, catching Faulkner on the left cheek with all the force he could summon. There was a metallic crunch, and the man fell sideways with blood leaking from the gash on the left side of his face. A shattered cheek bone was going to cost a pretty penny to put right.

Reaching down, Drake gripped him by his expensive suit jacket and hauled him to his feet. 'You're coming with us, too, you piece of shit. And you're going to tell us everything. Believe me, by the time I'm finished, you'll wish there was more to tell.'

–

Down below, a rusted old panel van was chugging along the main drag that ran parallel to the factory, moving with no great urgency, like most of the other traffic in this town. However, as it approached the main gate, the driver suddenly stamped on the accelerator, swinging the vehicle hard right and straight into the chain-link barrier.

'Hope you're ready for this, Ryan,' Mason muttered through gritted teeth, bracing himself and ducking down low in his seat.

There was bang, a crunch of metal and plastic shattering, and the gate sprang open, allowing the vehicle to barrel straight into the delivery yard beyond.

–

Up on the rooftop, Caitlin Macguire flinched at the sudden disturbance in the delivery yard below. Instantly her mind assembled the facts, arriving at a single irrefutable conclusion. It was a trap.

'Contact! Contact!' she cried into her radio, shifting her aim to try to get a fix on the driver of the van. 'Targets inbound!'

Sighting the van's windshield and bracing herself for the inevitable recoil, she pulled the trigger.

'Shit!' Mason cried out, ducking down as shattered glass rained down around him and a high-powered round thumped into the seat mere inches from his head. Pinned down, he could do nothing but keep his foot on the gas.

The rough engine roared and the vehicle shot forwards as if it were a wild animal suddenly set free, Mason steering virtually blind for fear of exposing himself to the deadly sniper fire.

The chassis thumped and clanged as more rounds slammed into it, but still he ploughed onwards, heedless of anything that lay in his path. He could only hope Frost had had the presence of mind to get out of the way.

This thought was interrupted by the sickening, crushing impact of the van slamming straight into the big sliding doors that blocked the main entrance, demolishing the thin metal walls and careening forward until it slammed into the unyielding mass of a support girder. Unrestrained, Mason was pitched forward with bruising force as the vehicle came to an abrupt stop, steam and smoke billowing from the crumpled engine bay.

–

'Fuck,' Macguire hissed, ejecting the spent magazine, which clattered to the ground at her feet. Wisps of smoke trailed from the barrel of her silencer, now red-hot after expending thirty rounds of ammunition in short order.

With the practiced ease born from long years of experience, she snatched a fresh clip from the pouch on the left side of her webbing, pressed it into the magazine port and gave it a tap to make sure it was locked in place.

Situated on the factory rooftop, she was oddly removed from the chaos unfolding in the square down below, though the added distance did little to improve her mood at that moment. She'd watched in disbelief as the van hurtled forward into the delivery yard, the driver seemingly having no regard for his own safety, until finally it had slammed right into the building itself, crashing through the corrugated steel wall and crippling the vehicle.

It was only then that she'd understood escape had been the last thing on his mind. Now that he was directly beneath her, she had no shot. And there was absolutely nothing she could do about it from her remote vantage point.

She was moving a moment later, abandoning her position and making straight for the stairwell that would take her down to the lower level, moving with fast, efficient strides. She preferred to keep her distance in situations like this, to strike from a position of total superiority, but sometimes there was nothing for it but to get up close and personal.

In any case, it wouldn't be long before the local police showed up. She intended to be well clear of the area before then.

Descending the stairs two at a time, she keyed her radio. 'Tarver, I've no shot from up here. Keep their heads down until I can flank the fuckers.'

Her terse command was met with nothing but static.

'Tarver, report in!'

Nothing. Macguire paused for a moment, quickly reconsidering the situation. It seemed Faulkner had underestimated their opponents, never guessing that Drake himself would have been capable of outplaying him.

Well, those were Faulkner's mistakes. She would put them right herself, one dead body at a time. Gripping her rifle tight, she hurried down the stairs.

–

Reaching up, Mason yanked open the passenger door and practically tumbled out onto the ground, battered and bruised after the crushing impact against the building. He was just in time to see Frost come darting over to meet him, clutching her silenced automatic.

'Nice driving, Cole,' the young woman remarked.

Mason glanced at her. His face was marked by several cuts where flying glass had caught him, but otherwise he seemed unhurt. 'Had to improvise,' he said by way of apology. 'And we needed the cover.'

'Someone's taking pot shots from up there. You get a fix on the sniper?'

Mason shook his head. It had all happened so fast, it was hard to take in anything beyond the split-second decisions needed to stay alive.

'Couldn't see him.'

'Fuck it,' she decided, removing the shotgun from the improvised sling across her back. 'We're in. Let's find Ryan and get the fuck out of here.'

Mason wasn't about to argue. Rising up from behind cover, the two specialists rushed forward, pushing deeper into the ruined factory.

Chapter 62

Drake was just heading towards the stairs with Faulkner in front, Cunningham and McKnight bringing up the rear, when he saw them. Several armed men, two in front and two further behind, having just ascended to their floor, no doubt to safeguard their commander. The two groups had literally walked right into each other.

Their reactions were creditably fast. Straightaway the two operatives in the lead went for their weapons, the one on the left dropping to one knee to present a smaller target while the second moved forward to close the range.

They were good, but they were a second too late.

The operative on the left was his priority. The other man was concerned firstly with protecting Faulkner, but his comrade was about one thing only – killing.

The world seemed to go into slow motion around him as Drake brought his sidearm up into the firing position, watching with a kind of curious detachment as the man's head slowly drifted into his sights.

There was no time to line up his shot. The man already had a compact little MP5K submachine gun in his grasp, and was turning the deadly weapon towards him.

Without hesitation, Drake pulled the trigger. The Smith & Wesson automatic snapped back against his wrist, the recoil travelling all the way up the bones of his arm as the round discharged with a thunderous crack.

His aim was true, and his target's head was knocked backwards as if he'd taken a haymaker punch straight to the chin. But there would be no getting up from this blow, Drake knew. As a cloud of red mist ejected from the back of his head, he stumbled sideways and collapsed.

One down.

Straightaway Drake shifted his aim to the second bodyguard, who had by now reacted to the danger and was bringing his weapon to bear. With no time to line up his shot properly, Drake opened fire, aiming to injure and incapacitate rather than kill. Either outcome was fine by him, as long as that submachine gun didn't start spitting fire.

His first shot missed, sailing past the man's right shoulder, but the second round found its mark, tearing into his chest and spinning him around with the force of the impact. Caught off balance, he toppled and fell backwards, but not before squeezing off a long burst from the MP5K that sliced through the air towards Drake in a deadly arc, shattering nearby windows and chewing up the wooden floor all around.

To stand in the face of such murderous automatic gunfire would mean certain death. Drake was forced to abandon his position and throw himself aside to avoid it. He landed hard on the unyielding floorboards, the impact bruising his already injured body while fragments of broken glass sliced into his skin.

Even as the gunfire continued, he caught a glimpse of Faulkner turning away from the scene and sprinting towards one of the broken windows nearby, moving with surprising speed for a man his age. Gathering himself up, he leapt through the gap without hesitation, disappearing into the open void beyond.

He was getting away.

Ignoring the stinging pain of his lacerated arms, Drake twisted around and loosed another couple of rounds at the injured bodyguard, though it was impossible to get a clear line of sight from his position and his shots failed to find their mark. The man was hurt but not fatally so, and he still had an automatic weapon that he was more than happy to use.

More rounds perforated the walls and floor around him, tearing through the soft wood and ricocheting off corrugated steel. Drake rolled sideways, trying to avoid the rain of fire, but he knew it was only a matter of time until he took a hit.

Then, suddenly, he heard the distinctive crack of another weapon. A semi-automatic, snapping off three shots in rapid succession. There was a cry, the dull thump of a body hitting the ground, and the submachine gun fell silent.

Chancing a look, Drake spotted the man lying unmoving on a bed of broken glass and pooling blood. Three gunshot wounds marked his chest.

'Get after him!' Cunningham called out, smoke still drifting from the barrel of his weapon. 'Get Faulkner!'

'Go, Ryan!' McKnight added, having taken cover to avoid the worst of the fire.

Drake knew there was no time to debate the issue. The other two operatives had retreated behind cover, but it wouldn't be long before they renewed the assault. Anyway, this was all for nothing if Faulkner escaped.

One way or another, this had to end now.

Casting one last glance at his former friend, Drake gave him a final instruction. 'Keep her safe.'

With no time left, he turned and sprinted off in pursuit of his enemy, launching himself through the window and praying there was something to break his fall on the other side.

Beyond lay a gap of perhaps ten feet, beneath which was another sloping rooftop, obviously an extension of the lower storey of the factory. Bracing himself, Drake hit hard, the aged steel bowing and creaking with the force of the impact, while his bruised and battered body screamed at him in pain.

Unable to find purchase on the slippery roof, he slid downwards towards the edge, and the ground lying an unknown distance below. He could only assume that Faulkner had descended by similar means.

His last thought as the roof disappeared beneath him and he pitched forward off the edge was that if the fall proved fatal, at least he'd have the satisfaction of knowing that Faulkner had died first.

What followed were a couple of seconds of uncontrolled, tumbling weightlessness, and then suddenly the dusty tarmac below rushed up to meet him.

The thing Drake had learned about landings during his days with the Regiment was the importance of absorbing the impact, reducing the sudden deceleration that was powerful enough to snap bones.

That was the theory at least. It was easy enough when one was at the end of a controlled descent by parachute, but not so much when falling off a factory roof. The reality was that the ground smashed into him like a hammer despite his attempts to cushion his fall, bruising flesh and tearing skin, knocking the breath right out of his lungs.

But he was alive. He knew that with absolute certainty when the first wave of pain hit, nearly causing him to black out. He'd put his body through a lot over the past few days, and though he was fit and hardened by past experience, even he had his limits.

He was lying at the edge of a wide service road that ran between this factory and another unit of similar dimensions. Disused pieces of heavy machinery and stacks of metal pipes had been left abandoned in the open space, slowly rusting and perishing in the desert climate.

Coughing bloody phlegm onto the ground, Drake looked up through bleary eyes, seeing a figure sprinting away from him, heading for the far end of the factory complex. A man, his expensive clothes torn and bloodied, but still moving with surprising speed. A man who was about to get away.

Taking a breath, Drake drew his weapon, rose unsteadily to his feet and sighted the distant target, aiming low to avoid hitting a vital organ. He needed Faulkner alive.

One shot. Make it count.

The crack of the single gunshot in the echoing space between the two buildings was enough to leave Drake's ears ringing, but still he heard the satisfying cry of pain as the round found its mark. Faulkner stumbled, falling to his knees for a moment amidst the windblown trash and discarded industrial machinery. But somehow the man was able to drag himself to his feet once more and carry on, limping heavily on an injured leg.

In a moment, he had disappeared around a corner.

'Fuck,' Drake hissed, taking off in pursuit.

No way was he letting the bastard escape now.

Chapter 63

Clutching his Sig Sauer automatic tight, Peter Boone advanced down the ruined, decaying corridor, heading for the stairwell that would take him to the upper level. The factory's ground floor was a maze of disused workshops and abandoned offices, any one of which could hold an enemy.

He was no stranger to combat like this, and knew all too well how easy it was to fall victim to an unseen ambush. Even now he could hear gunfire echoing down the empty hallways.

That stupid bastard Faulkner had led them to this. Instead of executing Drake when he'd had the chance, he had insisted on bringing him back here. For what? To gloat? To prove how superior he was?

Stupidity of the highest order. When you had a shot, you took it.

Reaching up, he touched his radio earpiece. 'All units, report in. Anyone transmitting?'

'Macguire,' came a female voice. 'Hostiles in the building. Unknown number.'

Tell me something I don't know, he thought. 'Got a location on Faulkner?'

'No idea.'

Her tone suggested she was harbouring similar thoughts to himself.

'Fuck him,' Boone decided, unwilling to lay down his life for such a man. 'We pull out, kill as many of those bastards as we can on the way.'

She didn't respond to that. She didn't have to.

Gritting his teeth, Boone pushed onwards.

–

Situated a few blocks away from the factory amidst the ancient ruins that stood atop the hill near the centre of town, Laila Sowan could hear the distinctive boom and crackle of gunfire as clear as day. Clearly a ferocious fight was taking place, and she was powerless to do anything about it.

Her captor, the young Tuareg named Amaha, was of like mind, judging by his anxious pacing and the tight grip he kept on his weapon.

'Your brother may need your help,' she said. 'He could be in danger.'

'We were told to stay here,' he mumbled, not looking at her. His mind was elsewhere. 'We must wait for them.'

She'd known he would say that, but it didn't matter. She didn't need him. Reaching down, she closed her hands around a large rock, perhaps once a piece of the great ruined temple in which they now stood.

Gripping it tight, she pulled it from its resting place in the ground, hoisted it above her head and took a step towards him. Preoccupied with the distant battle and his own dark thoughts, he didn't hear her approach until it was too late.

The impact sent him staggering forwards, crumpling beneath the blow like a rag doll. He shuddered once as if trying to rise, then lay still on the hot sand.

Wasting no time, Laila crouched down and snatched his weapon where it had fallen. It was an automatic handgun of a make she didn't recognize, but that didn't matter. She knew enough to use it.

And use it she would.

–

Rising from cover, Cunningham raised his weapon and sighted the new target. One of Faulkner's men – a short, heavy-set man with dark curling hair and pale skin – backed up against one of the cement pillars supporting the roof high above.

With Drake having escaped through the window, the two remaining operatives had turned all their attention towards Cunningham. His weapon was levelled, body already tensing up as he prepared to open fire, but Cunningham was half a second faster, emptying his remaining rounds at the man before he could pull the trigger, and forcing him to take cover behind the pillar.

Bullets ricocheted wildly off the stonework, shattering glass window panes behind him and throwing out clouds of dust and rock fragments, but failed to find their target.

The answering volley of crossfire from the second operative caught him exposed. He felt the thump of something striking him hard, like a fist driven right through his rib cage, followed a moment later by another strike to his left leg.

Letting out a groan of pain, he fell even as more rounds hammered off the wall around him. He was done, he knew in that moment. Out of ammunition, out of cover, out of time.

He glanced back at McKnight, crouched behind cover further down the corridor. Still clutching the laptop he'd given to her. The one thing on which all their fates hung.

'Get out of here, lass!' he called out to her, readying himself to stand up, to draw their fire for a few precious seconds. Perhaps it would buy her time to find another way out and escape with the laptop.

Perhaps it would even earn him some measure of redemption.

That was when he heard something he'd never expected. A boom; not the sharp crack of a handgun or rifle, but the heavy thud of a shotgun round, quickly followed by a second shot.

As he stared in disbelief, the first operative stumbled forward, a fine spray of crimson ejected from the shattered remains of his chest. His companion started to turn towards this new, unexpected threat, only to be cut down by a trio of silenced rounds – two to the torso followed by one to the head that finished the job.

As both men slumped to the ground, Cunningham almost laughed as Mason and Frost darted forwards; the young woman clutching a sawn-off shotgun whose twin barrels were still smoking.

'Clear!' Mason called out, scanning the hallway beyond while keeping his weapon up and ready.

Meanwhile, Frost rushed forward and knelt down beside him, quickly taking in his injuries. 'You're not dead yet,' was her only conclusion.

'Aye, I can tell you're pleased,' Cunningham said, managing a grim smile through clenched teeth.

'I don't believe it,' McKnight called out, rising from her position at the end of the corridor. 'What the hell are you two doing here?'

'Sam!' Frost cried, her face lighting up with utter relief. As McKnight rushed forward to greet her, Frost threw her arms around the woman and hugging her so hard that it prompted a groan of pain. 'Thank Christ. Are you okay?'

'I will be when we're out of this goddamn place,' McKnight assured her, grimacing a little as her injured ribs blazed with pain.

'No argument here,' Frost concluded as she snapped open the barrel of her weapon, the two smoking cartridges automatically ejecting. 'Where's Ryan?'

'He went after Faulkner.'

At this, Frost's smile faded.

'Goddamn it,' Mason said, shaking his head. 'Local police are going to be on this in minutes, and we've still got hostiles in the building. This is not a place we want to hang around.'

'You don't need to.' Reaching down, McKnight snatched up a weapon from one of the dead operatives, then thrust the laptop into Frost's hands. 'Everything we need is in there. Get it to safety, no matter what. Understand?'

'Of course. What about you?'

'I'll find Ryan.' Her gaze flicked to her two companions, giving them a faint nod of encouragement. She swallowed hard, taking a breath to psyche herself up for what was coming. 'Good luck. Both of you.'

'Sam, wait. You can't—'

But she had turned away before Frost could finish, limping back along the corridor and clambering out through the same window Drake had disappeared from. Within moments, she was gone.

'Goddamn it!' Frost hissed, making to follow her. Only Mason's strong grip was enough to pull her back.

'Forget it,' he warned her. 'She made her choice. We've got other problems to deal with.'

Swearing under her breath again, Frost reluctantly conceded to his point. With a vexed sigh, she turned her attention to the injured man. 'Can you walk?'

'Would you leave me behind if I couldn't?'

'Shut up, old man.' Inserting two fresh cartridges in the shotgun, she snapped the barrels closed. 'Get him, Cole. I'll cover you.'

Moving forward, Mason hooked an arm beneath him and hauled Cunningham to his feet; no easy task with such a large man. Groaning in pain, the injured man stumbled down the corridor, with Frost leading the way.

Chapter 64

Limping heavily on his injured leg, David Faulkner tore through back alleys and side streets, heedless of anyone who dared cross his path. His haphazard course was carrying him generally uphill, towards a rounded area of high ground that overlooked much of the town.

He couldn't see what was up there yet, but anything was better than what he'd left behind. Drake was out there somewhere, following him, hunting him. Fury and rage vied with something else he hadn't felt in a long time – fear.

Reaching into his torn and dirty jacket, he fished out his cell phone and quickly dialled a number from memory, unable to keep his hands from shaking. Blood loss was making him weak, slowing his progress.

The number rang out for several agonizing seconds before they at last picked up. 'Well, is it done?' his contact asked without preamble.

Faulkner let out a pained sigh. 'We've been ambushed. The location is compromised. I need transport out of the country.'

NSA Director Richard Stark paused for a moment or two. 'And Drake?'

'He's after me, for Christ's sake,' Faulkner said, pain and anger getting the better of him. 'I need extraction, now.'

He was almost there now. The crowded buildings were giving way to open ground scattered with the tumbled walls and leaning pillars of some kind of archaeological site. A wind gusted across the hilltop, carrying dry windblown grit into his eyes and forcing him to throw a hand up to shield himself.

'You've disappointed me, David,' Starke said, his tone sad and resigned. 'Remember what I said about the group and failure? Think on that.'

With that chilling proclamation, the line went dead.

'You bastard!' Faulkner hissed, trying to redial.

But at that moment he stopped in his tracks, his face frozen in shock and disbelief at what he saw. The phone fell from his hand and he took a step backward, staring down the barrel of the weapon now trained on him.

–

Together the small group emerged through the gaping hole torn in the side of the building, Frost leading the way and Mason supporting the injured man beside him.

'That's our ride out of here,' Mason decided, heading for the black Ford SUV that had brought Drake here less than an hour earlier. Mason doubted its original owners would mind if they borrowed it.

'Can you hotwire it?' Frost asked.

He flashed her a grin. 'Better than you can.'

Frost was just opening her mouth to retort when suddenly something flew through the air past her, thumping against the side of the wrecked truck before coming to rest on the ground nearby with a heavy metallic *thunk*.

She didn't need to look at it to realize what it was, just as she didn't have to think about what to do next. Reacting with the instinct born from long experience, she dropped her weapon and threw herself at Mason as if she were trying to tackle him to the ground, pulling him down with her just as the grenade detonated.

White light engulfed her vision just as a thunderous boom resounded in her ears, sounding like a thunderclap right next to her. Shaking her head, she blinked furiously in an effort to clear the splashes of light that danced across her eyes.

Her quick reflexes had saved most her sight from the flashbang, but Mason had taken the full brunt of it. 'Cole. Cole! Can you hear me?'

'Fuck! Keira? You there?'

It was obvious he couldn't see or hear a thing, and it would be several minutes before his senses returned to normal.

Several minutes they didn't have.

Raising her head far enough to get a bead on where the grenade came from, she was immediately forced to duck down by a burst of gunfire that slammed into the ground and the SUV that she was partially shielded by.

She twisted around, searching frantically for a weapon. Her shotgun had fallen beneath the car when she'd thrown Mason to the ground, and there was no time to reach for it now.

Mason's sidearm however was lying several yards away, knocked from his hand when the flashbang went off. Leaving her injured comrade, she crawled forward to retrieve the fallen weapon.

That was when she saw him. A lone man advancing from the ruined factory, short and wiry of build, with pale skin and buzz-cut red hair. A man armed with an automatic weapon, and a burning desire to use it on anything that stood in his way.

She saw him, and he saw her.

She wasn't going to make it, she knew then. He had the drop on her. All she could do was watch as he swung the weapon towards her.

She'd always said she'd wanted to meet death with her eyes open, without fear. She couldn't vouch for the second part, but she refused to close her eyes as he pulled the trigger.

But at the same moment, his right shoulder exploded with the impact of a shot, followed quickly by another. His weapon kicked back as his finger tightened on the trigger, no longer properly aimed, the round sailing harmlessly through the air.

Frost stared in disbelief as her would-be killer stumbled backwards and fell, never to rise again.

'What the——?'

'Keira!' a voice called out, slightly muffled by the ringing in her ears.

She turned towards the source of the sound, letting out an involuntary gasp of shock at the sight of Iskaw emerging from a building on the far side of the street, a sniper rifle up at his shoulder. His eyes met hers and, perhaps relishing the look of shock on her face, he smiled. That slightly lopsided, rakish smile caused by the scar on his cheek.

It was a moment. A moment she had never expected and would likely never forget.

A moment that was shattered in a heartbeat by the crack of another shot from up above. Staring in horror, Frost watched as the young Tuareg hunter jerked with the impact of the shot, blood painting his pale robes, before falling to his knees, the weapon clattering from his grasp.

'No!' she cried out as he slumped forward.

Glancing up, she spotted the distinctive, eager snout of a rifle protruding from one of the factory's shattered windows, along with the hand that wielded it.

Reaching out, she snatched up Mason's fallen sidearm, turned it skyward and opened fire, capping off four or five shots in short order, tears streaming from her eyes. She saw a burst of red, heard an agonized scream, and suddenly the rifle fell from the window, breaking against the tarmac below.

Dropping the now-empty weapon, Frost slithered beneath the SUV, reaching out until she felt her fingers close around the grip of the shotgun.

–

For the first time in a long time, Faulkner was stunned into silence.

Drake was standing before him, having emerged from behind one of the ancient pillars up ahead. Somehow he must have anticipated his course, circled around and intercepted him.

He was bruised and bleeding, his body pushed to breaking point by everything he'd been through over the past several days, but he was alive. And he was armed.

For several seconds, neither man said or did a thing. They remained frozen like that, poised in a moment of perfect balance, eyes locked in a final battle of wills.

But only one of them would walk away from this. Both men knew it, and both knew which one it would be.

'Wait,' Faulkner implored him, holding up a hand as if that could change how this was about to play out. 'You don't want to do this, Ryan.'

Drake said nothing. He just kept the weapon trained on his target, his vivid green eyes glimmering in the harsh sunlight.

'The things I've done… I haven't always been proud of,' he admitted, his voice betraying an edge of what might have been honesty. 'But if you really understood what was at stake, you'd know I did them for the right reasons. I'm trying to *save* lives, Ryan.'

Drake took a step towards him, prompting Faulkner to back up a pace in response, his hands held up to show he was unarmed – as if that mattered now. For the first time, he actually looked afraid. That mattered a lot.

'I underestimated you. That was my mistake.' He licked his dry lips, his eyes flitting left and right, always seeking an escape, an alternative, a way out of this. 'But I can help you, Ryan. I know things – things nobody else wants you to know. And I can tell you everything, but not if I'm dead. If you kill me, you'll never know what Freya was really involved in, who she was working for, why she really died. It's all gone if you pull that trigger.'

Drake could feel his muscles tensing up, his posture changing almost imperceptibly as he prepared to pull the trigger. With the careful deliberation that came from his years of training and practice, he took aim at Faulkner's centre mass, adjusting just a little to compensate for the recoil.

'I know about Operation Hydra, Ryan,' Faulkner suddenly blurted out, sensing what was about to happen.

Drake froze then, his heartbeat pounding in his ears, his breath coming in shallow gasps as the words sank in. Operation Hydra. The day his life had changed forever. The day that started him on the path to the dark, murky world in which he now lived, and where he might well die.

Hydra. The word he had come to fear and hate in equal measure. And the man standing before him knew the truth about it.

'I know what they did to you, and I know why,' Faulkner said, Drake's silence encouraging him to continue. 'It wasn't what you think it was. They lied to you, Ryan, to cover up what was really happening. They let you take the blame for it, but I know the truth. I can help you bring down Cain, bring down the Circle, put an end to the whole fucking lot of them.'

Drake's hand was trembling, his grip on the trigger growing tighter. A fraction of an inch more, and it would be done.

Yet he didn't pull the trigger. This man standing before him, bruised and bedraggled, who had tried to kill him and his companions several times over the past few days, who was responsible for sacrificing countless innocent lives to further his own goals... this man might just hold the key to his redemption.

This man had the power to help him.

'Talk,' Drake spat, hardly believing he'd just said it.

Faulkner let out a breath. 'First you get me out of here. Then I'll—'

His sentence was cut off suddenly by the sharp crack of a single gunshot. Faulkner stiffened suddenly, letting out a gasp of shock. His eyes were locked with Drake's, blank and uncomprehending, then slowly his gaze travelled down to stare in confusion at the crimson stain spreading out from the centre of his chest.

'No!' Drake cried out, even as Faulkner's legs gave way beneath him and he sank to the ground, collapsing in a bloody heap.

And behind him, revealed for the first time, stood Laila Sowan.

–

Clutching her maimed and bleeding hand, Macguire stumbled down the last flight of stairs and through the fire door at the bottom, kicking it open with savage anger to emerge into the service alley beyond.

The pain of shattered bone and torn flesh was intense now that the shock and adrenaline were wearing off, but it was nothing to the rage and indignation that now burned inside her. Thirty-two kill missions to her name, and not so much as a scratch until today. Fuck.

Given her injuries, it was fair to say that her career as a sniper was over. Whatever else she did with her life, it would have to be in a new profession, serving a new master. Faulkner had fucked up badly on this operation, leading the entire team into a trap from which none of them were likely to escape.

Even if the man himself somehow made it out, she wouldn't be making contact with him again. He'd already proven himself quite unworthy of her efforts, and she certainly wasn't going to risk her life for a man like that.

Her only regret was that she hadn't been able to take proper revenge on their enemies. Some of them at least were still alive, and that rankled her. She wasn't accustomed to leaving jobs unfinished.

So consumed was she with these thoughts of bloody revenge that she almost didn't notice the diminutive figure waiting for her in the alleyway. She froze, staring in puzzlement at the young woman she had previously seen only through the scope of her rifle.

Keira Frost.

In an instant, surprise gave way to survival instinct, and she went for the sidearm holstered at her thigh. Her enemy was faster, raising what looked like a crude sawn-off shotgun.

There was a boom like the discharge of a cannon, and suddenly Macguire went down, her left leg simply giving way beneath her as if it were no longer under her control. Landing hard on the dusty ground, she looked down in disbelief at the mess of shredded fabric and bloody flesh that had once been her left knee.

The first waves of pain were beginning to wash over her now as she glanced up at her attacker. Frost was walking towards her, not a trace of emotion on her face, as if this were simply some grim task to be completed as efficiently as possible.

The shotgun still had one barrel left to unload. She was getting close, making sure the short-ranged weapon was as effective as possible when she loosed her shot.

'Do it, then, you fucking bitch,' Macguire snarled, her teeth clenched tight. 'I'm not—'

Her final sentiment was interrupted when the young woman dropped the shotgun, drew an ancient hand-crafted knife from her belt and slashed downward with the blade, cutting Macguire's throat.

Her work done, Frost took a step back to avoid the resultant spray of blood, and watched in cold silence as the life slowly drained from the woman's eyes. She didn't cry out, either because she couldn't make the noise or because of sheer stubborn refusal to give in.

But at the end, in the final moments, Frost saw it in her eyes. The fear. The knowledge that this was the end, that death had come for her at last. Everyone, no matter how brave they might have been or how much they might have longed for death, felt the same way. When it finally came for them, they'd do anything to stay alive.

With a final gurgling groan, it was done. Frost let out the breath she didn't realize she'd been holding, wiped the blade of Iskaw's dagger on her trouser leg, and sheathed the weapon once more.

She couldn't protect him, but at least she'd answered his death in kind. Somehow she'd expected that to make her feel better.

It didn't.

–

Laila's expression was cold and hard, her posture tense as she stood over the mortally injured man, a pistol clutched in her left hand. Only her eyes betrayed the depth of her emotions, streaming with tears and burning with hatred and vengeance that knew no bounds.

Gasping to draw a breath that wouldn't come, Faulkner stared up at her, his face betraying his utter shock at what had just happened. Even now, with the woman standing over him, with his life ebbing away, he couldn't comprehend the events that were playing out.

'Tarek Sowan was my husband,' she whispered, her voice strained to breaking point as she struggled to maintain her composure. She raised the weapon once more, aiming for his head. 'I give you the death that you gave him.'

'Stop!' Drake called out, training his weapon on her.

Her head snapped around, dark smouldering eyes taking in the weapon now pointed her way. 'This man deserves to die for what he did.'

'I know,' Drake promised. 'Believe me, I know. But you can't kill him. I need him.'

'He sacrificed innocent lives, killed my husband, tried to kill you and your friends. He will do it again if we let him live.' She shook her head. 'No. It has to end here.'

Lowering his aim, Drake squeezed the trigger, sending a round into the ground at her feet. The report of the weapon made her flinch, and she looked at him not with anger, not with accusation, but with sadness. She was disappointed in him. He'd had a chance to prove himself a better man, and he'd failed.

'Would you kill me to save this man's life?' she challenged him.

'Don't force me to make that choice.'

That was when he saw it. A faint, bittersweet smile. The smile of someone watching a long-anticipated moment come to pass. Drake could sense what she was about to do, even as he prayed she wouldn't.

'Then I will make it for you,' she said, raising her weapon.

One shot was all it took. One shot to the head, and he put a stop to her.

Drake didn't watch her body crumple and fall to the ground. He couldn't bring himself to look. He could hate himself later for what he'd done – and he certainly would – but for now he could only afford to think of the matter at hand.

384

He rushed over to Faulkner and dropped to his knees beside the injured man, yanking apart his shirt to expose a gory exit wound from which blood was leaking steadily. He was conscious, barely, but how long he would remain that way was questionable. Every breath seemed to be growing shallower and weaker.

'Shit,' Drake said under his breath, trying to apply pressure to the wound. 'Stay with me, Faulkner. Look at me. Fucking keep your eyes open, you bastard!'

He was trying to speak. Drake could see his mouth moving, though his voice was too weak to project the words.

Leaning in close, Drake strained to listen, to discern the barely audible whisper.

What he heard sent a shiver through him, a chill of shock and disbelief as the man's final words hit home. 'I didn't kill Freya.'

'What? Then who did?' he demanded. 'Faulkner. Faulkner, listen to me!'

But there was no response. When he looked into the man's eyes, they were glassy and lifeless, his breathing grown still, his fight for life over at last.

Letting out a gasp of pain and grief and devastation at what he'd just heard, and what he'd sacrificed to get it, Drake sat back, staring off into the distance without seeing a thing.

'Ryan!' a voice called out.

Turning his head slowly, Drake watched as Samantha sprinted over, falling to her knees beside him. Straightaway she took in the scene, both Faulkner and Laila lying dead, and an injured and bleeding Drake apparently in shock.

'Jesus Christ,' she whispered, her expression betraying her sadness at the woman's death. Then, realizing the urgency of their situation, she turned her attention to Drake. 'Ryan, we have to get out of here.'

She tried to drag him to his feet, but she lacked the strength to lift him.

'The police are on their way. We have to go.' Moving around in front of him, she took his head in her hands and stared right at him. 'Ryan, we can't stay here. I need you to come with me. Please.'

At last her words seemed to reach him. She was right, of course. He wasn't sure he deserved to get away after what he'd done, but the rest of his team certainly did. He couldn't abandon them now.

Wearily he dragged himself to his feet and followed her, pausing only for a moment to look back at the two bodies he was leaving behind. Another two casualties in a war that was growing increasingly bitter and desperate.

It was almost a relief to turn and flee the scene, though he knew that he could never escape what had happened here today.

Chapter 65

By sunset that evening, the small group once again found themselves out in the desert, this time gathered around a small funeral cairn in solemn silence. They had retrieved Iskaw's body from the scene of the battle at Frost's insistence, refusing to leave behind the young man who had given his life to help a group of strangers.

After tending their own injuries, they had dug a shallow pit in the desert sand and lowered him in, placing him on his right side so that his body was facing towards Mecca as was the custom of his people. With this solemn task accomplished, they had piled sand and then stones on top to mark the grave site.

Leaning heavily on a stick for support, Cunningham stepped forward and laid the final rock atop the cairn, quietly reciting the *janazah* funeral prayer as he did so. Though not a Muslim himself, he understood the culture and its rituals enough to honour it as a mark of respect for his fallen comrade.

Amaha, his brother, watched on in silence, his head bound with a bloodstained bandage. He said nothing, but tears were glistening in his eyes.

The words seemed to catch in Cunningham's throat as he spoke, though with some effort he was able to regain his composure enough to carry on. Only when he'd finished the prayer did he step back and wipe his eyes.

'I'm sorry, mate,' Drake said, laying a hand on his shoulder. Whatever his own history with Cunningham, he recognized a man in mourning. 'He was a brave kid.'

'Aye,' the man agreed, his voice ragged with grief. 'But stupid. Always starting fights he couldnae finish.' His voice wavered and he looked away for a moment. 'I'm sure he's up there right now stirring up shit.'

Drake smiled, though the look in his eyes was serious as surveyed his former friend. Stricken with grief, injured and in pain, he was a far cry from the powerful, intimidating figure he remembered from his days in the Regiment. Then again, a great many things had changed since then, for both of them.

'You've given more than you had to,' he said quietly. 'Why?'

'Because you needed the help.' The older man sighed and looked at him. 'And because I owed you. Maybe I still do. I dinnae expect you to forgive me for everything that's happened, and I know you'll never call me a friend again, but... I'm trying, mate.'

Drake didn't know what to say to this. In truth, he couldn't make sense of his own feelings towards this man. This man who had once been a father figure to him, who he would have trusted with his life, and whose betrayal had cost the life of one of Drake's closest comrades. This man who had twice saved his life, and lost someone he cared deeply about for his efforts.

'Tell me something,' Cunningham went on. 'Now that it's over, are you still going to come after me?'

Drake shook his head. What was the point? He already had enough deaths on his conscience without adding another to the list. 'I can't say for sure about the rest, but you were wrong about one thing. You don't owe me anything now.'

Cunningham swallowed and glanced away, saying nothing.

'What are you going to do now?' Drake asked. 'Where will you go?'

At this, Cunningham managed a thin smile. 'You know me – I'll find somewhere. I'll make sure Amaha gets back to his people. He deserves that much, to tell them how brave his brother was.'

Of that, Drake had no doubt.

'What about you?' Cunningham asked.

Drake looked over at his three companions. All were hurt and tired after the ordeal of the past few days; their torn clothes, battered bodies and weary faces all showing the marks of what they'd been through. All had been tested, pushed to breaking-point, but all had come through it. His friends... his family.

They were almost the only family he had left now. He would die to protect them.

'We'll survive,' he said at length. 'It's what we do.'

His former friend nodded in understanding. 'Then I wish you luck, mate.' He reached out and clasped Drake's hand. 'If we somehow run into each other again, I hope it's under better circumstances, aye?'

Drake gripped his hand tight, meeting his gaze not as a friend or an enemy, but simply as an equal. They were both survivors, each owing his life to the other. No matter what else had happened between them, they were bound together by that at least.

Releasing his grip, Cunningham turned, mounted the SUV they had stolen from Faulkner's group, and fired up the engine. Amaha climbed into the passenger's seat.

Nearby, Frost was also watching the vehicle and its two passengers depart, though unlike Drake she made no effort to bid Cunningham farewell. Still, her gaze held none of the anger or animosity that it once had, and she made no attempt to stop him. She was unsure what to make of him, whether he was a good man or bad, whether he'd found some measure of the redemption he'd been looking for. For now, at least, she was content simply to let him leave.

When at last they had disappeared from sight into a shallow valley, the young woman turned her attention to matters closer at hand. With her head bowed, she approached the cairn and knelt down before it, staring at the low pile of stones for a long moment in a solemn, uncharacteristic show of respect.

'Here,' she said, laying her knife down beside the grave. The knife that had once belonged to her, and which he'd playfully claimed for his own. 'You earned it.'

Her expression was calm and composed when she rose to her feet and walked away from the cairn, though Drake couldn't help noticing that her eyes were red and glistening in the evening sunlight. He also noticed the *tellak*, the traditional Tuareg weapon that Iskaw had given her in return, was sheathed at her forearm as it was intended to be worn.

'You okay?' Drake asked as she passed him.

'Fine,' she replied, though she was careful not to make eye contact. 'But I'm ready to put this place behind me.'

He wasn't about to argue, but first he had another matter to attend to.

McKnight was sitting a short distance from the others, staring out across the desert at the setting sun. Only when Drake eased himself down beside her did she glance around, woken from her reverie.

'How are you holding up?' he asked.

She sniffed, reaching up to move aside a lock of hair that had blown into her face. 'I keep thinking back on everything that's happened. Everything we've been through.' She glanced at the funeral cairn. 'I keep asking if it was worth it.'

Drake wished he had an answer for her.

'Mind if I ask you something?' she asked instead, looking at him once again. 'Why didn't you do it?'

'Do what?'

'Pull the trigger,' she said simply. 'When we were out there in the desert, when there was no chance for us. Why didn't you end it?'

He looked surprised. Surprised, and perhaps a little ashamed. 'I didn't think you'd remember that.'

'I do.' Her memory of those final few minutes, as her conscious mind had faded out, was hazy and fragmented, but she did recall Drake reaching for the weapon and pressing the barrel against her. She'd welcomed it at the time; an easy way out for both of them.

Yet somehow life followed her around.

Drake swallowed and looked away. 'There was always a chance. I wasn't ready to give up.'

'No.' She shook her head. 'No, it's more than that. What really stopped you, Ryan?'

It was some time before he answered. Perhaps he didn't know how to put it into words, or perhaps it was hard for him to relive that desperate decision. Either way, his voice was tense and strained when he finally spoke.

'I couldn't do it,' he admitted. 'I knew it was necessary, maybe even the right thing, in some ways, but... I couldn't do it. I couldn't take your life, even if I'd wanted to. You're pretty much the only thing I've got left in the world, Sam. If I lost you, it would...' He shook his head, as if unwilling to contemplate it. 'I'd rather have died myself.'

She let out a ragged breath, his words cutting deep as she realized at last the depth of his feelings for her. She had done exactly what she'd been sent to do, and she hated herself for it.

Unable to look him in the eye, she did the only thing she could think of: she pulled him close and pressed her lips against his, her kiss hard and urgent as the conflicting emotions rose to an unbearable peak within her. Taken aback for a moment, he soon responded in kind, his strong arms encircling her and his hands travelling down her body.

Out here, under the stark beauty of the evening sky, it was almost possible to forget everything else.

Almost.

When Drake and McKnight returned to the others a short while later, it was with a renewed sense of purpose. There was something he had to bring before the others.

'I need to speak with you all for a minute,' he said, raising his voice.

He waited until Frost and Mason had gathered around, surveying each of his companions in turn. He was oddly reminded of their meeting in a pub in London that had kicked off this entire operation. It was hard to believe it had all happened less than a week ago.

'You all know why we're here,' Drake began. 'You all know what it took to get us here. We've got a choice to make now; all of us. And I do mean *all* of us. This can't be a majority decision, not for something like this. We all have to be behind it, one way or the other.'

He sighed, reached into a simple canvas pack and carefully lifted out the laptop they'd stolen from Faulkner and his men. The hard drive was still attached, decrypted, its secrets laid bare.

'So, the first choice is that we fold. We destroy this drive, go home, pretend the last few days never happened, and hope that somehow we can go back to the way things were. We'll be no closer to stopping Cain, we'll have gone through all this for nothing, and we'll probably have a lot of questions to answer back at Langley. And while we're busy forgetting it all, thousands of people will be dying here in a civil war we could have prevented.'

He paused, giving them a chance to take it in, to think it over. This was no time for making decisions based on a rush of emotion. It had to be done in the full knowledge of what their choice might mean.

'The other option is that we go all in. We give out all the information on this thing, we take down their entire operation. Destroy it from the inside.'

–

CIA headquarters – Langley, Virginia

Charles Hunt leaned forward in his chair, eyes glued to the pictures being transmitted via secure satellite link from the strike team's helmet-mounted cameras to his laptop. The effect was to make him feel as if he was almost there with them, getting ready for the assault.

But he wasn't. He was half a world away in a comfortable air-conditioned office, while they were skimming along at 150 knots, barely fifty feet above the surface of the Libyan desert.

The interior of the Black Hawk chopper was bathed in red light for night flying, making the heavily armoured soldiers look even more intimidating as they performed their final weapons and equipment checks.

'We're almost on station. ETA, sixty seconds,' Joel Paxton, the strike-team leader reported over the satellite link. 'Are we still cleared to move in?'

Another window on Hunt's computer showed him real-time satellite coverage of the target area, which he'd had specially retasked for this mission – no mean feat without drawing Cain's attention. But Hunt was a man with a long history in the Agency, who could still call in a few favours and draw on formidable resources when the need arose.

The strike team's target was a small, isolated compound located near the village of Eferi in south-west Algeria. Far from anything approaching civilization, and virtually unnoticeable unless one knew exactly where to look for it. Well, thanks to the information provided by Drake, plenty of people were now looking at it.

Not to mention a dozen other places just like it.

'That's affirmative,' Hunt replied. 'You're good to go.'

'Roger that. Gear up, gentlemen! Thirty seconds!'

Weapons and equipment shifted and clicked as final checks were made.

'I want a solid perimeter established as soon as we're on the ground,' he heard Paxton say. 'If they try to run, I want all escape routes covered. Force is authorized, but only as a last resort.'

'No sign of activity.'

'Ten seconds!'

One of the troopers leaned over and hauled open the sliding door, and then the cabin was filled with the rush of wind and the thudding of rotor blades. Paxton was first to hook on to the descent wire, and a moment later he disappeared out into the darkness. The rest of the team followed in short order, and for a few moments Hunt could see nothing on his screen except blurred movement as they slid down the wires.

The images soon returned to normal as each of the troopers touched down with a bump and unhooked themselves.

'Move forward! Go! Go! Watch that left flank! Get me a perimeter now!'

On the satellite feed, Hunt watched as the glowing blobs of his own troops fanned out to encircle the compound. Overhead, the Black Hawk peeled off to give the assault team room to work, and to make communication easier.

'Perimeter secure.'

He switched his attention back to Paxton's helmet camera as the man rapidly closed in on what looked like the compound's entrance. 'Walker, cover left,' he said, his voice tight with anticipation. 'DaForte, on me. Ready?'

'Roger.'

Paxton halted in front of the door, weapon at the ready. 'Go! Go! Go!'

In a blur of movement the door had burst open and the team surged in, yelling commands and calling out anything they saw.

'Get down on the ground!'

'Get down now!'

Hunt's heart was beating hard and fast now as the team spread out to comb the fortified compound. Even in the harsh glow cast by their weapon-mounted lights, he was able to make out containers piled high against the walls, frightened men with ghostly green eyes viewed in night vision, kneeling on the ground with their hands behind their heads while the assault team swarmed all around.

One of the troopers had moved in to investigate one of the containers, unlatching the metal clasps that held it closed.

'Paxton, give me a report,' Hunt commanded over the satellite phone.

'Jackpot, sir,' Paxton replied, a little out of breath now. 'You should see this.'

Sure enough, he was able to angle his helmet-cam enough for Hunt to make out the inside of the container. Neatly stacked in long lines were rack after rack of AK assault rifles, along with boxes of ammunition and spare magazines.

Hunt let out a breath, slumping back in his chair as the scale of what they'd uncovered settled on him. One of the biggest arms-smuggling operations in the past ten years, and it would all be attributed to him.

'Well done, son,' he said quietly. 'Clear up. I want this on record.'

–

'But you all know what it will mean. There'll be no such thing as normal lives for us after this. We'll be at war. Cain will be after our blood – he won't stop until he gets it, or we destroy him first. We'll have to go dark, sever all ties to the Agency and go underground until this is all over. We'll be branded as traitors and God knows what else, because he'll do everything in his power to take us down with him.'

–

Great Falls National Park, Virginia

Once more Marcus Cain found himself on the familiar forest trail in the woods north of DC, walking with NSA Director Richard Starke. But this wasn't like their last meeting. This was no thoughtful, composed exchange of information and ideas.

Starke's pace was fast and agitated, his head down, forehead creased by deep frown-lines. It gave Cain an almost perverse sense of satisfaction to know the man could be upset after all.

And he had good reason to be. Operation Antonia, the group's clandestine plan to incite an armed rebellion in Libya and install leaders friendly to their economic interests, had collapsed in dramatic fashion after a series of surgical strikes by

Agency assault teams. Strikes that were far too coordinated and precise to have been anything other than an inside job.

'Would you care to explain what the hell happened in Libya?' Starke demanded, wasting no time on greetings. 'You assured me the situation was being handled.'

'I did,' Cain acknowledged.

'So why was our entire distribution network wiped out in the space of a few hours?'

'I wondered the same thing, so I had my people do some digging.' Cain sighed, opening the folder he'd brought with him for their meeting. 'It pains me to say this, but it looks like we have a leak. Someone in the group isn't playing for our side.'

The surveillance photos thus presented were taken from long range, no doubt from a hidden camera, but nonetheless the two participants were easily identified. Ryan Drake, the operative who had gained such notoriety over the past couple of years, and who was now known to have played a key part in events in Libya. And seated beside him in the memorial theatre at Arlington Cemetery was Charles Hunt, Cain's predecessor as Deputy Director, demoted within the group to make way for Cain's rising star.

'According to our communication records, the strike orders originated from Hunt's office,' Cain added, his tone one of solemn regret.

Starke worked his way through the dozen surveillance pictures, staring long and hard at each one before finally closing the folder. Bowing his head, he let out a slow, pained breath.

'Thank you for bringing this to my attention.'

'We could bring him in?' Cain suggested. 'Give him a chance to explain himself.'

Starke shook his head. For once in his life, cold logic and reasoning had deserted him. 'Don't worry about Hunt. I'll handle him.'

It took some effort for Cain to hide his smile as they resumed their walk.

–

'That's the price. That's what we'll have to sacrifice to win. But in the end, everything he throws at us will be worth it. In the end, we'll win, and he'll lose.'

He looked at them all, seated around him. His friends. His family. The people who had stood by him through everything that had happened so far. Would they do it one more time?

'So... what are we going to do?' he asked.

–

For the second time in as many weeks, Charles Hunt found himself at Arlington Cemetery, sweating and out of breath after his ascent up the hill to the Tomb of the Unknown Soldier.

As always, the Marine honour guard were standing the post as he shuffled past, their backs ramrod straight, their faces as immobile as stone. He paid them little heed today, because in truth he had a more pressing errand here.

Passing through the great rows of stone columns that encircled the building, he found himself facing out into the open space of the Memorial Amphitheatre. Much as it had been during his last rendezvous here, the place was empty and unused.

Drawing on his formidable memory, Hunt counted along the rows of stone benches until he found the very one he'd sat on last time. Nothing about it was exceptional, nothing marked it out as different from the others, but he knew this was the place.

Taking a breath, he lowered himself down onto the hard, uncomfortable surface, then reached down and slowly, carefully, felt along the underside.

He frowned. Nothing.

Had he been wrong? Had he misunderstood Drake's instructions?

Hunt was just rising to his feet when he saw him. A small, innocuous-looking man with greying hair, standing on the other side of the theatre.

Richard Starke, the Director of the NSA.

'Richard, I—'

He never saw the operative come at him from behind, never had time to cry out before a plastic bag was thrown over his head and a taser jammed against his neck. He went down, jerking and shaking, unable to fathom how this had come to be.

But through the clear plastic of the bag, he was just able to make out the shape of Starke as the man turned and walked away, before the darkness closed in around him.

–

CIA headquarters – Langley, Virginia

In one of the New Headquarter Building's plush conference rooms, Marcus Cain took a sip of his coffee, watching the overhead satellite feed of a small encampment deep in the Libyan desert. Around the table were seated several of the Agency's senior directors, each making notes as the mission unfolded on the big screen before them.

One notable absentee was Charles Hunt, who had regrettably passed away from a suspected heart attack during a visit to Arlington Cemetery. Hardly surprising for an ageing man in poor health, who had just ascended the hill to the Tomb of the Unknown Soldier.

Should have taken better care of himself, Cain thought with a faint smile.

'Package is away,' he heard through the radio link to the pilot of the Reaper drone flying over central Libya. 'Time on target, ten seconds.'

With Operation Antonia effectively crippled by Hunt's interference, Cain had been able to persuade the group to adopt his own initiative. The objective he'd been pursuing since this whole thing began – the elimination of Islamic State's senior commanders in Libya. Cutting the head off a snake before it became a monster none of them could stop.

That was worth everything he'd sacrificed. That was worth the lives lost.

'Five seconds.'

It had been a difficult and dangerous path he'd walked, but it had been worth it. Drake had proven easy to manipulate in the end, giving him exactly what he wanted – an excuse to eliminate an old enemy within the group, and a chance to clear house. Now the man was on the run in the wake of his failure, but that didn't concern him. Cain had someone very close, keeping an eye on Ryan Drake.

'Impact.'

The screen was momentarily swamped by a bright green glow as the Hellfire missile impacted right in the centre of camp. As the flare slowly subsided, Cain leaned a little closer, surveying the scene of devastation with approval.

'And that's a hit,' he said quietly, to scattered applause around the conference room. Another little victory in their ongoing war; for him most of all. 'Good work, everyone.'

Leaving the conference room a short time later, he fished out his cell phone and dialled a number. A Libyan cell phone. It rang only a couple of times before it was answered.

'It worked, I assume?' Hussein Jibril, the head of Libyan intelligence remarked.

'Your intel was good,' Cain allowed.

'As was yours.' Not only had they eliminated an arms-smuggling operation with the potential to overthrow the Gaddafi government, but they had also provided Jibril with the names of key personnel within the Libyan military and intelligence agencies who were poised to play an active part in the coup. These demonstrations of loyalty had been enough to finally persuade Jibril to release the locations of the Islamic State commanders he had been secretly harbouring. 'I hope our relationship continues to prosper.'

Only as long as your intel holds out, Cain thought. Jibril was another loose end that would likely need tying up eventually, but for now he still might have a role to play.

'I'm sure it will,' he said instead.

–

Bishr Kubar blinked as the van doors slid open, allowing harsh sunlight to flood in, almost blinding him. Sunrise on a new day in Libya.

But not for him.

'Out,' the field operative beside him barked, shoving him outside.

With his hands bound, it took no small effort to avoid falling face-first into the dirt. He didn't want to die like that, on his knees. A real man died on his feet. That was how he imagined his father had met his end, such as it was.

'Forward, come on,' his guard said.

It didn't take much imagination to see where he was headed. A shallow pit had already been excavated in the desert sand. Another man was waiting for him there at the edge of the grave. Adnan Mousa; his partner, his colleague and perhaps, in a way, his friend.

But no longer. The pistol clutched in his hand made it obvious what was soon to happen, even if his eyes still harboured some trace of sympathy and compassion. A good man called upon to do bad things.

'Take it easy with him,' Mousa ordered, giving the field operative a warning look.

Sure enough, Kubar felt the grip on his arm ease. A lot of Mukhabarat men were being taken to places like this, and likely he wanted to avoid the same fate.

'Thank you,' Kubar said quietly, appreciating the gesture.

Mousa looked at him sadly. 'You know why you're here.'

'I do.' Resisting or even pleading for his life would be futile, so he simply walked right over to the grave and stood at the edge, staring down into the shallow pit.

Even now, he could scarcely believe how dramatically it had all fallen apart. The plan. The great scheme to rid Libya of Gaddafi and establish a new, truly progressive government, to rebuild this land into a modern and democratic country. The plan he'd persuaded himself could actually work, had risked his own life and killed to protect.

All gone.

It was he who had killed the man captured in Paris, slipping a cyanide pill into his food and ending his life before he could be tortured into compromising the plan. And he would have broken sooner or later. Every man broke – Bishr Kubar knew this better than anyone.

At the time it had been a necessary sacrifice. That was what he'd told himself. But now it was just another futile death in a country littered with them.

They'd come for him just after he'd sat down to start his work that day, his first cup of coffee still steaming on his desk. He'd never even had a chance to take a sip, he reflected as they'd led him away. Strange, the things one remembered.

'Why, Bishr?' Mousa was asking, disturbing his thoughts. 'Why did you do it?'

Kubar shook his head in sad resignation. Even now, the man still didn't understand. How could he, when he represented the very ignorance and unquestioning obedience that had brought this country to its knees, that kept the population cowed and fearful, that bred the kind of petty infighting that had claimed Kubar's own family?

How could he make his former friend understand that those same qualities would one day find him out here in a shallow grave just like this?

'It doesn't matter now,' he said instead, too weary to fight that battle.

Mousa took a step back, perhaps interpreting his words as casual dismissal of his last attempt to reach out to him.

'Do you want to say a prayer first?' he asked, his tone stiff and formal as if he were reciting from a script.

At this, Bishr Kubar did something he hadn't done for a long time. He smiled.

A prayer. To whom? Who would be inclined to help him now?

'Just get it over with,' he ordered. 'I don't have—'

His words were cut short by the crack of a single shot, and he pitched forward into the shallow grave.

Chapter 66

George Washington University Hospital

Dan Franklin was reviewing the daily briefings that he insisted be brought to his hospital room, wanting to keep himself in the game despite everything that had happened, despite the fact he still couldn't feel anything in his legs. More than anything, it was a way of keeping his mind occupied, keeping him from thinking too much about what the future might hold for him.

He was interrupted when the door to his room flew open and his private secretary rushed in, the look in her eyes bordering on panic.

'I'm sorry to disturb you, sir,' she stammered.

'What is it, Barbara?' he asked, wondering if her intrusion had been prompted by some kind of personal emergency. Normally a composed and efficient woman, he couldn't imagine anything less than the death of a loved one rattling her like this. 'What's wrong?'

'Sir, we've got a problem at Langley. Internal security teams just showed up, started shutting everything down. We're being locked out.'

Franklin felt his blood run cold. 'On whose orders?'

'Marcus Cain.'

His hands curled into fists, the blood pounding in his ears. 'Get me Cain's office. I want to speak to them now.'

'No need for that, Dan. We can take care of this right here.'

Franklin looked up as a tall, ruggedly handsome man strode into the room. Now in his mid fifties, he wore his extra years with the same easy confidence as his expensive, tailor-made suit. This was a man well used to wielding power and authority, and bending others to his will.

Marcus Cain.

Barbara shrank aside to make way for the pair of agents accompanying him. Their aggressive bearing made it plain this was no normal meeting.

'Please, don't get up on my account,' Cain said, his tone faintly mocking.

Franklin eyed the deputy director from his bed. 'What brings you here?'

'I'm the bearer of good news, Dan,' Cain replied, smiling coldly. His piercing blue-grey eyes were locked with his. 'From today, your workload's going to be a little lighter.'

Franklin frowned. 'What are you talking about?'

'I'm shutting down the Shepherd programme, effective immediately.'

Franklin stared at the deputy director in utter disbelief, wondering if he'd misunderstood. One look into Cain's eyes was enough to persuade him otherwise. 'That's ridiculous,' he protested. 'On what grounds?'

Aside from the fact that the Shepherd teams were a vital part of the Agency's internal security apparatus, one couldn't simply shut down an entire top-secret programme involving hundreds of support personnel and dozens of field operatives. It was impossible.

'Security concerns.' Reaching into his jacket pocket, Cain unfolded a printed sheet of paper and laid it down beside Franklin. 'I know you're trying to stay across everything, so here's another briefing for you. The programme's being shut down, pending official review.'

'Bullshit,' Franklin snapped, shoving the official orders back at him. 'You can't just shut us down. The Agency needs us.'

'No, Dan. The Agency needs field agents it can trust. And right now, that's not you. My people are already at Langley securing all your files and data, so it's up to you how you handle this. Personally, I thought you might like to keep some shred of dignity and give the order yourself. Then you can concentrate on… recuperation.'

Franklin's hands curled into fists as he stared at the deputy director. 'You son of a bitch. How dare you?'

Cain turned to his two bodyguards. 'Give us the room, please.'

Nodding, the two men turned to leave, making sure that Franklin's secretary left with them. As the door closed, Cain moved over to stand by the full-length windows, studying the panoramic outlook over central DC.

'I do miss my old office,' he remarked thoughtfully. 'It's the view. You can't put a price on a good view.' He smiled as an old memory surfaced. 'You know, the first place I ever owned was an apartment in Boston. Little one-bedroom place. Not much to look at, really. The heaters didn't work right and the windows rattled in their frames every time the breeze got up, but I didn't care. It was the view that kept me there – perfect, right on the ocean. In the evening, when the sun was going down, it looked like the whole sea was on fire from Quincy Bay all the way to the horizon. I used to sit there and just stare at it, imagining what was out there. I think that's what people like so much about a good view. Not what they can see, but what they can't. The possibility of what lies beyond that horizon, instead of what they're stuck with.'

'What the fuck is this about, Marcus?' Franklin demanded, in no mood for such philosophical reflections. 'We have a deal.'

Cain let out a faint sigh and turned away from the scene beyond the windows.

'*Had* a deal,' he corrected. 'You were supposed to keep your dog from biting anyone. Drake broke our agreement, went into Libya without authorization and blew a major operation in the process. Years of work has been lost because of that man.'

Franklin could feel himself paling. Libya, covert operations… Jesus, what the hell had Drake done?

'There must be another explanation.'

'Read the debriefing documents yourself if you want. I'm not going to sit around waiting for him to cause another disaster; not when there are lives at stake. This ends now,' Cain promised him. 'Whatever protection he had, it's over. As of today, he's an enemy – of the Agency, of the State, of *us*.'

Franklin's eyes were wide as he stared at his nemesis across the room. 'Wait just a Goddamn—'

'Time to choose a side, Dan,' Cain interrupted, taking a step towards him. 'You've been sitting on the fence for a long time now, playing both sides, waiting to see which one would come out on top. I can't say I blame you. You're smart, cautious, and you and Drake have a history together. Unfortunately, the one thing he doesn't have is a future. Only I do.'

'I could ruin you,' Franklin reminded him.

'And I could kill you and destroy your reputation forever,' Cain replied with a flippant shrug. 'Like I said, things are changing. It's a brave new world, but there's no room in it for men like Drake. Only one of us is going to be standing at the end of this, so it's time for you to choose. Are you with me, or against me?'

Franklin was shocked, stunned by the sudden seismic shift that had just taken place in his world. Just like that, the rules had changed. The game he had believed himself close to mastering had vanished before his eyes.

All that was left was Cain, the master player.

The last man standing.

'That's what I thought,' Cain said, turning away. He was just reaching for the door when he turned around and glanced at Franklin for the last time. 'By the way, I hope you feel better, Dan.'

As he closed the door behind him, leaving Franklin alone, the former director of the Shepherd programme clenched his fists and closed his eyes as utter defeat washed over him like a tide. It had all fallen apart. The shaky truce that he'd negotiated had at last come to an end.

Now it was war. A war that could only have one victor.

'Goddamn you, Ryan,' he whispered.

That was when he felt it. Movement.

Frowning, he opened his eyes and looked down at his bed covers. And sure enough, the fabric wrinkled slightly as his foot twitched beneath.

Chapter 67

Fifteen years earlier

Taking a deep breath, Drake knocked on the locker-room door. His aching hands were heavily bandaged up, and the impact sent a wave of pain through him.

It was a few seconds before a gruff voice answered. 'Yeah!'

The locker room was old, like the rest of the club in which they'd fought. It smelled of sweat and steam and worn leather. And sitting on a bench against the far wall, looking as tired as his surroundings, was his opponent.

The man was a mess, one eye swollen shut, face covered in cuts and bruises, swollen arthritic hands still taped up. He looked up and nodded.

'I thought I'd be seeing you.'

'You know why I'm here.'

He nodded again. 'You gave me a fuckin' good fight. Best beating I've taken in years. You should be proud of yourself.'

'But you wouldn't go down,' Drake said, an edge of anger and frustration in his voice.

The old fighter managed a wry smile. 'No, I wouldn't.'

'Why? Look at yourself. This wasn't a title fight. What was the point?'

At this, the man rose to his feet. Old, overweight, beaten and bruised he might have been, but he was still a tall, imposing figure. 'If you have to ask that question, you've got no place calling yourself a fighter,' he said, his voice laced with the pain and weariness and defiance and triumph of a hundred fights just like this. 'We don't do this for pay days or title shots. We fight because that's what we're born to do, because it still means something to get up when another guy knocks you down. Maybe one day you'll understand that.'

Drake backed off a pace, such was his shock at the man's words. But more intimidating was the look in his eyes – that hunger, that fierce burning passion for what he did. For all Drake's own training and finesse in the ring, it was something he'd never experienced before.

But he understood now. At last, he understood what it meant to stand your ground, to keep getting up when you were knocked down, to never submit no matter what was thrown at you. He understood now why his opponent had chosen to go out the same way he'd always been – as a fighter.

Without saying another word, he turned and walked out.

–

400

It was a warm spring evening, the sun just settling behind a blanket of thin cloud off to the west, its dying glow setting the nearby mountains ablaze in colour. Drake inhaled, tasting the scent of flowers and freshly cut grass. So different from the burning desert sands he'd left behind a week ago.

But as pleasant as his surroundings were, his thoughts were turned inward, contemplating everything that had happened in the week since their escape from Libya, everything that had fallen apart in such spectacular fashion.

They had been played, he realized now. Cain had manipulated them right from the start, using their efforts to overthrow him as a means of eliminating a rival programme in Libya. With their supplies of weapons and ammunition cut off, the attempted uprising had been aborted before it could even begin. A bloody civil war had been averted, to be sure, but Cain's crooked deal with the Libyan government remained intact.

For now, at least.

Drake sensed trouble ahead for that country. With or without the Agency's help, he knew that a war was coming.

As for himself, he had a different war to fight, and he was fast running out of allies. It was fair to say he couldn't expect any further support from Franklin, who he had effectively alienated by going behind his back and openly breaking their agreement not to move against Cain.

Hunt too had paid the price for his part in their little conspiracy. Drake had caught an obituary for him on the *Washington Post's* website several days ago, the brief article mentioning only that he had died of natural causes, and that he was to be buried at Arlington Cemetery. Another one of Cain's old rivals eliminated, and another name added to the list of people who had died from Drake's mistakes.

As if that wasn't bad enough, Faulkner's revelation about Drake's mother had shaken him to his core. Everything he thought he knew about her, every judgement he'd made, every assumption, every petty resentment, had just been called into doubt. How could he not have known? How could she never have told him?

And if Faulkner was right, if she had somehow been part of this deadly world of shadows and betrayal in which Drake now existed, then whose side had she been on? What was this mysterious group called the Circle that Faulkner had alluded to? And if Faulkner hadn't arranged her death, then who had?

There were answers out there; of that he had no doubt. But finding them was unlikely to be easy. And even if he did somehow fight and claw his way to the truth, there was a good chance he wouldn't like what he found.

But he would get there. He knew that with absolute certainty. He would find his answers, or he would die trying.

His only cause for comfort was that the rest of his team were safe, for now at least. They had gone to ground as soon as it became apparent their plan had failed, splitting up and travelling under false identities to avoid arousing suspicion. Each of them was a trained Shepherd operative, well versed in the processes and resources the Agency could call upon to hunt down targets, and familiar with how to avoid them.

They would survive, but they were shut out now. All of them.

So here he sat; a wanted man. Wanted by the Libyans, wanted by the British, wanted by Cain, wanted by the Agency. A man with a growing list of enemies and a dwindling list of friends, with few resources to call upon, facing an enemy whose power and influence was growing almost by the day. An enemy who wouldn't stop until Drake and everyone connected to him was dead.

He sighed, staring down at the distant farmhouse. The house that had once belonged to his mother, that Jessica had now taken over. The house where he had come to say goodbye.

He was just about to return to his car when a voice spoke up from behind. 'I'm sorry for being late. This was not an easy place to find.'

Drake smiled despite himself. It was good to know that even Anya had trouble navigating the Welsh countryside.

'Join the club.'

Her arrival was no surprise. She had contacted him several days previously, telling him little about her situation except that she wanted to set up a meeting. He'd suggested the time and place. Thousands of miles from the Libyans and the Agency, this seemed like as good a place as any.

Moving forward, she lowered herself onto the grass beside him. As she did so, he couldn't help but notice the bandage wrapped around her hand, the cuts and bruises on her face. She had worn makeup to disguise them, but seated so close to her it was easy to see that she'd been in the wars since their last encounter.

They both had.

She inhaled, tasted the scents of flowers and wild grass and growing things. 'This is a good place,' she decided, glancing at him. 'It means something to you, doesn't it? Did you grow up here?'

'No.' Though he was starting to wish he had. 'But it does mean something to me.'

He sighed, pushing those thoughts aside.

'Tell me, how did your… "business" work out?' he asked.

She shook her head. There was a flicker in her normally cool, steely blue eyes. A sadness, a pain that he rarely saw in her. She was hurting; not physically – pain like that barely seemed to trouble her – but deep inside.

Whatever errand had brought her to London a couple of weeks ago, it clearly hadn't worked out well for her. He caught himself wondering what exactly she'd been involved in, what secrets she had uncovered, or what she had lost in the process.

But as with all things, he knew she wouldn't tell him until she was ready.

'I'm done with the Agency,' he said simply. 'Finished. I can't go back to Langley.'

If he was expecting a look of surprise or shock, he didn't get it. Perhaps she knew already. Sometime he felt like she knew more about him then he did.

'What happened?' she asked, her voice quiet and subdued.

Drake snorted with dark humour. 'I tried to take on Cain, thought I could finish this myself.' He shrugged, reflecting for a moment on the full magnitude of his folly. 'I was wrong.'

And there it was, laid out in stark, simple terms. He'd gambled and lost, pitted himself against an enemy and come up short.

'So was I,' she said.

Drake glanced up at her, unable to hide his surprise. 'It's not often you admit that.'

'It's not often that I have to.' She drew her knees up to her chest, staring out across the fields and rolling hills with sadness in her eyes. 'But you were right, Ryan. Last year, when you said we needed to work together, you were right. But I was…' She glanced away for a moment, struggling for the right words. 'I'm not used to trusting people, even good men. I did not live up to that agreement, so I shouldn't be surprised that you didn't either.'

'Jesus,' he said in disbelief. 'First you admit that you were wrong, then that I was right. Whatever next?'

Anya's eyes were on him now. He couldn't tell if she was angry or faintly amused by his remarks. Perhaps it was a little of both.

'That depends on you, Ryan,' she said at last, her tone turning more serious now. 'What do *you* want?'

There was a tension in her, an uncertainty that he wasn't used to seeing. He sensed she was referring to more than just his immediate plans to tackle the threats they faced.

He stared back at her, once again questioning who she really was, what really lurked behind those pale, intense eyes. Anya, the woman who had turned his life upside down, who had lived through things he could scarcely imagine, whose real intentions and motives he could only begin to understand, and yet who somehow kept drawing him back no matter how far apart they were.

For the first time, he sensed those same doubts and questions and fears in her. For all her resourcefulness, her inner strength and her sheer indomitable will, she still sought in vain the one thing she'd never had.

Anya, if I told you what I really wanted, would you understand? he said to himself. Could you ever be like me, or I like you?

He reached out and gently touched her hand. For once, she didn't move it away.

'Remember what I said to you once? I made a promise that I'd be there for you even if you didn't think you needed me, that I'd do everything I could to help you, and that I'd never give up on you. Because this is my fight now as much as yours. That hasn't changed. We started this thing together, Anya,' he said. 'You and me. That's how we're going to finish it. Together.'

The woman said nothing to this, but at that moment he felt it. He felt her squeeze his hand just a little.

'I need to ask something of you,' she said at length.

'What is it?'

'A favour. Someone recently risked their life to help save mine. Now... she needs help, and I can't give it to her. But you and your... team, you have made a living out of helping people. If you can, I would ask that you bring her back.'

Drake was surprised. It wasn't often that Anya asked for help in any matter, and he could see how difficult she found it now. 'I'll look into it.'

He would get the details from her later. For now, he had other matters to attend to.

'Thank you,' she said, looking genuinely grateful. With the matter decided, she nodded towards the distant homestead that was the only dwelling in sight. 'That house. Your sister is down there, isn't she?'

Drake nodded.

'Then go to her,' Anya advised him. 'I'll be waiting. We can talk more... when you're ready.'

–

The house was in a state of organized chaos, with packing boxes everywhere, stacks of clothes and personal belongings waiting to be sorted, and furniture scattered around. Moving one person's life out of a place and another's in at the same time was a daunting enough task for a team of removal men, never mind one person living alone.

But Jessica was determined to tackle it alone, just like everything else.

For now, however, her mind wasn't on unpacking, sorting or any of the other work that still needed to be done. It was on her brother, who was standing by the kitchen counter with a cup of steaming tea in his hand.

He had finally returned after his abrupt departure a couple of weeks earlier, a different man from the one who had left. Whatever had happened out there had clearly left its mark on him, both physical and emotional. Only now, as he related the deadly events in which he'd become involved, was she able to form some understanding of what he'd been through. In particular, the revelations about their mother.

'I didn't know,' she whispered, shaking her head in disbelief. 'I never imagined... our own mother. I feels so unreal.'

Drake let out a breath and glanced away. She could see easily enough why this was so hard for him. She at least had had a chance to reconcile with their mother, put the past behind them and form a new relationship in her later years. Ryan had never had that, and he never would.

The knowledge that she hadn't been the person he'd long convinced himself she was only made it harder to bear.

Jessica swallowed hard, almost afraid to ask her next question. 'Ryan, these people she worked for. Who are they? What do they want?'

'I don't know,' he admitted. 'But I'm going to find out.'

'So you're leaving, then.' It wasn't phrased as a question. She'd sensed from the moment of his arrival that his visit would only be a fleeting one.

He nodded slowly, saying nothing.

'You know there's a place for you here, if...' She trailed off. Something about the look in his eyes warned her that things had changed. He had something to tell her. Something bad.

'Jess, it's not going to be like before,' he said, his voice strained, his body tense. 'I... I can't go back to the way things were. Cain's coming after me now, and there's nothing left to hold him back. I need to disappear for a while. I took a risk even coming here today, put you at risk as well, and I'm sorry for that. I really am. But... I had to come. If nothing else, I know what it's like to leave things unsaid. I wanted to say goodbye.'

His words were like a knife driven into her heart. She let out a faint sob, managed to regain her composure a little, then reached up and wiped a tear from her eye. 'Will I see you again?' she asked, her voice trembling.

Taking a step forward, he embraced her, pulling her tight as the tears finally came. He held her for a time in silence as she cried; cried for the loss of the parent she hadn't truly known, cried for the loss of a brother she might never see again, cried for the loss of her family that had been driven away.

Only when her tears subsided and he finally backed off did she see the glistening of moisture in his eyes, and knew that he felt the loss just as keenly as she.

–

Some time later, Drake emerged from the house into the glow of the evening sky. His parting with Jessica had been as hard as he knew it would be, made all the more difficult because of the uncertain future they both faced. But he had at least made peace with her, told her how much she meant to him and how she would never leave his thoughts.

That at least meant something.

He was just walking away, shoes crunching on the gravel drive, when he glanced to the right and spotted the garage where his father's car was stored. On impulse, he changed direction and headed for it, slipping the bolt open to swing the old wooden doors apart.

The Austin Healey was still there, paintwork gleaming in the evening light. Sighing, Drake reached down, allowing his finger to trail along the bodywork as he made his way to the driver's side.

Swinging the door open, he settled himself into the seat. He could taste the scent of old leather, oil and petrol in the air. Such a strange thing that his mother had chosen to hang on to this car, this fragment of their former life, paying money year after year to maintain and look after it.

He wondered suddenly whether he could run the engine over, just once, to hear the sound of it again. Surely there was no harm in it? Remembering Jessica's explanation from his last visit that the keys were kept in the glove box, he reached over and popped it open.

It was at that moment that something fell onto the floor. Something white and square. An envelope.

Frowning, Drake reached over and snatched it up. It was heavy and lumpy. Something was inside it.

A single word had been inscribed on the front in his mother's distinctive handwriting.

Ryan

'What the hell?'

Breaking the seal on the envelope, he reached in and fished out a slip of paper that had been folded inside. Feeling his heart beat faster, he unfolded the handwritten missive and began to read.

Ryan,
If you're reading this, then I pray it's because Jessica brought you here. It saddens me greatly that I was never able to do it myself, and that was my failing. I let you down, Ryan. In many ways.

I wasn't the mother you deserved. I couldn't be there for you the way I wanted to be, or tell you the things I wanted to, but never for a moment blame yourself. It was my fault – all of it. I don't expect you to forgive me, but perhaps in the end, you might understand.

I wish there were a way for me to explain everything that's happened, everything I did and everything I tried to do, but this isn't something I can tell you. The only way is to show you, and let you judge for yourself.

Always yours,
Freya

Drake leaned back in his seat, closed his eyes for a moment and crumpled the letter in his hands as the pent-up emotions he'd held in check since all this began threatened to break through whatever self control he had left. He could feel his eyes stinging, and reached up to wipe the drops of moisture away.

It had been there the whole time. Just waiting for him.

Looking at the envelope again, he reached inside and plucked out the other object that had been left there. A single piece of stamped metal that glistened in the sun's dying light, with numbers etched into its upper surface.

A key.

Epilogue

Seventeen days earlier

Yanking her arm free, Freya turned around to face her adversary, eyes gleaming with defiance. She wouldn't give them the satisfaction of putting a bullet through her head from behind.

'You look me in the eye, you coward,' she said, staring right at them. 'Look me in the eye when you pull the trigger.'

If she'd expected her words to strike a chord, to engender some kind of reaction, she was to be disappointed. A second came and went. A second broken only by the sigh of the evening breeze, and distant hoot of an owl, and the hammering of Freya's heart.

'You shouldn't have come looking for me.'

She saw the barrel of a weapon raised, saw the long snout of a silencer gleaming in the thin sliver of moonlight.

Freya let out a breath. 'Of all the people, I never—'

A 9mm slug passing through her chest silenced that sentence before she had a chance to complete it. She let out a strangled gasp, as if in surprise, then fell backward and collapsed to the ground, her body skidding down the rocky slope until it came to rest in the pool of stagnant water.

As darkness closed in around her, Freya's last thought was one of simple, heartfelt regret.

Ryan, I'm sorry.

Her killer lingered a moment or two longer, waiting to be sure the gunshot had done its work. Waiting to make sure her target really was eliminated.

'You shouldn't have come looking for me,' Anya repeated, looking down on the dead woman with a hint of regret.

Her work done, she turned and started her walk back to the waiting van.